THE FLAME QUENCHER

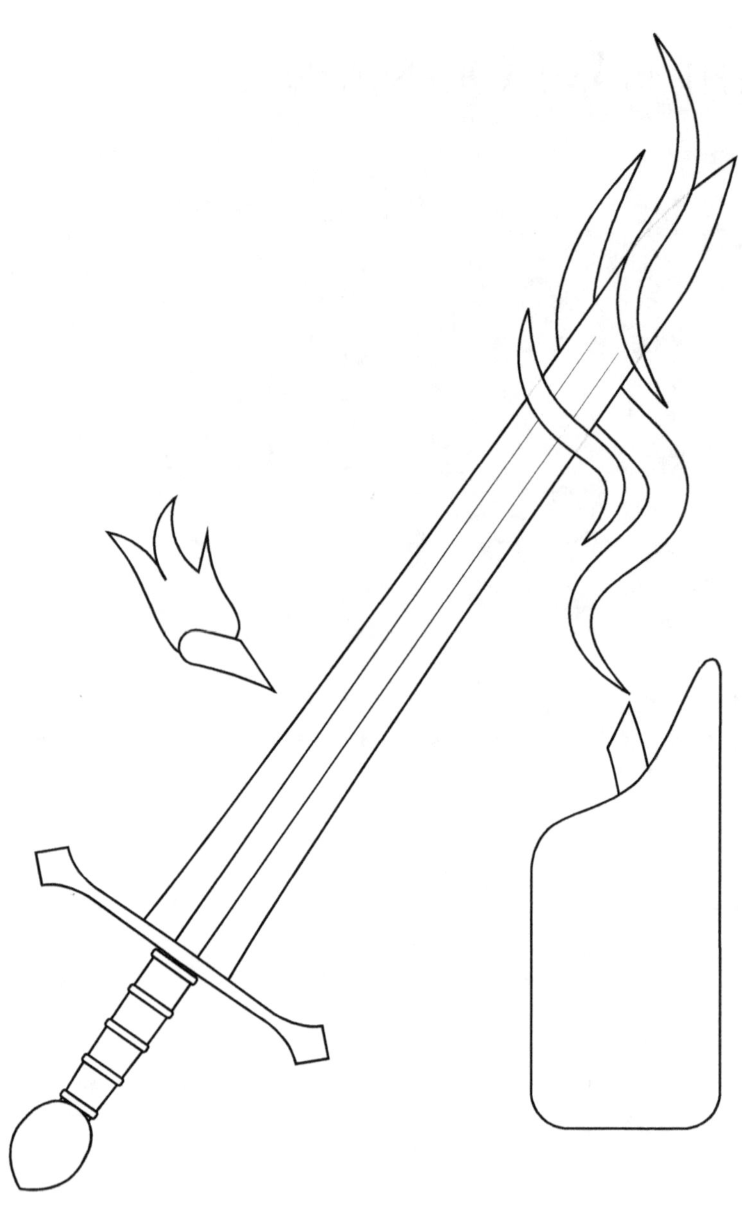

THE LAST STRANGE KINGS

Book Three

The
Flame
Quencher

Carla Fraga

Quills & Pixels

THE LAST STRANGE KINGS, BOOK 3

THE FLAME QUENCHER

Learn more about The Last Strange Kings series and download a full-color map:

laststrangekings.com

Follow on Instagram @laststrangekings

Published by *Quills and Pixels*

Seattle, WA

quillsandpixels.com

ISBN   978-0-9860686-6-9

Copyeditor: Kyra Freestar, Bridge Creek Editing

Design, map, and layout: Steve Laskevitch, Quills and Pixels

Por Los Padres

CONTENTS

PART THREE

*A plentitude of gratitude to my
sounding board SML3 and to beta
readers Diana Lull, Mario Baumann,
Wolf, KLH and most especially the
immensely sensible Jennifer Laba.*

Map: Eskalind and Surrounding Lands

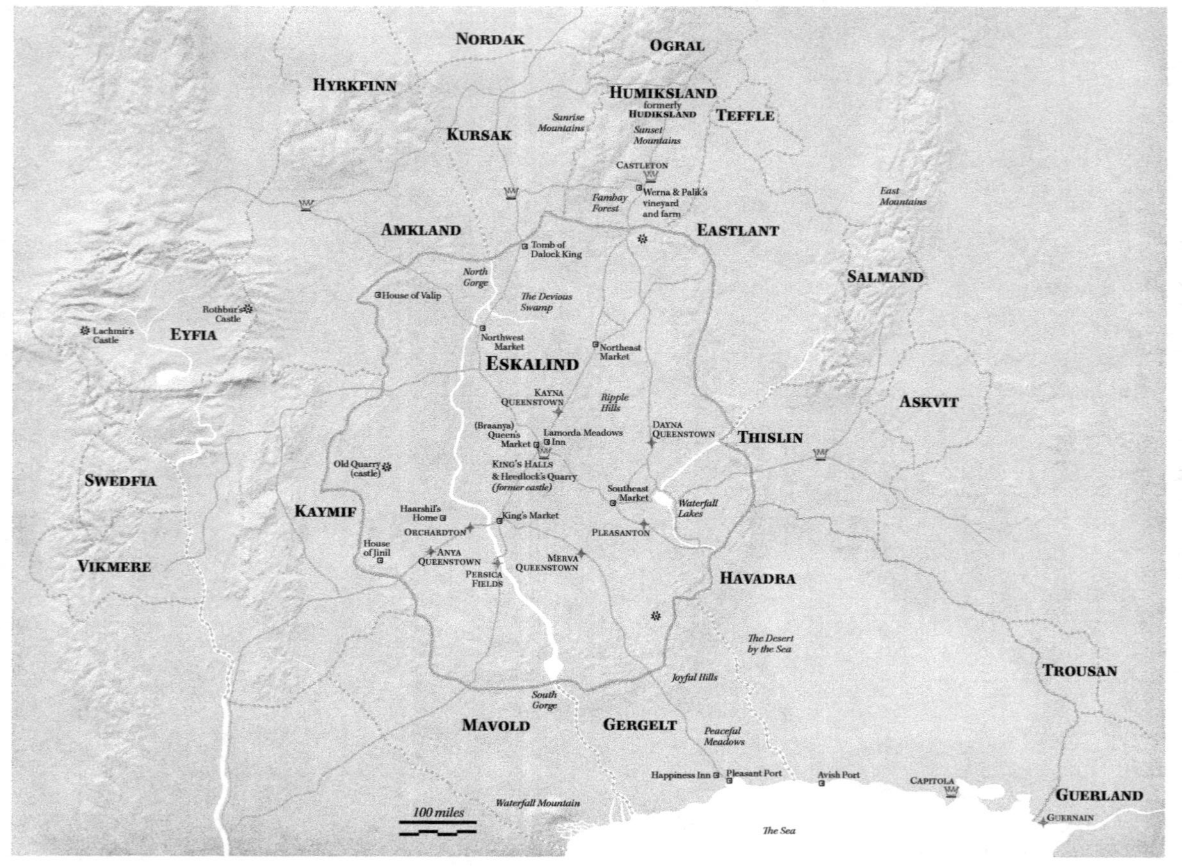

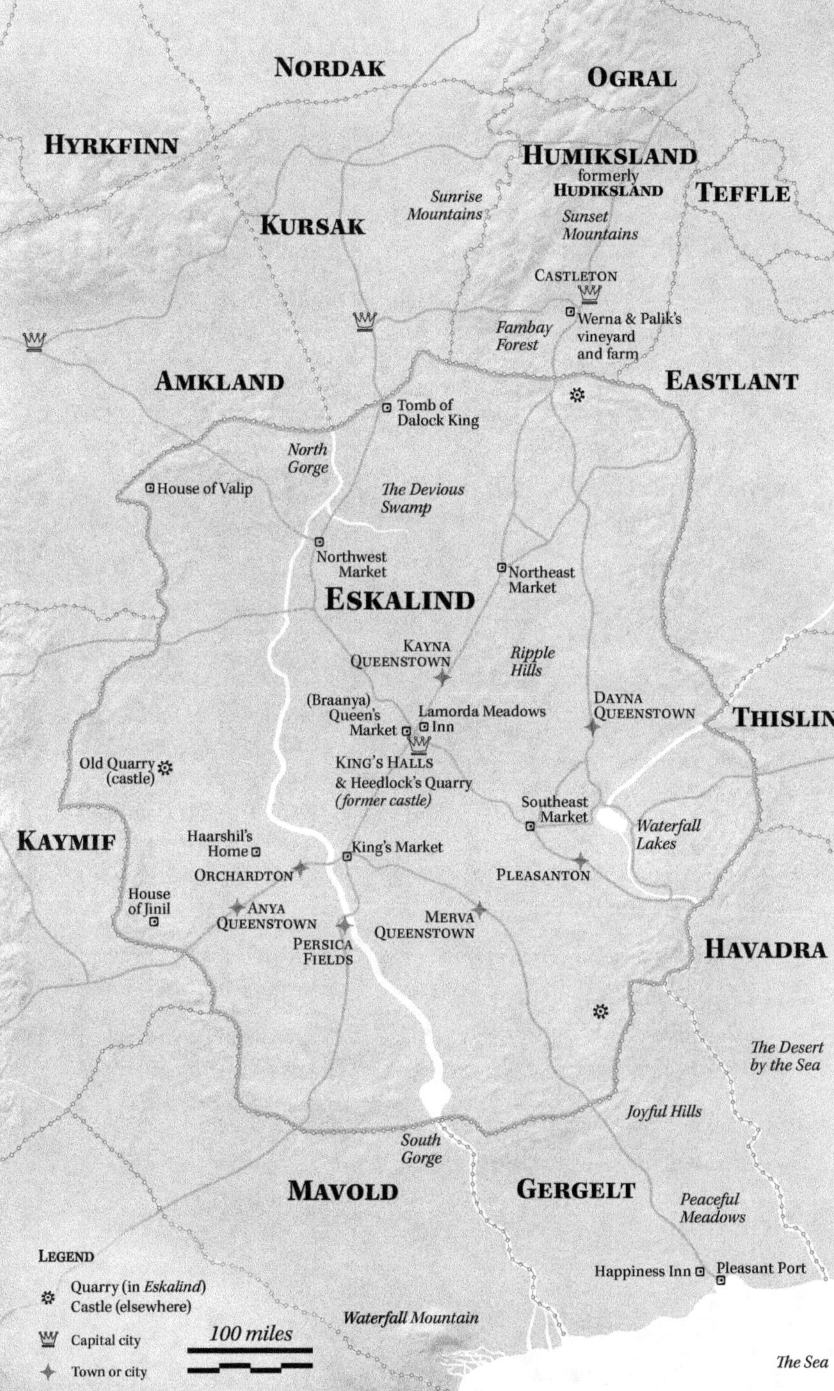

NORDAK
OGRAL
HYRKFINN
HUMIKSLAND
formerly
HUDIKSLAND
TEFFLE
KURSAK
Sunrise
Mountains
Sunset
Mountains
CASTLETON
AMKLAND
Fambay
Forest
Werna & Palik's
vineyard
and farm
EASTLANT
Tomb of
Dalock King
North
Gorge
House of Valip
The Devious
Swamp
Northwest
Market
ESKALIND
Northeast
Market
KAYNA
QUEENSTOWN
Ripple
Hills
DAYNA
QUEENSTOWN
THISLIN
(Braanya)
Queen's
Market
Lamorda Meadows
Inn
Old Quarry
(castle)
KING'S HALLS
& Heedlock's Quarry
(former castle)
Southeast
Market
Waterfall
Lakes
KAYMIF
Haarshil's
Home
King's Market
House
of Jinil
ORCHARDTON
Pleasanton
ANYA
QUEENSTOWN
MERVA
QUEENSTOWN
HAVADRA
PERSICA
FIELDS
The Desert
by the Sea
Joyful Hills
South
Gorge
MAVOLD
GERGELT
Peaceful
Meadows
LEGEND
Quarry (in Eskalind)
Castle (elsewhere)
Capital city
100 miles
Town or city
Happiness Inn
Pleasant Port
Waterfall Mountain
The Sea

Note: Eskalinders preceded by 🪶

Avnil, *First Sergeant of the Eighth Company*

Baavnif, *born of Thislin, famous Eskalind Loremaster*

Bafnil, *Secretary of Ambassador Moril*

Dalich, *125th King of Eskalind, husband of Damina*

Dalock, *124th King of Eskalind, deceased, husband of Marna, father of Dalich*

Damina, *Queen of Eskalind*

Dara, *Lady and Acta Sua* of the House of Naymil, Merlich King's Friend*

Deenofts, *Scholar and dye merchant of Havadra, brother of Samathe*

Edvain, *Mavoldian Swordmaster*

Favik, *born of Hudiksland, now Humiksland, Ambassador of Eskalind*

Fornil, *Ambassador of Eskalind*

Havnil, *Ambassador of Eskalind*

Humik, *king of Humiksland*

Jinilya, *Lady of the House of Jinil, Dalock King's Friend, daughter of Saralya, sister of Saril and Marnil*

Kaloft, *Lord of the House of Jinil, Dalock King's Friend, son of Marnil and Athla*

Kermon, *Merchant Master of Guerland, Scholar, cousin of Saralya*

Kostaza, *princess of Kaymif, wife of Moril, sister of King Moulai, mother of Elai*

Marna, *born of Hudiksland, now Humiksland, Scholars' Mistress, King's Mother of Eskalind, wife of Dalock, mother of Dalich, called the Bladesmith's Daughter by the Scholars*

Marnil, *Lord of House of Jinil, Dalock King's Friend, brother of Saril and Jinilya,*

Melande of Havadra, *daughter of Yirlofts, wife of Sirish, mother of Yirish*

Moril, *Ambassador of Eskalind, husband of Kostaza*

Moulai, *king of Kaymif, brother of Kostaza*

Narnik, *born of Hudiksland, Captain of Eskalind, nephew of Marna, cousin of Dalich*

Palika, *born of Hudiksland, Chief Scriptor of Eskalind, niece of Marna, cousin of Dalich*

Pamina, *sister of Damina Queen and Yamina, daughter of Gamin*

Radil, *Lord and Acta Sua* of the House of Valip, Palich King's Friend; Scholar, husband of Mayva, father of Amril*

Saralya, *Scholar, Lady and Acta Sua* of the House of Jinil, Dalock King's Friend, Mother of Saril, Marnil, and Jinilya, called Queen's Reader*

Saril, *King's Second and Lord of House of Jinil, Dalock King's Friend*

Sirish, *a colonel of Havadra*

Synya, *Librarian at King's Halls*

Trevil, *Dalich King's Guard, husband of Yamina*

Werna, *midwife of Humiksland, sister of Marna, mother of Narnik and Palika*

Yamina, *sister of Damina Queen*

Yirish of Havadra, *grandson of Yirlofts*

Yirlofts, *general of Havadra, father of Melande, grandfather of Yirish*

***Acta Sua,** *title given to the eldest member of a noble house of Eskalind*

PART ONE
2912–2915

Father says I have grown too big for his box. But he would rather keep me close and hire more men to carry us than risk me traveling separately.

In the dim light, Yirish watched his father, seated across from him. The padded container they traveled inside jostled from the steps of the men bearing them to their destination. Sunlight filtered weakly from dense screens at the top of the walls, the only openings. A carrying box was an anonymous way to travel and thus, in Havadra, the safest. Robbers and kidnappers never knew if a person of import and wealth occupied the box or merely a servant on an errand for his fortress. Outside the wooden walls, horses clomped and men yelled directions and stern warnings, a muted cacophony punctuated by the occasional pitiful wails of beggars.

Without asking permission, the boy maneuvered to his knees, reached for the handles near the roof, and craned his head close to the screen, squinting from the bright sunshine. The colonel inhaled slowly, a ragged sound given his crushed nose. "Hold fast to the handle, Yirish." The lad bobbed his blond locks in agreement just as he spied two carrying boxes identical to their own on the road beside them. Sunburnt men on horses cantered in all directions as beige-clad men on foot threaded through the chaos, one nearly trampled by a gray horse. The gray horse's rider shouted insults at the man on foot, who hurled angry words and flapped his arms. The mounted man reached for his sword.

"What's going on out there, Yirish?"

"Two men drawing weapons."

"Are they following us?"

Yirish watched as the men shrank from his view. "No." He slanted his gaze in the direction they traveled. Not far ahead, he could see the tall, rounded walls of his grandfather's fortress. The box shifted as the carrying men in front dodged an obstacle invisible to the eleven-year-old. He clung tight to the handles and nearly bumped his head.

Father banged the side of the box to express his displeasure. When Yirish looked out the screen again, he saw a scrawny, light-haired boy in a tattered silken tunic the color of fading sky, crying for alms by a dusty wall. A group of men passed by as if he were made of air; none acknowledged him. The sapling-thin youngster shrank to the chalky beige ground, brown eyes vacant amongst stark cheekbones. A sense of foreboding swept through Yirish. He lowered himself into his seat.

His father watched him. "What is it?"

"I saw him again."

"The son of the dead king?" Yirish nodded, his eyes adjusting to the interior space again, straining to see the catch on the door latch. "Why does the former prince's condition concern you?" his father asked.

The youngster rubbed his eyes. "I don't know." Suddenly mindful that this was not an acceptable explanation to his lord father, he spoke up, clear as a soldier giving a report. "It makes me sad."

Father frowned. "His family failed to keep their position. He's lucky he wasn't killed."

"What would happen if Grandfather lost his position?"

"You would still have me to protect you." The colonel ringed a finger inside the long sleeve of his tunic, adjusting the gold embroidery trimming its edges to cover the demarcation line where suntanned skin on his hands met the pale skin of his arm. "We make plans and work to see that we remain a strong family of high position." He crossed his arms. "Ask your mother to give you brothers to aid us in this endeavor."

"But the dead king was killed by his brother."

Father sounded ready for this retort. "Ask for sisters too. Women are great assets in bargaining." One thump sounded on the door. "We have arrived at the first gate. Confirm it." He pointed to the screen, his gaze impersonal and neutral as though already negotiating with Grandfather.

Yirish scrambled to his perch again and saw that they were passing through the gate of the first wall. "We're there," he whispered.

Merchants stood in the space between the first wall and the second, their wares spread upon blankets in neat rows. Some beckoned to the screened enclosure embedded in the second wall, where members of the household might be watching and evaluating the goods. A produce seller carrying a pole laden with oblong purple pods, glossy in the harsh sunlight, turned toward their box. He called out, but a male voice warned him away as the box lumbered toward the second gate. As it opened, Grandfather's guards poured forth in a swarm of stomping sandals, swords on their hips and short spears straight by their sides. These iron-helmed sentries surrounded the carrying men with their burden and escorted all inside the second gate. The carriers lowered the box to the dirt as ordered as the gate ground almost shut behind them. Then a guard shouted at them to leave the area, that they would reclaim their boxes soon.

Yirish whispered, "Wait, we are not being carried inside the third wall?"

"Not this time."

"Why?"

"We are breaking up the pattern." Father sounded weary. "Remember your lessons: we don't do the same thing over and over, in case anyone is monitoring our movements. An observer will think we're not important."

"Oh."

The carriers filed back to the area between the first wall and the second, and the heavy metal gate shut behind them with a thunderous clang. All of the guards except two turned their backs to the box in unison. The remaining pair approached. Yirish scampered down to sit on the bench. Someone tapped on the door. Father unlatched it with a quick flick of his hand, and it swung open slowly, like a servant gesturing at the inner entrance of a fortress, waving the way to a washing bowl. The lad squinted against the light. The pale earthen walls and foot-trammeled ground were all an equal shade of beige, as though made from the same material. For the first time, his eleven-year-old mind put together that each was indeed one form of the other.

The guard looked from boy to man, and Father nodded. Then the guard closed the box door and barked, "All sentries retreat." The guards stomped away to their posts inside the ring, pounding the packed dirt. The third gate creaked open.

"Time to see your grandfather."

The pair stood and left the box. Passing through a bare expanse unpopulated by men or beasts, they approached the tall walls of the innermost fortress. Green plants spilled flowers and a sweet citrus scent along the edge of one wall, which Yirish knew to be the women's quarters, where Mother had grown up. The rest of the building was enclosed by a smooth, high wall, occasionally pierced by square windows near the roofline. Not a single tree or shrub was at ground level.

Father spoke in a low voice, and the boy strained to listen. "See, this is a very defendable position. If anyone attacked, men on the roof would throw spears or rocks onto the attackers."

"Or pour boiling oil on them. Then drop lit torches." Yirish held his head higher as they approached the dark arch of the main door.

"Ah, you have paid some attention to your strategy lessons."

Yirish bit his lip at this backhanded compliment and fought the urge to lower his chin. He blustered forward. "Father, is it true that long ago, people were able to throw spears hundreds of feet?"

Father paused ever so slightly. "Where did you hear that story?"

Ah, he could see a spark of interest. "A legend Grandfather told me." Not certain this was something he should have revealed to his father, Yirish continued with, "That would make warfare very different than now."

"Indeed." He saw the slight muscle twitch in the lip, the slight downward movement. Best to remain silent when Father wore that face. Thankfully, there were only a few more paces to the iron-platted door, which swung open at their approach as if an invisible mechanism recognized them. As they entered the tile-lined open foyer, a male servant came forward, head bowed to avoid the guests' eyes. He offered them a basin of water for their hands and faces. Musicians began playing in the near distance.

They washed their arms and faces, the rose-scented water reminding the blond lad of his mother. Another servant stepped forth, his arms held aloft, a towel draped over each. A human towel stand. The towel bearer too kept his gaze upon their feet.

After they finished their ablutions and dried their hands, a third male servant appeared, brown eyes steady upon theirs. This was Grandfather's trusted man. He led them through the courtyard, past the splashing fountain and the patternless green fabric wall that screened the musicians: a drummer striking soft resonant beats, a fiddler playing long sliding notes, and a harpist strumming a placid cascade of notes. Not a single guard could be seen, but Yirish knew they were watching. Likely Grandfather was too, from above.

Up the wide stone steps to the second floor they went, to a long room with square windows high in the wall. The other end was open to face the courtyard where the musicians' tune droned. On the short end of the room, Grandfather sat at his desk, quill in hand. "Ah, my grandson," he called, replacing the green-feathered plume in its holder. He stood, opening his long arms like an eagle stretching.

Yirish grinned and walked forward for a fond embrace, crushing his cheek against the embossed leather of Grandfather's vest. The old man laughed and squeezed the lad's ribs hard enough to force the air from his lungs. "An enthusiastic greeting. Ah, you are pure love, my boy, a rare, fleeting thing." He patted the lad and released him. For a moment, Yirish felt dizzy, and he lost his footing, grabbing at the desk and bumping a small, gilt-framed painting. It teetered on its tiny stand toward the uncovered inkwell.

"Careful!" thundered Grandfather, catching the artwork with one hand, swift as a hunting bird diving for a mouse. He caught the painting before it fell and with the other hand seized the lad's shoulder to steady him. Yirish turned his head. "I'm most sorry, Grandfather." But the old man wasn't looking at him. Instead he stared at the painting. "By The Powers, you truly are a likeness of your dead grandmother." The boy nearly smirked, having heard this dozens of times. "Isn't he, Sirish?"

Father stepped forward and glanced from the child to the painting, the subject a bright profile against the smooth darkness of the background. "His resemblance to her likeness cannot be denied, General." The older man nodded, released the lad gently, and replaced the painting reverently onto his desk, alongside several small square boxes. "Yes. I hope, my sain, when you and my daughter parent more children, that a girl follows so I may gaze upon her likeness in female form again." He smiled slightly, none of the warmth or love in his voice that he reserved for his grandson.

"That is my wish as well, General. Yirish and I were just discussing the matter in our carrying box."

"Good. Though it would be better for you to pursue it with my daughter. At length." He chuckled. "Now, report, Colonel."

Father glanced at Yirish, who backed away. He dreaded this part of the conversation, though he had worked harder than a slave under a salted whip to please Father. The colonel asked, "Report upon our matters or—"

"The boy."

"The Kaymif master of the short sword has just administered his trials. Yirish performed exceptionally well for a lad nine years from manhood."

Yirish watched Grandfather, whose expression remained neutral as he said, "Excellent."

"He has mastered writing Thislin script and can quill as well as any accomplished adult. The writing master proposes he copy a book and see if a merchant can sell it at a fair price as a final test of his talents."

"Excellent. What requires improvement?"

The words must have been ready in his mouth before the question was asked, for Father replied with rapid diction: "Strategy. Negotiation. Diplomacy." He folded his hands together.

Grandfather looked to the lad, dark eyes narrow behind light eyelashes. "I wasn't very good at strategy when I was eleven." The hint of a grin played at the corners of his mouth. "There is much work for you to do, Yirish."

Yirish snapped his head in salute. "Yes sir. I work to be worthy of our family and our position." It was a rote phrase, much practiced, much used. But to his grandfather, he meant every word with all the innocent conviction a child can muster.

"Good. Now go sit over there while I talk to my colonel." The general squeezed the lad's shoulder, then patted it in dismissal. Yirish darted to the far side of the room, watching as Grandfather lowered himself into his chair. Father walked to the other side of the desk and stood, stiff and wary as a messenger imparting bad news to a lord renowned for slaying messengers. "Report," the general said.

Yirish slipped into the seat of the closest carved chair, still over a dozen feet away. He held himself in a trained meditative pose, elbows on the chair arms, fingertips touching, his face in profile to his sires', eyes straight ahead. But he attended to the men's movements and words, honing his thoughts upon them, pleased that no one told him to move farther away.

Then Father cleared his throat and turned slightly toward him.

"He can't hear us," Grandfather said, though something in his tone made Yirish think he would not mind it if he could. "Report, Colonel."

Father turned back to the head of their family, his voice low. "My Lord General, the experiments for developing long-range weapons have failed. Again. Twelve men lost, including my best engineer, Hamvish."

Grandfather made a sound between a sigh and a moan. "Hamvish was a genius. That is a loss." He paused, and in that pause Yirish felt a breath akin to an accusal. The older man continued, insistent with unspoken command. "You will keep working, Sirish. Find more men. There must be a way. You are the best man to find it." His tone darkened. "Think of how powerful our family would be if we—only we—commanded spears that flew on their own or a machine that hurled rocks long distances. Warfare would change completely; we would be at the helm of that change."

"It would unquestionably seal our position as the most powerful family in Havadra, and the kingship would be…ours." Father lowered his voice further, but the boy could still make out the words. "Yet after nearly a decade of trials, I wonder if there might be some reason, some explanation as to why this task proves impossible. So far."

His mother's father rose slightly in his seat and began, in a gruff tone, "I have thought the same." Then he slid into a confiding voice, empathic and nearly kind. "But Sirish, my sain, you cannot allow this thought to defeat you. Any reasonable man would acknowledge that the setbacks have been many. It is disheartening, but the prize, the prize is higher than we can imagine, if we can attain it. You must not give up."

He reached for his quill. "I will authorize more funds for you. Find more engineers, from other lands. Then, if we are wrong to continue, no more Havadran blood will be spilt. And if we find the way, we will rise above even our own borders." He looked pointedly at Yirish, then spoke loudly, like a man losing his hearing, "Perhaps my grandson can copy your letters of request in his exquisite hand. Yirish, come." He beckoned the boy forward and, turning his gaze back to his sain, said, "May the artistry of Yirish's hand convince the men we require to come to Havadra and work for us. Havadran beauty always astonishes outerlanders." He looked to the portrait of his dead wife and smiled, an expression both cunning and commanding. "Our entire family will work on this project. And reap its rewards."

Marna bent before the sputtering fire in her quarters' fireplace, sifting papyrus fragments and ashes with an iron poker in one pale hand and, with the other, holding over her nose a handkerchief in her son's colors, violet and black. No one would discover the content of the burnt missives now. If only the acrid scent would disperse.

Her gray eyes glancing at the hourglass atop her spacious and freshly tidied desk, she straightened her tired back. "Umpf." She laid the poker beside the carved stone framing the fireplace. How smooth the stones appeared next to the crinkling texture of the pale skin on her hand. She was in her fifth decade now, and perhaps it was time to utilize the moisturizing salves Lady Dara gave her on her last Naming Day. With a slight shake of her long, light locks, she folded the handkerchief into a pocket of her sable-colored smock. Just as the last dark sand grains fled the upper chamber of the hourglass, Marna sat with a thud upon the somber cushions of her chair.

The door on the far end of the long oval room opened, and a dark-haired Apprentice Librarian stepped forward and bowed hastily, in the manner of a shy person wanting to quickly accomplish a task that required others' attention. "The Queen's here to see you, my Lady King's Mother." Her hands fidgeted under her dark violet cloak, broadcasting ripples in the fabric.

The former Queen of Eskalind reached for a wand of fresh Lamorda sprigs tied with a purple velvet ribbon. "How punctual. Show in my son's wife." The Apprentice departed. King's Mother waved the aromatic flowers in the air, dispersing their pleasing rosy citrus fragrance. A new form appeared in the entrance.

"Maither," Damina Queen called in a fond voice from the far end of Marna's Library chambers.

"My dear daighter," Marna replied, lowering the Lamorda and rising from her chair. She came around her desk to greet the petite young woman midway through the long room, where they embraced warmly, the Queen's dark head not even cresting her elder's shoulder. Marna released her daighter and gazed upon the cream-complected beauty's sweet expression. "You look radiant, just as a newly joined bride should."

Damina's smile curved deeper at the compliment, as one would expect from a new Queen with only seventeen years of life behind her. "Thank you." Her smile dimmed as she caught her grammar. She corrected herself to Noble Speech. "I thank you."

"For those of us common born, Noble Speech is difficult to get used to, is it not?" Marna offered, a gentle hand on the petite Queen's arm. She led her daighter past the couches and tables to the chairs alongside the only small table not littered with books and scrolls. "Why, when I first came to Eskalind from my home country of Humiksland, I did not know that in Eskalind no one ever *asks* The Powers for anything. And it is a common expression in Humiksland. Eskalinders thought I had a Gift to say such a thing." She shook her head as the pair sat. "But since you are Eskalind born, that is not a worry for you."

Marna smiled. "I thought you and Dalich would want to spend more time together, since you were reunited and joined only two days ago."

Damina delicately fanned her silk skirt about her legs. "Oh, but we have spent much time together. Our joining night went on forever."

"Hmm, mine passed rather swiftly."

"It is not as though I do not want to spend time with Dalich. I do. Our thought connection was broken for eight long years, a lifetime! But you see, I thought we would spend our joining night in my father's inn. Instead Dalich insisted I lay down my beautiful Mavoldian linen scarf—with the velvet trim, the one you gave me for my sixteenth Naming Day—he wanted me to place it on the ground, outside."

"How odd." King's Mother leaned back in her chair. "Did you?"

"I did *not* want to, but when I did, it became this long, rippling carpet, and we walked onto it, and everything else disappeared—"

"How strange."

Dalich's Queen nodded. "And we stayed there for, I do not know, weeks, months, *forever*, and talked about everything we could think of until we grew tired of … talking."

"That must have been a Gift from The Powers." Marna placed a finger on her lips as she mulled this oddity. Scanning her son's bride's violet gown, which perfectly matched her eyes, she asked, "Damina, I just realized, you had a gown sewn overnight?"

"Aye, Lady Dara was sewing it for her niece. She insisted on altering it to fit me so I would have something suitable for my first full day at King's Halls." The Queen sighed. "Lady Dara is such a lovely, tall, elegant Lady. I hope to be like her when I'm, when I am, old."

Marna turned her head and quirked a smile. Dara was at least five years younger than herself, but she said nothing on the subject. "Well, my daighter, I was surprised you wanted to see me this morning, since you and Dalich arrived only yesterday."

"Oh, but I want to meet everyone and see all of King's Halls, even though I feel I already have been here. Dalich told me everything." Her radiant expression fell slightly. "I do wish he had corrected me more often on using Noble Speech. I still make mistakes."

A knock sounded at the door. "I hope you do not mind," Marna began. "I called for a special tea for us."

"Lovely!"

Marna smiled and turned to reach a nearby bellpull and give it a stout yank.

The door of her chamber creaked open, and an Apprentice Librarian, tunicked in Dalich's morose black, entered. He bore a tray, set with a tea service and laden with many small ceramic canisters, some bearing the King's emblem of parchment and quill. King's Mother gestured to the young man to place the tray on the table. "Bring my mortar and pestle," she commanded, pointing to another table. He rummaged around a stack of books and scrolls before finding the designated items hiding under a loose parchment. He brought them to her. "I thank you. You may go." The Apprentice bowed, sneaking a moonfull glance at his beautiful Queen. Marna could have sworn she heard him sigh as he left the room. Shaking her head, she poured small portions from each canister into the bowl and set to grinding them.

Damina watched intently. "Dalich told me you are a mistress of herbcraft, but everyone knows that. What is it?"

The scent of mint filled the air. "This is a special recipe of my own creation. I hope you will like it."

"I thank you, Maither." She reached for one of the cups and placed it before her, then flicked dainty fingers at the edges of her sleeves for a moment, which reminded Marna of how often her son exhibited the same gesture. The former Lady of Eskalind lifted the bowl, poured its contents into the Queen's cup, and placed the bowl aside. Lifting another canister off the service tray, she spooned its brown powder into her own cup, then poured hot water into each cup. "When the sediment settles, it is ready to drink. A quick stir helps speed the process." She turned a spoon around the inside of her cup.

Her daighter mimicked the action. "Maither, I must tell you, Dalich told me of your secret."

"My secret?" It felt like ice trickled through her brain as her thoughts raced to ascertain how much Dalich knew about the Scholars.

Two of the bells over the entry door sprang on their wires, ringing loudly. Damina nearly dropped her spoon, just as Marna spoke. "Ah, I am sorry about that, but it is the signal that someone special is here.

You were saying?"

"Special? Dalich told me you have very important meetings." Then the new Queen, whispered, "Might whoever it is interrupt?"

Marna nearly smiled at her young daighter's question. "Not until I give the signal. Please, go on."

Damina's voice was a bare whisper, and the Scholars' Mistress cupped a hand to her ear to make out the words. "I meant the secret that is now ours. About Dalich." Marna raised a questioning eyebrow, torn between fear that the Scholars were discovered and the sudden idea that her son had exhibited some unusual Gift on the mysterious scarf. Her daighter whispered, "How The Powers decreed that Dalich cannot leave Eskalind's borders."

Marna exhaled slowly, her eyes on the table, weak with relief. She spoke in a solemn voice. "Yes, dear, it is true. If you can think of any way to make this an easier burden for him to bear..."

The new bride giggled, then said in a husky voice, "I can think of several." The two women laughed riotously. Marna fanned herself as she sought to control her outburst, and Damina said, "See, I knew you would find that funny. Dalich thinks you are still uncomfortable with Eskalinder ways when it comes to bedchamber talk."

"Oh Daighter, that may have been true a long time ago, but I have had many years to adjust." Wiping a tear from her eye, she said, "Now, I think you may have an interest in our awaiting visitor." King's Mother reached behind her to yank the bellpull. A moment later the door swung open and her man entered, straight-backed, a clear gaze in his odd gray eyes, which swept the room as he approached. "My Ladies," he said, and bowed.

"Favik?" The young Queen jumped up to embrace him, and he laughed lightly as he looked over her shoulder to Marna with a "Well, what can I do?" expression.

Damina released him. "It is good to see you, but I am unused to you being this formal."

"When I tutored you, we did not often rehearse our current roles."

"Yes, but I always thought I would join with Dalich."

"That was the fond hope of all of us in this room," Marna said. Eyes on her daighter, she deliberately slurped tea from her cup. "Favik, would you like some tea?"

"I am afraid I cannot stay long." He placed a finger on his cheek for a brief moment, which signaled that he needed to speak to her privately. "There is a matter in the Scriptorium that requires your attention."

"I see." Marna watched as her daighter reached for her own cup and tried a sip of the specially crafted herbal blend. "Do you like it, Damina?"

The young woman nodded. "It is refreshing." She tilted the cup for a larger swallow. "I do like it."

"Aye, it is best drunk when fresh, though I am afraid I must be off with Favik in a moment." Marna stood and waded to her desk. She lifted one of books neatly stacked upon it. "Favik, I promised Palika I would bring her that copy of Haarshil I loaned you when next I returned to the Scriptorium. You know the volume. Will you help me find it?" She turned to the closest table and leafed though some loose papyrus sheets and scrolls. Finding a book she thought she had returned to the Library, she grasped it, then realized how still the room felt. She looked back at Damina. The Queen stared into the center of the room as though transfixed by something invisible.

"Daighter?"

The young woman did not respond.

Favik bent closer to Damina, and she twitched. "I'm sorry, no, *I am* sorry. Dalich asked me if I wanted to tour the gardens with him." The new Queen rose to her feet in one smooth motion as though some outer force had propelled her. "He's done, um, he *is* done with his council meeting sooner than he expected. Saril was quite surprised he made an appearance. Will I see you both at dinner in the Great Hall?" She blinked her violet eyes at Favik.

"Certainly, my Lady," and he nodded his loose blond locks.

"Maither?"

"Of course, dear child."

"Till then." She skipped out of the room, the door a gentle thud behind her.

Marna raised a gray eyebrow at her man.

"Well, my Lady, it appears their ability to speak to each other in thought has returned."

"Clearly." She walked to a library basket on the nearest window seat and placed the book in it. "How do you find her?"

"Amiable as ever, but she will require more practice in Noble Speech."

The former Queen of Eskalind sat. "Damina has been a royal for two days. At least, by our reckoning." She smirked, thinking of the scarf she had given Damina the year before that had apparently been Gifted by The Powers. "I hope she feels comfortable and free to make mistakes around us." The slight scold in her tone was clear. "I thank The Powers she is at ease with me. After the long months of Dalich's despondency, I welcome her open heart. I had thought it might be awkward between us, till we became better acquainted, but that is not the case."

Favik tilted his chin downward in agreement, then touched the Queen's teacup. "An odd-smelling brew. Might I ask what it was?"

"A concoction to mature her body."

"What, my Lady?"

"Just look at her—she has the bosom and hips of a girl, not a woman. If she were to already be with child, she would never survive childbed. And Dalich would collapse into his pit of despair again." Marna leaned into her pillows, then pulled back to examine them, for something had poked her painfully in the back. Finding the culprit, a large tassel that had broken free of its threads and draped itself in the middle of her pillow, she flung it away and reclined peacefully. "I am getting too old, too tired to run both this country and the Scholars. I pronounce that in this fifth month of 2912, it is the young people's turn." The Scholars' Mistress smiled. "To run the country. Come, come, sit, Favik. I am assuming this nonsense about the Scriptorium was a ruse."

"Indeed." Her man lowered himself onto the cushions and turned to face her. "I am curious what to make of last night, when Lady Saralya's young daughter squelched the flame in the air?"

Marna's eyes darted to the dead fire; it seemed an ember flickered. She held up a pale hand to stay speech, her index finger stained with dark ink that no amount of soap and scrubbing could remove. More than once she had been asked if she had burned herself. "Best not to speak of that now. Tell me, have you any Scholarly business to relate?"

His lips tightened for the barest of moments, but he said nothing to acknowledge her dismissal of his question. Placing his stubby-fingered hands together, palms facing, Favik made the gesture of opening a book. "Knowledge knows no borders, my Lady Bladesmith's Daughter."

"What news have you?"

"Scholar Lord Radil reports that two of his acquaintances, both Builders, have been contacted by the Havadrans to ply their craft in Havadra." He raised his blond eyebrows slightly. "The details of the project seem secret, as the letters of inquiry mention only salary and skills required, but no explanation as to the project's scope."

"Odd. Which faction of the Havadrans? Their current ruler or one of the rival families?"

Favik's lips pursed slightly. "Colonel Sirish."

"Sirish—"

"You know of his faither, General Yirlofts."

"Ah, the general. The only man in Havadra wise enough to not rise to the loftiest position in that viperous country." Marna studied the diamond-shaped windowpanes, the lower section of smoky glass up to the height of a person, for privacy, the upper panes clear but for stretched bubbles that sparkled in the sunlight and cast muted light upon the scroll and bookshelves on the opposite side of the room. "Hmm. Scholar Deenofts told me the colonel is joined to a daughter of the general, but is Sirish working for the general or himself? And any idea what this secret project is?"

"Speculation"—for a moment there was a hitch in Favik's voice, then he continued—"on both fronts. The letters were signed by Sirish. The only other fact via our Scholarly sources is that the previous chief engineer was killed experimenting with applying tension to sturdy twine. A strand broke, cutting him across the neck and nearly severing his head. A gruesome and most odd death. Difficult to believe."

The former Queen shook her head. "Not to me."

Favik looked surprised. She sat up and leaned toward him, speaking quietly as one who imparts a grave truth. "There is a secret Legend scroll that tells how, long ago, people had means of hurling spears and rocks great distances. They made fire that erupted at will. That is, until The Powers prevented such weaponry." She studied his face as he listened to her, his gray eyes, rimmed with a deep blue, intent. "Since then, anyone who strives to rediscover a way to make such weapons dies in the attempt. By the Will of The Powers." Marna glanced again to the fireplace, but saw neither flicker nor light.

Her man spoke. "The Havadrans would not want word of this to reach engineering recruits."

She chuckled. "No, but it may be that word that these weapons are possible has reached the Havadrans." She gave him her gaze. "Favik, years ago, whilst my dear Dalock still lived and not long after you were sent to Havadra as an Apprentice Ambassador, a Havadran delegation visited Dalock here, in his Halls. When they left, the Legend scroll I just mentioned was missing. Dalock had been reading it in his chambers, and then it disappeared, though no Guards saw the Havadrans climb the steps to Dalock's quarters." She shook her head. "That scroll has never been found."

Her man looked thoughtful. "Hmm, I recall that in Havadra our Ambassador Hornil made inquiries about a scroll before he died, but he never gave me details."

King's Mother's lips set in a hard line. "When Hornil died and you became Ambassador, Dalock did not want you to pursue the matter. I am not certain why. We disagreed about that." She rotated her right wrist so the strands of garnet beads draped around it vanished back under her sleeve. "Did you ever meet the general?"

Favik nodded. "It's many years since I saw him. He was a man who radiated power and control, though in private he was congenial and seemed to truly find a personal interest in me." He tapped his fingertips together. "General Yirlofts has a quality about him that can draw a person's confidence. As a trained Ambassador, I was keenly aware of his allure. Do you remember, when I was recalled to Eskalind, there was some question that Dalock King's summons letter had been tampered with—"

"I do."

"When I left Havadra, the general's departing words to me were, 'Thank you for your service.' Odd, as Havadrans never thank anyone for fulfilling their appointments."

"Maybe you did him some service you were unaware of." At this, Favik looked at her for just a moment, as though he readied himself to say something—perhaps a disavowal of having any hand in the scroll's disappearance. But in the blink of an eye, his expression resumed the steadiness of the consummate Eskalind Ambassador he was, though he had not served as such since she made him her sole Queensman over a decade ago. Now, as King's Mother, she could no longer call him such. She reached for his fingers and with both hands brought his open palms together. "I may require you to go back to Havadra and be my eyes there. I realize it is much to ask."

He smiled, and again Marna felt a secret significance. "If the Bladesmith's Daughter asks this of me, I will go." She squeezed his hands. "Though perhaps, my Lady," he said, "our Scholar Deenofts would, as a Havadran, draw less attention than this long-nosed, gray-eyed northerner."

The former Queen released his hands and leaned back, hearing a popping sound in her back. "I thank you, Favik. Your idea is sound. I will send Deenofts." Raising herself to stand with a small "Umpf," she continued, "Now, to keep up your Scriptorium ruse, I shall go there and also return a book to my niece."

Deenofts's sister Samathe raised her her blond-ringleted head from behind her painter's easel, brown eyes lit with joyous recognition. "My brother, here, in Capitola, in our very own fortress?" She dashed her paint-stained oversmock to the floor and rose to embrace him. "What a wonderful surprise!"

Deenofts chuckled as they hugged, feeling her wrists, but not her fingers, press against his back. "My ever cautious sister, not wanting to besmirch my robes with your paints."

They released one another and she smiled, the same smug expression she had bestowed upon him when he was a child and she'd played a trick on him that he had not yet discovered. Then Samathe reached up and swiped a finger across the tip of his short nose. "Oh, poor little brother. You will need a mirror to find out what color your nose is."

"Or," he said, making a grab for her hand. Samathe backed away, laughing like the teenager she had been some decades earlier, eluding him as always. She grabbed a clean rag by her easel and wiped her hands. With an adept flip, she flung the rag behind a large flowerpot in the corner. There it landed, perhaps to be found later by a puzzled maid.

"Sit and tell me everything." His elder sister beckoned him to the two chairs flanking a small table. "I have been lonely of late, alone in this fortress. Father has been away two months; he left in the fifth month for army duties."

"And our brother?" They both sat.

"The same, though he departed in the fourth month. Three months without him, and I am not complaining."

More than inclined to agree, Deenofts swept a glance at the back of her easel. "You appear to have work."

Samathe raised her hands in a broad gesture. "What do you think pays for all this?"

"Blue," he replied.

"What?"

"The finger you touched me with is blue. Therefore, my nose must be blue."

She leaned back in her chair, thin lips stretched in a smirk below her small nose as he leaned toward her. He continued in conspiratorial tones, "And yes, blue and red and beige and all the colors on your palette provide richly for the men of this family."

Sitting straight, he cleared his throat as if to make a solemn pronouncement. "Yes, dear sister, I acknowledge, as our father and brother should if they have not done so already, that your income keeps this household in the fine manner to which it has grown accustomed."

"You always were my favorite brother."

"That reminds me." He reached into his robes and retrieved a small, sealed envelope. "The fur of a Nordak lemix. Perfect for brush making. Finest quality, smooth as air." He placed it atop the table between them. "In a variety of lengths."

She reached for the envelope, her eyes on his. "Your status is not bound to change."

"Careful, careful when opening it. They are very lightweight and the slightest breath will scatter them." Here he sighed. "I speak as the voice of, ahem, experience."

"Oh Deenofts. You are the life in my days."

He wagged a finger. "Hold your praise. That envelope may be empty."

Her jaw dropped, and he winked. They both laughed, then she rose.

"I will call for food and sweet wine."

"Excellent." He pushed away a long strand of his straight blond hair and placed his hands in his lap. Samathe rose and returned to her easel, flipping its side arms around the painting, then unfurling the privacy cloth to drape over the structure, thus shrouding the image.

"Someday I may let you see one of my commissions, but not today." She lifted and rang the clangorous serving bell, then returned to sit by him.

"Sister, you are assuming I would want to break our land's customs and see these fine ladies that you paint," he teased, not certain how loud he was speaking, as he felt temporarily deafened.

Samathe fixed him with a steel gaze, but the corner of her mouth rose slightly.

At the sound of the latch turning, she resumed the neutral, passionless demeanor of a Havadran woman of standing speaking with what Havadrans called the household whore. Unrelated women and men in Havadran households were kept separate, and only the whore of the household could properly traverse and communicate between the two. Deenofts's brother found other uses for the poor woman. There were a myriad of reasons Deenofts did not relish visiting his homeland. But his mission was of great importance to Lady Marna, and perhaps the world.

The veiled servant entered the room, received her instructions, and left, only to return with a large platter of refreshments: bowls of dried and spiced fruits, cured meats crusted with seasonings, and a clear, silver-handled glass ewer sloshing with sweet wine. Deenofts raised an appraising eyebrow at the fineness of the silver chasing, the small squares dotting the handle in a precise march of pattern. He wondered how many trials the silversmith had spent reworking the line to attain such exactitude. Samathe's smile hinted there was more to come, which indeed followed when the servant placed before them two clear glasses, each in the bulbous form of a tulip flower and footed in silver, with a smaller, but equally fine, rendition of the pattern on the ewer.

As she raised the ewer to pour, he lightly touched the fabric covering her arm and asked, "Might I trouble you to tell me what color my nose is?"

The woman paused, though he caught no hint of her expression behind her mesh veil. "Reddish."

"A single patch?"

"No, like one who has been much in the sun."

Deenofts fixed his sister with a saucy look, which she ignored.

The beverages poured, the servant made to leave, but her mistress made one last request. "Have the fiddler play. Outside the door, behind a screen."

"Yes, fine lady." She departed.

Deenofts raised his glass, tapping the polished base. "Exquisite."

"And I attained them at a good price." The strains of the musician's tune began just beyond the door behind him.

"Your bargaining skills put me to shame."

"Ha." She sipped the wine. "So tell me, where have you been?"

"Here and there, and now I am here again. Do you know exactly where our father and brother are stationed?"

His sister waved her free hand as if swatting a fly. "Please. Those two never tell me anything."

"I understand completely. Well, I made inquiries the length of Havadra from Eskalind to here, with no success."

"You made the overland journey from Eskalind, through the desert?"

"And yet, arrived safely at your door, five hundred miles later." The Scholar dipped his head. Samathe shook her blond locks and frowned. Deenofts continued, "Of course, we have military camps along the southern coast, en route to Guerland, which is where I will journey next on business. I will inquire after our menfolk along the way."

"Well, at least that is a safer route than traversing the breadth of our land." She paused. "Guerland. Will you visit our aunt, or are you adding salt to your trade?" She laughed and flipped her wrist. "Ah, your business, my procurer of rare animal furs and unusual dyes for paints. You may go where you please." She sipped her wine again, then launched into, "I must tell you something now, while the fiddler plays. It's a mystery and a pain in my heart." Samathe drew closer to the table. "Oh Deenofts, do you remember my painting mentor?"

"I never met her, of course, but you told me she was marvelous teacher, a kindred spirit, a great influence."

His sister nodded, her eyes on her goblet. "All that and more."

He wondered what she would reveal, but her silence seemed complete. "I know you miss her terribly."

"I do." More silence. He reached across the table and touched her hand. "Careful," she said. "You may get blue on you. Or reddish." Her teasing lacked enthusiasm. He withdrew his hand.

"Samathe, you need not say more if it is a pain to you."

His sibling raised her brown eyes to his. "But you are the only one I can tell." She lowered her silver-footed glass onto the table. "I was hired to mutilate one of her paintings."

"Mutilate?" He kept his voice low.

"It's how it felt. The actual request was to alter an existing portrait of a deceased woman, because," her voice dropped in pitch, "she did not look how she was remembered." Samathe cleared her throat. "To change a normal-looking woman into a long-nosed, gray-eyed oddity." As she spoke, she bobbed her head as if mocking someone else's manner. "Oh, but the eyes had to have blue encircling the iris." A short pause. "Deenofts, are there people who truly look like that?"

There was no point in naming Favik specifically, so the Scholar replied, "I have never seen a woman like that, but with my own eyes I have seen a man. He was born in Humiksland. Maybe most Humikslanders look like that."

Samathe shook her head, her eyes glassy, and he thought it best to say nothing more, to let her continue, lest he stopper her outpouring.

"Oh Brother, I would have denied ... denied the commission, if I could, but they tricked me into thinking it was a normal portrait session. And the family is *too* powerful. The head of the household himself ordered the work."

His eyebrows rose in surprise that she had met directly with a man. It went against all Havadran mores, and the carefully negotiated rules of her trade. Deenofts wordlessly mouthed, *The king?*

She looked him in the eyes, and her lips silently moved in the shape of words: *The general.*

Aloud he asked, soft but insistent. "Were you harmed?"

She retrieved her goblet, swirling the amber liquid. "Not physically." He rose slightly in his seat; Samathe reached to stay him. "You must understand, asking me to butcher her work was like a knife in my heart. I wept for days, I could not work afterward." She held the goblet at an angle that threatened to pour wine onto her robes.

He gestured to it as he spoke. "Yet you completed the commission."

His sister righted the glass so it would not spill, breathing a reluctant, "I did."

"And you still have work."

"Much."

He neglected to say what he thought—that her alterations must have found favor with the general.

"One more thing, Brother. Not long thereafter, I worked on"—she leaned forward to whisper—"a double portrait. Mother and son." She leaned away, smiling. He could not restrain his eyebrows from puckering. "No, no, you know it is against our custom for me to paint a man. I painted the female side of the painting. The male's side was covered. But," and she pointed to her eye.

"And?"

She motioned him close, leaning forward and whispering in his ear, her breath hot as it was quiet. "A boy, maybe twelve, thirteen. His eyes, his nose, he looks *exactly* like the altered woman. His mother is wife to Colonel Sirish." Samathe leaned back, her chin dipped and a light in her eyes as she waited for him to put two and two together.

All of Havadra knew that years ago, Colonel Sirish had attempted a coup against General Yirlofts. To the amazement of their countrymen, the general, rather than eliminating Sirish, had combined forces with him by joining a daughter of his house to the colonel. It was one of the rare bits of family gossip that had percolated into the public sphere.

Deenofts pursed his lips, considering this information, and feeling as though a stone sank in his heart. For if the general discovered that Samathe knew his grandson looked like the altered portrait of his wife, her career, and likely her life, would end abruptly. And if Colonel Sirish knew his wife's mother did not in fact look like his odd-eyed son, he might question his son's parentage. Havadra could face another civil war.

He asked lightly, "Samathe, have you heard of the beauty of the new Eskalind Queen?"

"No, why do you ask?"

He could not help but smile. "I am hatching a plot to get you out of—" He swirled a finger in the air.

"What? Who says I want to go?"

He raised both eyebrows. "If you came to Eskalind with me, I am *certain* I could obtain a commission for you to paint their Queen." Let Samathe wonder how close his connections were to an Eskalinder royal. "An exquisite beauty she is, hair dark as a starless night, flawless pale skin, and the crowning glory of her face are eyes the color of"—he reached into his sleeve and pulled forth a capped glass vial of powdered amethyst—"this." Deenofts placed it on the table.

Samathe grinned. "I wondered what that lump in your sleeve was." She scooped the vial into her free hand and admired the color. "Your plan is for me to use this pigment for her portrait."

"No, I thought we could use it to bribe the inevitable bandit along the way."

She looked cross and sipped her wine. "I am not going anywhere, Brother. Traveling is most unsafe for a woman. Besides, my life is here, in Capitola, where there are so many fine ladies who want portraits."

His sister plunked the vial on the table.

He wondered how true that would be if what she had whispered to him were discovered. "You would have a comfortable life in Eskalind, and once you paint their Queen, all the noble houses—there are dozens—will be clamoring for you to paint their women. And men."

"I will *not* paint men."

"You painted me."

"Only because you are my brother, and it was before you were a full man of twenty, so it doesn't count." His sibling placed her emptied glass on the table and glanced at the full measure in his. "Deenofts, this is a fine vintage." He acknowledged her prodding with a nod and sipped as she spoke again. "How long will you stay?"

"Sadly, not long."

"Ah."

"I have some business to conduct here, some inquiries, but it may only be a few days."

Samathe stood, turning away. "Then I will make certain your room is prepared." She pulled her veil over her head and exited the room as swiftly as though a nonfamilial man had entered it. Deenofts sighed, long and loud and burning with frustration, for he knew she would not easily be swayed to leave.

Perhaps The Powers had directed her thus. Lady Saralya stood expectant, an ovoid cup of tea in her deep brown hands, gazing out a tall window overlooking the rust-colored gravel lane that led from the distant main road through her estate to the entrance of her house.

Outside, nothing more awaited the Lady than sunlight glimmering off the chestnut-toned leaves of her crimson-barked tree, unique in Eskalind and given pride of place at the center of the entrance courtyard. In Spring and the warmer months, when leaves were full, it was a natural embodiment of her noble house's colors.

The tree seemed taller than she recalled, though perhaps she had not given it much attention of late. Between Saralya's lively young daughter skipping through the passageways and her grandson discovering his voice, one could not describe the household as sedate. Hard to believe the pair were normally that boisterous as she watched them now, rounding the stone path into her view. Little Lord Kaloft sat upright in his babe cart, pushed by his Nurse with young Lady Jinilya alongside, brown fingers of one hand possessive on the wicker basket, the other hand smoothing a strand of her long black hair back into the scarlet band crowning her head.

Then the eight-year-old's attention snapped toward the road, and

Saralya, still sipping her tea, the bright scent of mint concentrated by the egg shape of the cup, looked for what drew her daughter's gaze.

The trio on the pathway paused just outside the elder Lady's window, and her daughter raised a hand to point. A rider, approaching, upon a gray gelding, which immediately marked him as not associated with her estate. For her noble house preserved the colors of Dalock King, the brown and the red, or the mud and the blood, as he had once said to her. Preserved too in her house were his symbols, the sword and the book, invented by his Queen, who was now known as Marna, King's Mother.

The distortions in the glass obscured the rider's features, and Saralya turned the window latch and opened it for a clearer view just as he dismounted and bowed with a flourish to the children. The distinct small nose and prominent brow marked him as the sole Havadran amongst her fellow Scholars. Deenofts.

Following Eskalinder custom, the Havadran addressed them in echelon order, his voice carrying clearly to Saralya's ears. "My Lady Jinilya, my Lord Kaloft, and Nurse." He inclined his head toward each in turn.

"Well met, Deenofts of Havadra." Jinilya spoke as properly as a Lady twice her age. A groomsman dashed into view, and the Scholar passed the reins of his horse to him. Deenofts approached the trio as Jinilya came to the other side of the babe cart, half facing Deenofts and half facing the window where her mother watched. "Have you come to see Mother?"

"Indeed, I have." As the groom led the horse away, Deenofts bowed his head to the girl. "You are most perceptive and wise, young Lady."

The studious expression in her daughter's green eyes struck Saralya in her heart, for in it she saw the fond face of her late husband. The child said, "I do not think it is wise to call a girl of eight years wise. It goes against the meaning of the word."

"You prove my point." From her vantage not ten feet away, Saralya heard the smile in Deenofts's voice.

"Da," squeaked the babe.

"Well said, my kind Lord." He patted Kaloft's shock of dark hair. "Now I must hasten inside."

The Nurse said, "I will announce you." She pushed the babe cart toward the main door.

"Deenofts," Jinilya raised herself on her toes and touched his arm to stay him. "Can you settle a matter for me?"

"I will do my best." He turned to face her and bent his knees, bringing him closer to her eye level. Saralya smiled as she watched their interaction.

"When we were both at court, when the royals joined—"

"You waited nearly a year to ask me? Young Lady, you have the patience of a Records Keeper. Why, you are even standing like one, on your toes. Have you decided upon a career as such?"

Her daughter's smooth brow knit and she lowered her heels. "This is the first we have spoken alone. I overheard some people talking—"

"Ah, you have discovered the best thing to do at court, besides eating and drinking. Oh and people-watching. And comparing the latest fashions."

The girl looked confused but charged onward. "Please, I have been waiting a long time to ask you. People said Kaloft was a Havadran name." Saralya wondered who had said that to her daughter, as the child asked, "Is that true?"

The Havadran narrowed his brown eyes. "It's your nephew's name, and he is an Eskalinder, like you."

"No. I mean aye, he is, but they said it sounded like a Havadran name."

"Tsk tsk, no no, young Lady." Standing to his full height, he waved his hands in the air as though he were a traveling player addressing a large crowd. "Those people have no idea what a Havadran name sounds like. Why, a true Havadran father would never name his son Kaloft. That is a good, strong, Eskalinder name. Lots of hard sounds with that *K* and that sharp *T* ending. Kal-oft!" On his lips it sounded like a military command.

Softening, Deenofts continued. "Havadrans, surprisingly, like softer sounds. *S*'s and *F*'s and endings like *-ofts* and *-ish* and so forth, so we can hiss." He shook his head vigorously. "I wonder how many Havadrans those gossips have met?" He lowered his gaze to face her. "Let me ask this, my little Lady. Next we are at King's Halls together, do point those people out to me, and I will educate them on this matter. Gently of course, and in a manner that does not tell, in any way, of your involvement. Most discreetly."

"You can be discreet?" Her daughter's voice rose with disbelief, carrying no hint that she realized the insult in her utterance.

"In important matters, such as defending your family, and Eskalind, yes. Very discreet." His eyes swung toward Saralya, observing from the open window, as though he had known she was there all along and chose this moment to acknowledge her. In his brown-eyed gaze was the sudden seriousness that was a hallmark of his personality and his fidelity to their Lady Marna's cause. Lady Saralya nodded in acknowledgment. Turning, she passed into her library and receiving chamber, telling a servant along the way to show in her visitor immediately.

Saralya had barely placed her teacup upon her desk on the far end of the oval room when the double door opened and Deenofts entered. He closed the red-lacquered doors and faced her.

"Acta Sua of this house and Lady Reader to our Lady Marna." He bowed his blond head low as though addressing that royal personage herself.

"Deenofts, I apologize on behalf of my young daughter for meeting your generosity with distrust." He raised his head, and Saralya beckoned him forward. He walked toward the middle of the room across a caramel-colored carpet ringed with interwoven patterns of *M*'s and *D*'s along its curving border

"Ah, thank you, my Lady." As he approached, he lowered his eyes and inclined his head, an aura of stillness, perhaps even resignation, about him. "I must say, your daughter does indeed possess your great beauty." He stopped before her.

"It must be rare for a woman of nearly fifty years to receive such praise on her appearance."

"Ah, dear Lady Reader, the stars are of countless years, and yet they glimmer brightly through the ages." He raised his brown eyes to her, in sudden seriousness. "I have just come from Guerland, directly from your blood cousin, the Merchant Master, discerner of truthfulness."

Saralya reflexively chewed her bottom lip. "You made the land journey from Havadra?"

"No, a most safe journey by sea. At our Lady Marna's behest, I departed for Havadra just after Dalich King and his Queen joined. After many, many months of fruitless research in my homeland, I sailed to Guerland, met with your blood cousin, then sailed to Gergelt and made the land journey from Gergelt to your door. A smooth passage, I assure you. Though I was threatened with dying of boredom on the road via Gergelt. But that is to be expected."

The half-Guerish woman smoothed the ruby-hued silk of her skirt. "Thank The Powers you are safe. How fares my blood cousin Kermon, and what news?"

Deenofts sprang to life, eyes bright. "He is as well as any man of, what, sixty that I have ever seen. And his ears are as sharp as ever." The Scholar raised his blond eyebrows and opened his palms before him as though they were the pages of a book. The Lady repeated the secret hand gesture of their order.

In unison they said quietly, "Knowledge knows no borders."

The Havadran began. "Our Merchant Master reports massive orders for kevelian twine from the eastern lands, and also orsblat wood, are filtering through Guerland to Havadra."

"Orsblat?"

"A tree that grows only in the far southern regions and is noted for both the strength and flexibility of its branches. A most unusual combination. Transport of both goods is purposefully being routed to skirt the Havadran capital, but otherwise it moves along the major caravan routes." He snorted. "I can imagine bandits finding those wares not worth the effort to steal."

"Goods are not all Havadran bandits plunder." Saralya's vocal cords tensed.

"Sadly true, dear Lady. Your blood cousin Kermon also told me he observed trade negotiations for supplies by a dozen engineers from the southern lands. They gathered in his town to await a caravan transport into Havadra. They were only gone a week, and despite never seeing the Herald, bandits ambushed them and, finding few goods worth stealing, slaughtered all but one engineer, who escaped. The survivor managed to return, giving his report before perishing of exhaustion."

Lady Saralya nodded her head slowly. "I am sadly familiar with this abominable situation. My mother was killed in a caravan traversing Havadra. We never saw the Herald either. They were just … upon us." She paused. Never had she told anyone a single detail beyond that, for she had been sworn, before she returned to Eskalind, to never speak of what happened. Though it often entered her thoughts to write of it. "As you can see, I survived."

"My Lady Reader, I am most sorry. I had no idea."

"It was a lifetime ago. Please, continue. It will distract my thoughts."

"As you wish." He leaned close, tipping his forehead toward her, his voice just above a whisper. "Kermon discovered that Colonel Sirish of Havadra is directing experiments with these odd materials. Sirish's builders have tried other materials in the past to no avail. It seems our Lady Marna was right in thinking that they are trying to create new weapons."

"By The Powers, I hope they do not meet with success."

"So far, my Lady, they have not." Deenofts's eyes scanned her face. He inhaled dramatically. "Kermon also says that this is all being done under—who else—the tutelage of General Yirlofts." The Havadran Scholar raised himself to his full height. "I even encountered news of outerlanders and Eskalinders with knowledge of building and materials being recruited."

The Acta Sua nodded. "When I was last at court, I met a Nordak engineer on his way to Havadra, though he would not divulge why he journeyed there."

"Now, what assistance could an ice stone miner lend in weapons creation?"

Saralya shook her head at the Havadran's joke about Nordak's most well-known profession. "I do not know, but perhaps there is some knowledge that may carry from mining ice stones to the potential creation of weaponry."

"Or," Deenofts paused, sneering, "they are getting desperate." He leaned close again. "Kermon fears they are, that this operation has been going on for many years, and that Colonel Sirish grows tired of this endeavor. Adding speculation to speculation, he fears the colonel will plot against the general again, as he did thirteen years ago in 2900."

"Which could destabilize Havadra."

"A fearsome thought. The general has kept the public unrest that was prevalent in my younger years to a minimum. Only when there's a change of kingship, now, does Havadra see much bloodletting, but nothing like the riots and blood baths in Capitola when I was a youth." He leaned back as though about to laugh. "There's a good reason Havadrans live in fortresses."

"May The Powers protect your people from such terrors." The Acta Sua shook her head. "I will see that these words reach our Lady." Her fellow Scholar nodded and closed his palms. She did the same. "I thank you for your news. Now, Deenofts, you must be hungry. Would you like bread and sauces and tea? Will you stay the night?"

Deenofts dipped his head. "You are most generous. Yes, I would enjoy your hospitality, Lady Saralya."

"Please, sit wherever you would like." The Acta Sua went to the bellpull and yanked the sequence for refreshments while the Havadran Scholar sat.

"And I do have some personal letters for your house from Kermon," he said, and he reached inside his tunic vest and retrieved several letters.

"So many!" She accepted them, sat, and quickly leafed through the envelopes. "How sweet, a note for each member of my house, even wee Kaloft."

"Belated First Naming Day greetings, I believe." She was aware that he studied her. "Lady Saralya, if I might ask one more thing?"

"Yes?"

"That exquisite red-barked tree growing in your front courtyard. Such a lovely shade! Would it be too much, too forward of me to ask for a small sample of the bark? Nothing that would harm the tree or even be in the slightest bit noticeable. I only ask as I think it might yield a most unusual and pleasing shade of red. Why, it may even save you the trouble of purchasing red inks from merchants such as myself if it proves a good source. It is growing right at your front door."

Saralya waved a hand. "Alas, Deenofts, while the bark is red, it does not give a red color when processed. My daighter's dressmaker tried to use the tree bark as a dye, and it shocked us all to learn that when immersed in hot water, the bark yields a most intense shade of green."

"Oh, how disappointing. Entirely unsuitable for your house." He tsk-tsked and shook his head. A knock at the door sounded.

The Lady called, "Come in." A servant entered, pushing a cart laden with breads and sauces and a tea service. "Please set it by me." He did as she bid, and Saralya turned back to her guest as the servant departed. "Still, you may find the bark useful to your trade. You have my leave to harvest a small quantity and see how the shade suits you." She reached for the tea canisters.

The Havadran bowed in his seat. "Thank you, Lady Saralya."

She spooned tea into each cup. "If it is a marketable color, perhaps we can come to an ongoing agreement. The tree is unique in Eskalind." She smiled but tempered her voice. "Our Lady King's Mother, whilst Queen, was granted a seedling too, but it did not survive the transplant." She poured hot water into each cup. "By The Powers, I was surprised, as she has a Gift with herbs and plants."

"How odd. Well, I would welcome the opportunity to sample a bit of the bark. I will use the utmost care to not damage this precious specimen." He dipped a spoon into his cup.

"And Deenofts…" The Lady leaned across the table toward him, and he stopped stirring. "When you next see the Bladesmith's Daughter, tell or show her of this unusual property of the tree. She may find it valuable knowledge."

"I will share with our Lady as you bid, even if I must cross many borders between now and then to bring her such knowledge." The Havadran smiled and saluted her with his teacup.

Marna paced the carpets of her Library office. "Well, Favik, this letter from Saralya is…" Her spoken words trailed off as the written message before her dominated her thoughts.

Perhaps a minute later, her patient man asked, "What does your Lady Reader impart?"

Favik standing before her, King's Mother settled into the chair behind her desk, her eyes lowered to the glossy red ink shining on the papyrus. "Our Havadran Scholar has news from Scholar Kermon in Guerland." She laid the bleached-brown letter atop the sable smock covering her lap. "The Havadrans are secretly pursuing a way to build weapons that fly through the air." Her demeanor darkened. "By The Powers, just as the Legend scroll told of, long ago. If only that scroll had not gone missing."

"Have the Havadrans been successful?"

"I imagine we would have heard from other sources by now if they had. Then again, Havadra is a very closed society."

"Indeed. I have some evidence of that myself."

The former Queen raised an eyebrow at this insinuation and invited him to sit.

He settled across from her and spoke: "I just received a letter from

Havadra, written by an Eskalind Builder. He claims he is held against his will there." Her man unfolded a heavily textured papyrus from inside his tunic and handed it to her. The black ink was smudged across the thick veins in the page, but still readable, in the flowing script of an Eskalinder.

> *4th Day, 4th Month, 2913*
> *Former Ambassador Favik,*
> *I am writing you in desperation. I am a Builder and answered a call to come to Havadra to assist in constructing a new palace for their king. For a year I am held here, wanting to return home to Eskalind, unpaid and poorly looked after. I have written pleas to Ambassador Moril at our Embassy in Capitola, but no relief or response has arrived. It is my hope that this note will reach you through subtle means. I beg The Powers that you or others of our countrymen will find a way to rescue me and the other Eskalinders trapped here.*
> *Livyak of Eskalind*

Marna pondered. "This raises many questions. First, Livyak is a very odd name for an Eskalinder, if he was born here."

"It is a backward spelling of Kayvil."

She smiled at this simple ruse. "An Eskalinder name. That solves one puzzle. Hmm, perhaps this supposed palace building was truly weapons building." She paused. "He does not say where he is being held, or who the other Eskalinders are."

"Nor does he bid us send word to any family members."

"If he is smuggling a note out via secret means, he may not want to explicitly mention any names, even his own, for fear of this note falling into his captors' hands."

"My Lady, why did he write specifically to me? Lord Saril, King's Second, was also once Ambassador to Havadra."

"Many puzzles. What do you propose to do?"

"First, find any information on this Kayvil of Eskalind."

"If you require any assistance with the Records Keepers, I hold sway over them. They scatter like children caught pilfering sweets when I enter their office."

Favik grinned. The former Queen glanced to the windows. "We will require eyes and ears in Havadra to discover more. If Havadra succeeds in making new weapons, we must know immediately. And if Kayvil is genuine, he must be found, rescued, and interviewed. Our Havadran Ambassador should be alerted. But." Here she waited. "Favik, no one else knows of this letter?"

"I have shared it with no one but you, my Lady, but it was not a sealed letter, it was merely folded many times. Others may have read it along its passage to my hands."

"Hmm. As he wrote to you in your capacity as a former Ambassador, the King, or the King's Second, must decide what is to be done." She faced him. "It is not just a matter for our Scholars, though we must now focus our attention on learning more about Havadran engineering."

"Of course, my Lady."

The bell signals rang, startling her. "By The Powers. That is the sequence for my son. Ah, or his Second." With a dexterous flip of her wrist, she sailed Saralya's letter into an open drawer, slid it shut, then rose to reach the bellpulls. She rang her acceptance, though her nerves tingled at the timing of this unexpected visit. She could not help but think The Powers were at work. "You know, Favik, I see more of Saril than Dalich. Usually Saril's visits are as my son's representative, and so I gave them the same signal." She smiled through her teeth as King's Second entered the room, his dark eyes making immediate notice of her man, who rose from his seat.

"My Lady. And former Ambassador." Saril bowed to her, a neutral, calm expression across his brown lips. It reminded her of his late father, a master diplomat and her husband's closest advisor, but not her favorite subject. The young man approached.

As Favik made his deference to Lord Saril, Marna rose, saying, "Saril, what timing you have. A letter pouch from your Lady mother just arrived." She walked toward one of the tables in the middle of the room.

"Of this, I am aware, my Lady," the dark-haired man said, in the manner of one who wants all to know that little slips his notice. King's Mother approached and embraced him, then gestured for him to sit nearby as she lifted a stack of three letters from the side table. Favik stood watching near her desk.

"Hmm, this one is for you from your mother, and another from your young sister—my, Jinilya's script is coming along nicely—and the last is for the Queen from your saister Athla. Would you like all of them, or should I have someone deliver Athla's letter for Damina?"

Saralya's son leaned back slightly; one of the broad curls in his hair shifted in the movement, "I have business with Dalich King in his chambers. I will bring it to him to give to her."

"I thank you." Marna smiled, sitting as she glanced to Favik. "Saril, Favik has just received an odd letter." With that she gestured for her man to produce the Builder's note, which King's Second read. "We think the letter writer's true name is Kayvil."

Saril cleared his throat. "Is this genuine?"

King's Mother replied, "We are not certain. I was about to send Favik to the Records Keepers to ascertain any information about this Kayvil, or other missing Eskalinders, to see if the story holds."

Lord Saril nodded, again a critical eye on her man. "If it proves true, our Ambassador Moril in Havadra must be alerted—in person. I do not trust such a sensitive matter to our normal communication channels." He turned to Marna. "My Lady, even for the Havadrans this would be an act unheard of, holding one of our citizens. The highest levels of their government," again a quick look at the blond man, "must be consulted to find this Eskalinder and return him home; others as well who may be held in similar circumstances. As Favik has served in Havadra before, I would send him to do the job, with the King's approval. Again, only if this proves true."

Marna inhaled slowly. "This is a very troubling matter, and I understand your reasoning." She placed her hands in her lap. "It is Dalich's decision, I leave it to him."

"I thank you, my Lady King's Mother."

Saril bowed to her; she smiled weakly, looking away as he left the room. Then her eyes found Favik's, and she did not hide the misting of her vision. "I would rather you did not go to Havadra."

He came to her side and knelt on one knee, voice gentle. "My Lady, it may not come to that. And if it does, I will be upon a diplomatic mission. No harm will come to me, for I will have the protection of Eskalind."

She tried to harden her manner, even as she accepted his hands. "And Eskalind will trust your eyes and ears to discover if the Havadrans are indeed developing powerful weapons."

"If I find that to be true, what would you have me do?"

"Tell me they break, they do not function," she jested, though there was truth in her words, for to The Powers, that was her hope. She glanced at the unlit candles. "Alert me, and then we will make our own plans."

———

Saril conveyed Kayvil's letter to Dalich King. He made no mention of King's Mother's pained smile at his suggestion of dispatching Favik to Havadra. It was clear she was not happy with her man being sent away. However, upon reading the letter, Dalich King agreed that sending Favik to Havadra was the best course of action in these unusual circumstances.

After a pleasant meal with the royal couple, Saralya's son returned to his quarters, easing into a seat before the lit hearth in his chamber. Holding the letters from his mother and sister in separate hands, Saril weighed which to open first. Jinilya was five months from her ninth Naming Day, and her childish observations of life on their estate were both sweet and surprisingly informative. Their mother entertained some unusual outerlanders at times, including a certain Havadran dye merchant. Yes, his sister was quite useful in expanding his knowledge of the doings of his mother and King's Mother alike.

My, he was thinking like a Havadran. It was distasteful.

The fire crackled as his thoughts drifted to that land. While most Eskalinders harbored keen dislike for that people, arising from coin-diminishing transactions with perfidious Havadran merchants, or from hearing such tales second- or thirdhand, Saril's Ambassadorship in Capitola had given him a lifetime's worth of direct involvement to cement his aversion. Juggling the Havadran king's machinations, the scheming claimants to the throne, the masterful General Yirlofts and his orchestration of his own rivals, even the ridiculous negotiations involved in a task as mundane as purchasing a meal at the market… Lord Saril's opinion was firmly sealed. The less he had to do with Havadrans, the better. He had not bedded a light-haired man since that time, nor even eyed one with interest. The association with Havadra was too strong.

It did not help that Havadra was where he had learned of Dalich's ascension to King. A thousand miles from his bereaved friend, and the only solace he could offer was via letters. Letters uncertain to reach their royal destination, thanks to the vagaries of Havadran letter bearers. Saril placed the unopened letters from his family in his lap and rubbed his hands together, watching the lit hearth.

It had entered his mind that General Yirlofts could be behind this strange letter from Builder Kayvil. The general. One of the few people Saril had never deciphered.

On his first meeting with Yirlofts, the Havadran had listed all the men who had served as Ambassadors from Eskalind during his tenure: "Lord Saril, Havnil, Kanil, Kinakil, Favil," the slightest of pauses, "Hornil, Vanip."

"Yes sir, though I believe you meant Favik, instead of Favil."

Yirlofts merely smiled, an appraising expression in his eyes. The conversation diverted to other topics. But the notion rang in Saril's brain that the general's mistake had called attention to Favik, and perhaps to his name, unusual for an Eskalinder.

Favik's name reflected his birth in Humiksland, his northern origins. Saril had observed enough about Havadran culture to know that their people did not trade or mix with others, unless business or ulterior motives demanded it. More reasons to dislike them.

Later, Yirlofts had referred to Marna Queen as "Eskalind's northern Queen." He said the words with such intent, the young Ambassador restrained himself from showing any interest in the phrase, while uncertain whether an insult were concealed in it or something else.

Saril watched the fire before him, still thinking of the past.

At the end of his Ambassadorship, Yirlofts had invited him to his fortress, and brought the Eskalinder to a private room where he was introduced to a ten-year-old boy. Saril's first thought was that the elder man was depraved, to offer him a child lover. But then the Havadran called the lad his grandson, smiled as the boy came forward to be introduced, a pale child's first meeting with a darker-skinned man. Saril counted it a customs lesson—until he saw the general's grandson's eyes, which possessed the same pigmentation as Favik's.

How the general watched him observing the boy, as the usual pleasantries were spoken. Saril knew better than to ask questions about a Havadran's family, much as he wanted to; he strove to appear to politely accept the relationship as presented.

Then Yirlofts said, "Do tell your Lady Marna, King's Mother, that even Havadran families have northern bloodlines." Saril had dipped his head, seemingly agreeing, in truth vowing to convey no such message to his former Queen. But he later told Favik obliquely that Favik's eyes matched those of the general's grandson. Favik's response: complete nonchalance. Either the man had no knowledge of the child, or he was the most self-controlled Ambassador Eskalind had ever possessed. Saril then thought himself perhaps a pawn of the general, that Yirlofts had been inserting a doubt about Favik that should not exist.

Today that doubt returned.

The fire crackled, a sound almost an echo of the word *doubt*. He blinked, staring at the flames. Favik and King's Mother, and something between them. Saril rubbed his eyes. He was still thinking like a Havadran, but the notion would not be quenched.

At the appointed hour, a carrying box arrived outside the general's first gate. One never knew who was in those beige boxes: a visiting merchant, a household whore returning from a trip to conduct business for the women of her fortress, or even the king himself.

This box contained its expected passenger—the general's daughter, wife to Colonel Sirish, named Melande by her mother and known as such only by her family. If she had lived the proper life of a proper Havadran female, no one else would ever have known her name, but this was not the case. She was very proud of this secret, for within it was her greatest success: the one time she had eluded her father's omniscient reach.

At the first gate, a guard opened the box door and, upon seeing a veiled person, allowed the carrying men to enter the second gate. There, guards with swords drawn ushered the carrying men back to the first gate, which shut behind them with a booming clang. Then they turned their backs as the whore of the household stepped forward and opened the box door to inspect its passenger. Melande moved her face screen aside for the woman to glimpse her. "Now you do the same," she ordered, for she would not tolerate an unknown escort. The slim dagger concealed in her robes offered minimal protection. But the servant did as she was bid, revealing the familiar mole by her nose, the dark eyes and unusually hollow cheeks. "Are you ill, Feethe?"

Melande covered her face and exited the box as the other woman replaced her own face coverings. "Guards, leave us." The men stomped away, and Feethe gestured with a bony hand for Melande to walk through the opening third gate.

"I am well, Fine Lady," she said.

"You do not look it." The women passed the third gate and approached the house, the soft orangey fragrance of flowering blooms at odds with eddies of dust swirling in a shaft of sunshine along the third wall. Melande could hear the musicians playing from outside the house, never a good sign. "How is my father today?"

"Well, Fine Lady."

"You always say that."

"He is in a *fine* mood, Fine Lady."

"An execution?"

"Precisely, Fine Lady."

Melande inhaled, preparing herself for a gruesome scene as the door swung open. A headless corpse, dressed in the green-trimmed livery of her father's servants, lay stomach down on the tile floor of the courtyard, the executioner carrying away the head by a snatch of blond hair. She caught a glimpse of a startled expression upon the dead man's face, perhaps the same expression he'd worn when caught in the midst of his transgression. She wondered what his offense had been, if he had even made one. A dotted trail of blood marked the exit path of the executioner.

Melande turned her veiled head to the male servants standing before her, anxiously proffering bowls of water and bowing.

The general's daughter rinsed her hands and dried them upon a soft towel draped over a servant's arm, then marched through the courtyard to mount the stairs, sidestepping the crimson river issuing from the body. All the while the musicians, from behind their screen, played a frenzied tune, music that demanded a swift pace, yet she moved with a stately stride as though preparing to meet her husband on the day they would sign the joining contract.

At the top of the stairs, another servant greeted her and led her to the general's office. Melande sat before her father's desk as the servant unfurled the standing screens, their broad, beige sides, decorated with box-shaped geometric patterns, creating a visual barrier in the room. As the servant moved to place the last screen, the general approached from the hallway, pausing to cast a stern glance down over the balustrade at the musicians, who altered their tempo and tune to a more soothing melody.

The general entered the room, a gray eagle, to her mind, and the last screen swung into position, blocking father and daughter from the sight of others. He swept a hand over his head, indicating that she should remove her veil, which she did. Her father's face lit with a broad smile. "Melande, my sweet," he said tenderly and quietly, in almost a purr, as he approached. She stood, exhaled, and embraced him. His arms were as strong as ever, and she silently thanked The Powers she had remembered to empty her lungs before encountering the force of his embrace.

He released her.

"Well, Father, that atones for my greeting downstairs. Why did you not save that show for Sirish or one of your men?" They sat in chairs facing one another before his desk, as though they were equals before an unseen master.

He chuckled, brown eyes knit into slits. "How fare your son and your husband?"

"Yirish's twelfth Naming Day is next week. He expects a true long knife, which he will receive, though it is scarcely a present; the amount of coin he has made from selling his copied books would pay for a set of them." She folded her veil into neat layers and placed it upon her lap. "If I had not seen him quill with my own eyes, I would never believe a boy his age could create such beautiful works." Melande smiled. "Sirish is off on whatever projects you have him scurrying over, and I am still unable to give him another child, it seems."

"I am working on a solution for you."

"For me? I scarcely dare to ask what that entails."

Her father looked hurt, and she opened her mouth in surprise at this unexpected emotion. One benefit of wearing the veil was one need not always hide one's expressions. But she was uncovered and felt like a small rabbit in a raptor's sights as he began to speak.

"Melande," and he laid a firm palm flat on his desk, "what manner of country is it that allows, even encourages, a man to give his only child to a rival to preserve his own position?" He leaned toward her.

"I don't know why you are asking me this."

"I had a chance once, as a new man, just twenty years old—how long ago that was—to emigrate. To Eskalind. Our lives would have been very different had we lived there."

"I can imagine, yes." The general's daughter placed both hands on her chair's arms, her jaw tightening.

"The Powers set things to rights there. People are led to their destined mates. Thieves do not come in the night to steal a man's household, take his daughters, murder his sons." He patted his palm on the desk, then leaned back in his seat. "I will set things to rights here, using the skills and the people at my disposal." He knit his fingers and regarded her closely. "The first step: I will send a healer to your household who specializes in your condition. That will appease your husband for a while."

"I see. Perhaps you should also engage a healer for your servant Feethe. She looks entirely unwell."

He directed a look at her that would pulverize a stone, but as his child, she had weathered that expression before. He continued, "The second step you will be aware of when I send for you again. You will prepare for a lengthy stay here, in your old chambers."

"What? When will that be?" Without a word, he was standing. "And what of Yirish? I cannot be without my son." She rose to her feet as well, clutching her folded veil in one hand. "Father, I must, at the very least, know what to tell my husband. Sirish will ask questions. He will expect answers. Believable answers."

The general walked past her as though his mind had turned to more important matters and paced halfway around his desk as though he might sit. Brushing a hand across the feathery plume of his quill, he tapped a small easel that displayed a painting. Its back was to her. The size of the artwork recalled a painting of her long-deceased mother. She had not seen that portrait in years.

"Father?" Gathering the gold frame in both hands, he placed the painting facedown with an unceremonious flip. Uncertain if this was a threat or an insult, Melande strove to keep her face neutral.

"I will make excuses to your husband when the time comes." He made for the screens blocking the room. "I plan to see you again soon, my daughter." He bowed, his brown eyes on hers, the cool raptor gaze lighting them again. She nodded, but raised a challenging gaze to meet his. The general opened the screen and slipped out, replacing it behind him.

Melande marched around her father's desk. Picking up the frame, she turned the image over. Her jaw dropped, for the painting bore little resemblance to her beloved mother, though the soft drapes of the gown, the delicate chin, the green jewels set deep into square-shaped earrings were all familiar elements of the painting she had assumed this was.

While the portrait did indeed portray a woman, what she saw in that face were the characteristics of the man who truly fathered her son—the handsome young Ambassador of Eskalind her father once hosted in his fortress. The name locked deep in her heart all these years escaped from her lips in a dropping whisper. "Favik." She collapsed into her father's upholstered seat, still clutching the painting, and realizing that all she thought she had concealed—taking the Eskalinder as a lover, finding herself with his child—was no accident. Her fortuitously convenient joining with Sirish had been her father's plan all along. And now some further scheme of his was to be unveiled.

If it involved the same Eskalinder, perhaps it would not be entirely unpleasant.

Someone padded along the stone path behind Favik. Marna's man lowered his book to the red-lacquered wood bench. He half expected to see young Lady Jinilya, trying to surprise him from behind again, but no telltale giggle squeaked a warning.

A visit to Lady Saralya's estate inevitably included the youngest Lady of the house shadowing the former Ambassador's every move. Jinilya trailed him about as though The Powers whispered that he would be her future husband. He made a mental note to be far away, if he could manage it, when she came of age in seven or so years. The last thing he wanted was a decades-younger female to show him her feet, desiring his attentions.

He turned to instead glimpse the one person he hoped to see, approaching up the slight hill, Lady Saralya's home in the distance below him. "Ah, Deenofts, the reason for my visit to this estate: to see my favorite Havadran."

The borderland Scholar gazed up at Favik as he ascended the path. "Truly?" He spoke with enough incredulity in his voice that Favik wondered if he could possibly know about Melande.

"Well, if we were in Havadra, I would amend my statement to say, 'Deenofts, my favorite Havadran after King—' Remind me who is high lord there now?"

Deenofts knit his fingers together, then sat beside Favik. "What do you think of the general?"

"To name the general as the true lord of Havadra would be … truth."

"And treason, if one is inside Havadra. Which, fortunately, we at present are not. But what if we were?"

"Then we would not be having this conversation." Favik smiled, wondering what his companion hinted toward.

The pair sat in silence a while. Since their former topic seemed to have concluded, Favik made the sign of the Scholars, resting his hands low in his lap so the signal would not be discernible by any chance onlookers in the distance. His companion mimicked him, and they both murmured the words "Knowledge knows no borders." Which, strangely, was a comfort to him in this moment.

"Deenofts, I am to journey to your homeland immediately. Dalich King sends me, and our Lady requires more information about possible weapons experiments."

His fellow Scholar wagged his chin. "I wish I could tell you and our Lady something of use. News was as sparse as sunshine during a Nordak Winter when I ventured to Havadra. I wish you better luck."

"Our mistress hoped you might have extra information, that you would not trust to a written message."

"Nothing having to do with Havadran weapons experiments."

Favik waited, but Deenofts did not elaborate. Rather, he said, "Let us continue in this vein, as Scholars."

His utterance hinted that there was something beyond the Scholars' business that he wished to impart, and Favik sought to conclude their official meeting swiftly. "I was sent a letter from an Eskalinder Builder being held in Havadra," he said. "This man claimed he was hired to build a palace, but our Lady thinks creating weaponry was the true purpose. Dalich King wants me to go as a representative of Eskalind, seeking to free this man."

"Is the letter true?"

"It appears so. The Records Keepers documented a man with the same name, Kayvil, and the same skills, leaving Eskalind in early 2912. Over a year ago, and no word since."

The Havadran nodded, but seemed unconvinced.

His message concluded, Favik stretched out his arms. "Perhaps you can come with me, hmm, Deenofts? We could visit your family." He grinned.

"You are mentioning, directly, to a Havadran, his family?" The sudden sharpness and rising incredulity of his tone concerned Favik. The fierceness of Deenofts's gaze did nothing to diminish that concern.

Marna's man raised his hands in the air. "Please, I meant no offense." But Deenofts folded his fingers together, shaking them slightly, as though he might burst.

"Let me tell you an odd story, my Scholar. True, but odd. My sister—yes, I have a sister," and he shot Favik a look that cautioned against interruption. "She is a portrait painter. In Havadra, women can interact only with other women, and thus only a woman can paint the likeness of a woman. I suppose you learned something of our customs during your Ambassadorship there?"

Favik, refusing to be offended, was yet apprehensive to answer given his companion's odd behavior, but this seemed an invitation. He said, "Yes, the separation of the sexes was well covered during my training—"

"I thought so," Deenofts said. "You Eskalinders are most thorough." The Havadran nearly laughed, and his attitude shifted abruptly to that of a Story Teller relating a tale so fabulous, he could not contain his glee, as he expected to relish his audience's surprise at the story's twists and turns. "Well, the usual procedure is that my sister and her supplies are brought to a fortress, fully draped, of course—her, not the supplies—and ushered to the women's quarters for the painting sessions."

Deenofts grinned, and Favik, feeling encouraged, asked, "Isn't there a lot of bargaining and negotiation?"

"Oh yes, yes, but that occurs before she even gets in the carrying box." He raised his eyebrows. "My sister is the best female portraitist in Havadra and is much in demand. She has associates who bargain for her." The look of pride on his face was unmistakable.

"So in this case," he continued, "she arrives at a fortress, the family home of her commission, and is brought directly to the head of the household, a very lordly man of high standing. Now this is against Havadran customs, but it happens on occasion in her field. In this case, she thinks he wants to put the fear of The Powers into her personally, so that she will not reveal who she paints in his household. And she is partially correct; he does make that demand of her. Not unusual in her field!" He held his hands up as though startled from behind. "You know, the existence of women in one's family is a very guarded secret in my homeland. I understand his concern. But then, suddenly, this lordly man, his manner becomes soft as a pillow," Deenofts gestured as though petting a cushion, "and he tells her in hushed tones that the subject is not a living woman, but a dead one, one dear to him and long gone. Now, how will the portrait painter paint someone she cannot view?"

Favik shifted in his seat. "I suppose she would ask for a description and make sketches from there."

"Her line of thinking as well. Here's the catch; he already possesses a painting of this woman, painted from life, but," Deenofts sat as bolt straight as if commanded to do so, "that portrait is not to his satisfaction. He claims it does not match his memory of her."

"So your sister was called upon to alter it."

"Exactly. And thus she makes a brown-eyed, small-nosed woman, typical of my race, into a gray-eyed lovely with a slender nose worthy of any northerner. Why, this person's eyes even sounded familiar to me." He wagged a finger at Favik, at eye level. "Yes, as though they were before me now." He leaned back and tilted his head quizzically.

A growing feeling of unease rose within Favik. Once, years ago, Lord Saril had told him that the Havadran general's grandson possessed gray eyes. Favik had realized then that the child must be his and Melande's. The lordly man described in his fellow Scholar's tale could be the general. But the general altering a woman's portrait to look like Favik, this hinted at a greater deception, an ingenious way to explain the boy's unusual looks to a suspicious husband. Favik could not let any hint of this notion trickle to Deenofts. "Let me verify that I am following your tale," he said. "This man of high position—"

"Very high position."

The former Ambassador aimed to sound impartial, logical. "If the woman in the painting was his wife, then he joined with a foreigner."

"Oh, did he?" Deenofts's brown eyes seemed to shrink under his protrusive brows as though his effort of thought required it.

"Or he wanted someone to think he did."

"Hmm, possible, extremely possible. Especially," and Deenofts paused, his shoulders rising and his voice lowering in comic reenactment of the way Eskalinders said the damning phrase, *"in Havadra."*

Favik laughed, shaking his head at his colleague's delivery of this familiar refrain. "I do wonder, why would the general do that?"

"Whatever the reason, you did not hear it from me," said the Havadran, a twinkle in his eye. Rising to his feet with a bounce, a pleasant smile on his face like that of a schoolmaster elated with a pupil's progress, he said, "I must be off, and it sounds like you are departing soon as well. Goodbye, Humikslander."

Wondering what new information lay concealed in this unusual salutation, Favik said, "Deenofts, I have lived in Eskalind since I was a lad."

"But you look like a Humikslander, as I look like a Havadran, and there are those in this world who will never let us forget our southern, or northern, place of origin." He grinned, his eyes small and bright under the ridge of his brows. Then he turned and made for the stables, calling behind him, "Cautious travels to you. It is an old Havadran saying."

"Sir?"

Colonel Sirish of the Havadran Army glanced up from the report before him. His brown eyes narrowed into the universally recognized expression of annoyance at this unexpected intrusion.

"Very sorry, sir." The soldier stepped back and bowed as though about to leave the tent. Something in his demeanor, or perhaps the way he had momentarily made eye contact with his superior, intrigued the colonel. It was not the behavior of a commonplace man of no rank. There was something intelligent about his servility.

"Who were you looking for?" Sirish raised the report off the table at a slight angle so that a bit more light reflected onto his eyes. He believed this gave him a more commanding look—and drew attention to his wrecked nose, which could distract his subject to his advantage. Useful when examining a man who might be one of the general's roving spies.

"I was told the general was here, my lord."

"He is not. I am the general's chief representative at this camp. Conduct your business through me. I will relay it to him."

The man said nothing, but his brown eyes appeared to hold internal counsel as he no doubt wagered on the truth in Sirish's words.

The colonel leaned back in his seat, gaze steady upon the soldier. He reached for a stack of papyruses. Sliding his hand under the pile, he hefted it as though it was a great weight, then slapped the stack with a satisfying thump over the report he was reading. "If you truly work for General Yirlofts, as you claim, you will recognize his signature and seal on every one of these command missives, all addressed to *me*." Leaning forward, he flipped through the bottom third of the letters, revealing a dizzying march of the general's green wax seal and quilling in his scrawling hand. His son's talent for drawing and quillmanship certainly did not come from the maternal line.

Fending off a smirk, he rotated the stack and leafed through the top of each letter. "All addressed to Colonel Sirish."

"I had no doubt you were Colonel Sirish, sir."

Sirish smiled grimly, wondering what the man was playing at besides the obvious observation that his was a recognizable face. "Make your report." He slid his free hand to the dagger hilt at his waist. If this man was not a messenger, perhaps he was an assassin. Best to be prepared.

The man nodded and stretched his arms toward his superior, palms up and fingers splayed to show respect. And that he held no weapon. "Colonel Sirish, I report to you news for General Yirlofts. A man, fitting a description that border and port guards were bid to watch for, has entered Havadra at Avish port."

"The man's description?"

"The looks of a northerner: tall, blond, well proportioned, long nose. Distinguishing feature is gray eyes with darker blue where the color meets the white."

The colonel nearly muttered aloud, "That could be my son." Perhaps the man was a relative of Melande's mother. It would not be surprising for the general to have made strategic, familial ties to other lands. An excellent way to avoid Havadra's interfamilial power struggles, or to have a place to escape to should the struggle be lost. Sirish had always wondered about his long-dead maither's origins. He asked, "How old?"

"We were told he would be aged about thirty-five or forty, and likely from Humiksland or Eskalind. The man in question fits the description."

"When did he enter and where is he going?"

"He entered less than a week ago, with Eskalind papers directing him to King Astofts in Capitola. He comes on business for the Eskalinder King." The man swallowed. "His ship was forced to dock for repairs at Avish en route to the port at Capitola."

The general's sain tapped a finger on his desk, considering the veracity and hidden meanings in this report. He replied, "I will alert the general and give him a word-for-word report." He watched to see if the man might give any indication of hesitation, but he did not. "You are dismissed." The man lowered his arms, made his deference, and departed, leaving Sirish to sort through his options. Arising, he called for his trusted man and then returned to his desk to quill upon a papyrus. When his man arrived, Sirish lit a candle. "Hazish, our immediate lord may be summoning assistance for our works from outside our borders. See if you can find out anything, *anything*, about his wife's family."

"The general is joined, Colonel?"

Sirish shrugged. "Any information on any wife he has or has had." He tapped the ink lightly with his fingertips, and finding it dry, folded the page into a square. "This note will find itself delayed en route to the general, but it will reach him." Inserting the missive into an envelope, he dripped candle wax along its folds to seal it.

"How long a delay would be appropriate?"

"Three days at a minimum. Use the time in Capitola to learn what you can about his wife."

"Yes, Colonel."

After a late afternoon visit to the Kitchens, Marna entered her Library office, closing the stout door behind her. Turning, she paced to her desk through long shafts of sunlight, streaming through the glass windows as though light were a liquid pouring out of the air. A lovely phenomenon, at its peak in this sixth month of the year. But when she blinked, it was not from the beauty of the sight but rather in wondering if her eyes were playing a trick upon her. The Bladesmith's Daughter was certain that not a single book or papyrus had littered her desk when she last occupied the room. Yet there, perfectly placed in the center of her desk, as if someone had calculated the distance to each edge and laid it in the exact middle, rested a lone sheet of parchment.

She drew closer. It was clean of any quilling.

"I did not leave that here. Who has been in my chamber?" Before she could yank the bellpull, the errant sheet began to glow, with the faintest green tinge.

King's Mother inhaled sharply. Not certain she could trust her eyes, she glanced about, nervous as a new Apprentice Librarian uncertain where to file a scroll. Then the former Queen reached with a hovering hand to the parchment and nudged it.

Nothing happened.

With a pale finger, she touched it.

Nothing happened.

She lifted it into the shade and inspected its backside.

Nothing happened.

Marna replaced it upon her desk, directly beneath a bright beam of sunshine, and letters, forming words, appeared as though an invisible presence quilled upon the sheet.

> *Earth is for us*
> *Fire is against us*
> *Water is with us*
> *Air is everywhere*

"What … what does this mean? Who is this?"

No response came.

She grabbed the parchment and brought it closer to her eyes, but the instant the sheet was removed from the sunlight, the text evaporated.

In disbelief, Dalock's Queen sat heavily, her chair creaking from the unexpected intrusion. Placing the clean parchment back into the sunshine, she waited a moment.

Fresh words appeared.

> *Do not speak aloud*
> *Write your questions*
> *Never burn this parchment*
> *or show it to flame*

With one hand, Marna unstoppered her inkwell; with the other she plucked a sable quill from its holder. She scribbled,

> *Who is this?*

A response appeared.

> *Doubt will come by flame*
> *By candlelight*

Marna leaned back, her breath quickened. She quilled,

> *The green-clad Lady who appeared to me in Dalock*
> *King's chamber?*
>
> *Yes*

In the eleven years since that incident, many questions she wished she had asked that Lady had loomed in her mind, and the foremost among them she wrote now:

> *You told me then that war was brewing between The Powers,*
> *that they no longer followed the rules upon which they agreed.*
> *What were the rules?*

She lifted her black feathered quill, and instantly, writing appeared in answer.

> *Air*
> *Confinement of ice to the*
> *most northern and southern*
> *regions of the world*

Why The Powers had thought this a necessary thing to do, Marna was uncertain. Perhaps the world had once been much colder. She wanted to ask, but the writing continued.

> *Water*
> *All peoples speak the same tongue*

Again, this seemed odd. Of course everyone spoke the same words. Styles of handwriting varied, yes, and spoken inflections and accents as well, but still, never once had she read, even in a Legend scroll, that this had not always been the case.

> *Fire*
> *Banishment of all weapons*
> *that reach a range beyond*
> *what a person can throw*

A small sound escaped her throat. So the Legend scroll was true: there once had been weapons that flew through the skies. And The Powers had suppressed these frighteningly lethal arms. Now, if Fire was against them, the limitations on weapons might not last.

Marna pressed her quill nib against the parchment. A capital letter *E* had just formed on the page, but she wrote over it.

> *If Fire is against us, and Fire prevents terrible weapons, then*
> *Fire will no longer prevent these weapons?*
> *Perhaps*
> *Write swiftly*

Marna quilled,

> *What can I do?*

> *Use the Scholars and wait*
> *I am at work*

The parchment seemed to dim, and she hastily responded,

> *How?*

The silence in the room seemed to magnify the page before her. No fresh text appeared. Again, she wrote,

> *Please tell me.*

The Scholars' Mistress waited a moment to see if there would be more, feverishly formulating questions. But nothing followed.

Feeling powerless, she groaned, leaning back into her chair and shutting her eyes tight, hands flat beside the parchment. Soon the warmth of the sunlight faded from one hand, and opening her eyes, she saw that a section of the parchment lay in shadow. The writing in that area faded, shrank to nothingness. With a nod, she moved the entire page into the shadow, and all the green-clad Lady's words vanished.

Outside, the day was being chased away by night, and soon one of the Apprentices would knock, wanting to light her candles. After her last encounter with the Lady in green, the former Queen had forbid open flame in her chambers during daylight. She rubbed her hands on her smock, pondering how to use the Scholars to stop a Power's Will.

Then, quick as a spark jumps from the fireplace, it occurred to her that she now knew something perhaps no one else in the world knew, or perhaps had ever known. For all Marna's poring through Legend scrolls as ancient as could be found, and even the secret chronicles of the Strange Kings and their Queens, she had never unearthed this knowledge: The Powers numbered four, and each had established a rule that governed the world. She stared into the darkening room, reviewing their mandates in her mind. But she had learned only three rules, not four—and with a silent curse, she realized she herself had stymied the Lady's disclosure of Earth's rule.

How odd and yet familiar it was to approach Eskalind's fortress Embassy, where Favik once resided. Over a decade had passed, and another Ambassador now called this his heart-held piece of Eskalind in Havadra.

Little seemed changed from the outside. The sand-beige walls remained the color of Havadran earth, the Guards' faces bore the same stern expressions. Only the current King's colors had changed, the pennants now black and violet for Dalich King, no longer the red and brown of his Lady's late husband. The rooftop flagpole bore both the colors of Dalich, Eskalind's 125th King, and the red and white of Heedlich First King.

Inside awaited a hybrid Havadran-Eskalinder household, servants greeting the visitor with glistening bowls of water and soft drying cloths, the trusted man at the ready to escort the visitor to the head of the household—but all these people met his eyes, and the trusted man was a recognized face. "Bafnil? Many years since we chanced one another's company."

Dalock King's former Page replied, a grin upon his thin, still-boyish face, "Good to see you again, Favik Queensman."

"It's long since I answered to that distinction."

"Ah, then are we to call you Ambassador again?" The younger man glanced back to the elder whilst he led the way through the main meeting hall, and Favik merely pressed a single finger to his lips as though containing a secret. Bafnil, with a mischievous spark in his brown eyes, replied, "Ambassador Moril will be very pleased to see you." He opened a door that led to a garden courtyard and announced the freshly arrived Eskalinder.

Ambassador Moril rose from his seat by a small table in the midst of the greenery to greet his guest. "Well, well, Favik, my fellow Page to our royals, well met! Why, this is a room full of former Pages." Bafnil bowed and left as the two older men strode across the marble floor and embraced. "By The Powers, who would ever have thought, back when we two were lads, that we'd meet again in Havadra?" Moril laughed lightly, and Favik chuckled too, noting gray threads in Moril's dark hair.

"Good to see you in health after these many years, Ambassador," Favik replied.

"My health would be much improved if you were to tell me you have come to replace me, ha!" They both laughed as the current Ambassador led the former to a pillowed bench. "Or that my next posting was, say, Gergelt. The one borderland I have not yet served as Ambassador." He spoke as though recalling a dear, departed companion.

"Alas," Favik said, "while Dalich King has sent me, it is not because he has drawn the tiles."

"I see." They sat, and here Moril's demeanor changed to that of the patient diplomat, neutral in face, slightly aloof, expectant in a way that could draw his audience to reveal more than they planned. The transformation was sudden, like a candle unexpectedly burning out, and Marna's man nearly forgot the congenial Eskalinder of a moment ago. Then Favik nearly smiled, for Moril's transformative talent had earned him high marks whilst the pair were Ambassador Apprentices together, and as a youngster, Favik strived to mimic the slightly older Moril's aptitude. His efforts had not been without success, but his true talents lay elsewhere.

Favik imparted the story of Kayvil's letter, Moril duly questioned the veracity thereof, and the former Ambassador confirmed it from his study of the Records Keepers' dossiers.

Moril asked, "Does this man have family?"

"None. Raised in a King's House."

Moril nodded, "Like us." Favik was about to correct the Ambassador, but Moril realized his mistake. "Forgive me, I recall now. You came to us with King's Mother, when she was King's Betrothed, after the battle in Humiksland. While it was still called Hudiksland, aye?"

"Indeed. That was not long before King Hudik died, and the country of my birth changes its name with each change in kingship." Favik placed a hand upon the black cushions and leaned back, gazing about the garden. A small red bird flitted by, a burst of contrast amidst the green hanging plants.

"Humiksland has been an exemplary nation since then, at least as we Eskalinders consider such things, yes?" Favik returned his gaze to his colleague. "Good governorship, its people well looked after." Moril's expression hinted at a smile. "May I see the document?"

Favik produced the letter, and Moril opened and examined it, his expression unchanging. He licked a finger and rested it upon the ink, then licked the finger again. Having never seen this before, Favik asked, "What are you doing?"

The Eskalind Ambassador made a motion like chewing, then said, "It is indeed Havadran ink. Their ink always has a smoky aftertaste. Eskalind inks have floral notes."

"I must have missed the day at Ambassador studies when that was taught."

Moril grinned. "My own discovery. I have found it useful here."

"You're not concerned about poison?"

"Not unless I suspect it came from a high household. Sometimes you can smell the smoke scent without tasting." He studied the text. "What does our Lord Dalich King want done?"

"He asks that you meet with the Havadran king and insist that this man be found and returned to our Embassy. And find out if there are more Eskalinders being held in Havadra against their will. If they are, than they also are to be released."

"And what is your role, other than trusted, face-to-face messenger?"

"To assist as required, and possibly travel to the site where Kayvil and any others worked, to determine if any other Eskalinders, and possibly other outerlanders, are being held."

Moril nodded. "The Havadrans will not like these accusations, but," he tapped the papyrus, "we have sound evidence. Fortunately, I understand how to deal with King Astofts. Well, I think I do." He leveled his eyes at Favik. "This being Havadra, one never knows for certain. But I will strive to meet with him tomorrow and see what can be done."

A blond woman, unveiled and dressed in a high-necked, flowing blue gown, entered the courtyard, and Favik's first thought was to turn his head away as though he never saw her—this the required etiquette in a Havadran fortress when a member of the opposite sex was inadvertently encountered. His second thought was a brief and unrealistic hope that the woman might be Melande, for she appeared close to the same age his lost love must be now: not long past thirty. Looking at her closer, he decided she was perhaps a bit younger. It troubled him how richly the image of Melande remained still in his mind.

As this was an Eskalinder household, the pleasingly proportioned female strode toward the two men without any hint of a pause. The Ambassador called to her, all warmth returned to his voice. "Kostaza, come, meet Favik. Favik, meet my beautiful wife, the former princess of Kaymif."

Now he recognized her! Favik rose and bowed to her, and she smiled at him. Her dress was a perfect match to her eye color. "Well met, Favik," she said.

He declined to mention that they had occupied a room together once before, nearly ten years ago, on the occasion of her mother's exile. "An honor, Lady Princess."

She smiled in return as Moril placed an arm around her waist. "Oh, if you could have seen," Moril said, "the diplomatic skill required to convince her brother, King Moulai, of the fact that in Eskalind, a joining babe is considered a grace from The Powers." His boyish grin belied his nearly four decades as he kissed her blond brow. "How fares our wee lad?"

"Finally asleep."

"Speaking of sleep, I must show Favik to his quarters."

The tour of his chambers concluded quickly, for the former Ambassador found himself staying in the exact room he had resided in during his tenure as Ambassador, and he was thus familiar with the arrangements. He had never felt comfortable in the designated sleeping chamber for the Eskalind Ambassador: finding his predecessor sleeping his final sleep in that bed, the bed Moril and Kostaza now shared, had left him disinclined to inhabit that space, and he had resided for his entire term as Ambassador in the smaller apartments appointed to him now.

But this time he did not stay long. The next day, Moril returned from his visit with King Astofts, and the pair met alone in the Ambassador's private receiving chamber. The elder Eskalinder shook his head. "Astofts claims not to have started any palace building since his reign began, but there are a few projects his predecessor began that he has continued. Perhaps Kayvil was caught in unfortunate circumstances at one of them."

Kostaza entered, blue eyes intent upon not the current but the former Ambassador. "Favik, this is for you." She placed a written message onto a tablecloth embroidered with their Lord's emblem of quill across a blank sheet, an almost ironic reference to how the note was created. "Moril's Secretary, Bafnil, said it just arrived."

He thanked her, picked up the note, and slit the green wax seals, which felt sticky. Inside the tan envelope was a formal invitation from General Yirlofts to reside in his fortress while making his investigations, in the hope that the general "might assist in any manner possible" in the search for the missing Eskalinder. Kostaza and Moril stared at him as he read the note aloud.

"One moment. I was just at the palace," Moril exclaimed. "The general was there and made no mention of you visiting his fortress. He only told King Astofts he had firm ideas on how to help in this search."

Kostaza added, "Favik, he must have known you were here."

"Known I was here and what my mission was, it seems. Prior to Ambassador Moril disclosing it to King Astofts."

Moril nodded. "Perhaps it is time for a replacement of staff in this household." His wife frowned.

"Well," began Favik, a tinge of giddiness in his heart at the chance to enter Melande's former home, where some hope of seeing her lingered, "I may have deeper access in the search for Kayvil if I stay at the general's."

The Ambassador frowned. "Or the general is thinking of a divide-and-conquer mission."

The former princess interrupted, brushing nervous fingers through her hair, "By The Powers, you are not thinking of going in his stead, are you?"

"No, 'Staza, no. That would be like asking a Havadran to eat his siege rations when the gate is open." Her fair brow knit, and Moril continued in a softer voice, "I would not leave you and our son alone here, or bring you there. If one of us goes, it must be Favik. Besides, the invitation was addressed to him." Moril's clear brown eyes were an ocean of calm, as though he could immerse his wife in a sea of tranquility.

Favik had his own ideas. "I have been a guest at the general's before, I do not fear the place."

The former princess opened her mouth, but her husband spoke first. "Still, an extra measure of caution is warranted. I hope to The Powers you find our missing Eskalinder before whatever scheme the general plays at unfolds."

Favik replied lightly, "He undoubtedly has one, or he would not be the general." He smiled to reassure his hostess, but she turned to her husband.

"Moril, please, how much longer must we remain in Havadra?"

Inside the inner wall of the Eskalind Embassy compound, Favik and Ambassador Moril appraised the two carrying boxes that rested atop the beige dirt, pale dust settling from the tromping feet of the just-departed carrying men. Moril shook his head. "See here, this scratch distinguishes this box from any other."

The former Queensman noted the long, narrow nick in the tan paint, a thin heart of wood showing through. "Indeed."

"It's entirely unsafe to travel the streets in a recognizable box. I'll call for another carrying box for you and your luggage." Moril nodded as though agreeing with himself and barked the order to Bafnil, who stood nearby.

The elder Eskalinders returned inside, where Favik spent an anxious hour in polite conversation with the Ambassador and his wife. Their babe-in-arms son, who had just discovered the sound of his own voice, constantly exclaimed his joy at this event with arbitrary, hearing-numbing shrieks. The parents encouraged the babe's vocal exercises, oohing and aahing as though they thought by doing so they could encourage him to graduate to full sentences in no time. For a brief moment, Favik considered himself fortunate for missing this stage of his own son's development. Then the realization of how much time had passed since the boy's birth rushed upon him, engulfing him in a silent sadness that progressed to doubt as he wondered whether he did indeed have a child by Melande.

The present wee lad exhaled another squeal, and the former Ambassador considered that The Powers Themselves were conspiring not only to keep him from the general, and any hope of seeing Melande and meeting his son, but to render him deaf as well.

At last, two unscathed carrying boxes arrived, replacing the former specimens. Favik stowed his luggage into one, himself into the other, and the pair began the journey to the general's fortress, the carrying men lumbering through the maze of streets with their load, beggars calling for alms, and the boxes once chased by a merchant calling, "Fine Lady! Fine Lady! Beautiful scarf for you! Excellent price!"

The carrying men paused, as if to allow the box's occupant a moment to ponder this offer. Not for the first time, Favik wished the ventilation screens near the roof were placed lower, to allow a view of the outside. His nerves tensed as he considered the possibility this might be some type of attack, and he drew his long knife, just as the carriers resumed their pace. The Eskalinder breathed out heavily, glad no one could hear him through the cacophony of the streets. He nearly cut himself replacing the blade into its sheath in the swaying box, cursed, and with that near miss, settled loosely into the cushions for the rest of the journey.

He did not know what awaited him at the general's, other than his continuing role as a soldier in the battle to find the missing Eskalinder and bring justice to his cause. His thoughts turned to memories of being a young boy, before his father was killed. Then he had spent sleepless nights wishing to The Powers for his mother, whom he had never known. After his father's death, Marna, King's Betrothed, soon to be Queen of Eskalind, accepted him as her Page, and by this unlikely and strange circumstance, he felt The Powers answered his earlier pleas. The Lady's kindness, confidence, and affection radiated into his own being, much as he imagined a mother's love would. Only with Melande had he felt a deeper attachment to another person, and now again he hoped to The Powers that he might somehow see her again, soon, whatever plan of her father's unfolded. For if he could, he would bring her and their son to Eskalind. At any cost.

Stern shouting signaled his arrival at the general's fortress as the carriers were ordered to enter the first gate and place their burden before the second wall. Once the box was lowered to the ground, Favik chanced standing to view what he could through the thin mesh of the air vents. He watched as a cadre of green-capped guards stepped forward and motioned the carrying men aside. They surrounded the box, spears upright in one hand, the other near their blade hilts, which alarmed him, but then they approached the box with their free hands outstretched, and he realized they intended to carry it. He sat down just as the box was hoisted from the ground and lurched forward, swaying clumsily from their inexperienced gait. It was a brief journey before they placed the container on the ground again, and the Eskalinder suspected that they must have passed through the second gate.

He heard a dim knock, then a firm thump thudded upon his door. "Who are you?" a male voice asked.

"Former Ambassador to Havadra, Favik of Eskalind, come at the general's invitation."

"I'm opening the box." The man did as he said, and Favik squinted against the light. The general's man gave a firm nod. "Who's in the other one?"

"My luggage."

"Wait." The door closed. Favik stood to watch through the ventilation screen as the second box was opened. The man leaned into the container, pawed at the bags, shut the door, and barked, "Clear." Favik sat again quickly, but nothing happened for a moment, except for the unmistakable reverberation of a large door or gate grinding open. Then his box was lifted and carried maybe thirty steps before the men lowered their burden. He must be inside the third and final gate, though if he recalled the layout of the general's fortress correctly, there had been enough space left between the third, inner wall and the residence for a fourth wall to be built.

"Ambassador, wait until you are called." The guards marched away, then there was the low rumbling hum of the gate closing.

He waited. And waited. The air in the box grew warmer. And warmer.

"Ambassador Favik, come out."

Grateful to escape the stifling container, Favik pushed the door open.

There across the beige dirt stood none other than the general, the lines in his face set deeper than at their last encounter, well over a decade ago, but otherwise looking remarkably unscathed for a Havadran who had spent an unprecedented length of time at the apex of his society. A dozen feet away stood his broad-shouldered trusted man, the slight lowering of his gaze upon Favik's person a perfect execution for a man of his station: watchful, wary, and above all, protective of his lord.

"General Yirlofts, Supreme Commander of Havadra, sir." Favik dipped his head in accordance with his highly formal greeting, all his senses and instincts concentrated on this moment. He heard the sounds of music growing louder. He held his hands open to the general and his man to show he carried no weapons.

"Welcome to my fortress, *again*, Ambassador Favik."

Melande's father nodded to his subordinate, who stepped back to the metal-plated wood doors that marked the entrance to the abode. The rest of the open yard was vacant of man or beast, insect or plant—extinguished of all life. The general walked forward and spoke low. "I am told you seek a missing countryman."

"I do."

"Kayvil of Eskalind?"

"That is his name. He is a Builder."

A slight change of expression, perhaps a twinge or the beginnings of a smile crossed the general's face. "In Havadra, we prefer the term *engineer*. Builder implies only the making of things. Engineers have many uses. But, I will aid you in your search." He raised his voice a notch. "You are aware of the sad fact that foreigners traveling in my country, especially across longer distances, can fall victim to plunderers … bandits … killers."

Favik kept his voice steady. "That is why my King asks that military escort and protection be provided to me as I search."

"It will, if my investigations are fruitful and there is requirement for you to leave my fortress." Here the general smiled, ever so slightly, but his eyes were serious, and Favik met his gaze with an even demeanor born of patient practice and discipline.

"Sir, freedom of movement is a hallmark of Eskalind society. I understand that precautions must be made in dangerous situations," and he inclined his head slightly as though offering his deference, "but my King expects I will be granted access wherever I need to go to locate his subject, Kayvil the Engineer."

The general spoke in a hushed tone, with the abruptness of a man proposing his final offer. "I will grant you full access to my fortress and its occupants."

Doubting his ears, Favik began, "With respect, as a foreigner perhaps rusty in my understandings of Havadran—"

The general's voice dropped to a controlled whisper. "You had the same privileges when you visited last. I suspect you would like to enjoy them again."

Favik stared as the most powerful man in Havadra stepped forward a pace so their noses were but a hand's breadth apart. "Nothing happens inside my walls without my knowledge."

The former Ambassador craned his neck slightly, holding his facial muscles steady as he processed this information, not quite believing what the older man was offering. The thought that his clandestine affair with Melande has been condoned by her father had never occurred to him, but it made a strange sense, given the general's reputation as a master planner and strategist.

"Ambassador, do we have an agreement?"

It was Favik's turn to allow a slight smile, though he tempered his voice to belie his rising enthusiasm for the scheme. "If I am promised safe passage from this fortress when I leave, then I believe we do."

"Eskalind is Havadra's border ally. Eskalind is guarded by The Powers, as Legends tell. The Powers' Gifts run through the royal family line; is that not true?" The general smiled as though he had won a long-sought prize.

"That is the belief of Eskalinders, but stating it does not answer my question."

"I would never harm you, Eskalinder born of Humiksland, save you were to harm me or one of my family." Here he turned his head at a slight angle, a stern but quizzical expression that taunted Favik to decipher a hidden meaning.

"I have your word then, General."

The older man turned to his trusted servant. "Show him his quarters."

On a long table by the grand bed rested the black leather bags that served as his luggage. Favik sat on the periphery of the bed, exiled to the edge by the many pillows that adorned it. He regarded the cinched purple cords knitting his bags closed, the dark leather enveloping his possessions, protecting his writing kit, his dress tunics, his boots. All nestled in the embrace of Dalich King's colors, as though his Lord's symbols were a citadel against dust or thieving hands. He wondered how well protected he was inside this room deep within the general's fortress. The very air felt stifled, as though it too recognized its confinement inside triple gates and stout walls.

He pondered why the general had allowed him access to Melande those years before, why her father now mentioned the Gifts of the Eskalind royals to him. He could not fathom the connection or reasoning.

Upon the longest wall of the room hung a display of several short, decorative carpets, all featuring square-shaped patterns in graduated shades from tan to an uninspired green. Then the middle wall covering swung into the room, and he realized it concealed a door that was opening. He stood, casting a quick eye to his unsheathed long knife, stashed atop the pillows. There had been an intention in his mind to polish it when he sat down earlier; now his thoughts strayed to more immediate uses.

A draped figure embarked into the room through the hidden door and with a gloved hand shut it. It spoke in a woman's voice, low and timid. "The master bid me to look after you."

Likely she was the go-between, the female servant of the house whom Havadrans called 'whore', who perhaps offered more service than fetching tea. "I have all I require at the moment," he said, letting the words hang in the air as she stood silent, facing him. He warily watched her, noting a small dark spot on her face covering he was certain had not been there a moment ago. It grew larger. Then she choked back a quiet cry, voice breaking free in a higher tone. "Oh Favik, how did you come here?"

"Melande!"

She backed away, then reached to tear away the veil. Her blond hair was braided in small ringlets around her face, her brown eyes glossy with tears, but she looked as he remembered her: beautiful and strong, even in her distress. "I never…thought I would see you again."

He lifted his arms to embrace her and walked forward. She started to smile, but her eyes hardened, as though caution whispered in her ear. She did not step back again, but something about her manner seemed to pull away from him. "How did you come here?"

He stopped before her, lowering his arms but giddy, all Ambassadorial restraint fled from his marrow. "I hoped for years to come back to Havadra, to try to see you. I am on a mission from my King; your father offered quarters for me during my stay."

His lost beloved watched him, cautious deliberation in her high shoulders and hardening gaze. "My father invited you?"

"He did. I just spoke with him, inside the third gate."

Now she smiled. And laughed, the coy laugh of a woman with a secret.

"Melande, this amuses you?"

"Oh, you have no idea. Come, let us sit and I will explain."

To his great pleasure, she gripped his hand and led him to the floor pillows clustered around a low dining table. She released his hand and they sat. The general's daughter tapped her fingers together. "What an odd circumstance to tell you this." She adjusted her robe and tucked her feet under her. "I always thought ourselves ferociously clever, never being caught abed when you stayed in this house. For once I had tricked my father, I thought." She smirked. "When Father sent you back to Eskalind, I was with child, but I didn't know."

"Oh, Melande."

"Wait, let me continue. My nurse examined me and told me." His lost love glanced at the door she had entered through, perhaps recalling their past clandestine meetings. "I thought I would die by my own hand, rather than face Father's wrath. But lo, with no prior word, he had arranged a husband for me." She met his eyes. "I bore your son. My husband believes the child is his own." She watched him with a gleam similar to her sire's. "And ever since Yirish's birth, I have been unable to get with child."

"But our son, Yirish? He is healthy?"

"He thrives." She was smiling.

"And you have had no other children?"

Melande shook her head, her expression bordering on amusement. "Do you see Father's plan in bringing you here?"

Favik did, but despite his willingness to participate in it, his exit strategy differed from the general's. "I may have a plan of my own."

"What?"

"Melande, I don't want to leave you again." He reached for her arm, tracing his fingers to her elbow, grasping it as gently as he could through the folds of fabric enshrouding her body.

She looked away. "We have been apart many years. How do you know you still like me?"

"Because you, Melande, have been all my thoughts these many years." His words burned with the fierceness of his desire, then lightened. She had confirmed what he had long speculated. "And we have a son.

A son I long to meet. What does he look like?"

"Have you a mirror?"

"What is he like?" He laughed quietly, joyful in The Powers' benevolence for reuniting them. "Why by the laws of Eskalind, by the laws of The Powers Themselves, we are joined. We should be together."

"A problem, in that we are not in Eskalind, and I already have a Havadran husband." Melande ran a finger by her ear. "We are different people than we were. If you are not, well, I most certainly am." She lifted a hand to touch his cheek. "There is much to discuss, but quick, let me show you the passageway to my new quarters."

"Colonel Sirish?" Hazish's familiar face poked through the tent entrance.

Sirish dropped his chicken leg onto the plate before him and beckoned his trusted man to sit. Gesturing to the food, he said, "Eat. Tell me what news you have."

Hazish reached for the basket of round rolls and tore one in half. "Despite much effort, no word can be discovered as to the general's wife or wives, past or present." He bit into the bread.

"As it should be, if Havadrans are to remain Havadrans."

His man grinned and said, "I did speak to an old midwife who claimed she served at a birth in the household, some thirty years ago, but she could remember nothing about the mother, save she was a fine lady and it was a girl child."

The colonel shrugged. That child was likely his wife. Melande had never told him whether she had siblings, but he believed she did not, given that no stories had ever surfaced about them. He could fill an evening with tales of his brothers from when they were children. His long-dead brothers. He reached for more chicken.

"Sir?" A guard ventured into the tent, and quick as a spark leaps from a hearth, Hazish leapt from his seat to guard his lord's side.

Sirish drew breath through his nose slowly. "What do you want?"

"Sorry to interrupt, sir," the soldier dipped his head, "but one of the engineers has found a way to make fire fly through the air." The man's voice rose with excitement. "I saw it with my own eyes!"

"That news is worth interrupting a meal. Come, show me." Sirish led his men from the tent, biting a large chunk of chicken from the bone as he went and hurling the rest to dirt. He swiped a hand across his chin. Ahead, the engineer trembled like a youth ill-prepared for the fight that would earn him his manhood.

"Colonel, sir, come see!" His teeth flashed white against the deep umber of his lips and face; his accent sounded Guerish, which would explain his tight-fitting tunic and breeches. "Come, see what I have done for you." He led the colonel across the camp toward a black plume of smoke in an area of flattened dirt sometimes used for marching drills. On the far end of the smooth expanse, about a hundred feet away, four staked mannequins, made of twigs and straw, were aligned at even distances. Orange flames consumed one.

"Come, come here," said the Guerlander, waving. He led them to a rough table covered with polished sticks of browned wood, sitting beside a bowl of dark tar. To the side, a grinning soldier stood next to a lit brazier atop a tripod. "That fire was set from here. Let me show you." The Guerish engineer gestured to the soldier, who carried what appeared to be a curved wooden rod of white orsblat wood, strung with a taut ribbon of twine. The soldier grabbed one of the sticks from the table, laid it perpendicular to the curved rod, dipped the end into the tar, then the fire. Pointing the flaming stick at the mannequins, he pulled the twine, and the stick flew through the air, flames intact until it struck the mannequin next to the one already burning. Sirish gaped as the figure caught fire.

"By The Powers, this is it." He turned to the soldier. "You, show Hazish how to do this."

The man nodded and handed the bent wood to Sirish's trusted man, explaining how to ease back on the twine. The engineer clapped his hands like a child overwhelmed with Naming Day presents. Hazish's brown eyes were intent as he followed the instructions, sending an untarred stick only a few yards on his first attempt.

"Go on!" Sirish encouraged, gleeful. Thoughts of how he could use this weapon to rain fire from the skies upon all who stood in his way to the highest lordship—the king and his wife's father topping his list—swirled like too much unwatered wine in his brain. For a moment the imaginings of his plans obscured his vision, till he realized that Hazish's second try had traversed halfway across the field.

"Try again, Hazish, again." Sirish slapped his trusted man on the back as more soldiers gathered behind. This time he would concentrate on the moment at hand.

Hazish flicked back a wisp of blond hair, dipped the end of the stick into the tar, then into the fire—as though the action were one he had practiced all his life. He pulled the twine toward his chest and released the burning stick. It sailed across the distance toward the mannequins, a thin trail of smoke in its wake. The gathered crowd breathed as one at the spectacle, but the flaming brand dove short of the mannequins and instead pierced the bare earth. The flame fizzled and died.

The colonel opened his mouth to exhort his man to try again, just as the ground where the last stick had landed trembled, undulating like water in a washing bowl.

No one spoke.

A jet of water-dark mud erupted skyward from that spot, rising higher and higher, towering overhead as though it would spike the sky. Someone screamed behind him, but Sirish only stared, rooted to the spot as the frothing geyser spread sideways, a trench opening from inside the earth, splitting the marching ground, engulfing all four mannequins. He was struck from behind by an unseen force, like a gale of wind but hard as a shield, and fell upon his face, raising his forehead just in time to see the geyser blown back as though a great hand of air pushed it away.

"Colonel! Sir! Are you all right?" Recognizing Hazish's voice, he turned to see his trusted man close by, crawling toward him. A splotch of dark tar coated one side of his face.

"I think I am." He made to stand, but Hazish screamed, "Stay down!"

Sirish turned toward where the mannequins had been. A curtain of flame, a vivid, pulsating rain of orange and red, fell from the sky and swept toward them. He dropped to the ground shrieking and pressed his hands over his face as the heat seared over him.

"Mmm, are you still reading that?" Melande rubbed her nose against the bare skin covering Favik's ribs.

"You fell asleep." Favik closed the book and nudged her away across the warm sheets. "That tickles."

She laughed and sat upright, framed by the curtains canopying her bed, blond ringlets amazingly intact despite recent activities that should have disheveled them. He did not reopen the book but rather gazed upon her bare torso. Then he realized she was talking.

"Aren't Yirish's skills amazing? He quilled all the text in that book, and made the drawings as well. He thinks he snuck out unawares to sell them to booksellers, but of course I had a trusted man follow him there." Her voice lilted into a sigh. "I love the delicate curves of the scrolling ribbon on the frontispiece."

"Mmm-hmm," Favik replied, laying the book on the opposite side of the bed with one hand and reaching to stroke the curve of her hip with the other. Then he shifted his hand to stroke the smooth skin on her belly.

"Now you are tickling me." She held her ground on the sheets.

"I'd rather be kissing you. Again." He pulled her toward him and her lips found his.

The distinct tingle of her servants' bells rang, and they both opened their eyes, two shocked faces mirroring one another. But they had rehearsed this.

"Hide!" she commanded in a voice worthy of her father. Favik sprang from the bed, snatching the tidy pile of clothing he had left by the bedside in case they were interrupted. The former Ambassador bolted for the screened room, an inner chamber of Melande's expansive bedroom. His lover came behind him, the bedsheets bundled in her arms and billowing like an exotic costume from the outerlands to cover her nude form. She threw the soiled cloths to him, then returned to the main room to don a pale robe as she marched to the opaque folding screens shielding the door. "Why are you ringing? I'm not to be disturbed." Her crossed arms and irked tone reminded him of his Lady dismissing a troublesome Apprentice.

A female voice called from the other side of the door, "Fine Lady, your pardon. Your husband is here and will see you."

Melande glanced to where he hid behind the mesh screen, motioning him to get down. He did. She replied to her servant, "Ah, very good. I require a moment to prepare."

Favik heard water sloshing in a bowl, the squirt of a perfume canister, and feverish footsteps padding about the room, leading back to the bed. A weak plopping sound he eventually realized were pillows falling to the ground. A knock on the door, and then it opened.

"Sirish, what a surprise. I was in the midst of a treatment, but am very glad to see you, husband."

The door thudded shut. Favik held himself steady, wishing he could watch their interaction, but considered it too risky to raise his head to look through the screen.

"I wanted to see you." Sirish had an oddly ragged inhale that made him sound winded, though his voice was strong. Then Favik recalled that the colonel was famous for his smashed nose. During his own Ambassadorship in Havadra, it had been a topic of great debate as to how the injury occurred.

"Sirish, what's wrong? You look … distressed."

A pause, and the crushed inhale. "There was an accident at camp. Many of my men were killed."

"Were you hurt?"

"Not much, but Hazish was burned across his face. I thought he would die."

"How terrible. What caused it?"

The man's voice shifted, as though he had turned away. "I would rather speak no more of it. Come, sit by me. Tell me of your time in your father's house."

She laughed. "Oh, this healer Father has for me. You would not envy the concoctions she has me drinking. Or the postures she has me doing."

"Postures?"

"They are not very flattering."

There was a brief pause in the conversation. The colonel said, "Why is your bed stripped?"

"I am surprised you noticed. Did you have an intention?" The general's sain made no answer that Favik could hear, but Melande laughed. "Oh, I see you do. Well, my treatments are at very particular times," he could hear her moving through the room, "and my maid wanted to replace the bedding, but I sent her away since I was in the middle of my exercises. See all the pillows there? I am supposed to lie nude upon them in different postures—"

"Show me." Sirish's voice was insistent, tinged with a lustful fire. Favik's heart chilled; murderous thoughts rose in his mind. By rights it was *his* wife on the other side of the screen, not the Havadran's.

"Husband, the timing isn't right. We're supposed to wait until the healer says I am ready for you."

"I say when the timing is right."

A long pause. Favik wished he could see the pair and study their expressions. The colonel spoke again. "Melande, what's the point of going through this nonsense if there is no chance for your husband to impregnate you?"

"It's not nonsense. I want this to work. I want another child. I thought you did too." Another pause. "How is Yirish?"

Sirish murmured something.

"But I've never been away from him this long. Oh. Oh my." Her voice dropped into a moan, whether of pleasure or pain, he could not tell.

Silent as vapor, Favik rose until he could see them, through the mesh screens, lying on the floor by the bed. Sirish's naked back was toward him, Melande's torso and head obscured behind it. Her pale arms lay across the beige pillows. Her wrists rotated and she clenched the cushions.

Sirish growled, "The healer better approve of this posture."

Melande moaned again, a familiar ring of delight in the depths of the sound. Favik bit his teeth, wishing for a weapon to skewer the man. Then an odd snorting noise redirected his attention. It sounded more appropriate to a barnyard than a bedroom, and he scanned the room in dismay, wondering if some sort of Havadran livestock might have wandered inside. But it was Sirish, breathing heavily, rhythmically, through his crushed nose, a hideous, grinding snorting that invited disgust and pity. Poor Melande, braving that racket for years. Favik sank to the floor, stuffing his stubby fingers into his ears.

He did not stay there long, for the sound tapered away. The hidden man unstoppered his hearing.

Melande whispered words he could not distinguish, and then Sirish was speaking. "It was horrible, water and mud shot out of the ground, you could never have imagined anything like it." Favik rose again and gazed out the screens, intrigued by this odd pillow talk. The general's sain continued, "Then a wall of fire came out of the sky, burning everything. All the weapons, all the research. Ashes. Again my work crumbles to nothing." He paused. "Twelve years wasted."

The hidden man inhaled as slowly as he could while he digested this portentous news. Marna, King's Mother, had long suspected that the general and his sain actively sought new instruments of death. Here was a confession of utter failure, and a confirmation that it was not the first such fiasco. His Lady would rejoice to have this information, though what it boded for the future was another matter. And he still did not know when he might be able to safely relay this news to her.

Melande murmured something, the familiar, soft sound drawing his attention. He saw her hands caressing Sirish's back. The colonel replied in a defeated voice, "No, I'm not certain I want to try again. All the wasted time."

Now Favik could distinguish Melande's speech. "Sirish, I meant *we* cannot try again now. I have to execute the postures the healer gave me for after we lie together. Let me get up. Quickly." Sirish moved, and she scooted away from him, rising to stand by the wall. She turned her back to it and walked a pace away, then leaned backward, reaching overhead to the wall whilst dangling her head to the ground. A slim strand of hair stuck to her shoulder.

The colonel stood. "What are you doing?"

"The postures. They are to flex the womb and aid conception. There is a sequence I must go through immediately." She brought herself upright, then laid on her back upon the pillowed ground and held her arms at crossed angles overhead. He saw her feet lift and lower several times. Then she scissored her legs.

"That looks ridiculous."

"There are several more."

Sirish turned toward the door. "I'm going." The general's sain lifted his tunic and trousers from the floor and dressed. Melande rose on all fours, bobbing her head from side to side. The colonel adjusted the gold-embroidered cuffs of his tunic and made for the door.

"Give Yirish my love," called Melande. She lay on her stomach and stretched her arms before her, then to her sides, over and over as though the pillows were air and she a flying creature.

"Uh-huh," intoned Sirish with a grunt. He paced away, as eager to depart as an Ambassador at an unpleasant posting who had just received orders to return home. The door thudded shut behind him.

The general's daughter ceased her motions and exhaled, a long, clean sound. Climbing to kneel, she looked to the screened room. After a moment, she glanced at the screen by the main door, then motioned Favik to come out.

The cloistered man entered the main chamber, as nude as she was, and faced her.

She smiled weakly. "I'm sorry you had to witness that." She sat back on her bottom.

"I'm sorry you had to go through with it."

"I saw no choice. He—"

Favik interrupted with a snort in a weak imitation of Sirish. Melande opened her mouth. He grunted, then inhaled roughly as he sat next to her. "I think, with practice, I could mimic that perfectly, if you would find that pleasing." He grinned and made another attempt.

She leaned back onto the pillows, lovely brown eyes to the ceiling. "By The Powers, no!"

The hidden door in his Havadran chamber swung open behind him. Favik turned in his desk chair to face the intruder, placing one hand on the cool ivory of his chair back, the other reaching for his long knife, scabbarded at his waist. It was a veiled woman, Melande by her strong posture, a stance he now felt he would recognize under a dozen veils. She peeled the head covering away, a sly expression gracing her face. "I am not used to seeing you dressed."

"That is easily remedied." His smoke-colored tunic and breeches contrasted with the beige tones of the chamber he had quartered in for some weeks, but as an emissary of Dalich King, he wore his Lord's colors. When he was clothed, of course.

Before he could act upon his statement, his beloved came to his side. Kneeling by his chair, she placed a pale hand upon his sable pant leg, her expression far away yet inward, as though silently conversing with herself.

"Melande, are you all right, my love?" He touched the soft fabric draping her shoulders, one finger grazing the smooth skin of her bare neck.

She shook her head, glancing at the desk. "I feel … strange. I am not certain how to characterize it, other than I have not felt this way since I was with child, when I carried Anish."

Fighting the urge to straighten in his seat, he asked in his best Ambassador's voice, "Anish?"

She brightened, looking into his eyes. "I cannot believe I never told you." Dropping to a whisper, "Anish is what I call Yirish, but only when we are alone. Even Sirish doesn't know it. I would have named him Anish, but in Havadra boys are named by men."

His love spoke a bit louder. "Usually the first male babe is named after the head of the family, but Sirish combined my father's name with his own." Her gaze became dreamy and she moved her free hand to her belly. "But mothers name daughters."

"Are you saying you think you may be with child again?"

"I've told no one, but yes. I am certain."

"Ah." He wanted to embrace her but hesitated, uncertain what this would mean for their future. Then he gave in to his heart and leaned toward her, encircling her shoulders with his arms. His heart's light drew close and laid her ear against his lap. They stayed a while in this great comfort. But he knew it would be short-lived if they did not act.

Kissing her head, he began, "Melande, I want you to come with me to Eskalind."

The general's daughter answered immediately, as though she had read his thought and prepared for it. "My husband would hunt us down."

"By the laws of Eskalind, *I* am your husband."

She pulled away and would not look at him.

"Melande, we would be protected there. I am in service to Marna, Dalich King's Mother." She raised her eyes to his, her expression hinting at recognition. "I am highly favored by her. She has many who work for her, who would protect us. In Eskalind, we would be safe."

She stood, steady in her slippers as though drawing strength from the earth. "You do not know Sirish. He would, by sly and subtle means, come after us when we least expected it."

Favik rose to his feet as well. "Dalich King's Halls are well guarded. Or we could stay at an estate remote to Havadra, where outsiders would be detected instantly. Please, Melande. We need only cross into Eskalind and show Anish to a Records Keeper."

"What?" She crossed her arms, brown eyes igniting with suspicion.

He continued, mild as a tutor explaining a subtlety to a discouraged pupil. "There is an Eskalind saying, 'The face proves the father.' When parentage is in doubt, the child and potential fathers are brought before a Records Keeper for judgment. You have said anyone with eyes can tell Anish is my son. And the fact that you have borne no more children to the man you were forcibly joined with is further proof." He drew close to her, close enough to sense her body heat. She did not retreat. Threading his fingers delicately through her ringlets, he whispered, "You, our son, and the newbabe would be granted asylum." Her lower lip trembled. "We would live together as a family, as The Powers intended."

His son's mother gazed at him, intent. "I would come with you, but Anish cannot."

"Why not?"

She sighed. "Havadran children are the property of their father. I have lived with that fact since he was born." Melande pulled away, gesturing with her hands. "Do you not see? Sirish believes Anish to be his son—if we bring Anish with us, there is no doubt Sirish will follow, to kill us and reclaim the child he believes is his. But if Anish stays here, he has the life of a lord of Havadra, the sole son of a prominent house."

"We both know how short a career that can be."

Her eyes narrowed. "Favik, if I alone leave, Sirish may come after me for revenge, but he *will* find another wife and perhaps father children. Still, Anish will be the eldest by far and in the best position to inherit everything."

"Or the new wife might kill him."

She crossed her arms again. "My father would protect him. No family in Havadra would risk the fury of both the general and Sirish."

Favik smoothed his voice. "If our son comes to Eskalind, he will live in a peaceable kingdom, free from the political machinations and terrors of this place."

"This place is his home and all that he knows. Do you expect him to blindly depart his homeland with you, a complete stranger?"

"I am his father."

"Oh Favik, he can never know that. It is the only way to protect him, and us, from Sirish's wrath." She turned and marched toward the hidden door. "I have an appointment with my healer, I must go."

Every ounce of him wanted to grab her, restrain her, but he would not be that manner of man. "Melande!"

With one hand upon the slim door handle, the general's daughter faced him, cheeks flushed as though they had just lain together. "Find a way, Favik, find a way for me, just me, to journey to Eskalind soon, and I will go."

Favik tried to smile, to reassure her, despite wanting to argue his point further. "I will. And in Eskalind, both parents name newbabes, be they male or female."

His beloved's expression lightened and she flew to his arms, laughing or weeping he could not tell, for he too was caught in a joy so rich it brought tears.

His daughter's healer departed the general's office in a sway of beige drapes, the clink of coins muffled in her closed hands. The musicians in the courtyard below hammered a rousing tune, in sync with their master's mood. His trusted man entered, pulling the screen closed behind him. Cutting his eyes to his servant, General Yirlofts spoke from his seat. "Time to procure a body from out of the walls."

The man nodded. "Burn it well?"

"Yes. Even if the Eskalinder examines it closely, he shouldn't be able to discern if it is the engineer that he seeks." A crisp salute, and the trusted man departed, leaving the general alone with his furnishings.

Reaching to one of the many small, square boxes on his immense desk, Yirlofts pressed the pads of his fingers tight upon the smooth stone surface. Faint green traces in the creamy stone referenced his loyalty color, a subtle reference to his family. For a man too clever to inscribe plans upon papyrus, each box housed objects that denoted steps in a scheme, their true meaning opaque to anyone but himself. The plot contained within this box needed no such mnemonic device, but habit allowed this indulgence.

Lifting the cool lid, he beheld the contents laid in horizontal order. First, a small vial made of glass and stoppered with a pure Nordak ice stone. Inside it, the pale yellow soil of Eskalind. Next, a stone marble, followed by a bent carpenter's nail. Lastly, a double seed of an orsblat tree. Items confounding to anyone but Yirlofts, who had invented their symbology.

Placing the lid aside, he lifted the vial by its base. This represented Favik, secret son of Eskalind's former Queen, in whose line ran Gifts from The Powers. Years ago, his spies at King's Halls reported the similarity of his looks to hers, their familial closeness. Havadrans noticed everything, especially the things Eskalinders were too blind to see or acknowledge.

The stone marble, threaded with gold, a favorite toy of his daughter as a small child. How she would giggle, rolling it down stairs and tables, chasing it to and fro as it clanked from one surface to another in the women's quarters. His wife once remarked that it must be under The Powers' protection, for it never once cracked or flaked, despite Melande's rough handling.

The useless nail represented the dead engineer, the pretext bringing the two together again.

Lastly, the twin seed for the newbabe and Yirish. If the newbabe were a son, it would serve as a second to its brother; a girl would be useful for alliance building.

Yes, the orsblat tree was renowned for its strength and flexibility. Useful qualities for surviving near the apex of Havadran power. Someday Yirish would serve at his side, once he matured and Sirish was eliminated. Grandfather and grandson would then align to maintain their family's position. May The Powers send the lad swift maturity.

———

Favik did not see Melande the next day or the next. It was the ninth month of the year, two months since he had arrived in Havadra. With Melande carrying his child, he must return to Eskalind swiftly to put a plan in motion to bring his family home. But first he must escape the general's mighty fortress.

Wandering the courtyard and garden in a haze of plots and possibilities, Favik settled on withholding his daily note to Ambassador Moril, thus failing to apprise him of his well-being. That produced the desired effect, for on the second day, a note from Moril arrived with an urgent request for word from the Eskalind emissary. The note was well sealed, but the wax not quite as smooth as the globules sealing the other messages from Moril. Favik suspected tampering.

He folded the note, just as the tiptoe echoes of a servant pacing across the paving tiles came toward him. He turned to see a serving man with downcast eyes.

"The general has news for you, Ambassador. Follow me." The Eskalinder obliged.

The pair made their way from the sunlit air of the courtyard, with its citrus scents, through a labyrinth of passageways leading down to cool darkness. The passage ended before a torchlit door. A large man stepped from the shadows. With a gesture and a piercing gaze in his sharp brown eyes, he demanded Favik's weapons.

The former Ambassador smiled as he unbelted his long knife. "If the general is on the other side of this door, I do not think I will require this." He handed the scabbard to the guard, who passed it to the servant. The guard opened the door, and Favik entered a long room. Square recesses lined one wall at eye level, each with a lit candle, thin threads of smoke trembling upward to soot the alcove. Crates and goods lined the opposite side of the room. A wide passageway lay in between, some items littering the floor, difficult to identify in the dim light. An odor, not of waxy soot, but of acrid smoke, grew as he stepped cautiously forward. The door behind him closed and another on the far end opened. A man entered.

"Ambassador Favik," the man called in the general's clipped bass.

"Sir."

The general stepped forward, the recessed candles rendering his leathered face menacing in their light. He carried a dark, amorphous bundle near his waist. "I have found your missing Eskalinder Engineer."

"Excellent. I shall meet with him at once."

The most powerful man in Havadra replied, "He is there, by your feet."

Gazing toward his shoes, Favik's eyes adjusted to the gloom near the floor. He saw a long beige form. He reached for a candle and brought the light toward it. Bending forward, he saw the shape was tightly wrapped in rough Havadran cloth. The scent of smoke grew stronger, and Favik glanced about, half worried that an unattended fire burned in the chamber.

One end of the draped figure's wrap was bunched loosely. Peeling back the fabric revealed a human head—charred, sticky, devoid of hair, even the maniacal grin of the teeth blackened. Whether it had once been Eskalinder or Havadran, it was impossible to tell. He stood, placing the candle on a crate, and inhaled, glad for purer air at nostril level. "What proves this is Kayvil of Eskalind?"

The older man watched him closely. "This." He hefted the item he held in his hands, walked forward to no more than a dozen feet away, and placed it on a crate with a clanking sound akin to wood pieces knocking together. The Havadran patted the bundle. "His personal effects, though not all had always belonged to him, I gather. Your Lady will be pleased by their return."

"My Lady Damina Queen?"

"No, her maither, your Lady, your royal Lady." His tone pressed with hidden meaning, begging Favik to inquire at what he hinted.

The former Ambassador countered with his own agenda. "Are any other Eskalinders serving as Engineers in Havadra?"

"My land no longer requires outside workers. King Astofts will delay any building projects for the time being."

"Perhaps they are required for other projects."

"No." The general's brow lowered over his brown eyes. There was nothing in his face at this moment that recalled his daughter, but her memory spurred the Eskalinder.

"And have I done you good service?"

A slow grin broadened Melande's father's face as silence fell between them. "I believe so. We await the final results."

The general's voice bore into him, prying, insistent, and for an instant Favik imagined his love alone, the pangs of childbed upon her and he a thousand miles away, unable to offer comfort or support as she brought another child of theirs into the world, without him.

The Eskalinder stepped forward. "Why? Why are you doing this to us?"

The slick shiver of a long knife tinged the air as the general drew blade. The candlelight flickered along the sharp metal as Favik fought instinct to draw back. He stared hard at Melande's father, who spat, "Ask she who bore you, when you show her this." He punched the Engineer's bundle with his free hand. "You're dismissed from my fortress." The Havadran exited the room through the door he had entered.

Favik stood aghast, muttering to himself, "She who bore me? What? He cannot think my Lady Marna is my mother." It made no sense, unless it was a calculated deflection on the general's part.

But it could explain the general's odd utterance, when Favik first entered the fortress several weeks ago—his enigmatic reiteration of Eskalinders' belief that The Powers' Gifts ran in the Eskalind royals' family line. If the general thought Favik part of that bloodline, it could explain why he would allow him access to his daughter. Twice.

If that were true, it also gave Favik power over the general, for the Havadran would not dare harm a man he thought was Marna's son. The Havadran general would believe it would bring certain war between their countries.

Not that Favik would use that power; he would not risk involving the Bladesmith's Daughter in the rescue of his family. Such a move could expose the Scholars and their secret works. He recalled how Lord Saril regarded him of late, the suspicion in the man's eyes could not be masked. The Lord must have passed his poison to Damina Queen, who now treated Favik coolly, as though their years of closeness during her childhood had been erased.

No, to spirit Melande and Yirish to Eskalind, he must devise an independent plan.

Marna, King's Mother, contemplated the tea canisters aligned neatly as books on the tidy shelf set on the polished ebony table. The shield-shaped table's glossy surface reflected the glazed pottery so truly that there appeared a mirror twin of each container, in exactly the same distinct shade. They ran the gamut that Dalich King's colors of black and purple allowed: from lavender to deep violet to deepest sable. The bell rang, in a sequence she had not heard since fourth month. "Favik is returned?" Marna stood and rang the answering bell. The door swung open, and her man entered the room, bowing.

"My Lady."

"Oh, my dear Ambassador! Safely returned from Havadra, how good to see you. How has it come to be so long since you left King's Halls? Your note said you would reveal all in person."

She smiled hugely at him as he approached, but she noted that while he smiled as well, something about him felt removed, hardened. As though he were before and yet somehow not before her.

"My return journey from Capitola was much delayed. First the ship that was engaged for me detoured to Veranga—"

"Veranga! That is far to the south of even Guerland." No wonder the journey had consumed months.

"Indeed." Her man stopped before her. "It was not my plan. Then in Veranga I found another ship, which brought me back north to Guerland, then to Mavold." He seemed done with the tale, his eyes sad.

Marna placed a hand along his cheek. His gray eyes brightened slightly in surprise. "Tell me, Favik, what has happened?"

"There is much to tell, my Lady." Now there was urgency in his voice and gaze. She nodded, indicating he should sit.

"Your Lady wants to hear it all, but unfortunately at the moment we do not have much time; I am expecting Damina for tea. The timing, the freshness of the herbs are all specifically important today." As she spoke, he removed a leather shoulder bag and opened it, pulling out a faded red parchment scroll. It was wound unevenly, more parchment on one tube and less on the other. "Is that—?"

"The Legend scroll stolen from King's Halls before I left for Havadra as an Apprentice Ambassador those many years ago."

Dalock's Queen lifted the scroll, untied the binding ribbons, and unfurled the parchment enough to ascertain at which section the last reader had abandoned it. Before her, an illustration of a group of men, each holding what appeared to be the outline of a brown triangle, the extreme point facing away from them. A small, sharp, pointed spear was notched at the point of the triangle, directed toward a stone-walled fortress. In the next illustration, the small spears flew through the air to a high-walled building.

"Yes, the Legend scroll made in the time of Keernlich King, the sixty-second—or was it sixty-third?—King." Her voice softened with sadness for all things lost. "A copy of an earlier scroll, abandoned to time." Hardening her manner, she asked, "Who had this?"

"Supposedly Kayvil, our missing Eskalinder Builder. The general himself showed me a body, one that was charred worse than an exhausted hearth log. He claimed the body was Kayvil and gave me a satchel he said belonged to the Builder. This scroll was in it." Her man sounded much more like himself.

"Ah. So the Havadrans know of these ancient weapons." She drew a ragged breath. "Oh Favik, if they use this knowledge…"

"My Lady, they have tried for years to re-create them, to utter failure and ruin. I overheard the tale with my own ears."

Weakly, the Scholars' Mistress whispered, "The Powers still preserve us." She lowered the faded scarlet parchment to her lap, noting that the gold decorating the finials had worn unevenly through to the wood. "How did you overhear this?"

"I stayed as a guest of the general at his fortress and found a hidden passageway."

She raised an eyebrow. "Could the general have meant for you to discover this hidden way?"

"He most certainly could, but what I saw and heard was a moment of pure emotion, of desperation." He leaned closer. "It was the general's sain, Colonel Sirish, conversing with his wife."

She thought she detected extra emphasis on the word *wife* but listened steadily as Favik reported how fire had rained from the sky at Sirish's weapons camp.

"Fire, you say?"

"Indeed. A great wall of flame swept across the colonel's weapons camp and obliterated men and weapons. Sirish barely survived, and he said it was not the first time his research efforts had been destroyed. The man was utterly distraught."

"Fire. That is good news." She glanced to her desk, to the plain piece of parchment she used to communicate with one of The Powers that lay atop it. Raising her chin, she inhaled deeply. "I thank you for your report. It cheers me immensely, as it does to see you finally home and safe. I will relate to my son that Builder Kayvil died in Havadra in a fire." She looked back to her man. "Ah, were there any other Eskalinders held in Havadra?"

"None that I could discover, my Lady, but I fear there may be. I was unable to leave the general's fortress the entirety of the month and a half that I was sequestered there."

Her whole body tensed. "You were not granted freedom of

movement?"

"No, but had I not stayed there, I would never have overheard that conversation I mentioned earlier." He paused, inhaling, his chest slowly rising. "I ask, if you do not require me for other tasks," her man bowed slightly, then raised his eyes to hers, "that I may search the Records Keepers' local offices for any documents pertaining to Eskalinder Builders journeying to Havadra."

Marna knit her brows. "But Favik, you searched the records here at King's Halls. All the duplicate documents sent from the local offices and the border crossings are kept here."

"Indeed, my Lady. But," he paused, "something in the general's demeanor makes me suspect he knew of more Eskalinders held there. I also think it was a scheme of his that sent my first ship to Veranga."

"But why would he want to delay you?"

"I had much time to think on it, and I have several theories." Favik nearly smiled. "Given who he is, I mainly suspect it was to demonstrate that he is the one who controls the situation."

Marna nodded, tapping the scroll knobs with her fingertips. "A demonstration of power."

"Yes." His demeanor softened. "If I find any documents proving that more Eskalinders, even one more, traveled to Havadra—documents that were not copied or were misfiled—it would mean one or more of our citizens, even children, may still be trapped in Havadra."

She sighed. "You are correct, that would not be acceptable. We"—she turned her thumbs away from each other in a subtle mime of the Scholars' secret hand gesture—"still must keep close watch on the Havadrans and their weapons schemes. As well as ensure that none of our citizens are held there. I want you to bring this," and the former Queen rolled the scroll back together, "to our Scholar of ancient texts at his estate. Have him make a copy by his own hand, for his research and personal library. No one else must touch it or see it but you and him. Then bring it back to me." She retied the ribbons and set the ancient volume into her man's stubby fingers.

"To Lord Radil in the far north." The hint of resignation in his tone was unmistakable.

"Whilst Radil copies the scroll, visit as many Records Keepers offices as time allows." She smiled. "I am sad to send you away again." Then, lightening her voice, "But the northwesterly reaches of Eskalind are lovely this time of year."

"The great greenery of Eskalind is a sharp contrast to colorless Havadra." Favik's gray eyes focused upon her. "My Lady, if I may ask, where is Deenofts these days?"

"In Kaymif, then to Saralya's estate, I believe."

"If I come across him, should I relay this news?"

"Wise of you to ask. He may have more information in this regard, given his frequent visits to Havadra. But tell him only if you meet in person. I trust none of this to correspondence."

The bell tolled, signaling the arrival of the Queen. "That will be my daighter." They stood and turned toward the entryway, both assuming an expression of pleasant expectation. The door to King's Mother's Library chambers swung open. "Come in, Damina. My, it seems you have grown even taller since I saw you last. Or are you wearing elevated slippers?"

The dark-haired Queen glided toward them, giving Favik a slight nod of acknowledgment. He stepped back.

The Ladies' heads were at nearly the same height, and the Queen scolded her maither as they embraced. "Just flat shoes, Maither. If you would only feast with the rest of King's Halls, more frequently than on Naming Days, we would enjoy your company more often and there would be nothing new to remark upon." The pair released one another.

"Favik was just leaving." Marna nodded to her man, who bowed to his Queen.

Damina lowered her chin slightly. "Of course."

"My Ladies." He departed, his face a mask of neutrality with a hint of Ambassadorial deference. The scroll remained unseen, tucked into his bag, Marna presumed. Damina watched him depart, her lips puckered slightly.

It struck King's Mother as odd that Damina acted so coldly to her man, and she touched the smooth linen covering her daighter's elbow. "Is everything all right?"

"Oh yes." It was an affirmation in word only, for her tone hinted at skepticism.

"Then come to the tea table, dear. I have prepared something very special for you."

Her son's wife paced alongside her, violet eyes searching the room as though she might discover some evidence of wrongdoing in plain sight. "Dalich and I are sad that you spend so much time in your chambers. We miss you."

"Now now, the Library and Scriptorium and all their attendant Apprentices require vast amounts of my attention. It seems everyone in Eskalind wants to be a Copyist or a Scholar of this or that knowledge."

"Hmm," intoned her daighter. It was a sound that begged consideration of its meaning.

Marna turned her full notice to the young woman. "My, another new gown? You keep the dressmakers busy."

The corners of the Queen's rosebud lips lifted. "Lady Dara said there were many pieces left over that will make fine bindings for your books."

"Ah, we know each other's weaknesses." The two women laughed, and the odd tension between them seemed to dissipate. With her hands flat upon the table, King's Mother lowered herself into her chair. "Your gown does show your figure to fine effect."

Damina fluffed the edges of her skirt around her hips as she sat, which made her petite waist appear even thinner against the swell of fabric around her round hips. "Dalich agrees. Though he made a comment that he preferred it rumpled on the floor next to the bed." The pair looked at one another, both snickering.

Marna turned to study the tea containers. "How fares your sister?"

"Yamina? Laden with child; the newbabe will come any day now, and her little daughter could not be more precious." The Queen sighed.

"How is it my sister has two children after being joined but a year, and here I am, still childless after years with Dalich."

King's Mother smiled slowly. "Now dear, it is not quite a full two years since you two were reunited and joined." She reached for a tea canister she had never served before and spooned its contents into her daighter's cup. "First we worry about whom we will join, then we worry about when we will get with child, then we worry how the child will fare; there is no end to worry, my daighter." She poured hot water into the ovoid cup, its shape reminiscent of a ponderous water droplet swelling in readiness for its imminent plunge to earth. "I fretted as a fresh bride on this very topic, as did the Queens before me who did not bear a joining babe."

"Maither, I am no longer a new bride."

"You know, my husband's parents waited nearly thirteen years for his arrival."

"Oh, by The Powers, I cannot wait that long. How miserable."

"Now now, you know it is mostly in Their hands." She gave her daighter a reassuring smile along with the smooth cup of tea. "I find the best antidote for worry is to plan and prepare."

"This tea smells different from the ones you poured me before." The Queen sniffed the cup, its potent, zesty scent rising in the air.

"A new formula of mine."

"My, the herbs settled quickly." She sipped. "Mmm, it is good. Spicy even."

"Excellent. Although it appears there is not enough hot water for tea for me." The elder royal reached for the closest bellpull and yanked the signal for hot water. Her gray eyes roved Damina's violet gown, the bodice a great exhibit of her generous cleavage. The long, elegant sleeves, trimmed in black Mavoldian linen, ended in a swirl of small lilac-colored gemstones decorating the cuffs. They looked familiar. "Have you no use for a bellpull in your quarters?" Marna asked as she recognized the rounded amethysts.

"Oh, I have a Page I can send for things. Or one of my Ladies,"

Damina began. She ran an admiring finger over the smooth beads. "And these were so pretty, I thought they would look lovely on a dress. You should come dine with Dalich and me in our quarters sometime. I know they were yours and Dalock King's; perhaps it is difficult to see how they have changed, but I would very much like to entertain you there, someday soon, if you would make the journey."

"Up that endless stairway?" Marna shook her head. "I appreciate the invitation, but even the thought of climbing those hundred steps makes my knees ache. But I will not speak of that. I promised myself when I was a girl that I would never make tedious conversation about my aches and pains as many older folk do."

She had not noticed the Apprentice Librarian enter the room, but the young woman came forward silent as a shy forest creature and deftly exchanged the depleted tea-water pot with a fresh one. Normally such action would earn no comment, but the Scholars' Mistress was always on watch for those with a talent for being unobtrusive. Many a Scholar's mission demanded it; Deenofts being the exception that proved the rule. "Dear," called King's Mother as the Apprentice reached for the door, "remind me your name."

Her eyes downcast, she bowed her blond head. "Layda, my Lady."

"Very good." The youngster departed. Marna placed powdered herbs into her own cup and poured the water, fighting a cramp in her fingers.

Damina's forehead knit. "Something ails you, Maither?"

"Nothing to worry about." But she nearly lost her grip on the pot as a painful twinge radiated across her back. "Umpf!" She gave up pouring the water and settled back into her chair, pretending nothing had happened, stirring her sludgy tea with a spoon with one hand and picking a silvery hair off her smock with the other while the tea settled.

Damina gazed at the sable-colored cup in her hand, but Marna felt her daughter's thoughts lay elsewhere. King's Mother sipped from her cup loudly, hoping to encourage her son's wife to drink more. Damina glanced at her and smiled, as though waiting for something.

Marna adjusted her position in her chair, the muscles along her spine relaxing. Indeed, she felt better all over, even in her knees. "My tea has never had this effect before."

The Queen grinned. "Oh, do you feel better?"

"Better than better," she admitted. "And all of a sudden."

"I asked the King to heal you," Damina said, a proud smile expanding across her fair face.

"What?" Marna asked, even as she realized what had happened. Under her breath she whispered, "What a fool I was never to think of that." She cleared her throat and settled comfortably into her chair. "Oh Damina, that was wonderful of you."

Her daughter blushed and sipped her tea. "I have been helping Dalich with his healing." The tone of love in her voice when she said her husband's name was endearing. "Yamina had a wonderful idea, that we two review all the letters he is sent requesting healing, then we make a list of each name and ailment."

Marna nodded. "Yes, I had thought of doing that myself during Dalich's … confinement, but I decided against it then. I thought the attention to reading each letter would help him feel needed. Of course, things are different now. He has you." She patted her daughter's sleeve, mindful of the purple beads.

"Yes, and whenever Dalich has time between his other duties, I ask him to heal then. It frees much of his day. Oh Maither, I love to help him and to help our people. That reminds me, I had not seen Favik in a long while." She looked over her cup as she sipped, the glossy black glaze as wet and radiant as her violet eyes, and somehow it made her observation seem more innocent than Marna felt it was.

King's Mother met the young woman's gaze. "He is just returned from a very long journey on your husband's business. Do you know when I might speak with Dalich? He will be very interested to hear it. Though," she glanced at the Queen's cup, "it may be a better use of his time if you were to visit him soon, privately. Very privately."

Damina glanced at her cup. "I see we are helping one another." Her violet eyes darted to the former Queen's. "Dalich always says you have a Gift for herbcraft." She stood, a sudden bout of giddiness upon her. "Oh, I thank you, dear Maither. I cannot wait to be a mother!"

"And I, a grandmother." She was not certain if her daighter heard her, for the young woman's expression had transformed to the curiously removed look she exhibited whilst in silent communication with her husband.

Then her aspect relaxed into a joyful smile. "He is alone!" She bounded from the room like a youngster promised a favorite treat on the other side of the door.

"Well," said Marna to the empty room. "Now we wait, and hopefully, in the eight month of next year, King's Son will appear."

The breads and sauces arrayed upon the table carried aromas of sage and smoke, but upon the tongue tasted flat and flavorless. Favik dipped a thin crust into the brown sauce, hoping the black flakes suspended atop it were pepper. Eskalinder food tasted ho-hum ever since he had returned from the spice paradise of Havadra. The short visit to Lord Radil's estate had not helped. The Lord's maither ran the kitchens, and her cooking reflected her Nordak heritage: spare the spice, forget the flavor. There was a reason Nordak was renowned solely for ice stones. Any mention of its cuisine was met with silence and knowing looks.

The Scholar leaned against the hard chair back and glanced out the Orchardton Tavern's window just as a gray-horsed figure rode into view. "By The Powers!" For it was none other than Deenofts, whom he had hoped to meet along the road south. It was already Winter, and after nearly two months spent attempting to return to Eskalind from Havadra, followed by his Lady Marna sending him to Lord Radil's estate in the farthest northwestern corner of the country, he felt that at last The Powers smiled upon him and he could put his plans into play.

The Havadran entered the room not long thereafter, sharp brown eyes immediately alighting upon Favik, who sat with one finger upon his cheek, staring at him. Deenofts approached and sat opposite him. Favik lowered his hand to the table.

Deenofts folded his hands together under his chin. "I see you use the classic gesture of my people."

"I wanted your attention."

"You have it." He unfolded his arms as though he were a giant bird about to ascend into the air.

Favik laughed. "It's good to see you."

His fellow Scholar dipped his prominent brow and brought his hands back to the wooden table. "And you as well, survivor of yet another sojourn in Havadra."

"Yes, and some of it was even spent inside the general's household."

"Indeed. Just a short ale, please." He preempted the bar man who was shuffling toward them.

"Only if you pay first, Havadran." His voice was gruff, like he needed to clear his throat.

"Damnil, you know me."

The man slapped a hand on the table. "Aye!" he guffawed, and he toddled off to retrieve his customer's beverage, waving a hand in the air as if pleased with his joke.

Deenofts shook his head. "You see what I must deal with here?"

"Just wait. You haven't tried the food yet." Favik glanced at the flavorless fare on the table.

"Oh, but I have." Deenofts pulled his head away from the table as though a foul odor emanated from it. "I stop here every time I leave Lady Saralya's estate. Ever since Damnil's wife became the brewer, he's been the cook. A sad day for the kitchen, but a *glad* one for the brew." He gazed at the approaching mug of beer as though he were a new father being brought his firstborn. "Best in Eskalind," he proclaimed as the Tavern Keeper placed it before him, a slight slop of foam dripping on the table. "Oh no, not to waste!" Deenofts cried, flicking his fingertips over each errant droplet and bringing them to his lips.

Favik chuckled at this display, glad for a light moment. Relaxed, he gazed about, and his eyes alighted upon a figure entering the tavern. For a moment he thought time had gone backward. It was a man dressed in a Chief Records Keeper's robes and headwrap, yet not the purple and black of Dalich King's officials, but a red robe and brown headwrap as seen in Favik's younger years, during Dalock King's time. The man grinned through his bushy beard as he noted Favik's expression. He passed by the pair, his ruby-hued robe long and flowing, then paused to ask, "Have you come for my story-telling?"

Marna's man wondered if this fellow was indeed a Records Keeper, one who enjoyed story-telling as a hobby. It seemed unlikely for a staid, exacting Records Keeper, but then again, Deenofts's penchant for dramatic gestures and outrageous behavior masked his observational abilities—and secret-keeping talents that even an Eskalind Ambassador could admire. "You are a Story Teller?"

"Yes, and I always dress my part." He gestured to his brown headwrap. Favik kept the thought to himself that the spread of the man's beard was worthy of an Amklander. The Story Teller continued to the back of the room and mounted the steps of the raised platform.

Favik turned back to his tablemate as the Havadran spoke over his mug. "He's playing the part of Daavil, a Records Keeper during the time of Haavlock King." He swallowed. "I've seen this costume and performance before. But last time I was here, he dressed as Braanya Queen to tell the tale of her founding Queen's Market."

"A bearded Queen?"

"He was *very* convincing." Deenofts stood and came round to Favik's side of the table. "Come, we must be civil and pretend to listen, if I hope to drink the exquisite brew here again without undue fuss." He pulled his chair beside Favik to face the Story Teller. The former Ambassador rotated his own seat. Side by side, the pair watched as other tavern patrons moved to sit closer to the entertainment.

The Story Teller began with an introduction that the gathered crowd found favor with, for the foot stomping that showed their approval rattled the tables and chairs as far back as the seated Scholars. Deenofts leaned toward his ear, "Now would be a good time for us to talk."

Favik held his hands in his lap in a loose rendering of the Scholars' gesture. His companion mimicked the subtle display as they both murmured, "Knowledge knows no borders." He could barely hear the Havadran over the Story Teller's voice. The former Ambassador to Havadra began quietly. "Where have you been?"

"Kaymif. No news there, but I made more merchant connections for my dyes. Then to Lady Saralya's, again no news. Most unusual. Now I'm en route to King's Market to raise some coin from my trade." His brown eyes watched the Story Teller, who held aloft a wooden blade in one hand and a furled scroll in the other. Deenofts rolled his bottom lip. "I had forgotten this part. But tell me your news."

Favik whispered of Colonel Sirish's failed weapons research and the discovery of the stolen Legend scroll. "My, that is momentous," Deenofts said. "Our Lady has the scroll?"

"No, its current whereabouts is over three hundred miles to the north."

"With Lord Radil?"

"Aye. I am to retrieve it when he finishes copying it, but he said that may be three weeks in full."

"Well, he is known for being extremely exact in his work."

Favik continued. "Radil's estimate gave me enough time to use the Swift Riders' horses to journey here and hope to meet you, and to make a trip to the local Records Keepers."

Deenofts seemed unconvinced. "Two questions. Why me and why the Records Keepers?"

"Our Lady wanted you to know of the news regarding Havadran armaments."

"I see." He reached to the table and retrieved his beer mug, resting it on his leg.

"Also, the missing Eskalinder Engineer I sought turned up dead in Capitola, and I fear there may be more Eskalinders trapped in

Havadra. Since I am here and have found you, I will check the local records and see if they yield any news. But you are wanted for a different mission." He turned to look Deenofts in the eyes. "When are you going to Capitola again?"

The Havadran nodded ever so slightly. "I have the feeling I may find need to journey there soon." He sipped his beverage.

"When you are there, see if you can find any information about a youth named Anish." He felt breathless saying the name aloud. If only he could tell Deenofts the full truth, but that must wait until Favik's family was finally in Eskalind. "Anish is a Copyist of immense talent, and he isn't even thirteen years of age. Not only can he form beautiful letters, but his drawings are stunning."

"This is more important than new weapons?" The Havadran placed his mug upon the table.

Favik chuckled. "Your ears must be open to any word about weapons too."

Deenofts looked unconvinced. "You sound familiar with this Anish's work."

"And impressed beyond words."

"Am I," Deenofts lifted his hands to draw attention to them, "to recruit him?"

"Not as one of us, but you can imagine how a talent such as his would be most welcome in our Lady's Scriptorium."

"To say nothing of his talents at forgery? I assume he is skilled in that area as well."

The audience stomped their feet, and Favik bent closer to his fellow Scholar. "Anish's skills can be applied where required." He glanced to the Story Teller. "The youth is still years from manhood and very close to his mother. He will not leave Capitola without her."

"What of his father?" Deenofts's brown eyes were keen.

"His father wants him in Eskalind, but only if he is absent when Anish and his mother leave Capitola."

"Is the father highly placed?"

The words were in his mouth ready to burst forth, but again he must keep silent. The less Deenofts knew of the true situation, the better. For now.

Favik answered the Scholar's question with a mere "Yes."

Deenofts chewed on this information. "Families of high standing are always in a precarious position in Havadra. At least they were before the general's sway stabilized the constant civil wars. Now it is just the families of grand ambition that need worry." He nearly sighed. "Favik, why would this youth and his fine lady mother want to accompany me, a complete stranger, out of Havadra?"

"Because you are offering them what every Havadran wants."

Deenofts pursed his lips in a quizzical *O*, then said, "Go on."

"You yourself told me every Havadran wants to leave Havadra."

Here Deenofts grinned, his thin lips stretched, almost showing his teeth. He spoke rather loudly. "Indeed." A woman in the audience turned and looked at them. The Scholars sat quietly with patient eyes upon the Story Teller. She returned her attention to the performance.

Favik placed a curled finger above his upper lip to conceal his mouth. "And you will be offering them a chance to emigrate to Eskalind, where the lad will work in our Lady Marna's renowned Scriptorium."

"And our Lady will fund this?"

"I will give you the coin myself. Now."

"Coins." Deenofts murmured the word slowly and lingered on the *S*. "Favik, I can manage on my own well enough, but if I must buy passage on a ship for, what, three people?"

"You, Anish, and his mother."

"Three, including a fine lady. A Havadran fine lady, who must not only be quartered separately from unrelated men, but in splendor away from common women as well. Likely with what Eskalinders call a woman servant. Or two. *That* will be an expensive passage."

"Deenofts, are you turning this into a Havadran negotiation?" The Scholar next to him shrugged as though offered a morsel not to his liking. Favik pressed. "As she is escaping the country by our Lady's grace, perhaps she will make some accommodation." He smiled, an expression that bordered on a smirk, for he believed the general's daughter to be tougher than her soft exterior might indicate. "I have the coins here for you. Now, if you have any word of Anish or happen to encounter him in Capitola, offer him and his mother passage to Eskalind. Our Lady will be most pleased if his talents are used in her service."

The Story Teller held his arms aloft, then made a sweeping gesture toward the entrance door. All the patrons rotated in their seats to watch as a woman dressed neck to toe in brown ran into the room, toward the Story Teller, and jumped into his arms. Everyone stomped their feet as Favik called to Deenofts. "This is more like a traveling players' show."

"He combines Story Teller and traveling players antics in his per-formances. A hybrid of the usual forms of entertainment, if you will." The Havadran Scholar lowered his chin slightly. "I wish … my sister also would leave Capitola." He reached a finger to his neck and pulled forth a black necklace cord. "She gave me this, last I saw her." He held the pendant for Favik to view. It was gold, a thick outline of a square, and perfectly smooth. The Ambassador calculated that it was worth more than all the coins he had just given the Havadran.

"My. Your sister must adore you."

"How could she not?"

Favik shook his head. "Bring her to Eskalind too. Why, she could act the part of the fine lady's companion, if required."

"She won't come. Earns too much coin to leave." His flicked the pendant under his robes, eyes narrowed on Favik, and spoke quickly, as though wanting to forget what he had just admitted. "How am I to find this Anish?"

"I have word he ventures from his family's fortress to anonymously sell fine books to the booksellers in Capitola. You may encounter him there. Here." Favik reached to the seat next to him and brought forth the thin book Melande had given him as an example of their son's craft. "He does not sign his name, just a symbol." He passed the book to his companion.

"Standard Havadran practice." Deenofts flipped through the pages, nodding his head and unable to resist a quiet aah over the quillmanship. "And not quite thirteen? Most impressive." He made to give the book back to Favik.

"Keep it. It may help you find him."

"And if the journey's expenses rise, I could throw this into the bargain." The Havadran grinned like he had triumphed at a heated negotiation. Favik smiled too, hoping his eyes did not betray his fervent hope that this scheme would work, though he was devising other plans as well.

After departing Deenofts's company, he made for the nearby Records Keepers, located conveniently alongside the Swift Riders' stables. Eskalinder planning and efficiency demanded this arrangement, for a message could be dispatched from King's Halls via the Swift Riders to reach this office in three days' time, despite the distance of nearly 250 miles. Not that the records here were usually of great importance, but to Favik, they were the first step in a journey he had never thought he would make.

Two black-berobed and purple-headwrapped Records Keepers greeted him from behind the long wooden counter, a man and a woman with a chill manner so identical it was as though one impersonated the other. The man ushered him into the horseshoe-shaped Records Room. A younger man in black robes, but without head covering, which marked him as an Apprentice Records Keeper, sat at one of the two tables in the center of the space, copying a densely scripted document with such speed Favik wondered if some wager for swiftness was at stake. Maneuvering to the shelves lining the room, his guide inhaled, raised a hand, and with a stiff gesture called out what each shelf encompassed. "There the military records from the later reign of Dalock King—anything earlier we must pull from storage. Next, military records from Dalich King's reign, there the current and five-years-prior census of the nearest estates and towns, next correspondences relating to taxes, then tax records for the past twenty years, followed by property records, and lastly," he inhaled, "passage records for all foreigners who have passed through this region since Dalich King began his reign. You were an Ambassador, were you not?" the man asked, a bit red in the face from his nonstop monologue.

"Yes. It is why to this day some people address me as former Ambassador."

"Hmm, well, since you have their memorization training, you should have no difficulty recalling what I have just told you. Or ask young Laglil here." He bowed, slightly, though with his voluminous sable robe it was difficult to discern his exact posture. The Records Keeper departed, leaving Favik alone with the fast quiller, who drew air through his nose in a conspicuous manner as though the act of inhaling would speed his progress.

The Scholar acknowledged him with a nod, then turned to gaze at the towering shelves stacked with compartments laden with beige, brown, and lilac-colored parchment and crinkle- edged papyrus. He stepped to the section with passage records and browsed the top document on each shelf. Many of them bore an inked *C* in a circle in the lower right of the page, which meant this was a copy of an original document. As a former Ambassador, in service to King's Mother and, for this mission, to King's Second as well, he might be given liberty to bring away originals, but still, copies must be made. Grasping a stack of documents, he removed them from their cubby, placing them upon the empty shelf used for reading. Favik then leafed through each sheet, familiarizing himself with the protocols of language and subtleties of quillmanship, repeating the same actions with sheaf after sheaf of records. He began a separate pile of records he would like to peruse at length, perhaps even copy. Whilst he labored, the sunlight shifted from the near window to the far, the day departing at its own pace, regardless of whether people toiled or sat in sloth.

Behind him, the swift-quilling Apprentice sighed, long and drawn out like a death rattle. Favik turned to him as the young man massaged his wrist and groaned. "Oh, sorry," Laglil said. He had a thin beard that did not quite reach his ears. It was debatable if that was an intention on the part of the razor's wielder or a matter of hair refusing to populate the area.

"No matter," the former Ambassador replied. "I would like these documents copied."

The Apprentice looked at him as though responding to a request to stone a puppy, then his expression stiffened into the purposeful but neutral Records Keeper guise. "Of course, Ambassador."

Favik smiled. "If it were not a bother to you, I could assist, though I may require some pointers on the appropriate forms."

The barely bearded one's eyes shifted toward the direction of the main office. "I think we could do that." His gaze shifted quickly from side to side as though scanning an unseen list. "Yes, it is in the protocol, as you are an Ambassador of Eskalind." He shook his wrists and for the next two hours assisted and instructed the Scholar in copying the documents, explaining the purposes of the different types of parchment and papyrus. Just as the sunlight started to fail, they completed the last copy. Favik blotted clean the quill the Apprentice had loaned him. He handed it to the young man just as the door swung open. The female Records Keeper entered the room in a sweep of black robes.

"Laglil, have you finished copying *all* the documents I gave you this morning?"

The Apprentice dipped his head and motioned to pairs of documents lined upon the table, every other document bearing a *C* in a circle in its lower corner, but lacking the seal of a Records Keeper.

The former Ambassador interjected, "And these for me as well." He pushed the parchment and papyrus copies forward.

"Indeed." Her eyes roved the documents. "Well, Laglil, this is impressive." Nothing in the Records Keeper's voice betrayed any hint of what the adjective conveyed. "Your final Apprentice tests must be scheduled. Congratulations. I will retrieve the wax and affix my seal."

She departed the room, and Laglil whispered to Favik, "Thank The Powers and you. No more torturous copying tests."

The Scholar leaned back into his chair, his eyes upon the perfect duplicates. "No, thank you."

"Uncle Favik!" The blond boy zipped toward his knees, clamoring to be hoisted to eye level for their usual greeting. His father, Lord Radil, chuckled at the scene, but his gaze portended serious matters awaited.

"Am I uncle now, Lord Amril?" Favik swung the lad in a full circle above the yellow marble tiling the foyer, careful to position the child to his left side so that he wouldn't crush the rolled papyrus in his pocket.

"Again!" laughed the little Lord, his head tossed back and his red velvet cap teetering toward the floor.

"Come, Amril, that is enough," his father said, stepping forward and repositioning the hat at a secure angle. "Welcome back, Favik."

"It is good to be returned to your home, Lord Radil." The former Ambassador lowered the child until the soles of his maroon shoes safely met the floor.

The boy clasped his hands together as if excitement were a small thing he could cage behind his fingers. "Uncle Favik, you came for my Naming Day?" His blue eyes shone bright at the prospect of the anticipated affirmative.

Marna's man glanced at his fellow Scholar, who mouthed, *Five. Tomorrow.*

"Indeed," the honorary uncle replied with a wink to Radil. "Why it seems not long ago you were just a wee babe, and tomorrow you will leave the nursery."

Lord Radil stepped forward to grasp his hand in greeting. "Do not make me feel old."

Favik chuckled. "I'm on the opposite side of thirty from you. The wrong side."

The Acta Sua grinned. "We are all glad you are here. I am not certain where my wife is at the moment, but she can explain the custom, from her mother's land, of calling close companions relations. Nordakslanders are the opposite of Guerlanders, with their special designation for blood relations. The northerners are more free with their terms." He smiled.

Favik assumed his best neutral Ambassador's expression. "This meets with your approval?"

Radil clapped him on the back. "As the sole child of my house for a generation, I welcome all the family I can collect, especially this honorary uncle to my son."

It warmed Favik's heart to hear these words. He wished Melande and Anish were with him to complete the family, though he wondered how Melande would harken to companionship with the Lord's wife, Mayva, who had been a servant in the Lord's home before getting with his child.

That child hopped along the corridor, running a small hand over the carved wood paneling, painted in his house's colors of red and yellow, with accents outlined in gold. Favik smiled, coming to the conclusion that Melande would simply have to grow accustomed to how Strange Kingdomers lived their lives, free from the scheming and corruption of Havadra. The daughters of Innkeepers and Blade-smiths joined Kings, and nobles joined servants. It was the way of things in Eskalind.

His fellow Scholar spoke. "Son, go find your mother and let her know Uncle Favik has arrived, that we will be in a private meeting in my library." The boy scampered off with no indication he had heard his father's directions until halfway down the corridor, when he shouted, "Mama! Mama!"

Radil shook his head and led his companion to the appointed room, opening the door and inhaling slowly. "Ah, the scent of old scrolls and new books. I will never tire of it. Are you hungry or thirsty from your journey?" Favik declined, and the Lord paced around several tables clustered haphazardly around the central area of the ovoid room. From high tapered windows filtered a pleasant glow of warm daylight. The sides of the room were lined with the traditional assortment of shelves and cabinets, but the open floor space contained not a single couch or seating area. Instead, tables of varying sizes, covered with bare parchment, quill trimmers, inks, dyes, used quills, papyrus, scroll finials, and rods, lay scattered about with no apparent logic to their placement. The Lord Scholar laughed. "You can see why I forbid Amril from entering this room without direct supervision."

They approached a table heaped with parchments. Radil gathered several and pinched the opposite corners with his long fingers to lift them without causing any crease or indentation. Two scrolls, each with faded gold finials, lay harbored beneath them. "You may recognize one of these." He placed the parchments on a near table and unfurled said scroll to a section marked with a red ribbon.

Favik noted the now-familiar illustration of men shooting short spears into the air. "Ah, the recovered Legend scroll from the King's Library."

"Or is it its copy?" The Lord Scholar swept the second scroll open, revealing a precise drawing identical to the first. Marna's man squinted to find any nuance of difference.

Radil smiled, the prideful craftsman before his masterwork. "Yes, this came out better than I hoped." He tapped a finger upon the first scroll. "Fortuitous that this original scroll was quilled during the reign of Keernlich King, whose colors were the same as my house. I had many old parchments to choose from. Perhaps The Powers planned this coincidence." He tapped the newer scroll. "Of course I made note that this is a copy, with our Lady Marna's permission, at the beginning and at the end of the scroll. I will keep this in my vault, to which only the Acta Sua of this house—me—has the key."

"She will be most pleased to know there is a copy safe in your Library. And I would enjoy studying these further, Lord Radil, but I have another matter to discuss with you whilst we are still in confidence." From his coat Favik retrieved a rolled papyrus sheet. "I found this at the Records Keepers at Northwest Market." He handed it to Radil, who uncurled the thin sheet upon another table. "As you know, both Lord Saril, King's Second, and our Lady tasked me with finding missing Eskalinders held in Havadra against their wishes."

The Lord reached for a set of sand-filled cushions and anchored one at each corner of the document as Marna's man continued. "The papyrus is a summons from Havadra—"

"You found it in this state? Flat?"

"Yes. I rolled it for transport."

"Then it is not from Havadra. The Havadrans fold documents into squares; this has no remnant creases. Did you not learn that in your Ambassador training?"

"I must have been ill that day." When Lord Radil's jaw dropped, Favik grinned. "No, Radil, I knew that. But look closer. Is there anything else your expert eye detects about this document?"

"Mmm, a dull blade trimmed the quill that was used on this final paragraph, see how the ink scatters ever so slightly more than here?" He pointed as Favik leaned closer.

"Now I do." He made a mental note to sharpen all his quill-cutting blades. "But that has nothing to do with the supposed Havadran origin of this document."

"True. The letters are formed in the manner typical to Havadran quilling. See the squareness of the letter *O*, here? And the hard right edges on this numeral *8*? This is normal for a document of this type."

"What about the ink?"

Radil placed his cheek alongside the document, his eyes cut to its surface. "Nothing unusual that I see."

"While you are in that position, how does it smell?"

Radil looked at him crossly as he raised himself to his full height. "Are you jesting?"

"No, my dear Lord. Ambassador Moril told me that Havadran ink has a smoky taste."

"Brave man. I would never taste Havadran ink; it might be poisoned."

"I concur, yet I tested his theory whilst in Havadra, and I found him to be correct. Most documents carry a slight hint of smoke, even in their scent."

The younger Scholar lowered his nose to the papyrus and sniffed loudly. "It may. But," he rose to Favik's eye level, "we already know it is not Havadran from the lack of creases caused by folding."

"Indeed."

"Still, it is good to know Moril's observation about the scent of Havadran ink." Radil stared at the document. "It is an odd thing. The text summons a Kaymiflander to Havadra, for the purpose of building… well, it does not say what."

"According to another document I read, this man from Kaymif had been firmly settled in Eskalind for over three years, and bought property, but had not quite found the time to apply for Eskalind citizenship…"

"Or serve the requisite five years of military service that would entail." Radil nodded. "You think the Kaymiflander created this document as an excuse to leave Eskalind without penalty?"

"Perhaps. It was very strange, and I wanted to hear your opinion on it. Thank you." Favik bowed slightly, summoning all his Ambassadorial skills to hide his glee. For this papyrus was one of his own hand, in an attempt to ascertain what a skilled evaluator of documents might discern as unusual or wrong in a Havadran document. Now he would be able to continue to the next step in his second plan for freeing Melande and their son. His companion interrupted his thoughts.

"Do you know what happened to this Kaymiflander?"

"No, but when I next find myself near the Havadran border, I will see if the Records Keepers there have any word."

Radil nodded, dipping his voice to a conspiratorial tone worthy of Deenofts at his most dramatic. "If this is concluded, allow me to share with you my newest prize."

Favik raised his eyebrows. "It is."

"Then follow me." Radil went to a cabinet with a high latch on the farthest end of the room, stopping first to lift what appeared to be a pair of folded red table napkins from a stack of same. He passed one to the former Ambassador. "Here, wear this over your nose, like this." Lord Radil placed the cloth over his nose and tied it tight around the back of his head. His blue eyes shone with a serious light above the red fabric.

"Are you jesting with me?"

"I am as serious as The Powers, for this concerns Them." His voice dropped to a whisper. "This may be the oldest document you ever lay those gray Humikslander eyes upon."

Favik fastened the cloth over his face. Radil turned to the cabinet, flipped the latch open, and drew back the doors to reveal several long, shallow drawers. With both hands he removed the uppermost slender rectangle and brought it forth. "Pull out one of the table drawers," he whispered. "The round gold knob. Either will do." Favik did as he was bid. "No, that one is dusty, try the other." Again, Favik complied, though he wanted to rib his companion for his after-the-fact fastidiousness.

The Acta Sua lowered the drawer he held, which was lidded with a thin sheet of red fabric covered wood. "Breathe very, very gently." He lifted a short ribbon to pull the wooden sheet away. Inside the tray lay a crumbling sheet of vellum, its edges rough and notched; faded brown ink that may once have been black lay in flakes like breadcrumbs atop the pale parchment. "Can you read it?"

Favik nodded, though the letters were faded; barely a whisper of dark ink lingered atop the yellowing animal skin. Radil covered his prize and replaced it in the cabinet from which it came. He pulled off the red napkin and gestured for Favik to do the same.

Favik spoke. "I read it, but do not comprehend it. It said that there were once many different speeches that people spoke, until The Powers decreed that all would speak the same tongue. What does that mean?"

The two Scholars paced slowly away from the cabinet, through sunbeams that raked across the room from the high windows. Radil replied, "I have thought long about it since I read it the first time. Let me tell you this." He paused his steps, and Favik did the same, meeting his companion's intense gaze. "When Amril was learning to talk, he would babble sounds as he tried to make words. I thought, what if that babbling was another form of speech? A form of speech we do not understand. How would one communicate with one who speaks a different speech? Pointing and hand gestures would have to suffice for communication. Think of how frustrating that would be, treating a grown person like a very young child." Radil shook his blond locks. "If this is how people once lived, perhaps The Powers did this to make communication easier between everyone. It would certainly save a lot of confusion."

Favik scratched his head, trying to understand. It was so odd. "I think I see what you are saying. How did you come across this document?"

The Acta Sua resumed walking. "It is ancient, from the time of Heenlock, our seventh King. You know my father was a military man." He stopped in front of a shelf crowded with small frames encircling the likenesses of his noble ancestors. "But his father shared my passion for our Legends and Legend scrolls, though he died when I was quite young." He lifted a miniature portrait of a man with dark hair and gazed at the image. "That vellum was his, the prize of his collection, hidden in a locked drawer. In his last testament he said it could be read only by me, and not until I reached my twenty-seventh Naming Day, which was last week."

"That's right, your Naming Day is in the First Month. But why wait until twenty-seven? A dozen years past when a youth qualifies to be a man? How odd."

"True." Radil placed the glossy yellow frame upon the shelf. "Perhaps The Powers somehow directed him to make this stipulation. Perhaps for some reason They wished this knowledge saved to be revealed at this time." He leaned close. "You must share this with the Bladesmith's Daughter, in private, in person. I feel she may find it of some use, and perhaps comfort."

"Comfort?"

"In The Powers' benevolence." He went to a nearby table and grabbed a rolled parchment, sealed with a precise circle of wax encasing a braided ribbon of red and yellow threads. "When you tell her, do so after she reads this document." The younger man passed the parchment to the elder. "The fruits of a research she tasked upon me."

Favik tilted the parchment end as though trying to look inside. Radil shook his head and held up a hand. "It is a matter concerning the royal family's relations. You know King's Mother has a sole sister, who is mother to eleven children."

"Yes."

"And yet our former Queen writes me that none of her sister's children have parented a child. Well, neither did Treya Queen's brother or Farlich's Queen's cousin—"

Marna's man held up a hand to stay what would surely be a lengthy recitation. "You are saying that once a woman joins the King of Eskalind, her family members will have no further progeny?"

"Maybe not none, but in a generation, or at most two, the Queen's family line will die out. I researched back twenty generations. The only descendant who remains is King's Son."

"Damina Queen's sister Yamina has two children."

Radil shook his head sadly. "According to my research, they will either never mother a child, or any children they bear will be childless."

"I would rather not be the one to tell that to Damina Queen or her sister."

"Yes, and if The Powers Will that I father a daughter, I will advise her to never show her feet to King's Son, when he comes." He raised his blond eyebrows. "But, if that be The Powers' Will..."

"You are getting ahead of yourself."

"Far, far ahead." Congenial laughter followed, though Favik wondered how his Lady Marna would process the news, and if carrying it might further delay him from his designs.

Lord Marnil, a First Sergeant of the Sixth Company of Dalich King's army, but for the next few weeks its Acting Captain, stood facing the taut canvas strung across one side of the commander's tent. Upon it, a rendering in dark inks of the southeastern corner of Eskalind, its border with Havadra and Thislin, and the entirety of the region under his charge. Beyond the depiction of Eskalind's borderwall was shown the interior of each Ever Allied nation. Those inner territories were not well-known to most Eskalinders, who tended to stay close to their peaceful homes and hearths, except during military service or if employed as traveling merchants. Even those born outside of Eskalind tended to remain in their adopted homeland once they gained their citizenship. Only Eskalind enjoyed The Powers' protection from the vagaries and cruelty people could visit upon one another.

Marnil's brown eyes darted to the long desk: a letter from his wife, Lady Athla, lay unapologetically unfolded upon it, as though it could impart its domestic messages through the air to his ears. He closed his eyes, could almost hear her voice reciting her lines, her excitement that later this year, their Lord and Lady would welcome their own son. Opening his eyes and glancing back to the dots depicting the Eskalind border, he wondered how The Powers discerned the boundary of their protection. Did They see it as a crumbling jumble of rain-rounded rocks? Perhaps in their vision it was a soft ribbon of light traced across the land in a permanently fixed position, according to Their design.

Someone entered the tent behind him, and given the brisk sound of the canvas flap being shoved aside, it was someone of authority or firm intent. The First Sergeant turned, a quick hand hovering over the hilt of his long knife, bestowed upon him by Dalock King at the granting of his noble house. In that instant, he half expected to face his brother Saril, or even the King. But it was someone else associated with his childhood home of King's Halls.

"Ambassador Favik. Well, this is a surprise." He lowered his hand.

"My Lord Captain." The blond man bowed, his eyes alighting on Marnil's purple tunic.

"Acting Captain, at least until Captain Sakil's child is born and named and Sakil returns to us. Which may not be till the third month. What brings you to this far corner of Eskalind?"

"Sadly, not a holiday visit to the waterfalls." Favik smiled slightly, the skin at the corners of his eyes holding their creases after the smile had passed. "Time is of the essence. Your Lord brother tasked me with finding evidence of Eskalinders held against their will in Havadra." He unfolded the papyrus in his hand. "And I have. This document," which he passed to the young commander, "outlines the sad tale of an Eskalinder living in Capitola along with his Havadran wife and son. The family wants to leave together, but while the man has been granted passage, the woman and child are held against their will."

Marnil scanned the papyrus. "So, the son is a master copyist and held for his skills, in service to a Havadran lord." He handed the document back to the dark gloved hands. "But if the son was born in Havadra, of a Havadran parent, the Havadran king will consider him one of his countrymen, to dispose of how he likes. I do not see the problem."

"Sir, under our law, the spouse of an Eskalinder can be considered an Eskalinder. And the child of an Eskalinder, even one born beyond the borders, can claim Eskalind citizenship."

"Can claim but cannot commit; if he is trapped in Havadra, how is this son going to complete the five years' service required to fulfill his Eskalind citizenship? He cannot. Now I see your point." Marnil paced to his desk and sat, pulling Athla's letter aside to make a clearing upon the leather surface.

The Ambassador approached the far border of the desk. "As a father yourself, I am certain you can appreciate how an Eskalinder parent would want his child to live within the safe confines of our border. Havadra is known as a treacherous place for good reason. The lord the youth works for may be toppled tomorrow and all his household with him."

Marnil folded his hands, sliding a forefinger over the points of the *M* carved into his signet ring. "This Eskalind man joined with a borderland woman and settled in her country. That makes them and their offspring subject to the laws of that land, however unjust those laws might be in our eyes. I do not think we need to call a Records Keeper to confirm that." He leaned back in his chair, eyes fixed on the standing former Ambassador, who tilted his chin in the same manner that Saril did when he was not quite in agreement, but wished to appear so. It must be a gesture learned in their Ambassador's training. Marnil much preferred the army's straightforward ways. Decisions. Commands. Actions. No verbal dancing.

Thank The Powers his parents had foreseen his aptitude for a military career and acted upon it.

"My Lord Acting Captain, I have studied our histories and laws. There have been cases where Eskalind sent aid to Eskalinders held abroad against their will."

"Indeed. As you must know, the procedure is to start with the Ambassadors and see what work they can do to extract our citizens."

"Aye. I recently spent months in Capitola on that exact errand. It may not surprise you to learn the Eskalinder who petitioned at that time for rescue conveniently died before he was returned to us."

"The Powers take those Havadrans." Marnil unfolded his hands. Palm up, he tapped the flat face of his signet ring upon the leather desktop. "My understanding of the law is that this document alone is not enough. But, if the husband returns to Eskalind and petitions a Records Keeper in person, the force of law may be called upon. Then the military may act to extract the wife and son. A quiet mission, of course. And it would require Saril's, it would require King's Second's approval."

"Certainly."

"Do you have a clear way to communicate with the father?"

"I do." Favik seemed very certain of himself.

"Good. Make use of it." Marnil stood. "May The Powers help us to bring this family together to Eskalind."

Favik nodded. "That is my wish as well, Acting Captain."

Making his deference to the young man, Favik turned and strode from the commander's tent. Once outside, he continued, his feet passing the flat sparring ground where a line of new recruits practiced their drills with swords and shields, the shouts of their Sergeant coaxing them to swing harder and higher. Spring came faster in this southerly part of the country, and even in the third month of the year, a nearby cluster of trees sprouted tender green leaves. A Healer, her long dark hair tied back behind her head, darted past him, racing toward a Soldier with a bleeding arm. She was garbed in the traditional Healer's red apron dress with white undertunic, the insignia of Heedlich First King, a white-petaled flower with a red center, above her heart.

Marna's man continued till he came to the knee-high stones of the borderwall, stopping with the tips of his shoes just short of the shadow-dark rocks. Across the beige expanse on the other side, miles beyond, somewhere in that great colorless expanse of wave-shaped dunes, was the western edge of Capitola, and somewhere within its walls was Melande and their son. Their life and his were a great stretch apart, and how to yoke them troubled him. He wondered what new illustrations Anish might be drawing this very instant, how Melande fared as their child grew within her.

His face turned away from others, in a solitary moment at the edge of Eskalind alone and with an army behind him, he considered what to do.

He had consulted every scroll about childbearing he could study in deepest privacy. His love must be well into her seventh month with child, and traveling would soon be unwise for her, especially with traveling conditions unknown. He would not put her or the babe at risk. But if his only hope of conveying them from Havadra was a clandestine military mission, he would carry through with that plan.

Favik imagined the moment Eskalind Soldiers appeared to them, and he knew they would not go with unknown people without a struggle. Melande kept a dagger in her robes and another strapped to her thigh. She had never explicitly told him of this, but he had seen the leg knife in brief glances when she undressed before him, felt the indentations left by the scabbard cinched to her moon-white skin, weighed the heft of the blade within her cast-aside clothing.

What she had told him was that Anish had had defensive training since he was old enough to walk. It saddened him to imagine his wee son learning to hide or dart away from attackers at a tender age. But in sooth, it was the nature of the youth's birth country to prepare for such. The general's grandchild would make a valuable prize.

However, the lad was old enough now to fight back. Favik would need to appear to Melande first, then have her convince their son to flee with them. If she would agree to it.

Placing his hands behind his back, the former Ambassador thought through the possibilities. Yes, it would be better to bring them to Eskalind whilst they were still a pair, rather than a trio; traveling with a newbabe would add extra difficulties. It was difficult to imagine a safe outcome for all concerned in a removal by military means, even if he could be there. If only Deenofts could find them, and convince them to flee. But the odds of that were likely as high as those of finding a lost ice stone in the expansive desert wastes before him.

How he wished he could ask his Lady Marna for assistance, to explicitly use the Scholars to help. But given King's Second's cutting words and coy looks, Lord Saril had some inkling of the Scholars, at the least he suspected Marna and Favik of malicious actions. The great favors that Favik might ask of his Lady to save Melande and Anish might capture the Lord's notice.

How Saril reminded him of a creature coolly studying its prey: vigilant, coiled to pounce, and confident that moment would arrive. Favik's actions and decisions must be completely separate from his Lady's, for if Lord Saril were to say anything to the King, that posed a greater risk for King's Mother. Once, when Dalich was new to his reign, the young ruler thought he discovered his mother and Favik in a lovers embrace, when she was merely comforting him. The outcome was Dalich alienating himself for months, leaving Lady Marna to perform all her son's duties as the young man shut himself away in anger. Favik would not have her suffer such an estrangement again.

And Deenofts. If only Favik could have told him his true purposes, but alas. So loyal to their Lady the Havadran Scholar was, he would certainly tell her everything the moment they spoke in private. Favik would rather tell Deenofts the true tale later, however it might damage their relationship. Surely the man would eventually understand that Favik did this only to rescue his beloved and their children.

A notion crept forth. Lord Saril had agreed that Eskalinders held in Havadra should be freed. If Favik brought Anish to a Records Keeper, he would surely be judged the youth's father. That would make his entire family eligible for Eskalind citizenship, and thus Eskalinders who deserved rescuing. So he must appear to a Records Keeper and reveal himself as the husband and father, then proceed with the Sixth Company to save his loved ones. But once it was known that his wife was the general's daughter, and called wife by another—a Havadran colonel—there would be no chance of a rescue. Such an operation could cause war between Eskalind and Havadra.

Unless the general wanted him to spirit them from Capitola; Melande had told him her father seemed to regret not emigrating to Eskalind as a young man. General Yirlofts might even aid them in the endeavor. It would be the ultimate insult to his despised sain.

Favik dug his toes into the soles of his shoes. It seemed an impossible position, the worst Ambassador's conundrum he had ever faced. There was no clear, safe way out. Unless he could write or visit Deenofts. Perhaps the pair of them, together, in Capitola, might find a way. But that could be months. Maybe Melande was right, maybe there was no way to bring Anish with them. She and the newbabe, only.

No, that was not acceptable.

He wanted to cry to The Powers for help, yet he felt the only assistance to come would be of his own device and design.

Kicking the mustard-yellow dirt at his foot, he made his plan. Following Lord Marnil's idea, he must petition a Records Keeper for his family's rescue. But if he petitioned as himself, his name would enter the records, which were publicly available, with multiple copies kept: one at the office where they were made, another at King's Halls, and, when the records concerned passage from Eskalind to another land, a third copy at that border's main crossing. Colonel Sirish would doubtlessly send men to find his wife and supposed children. They could find a copy of the records wherein Favik, as himself, claimed them as his own family. Even the general might then attempt to retrieve his daughter and grandchildren; he would at least make a show of it to Sirish.

Given that the general might possibly think Favik to be Marna's son, it seemed unlikely he would mount a true retrieval mission. He might even be counting on King's Mother's protection of his offspring in Eskalind.

So. It became clear. He would disguise himself, petition a Records Keeper on the western side of the country, far from Havadra, unlikely to be found by Havadran spies. He would return to the Sixth Company as himself, with a copy of that petition. But first he must forge a record of military service and of travel to Havadra for his bogus Eskalinder, then plant those records in King's Halls' Records Keepers' offices. As a trusted former Ambassador, it would not be difficult to sneak fraudulent records into the masses of documents. He must also show the documents to Lord Saril to earn his nod for the mission.

Lastly, Favik considered what to do with Melande and Anish and the babe once he brought them to Eskalind. Here he smiled. Melande would be more comfortable amongst a household of noble women as she transitioned to her life as an unveiled Eskalinder. A sojourn at Lady Saralya's estate seemed a good choice. His fellow Scholar had a kind heart and would be unlikely to refuse a woman with a newbabe in her arms. Anish would revel in Saralya's library.

Why, the boy and Lord Radil would have much in common as well, and perhaps for a time the trio could shelter at his estate—about as far from Havadra as one could get inside Eskalind—at least until it seemed safe for them all to live freely as a family. While they waited, Favik would travel the land and destroy the records of his nonexistent Eskalinder.

Yes. He would sequester Melande and Anish at Lady Saralya's, then Lord Radil's as a secondary or a later plan. Smiling at the desert expanses, Favik calculated that at some point in the next ten years, the general would lose power. Sirish might attempt the kingship, and that quest never lasted long in Havadra. Then Favik and his progeny would appear to Records Keepers, who could judge him the father, and thus the lawful husband of Melande. Time would solve this problem, as it does all problems. Then he and his family could live openly in Eskalind.

"Portnil of Eskalind, you appear before me, Abya, Records Keeper of the town of Haarshil's Home, on this fifth day of the third month, in the year since the founding of Eskalind 2914, to make claim that your Havadran-born wife and Havadran-born son are held in Capitola, the chief city of Havadra, against their will and yours."

"I do." The petitioner kept his eyes on the parchment stretched on the desk between them, upon which were quilled the requisite lawful words interspersed with the situation's specific names, awaiting only the Records Keeper's seal and signature.

"Furthermore, you state that your son, Anish, is held at Colonel Sirish's fortress, where he is stayed because he is a prodigy Copyist."

"Yes."

This was the first time Abya had served as an adjudicator in a matter as troubling as an Eskalinder family forcibly confined in a borderland, and she thought a parent might exhibit more emotion during such a proceeding. The child's future as a free Eskalinder, or as a Havadran bound in service to a fickle master, hung in the balance. Then again, the dark-haired man standing before her exhibited a quiet solemnity that could be born of long suffering during his struggle to rescue his family.

Family. A topic much on Eskalinder minds these days, as the Queen was with child. Another generation living under The Powers' protection.

The Records Keeper rose to her toes. A section of her purple headwrap shifted as she did so; for a moment she thought it might tumble apart, but the cloth remained stationary.

"All your paperwork is in order, all proof supplied and measured. I now sign this document and its copy." She reached for her quill, with its black feather slightly curved at the tip, an exotic and no doubt expensive present from her proud parents upon her promotion to full Records Keeper. She had used it only thrice before. Signing and sealing a document whilst elevating herself on her feet was still an unfamiliar habit, but she laid her name to the parchments with a flourish and poured the violet wax at the most solemn pace the molten goo allowed. Impressing the wax with her seal, Abya lifted the parchment by its far corners and passed it across the table. Lowering her heels to the ground, she said, "May The Powers lead your family to the safety of Eskalind."

The man nodded, his head bent slightly, beardless chin angled to the ground. A strand of dark hair lay across an ear. Portnil's eyes appeared heavy lidded, almost as though he were sleepy, but Abya guessed they were intent upon the document—as though it threatened to flee on its own accord. Then Portnil reached for the document and lifted it from the table.

———

Favik paced from the Records Keepers' office at a sedate walk, the document suspended between his fingers. He calculated the pool of wax holding the seal to be an inch and a half across and likely to require another few minutes to cure and harden fully. Slowly he walked to the tavern, and once inside, laid the document before him on a table, watching the seal as though it might speak to him. It might whisper that he would be lawfully banished forever from Eskalind if his deception were revealed. How fortunate to have a newly made Records Keeper judging his case. The woman seemed more concerned with uttering the proper words and stamping the documents in the proper manner than with investigating his cause. Perhaps his scheme would carry through.

After nodding to the Tavern Keep's offer of bread and sauces, he touched the purple wax with his fingernail and judged it firm, but he did not fold the parchment until his meal was reduced to crumbs and empty bowls. Speaking to no one, he left coin upon the table and rode away, turning off the road to follow a small stream threading through thickening trees. Tying his sable horse to a stout branch, he retrieved his grooming kit from his pack and set to work cutting the dark-dyed locks on his head, then shaving away any remaining stubble. Surprised by how cool his bare skull felt, he was glad he had brought a cap. Across his face, there was a whisper of roughness as his beard made effort to reclaim his chin.

The former Ambassador continued his trek off the main road for over two hundred miles to his next destination. For several days he spent his nights camped where he could, frequently giving in to the urge to touch the unfamiliar territory of his cranium. At last he reached Pleasanton, on the twentieth day of the month.

Entering the Swift Riders office, he presented himself as Favik, former Ambassador on a mission for King's Second. He requested a fresh horse for his journey to the Sixth Company, which was granted. Before leaving, he visited the local Records Keeper, who made a copy of Portnil's document. Favik meanwhile quilled a letter to King's Second, outlining his discovery of firm evidence of another Eskalinder family trapped in Havadra. Both his letter and the copy journeyed by Swift Rider north to King's Halls, whilst the Ambassador headed east.

Four days and nearly a dozen exchanged horses later, he entered the Sixth Company's camp, tired and sweaty and seeking an immediate audience with the commander. Captain Sakil had resumed his post, and Favik found the army man standing in the exact same place in the commander's tent that Lord Marnil had occupied during his last visit.

"Ambassador Favik," the much taller man greeted him, gesturing for him to come sit by the desk. Sakil wore a puzzled expression. "What happened to your…" He waved a finger along his brown hair.

"Ah, a wager." Favik sat and smiled weakly, the expression of a man defeated by a silly embarrassment. Even with both men seated, Favik found his chin rising to meet the Captain's gaze.

"The Ambassador gambles?" Sakil grinned, clearly expecting a tale.

"Only when circumstances call for it." He cast his eyes to the documents pouch on his lap and undid the clasps with efficient aplomb, his lips set in a neutral line.

Captain Sakil read the cue and moved to business. "First Sergeant Marnil told me of your visit on behalf of an Eskalinder's family trapped in Havadra. Is that what brings you back here?"

"Yes, and I now possess the legal documents that substantiate the claim." He produced the parchment for the Captain to review.

Sakil held the document in both hands and said nothing for several moments, even after his eyes ceased scanning the lines. At last he lowered the petition to the table. "Extracting this boy and his mother from Colonel Sirish's fortress will be the toughest operation my people have ever faced."

"I understand, though it may not come to that. I have a Havadran connection that may benefit this operation."

"I want to hear all of it, but even assembling the team will occupy some weeks."

"Weeks?" He was too late to suppress the shock in his voice, for the word had already escaped.

Sakil nodded. "A rank that held some of my best people for just such an operation was recently transferred to the Eighth Company."

Favik's heart sank. "Isn't the Eighth stationed at the border of Amkland and Kursak?"

The Captain cast his brown eyes to the large map draped across the long wall of the tent. "At the moment, yes."

They could not be farther away and still tread Eskalind soil. "And you must have these, eight, twelve people?"

"Half of them will do, but the best chance of success lies with them. One is half Havadran and easily passes as full. He has even spent time in Capitola; we will need him to navigate the city." His last sentence was spoken with the authority one expected of a Captain of Eskalind. "But, Ambassador, tell me of your Havadran connection."

Fighting the despair growing in his chest, Favik replied steadily, "I have a contact whose sister has access to high households. She could enter Sirish's fortress under pretext and communicate with the wife, making arrangements for the wife and son to depart the fortress. Your team would pose as carrying box men, and bring them in boxes to board ship in the harbor, then escort them safely to Eskalind."

"I thought the son was held against his will in the colonel's fortress."

"My understanding is that he is trusted enough to leave briefly to purchase inks and parchment for his trade. Like all in Capitola, he travels anonymously in a carrying box. A youth of thirteen cannot be expected to escape Havadra on his own, and his true father has limited means to help. More people are required for this to be a successful rescue." His throat wanted to tighten as he spoke, for discussing his wife and son in such impersonal tones brought pain to his heart. "The mother will be veiled, thus a swift change of clothing in a carrying box will render her untraceable. The boy can be hid in a padded barrel or luggage for placement aboard ship, or dressed as a veiled female."

"And how will you see to it this happens?"

"I will journey ahead and send word back as to how our plan progresses. We should rendezvous in Gergelt, but as their main port likely brims with Havadran spies, I recommend we rendezvous at the inn that is just a day's ride north on the main road."

"All right. I will send word there."

The letter from Humiksland rested face up on a shaded part of Marna's desk, laid there half in the hope that the ink would fade immediately and somehow render the words untrue. It pained her to read them, but the news must be shared with her niece Palika and Palika's two brothers who resided in Eskalind, for they must be informed of their mother's death.

"Mother of eleven, grandmother of none. By The Powers' Will, it seems Lord Radil is correct." The former Queen sighed, her heart a great weight within her chest. The last letter her sister had sent bemoaned her plight, in light of Marna's grandchild's birth coming in a few months. "But Werna constantly complained about everything," Marna murmured, "ever since I left her household. No matter how much I tried to help, sending her servants and horses and ..." She looked away and sighed again, grateful to be alone in the morning quiet.

As though her breath had propelled it, the bell rang. Closing her eyes with a groan, she lifted the answering bell on her desk and rang the response. "Well, this will move my mind to other matters." The former Humikslander leaned into her chair, the long braid draped down her back a poking lump of discomfort. Resolving to return to her usual style of loose hair, she watched the door.

"My Lady!" An Apprentice entered, her eyes bright and wide. "My Lady, the Queen is in her pains."

"It must be false pains; the babe is not due for another three months by my calculations."

"She says the babe is coming."

Marna jumped to her feet. "Where is she?"

"In her chambers, my Lady. She calls for you."

Her passage to the top steps of the Royals' Tower was a blur, thoughts racing faster than her feet could carry her, the Apprentice at her elbow as they hurried to the Queen's quarters. They entered huffing and puffing.

Damina lay sprawled and writhing across the Queen's bed, her face contorted and red, tears streaking her cheeks, blankets and sheets strewn everywhere like haphazard hillocks. Her sister Yamina crouched at her side, tenderly attempting to pull long strands of dark hair from the Queen's eyes.

"Sister—breathe, try to stay calm. See, your maither is here, she will—"

"Help me!" Damina cried. "Maither!"

"Pull these blankets away, let me examine her," Marna ordered. "Has the Midwife been called?"

Yamina answered, "Yes, my Lady." She lifted the sable sheets covering her sister.

"It is too soon, too soon, my poor babe," wailed the Queen. "The Powers are punishing me."

"Shh, you both will be fine, dear. I know you are in great discomfort, but you must concentrate on breathing calmly," Marna soothed. As the last covering was flung aside, she could not believe what she saw. Damina's belly had grown large enough to house a full-term babe. She stifled an exclamation.

Damina's violet eyes glistened wet and unfocused. "Maither, I have wronged you, I am sorry. The Powers are punishing me."

"My sister," Yamina interrupted, "calm, calm."

"I must tell her!" Damina winced.

Yamina told the Apprentice, "Go see when the Midwife will be here." The girl ran to do her bidding, though her eyes trailed to the bed as she made her way to the door. When the door shut, the Queen's sister said, "Damina, I told you it's nonsense."

"What are you talking about?" Marna demanded.

Yamina shook her head as her sister began, "I am sorry I doubted you." Damina reached for Marna, who sat by her side. "Saril thought you and Favik, that you two were up to something without the King's knowledge."

The former Queen patted her daughter's arm. "Conspiring on Dalich's Naming Day present, perhaps?" She smiled. "There's no need to trouble yourself now; you have something more important to do right now, and that is to let the babe come."

The young mother-to-be inhaled so deeply, for a moment Marna thought the child might spring forth on the exhale.

"We are all here to help you, my sister," Yamina soothed.

"The Midwife's here!" the Apprentice called from the door.

King's Mother moved aside, allowing the Midwife and her assistant access to their patient. Wondering why Dalich had not used his healing Gifts to reduce his wife's suffering, she made for the door joining the royals' chambers. Yamina stayed her exit. "My Lady, will you remain? It would quiet her to have your skills present. Damina told me you delivered some of your sister's children." Her plain features magnified her concerned expression.

The former Queen closed her eyes. "I have not attended at childbed since the birth of Lady Jinilya, nearly ten years ago." Opening her eyes, she reached for Yamina's hand. "I just received word of my sister's death. I am not certain I will be of much use."

"Oh, my Lady, I'm most sorry for your loss."

"Dalich, help me," Damina whimpered, drawing her sister's attention.

Yamina turned to the former Queen again, still holding her hand, and squeezed. "My Lady, as the King can heal with his thoughts, could he reduce her pains?"

"I am on my way to ask him." Marna released Yamina's hand and achieved the door joining the King and Queen's chambers. Finding it unlocked, she entered her son's quarters. She thought she saw a dark head on the other side of the expansive bed. "Dalich?" she called. "Are you on the floor?"

"It is Saril." He rose and she saw Saralya's son, his coloring oddly pale despite his dark complexion, his expression equivalent to that of a lost child. "The King..." He gestured to the floor, his voice just above a whisper.

She closed the door behind her, bolted it, and stepped forward. "Where is he?" Her voice quaked with barely controlled anger and fear.

"My Lord, please, please wake up," Saril choked, as he bent to the carpet again. Marna's heart sank at the prospect that awaited on the other side of the bed.

There Dalich lay sprawled, face up, eyes closed, mouth trembling.

"Son?" She knelt by him. He did not respond. "Saril, what happened?"

King's Second blubbered sounds she could not interpret, as though all the world were lost, along with his reason. King's Mother barked, "Be useful. Help me sit him up."

That spurred him to action, and the pair lifted the King's head and shoulders from the carpet. He moaned as though stabbed. "Dalich," his mother asked, "are you hurt?"

"Damina...," he whispered, spit dripping from the corner of his mouth.

"Saril, position him against the bed. Do it." They dragged the King to sit upright as Dalich grimaced. "Get water and a cloth," Marna ordered, her voice firm, partly wanting to give Saril something useful to do but also to keep him away from her, for she feared saying something she might regret about Damina's confession.

King's Second crawled to his feet to fetch Marna's requests. Dalich groaned.

"My son, what is it, what has happened? Please, can you tell me?"

"I...feel her pain."

King's Mother processed this information, murmuring, "Could the herbs I gave Damina have done this?" Saril returned with a cloth in cool water, concerned eyes intent upon his Lord.

Marna dabbed the drool and sweat from her son's face as King's Second spoke. "My Lady, we were in counsel together when he felt her labor begin." The King made a soft sound. "He planned to extinguish her pain when the time came, but he was—" Saril's voice quaked. "Overcome."

Dalich opened his eyes, gray mirrors of his mother's. "I feel everything. Magnified."

Saril roped an arm around his Lord's shoulders, speaking in a tender manner. "Try to ease her discomfort, then you will feel better as well. Remember, when your son arrives, you must name him in the open air before The Powers as soon as possible." Marna's Reader's son smiled, his usual silvery tone returning. "I would be neglect in my duties as King's Second if I did not remind you."

"I know our custom," Dalich retorted, a flicker of defiance in his voice, extinguished the next instant as his eyes bulged and he choked, neck muscles tense. He leaned against Saril, who looked at Marna as though she were the only person who could rectify the situation.

She smoothed a hand over her son's slick forehead. "I will send for herbs to calm you and to ease Damina's suffering. Hopefully the babe will come soon."

But hours later she found herself saying the same words as she sent for yet more herbs, none of which yielded even the slightest efficacy. She considered retiring to her chamber to ask for guidance upon The Powers' parchment, but every momentary lull was countered with a fresh crisis. Instead Marna remained in the Royals' Tower for hopeless hours upon hours.

Thankfully, the Midwife reported the babe still vital inside the womb. Then night turned to day and exhaustion claimed the first Midwife, who was replaced by a second. Marna wished fervently for The Powers' continued benevolence upon her family as her pain-racked son sank into his bed, still as a corpse save for dripping perspiration. In the next room her poor daighter lay breathing raggedly, unable to eat, drink, or rest.

Through all of this, Lord Saril would not leave his King' bedside, nor did he betray a hint of suspicion of his former Queen. His steadfast attention and continual encouragement of Dalich bolstered Marna through the trial. At last, in the darkening of the day, King's Son was born, to the relief and joy of his mother and all around her.

The Midwife declared him hale, and remarkably equal in size to a full-term babe, whilst his vigorous, loud cries smothered any shadowy fears as to his well-being. King's Son was then presented to his grandmother, who after a sleepless night noticed first that he, disappointingly, had not inherited his father's and grandfather's lovely long fingers. She carried the wee babe across the threshold to his father's chamber.

The room stank of sweat. "Your son, Dalich. It is time to stand and name him outside before The Powers, before our people."

He barely opened his eyes. "Cannot move."

She hoped he fathomed the urgency in her voice. "You must. The Naming must be done outside, as soon as possible after King's Son is born. By *you*. For his protection and this land's. It is *vital* that you do this." She feared that every moment slipping by might bring a diminishment in The Powers' protection of the babe.

The lit candelabra by Dalich's bedside dimmed ever so slightly.

"Your mother is right, my Lord." Saril's smooth voice gave no hint of the exhaustion he must surely feel. "All our Legends tell that to enjoy The Powers' protection, the Naming must be done immediately." He glanced at Marna, who nodded. "My Lord King, let me assist you to your feet; lean on me as I see you to the terrace. Our people and The Powers await." He reached under Dalich's back and hoisted him into a sitting position. Dalich's pale face slumped against his Second's shoulder, his cheek contouring to its shape. Saril whispered, "My Lady, would you call a Guard to help?"

Marna carried the wee babe to the main door and opened it to find the Queen's braither, husband to Yamina, standing outside. "Trevil, help Saril assist the King to the Naming Ceremony."

The Guard's green eyes darted to the infant in her arms, and he nodded. She stepped aside to let him into the room, then began the long trek down the stairs, careful to hold the child with a firm grip. At the bottom she waited. It seemed forever before the sound of panting and heavy footsteps echoed along the spiral of stone walls. She nearly called back to them to hasten, even as Saril's voice came fast, like a held-back confession.

"Recall, my Lord, that my father, Jinil, accompanied your father to the Naming Ceremony when you were first born. I thank The Powers to be with you"—Dalich moaned, but Saril continued, soft as a lover—"at this momentous occasion, my dear Lord."

Members of King's Halls and the household trickled toward King's Mother, Lady Dara first among them, her bewildered expression lighting with joy when she saw the bundle in Marna's arms.

"Oh my Lady, King's Son! Oh, I have never beheld a babe as new as you, my Lord. Oh, except for your father!" She cooed over the child as others streamed forward, a gathering wave of people: Pages, then Cooks, followed by Ladies, groomsmen, the Mavoldian ambassador, a Nurse cuddling her charge (who was perhaps a week older than King's Son), various Lords and Gardeners, Apprentice Librarians, the wife of the ambassador from Kursak, all crowding the corridor for a glimpse of Dalich King's son. A misguided merchant from Thislin, bedecked in her people's famously brown garments, erroneously remarked that the other small babe was King's Son, and was quickly put to rights by the voices of many Eskalinders calling a correction to her error.

Amidst the bustle of onlookers threatening to engulf her, Marna spied her niece Palika waving from farther along the passageway, but the new grandmother dared not lift an arm in greeting. Nestled in his swaddles, her wee grandson slept, oblivious to the adults around him. At last, Saril and Trevil reached the bottom stair and brought the King forward, Lord Saril calling in a stern, commanding voice for people to make way. The crush of spectators parted, many holding hands to their mouths as they gaped at their Lord, who slumped between his men limp as a dying Soldier borne from the battlefield, his cheek still resting upon Saril's shoulder.

Marna allowed the men to pass and followed close behind their heels, mindful that if she did not, the crowd would sweep behind them and she and the still-unnamed child would be further delayed.

Slowly, this odd procession crept its way to the torchlit terrace. The flames in the brazier sputtered, then danced high in their bowls against the black of night as the murmur of many voices rose. Approaching the balustrade overlooking the courtyard, she could hear the crowds cheer at the royals' approach: three generations of Eskalind's Kings represented by Dalock's Queen, Dalich King, and his newborn son. The King found strength to lift a hand, with Trevil King's Guard standing behind to steady his Lord.

Saril called for silence, and Marna stepped before King's Second to hold the newbabe before his father, clinging fast to the blankets cradling the soft weight of the child.

———

"This is my son," called Dalich faintly. At last he beheld his child. He reached to touch the babe's wee head. Such a small form, that had already caused so much pain. A future warrior who would visit death upon many mothers' sons. May The Powers forgive him the thought.

He could feel Damina, as if to comfort him, dreaming a peaceful sleep, his healing Gift returned and restoring her as she slept. Still, weakness shadowed his muscles, his arm held out to touch his son strained with effort as though he bore a dozen long swords in hand.

His mother's gray eyes were keen upon the child in a maternal lock. Perhaps she had once gazed upon him in the same manner. Dalich felt he could peer into her heart for the briefest of moments, and there he spied all her care and concern for himself, his family, and their people. He sensed Gifts within her he could not comprehend, as though his vision were obscured by a gauzy curtain, but he felt certain that wonders lay upon the other side.

Saril whispered, "His name, my Lord."

It seemed an invisible signal gave direction then: Everyone assembled on the terrace, below and above, leaned forward to listen to his pronouncement, breathless for a moment as though their stillness might amplify the King's voice.

"On this day of the fifth month of . . ." Dalich could not recall the actual day, and no one made to inform him. "Of the year 2914, I name my child Namlich, King's Son. May The Powers protect him and Eskalind, forever." Some in the assembly began hooting and clapping, others asked, "What was the name?" and yet more stamped their feet and shouted thanks to The Powers for Their continued protections.

The orange flames of the braziers pulsed—whether in accord with or defiance of Dalich's words and the people's glad shouts, Marna did not know. King's Guard Trevil steadied her son, leaned toward the King's ear, and spoke. Dalich turned to reply as Marna heard Saril say, "May The Powers always protect us . . . ," his lips were inches from Marna's ear, and his dark eyes swung to meet hers, his tone shading from solemn to suspicious as he finished, "from whatever plans and machinations are afoot."

Ignited by his implication, she leaned away from him, pulling her grandson close as if to shield the babe. "Eskalinders always strive to protect our people and borders," she replied, voice chill as a Nordak Winter. "With or *without* The Powers' protection." She gave him her gravest look and hoped he understood the gravity of what they faced.

Lord Saril met her with a steady gaze and the barest of nods. Then someone touched her arm and she turned abruptly, hoping the long braid of her hair might smack King's Second in the face. Greeting her were the happy faces of well-wishers, a multitude crammed onto the terrace, a great clatter and racket of shouted praises and glad greetings to the newbabe and his family.

The general's sain knit his brows and stood as his wife lumbered into his study, her swollen belly apparent even under her voluminous robes. "Melande, it's early, you should be resting. The babe will come soon. You need your strength."

"Walking the passageways helps. The pangs have begun, but they are slight."

"I will have the whore call for the midwife."

She sighed. Before she could protest he asked, "Where's our son?"

"Don't send for Yirish. He's readying for a tournament at his sword-master's fortress. Let him come home this evening to find his mother and new sibling freshly scrubbed and presentable."

Here he would acquiesce. "If you wish."

His wife waddled to the door that connected their private chambers, leaving the room with another long sigh. The bell rang, signaling that Hazish requested entry. The colonel strode around the screen blocking the main door to find his trusted man standing at the opened outer door.

"Sir, a woman claiming to be the general's household whore is here to see you. She described the interior of his fortress accurately."

Sirish nodded. "Show her in. Have our whore send for the midwife."

A moment later, a veiled woman entered his study, followed by Hazish. His trusted man stood behind her, a hand on the handle of his long knife. The colonel addressed the woman. "You are the general's whore of the household?"

"Yes."

"Show your face."

She doffed her veil overhead with a gesture that told she found the request tiresome. Sirish noted nothing remarkable about her features, save a small, crescent-shaped mole near her nose. He wanted to mark her face.

The woman tucked her veil into the belt of her robes and lowered her brown eyes. "Sir, the general sent me to ascertain his daughter's condition."

"Her pains have begun. I will send news when the child comes." He waved for her to leave.

"Sir …" She paused. "I'm also here on another, personal mission, that you will find of interest." The woman raised her gaze.

"What of it?"

"Do you know a foreign man guested at the general's fortress during the same time as the fine lady?"

"By fine lady, you are referring to my wife?"

"Yes, your wife, the general's daughter." She swallowed, her eyes keen. "Sir, I have spent many years in the general's household. I knew the fine lady's last nurse. She told me an Eskalinder man, blond with gray eyes, guested at the general's before the fine lady joined with you." Her jaw jutted forward slightly. "The nurse told me she showed this man to the fine lady's bed." She raised her hands, open palmed, and lowered her eyes. "I have seen this man with my own eyes, and I have seen the fine lady's child. The two are alike as father and son."

A chill swept Sirish. This was why the general had men at the border and ports watching for a slender-nosed, gray-eyed foreign man. His faither had played him the ultimate fool. If it were true. But maybe this was some odd ruse of the general's, or his servant's. "Why do you tell me this? What do you stand to gain?"

"The general is an old man. He cannot stay in power much longer." The blond woman lowered her gaze further, tilting her head to the floor. He had half a mind to signal Hazish to sever her neck until she said, "I know all the passages of his fortress, many of them very well hidden."

So. She offered guidance were he to possess the general's fortress. That might be useful. "Again, you are telling me this why?"

"I wish to be well placed when the time comes."

A slight aspect of anticipation in her posture caused him to ask, "And?"

She turned her head slightly as if responding to a touch. "He killed the man I love." There was a hardness mixed with restrained emotion in her utterance that was undeniable.

Sirish looked to Hazish, then back to her. "Return to your current master. I may send for you." She bowed low and departed, eyes cast to the tiled floor as she paced away, plucking at her waist to free her veil and cover her head. Hazish followed her behind the screen to see that she departed the room. The door thumped shut behind her; Hazish turned the lock and returned.

Drawing his man close, Sirish ground out the words, "We will make two plans."

The youths arrived one by one in carrying boxes, their manner of disembarking a herald of their respective ages. The lads of younger years, eleven and twelve, leapt forth in a display of eagerness the moment the box lowered to the dirt. Those closer to their twentieth birthday, the age at which they could qualify to become a man here in Havadra, stepped forth at a regal pace.

This gathering of the sons of the most powerful families in Capitola, and thus their nation, gave the youths a chance to test their skills in combat and strategy against others of their class and age. A rare opportunity unless one had brothers or cousins. Possessing neither, Yirish viewed the event with intense interest. It was a chance to practice his studies in diplomacy and observation and perhaps form alliances with, or at least opinions of, his peer group. These would one day be the men with whom he would contest for power. For now, he noticed that some of the younger participants had forgotten to switch from the plain clothes one often wore in a traveling box to the elaborately cuffed tunics popular amongst those with the coin to finance intricate gold embroidery. He nearly grinned, wondering when they would think to change without their mothers or whores to guide them.

The swordmaster of Capitola, a lean man with sculpted arms that begged to be immortalized with quill and ink, assigned each contestant a number according to his order of arrival and barked orders to servants to bring refreshments for the guests. Standing under a covered pavilion, Yirish—or Two, as he was designated today for arriving just after the first attendee—watched the later arrivals gather and stand on the foot-trammeled earth of the large courtyard. Other young males stood nearby, brown eyes observant and watchful. A strange, quiet assembly of cautious Havadrans, each studying the others. Even those who were related to each other were careful not to reveal familiarity or mention a true name. Over the course of the tournament this might change, but not now.

Six lifted his long arm in a sweeping gesture toward the new arrivals. "There, the taller one, that's Twelve. I hear he turned twenty in recent days."

"Then what's he doing here? He could be killing a man to earn his sword, rather than fighting us youngsters," sneered Eight, his long light locks pulled tight in a knot on the back of his head. It gave him the appearance of a pet animal yanked on its leash.

A smaller youth, his face still babe-fat chubby, whispered, "Maybe he thinks to kill one of us to earn his man sword."

Someone standing beside Yirish grumbled in a voice of utter confidence, "Twelve cannot become a man unless he kills another man, and none of us here are men. Yet."

Not recognizing this youth of his same height, and with no memory of seeing him disembark, Yirish gathered that this one had been the first arrival. The general's grandson countered, "He could be sent by his house to kill a rival house member."

"That could happen to any of us, Two, or should I call you Long Nose?"

Aware of the distance between them, calculating how quickly he could draw his long knife, Yirish faced the other youth, whose brown eyes glistened over dark brows as he swiped a finger along his equally lengthy nose. "I see we share a characteristic unusual for Havadrans. Is there northern blood in your line?"

Recognizing this as a crafty way of inquiring about a taboo topic, one's family, the general's grandson deigned to make a cautious reply. "Perhaps." Thinking to meet a strong inquiry with a strong question, he asked, "And yours?"

A servant called the youths forward.

One held up his hands as though studying them for the first time. "I am not just browned by the sun." As the last youngster stepped away from them, the blond youth called One grinned, his ear tipping toward his shoulder in a side nod toward Yirish. "Did you know that before the snub noses came, another people claimed Havadra under the grace of The Powers? These people thought The Powers protected them. But the snub noses proved that wrong." He glanced to the assembly yard, where the swordmaster was gathering his students.

Yirish studied the youth's profile, noting that his hair, while a light color, seemed different. The texture was not fine like silk strands but coarser, wiry even. Just above the ear, at the hairline, there was a slight darkening in tone. He puzzled over this as the swordmaster barked, "One! Two! Out of the shade. The first to arrive need not be the last to gather. Come."

As the pair trotted across the beige dust, One laughed. Yirish accepted the bait. "What's funny?"

"You are Two and I am One."

"Yes?"

"Are you not the general's grandson?"

Yirish replied with a slight narrowing of the eyes that he hoped was akin to his grandfather's most commanding expression.

"Do you see?" the other youth continued. "Our numbers mirror our families' position."

The general would have been proud of his grandson's deduction. "Then I should call you, with respect, Prince One."

"Prince Sastofts will do."

They had just reached the huddle of gathered youths, thus when Yirish halted in his tracks, it appeared to be a natural stop. But it was not, for the king of Havadra's son had just told him his name. The general's grandson knew not what this portended.

"She is in her studio, sir," replied his sister's whore when Deenofts asked where he would find his eldest sibling. The Scholar strode toward the door of the painting room, the two musicians just outside the room, behind their screen, playing a tune loud enough for him to consider plugging his ears. At least if he did, he need not worry about insulting them, since they could not see him. Turning the door handle, he realized the original smooth polished stone knob had been replaced with a worked metal knob, possibly made of silver, etched with square patterns. He shook his head at its finery and entered the room, coming around the screen to find Samathe at her easel.

"Brother!" she all but shouted over the din. "You left early without saying good morning. I thought perhaps the Herald had come for you."

"I had an early appointment with a bookseller and must obey my clients' whims."

She laughed, wiping her hands with a rag. "That I understand."

"Why?" He twirled his wrist near his ear. "So loud?"

Samathe motioned for him to slide the bolt in the door. He did, noting that it also was of a much thicker heft than he remembered from his last visit to her studio. Returning, he found her standing midway in the room, her uncovered easel behind her. His sister drew him close, her demeanor reminiscent of the times she would scold him as a child. "We must talk. You know that neither of us has had word from our father or brother in over a year."

"Mmm."

"If they are dead, then you are the head of the household."

"Why are you speaking of this now?"

"I must be blunt. You are often gone for months at a time. I am here alone, with servants who I am certain are grumbling about serving a household run by an unjoined woman."

"Then perhaps you should join."

"Ha!" Her expression lightened a bit. "You know that would mean I must then leave this household and hand all my income to my husband. If he allowed me to continue to paint."

He gathered her hands in his. "I have a wonderful idea. Come to Eskalind with me."

"I have another idea." His sister pulled him toward her easel. "Could you see yourself joined with a woman who looked like this?"

Deenofts blinked in surprise. She had never allowed, let alone offered, to show him one of her paintings before. Craning his neck, he leaned to view the canvas. There from the smooth surface, the visage of a woman with heavy, hooded brown eyes and a dark halo of poofy hair gazed at him with the appraising manner of a person of authority over others. Nothing marked her as Havadran, for besides her odd hair, her skin was a deep tan and her nose was of a length that marked her as an outerlander. "She's lovely, but unusual looking for a Havadran."

"Not her. She is already joined." Samathe raised a finger over her head to gesture to the ceiling.

"I must assume this woman is joined to a high lord."

"The highest."

Deenofts whispered. "She is our queen?"

His sister nodded. "But she has a fellow countrywoman she would see safely placed."

"You mean outside the king's fortress and out of harm's way were the balance of power to change."

"Perhaps."

"And perhaps a safe haven for this woman too." He gestured to the portrait and raised his eyebrows.

"Ah, you think this fine lady might hope to harbor here if her husband lost his position."

"Given the history of Havadra, she must make a plan. And how many people would she bring with her? Children, servants, companions? Are you certain we have enough rope and siege rations?"

Samathe crossed her arms. "We are very well provisioned. The whore and I check and replenish our stocks every month on the fifteenth day, just like Father did. The schedule keeps the servants calm."

The music outside stopped and the siblings stared at one another a moment. Deenofts shook his head and walked away from the easel to the pair of beige chairs separated by a table, the only other furnishings in the room. He sat, straightened his robes, and tsk-tsked as he noticed a slight stain near the knee.

A voice called through the door, "Fine lady, should the musicians continue?"

"Yes," Samathe stated, loud enough for the servants on the farthest corner of their fortress to hear. She followed her brother and sat as the music resumed.

He leaned forward. "If I join, how does that improve your position?"

"There will be a joined woman in the household when you are gone, acting on your authority in your absence. A proper household."

"Samathe, by our custom, in my absence you too would have to answer to her rule."

Her brown eyes flashed. "I would rather that than worry about the servants wanting to overthrow me. Besides, if needed, you would correct your wife when you come back." She raised her hands in the air. "I just want to paint. And for there be someone else to talk to when you are gone." Her cheeks reddened. "And nieces and nephews to spoil."

He narrowed his eyes. "Our brother was the one who should have joined if you wanted children in the household."

"Well, Father never saw to it."

"Yes, too busy furthering their military careers." He glanced at the back of the easel, anger flooding his heart. His next utterance was strained through his teeth. "Samathe, I will consider this, but I ask that you also consider, deeply consider, removing to Eskalind. You would be safe. You would have work. It would solve all of our current problems." She opened her mouth, but he stood and continued, "Think on it. Now, there is another appointment I must keep." He walked to the door at a pace that by its momentum would communicate his intention of leaving the room, no matter what his sister said next.

"What? Where?"

"To another bookseller, then to the harbor to price passage to Eskalind." He unbolted the door. "I will see you later tonight."

"Deenofts!" If she said anything else, it was difficult to tell over the din of the music. He shut the door. This time, the Scholar stoppered his ears directly as he marched to the main entrance, unplugging them only to grab his satchel bag and to retrieve and belt his long knife on his way out.

The thick doors of Sirish's study swung open, and around the screen door came the veiled whore of his household. She entered the room with a slight bend in her posture and bowed low. Sirish rose from his seat behind his desk. "What news of my wife?"

Even under the fabric draping her face, Sirish could sense her hesitation. "Sir … the fine lady lives but the midwife was … insufficient to her task. The girl child did not draw breath."

The colonel nodded, his tone cool. "Bring them to me."

She raised her head slowly, the purposeful motion typical of a Havadran servant afraid to ask a direct question. Sirish repeated himself. "The child and the midwife. Now."

She departed, and he followed her path to the door, ordering the male servant waiting there to fetch Hazish. Returning to his study, he walked to his desk and drew a finger over his wrecked nose. Even a dead babe must be judged.

His trusted man entered the room. Sirish leveled his eyes at his man as the veiled midwife entered, carrying the child with one arm, tearing at its swaddles with the other, speaking without breath. "Sir, see, it is a girl, a small matter it died––your wife is healthy, she will bear you a son next time. Many more living sons will follow."

"Quiet." Sirish gestured for Hazish to stand behind the woman. He could hear her teeth clicking against one another, then she stammered, "It's just a girl." She held the naked newbabe toward him as though it would shield her from a blow.

"Let me see it close." Sirish gathered the child from her. Turning his back to the midwife, walked to a shaft of light falling from the high windows lining the room. Into the bright beam he stepped, holding the still warm newbabe before him in his tightening fingers. Gripping her in the light, he peered at her wrinkled face, studied her peaceful features.

Her nose was rather like his wife's or his own. For a moment Sirish thought he saw a hint of his own mother's features in the lips, and his gaze softened. He had not thought of her in years. Surely the babe was his if it resembled his mother.

Sadness flushed through him at the loss of a daughter of his house; he should be naming her, naming her for his mother, rather than mourning. The midwife would pay with her life.

The colonel turned to his trusted man, standing behind the woman, who trembled under her veils as though she read Sirish's thoughts. Hazish raised a finger to his eye and tapped beside it. The eyes, yes, he should check the babe's eye color.

Returning his gaze to the still newbabe, with two fingers he pushed the skin under each brow upward to reveal clear gray eyes.

So. The general's whore spoke truth. There was nothing in this child that was his. His wife, his faither, had tricked him all these years and thought they had tricked him again. It was they who would pay.

"Go," he ordered the midwife. "And speak none of this to anyone. Ever."

———

The general, sitting behind his desk, opened his eyes from a resting state, aware of the footsteps rapidly mounting the stairs that led to his study. His long knife lay unscabbarded atop the geometric shapes carved into the wood. The screens shielding his office fluttered slightly as the person approached. His servant entered. "A note from Colonel Sirish, sir."

At last, word of Melande. It would have been better to host his daughter in his own fortress for the birth, but he knew his sain would never allow it. Children must be born in their father's home. He smirked. Beckoning his man forward, the general accepted the sealed note, and motioned the servant to go. For a moment he studied the envelope, pondering its relative weightlessness and hoping it did not contain weighty words. Then he ripped the seals.

Come see your daughter and granddaughter.
S

"As I hoped." He smiled and glanced at the gold-framed portrait by his elbow. Standing, he scabbarded his long knife to his waist and spoke to the painted figure. "Thank you for your service. It is tempting to call upon you again." Chuckling, the general strode to the screens, opened one and called for his finest horse to be readied in full regalia. Within the hour, he rode through his three gates upon the dark bay, with one of his men on each side of him, one before, and a fourth behind. The polished copper beads in the gelding's mane sparkled in the sunlight like bright constellations. Through the clamorous streets the small contingent traveled to his daughter's fortress, past gaping onlookers shocked to see this famous man riding openly in the streets of Capitola. Many raised their hands overhead to clap in a show of approval. "Long live the general!" they called, their cries ringing over the shouts of beggars and food vendors. The tempting aroma of grilling meats rose, but they trotted onward to their final destination.

The gatemen at the first gate allowed them entry. They dismounted and were allowed passage through the second gate. The general strode to the opening front door of the inner building as male servants offered bowls of water and fresh scented towels. The servants' eyes were intent upon the floor tiles as though they would face certain execution if they did not memorize the pattern. Then the whore of the household entered, her veiled head bowed and a hand held aloft. "Come this way to see your daughter, sir." She sounded afraid; her gait was stiff, formal, and timid, but the general was well associated with this reaction to his presence.

"Why isn't my sain here to greet me?"

"He is with his wife, sir."

As if struck by The Powers, he considered that the happy outcome he anticipated might not be what was to greet him. Instantly on alert, he motioned his guards to come with him. The five men followed the veiled servant through the colorless, still corridors till they reached a closed set of double doors on square hinges. "Please tell your men to wait outside, sir."

"They will enter with me."

"But sir, there is a fine lady inside." Her voice trembled as she spoke.

"They can avert their eyes." The general rested a hand along his long knife's hilt. His guards mimicked his motion.

She cowered by the sand-colored door, the drapes and folds of her garments an identical match to its shade but a contrast to its flatness. Her pale hands fumbled upon the latch. The door opened. A large white screen blocked their view of the room, as was traditional in private chambers.

"You go first," the general ordered the woman, sweeping his eyes to each side. She wobbled forward, breathing in short bursts audible though she was facing away from him. He signaled his men to split into pairs and follow.

Passing the screen, he entered the chamber to find a large bed on the far end. Upon it lay the butchered forms of his daughter and granddaughter. Melande's brown eyes gazed blankly at him. He could smell her blood.

The general grabbed the whore with one hand and drew his long knife with the other. "Who did this?" His guards surrounded the pair, their backs to them and weapons at the ready.

The woman wept. "Colonel Sirish. I couldn't stop him. I tried! No, please don't kill me. Please don't."

He yanked her arm with such force it dislocated from the shoulder. She screamed, pawing at the injury just as Sirish's men poured into the room from the doorway, at quick count, ten in total, with knives and swords aloft. The general released her as his guards stood to fight, while he looked for another way to escape the chamber. "Make for the curtain," he shouted, figuring the wall hanging sheltered a servants' entrance. But even as he spoke, the curtain parted, and one, two, three more armed men leapt forth.

The general backed away, his guards before him engaging the horde, and seeing no other way out, he stepped forward to growl and fight and avenge his progenies' death by slaying as many of Sirish's men as The Powers would allow. Forward he charged and swiped and cut and parried, suffering men half his age to fall with death writ upon their faces. Until a point just above his left kidney, a hitherto unremarkable part of his body, exploded in pain as an enemy blade pierced him from behind. He turned to fight the blade responsible, even as a blow landed upon the side of his head. His foot slipped on the blood that coated the floor, and the general fell, landing atop a body, facing his dead daughter, as the last of his guards dropped behind him. His sain paced into view, a clean long sword in his hand.

"When my men find Yirish," he said, his eyes narrowed in hate or triumph, "he will meet you wherever The Powers see fit to send you lot."

"Why?" croaked the general, blood flooding his mouth. He rooted in his belt for the hidden short knife he concealed there, striving to make the gesture look like he was beckoning. "Come, tell me."

His sain shook his head. "I give you a death suitable for an animal. From a safe distance." With that, Colonel Sirish swiped his sharp blade across the general's neck in a deft enactment of the butcher's craft.

———

Sirish raised his gaze to his men. Some held hands over wounds, one had collapsed to the floor, all stared alternately at his slain wife and the newbabe or his fallen faither. Three generations dead in one room. "I require the least injured of you to come with me. We will lay hold of his fortress." His trusted man stepped toward him, and Sirish nodded.

Hazish gestured to the bodies. "Spread the word."

The Havadran Scholar watched closely as the bookseller slipped his fingers over the fine script that covered the parchment pages of the book. The stall was dimly lit with candles, the fabric walls lowered to cancel out the harsh sunlight.

"Yes, I recognize this script. My colleague purchased a book from a lad who quilled with this symbol. Three nested red squares." He flipped to the second page of the book, where Havadran copyists left their mark. "Yes, the same marking that book bore. Are you considering selling this book?"

"Perhaps. Is there anything you can tell me about the quiller?"

"Mmm." It was the sound a Havadran made when he knew something, something he would only share for a price. "My colleague dealt with the seller; I'm not certain I remember him saying anything about him. But I might." He slowly flipped through the book, whether to give Deenofts time to make an offer or in appreciation for the quillmanship, only The Powers knew. The Scholar waited, patient as a man with no agenda. After a while, the bookseller raised his head and sniffed pointedly. "Do you smell smoke?"

Sensing a ruse, Deenofts countered, "Perhaps a candle snuffed itself." He did not turn to see if his guess were true; he watched the man intently.

"That is not candle smoke." The book merchant closed the book and handed it with one hand to Deenofts. With the other he pulled open the fabric walls of the stall. Beyond the yellow-gated fortress across the open square, a fluffy pillar of dark smoke rose into the blue sky. "That is a scent I have not smelled in years. Like a fortress burning."

"Whose?" asked Deenofts as he clutched the book.

"It cannot be." The man turned to Deenofts. "That's the direction of the general's fortress."

"Ah." Deenofts stowed his book in his satchel. "It may just be a fire of another sort. But to be cautious, I must return to my fortress straight away." He hoisted the bag over his shoulder, wondering if his impending exit might hasten the man to bargain further with him. The bookseller opened his mouth just as a group of soldiers wearing red hats swarmed into the square. "Red. That's Colonel Sirish's color," murmured Deenofts. Some of the men had dark stains on their beige robes, as though they had been splattered with mud. Then one of the men turned toward them, a red gash dripping across his forehead.

The bookseller dropped the fabric. "That man was bleeding." He shook his head, as though disbelieving the image. "My stock? What will become of it? My colleague has the cart and isn't coming back for hours."

"Grab what you can, run to your fortress."

"And hope for the rope." The man looked as though he would weep.

For a moment Deenofts considered helping him. Then he remembered he was in Havadra, not Eskalind. The man would likely turn on him. "If this war is just starting and you are quick about it, you may reach your fortress before the gate is shut and barricaded." The man nodded as though he had had the same thought and automatically began loading books into a slack bag.

Deenofts watched a moment, beholding the numerous, hand-copied books that would be left behind if only one man carried them. He thought of the thousands of hours of labor, of the artisans and copyists, of their crafts perishing in fire or under the careless marauding of vandals. He could not allow that to happen. "Is your fortress nearby?"

"Yes."

"Give me another bag and I will bring as much as I can carry to your fortress."

The man turned to him. "At what price?"

The Havadran Scholar smiled. "Can you remember anything about the youth who made my book?"

The man considered. "He was young, about sixteen." He paused. "Has a limp. That's all." He retrieved a bag from behind the counter and laid it flat on the floor and began filling it.

Deenofts assisted him. "Which way is your fortress?"

"Opposite direction of the general's."

Dousing the candles, the pair lifted the swollen bags that bordered on being too heavy to carry and departed. Deenofts went ahead of the bookseller, who called directions. It was difficult to hear from his labored breath under the weight of easily two dozen books. They rounded a corner to face a fortress's gate sweeping closed. "That is mine!" called the bookseller. "Wait wait!" the man shouted. "I live here." Two men, one holding a long spear and the other a sword, fit themselves into the gap between the door and the wall.

"Cousin," the spear bearer called. "Hurry!" The bookseller dashed ahead of Deenofts, toward the fortress, the heavy satchel of books on his back rising and falling clumsily as though beating him in slow motion. Deenofts approached cautiously as the book merchant passed through the opening of the fortress. "Who are you?" challenged the spear man.

"He has my books!" the merchant cried, in the aggrieved voice of a man watching a thief make away with his goods.

The Scholar stopped. "Yes, I do. I carried them for you. To help you."

"He doesn't need your help anymore," stated the man with the spear. He raised his weapon. "Drop them or I will . . ." He shook the spear. Deenofts lowered the heavy satchel to the ground. "And the little bag too."

"This one is mine."

"Not anymore. Drop it."

"Get his long knife too," clamored the merchant. "I saw it close, it looks valuable."

Deenofts blew air through his nose. "First you rob me, then you leave me out-of-walls without a weapon? You might as well just kill me."

"If you are quick about it, you may reach your fortress before the gate is shut and barricaded," taunted the bookseller.

"Shut the gate!" called a male voice inside the fortress.

"Wait!" called another.

The man with the spear approached. "Hands in the air," he ordered. Deenofts stepped back but complied.

"By The Powers, shut the gate!" A woman's voice this time.

"Shut the whore up." The spear man held the metal tip inches from the Scholar's chest and reached with his free hand to unbelt Deenofts's scabbarded long knife. He flung it behind him, toward the fortress. The bookseller bent and snatched it from the dust. The spear bearer backed away from Deenofts and drew a short knife. Pointing the spear at the Scholar's neck, he reached with his knife hand and cut the satchel strap. It fell to the ground as though relieved to be free of the dispute over its ownership. Deenofts stared hard at the man, who said, "Now you can go."

The Scholar marched backward, away from his possessions, his departing curse rising like vomit in his throat. "Havadrans!" Deenofts bellowed, facing his robbers, who gathered his goods and scurried into their fortress. "Havadrans! The Powers take you all. Take you all!"

———

Even in the waning light of sunset, even in the darkened enclosure of the carrying box, the smooth inlaid pearl of the dagger's hilt gleamed in Yirish's hand. He admired his prize, smiling as he stroked the sea jewel, eager to tell Mother and Father of his victory in the tournament.

How proud they would be to learn their son's performance had earned him this trophy in his age group. Hopefully, his plan to present Mother with the dagger as a present would direct her attention away from the bandage on his leg, the embarrassing result of backing into a piece of metal protruding from a wall. It no longer hurt, but the bandage looked like it shielded an impressive injury. Perhaps he would remove it before he entered her rooms.

Stowing the small knife in an inner pocket of his satchel, the youth pulled his dress tunic over his head, the cool metal of the gold-embroidered collar sliding over his forehead like a caress. Bundling the fine garment into the bag, he dressed again in the plain, rough fabric tunic favored by his countrymen for anonymous travel. He patted the scabbard of his long knife, tied to his thigh, to make certain it had not loosened.

Someone shouted outside the box. Yirish stood, gripping the handle to steady himself, hoping to peer out the screen lining the tops of the walls of the box.

His face hit the wall, sudden, hard, as the container thudded to the ground. "Aw!" He blinked from the blow, swiping a finger over his nose, which felt wet. "Hey!" Yirish yelled, throwing open the door. It was darker outside than he expected, but even in the glooming of the day he did not see a single carrying box man. Instead, a stampede of men approached, the man at the lead carrying a sword and screaming unintelligible words. Yirish ducked back into the box, nearly tripping on his satchel. He threw it over his arm and bolted out the other side, dashing in front of a charging horse close enough to feel its breath. Turning, he saw its rider slumped forward in the saddle, a spear in his back. Yirish gulped and scrambled toward a tall mud wall, pressing his back against it as he surveyed the scene.

He was in a broad passage between fortresses. In the distance, fires burned, a halo of orange light against the dark blue of the deepening night sky. The lad inhaled and spat, copper in his mouth. He wiped the back of his hand across his lips and nose, seeing blood coating his skin. To The Powers, Yirish hoped he was the only one in his family trapped out-of-walls. But now he must concentrate, must get home to his fortress. Years of drilling for a moment such as this calmed his mind even as his heart raced.

Glancing at the sky, the general's grandson tried to read the stars to find his direction, but their white points wafted in and out of sight as clouds of black smoke smudged their beacons. If he could raise his viewing position, the landmarks of the king's fortress and Grandfather's fortress would guide him to safety. A man pushing a cart ran by, its wheels creaking. Shouting and a boom like a great door falling echoed in the distance. He moved along the passage, coming to an open area lit by staked torches. One of the torches lay sputtering on its side like a gutted animal quivering in the dust. Spying a stout, lidded carrying basket adjacent to one of several canvas-walled out-buildings, the youth dashed toward it, slinging his satchel strap over his head and behind his back. Scaling the sturdy basket, Yirish pulled himself to the tiled roof. To the south he saw the port, a dark patch ringed by the lights of the lesser fortresses of the craftsmen's guilds. Gazing north, the king's fortress, marked by a tall tower. It was too dark to see if the blue of King Astofts's pennants fluttered atop it, but what drew his attention was the fire in a fortress to the west, exactly where he expected to see Grandfather's fortress. He raised himself as high as he dared for a better look. One, two, three outer rings of the structure were visible. There could be no doubt that the general's seat was aflame and likely conquered. Still, Grandfather had escape tunnels, he might yet be safe.

Yirish sat upon the roof, trying to becalm himself and strategize his next move. "Breathe. Think. Plan." He lowered himself to the ground. He heard men talking and glanced about, trying to locate them as he slipped alongside the fluttering canvas walls.

Cursing and shouting came from the opposite side of the open area, and he could just make out three men kicking a bag on the ground. Then the youth realized the bag was a man, who howled and begged for mercy.

He slunk back against another fabric wall, hearing the animated murmur of two men arguing inside.

"May this day end soon. It's cursed luck to be caught out-of-walls in a civil war."

"Quit jabbering; let's make a plan. We must get to our fortress and hope for the rope."

"You're too fat to be pulled over the wall."

"Ha, you should talk. Grab as much food as you can. If we get stuck in a callers' camp, we'll have enough to eat while we wait this out. And we'll have something to bargain with too."

Yirish cautiously pulled the cloth away from a post and peeked inside. The pair had their broad backs to him, limp satchels at their feet. One of the men dropped a laden bag on the floor and grabbed an empty.

"I told you this would happen again once the general died."

Yirish covered his mouth.

"Colonel Sirish has set a place for himself in the histories. Kills his wife, her father, even his own babe."

Yirish gasped.

Both men swiveled toward him.

"You, what do you want?" The youth tried to speak but could not. His vision blurred, but he saw that the man who addressed him had grabbed a long knife. "Get out of here. This is our food."

The other man drew blade too. "Go away, Blood Face. Get lost. Or do you want to bleed some more?"

Yirish dropped the fabric wall and stumbled away.

A swirl of conflicting thoughts held him, but one thought emerged clear. If his father had killed his entire family, and only he was left, then his father would likely kill him too. But he had no idea why. Yirish staggered into the dark, then crouched in a corner near crumbling wooden stairs. There he wept, unmolested, till the sun rose, pale in the smoky sky.

Hoofbeats startled him. Several riders approached the open area.

The lad withdrew under the stairs, watching through gaps in the worn wood. These riders wore blue caps, marking them as loyal to King Astofts. Only in times of war, or during processions, were such displays common in Havadra. Anonymity was usually prized instead, unless one found himself amongst a large group of fellow supporters.

From the opposite side of the square a new contingent of riders approached, red caps atop their heads. His father's color. Yirish drew further into the crevice under the shadowed steps. The leaders of the two groups spoke to one another, and the king's men turned to leave. Then some of the red caps threw spears at their backs and charged.

Yirish bolted from his hiding place and ran in the opposite direction, along fortress walls, past overturned carts, dead horses, piles of shapeless debris. The sound of women wailing punctuated the air. Passing through smoke and dust, a male voice called, "Fastofts? Fastofts? Are you here? Fastofts?"

A man was standing before him. "Have you seen my son? He's about your height, wears his hair short. Have you seen him?"

The man grabbed his arm, but Yirish yanked away. "No!" The desperate concern in the man's eyes made him angry.

He came to another wall, where two veiled figures sat, still as the wall itself, as though they willed themselves to become it. Their draperies made him think of his mother, and he marched away, eyes darting right and left as more voices called in the dust. A pale youth ran into him, then backed away into the smoky dust as though he were part of it.

Finding another wall, Yirish sat, untangling his satchel straps to hug the bag to his chest. He pulled his rough tunic by the collar to cover his nose, filtering out the dust in the air, and lifted an arm to stretch his tense muscles. It bumped something warm. He turned and saw a figure propped against the wall next to him. It was stripped of all clothes but a breechcloth, and blood and bruises dotted its chest along with small, dark swirls of hair. He had never seen such hair before.

One of the closed eyelids was puffed and swollen, but the face looked familiar. "Sastofts?" he asked. A dark-irised eye opened.

"Two."

"What happened to you?"

Blood flowed from his ear. "Beaten. They stole my fine clothes."

"At the swordmaster's?"

"Carrying box. I didn't change in time." He rolled his neck slightly toward Yirish. "You look bad."

"Do you know a safe fortress we can go to? Sastofts?"

"The Powers are punishing me."

"What?"

"I mocked them, at the tournament. I said my mother's people were wrong to think The Powers protected them from the snub noses. They are punishing me."

"Then they are punishing me too. I overheard my whole family is dead." The prince stared, his injured eyelid a weak droop of flesh. "Sastofts, we must hide or get behind walls. You need a healer."

"Mother always said when this happened I should go to the Shinglo, they would see to me." The prince leaned his head against the wall, seeming content to rest there as though it were a comfortable, pillowed couch.

"All right, which fortress is the Shinglo's?"

"No, they live in the desert. Hidden."

The general's grandson whispered, "How does a woman of a hidden people come to be joined with the king?"

"Ah, you ask about my family." Sastofts coughed. "Impolite." He coughed, then coughed again, a pained, hacking sound. Yirish placed a hand on his shoulder, wanting to offer comfort. Moments passed. The youth made a horrible gurgling sound.

"Sastofts? Sastofts?" He gently shook the youth's shoulder, not wanting to cause him further injury, but Sastofts slumped slack against him and he knew the prince was dead. Yirish stared hard ahead, for how long he did not know. At last he held up his free hand, counting the deaths.

Mother. Grandfather. The prince. The sibling he never met.

There were five fingers on his hand, and four were accounted for; he vowed not to raise the fifth. He would not be the fifth. "No more," he muttered, as he made his plan. He would escape Capitola, find the Shinglo, and live with them in the desert.

Hours Deenofts walked and hid and walked, half wanting to punch anyone or anything he came across, lacking any direction in the smoke and dirt that filled the air from what source he could not tell, though it smelt of wood and burnt flesh and things unimaginable. Night came, then evaporated as the sun rose grimly upon his homeland. Exhausted, the Scholar sat against a hard surface. When he woke, the light was brighter and his thoughts calm enough to plan a route home. He heard a man approach, calling hoarsely, "Fastofts? My son, Fastofts, has anyone seen him?"

Deenofts rose, replying, "Anish? Anish?" The name Favik had given him for the prodigy copyist became a password that would allow him safe passage home, without weapon or coin. "Anish?" he called, stronger now. No one wanted to be out-of-walls in a civil war. Those who intentionally ventured forth did so to plunder or settle old scores or muster an attack on a rival's fortress. But callers were somewhat immune, forced by love and circumstance to seek missing family members, choosing to be out-of-walls in a desperate effort to retrieve a missing loved one. "Anish?"

Out of the smoke, a veiled woman stumbled by him, and he instinctively turned his head away from her, only to see three battle-hardened soldiers approaching him from the other direction, knives drawn and bloodstained. The blade color matched the caps upon their heads. Colonel Sirish's men. He had nothing to give them but his life. Or annoyance.

He paused, wanting to flee, but played his part as a pitiful searcher, hoping they would ignore him and abandon him unharmed. "Sirs, I am seeking my cousin, Anish. Please, have you seen him?"

This did not provoke the desired reaction, for the largest asked in a rough voice, "Have you come across a long-nosed youth with gray eyes?"

He stared. It was nearly the description Samathe had given of the general's grandson. "How odd. Some foreigner? No. I would remember a face like that."

"He's about thirteen, but looks older. Name's Yirish. There's a reward for him, dead or alive. Alive, even more."

The shortest man grinned, scratching a blond eyebrow. "It's a lot of coin."

"Well, we all are interested in coin, and I would certainly remember a face such as you describe. Now, my cousin Anish is sixteen. He has a slight limp. Recent accident caused it. The healer thinks he will get better and walk normally again." Their attention faded as he spoke, like a thin cloud evaporating on a hot day. "You see, he was standing on a three-legged stool, which was not very stable to begin with, but I was not there to tell him that, and…" The men had left him in the dust and smoke. The Scholar exhaled slowly, then resumed his calls. "Anish?"

A square, blue-tiled fountain appeared before him, the tinkling water soft as a lullaby. He leaned into it, washed his face, and drank a bellyful. Then he recalled having seen this fountain before. He was near the harbor. Thank The Powers.

He could leave for Eskalind straight away. But the port was surely clogged with Havadrans with more coin than him, also seeking to flee. "Anyone has more coin than me at the moment," Deenofts murmured. "May this day end soon." The unique fountain served as a landmark, though, guiding him in the right direction to reach his fortress, and he walked with purpose in his steps. Not for the first time, plans to forever leave Havadra consumed his mind, unfurling like a lengthy scroll displayed upon a banqueting table. But making an overland journey without planning and provisions would be a quick trip to The Powers. If he were ever to get back to Eskalind, his first step must be to harbor at the family fortress till the chaos was over. He would use the search for Anish to get him safely there, whether he found the lad or not. Thank The Powers for Favik giving him this excuse to be out-of-walls. "Anish?"

"Did you say Anish?" came a young voice, close by.

He stopped. "Anish, is that you?" He scanned at eye level, and seeing no one, lowered his gaze to find a youth with downcast eyes, crouched as though ready to run. The lad held an arm across his nose. "Anish, look at me."

The youth lifted his head slightly and gazed up at Deenofts. His eyes were gray, as alike to Favik's, with their darkened-blue rim around the iris, that he felt he was gazing at a younger version of his fellow Scholar. Even the brow was the same. A noise escaped the Scholar's lips as the thought came that this was the lad the soldiers sought, dead or alive. Deenofts lowered himself for a closer look.

Anish shifted on the dirt. "How do you know to call me Anish?"

"I was sent by my fine lady, at least I thought by my fine lady, to find you and bring you to Eskalind. I wager Eskalind sounds very appealing right now. It certainly does to me."

The lad said nothing, just watched him with a thoughtful, suspicious gaze.

Deenofts settled next to him, holding his hands palm up. "Look, I am unarmed, I have nothing of value save my life. I want to make certain you're the lad I seek, Anish." The youth pondered but said nothing. He moved slightly as though he might dash away.

"Did you once sell a book, copied by your own quill, to a bookseller by a yellow-gated fortress?" Deenofts asked.

The gray eyes grew wide. "I never told anyone I sold a book there last year. I went alone in a box. Did she have someone following me?"

Uncertain how to answer the question, Deenofts replied, "I was at that bookseller's just before Capitola became … this," he gestured to the smoke, "showing a book, that I believe you copied, to the merchant."

Again the suspicious stare. "My mark is three shapes."

"Red, nested squares?"

"Yes."

"Then it *was* yours. We must get behind walls." He noted the bandage on the youngster's leg. "How hurt are you?"

Anish pulled his arm away from his face, revealing dried blood splattered about his nose and around his lips. At a quick glance, his nose appeared smallish and typical of a Havadran, but then Deenofts realized the dark bloodstains made it look smaller. "I know there's blood on my face, but it doesn't hurt. And my leg is all right."

"You don't have a limp?"

"No." This seemed to puzzle the lad.

Deenofts gathered that the bookseller had lied to him. How surprising. "Anish, can you stand?"

The youth nodded and rose to his full height as Deenofts did the same. Anish stepped squarely, no hint of hobbling or injury. The elder Havadran pointed to the leg dressing. "If we run into any men wearing red caps, start limping and keep your head down, eyes to the dirt. Keeping your head down all the time would be best. Yours is a distinctive visage." He gestured in the direction they should walk. "We will go to my fortress, on the east side of the city, to wait out this war."

The youngster turned back as though reluctant to leave something behind, then faced the Scholar. "Did my mother have you watching for me?"

"No, I was sent to bring you and her to the safety of Eskalind."

The youngster withdrew slightly. "She can't come. She's dead." He spoke in a stout voice, but his eyes watered.

Deenofts reached to touch the lad's shoulder. "It is a great sadness to lose one's mother." He spoke from the heart, hoping his empathetic condolence would bolster the youth, but instead the teenager bowed his forehead and blubbered, "And my grandfather is too. And the babe my mother was carrying. And…" He lowered his head into his hands.

"Come, Anish, we must get to my fortress." Deenofts gently guided him through the street. "We will be safe there. It's been a long time since I ate. How about you, hmm?" The youngster did not reply. "It's good that you're keeping your head down," he murmured, deciding that silence was their best defense. Wordlessly, they rounded the corners of passageways and passed quiet as air through desolate open squares, past burning carrying boxes, around a horse with a twisted leg whinnying atop its crushed master, who lay staring dead-eyed skyward.

After some time creeping through the city, Anish tugged his arm. "Did you get a good price for it? My book?"

"I did not intend to sell it. That bookseller stole it from me. And my long knife. And my satchel. And my favorite quill sharpener." Deenofts spat on the cursed Havadran earth as he recounted his losses. He heard a sound nearby and glanced about, for a moment thinking someone lurked behind them. But the dust and smoke had settled and he could see farther ahead and behind now. Only the pounded flat dirt of a familiar street and fortress walls met his eyes. "My fortress is just ahead. Play the part of my young cousin. I will give the signal by the rope wall, and when the rope comes over, you climb first." Anish inhaled and nodded. "When you come over, there will be men with weapons drawn. Tell them Deenofts is behind you, keep your head down, your hands up, and your gaze to the dirt. Do not let them see your eyes."

"Why?"

He lowered his voice and drew close. "Before I found you, some men asked me about a gray-eyed youth fitting your description. But they said the lad's name was Yirish."

The youngster started and his lips parted, but he said nothing.

Deenofts led him to his fortress wall and whistled the signal. Silence, then chattering. He whistled again, but nothing happened. He waited. Fear grew in his heart that Samathe had been correct in her suspicions, that the servants had launched their own coup within the household.

Anish looked at him. "Why aren't they responding?" Just then the answering call came, clear and loud. The Scholar gave his unique final response call, and the gladdest sight an out-of-walls Havadran could wish for came into view: a stout rope arched over the wall and hung within grasp. "Thank The Powers, they are still loyal," he murmured, gesturing Anish to come close.

Deenofts helped the youth to the rope and gripped the end tight. "Remember, gaze down, hands up once you're off the ladder."

Anish scampered up the rope as though he had trained over and over again for such an exercise. He disappeared over the wall and a grumbling voice was heard. Anish cried, "Deenofts follows me. Deenofts is behind me!" More grumbling, and a snapping sound, like bones breaking. The Scholar cringed. Then he too clambered up the taut rope, pulling himself up and swinging a leg over the wall. Glancing into the dirt courtyard far below, he saw Anish facedown on the dirt, legs and arms spread, the veiled whore of the household training a spear on his back.

A male servant stood with a drawn long sword next to the rope-anchor rock, about to slice the cord, until his eyes met Deenofts'. "It's the young master."

"Thank The Powers it's you, sir," the woman called. Behind her, another male servant dashed to the wall, bearing another ladder. The men erected it to rescue Deenofts from his perch.

As he alighted from the ladder onto the safe dirt of his home, he spied shards of wood and two long poles on the ground. "I see the first ladder broke. Anish, are you all right?" He stepped toward the prone youth.

"Bruised, nothing broken, I think. Can I move now?"

Deenofts waved the maidservant to put the spear aside. "My cousin will harbor in my room till it is safe to go out-of-walls."

"Yes sir," she replied. "With your return, everyone in the household is safe within walls."

He reached and pulled Anish from the ground, laying a hand at the base of the youth's neck in a gesture that might read as affectionate, but was meant to angle his head so that his unusual face was shielded from the servants. Now that the order of the household was restored, the two men and the woman gazed at the ground, perfect dutiful Havadran domestics. Deenofts led the lad inside.

Chapter Twenty-Eight—A Letter to the Dead

Brother,

*I know not whether you still live, though I and Samathe suspect
not. We have had no word from either you or Father for over
two years. Pity. Our sister's hope dims and she makes a plan for
me. Hope does not dim in me, for my greatest hope was to see
you dead, my second to see her and I both removed to Eskalind
and rid of our homeland. Since I believe I have won the first, I
strive for the second.*

*As you were the first to trouble me, I will continue to write
you to solve the dilemmas that plague my days. Days that are,
thank The Powers, free of your presence, though I cannot shake
you from my mind. Especially here in our household.*

*So, there resides in our fortress now a youth whom I am calling
cousin but who is not. He stays in my room and I in yours. My,
I feel our roles are repeated, with him as the much younger
brother and I the elder. I can imagine you laughing at this
situation, for I know how you would make advantage of it. But I
will never touch his flesh as you touched mine.*

*The lad of about fourteen years—my, this sounds familiar,
does it not? He is a marvel with ink and quill, he has drawn a*

likeness of me more distinct than a mirror. Even Samathe was impressed. But that is not why I write this, to expound upon his talents. I found him in the streets when I was out-of-walls during our latest and ongoing civil war.

I watch him through the screen adjoining our rooms, and in his countenance I see one I know in the far lands, the one who gave me the mission to find this lad, and I am afraid. Afraid for this man when I see him next, and whether I should thank him or slay him. For this lad is hunted, he is the prize of our current lord, King Sirish. His presence endangers the entire fortress and all the lives it shelters. If one of the servants were to discover who he truly is and seek the reward for his return…

Yes, into our fortress I have brought this most wanted child, on the behalf of a man I trusted. Yet by strange coincidence, the search for him brought me safely home whilst I was caught out-of-walls. You would ridicule this, I know. I know what you would do. On a dark night you would lead him from our fortress, slay him in some forgotten corner, then return home as though nothing happened. Why, it would merely be a repeat of how you killed my first chosen lover. Most convenient that everyone assumed our servant merely ran away.

But that is not what I will do. I will shelter him, feed him, and show him every kindness. And once it is safe to go out-of-walls, I will arrange an overland passage with him to Eskalind. I will make the desert journey with this fugitive, whom I am growing to love, as an older brother should love a younger.

Everything I write to you, I burn. This papyrus sees flame before blotter.

And so, to the flames it goes.

Deenofts, head of what was formerly your household

The Havadran Scholar watched his letter burn, the flames evaporating the papyrus into deckled edges of char. He flicked scented water about the room to disperse the nose-puckering smell. The last thing he wanted was his sister storming into his quarters complaining of acrid scents. How she could tolerate the odors of her paints was unfathomable.

Deenofts folded his fingers and composed his thoughts. "And now I will write Favik. What I would not give to ask him many questions in person. Ha!" He shook his hands, returning his focus to his task. "Once the fog of civil war clears, the letter bearers will clamor by the wall for food or coins in exchange for carrying missives. I will make several copies." He grunted a cynical tsk, for he knew that when the letter bearers made their rounds, the new king's men too would pelt the city with their cries of reward for the deliverance of sheltered enemies. At the soonest opportunity, he must whisk Anish away from the fortress.

The Happiness Inn. Only in Gergelt would such a place name occur.

Favik gazed out the open window of his rented room to the flower-strewn meadow across the dirt track from the inn. Two men lay nude upon the grasses, asleep in the warm embrace of the sun, whilst nearby, a reclining woman wearing only a skirt laughed while her lover ran his hands over her bare toes. Then Favik reconsidered. The pair might not be lovers; perhaps they were merely companions. In Eskalind, the sight of a woman's bare feet was an invitation, but in Gergelt, it merely meant she enjoyed treading the earth without the encumbrance of slippers. Grinning, he wondered how Melande would react to these lands and customs, so vastly different from those of her homeland.

In this temperate region but a day's ride from the ocean, the cherry trees had long since imparted their fruits to the hands and mouths of the local citizenry. It seemed early to the Eskalinder, but heavy peaches blushed upon drooping tree limbs, an invitation to a juicy, sweet feast.

In Havadra, Melande had likely brought forth their child. Without him, despite his efforts to free her over the months since he had seen her last. He stood alone with his thoughts and plans and secrets, still waiting for Captain Sakil's contingent to arrive or for word from Deenofts. Dressed the part of a man traveling to Havadra, the former Ambassador adjusted a sleeve on his beige tunic, then exited the room, passing through the corridor and its cacophony of paints in orange, blue, red, green, purple, yellow, and a pinkish silver. Gergeltish paintsmiths and decorators shared a common aesthetic: to exclude no color that could be conjured from the earth's trove of minerals and dyes.

Entering the inn's common room, he found what appeared to be an impromptu market. Goods covered several of the long tables usually allotted for dining. Several people traipsed by as a man called, "Foot stones, get the best foot stones here." A young man dashed past the Eskalinder, followed by another, and soon an animated crowd bobbed in front of the rock merchant, clamoring for his wares. "Touch them, feel them, enjoy! Get and give the best foot rubs with these river-smoothed stones," the stone peddler beckoned.

In the far corner, a drummer tightened the skin of his large instrument, then pounded resonant beats. Favik distanced himself from the crowd, approaching a table laden with a globular green fruit never before seen by his eyes. He reached to touch one as someone tugged his sleeve. He turned his attention to the tugger, a small girl of about six years of age.

"Do you have a little girl?" she asked, brown eyes bright under a floppy hat constructed of the rainbow's hues of yarn.

He smiled. "I might."

"She needs a bonnet." The girl drew him to a thick-boarded table that was just above her eye level. She lifted what he would call a knit cap, of similar color scheme to her own but of newbabe proportions. "Would this fit her?"

"I'm not certain."

A gray-haired woman, perhaps the child's grandmother, sat watching from the opposite side of the table, a slight grin on her weathered features. In her hands, knitting needles clicked as she crafted a rippled swath of fabric reminiscent of the child's hat brim.

"If it doesn't fit her, it would fit her doll."

He considered that this might be a well-honed merchant's ploy, but the girl spoke with the sincere, innocent confidence only small children can convey. She continued, "I think she would like it."

"I'm certain she would." He reached for the coin purse belted at his waist, but the woman interrupted.

"Oh no, she wants to give it to you. Please, it's yours." He fixed her with a quizzical look as the girl scampered to her side. "She told me before she went over to you." The girl roped her brown arms around the woman's broad shoulders and hugged her, all the while beaming at Favik.

"How can I refuse such generosity?" He reached for the cap. "It's lovely." The tiny garment weighed nothing in his hand. He found this oddly troubling. "Thank you."

"Enjoy!" replied the woman. He stepped aside and waved goodbye at the girl as a pair of women, dressed in colors that identified them as the perfect audience for the knitter's wares, crowded forward to examine her items. They oohed and aahed over the knits as he pocketed the tiny cap. Through the front door, a rotund man whom he recognized as the proprietor entered the room, though the last time Favik saw the man, he was wearing clothing.

"Hullo, Favik. Do you know how much longer you will be enjoying with us?"

"The last note from my companions said it may be as long as two weeks before they arrive. I hope to stay till they journey here, if I may."

"Not a matter, not a matter. A trader just arrived, said we will be seeing a great increase in business, but not a matter, we will find room for everyone. My inn is bigger than it looks. I could say the same for my belly." He laughed and waved. "Enjoy!"

Shaking his head, Favik walked outside to the bare earth road. A brown-haired man was dismounting a worn-looking chestnut gelding. The human wore sweat-stained, loose-fitting long robes of beige-hued

Mavoldian linen, but cut in the Havadran style.

"I gather you are not the stable boy the naked man sent for." His tone was clipped and weary. He turned his attention to untying one of the several leather packs burdening his beast.

"No. Too old, and likely too dressed."

The man acknowledged his jesting with the barest, bored twitch at the corner of his mouth. Ah, a humorless Mavoldian. "Where are you traveling from?" Favik asked.

The trader lowered the packs to the ground and came to the other side of his horse, undoing the clasps of a sagging satchel, his thin lips set in a grim line. "Havadra. The Powers be thanked; I was lucky enough to buy passage on a ship. My visit was cut short when war erupted whilst I was in the port at Capitola."

"War in Havadra? What happened?"

The man shook his head. "I don't know. I saw flames in the city proper, but my ship departed quickly. Not a man or a woman on my ship knew anything about what was happening. Other than that it was a good time to leave." He lowered the pack to the ground. It clanked like it was full of rods of metal. The Mavoldian shifted around the horse again to reach the last of the untouched baggage in a carefully choreographed unpacking procedure. "Our ship was the first to land at the port in Gergelt, but there were many more just behind us. The port is swarming with people who fled Capitola. There are more behind me." He glanced at the south road, then the lodging house. "I hope this inn has a lot of available rooms."

A youngster of indeterminable gender and wearing only a skirt loped toward them, grabbing the horse's reins. The merchant gathered the last of his packs and trudged toward the inn. Favik followed. "Did you learn anything more about the Havadran war? When did it start?"

The Mavoldian stopped and faced him. "Sir, I am tired. I want a bath and a bed." He turned to leave.

"My family is there, please, any news." He grabbed the man's elbow. "By The Powers, anything you know."

The Mavoldian trader swallowed and shut his eyes as though stifling a deep pain. "I will not repeat hearsay. I have no way of knowing if the news is accurate."

"I don't care, tell me what you heard."

The man opened his eyes and glared. "All I know with certainty is that I left two weeks ago. Now, look, here come some men from Thislin." True enough, a pair of horses trotted toward them, the riders clad in the warm brown shade synonymous with Thislins. The pair slowed their beasts to a halt. The Mavoldian continued, "Their country folk are renowned for loose tongues. I am sure they will tell you everything they think they know and more that they have made up." He shook his elbow free and marched toward the inn.

Favik waved to the new arrivals, addressing them in respect to their country of origin. "With your permission, sirs, have you news of Havadra?"

"Yes, we fled there after the fighting began," began the more oval-faced man of the pair in an eager tone. "Allow me to tell you." With that the Thislins traded accounts of horrific tales: the death of King Astofts, the rise of King Sirish, the surprising demise of the general, the horrific annihilation by Sirish of his family. Favik sank to the ground; the men's voices came from far away. Another traveler arrived, and he glanced to her with hope, but her reports outstripped the men's in appalling detail. Favik turned away in silence.

Someone carried or dragged him to his room; he remembered not how he came to be looking out the window again, a new day dawning, brimming in warm orange rays, the trees shimmering in the sunshine as though playfully tickled by the light. The Ambassador felt himself an immovable stone that time flowed past, unblinking, unfeeling. It did not matter if he breathed or not, nothing could be more still, more empty, he was an utter void of sensation. Then his gut twinged, his throat tightened, and he rose to his feet, shuffling fast for the privy, uncertain whether his backside or stomach would empty first.

At length he found himself in his rented room again, sitting on the bed. The chamber rumbled slightly as someone walked through the corridor outside. Beyond the wall adjoining another room, a voice giggled, then moaned rhythmically. Favik reached for the chair by the table. He lifted it toward the ceiling and brought it down, smashing it against the table, then the wall, then the bedpost, then the table again, till it lay in wreckage, collapsed to the floor, a cowering hulk of fractured wood. Favik pounded and hammered and beat till the flat chair seat broke away, he battered and pummeled till the wood clutched in his hands was nothing more than spindly pointy fingers of jagged sticks. His ears reverberated with crashes and thuds and he could not distinguish if the sound came from memory or the present moment. He lay on the bed amongst the splinters and wept till his eyes emptied of tears.

He lay in misery he knew not how long.

———

Favik heard a slight tapping on his door. He tried to open his eyes but hardened tears sealed them shut. He rubbed then scraped at his stuck eyelashes, prying them apart. It was brighter in the room than he had expected. The tapping continued. Standing, he went to the door, his throat parched. "Yes?"

"Favik, there's a note for you. Are you all right?" It sounded like the innkeeper.

"No." He opened the door, leaning his body heavily against the door frame. The innkeeper stood before him, clothed, his dark brows furrowed.

"We heard a lot of noise." The man's brown eyes shifted into the room. He gaped.

"I'm sorry for your room. I will . . . pay for the damage." His own voice sounded unrecognizable to him.

The man stuttered, "What happened?"

"I received a lot of bad news."

The Gergelt's eyes softened into kind concern. "Then I hope this has some good news." He made to hand Favik an envelope, reaching out, then stopping mid action as though he realized he might instead add to his guest's misery by delivering the message.

The former Ambassador accepted the missive, but did not look at it.

"It was in a message satchel bound for Eskalind. I saw your name on this one and pulled it out." The innkeeper scratched his head deliberately, as if the gesture would provoke his next thought. "I've lost track of how many days you were in here; we've never been this busy. Let me bring you a meal."

"I am at a loss … you are most kind."

"Not a matter, not a matter." The Gergelt waved and departed.

Favik shut the door, threaded his way through the debris toward the window, the envelope rough between his fingers. A distant sensation came to him, like a call half-heard that jumps to the front of one's mind.

This envelope was rough-textured. Havadran papyrus. But not folded square. He raised it to his nose. Smoke-scented. He read the direction:

Personal to Ambassador Favik, Dalich King's Halls, Eskalind.

Deenofts's quilling. He gritted his teeth and tore the envelope asunder.

Ambassador,
Due to the recent civil war that saw the deaths of King Astofts
and General Yirlofts and the crowning of King Sirish, formerly
Colonel Sirish, I regret to inform you I have only half of your
requested order, which I will deliver to you in Eskalind. Due
to the above-mentioned events, the other half is permanently
unavailable.
Yours,
Deenofts, Merchant

"Half my order?" he blubbered. "I sent him for Melande and Anish. Then one of them is alive? But which . . ." Favik sank, sliding upon a broken table leg to the hard flooring. "The reports were explicit that Melande and the babe were . . . slain." He shut his eyes. "It must be Anish who survived. My son. My son who does not know me." He clutched the letter to his chest. "My son who is half . . . her."

Chapter Thirty—A Visit to King's Halls
Seventh Month, 2914

Dalich King patted his Second's arm as Saril drew breath through his teeth. "Saril, you need never fear a lasting injury from this sparring partner."

The pain subsided as Dalich had promised it would, and Saril stretched and turned the healed limb without ache or twinge. "It should not even bruise," his Lord promised. The pair sat together on a stone bench in the quiet privacy of the royals' sparring courtyard. Above them, a banner of the King's peaceful emblem of parchment and quill hung serenely amidst the weaponry crowding the walls.

"Then I have nothing to show for our first sparring match in months?"

Dalich's gray eyes sparkled bright as midday sun over a lake. Any observer would at that moment find it difficult to recognize the duo as the most powerful men in Eskalind. Rather, they appeared only as the fond companions they had been their entire lives. "Well, I could refrain from healing you next time."

"Who says there will be a next time?" Saralya's son lifted his wooden practice blade. The pair laughed, but then the King's demeanor changed.

"By The Powers, I cannot believe I was abed over two months. My son does not even look like a newbabe anymore." Dalich glanced to the Royals' Tower, then back to the stone-paved courtyard.

"But now you are returned to health."

"And strength. I am sorry I knocked your arm so."

"Knocked? My Lord, *broke* would be the term a Records Keeper would use. But it is better. I think." Saril lightly tapped his forearm, like a Healer evaluating an injury, and grimaced. Then he winked at his Lord. "It will be good to confer together again."

Dalich laughed. "Perhaps I should apologize for leaving you in Mother's hands whilst I was unable to work."

"My Lady King's Mother has a way of getting things done, despite the circumstances." King's Second lowered his voice but turned his gaze away. "Though some wonder if she has more important matters to attend to." He felt Dalich's gray eyes turn upon him as though he were a messenger bearing unwelcome news.

"Would 'some' in this case mean Lord Saril?"

He turned to face his King. "My Lord, I meant no offense."

"Good." The King stood, or rather erupted, from his seat, reaching a gloved hand to pull his man to his feet. The pair circled one another, dull blades at the ready. Marna's son charged twice but his Second blocked each blow deftly, all his thought upon his opponent's sparring sword, the grain in the wood apparent as it hovered steady in the air, then vanishing into a blur as its master thrust it toward him. Another pause till again the King made the advance that again was countered. "Saril, you are holding back."

"I do not want to try you too hard, my Lord; you are just come from sickbed."

Dalich stepped back, lowering his blade. "You are holding back on saying something."

Only the King could read him like this. "I do wonder, my Lord … all the comings and goings in the Library and the Scriptorium. Many borderlanders and outerlanders pass through…"

"Ah." The King's shoulders lowered, and he beckoned, slipping a hand to Saril's arm, the flesh still tender under the other man's touch. Dalich spoke quietly. "Let me tell you what my father once told me, in greatest confidence, my Second."

"Certainly."

The Lord of the Strange Kingdom leaned to his companion's side, his voice soft and intense. "Father said the women in my family often bear the greatest Gifts. You know his mother saw The Powers." It was not a question but a statement of fact. His gray eyes cut to his Second's.

"I recall that from her Legend."

His steady assent seemed to please his Lord. "Saril, I choose to not acknowledge my mother's dealings. Perhaps The Powers sway my thoughts this way. I do suggest you consider the same course of action." He flicked a thumb along the carved *D*'s of his pommel. "When does your family arrive to meet my son?"

"Marnil later today, and the rest of the family, including wee Kaloft, tomorrow."

"It will be good to see them again."

Saril knew the conversation had circled to its end, though in the end his Lord's suggestion would not root as the King hoped.

———

The next day, along the road leading into King's Halls, the sturdy, heavy coach of the House of Jinil approached. Inside, ten-year-old Lady Jinilya sat still, but eager-eyed, as she viewed King's Halls. How different it looked from the structure of her tidy, uniform home. For the royals' residence had windows of varying sizes and shapes, roofs of thatch and stone and wood, and sides of plaster, of rounded rocks, and all types of shapes, materials, and textures she did not recognize. It was as though a most indecisive person had chosen every option a Builder offered.

Spying familiar faces, Jinilya bounced from her seat to the carriage window. "Look, I see Saril! And King's Mother is with him!" She jostled with her little nephew to wave from the open space above the half door, while Kaloft jabbed her hip with his small elbow and giggled.

Her saister Athla cautioned, "Children, be careful. Come sit, we are nearly at King's Halls, and you must be calm and presentable."

Jinilya looked to her mother, whose steady gaze imparted the same message. She sank into her seat. Athla corralled her child, gathering him into her ruby silk clad arms. "For the greetings, we will arrange ourselves in order of age. Is that not proper, Maither?"

The Acta Sua of their house replied, "Aye. Two weeks journeying." She smiled at her daughter. "How glad it is to finally arrive."

The wee boy interjected, "Hungry!"

The carriage stopped and a servant opened the door. As decreed, Mother stepped forth first. Gray-haired Lady Marna, King's Mother, embraced her.

"Saralya, my dear Reader. How wonderful to see you and your beautiful family."

"Well met, my Lady. Now you too know the joys of grandmotherhood."

Behind the elder Ladies, her brother Saril stood observing them, hands behind his back. It seemed to Jinilya he studied the two women with extra attention. It reminded her of her writing tutor lurking over her quilling, finger wagging, ready to point to any imperfection.

Her mother stepped to Saril and they embraced, but when they broke apart, he laid the palm of his hand alongside her cheek, speaking softly to her. The girl leaned from the carriage to listen, but Athla was departing King's Mother and urging Jinilya to grasp Kaloft's hand and step forward. The great Lady beckoned the young girl into a fond embrace. "How tall you are for your age, Jinilya. You are growing nearly as quickly as my grandson."

Uncertain what to make of this last statement, the girl replied, "I thank you, my Lady. I am very happy to see you." She curtsied, and King's Mother bent to place a kiss on her head and then on Kaloft's curls.

After the greetings, servants led them to the quarters reserved for their house. Jinilya was sad not to find her brother Marnil there, but the Door Guard reported he would be there soon. Kaloft begged for a bite to eat, and Athla led him to the kitchens, leaving Jinilya alone in the room she would share with her nephew unless her saister insisted he stay with her. At King's Halls, Jinilya would not have her own room until she was of age, but that was six years away.

Whilst she was tucking her favorite doll into the bigger bed meant for her, Saril entered the room, the dark curls on his head a striking textural contrast to his smooth black doublet. "How fares my sister?" He closed the door.

"Tired. Athla was talking and talking and talking." She positioned the doll's raven braids along its shoulders.

"Well, we do not have much time alone, thus I will make this quick. I want you to be more affectionate with Mother."

"What?" She turned to her eldest brother.

"I will speak plain. Mother is a widow, and whilst none of us can fill Father's place, she needs to know we love her." Saril smiled, and for the first time she realized there were different types of smiles. His expression struck her as an attempt at warmth, but studied, honed to the moment at hand. Young Jinilya found this curious, for she could think of nothing in her reasoning that made his utterance suspect, despite being odd and unexpected. Yet something tugged at her to notice.

Her elder continued, "You can be cold sometimes, sister." The young girl, hurt to her heart, opened her mouth to protest.

"Jinilya, calm. I merely ask that you show her more warmth. Do you know what I mean? Touch her arm, embrace her, put your head in her lap, stay close to her. Mothers like that. It will make her happy. Now, I will see you at dinner in the Queen's chamber." Saril nodded to her, a curt, quick dip of his chin, and then turned, soundlessly rotating the door handle. He departed the room.

The girl stood slack-jawed as he exited, then burst into tears.

———

Lord Marnil smiled, watching his beautiful wife Athla lean close to the wrapped babe Namlich in the Queen's arms, the child's small profile pale against its father's colors. The young women exclaimed endearments over the infant, whilst his mother and King's Mother flanked their daighter's sides on the large couch in the Queen's quarters. They too cooed over the babe. His two-year-old son Kaloft stood by Athla's knees, gripping her ruby-hued skirt, his bottom lip turning downward. Jinilya sat draped tightly against her mother, eyes upon their brother Saril.

Marnil leaned into his chair and watched his elder sibling, an entertaining prospect whenever Saril thought he escaped notice. The oldest son of the House of Jinil trained his gaze on Lady Marna, which seemed odd to his brother. Marnil turned his attention to the King, only to find his Lord staring at Saril, a warning in his royal gray eyes. Wondering what to make of these potent gazes, he heard his wife say, "Such a lovely, healthy babe, my Lady. Only two months old and very sturdy."

"Yes, the nurses say he is big for his age. Athla, would you like to hold him?"

His Lady wife's voice trembled, "Oh, how I would love to!"

As the swaddled child was placed into her waiting arms, their son began an anxious sob. "Mama—" Saralya reached for her grandson and tapped his shoulder. The little lad turned his brown orbs to her, and she pulled him into her lap, just as a knock sounded at the door.

From his chair opposite Saril, Dalich King called, "Enter."

The knocker complied, and Favik stepped into the Queen's chamber, clutching a tan envelope with two seals of glossy black wax like fixed dark eyes appraising the room. Marnil looked to Dalich, but like when a candle suddenly intensifies its flame, his attention was caught by the brightened expression of his sister, whose sweet young face shone at the sight of the blond man. She looked as though she expected to receive a longed-for Naming Day present.

There was a leanness to Favik's face and demeanor that was new gained since Marnil saw him last at the Sixth Company's headquarters. The former Ambassador addressed the King in a perfunctory tone, as though he had said the phrase many times over: "My Lord, a letter from Ambassador Moril in Havadra." He placed the document into his Lord's waiting hand.

Dalich spoke. "At last, direct word from my Ambassador in Havadra. After, what, a full two months since their civil war started?"

Saril spoke, his gaze upon Favik. "As it was reported."

"Odd that this envelope is not in my full colors." The King's dark brows knit as he examined the seals. He opened the missive, eyes swiftly studying the quilling. Damina Queen's lower lip dropped, then she muttered, "Thank The Powers." The King slipped the sheet to his Second, who read it in silence. Then the two men stared at one another like Records Keepers pondering evidence at a tribunal.

"Well, what does it say?" King's Mother's tone reminded them that the room was populated with more than just the serious pair.

Dalich turned to her. "Ambassador Moril reports our Embassy in Capitola is a locked fortress due to the unrest. Moril mentions, thank The Powers, that their stores are plentiful and they can safely wait it out." He glanced to the other Ladies. "The letter is dated a month ago, but that is understandable given the distance." Looking to his Second, he said, "Moril says this is the fifth note he has sent."

"Yet it is the first Ambassador's letter to arrive at King's Halls." Saril placed the document on a low table.

The Queen spoke. "Dalich, tell everyone how fares his wife and their little son." She touched her friend's arm. "Athla, their boy Elai is close in age to Kaloft. No, he is younger. Between Kaloft and Namlich in age. But closer to Kaloft."

"Yes, they are all in good health and managing well." He smiled at the Ladies, leveling his reassuring gaze at the youngest.

"Perhaps," Saril began in a smug tone, "we should send someone to rescue them." His eyes roamed to Favik. Marnil pressed his fingernails into the leather upholstery of his chair's arms. To The Powers, he could not believe the audacity of his brother. It was not Favik's fault the Eskalinder family they tried to save was lost.

Favik's gaze pivoted to the King. "Should I prepare a response"—he paused for half a breath—"to Ambassador Moril's letter?"

"Not at this time. You may go."

The blond man bowed and departed, watched by Jinilya, who breathed, "Is Favik going to rescue them?"

Saril looked to their sister. "I am afraid that is not something at which he excels."

Marnil glared at his brother, but it was King's Mother who spoke. "It is my understanding that the great distances involved and the delays they engender led to the very sad events to which you refer." She raised a gray eyebrow as Marnil nodded his agreement.

"As you say, my Lady." Saril dipped his head, the perfect acquiescing courtier. Marnil half wanted to strike him.

"Kaloft," said the King, gesturing grandly to the youngest of the family as though the action could erase the strain in the air, "it is my great pleasure to see all your house gathered in private quarters to meet King's Son." Marnil's sole child looked from his grandmother to the Lord of Eskalind, who continued, "It is my hope that the two of you shall be as close in companionship as I have been with your father and uncle."

Saralya smiled. "What do you say, Kaloft?"

"Please?"

The adults laughed. Marnil shook the tension from his fingers.

———

The next day, Marna sat companionless at her desk in her private Library office. Glad beams of sunlight lay full upon The Powers' parchment before her, and she brought quill to ink and wrote:

Why is my grandson growing at such a fast pace?

She waited. And waited. No response emerged. Again she quilled,

Did the herbs I gave his mother to mature her body cause this?

Again, nothing. The former Queen sighed, but pressed forward, writing,

> *Does he need to grow swiftly to protect Eskalind, like his forefathers Karlock King and Saanlich King?*

Counting her breaths, her eyes held fast upon the sheet for such a length of time that when she closed her lids, a dark, letterless, parchment-sized shape floated in her vision like a cruel taunt.

Watching the sheet, Dalock's Queen lifted it and passed it into shade, her quilling evaporating like raindrops under the sun's stern gaze. "Well, perhaps all will be well and good as the Legends tell. Ha." She laid the parchment flat upon the desk, placing a hand upon it and gazing at the ropes of veins branching over tendons, the dull brown spots emerging amongst deepening pores. It was the fourth year of her widowhood. Only four more years till she reached her sixth decade. In this moment, the Scholars' Mistress felt the burden of her offices hard upon her. Marna could not remember ever possessing smooth fingers or taking her husband's warm hand.

She closed her eyes, and a returning vision sprang forth in her mind. That same hand upon a scarlet coverlet, trembling, weak, skin stretched thin with great age. Diamond-windowpane shadows moving slowly across the bed.

Marna opened her eyes to view her private office, just as the bell tingled the welcome arrival of Lady Saralya. Marna rose with happy haste to ring the entrance signal.

Saralya opened the door and stepped into the carpeted room. But she was not alone, as expected; behind her traipsed her daughter. Jinilya looked to Dalock's Queen with anxious eyes from her position beside her mother.

"My dear Reader, look who you brought with you," the Scholars' Mistress called as she walked to greet them.

The women embraced, and Saralya whispered, with an apologetic sigh, "She has become my shadow."

Marna smiled, an idea forming as she looked to the young girl whom she had secretly named Flame Quencher. "I am pleased to see you for the first time in my chambers, Lady Jinilya. Come, your mother has some letters to read on my desk"—the women exchanged meaningful glances—"while you, dear, will help me make our teas." She led her charge to the tea-making table, lined with porcelain canisters in her son's colors, and lit a short candle. Saralya went to Marna's desk and sorted through the missives there.

The girl watched her mother. Marna made advantage of the child's inattention to hide the candlesnuffer. She cleared her throat, and Jinilya turned her green eyes to the teacups. "Do you like mint, Jinilya?"

"Yes, my Lady."

Marna spooned herbs into two of the teacups, then lifted the lid on a third canister for the child's tea. "Oh, what was I thinking?" She turned her head slightly away from the girl and stepped a bit aside, using her body to block Saralya's view of her daughter and the candle. "It is bright enough without this candle. Put it out for me, would you, Jinilya? And be careful that it does not smoke much. I cannot abide the scent."

"Aye, my Lady." Her eyes darted about the table.

The former Queen measured out the herbs. "The correct proportions are very important. I must count every grain."

Jinilya made a quick glance at the former Queen, who pretended to be engrossed in her task. The girl then reached a bare hand into the flame and closed her fist around the burning wick without a flinch. When the child pulled her hand away, not a hint of smoke or its acrid odor was apparent. Marna glanced to her, serious and steady, "I thank you, dear."

The little Lady looked to the floor, lips closed tightly.

"Now, here is a tea for you." Marna slid the ovoid, sable-hued cup toward the girl's brown hands. Jinilya reached with outstretched fingers, displaying an unblemished palm on the hand that had extinguished the lit candle.

Well, confirmation.

"And these two are for your mother and myself." Marna lifted the remaining cups, each a pleasing purple shade, and called to her Reader, "Saralya, we shall sit on the wide window seat by the door."

King's Mother led the way, the guests following, and the trio nestled into the comfortable pillows, the women side by side, Jinilya hipped opposite against her mother. The youngster sipped her tea, then glanced at the cup as though it commanded her attention. Marna asked her friend, "How fare things at your estate?" Thus began a few minutes of idle banter, whilst the girl drained her drink, placing the cup on the window ledge. She lowered her head to her mother's thigh.

"Daughter! What has come over you?"

"Very tired, Mother."

"Let the child rest," Marna soothed, pleased at the efficacy of the sleeping herbs. "All the excitement of being at King's Halls can be overwhelming for a youngster. Or perhaps it is anticipation for her Naming Day. Only three months away." The former Queen tipped the last of her tea past her lips as Jinilya's eyelids fluttered closed.

Saralya stared at her offspring, who breathed as though dreams claimed her. "I cannot understand what has come over her since we came to King's Halls," she whispered. "She clings to me like a starving babe at the teat. She is normally very independent and never acts like this." Her Reader paused. "Unless she has been frightened by something."

"But what would frighten her so?"

"Oh, a nightmare." The Acta Sua of the House of Jinil closed her dark eyes. "This started just after we arrived. I found her crying alone in her room. I think she had been napping." She opened her eyes and glanced at her child, then stroked the girl's smooth black hair. "It must be difficult for her to adjust to being away from home."

"Poor dear." Marna wondered if something else were amiss, but dared not breathe that she feared The Powers might have a hand in it. After a fond gaze at the young sleeper, she ventured, "I wonder if you and I might remove to the far window seat and converse more." She placed her palms together, then flipped her hands apart in an abbreviated mimic of the Scholars' gesture.

"Of course, my Lady," Saralya responded, cupping her hands under her daughter's head and sliding away from her, careful to set her head upon the cushions. The two women rose and walked across the long room to the other end. Marna gathered a pair of wax tablets and styluses along the way, of the type usually used for teaching writing without wasting papyrus or parchment on one new to quilling. They sat side by side. Marna handed one of the tablets to Saralya, then wrote on her own,

The Powers destroyed the Havadrans' weapons research.

The half-Guerish woman's dark eyes seemed to magnify. "How?" She breathed. Dalock's Queen scrawled her response, and her friend whispered, "Thank The Powers! Did you have word of this from Deenofts?"

Marna scraped her lettering from the tablet, speaking quiet as she was able. "No, no direct word from him in months. But, our Havadran wrote Favik that he would return to Eskalind soon." She thought she heard the child snore and glanced across the room, then back to her companion, leaning close. "Favik was in Gergelt, preparing to rescue an Eskalinder family, a mother and son, trapped in Havadra. It is the incident Saril referred to earlier."

"It did not end well?" Saralya's brow knit tightly.

The former Queen spoke a bit louder. "Men from Marnil's company were to rendezvous with Favik in Gergelt and assist, but their journey to Gergelt was delayed. Whilst he waited, Favik had word that the mother and child in question"—she dropped her voice to the slightest hushed tone—"were slain."

"By The Powers, how horrible!"

"Yes, it was quite a blow. He feels personally responsible, despite my counsel that he did all he could. He wrote begging that he alone journey to relate the news to the father, in person. He is just returned from that sad mission. I tell you, Favik has not been the same man since."

Saralya's dark eyes widened. "And Saril rebukes him for this? Oh my Lady." Her shoulders drooped.

"But there is more to tell. Lord Radil has made a discovery on an ancient vellum…" She wrote upon the freshly scraped tablet Favik's news from the northern Scholar:

Before the founding of Eskalind, not all people spoke words understandable to each other. There was much confusion in the world. Till The Powers decreed that all must speak alike.

Her friend puzzled this as Marna continued, "I have independently verified this through my research here in King's Halls, via documents hidden from the eyes of all others."

"The Cabinet of Trelich King?"

"Yes, it has played a hand in these discoveries. Saralya, this is very exciting." She wiped away her lettering on the tablet and scrawled afresh,

I am discovering the Rules of The Powers.

The Acta Sua brought a hand to her mouth, studying the text with her dark orbs. "My Lady, you are richly Gifted." She pondered a lengthy moment. "I, what would you have me do, about any of this?" She lifted the wax tablet.

King's Mother laid a hand on the scarlet silk sleeve of the Acta Sua's gown. "Keep vigilant eyes and ears for any fresh news that may pertain to what we have discussed." She scraped the wax away. "Beseech your blood cousin Kermon to do the same. Send me reports when you return home. Not that I want you to leave, dear friend."

"I thank you, my Lady. I am happy to be in your company as long as I am able, but I may be of more use," and she gazed at her hands as though they held a book, "in the south at my estate, closer to the borderwall. As long as I need not cross it." Saralya turned her attention to the far end of the room, to her daughter. "And I think for now Jinilya would fare better at home. Though one day she may want to apprentice in your Library." She smiled, though Marna sensed that the girl's mother found the thought of separation from her youngest painful.

"I would welcome her. Of course, only when you think the time is right."

"I thank you, my Lady."

———

An hour later, Saril, alone, rounded a corner near Dalock's Queen's doors. A lone candle burned in an alcove, and something about it demanded his attention. For a moment he did not breathe, but an intention was hard upon him. He made for the former Queen's private Library office. "Announce me," King's Second ordered the purple-becloaked Apprentice staffing the closed door.

The young man touched the black threads of the scroll embroidered upon his cloak as though it might summon The Powers to his aid. "My Lord, sir, King's Mother departed a while ago. Sir." He cowered as if this situation was unique in the annals of the world and bewilderment the only course of action.

"Then I will wait inside." Saril marched around the Apprentice's desk to the door and opened it. He shut the door, stifling the weak protests of the young man. A feeling of certainty pulsed in his veins. Something in her chamber would reveal the root of her schemes.

At that moment, The Powers saw fit to grant a great deal of sunshine to the long room, though when he had last peeked out of doors, a gray sheet of cloud had blanketed the sky. Hands behind his back, he strolled amidst the furniture and tables, glancing at scrolls and an open book of herbcraft, which exhibited an illustration of a mint plant like enough unto life that it seemed one could pluck the leaves from the page.

Crossing the room to its far end, Saril rounded the large desk anchored there, dark eyes alighting on a blank sheet of parchment at its center, faintly glistening in the rays of the sun, as some high-er-quality parchments do. He had thought it was blank, but even as he gazed at it, letters appeared upon the sheet as though they seeped forth from a hidden source. He leaned closer and read.

Brother of Jinilya

Standing to his full height, Saril glanced about the room, wondering how King's Mother played this trick upon him and why this strange form of address. Perhaps his sister had told the Lady of his suggestion that she keep close to their mother. One never knew what children might say to their elders. Or what machinations their elders might let slip around a child. Again, fresh quilling appeared, writ by an unseen hand.

Do you serve the royal
family of Eskalind

Ah, so she of all people questioned his loyalty. Then again, the let-tering was more finely wrought than any he had seen by her hand. Trying to discover the mechanism producing the quilling, he passed a hand over the sheet to touch it. As the shade of his hand shielded the light, the words evaporated. Saril pulled his hand away quick as though burned, but the text did not reappear. He whispered, "How is—who is doing this?"

You love Dalich King

Yes, he had always loved his Lord and friend, but something in these words, in this moment, imparted the gravity of feeling that he hid in the deepest reserves of his heart. If this precise statement and its sen-timent had occurred in the midst of his Ambassador training, whilst former Ambassadors and Records Keepers were evaluating every twitch of his muscles, every stitch in his speech, there never would have been an Ambassador Saril of Eskalind. His hands trembled, and a sudden river of sweat slid along the back of his neck as he blurted, "Yes, I, I serve him. Who is this?"

Loyalty to all My family is required

Saril backed away, hands at waist height as though to push away an unseen foe. Dalich was right. The women in the royal family possessed unexplainable Gifts. "I have no argument with you, King's Mother," he whispered. "None at all."

"Are you both truly leaving?" Samathe asked in a tight, anxious tone from the doorway.

Only half-awake, Deenofts placed the cloth-wrapped dried bread at the top of the worn but sturdy satchel he used for journeying. He pulled the closure tight. "As they say in Eskalind, aye." The Havadran smiled at his sister, but could not read her expression, as she had veiled herself to traverse their home to the male family members' quarters. Only two small candles were lit against the predawn dark.

Samathe moved closer, whispering, "I have waited for this day for two prolonged months. Ever since you brought our so-called cousin here. Will you finally tell me why?"

"I told you, I thought you would like a companion to sketch with." Deenofts could almost sense her rolling her eyes behind the cloth draping her face. He turned his attention to his pack.

"Then this is goodbye, for now."

"Most certainly."

She pulled aside her veil. "I wish *you* wouldn't go. I can still find you a wife, though I grow tired of saying it."

The Scholar sighed loudly. "I wish *you* were going with us, though I grow tired of saying it."

"Are you certain it's safe?"

He quirked his mouth at his sibling's sudden change of tack. "My excursions out-of-walls indicate that the war is over and life returns to normal."

"But that could change."

"Samathe, the siege rations are replenished, and since they cost us less than one of your paintings, it is clear that even the food merchants are wagering that Sirish's kingship is acceptable for now. He may be king a long while."

His sister nodded. "I cannot believe you are not buying passage on a ship."

Deenofts nearly guffawed. He would not risk bringing a hunted fugitive to the port. Aloud he countered, "It's too expensive."

They spoke over one another, she saying, "I have the coin," and he, "Traveling on the back of a droma over the desert isn't that bad."

His sister waved a hand in dismissal. "Come to my rooms before you say goodbye."

"I will."

Samathe departed, and Deenofts glanced about the chamber. Nothing remained that he wished to carry on the long overland journey. Thus he went to the screen that connected his room to Anish's and called, "Cousin, come to my chamber when you are ready." A moment later his door opened and the youth entered. "My, you are quick."

"I packed last night." Anish's satchel slumped to the floor by his feet. He held it by its long, slender cord.

"Everything on the list I gave you?"

"All of it. And some of my drawings."

The Scholar nodded in approval. "After two months sequestered here, you are doubtless more than ready for our next adventure. Now, as the Thislins say, allow me to review our plan. We will depart this fortress, walk until just before dawn, then hire carrying boxes to travel to the western edge of the city. There we will pick up our dromas—"

"Can we just hire carrying boxes to bring us from here?"

"After we are far from this fortress, then we will get a box," and Deenofts swiped a finger along his nose in the silent code the pair used to refer to Anish's fugitive status. "No one must mark you as coming from—" He pointed to the ground.

"Go on," the young Havadran grumbled.

"Let us make a plan." The Scholar cleared his throat, half hating that he used this favorite phrase of his countrymen, though its usage here was most appropriate.

Anish interrupted, "Are you going to tell me what to do if we see the Herald?"

The Scholar raised his blond eyebrows. "In nearly a dozen trips across the desert, I have never once seen the so-called Herald of Death. I am well past beginning to think it is merely a story made up to keep children—and merchants—out of the desert. You know, the overland journey can yield much higher profits to those willing to make the traverse. Well, you probably did not know that." The youngster looked to the floor tiles. "Now, if we are separated, a youth such as yourself alone is likely to attract all manner of maleficence." Deenofts retrieved a small flask from his robes. "Use this to keep others away from you. If, and only if, we are separated, spread this on your upper arms or any large area of your body where you are normally covered. But be certain it is an area you can easily display. Do not use it on a small area: that will cause harm."

"Why? What is it?"

"That is a formula of a rare tree's bark, red in color, which, oddly, becomes green when distilled. That bark is mixed with crushed and strained Lamorda seeds, a very involved process, then a drop of . . ." His eyes scanned Anish's benumbed expression and he tsk-tsked. "I forget you have had an entirely Havadran education, which neglects herbsmithery, except for poisons and antidotes. Well then, it is an irritant. It causes an ugly—but painless!—rash when spread over a large area of skin. Counterintuitive, but true. On our journey, I will tell you the long tale of how I made that discovery." The man's eyes darted about to make certain none of the servants had crept near, then he lowered his voice. "If we are separated, you must get to Eskalind on your own." He draped his free hand across his forehead, mimicking a swoon. "Claim you are ill with no hope of recovery except by healing from Dalich Strange King." He glanced at the egg-shaped flask in his palm and lowered his hand. "No one will touch you—they won't want to contract your highly contagious illness."

"It's contagious?"

"Say it is." Deenofts pushed the bottle toward the youth.

Anish grasped the base and cork of the bottle using only the tips of his stubby fingers. "Um, how long will the rash last?"

"Long enough for you to journey to Eskalind. When you get there, Border Guards will bring you to a Records Keeper. Do not mention your hidden rash, but say you seek political sanctuary. Do not give your true name; use another name that suits you." Deenofts lifted a corner of his mouth in the slightest of sneers. "And, *Anish*, do tell the Records Keeper of your skill in copying manuscripts. That should land you a position in the King's Mother's Scriptorium." Here he smiled. "And I will see you there."

The lad's gray eyes lost their focus, and for a moment the Scholar wondered if he might faint.

"Remember!" Deenofts continued, in a manner as cheerful as offering sweets at a Naming Day celebration, "that is our second plan, only if we are separated." He slung his satchel over his shoulder and laid a gentle hand on the youngster's arm. "The first plan will work. We journey to Eskalind together; you pretend you are my servant till we leave Capitola. Play your role, keep your head down, hood up, and let's go." He removed his hand and patted the hilt of his new, much plainer, long knife.

Reaching into his satchel, Anish scooted aside several tightly rolled drawings as he stowed the flask. "My . . . grandfather always said to have at least two plans." His tone suggested a third plan might be in the offing, but he said no more.

"Yes, a wise man, your grandfather." Deenofts snuffed out the two candles, not wanting the servants to have any last glimpse of the fugitive. "Now wait here quietly while I speak to my sister."

After that final goodbye, the pair slipped forth from the fortress, leaving Samathe behind. Traversing the pathways that threaded around fortresses, they trod the hard dirt, pocked here and there by The Powers' only knew what accident or catastrophe during the recent civil war. Even at this early gray hour, workmen put brush to wall as they painted over sooty burn marks on the side of a fortress. Deenofts glanced sidelong at Anish, pleased to find the youth did as he'd been instructed, angling his head to the dirt like a serving lad, the fabric of his hood draping his face.

After nearly an hour on foot, the thin high clouds above turned pink in welcome to the sun, and the city gradually came to life as men began their daily business. The Havadran Scholar attempted to hail a carrying box, but the carrying men balked at fitting a man and nearly adult-sized youth into one box. Thus two boxes were procured, and the pair continued their journey.

Inside his box, Deenofts knit his fingers, uneasy about the separation and the usual Havadran attempt to squeeze more coin out of a fellow citizen. Leaning forward slightly, he closed his eyes as the box lumbered left then right, counting each turn in his mind to ascertain their position and direction. All seemed right, and when the box lowered, he opened his door to see Anish emerging from another box. A quick glance determined that this was indeed the westernmost square in the city, notable for the sizable fortress of the Santris family, with its huge purple-painted door, dominating the scene. "Thank The Powers, as they say in Eskalind," he murmured as the youth stepped toward him, flanked by one of his box's bearers.

The lead carrying man of Deenofts's box held a cupped palm to the Scholar's face, the characteristically unsubtle Havadran way of demanding payment. He reached in his robes for his purse of small coins—the only purse he exhibited whilst traveling out-of-walls. Then he became aware of the unnatural quiet that inhabited the air like an invisible living thing.

The man with the outstretched hand turned his gaze, and Deenofts followed. Arrayed in the blue shadow of the enormous fortress were men on horseback, dozens of them, each armed with a long spear and blades belted at the hip and saddle. A steady stream of stealth-sandaled men filtered forward, falling into ranks across the beige sandstones paving the square. They too bore long knives and swords and steel weapons of lethal description, sharp and of honed points. One of Deenofts's carrying men bolted and dashed eastward, back toward the center of the city. A mounted man rode forth in a sudden thunder of hooves and ran him down. The other carrying men dropped to their knees and bowed low, an instant exemplification of submission. Anish cowered near Deenofts's side. "Get down, servant," he muttered to the youth, who dropped to the dusty stones.

The mounted man returned, his horse clomping toward the Scholar. The man pulled the reins with his free hand and halted his mount, the long spear in his other hand held vertically and dripping blood along its shaft. It seeped into the purple leather of his tight-fitting gloves. His brown eyes narrowed on the Scholar, an evil flash in them that echoed in the glint of gold surrounding the clear, square-cut amethyst jewels set in his ears. "What is this deputation you bring to my walls?"

"No formal mission at all, sir, save my chance hiring of these men to bear me to the Western Wall." Deenofts slowly raised his arms, empty palms open, and tilted his head, keeping his eyes on his inquisitor. "I am Deenofts the dye merchant, traveling overland to Eskalind. I am to finalize the purchase of my dromas at the wall." The man stared hard at him, a decision turning in his mind, then he swirled a finger at some of the foot soldiers. Several of them approached, long spears sky-pointed, purple armbands tied tight over their taupe robes. Deenofts inhaled. "My business is to the west, far, far across the sands; I can imagine yours lies in a different direction." He smiled slightly.

The man grinned wide, baring his teeth to exhibit another purple jewel implanted in an incisor's enamel. His soldiers arrayed themselves beside him. "Cage the carrying men. Let this merchant go west. You two follow him. If he attempts any other direction, kill him."

"Yes sir."

The Santris man continued, "Merchant, when you reach Eskalind, you will be the first to tell them there is a new king of Havadra." He tossed his head, eyes aflame with schemes and intentions, and laughed, turning his horse back to his army.

Deenofts yanked Anish to his feet, and with two Santris soldiers steps behind them, the pair fled to the Western Wall. There, they stood in the doorway as the droma merchant denied the agreed-upon price, haggling for a larger amount of coin. Anish cowering at his elbow, the Scholar ground through his teeth, "Fifteen total for three dromas, as we agreed." The animal seller continued his haggling.

One of the soldiers said to the other, "Let's go, or we'll miss everything." The other must have agreed, for the first called out, "Remember your agreement, merchant." They paced away.

Making advantage of their departure, Deenofts growled low to the droma seller, "Yes, remember your agreement and I may throw some advice into the bargain that will save your life."

The man blew air through his lips and tapped his fingernails against one another. "Oh, you threaten me, bringing those men with you."

"Listen, you greedy idiot, at this very moment there is something afoot that will leave you wishing you'd stocked more siege rations. Now sell us our dromas and let us be out of the city's walls."

The man cocked his head slightly and whispered, as though the two were intimates, "The Santris family?"

The Havadran Scholar maintained a neutral expression. Beside him, Anish shuffled from one foot to the other, his hood pulled low over his forehead. It seemed impossible that he could see anything. "Fifteen total," Deenofts said. "That includes full water bags that do not leak, made of a sturdy material, preferably leather. And feed for the dromas."

"Agreed."

Deenofts began counting out his coins, and the beast seller leaned close, eyes locked on the Scholar. "Is it the Santris?"

The last coin accounted, the dye merchant placed the lot in the other man's hand. "It is."

"I knew it. I knew they would go after King Sirish. I have won a wager, a fat one, ha ha!" He squeezed the coins in his fist, blind to their worth in his gloating. "He should have stayed a colonel, ha ha!"

Shaking his head, Deenofts led Anish to their animals. He set the boy to filling the water bags as he checked each droma's feet and their food supplies. Everything seemed in order. As the Santris army crept east through the city, the pair departed through Capitola's Western Wall. The dromas of the Scholar and his fugitive charge trotted at a quick pace over the sands, bound northwest in a straight line as though Eskalind could reel them toward its borders.

"Stop!" Deenofts called as they approached the last rise overlooking the city.

Capitola shrank beneath them as though reminded of its own insignificance by the vast dusty wastes. Anish easily cantered his droma to the Scholar's side, an unexpected adeptness in his handling of the reins and seat. "Is there no end to your talents? Who taught you to ride a droma?" Deenofts asked.

The youth smirked, turning his gray eyes toward the Havadran capital, where the major landmarks were barely discernible against the pale blue vault of sky as smoke rose in billowing columns from the city, soot-dense in the vicinity of the king's fortress, though the king's tower stood proud and clear. "A dead man." He gave a self-satisfied nod.

Deenofts squinted at the city. "Do I see a purple flag atop the tower?"

"Yes. I hope the whole city burns." The bitterness in his voice would curdle milk.

"I do hope you exclude my sister and household from your statement."

Anish looked to him, slack-jawed. "I'm sorry, I didn't mean her. It was … it was kind of her, and you, of you both, to shelter me in your fortress."

"Well, you are most welcome, Yirish." Deenofts raised his eyebrows.

The youngster turned away, his aspect inward, pouting, like a small child deprived of his latest demand and threatening to cry. "Don't call me that. Ever."

"But that is your given name, is it not? Are you not Colonel Sirish's fugitive son?" The youth said nothing, though his demeanor hardened, and Deenofts felt he caught a glimpse of the man he would become. "Am I right? We might as well air this, and what better place?" He swept an arm at the desolate dunes. "No one can hear us here. Yirish, you are no longer a fugitive if the man who hunted you is dead."

His companion chewed his lip. "I cannot call the man who murdered my mother Father." Angry tears stood in his eyes. "She was with child. How could he kill her when she was about to bear his child?"

The Scholar withheld the numerous retorts that surfaced in his mind, the foremost that, given Favik's recent visit to Havadra, he suspected the babe was not the colonel's. But, better to let the former Ambassador explain that to the youngster. Deenofts hoped the lad had not overheard the servants' gruesome reports that Sirish had stabbed the babe in its mother.

Havadra made him sick.

"I too will be glad to be rid of this place." Deenofts touched the shape of the square gold pendant Samathe had given him, hidden under his high-necked robe.

The former fugitive continued, "The colonel called me Yirish, but I have changed my name to honor my mother." His gray eyes swung toward Deenofts, a raptor's fire in their gleam. "Anish, she called me, and Anish I am."

Deenofts nodded. "Then come, Anish. Eskalind awaits."

That night the pair made camp in a shallow valley, a solitary dune away from a small watering hole. In the sober, graying light just before the sun roused itself, Deenofts crept to the peak of the rise and scouted the dunes for any trace or track of travelers or bandits. Spying none, he gestured to Anish to bring the dromas up and over to the watering hole. Once there, he poured water through his hair.

"Why are you doing that?" asked the youth.

"I always forget what an annoyance sand is on one's scalp. And that the best place to hide anything of value is in a headscarf." He removed the pendant Samathe had given him and placed it, along with his stash of gold coins, into a secret pocket in the seam of the long strip of cloth that would serve as his headscarf. Anish watched with a critical eye as Deenofts bound the cloth atop his head.

"What if it blows off?"

"Chin strap." He wrapped the tail of the cloth under his jaw and held it in place.

"That looks stupid."

He dropped the strip of cloth. It dangled by his ear. "How old are you?"

The lad raised his chin. "Thirteen."

"Ah. You look older, but your speech betrays you."

Anish made a sound like a stifled inhale.

"Listen, when the moon returns to the night sky, we will travel by its light. For now, we go as far as the sun allows. Once it is burning a hole in the sky, we seek the shade of our dromas or a cave." His companion said nothing. "Anish, did you hear me?"

The youth turned steel eyes upon him. "The desert steals water. The more you talk, the more water you lose."

"Thank you, my dear expert traveler of the great expanses. Please, do feel at liberty to share all your more correct knowledge with my ignorant self whenever it pleases you." Deenofts drew air through his nose and tucked the cloth dangling by his ear amidst its fellows. "I suspect this will be a most entertaining trip." He tugged his droma forward.

———

Days later the pair rested in what Anish now understood was Deenofts's favorite place to hide in the desert: any deep depression amidst towering mountains of pulverized sand. The pair sat, stinking and deflated, the tedium of the journey seeping into their shoulders like rough hands pressing them into the yielding ground. Behind them their dromas sat as well, eyes shut in slumber.

Deenofts glanced at the hard bread in his hand. "How I miss civilization, where I can give a man a coin and in return he will give me a nice steaming bowl of tasty stew or filling soup, or broth with noodles, flecked with spices that would send a Nordaksman into a stupor."

"What are you talking about?"

"I miss buying things, Anish, particularly food. Out here we make do with what we carry with us or discover. Coin makes everything easier. As does a stable, wise system of government. Ah, Eskalind."

The youth sighed and rose to his feet, sucking bits of dried bread from his teeth. Or perhaps it was dust. It was difficult to tell. In this basin between dunes, the world was soft ripples of beige beneath flat blue. He traipsed the steep sand dune before him, pleased to mar the wind-sculpted grains and introduce chaos into the sameness. The dye merchant called, "What are you doing?"

"Having a look around, since you aren't." He marched with determined steps to the peak of the rise.

"Oh ho, two can play at this game." Deenofts tramped fast behind him, cresting the dune simultaneous with Anish. "Come, listen to me, young Havadran, born and raised to commandeer and to plot, to reap and to profit from the sweat of every man you can plunder or outwit—"

"What?" Anish backed away, eyes furiously studying the older man as though he bore arms against him.

"You are afraid of this notion? Have you not already seen it in motion, Anish? Seen it in the commands of your parents, the discipline and teachings of your tutors, in the very way our people live?" Deenofts's glare was murderous. "We are born and raised to be killers, for is not a Havadran male not accounted a man until he has slain another?"

The youth stared, his mouth slightly open, wide fear in his eyes. The dye merchant's bearing softened. "None of this was your doing, Anish, but it was to be your inheritance. You are saved from that now; we journey to Eskalind and the best life The Powers can offer." His gaze traveled in a quick flick over the youth's shoulder. "Ah." It was a falling sound, like accepting a failure.

Anish followed his eyes. All along the horizon, a billowing brown cloud rose from the ground, as though the sky had rubbed into the dirt and emerged filthy with it.

"Oh no," the youngster breathed.

Deenofts said, "Sand storm. How far away would you say it is?"

"Um."

The man placed a hand on his shoulder, brown eyes sharp and intelligent under his protuberant brow, a paternal calm in his manner. "It's always closer than you think. Soon a finger of dust will reach forward to claim us. We, Anish, must *preserve* ourselves and *prepare* to *prevent* our demise. Back to the dromas!" He raced down the dune.

Anish followed, slipping and sliding in his haste. At the bottom, Deenofts shook sand from his robes. "Why am I bothering? Ha!" His voice awoke the beasts, who stood. Anish skittered to his side.

"Anish, the dromas," he reached for the closest's rope and handed it to the youth, "are our first line of defense. We turn them to block the wind and stand against them. Standing is important, Anish: Do not sit down until it clears, no matter how tired you become. If you sit, you may be buried. Or the droma may step on you." The words came fast but clear, born not of panic but preparation. "Cover your mouth, eyes, and ears, and hold tight to your droma's rope. I will hold the other two. These storms can be very disorienting. Touch the droma's body to be sure it is still there."

Even as he spoke, the sun dimmed behind the puffing mass of dust that expanded above like a flowing robe across the sky. "And we cannot stand too close to each other, for if a droma panics, it might trample both of us." Anish gulped.

"Come." Deenofts nodded at him, and they pulled the dromas into position, the beasts blinking their long lashes and jerking their heads against the rope. "Cover up!" the man yelled, and Anish did, his last sight his companion's dark eyes locked upon his own as he too pulled cloth to cover his mouth and ears.

Eyes shut and bandaged against the sand, the general's grandson leaned against his droma's fuzzy hide, the stubby texture of its fur thick enough to feel even through the fabric draping his face. He clung fast to the rope with one hand and pulled an arm across his nose as stinging specks of sand bit into his fingers. He would not let go, would not be defeated.

The howl of the wind droned for what seemed hours. Standing tight against his droma, the youth threw his mind to faraway places. A warm bed, a soothing bath, the look of pride and approval his grandfather would bestow upon him. Pleasing curves of ink recording his movement of the quill. The sweet, citrusy scent of his mother's perfume that would linger after her embrace. In his throat he mimicked the sounds swirling around him. at times a wailing cry, at others a long moan. It seemed he was marching inside the sound.

Then it stopped. He was not certain when, but a ringing silence filled his ears. Anish squeezed tight on the droma's rope, but it was not in his hand. He felt for his droma and scraped air. Pulling off the dusty cloth binding his head, he choked and sputtered till it came loose. It was dark and still as though there were no world. "Deenofts?" he choked.

One of the cords of his satchel had come loose, but the sack still hung from his back. He adjusted the cords and swallowed hard, trying to moisten his throat. "Deenofts?" The youth wiped his eyes, and small lights appeared in the dark void. Stars, that disappeared into a curve of darkness.

Anish climbed up the darkness till he saw a fire, small but bright, burning in the distance. He wondered if he might be dead, if his mother and grandfather were there, by the fire, awaiting him. He had no idea where this notion came from but it compelled him forward. Trudging onward, feet rising and falling through the granular remains of pulverized mountains, he traipsed toward the flickering orange beacon. The stars hovered overhead, now mere pinpricks of light. At last coming to the rim of the fire's glow, he called for his companion again. Waiting, he sank to his feet and closed his eyes.

He awoke to daylight and an odd shiver of light at his throat, a blue blade, sky-reflecting, held by a Havadran with big teeth and leathery tan skin who said, "Don't move."

"Did you cut him?" called another male voice. Anish could not see the speaker.

"Not yet."

A shorter man arrived by the shoulder of the first. A shade or two lighter in skin tone, with small nostrils wet and prominent in his face. "Good, bring him in the cave."

"Get up, boy." The long knife hovered under his chin, nimbly tracing Anish's rise to his feet. "Hands up where I can see them." He complied, hanging his head as he realized his only weapons were in his satchel.

"Cut the bag off him first," ordered the shorter bandit. His captor flicked the blade by the youth's shoulder, and the bag slumped heavy on his back, toward the remaining strap. Anish inhaled, sharp and instinctual at anticipated injury, then saw that the accuracy of the bandit's aim had left even his robes unscathed. The man bared his large teeth. With his free hand, he lifted the satchel and sliced the other strap. He gestured with his long knife toward the shorter man, who led the pair into a low cave, flickering with firelight.

On the rise above, Deenofts poked his head over the dune, seeing the bandits march the youth into a cave. If he had more water in him, he would cry at this miserable turn of events. "Separated in a dust storm, and that's when we stumble upon bandits. At least I found Anish. May The Powers help me talk our way out of this." He rose to his feet. "At least there's no sign of the Herald." The Scholar followed the trio.

After a scalp-scraping entrance, the cave opened into a large space strewn with the detritus one would expect from men of this rough trade: crushed baskets relieved of their goods, wooden boxes with locks pried apart, filthy bits of straw, stray cloth, slit satchels, and bones that Anish hoped to The Powers came from animals. "Tie his hands, give me his bag. Let's see what he has."

The larger bandit followed the shorter man's orders, then shoved the youth against the wall.

A fourth person entered the open space. Deenofts's smooth voice echoed in the cave. "Gentlemen, I see you are men of business."

"Who are you?" The shorter man threw the satchel aside as he drew the long knife scabbarded on his thigh. The cloth bag skittered across the sandy floor toward Anish.

"Why, a humble, but well-traveled, dye merchant, seeking the return of his nephew." Deenofts swept a hand toward Anish. "Good, I see he is still alive. Now, I have a business proposition for you two—it is just the two of you?—and some information you may find useful." The bandits glared at one another. "If you know of any minerals that are a source of purple—"

The smaller man interrupted, "What are you talking about? What are minerals?"

"Rocks. Minerals are rocks that can make dyes, and as I said, if you know of any sources, minerals or not, that would yield a purple color or stain, I know some Eskalinders who would pay heavy coin."

The bigger bandit said to his companion, "We hadn't gotten around to asking the boy where he was going. Sounds like they were heading to Eskalind."

"Who cares?" muttered the other as Deenofts held up his hands.

"Oh no, no no. I am avoiding *that* border at all costs." He lowered his voice. "You see, there is a merchant there that I promised purple paint and ink, when I find them, and I have not found them yet. I cannot set foot in that land until I have merchandise for the client. Do you know how difficult it is to get to Mavold from Havadra when you cannot traverse Eskalind? You must pass through Gergelt. Gergelt! The worst country in the world. The most gullible, giving people on earth. A Havadran would perish of boredom, his mind collapsing under the strain of nothing to plot or plan for, before he reached their far border." Deenofts tsk-tsked.

"Hmm." The larger bandit rubbed the side of his mouth, where a chalky tooth protruded from his gums. "Maybe we should go there." He lowered his blade.

"Only if you like to eat your fill every day, all day, without dropping a coin."

"You make it sound like paradise." The smaller man sounded suspicious.

"Only if your version of paradise includes women—or men—rubbing your feet all day in tireless labor. Giving foot rubs is the national pastime of Gergelt. Oh yes. They love rubbing the body." He glanced at Anish, a silent command in his eyes. The youth realized he should recover his satchel, and the flask stowed within it. He dipped his head slowly in a half nod. Deenofts returned his eyes to the smaller man. "Gergelts are very free with their favors, if you understand me."

"Ugh, I don't believe it." Yet he too lowered his blade, his brown eyes intent on the merchant. As slowly as he could, Anish crept crabwise toward his satchel.

"No, no one does, until they see it with their own eyes and taste the full glory with their own mouths. But by then, oh, it is too late. Their minds have turned to mush from all the pleasure. I was lucky to escape with a modicum of reason." Deenofts lowered his tone to one of grave advice. "There's a reason you never hear of anyone coming back from Gergelt—it's far too tempting to never leave!"

The smaller bandit lifted his long knife. Deenofts's eyes were keen upon the blade as though nothing else existed. He opened his mouth, but the bandit barked, "You talk too much," and lunged. The merchant tried to step back, too slow. The blade found his throat, cutting deeply.

The taller bandit guffawed. "I get to kill the other one." Deenofts fell.

The murderer glanced at the youth, who trembled and retched under his glare. "Strip the dead one first. See what he has of value. Don't try to pocket anything. You will be under my knife."

The second man growled but did as he was bid, the pair turning their backs to the youngster.

Fear squeezing his windpipe, Anish shrank to the ground, which was wet, for he had lost command of his bladder. His satchel was behind him, his wrists aching from the tight bonds. His hands touched a smooth cord and he fumbled for the end, not certain if it was the tie to his bonds or the satchel. At last pulling open the bag, his fingers felt something smooth and stoppered: the flask Deenofts had given him.

"What's that?" One of the bandits said. Anish froze.

"Coins. Gold coins." The bound youth heard the distinct clink of metal.

"Best music in Havadra." The pair laughed.

Anish struggled to pry the cork with a fingernail, his hands sweating, his grip loosening on the glazed bottle. A muffled pop and cool liquid doused his quivering hands. Then came a searing pain. He dropped the bottle onto the sand, a whimper escaping his lips.

The bandits turned to him. "You'll be crying out soon enough, boy," joked the shorter man.

The other stuck out his tongue and stroked a finger down the middle of it, a wicked fire in his eyes. "Mmm, we should sport with him first."

"He's smooth enough to look like a woman." They cackled.

Tears frosted Anish's vision as one of the men yanked him by the shoulder, forcing him to his feet. He lost his balance and fell, pitched forward on his face, unable to break the fall with his hands, which were still tied behind his back. He rolled to his side, moaning, his back toward the men.

"Ugh, his hands … Look, he's got the scourge!"

"Didn't see any red on him earlier. You trying to trick me, huh?"

"See for yourself. I'm getting out of here. He's got it, that means the dead one may have it too. That's why you had me search him?"

Someone paced close to Anish. "Ugh, he does have it, has it bad. It's at the bleeding stage. Powers take you if you infected us." The man spat at Anish's back.

The youth quivered on the dirt, his eyes shut tight, expecting a deadly blow at any moment. But instead he heard scurrying behind him, then quiet. He sucked air through his teeth and rotated toward where the bandits had been. Deenofts lay on his side, dead eyes open, beginning to cloud, an expression of surprise and pity writ across his familiar features, his final face an apology. Anish looked away, fighting down bile in his throat. Anger gripped him. He rolled and then scooted on his rear end to his satchel. The bottle lay overturned, emptied out. There was no chance of applying the ointment on a larger area of his body now. Leaning forward, he used his teeth to pull the bag open wide, holding the other end with his knee, rooting for the pearl-handled dagger he had won at the swordmaster's tournament. The prize he had intended to give his mother.

The general's grandson drew the blade from its scabbard with his teeth, dropping the knife to the dirt and rotating so his back and tied hands faced the handle. His fingers felt stiff, immovable, but somehow he managed to purchase a grip and cut the bonds tying his wrists without nicking or cutting his skin.

He shook his wrists and shoulders, brought his hands to his eyes. Glossy pustules dripped blood and frothy fluid; his fingers curled palmward like claws. Reaching with a knuckle, he straightened a finger, surprised that it did not hurt, though it moved stiffly. Stiffly replacing the blade in its sheath, he rose to his feet, paced to Deenofts, and closed the eyes. Tears clouded Anish's vision, and he muttered, "No, I must flee in case they come back." Inhaling, he patted Deenofts's robes, searching for a weapon or water sack. "Nothing. He must have stashed everything with the dromas. They must be not far away. Or the bandits will have gotten it all."

A glimmer of gold protruding from the dead man's headwrap caught his vision. He gently removed the cloth and unwound it, finding the gold coins and pendant Deenofts had stashed there. It pained him to pocket them, but he did. He unfurled the cloth to make a shroud, then stacked rocks around the body. Gathering a water sack and some dried meat left by the bandits, he replaced his satchel with another sturdy strapped bag lying amongst the detritus of the thieves' lair and filled it with his goods. "Goodbye, my only companion," he whispered to Deenofts, then crouched to exit the cave.

Outside, Deenofts's last journey was writ in the sand across a nearby dune, the bandits' tandem tracks leading in The-Powers-be-thanked opposite direction. Anish mounted the dune from whence Deenofts came with a wary look over his shoulder, from that height spying the men shuffling away at a swift pace. On the other side of the dune, he found two of the dromas purchased in Capitola, roped and waiting. Deenofts's long knife lay secure in its scabbard on the saddle of the larger.

The youth inhaled, clumsily untied the bonds with his curled fingers, and secured the weapon on his thigh. Climbing aboard the smaller droma, he led the pair to the top of the opposite rise, slugging water from the sack, the cheerful slosh of plentiful liquid a boon to his heart. He sucked more fluid, the sack filling his vision for a moment. Pulling the sack away, he hammered the cap home and raised his eyes. A man in rippling robes stood nearby, his hands behind his back. Dark, wiry hair was pulled tight, away from his deeply tanned face.

The lone figure in the desert. The Herald of Death every Havadran feared from cradle to end.

Anish froze, but the man's features looked familiar, almost as though he knew him. "You are Shinglo."

The dark, hooded eyelids lifted slightly. "You are not a snub nose."

Anish's brows knit. "I...I am heading to Eskalind."

"What do you know of Shinglo?"

"I had a companion whose mother was Shinglo. We planned to run away to the desert together and find you."

The man tilted his head upward, but his gaze stayed level with Anish's. "Where is this friend now?"

"Dead. Killed by Havadrans. My other friend, he was just killed by Havadrans there." He gestured. "In the cave below this rise. The men who murdered him are running that way." The youth pointed. "You may want to be cautious of them."

The man grinned, slowly, as though relishing a secret. "I do not fear dead men. Or snub noses." He glanced away from Anish, who turned to see several cling-robed figures approaching over the rise with long blades aloft, some bloody. Anish's droma stepped sideways at the sight, and he checked the reins to calm it.

"You do not try to flee," the man said.

"We are both against Havadrans," Anish stated, a cool gamble worthy, he thought, of his grandfather.

"Then you will come with us."

"What of this?" The youth held up a hand, the blood still wet, the skin angry. "Do you want my contagion? It would be better to let me go."

"It is no matter. My people believe The Powers protect us from such illnesses. Besides, you are a curiosity. I want to learn more about you." He held aloft a hand and fluttered it in the air as though it were a bird. The warriors fanned around the dromas. "Follow me."

———

Still atop his droma, Anish was escorted by the walking Shinglo along a trail, invisible to him, that ribboned along the crests of dunes till it descended into a wide valley. Spying nothing of interest about the place, he studied the beige-robed figures before him, their ropy hair constrained with braided straps. The same straps tied their clothing close to their bodies, for all except the first man, whose attire rippled and flowed with his movements. Behind, his brethren trailed, the last leading Anish's second droma. Studying their movements, he wondered if there might be a woman or two amongst them. One in particular had a bit of a swell and sway to the hips.

A slit of darkness appeared before them, and he stopped short. The shadowy slot enlarged, and he realized hands were at work furling a cloth that, peeled away, revealed a cave entrance. The group approached, single file, and entered. After the third person had entered, hushed voices echoed ahead. The line stopped moving. The cloth sealed shut. Someone behind him said something, but too quietly to distinguish the words.

Training his eyes upon the curtain, Anish was amazed that even at this near range, it closely resembled its sandy surroundings. Unless one were direct upon it, the entrance was camouflaged completely. This must be how the Shinglo hid themselves from passersby.

The first man he'd talked to emerged from the screen. He beckoned the youth down from his droma. "I must blindfold you. It is temporary."

Anish nodded. A soft fabric draped his eyes, then tightened around his skull. It felt clean and smooth against his dusty face; it was scented with an herb he could not name. Someone led him forward. Behind, the droma made a hiss of protest. The air cooled, and he gathered he had now stepped through the concealing curtain. A hand, the fingers spread wide, touched his head and gently pushed him down. "Sit here." He did. Sounds like shuffling feet and then the distinct smooth swish of parchment laid open by a hand sweeping across it. Murmuring. He sat a long time, it seemed.

"Unshield your eyes." He struggled with the knotting. Someone behind him assisted. His eyes uncovered, he saw an unfamiliar Shinglo man sitting before him. Behind the man, in the cave wall, was a metal grate covering a dark area. Soft air flowed from it, animating a few strands of the man's dark hair. Sconces carved into the walls gave a warm light to the room. Anish's long knife, the prize dagger, his coin purse, and his fine shirt lay to the side as though they were of little import.

Standing beside the seated man was the Shinglo he met on the dune. He held aloft the parchment drawings Anish had crafted whilst harboring at Deenofts's fortress. "Who are these people?" asked the seated Shinglo.

The blond youth replied as each drawing was unfurled. "My mother." Fine lines detailed her hair; the shading around her lips was not to his satisfaction, as it lent a slight pout to the expression. "My grandfather." Two views, each three-quarters of his face. One a kindly look of approval and the other stern. "My friend who I just buried." The lively expression in Deenofts's drawn eyes tore his heart. "My friend whose mother was Shinglo." Prince Sastofts looked out from the parchment with a regal authority in his eyes, his long nose held high as though he might bestow favor upon those who met his gaze. Anish had forgotten the commanding expression he had given the slain royal, which seemed to meet with approval in current company, as those standing behind him leaned forward for a closer view.

The last illustration was a silhouette of a small-nosed woman great with child. "My brother or sister. My mother was killed when she was with child." He looked at his hand, the fingers bent and stiff, and tried to lift each digit in a silent count to five.

The man in command gestured for the parchments to be put away.

His dark eyes were expressionless, their only outstanding charac-teristic that the outer edges were sloped slightly toward his ears so that he must view the world in a perpetual squint. "You show us a mother and grandfather with the features of the snub noses, yet you do not look like them."

"My family always said I looked like my mother's mother."

"Your mother's mother." A shade of reverence inhabited his voice.

"Havadrans, snub noses, killed my family. My friend was bringing me to Eskalind to work in the scriptorium there. These drawings show my skill."

"Scripto…?"

"A place where one draws and writes, makes scrolls and books."

The man's eyes narrowed critically and fell to Anish's curled fingers. "You made these drawings?"

"I did, before this happened." He raised his hands. In the cool air of the cave, the skin burned less and the blood was hardening into thick scabs. "But now, I don't think I can even write my name." The youth lowered his gaze to the dirt, wanting to crawl into it and close his eyes forever against this ceaseless misery.

A hand touched his shoulder from behind and handed him the blindfold. "It is temporary."

The door clapper stood still in its bell, but its metal ring hung in the air as Favik entered his Lady Marna's Library office. The former Queen sat at the far end at her desk, leaning into a clear beam of sunlight, an inked quill in her hand. The parchment before her cast a gentle light onto her features, her chin line drooping slightly as one would expect from a person approaching her sixth decade.

She raised her other hand to shield the light and squinted at him. "Ah, Favik, good. It is you, at long last. I lost count of the signal. No no no, do not come all this way, sit in the middle, anywhere is fine."

He glanced about for a seat for two, but most every chair and couch was laden with books or loose parchments. He looked back to his Lady, whose gray eyes scanned the page before her as intently as though she expected it to speak. "It is no use," she murmured, and cast the parchment aside onto the shaded side of her desk. "At least they guide Dalich."

King's Mother stood and came to him as he waited next to one of the few unencumbered chairs. She bent and pulled a short stack of books from the seat of a black leather chair, piling them upon others resting on a table, spines in a teetering frozen cascade that threatened to spill forth at the slightest motion. She sat with a heavy finality, as though expecting bad news, then bid him to seat himself. "Any news from the Records Keepers?"

"None, my Lady. I have been to the offices along the Havadran and Gergelt borders, and no record is found of Deenofts entering Eskalind this year."

"And I have checked the copied documents kept here in King's Halls—especially the Mavoldian border ones, in the hope he might have boarded a ship in Mavold—with the same results. You visited Saralya?"

"Yes. She and her family are well, but no word from Deenofts."

She closed her eyes. "It has been over half a year since you had the note that he was returning to Eskalind."

"Nearly eight months to be exact, my Lady."

"Perhaps he is lost to us."

It was not a possibility he wanted to acknowledge, but after these many months, it seemed the most likely. His scouring of the travel records yielded nothing about his son either. He felt as though someone had tied a stone to his heart. Then his Lady was speaking again.

"We will never find a Havadran as trustworthy as Deenofts. Unless Scholar Kermon's Merchant Master Gift discovers another. But I was very fond of our lost Havadran. Very fond. He was unique." She sighed, the sound of one reluctantly turning her attention to other thoughts. "My son has asked something of me that I am most hesitant to oblige." She held a hand over her graying brows. "Ambassador Moril and his family are still in our Embassy in Capitola, having weathered three, or is it four, changes of kingship in Havadra?"

"Four, my Lady."

"Yes. Astofts, Sirish, and the two Santris brothers." She massaged her forehead, the permanent dark ink stain on her index finger a sharp contrast to her pale skin. "Dalich drew the tiles. Moril's name and Eskalind came together. Havadra and the blank tile came next."

"No designated Ambassador for Havadra?"

"None. Dalich wants Moril and his family and staff retrieved and brought back to Eskalind. My son says The Powers have spoken his mind: that given the constant unrest, we cannot leave our people there." She lowered her hand. "Dalich wants you to retrieve them."

"Me, my Lady?"

"Dalich wants you to guide a rank of Soldiers to rescue our people. But I believe King's Second has other reasons to send you on the mission." A look of disapproval toughened her features. "Perhaps he senses I do not want you to go."

"But if the King commands it—"

"He does."

"Ah." He ran his hands along the sable-colored linen of his trousers, stopping at the kneecaps, and leaned forward slightly, eyes on his lap. An idea bloomed. "My Lady, there may be an advantage in my going." He glanced at her. "Deenofts has a sister living in Capitola. If I can make contact with her, I may learn something of his whereabouts."

Dalock's Queen watched him, the sudden keen gaze one he had not suffered in a long while. "While I will welcome any word about our Havadran, it must be a secondary mission. Securing our Ambassador and staff must come first."

"My Lady, I would see first to Dalich King's wishes, then pursue our Scholar's whereabouts." He dipped his head, eyes still upon her.

"Yes. That would be good." His Lady's lower lip dropped slightly. "Oh Favik, do be careful." She touched his cheek, and he closed his eyes, silently hoping to The Powers to not fail in either mission.

Eyes closed, Anish lay on his back against the hard earth of the cave floor. Over the many months of his tentative sojourn amongst the Shinglo, the long sleeves of his tunic had worn through. His elbow met the ground. Nearby, a dozen dark-haired Shinglo youth lay in similar postures, their bodies clothed in the austere, snugly wrapped robes of their people, held in place by cinched cords. All thirteen of the youngsters rested their bare hands and wrists palms upward on small pillows. Amongst them walked a man intoning in a soothing voice, "Air moves on your skin, on your wrists. Air carries sound. Listen." The soft slow swoosh of his steps as he moved crescendoed as he paced close to the Havadran. "Long ago Shinglo ruled this land. Snub noses stole our lands." He stood over the blond youngster. "Air keeps us strong. Breathe slowly. Listen for The Powers." His voice faded slightly as he turned away to address his people. "Shinglo will regain our land one day. Listen for The Powers."

Anish did not hear The Powers. He heard the Shinglo youths' long inhales as though a giant beast lay awake and aware, ready to pounce upon him. Every time they repeated this ritual, he imagined that the moment he closed his eyes, the Shinglo turned, en masse, into some fantastic creature that regarded him as a tasty morsel. Fear tightened his vocal cords. He heard, very, very softly, a metallic clang. Something squeaked. He thought the sound emanated from his own throat, as all his nerves were tense and on alert. Then a noise like a pebble dropping. Anish risked opening his eyes. Nothing had changed in the main room, and the man's back was to him. The youth looked toward the earth-carved room's walls. There, against the wall he lay closest to, the air grate was dislodged. Two small upside-down feet poked out.

He blinked. The scene did not change. Rising to his feet, he dashed to the grate and grabbed the ankles of a child, drawing it forth. Behind him the Shinglo youths opened their eyes. Some sat up, watching. Their adult leader hurried toward Anish just as he placed the child upright on its feet, facing the rest. A girl rose and came forward, and the child held its arms out to her. "Ball went down," it said to her.

"Is your brother all right?" the man asked the girl.

She smoothed her hands through the lad's mass of thick curls and brushed dust from his cheeks and chest. "I think so."

"Get it back!" clamored the little boy. He pointed to the grate.

Anish turned to gaze down the air shaft. He reached a hand through the small opening and felt for the ball. Nothing but empty space met his hand. Another adult came and ushered the youths and child away whilst Anish fumbled in the dark, cool air for the toy.

"Get up," a male voice said behind him. He retracted his arm and rose to his feet, eyes to his shoes. As he expected, a cloth was thrust over his vision.

They led him down corridors and eventually allowed him to sink to the floor. Someone removed the head covering and brought him a ladle of water. It tasted cool and mineral. The cloth went over his head again. He slept, and when he awoke, it was to a quiet stillness as though he was still asleep in a pleasant dream. Or dead.

Someone approached and raised him to his feet, then led him through more twists and turns. "Sit," a male voice uttered. He lowered his bottom to the hard dirt. Someone came behind him and undid his blindfold. A woman was seated on the ground before him, her hair covered in light dust, her face lined heavily, as though a black crayon had traced the creases. Candles glowed steadily at her side.

He studied her features, realizing it was not dust in her hair, but light-colored strands, perhaps gray, maybe white. In the still, golden glow of the candles, her hair could be mistaken for blond. Her lips were thick, the dark eyes tapering toward the temples. They appraised him with a formidable look, even worthy of his grandfather.

"What do you want most?" It was a question, but it carried an air of command and kindled his heart.

"What I have lost, my family."

"You are young, you may make a family of your own someday." Her words stung, though he saw her truth. If he lived long enough.

He swallowed. "I want to continue my journey to Eskalind and to live there."

"If I allow you to go, you must tell no one of us."

"I knew of the Shinglo before I came here and told no one. I can keep silent again."

She nodded. "What else do you want?" It seemed he had earned much dispensation.

"My possessions, the dromas, the satchel bag I came with, everything in it."

"The things have always been yours. We held them while we evaluated you. The dromas are free animals, we do not keep them. Neither shall you. And?" She seemed to expect him to ask for more, though her voice carried a hint of impatience.

"I don't know if you can answer this, but I have wondered how my friend's parents came to meet, a Shinglo woman and a snub nose man. My friend laughed when I asked him."

"There are different Shinglo. My Shinglo kill snub noses we encounter." Her eyes wandered about his form as if to reassure herself he did not belong in that category. "It is known to me that another Shinglo had a woman volunteer to be the Harbinger, but as she stood alone on a dune overlooking a caravan of snub noses, one short nose came to her unarmed. She stayed her warriors and let him approach. He told her he had dreamed of her his entire life. After they spoke, she left her people and went with this man willingly." The crease at the corner of her mouth deepened. "Later she returned and called women to follow her, those that would come. They were fools to go with her, but it was their choice. Were I their leader, I would have learned all I could from her, then ground her into the sand."

Anish said nothing, though he wondered what Sastofts's mother might have revealed about her people to her husband, or how he might have retaliated were she harmed when she returned to them. Then he realized he was assuming the husband cared for the wife. He felt a sudden, immense sadness.

"A man will bring you somewhere near the Eskalind borderwall." She raised her hand and flipped her fingers in the air, a supremely dismissive gesture. Someone approached from behind Anish and draped a blindfold over his eyes again. The cloth was stiff, as though it had been dried quickly in hot sun and not beaten soft. He was pulled to his feet.

So began days of covered eyes and ceaseless walking, punctuated with the occasional rest or sharp command—"Steps leading down" and "Stop" and "Hug the wall or fall for a long time"—all given by the same voice. The Shinglo world was a deep warren of dirt-pocked tunnels and narrow tubes, passageways from one sect to another. "Sit and wait," his guide would say, then distant murmurings of conversation would waft to his ears, bouncing against the rock walls. Once the talk became heated. Pounding footfalls and a growing warmth approached him. Someone snatched the cloth off his eyes, pulling it roughly over his forehead through his hair. The world erupted in a blaze of torchlight. A man with a sweaty face and the narrowest sloped eyes Anish had ever seen regarded the youth's face with death in his eyes. He seemed a mythical beast conjured from darkest nightmares. Anish tried not to shudder.

The fiendish man grunted. "Not a snub nose. Go on." He tossed the blindfold to the earth. Another man came forward. Anish recognized him as the very first Shinglo he had met, out on the dunes just after Deenofts was slain. "It is temporary" he said as he replaced the youngster's blindfold. They then passed through what felt like large rooms, and he heard the breathing of many quiet people and a distant hum of activity. Then the sounds dissipated and all he could hear were the steps of his guide.

Anish stretched his arms long by his sides and felt rock walls again. They walked for a time. The walls tapered closer to his body, and he had to adjust his satchel.

"Untie the blindfold," he heard. Anish fumbled with the knot. "You won't need it for this part of the journey." He heard a sizzle.

Uncovering his eyes, he squinted in the harsh brightness. Twin torches were lit. "Where are we going?"

"To the Eskalind wall." The man handed him a lit torch. "It's not far. Leave the cloth here."

They passed through long, narrow tubes cut from beige rock, the pattern of chisels and hammers writ upon the stones. Their footfalls echoed dully against the powdery dirt at their feet; his soles felt worn in their shoes. Just as the youth opened his mouth to beg for a break, he saw darkness ahead that did not yield to the torchlight. Then the tunnel opened wide on both sides and the path ended, at an odd blackness that reflected the two figures and their torches in a fractured patchwork.

"What is it?" Anish asked. In the reflection, he saw his Shinglo guide bend to retrieve a stout stick from behind a rock. He hefted it to rest upon his shoulder. Anish backed away, but the man laughed.

"Watch." He came forward, the stick in hand. It was an old torch. The Shinglo thrust the stick at the black. It made a horrible crunching noise. The end of the wood crumbled into toothy jags of splinters, but the glossy blackness was unaltered. "The Powers made this wall. It rises above our heads to Their border fence. Not even Shinglo can dent it or tunnel through." He waved his torch toward the ground, and far from their feet Anish saw irregular black holes in the dirt, against the wall. "Attempts to dig deeper, see?" The Shinglo traced the stick along the wall. It made an odd, hollow sound.

"Most Shinglo believe The Powers protect us. I believe they did protect us, but long ago. Then something changed. Maybe we did something to anger them. I don't know. But the snub noses came from the north, they came from the east, from the unknown lands, and they conquered our cities, when we lived above." He tossed the stick aside. "It was long, long ago. Most Shinglo do not realize that The Powers transferred their protection to Eskalinders. But some whisper it. Once I saw this wall, I knew the whispers to be true." The Shinglo reached to touch the glossy blackness, a loving expression on his face, as though he hoped it might yield. His fingers met the stern black sheen. "It is smooth or sharp, and impenetrable." His dark brown eyes swung to Anish. "Let us go back."

The pair turned their backs to the wall and marched away with their torches, leaving the barrier in the lightless underground dark. When they reached the abandoned blindfold, the guide glanced at the youth, and Anish knew he must cover his eyes again. He handed his torch to the man, who rubbed it dark in the dirt. After tying the blindfold tight, the man grasped Anish's sleeve and led him forward, then up many stairs. They came to a landing and sat to rest. Anish removed his satchel. As he had done many times before on this traverse, he felt about himself to ascertain the size of the area, then removed the rolled parchments of his drawings, sat them aside, and fluffed his unworn fine tunic, the one with the gold-embroidered cuffs, finally placing it back in the bag to make a comfortable pillow. He patted the soft leather bag that contained Deenofts's pendant and gold coins. It still surprised him that the Shinglo allowed him to keep his finery, but they seemed to have no use for such things. Never knowing how long these pauses would last, he fell fast asleep.

After resting, the pair continued upward. It felt brighter and warmer as they rose. Murmuring voices, a dusty scent in the air, then they stepped into heat. Anish's feet sank into soft sand, which felt oddly unstable after months of walking the foot-battered floors of the Shinglo caves.

His guide came behind him and untied the blindfold, and Anish kept his eyes closed against the blinding sun for a moment. He raised a hand to shield his vision just as the man spoke. "From the top of that rise"—the Shinglo pointed away from the sun—"you will see the Eskalind borderwall and Guards." He reached into his own satchel and retrieved Anish's scabbarded long knife and the small dagger with the pearl handle. "Your weapons." The Havadran youth stowed them away as the man turned to leave.

"Wait," called Anish. The man halted and turned to face him, his head marked by a halo of light as the sun silhouetted the soft fuzz of his pulled-back hair.

"No one ever told me their name."

The man smiled. "To know one's name is to know one's nature. Goodbye, Not-a-Snub-Nose."

"Goodbye, Shinglo."

From the approach to the harbor, the beige walls of Capitola glimmered in the risen sun. Favik leaned against the ship's railing, the ship's Mavoldian captain, Madain, by his side. The man said, "The Santris color is purple, but a red flag flies from the king's fortress."

"Another change of kingship, then." Favik ground out his next utterance. "King Sirish's color was red, was it not?"

"True, but all reports say he was killed months ago." The Mavoldian shook his head. "The Powers be thanked we are not Havadran. There are more factions in Havadra than there are colors."

"It may be one of his men seizing power."

Madain glanced down his lengthy nose and raised his thin eyebrows. "My people abhor speculation."

"Speculation may soon be replaced by knowledge, Captain." The former Ambassador nodded to the approaching small boat, filled with black-clad Eskalinder Soldiers under his charge for this mission. The boat's oars churned the blue waters as the dark-hulled craft pushed toward the larger ship. Within minutes, First Sergeant Avnil of the Eighth Company and his recognizance team clambered up the rope nets to the ship's deck.

Avnil made his report, his cheeks reddened by the sun. "Ambassador

Favik, the streets are quiet, but cluttered with debris and bodies. We found only a couple men who would speak with us. The story given is that the Santris king has just been overthrown; the tale varies as to who is the new ruler."

"More reason to get our citizens out of here. Can we extract all our people from the Embassy?"

"If the entirety of our rank goes, yes. We saw no large armed groups. Packs of three or four at most. Still, I advise everyone carry their weapons unsheathed."

"Then let us review our final orders." Favik led the First Sergeant to an unoccupied corner of the deck and retrieved from his satchel Dalich King's envelope with their final orders. Breaking the dark seals, he read silently.

Tenth Day, Second Month, 2915
Ambassador Favik,
Upon arrival in Capitola, learn what you can about the
political situation in Havadra.
Offer passage to Eskalind to all members of my Embassy staff,
including Havadrans and their families. Abandon the Embassy.
The Havadrans will supply us a new one when they sort out
their government. It is The Powers' wish that Eskalind not come
to their aid until they do.
Dalich, 125th King of Eskalind

"What does it say?"

"That someday Havadra will buy us a new Embassy." Favik grinned wryly. He handed the note to Avnil. "We abandon the Embassy, bring everyone home who wants to come, staff included."

"Everyone? That could be a lot of people, sir."

"Indeed. Our ship's captain has said he has room for twenty passengers beyond us and our Soldiers." Favik glanced about the beige skyline of Capitola. He could not locate Melande's father's fortress, once prominent above the others. "Let us find out how many there are, first." The former Ambassador lifted his satchel from the deck and placed it over his back. After arranging the signals with the ship's captain, the ship approached the pier, arriving to a handful of clamoring people on the dock begging for passage. One Havadran man's voice rose above the others in anxious pleading, but Captain Madain would hear none of it.

"I await Eskalinders only," announced the Mavoldian in clipped tones. "From the open harbor." Madain then gave orders for the boat to remove from the dock. With First Sergeant Avnil and Favik leading the full rank of a dozen Eskalinder Soldiers, the group was fourteen strong, with fourteen blades drawn. They marched the long dock to the first market square.

Smoldering ash lay in the middle of the paved open area, centered as though placed through precise measurements in the exact center of the square. Following the former Ambassador's direction, the group turned and wound past a blue-tiled fountain and through passageways marred with burn marks, encountering the body of a man, face to the dirt and a spear staked through his back. Despite hearing the patter of feet and a horse whinny, they saw no living thing on the tense journey.

Arriving at their destination, Favik hammered on the stout wooden gate shielding the entrance. It bore a deep gouge as though a giant had tested it for carving.

"Ambassador Moril. Favik and Eskalind are here." His Soldiers formed a protective half ring around him, weapons pointing toward the street. The passageway was anxiously still, as though the air lay a wager with itself that it could hold quiet indefinitely.

Then a distant scraping sound, muffled, echoed from the other side of the enclosure. "Is that truly you, Favik?" came a clear voice, breathless with relief, from above. Bafnil's thin face poked over the wall.

"Indeed. Let us in, then we can let you out."

The young Eskalinder grinned, but the expression hinted that it had been a long time since he had done so. He disappeared from view.

A few moments later, a hand-sized piece of the gate opened at eye level. A pair of darting brown eyes appeared briefly, scanning the scene outside the Embassy. Then a man-sized door, cleverly concealed by the design on the outer gate, opened. Bafnil beckoned them through.

Entering, Favik sheathed his long knife and stepped into the courtyard to face half a dozen lean, muscular Soldiers outfitted in Dalich King's sable uniforms, swords drawn. He raised his empty hands, but the Eskalind Soldier following him kept his blade at the ready. The Embassy's Soldiers pivoted toward the entering Soldier as though he were prey.

"We are all Eskalinders," Favik intoned. "Here to bring you home."

"Always best to be cautious in Havadra," came a familiar voice. He turned to see Moril approaching, his brown hair muted with gray. It had been less than two years since they had last met, but from Moril's appearance, it could have been a dozen. His forehead bore worry creases never present before.

"Let them all in," the Ambassador ordered his Guards. He raised his arms in greeting to Favik, and the pair embraced. When they released each other, Moril asked, "Has Dalich King drawn the tiles?" The question sounded like a statement at first, with a sprinkle of levity at the end as though he remembered this was a question and could be a jest. Yet Moril's brown eyes remained serious and remote. "I have not had word from Eskalind since Sirish was king."

At the mention of his beloved's murderer, Favik turned away, to see his last Soldier entering the fortress. Bafnil shut the door and threw the steel bolts, and the Embassy's Soldiers hefted a huge timber across the entrance. Some of Moril's Soldiers recognized some of Favik's, and fond reunions rang through the courtyard as they exchanged greetings and tales.

Favik began, "Our Lord has drawn the tiles. Yours with Eskalind, Havadra with no one."

"What? There was a blank tile in the Ambassadors' names basket?

It's unheard of."

"And yet true." Favik handed the Eskalind Ambassador to Havadra the note from their Lord.

"Abandon the Embassy?" The elder Ambassador sounded incredulous as he scanned the quilling.

"Dalich King believes the situation warrants it."

"The Powers must agree. Well, there have been two attacks upon us in the past week. And I lost two people in the streets when the second Santris king overthrew the first. To my everlasting regret, I unknowingly chose the day of a coup to broach a diplomatic visit." The Ambassador's eyes hardened. "We are just past our last rations, and two days ago a flaming spear sailed over the wall and set the stable alight. Made it seem fortunate that none of the animals were left." He threaded his fingers before him and rose on his toes like a Records Keeper making a pronouncement. "I thank The Powers for Their direction. For the sake of the Eskalinders under my protection, abandoning the Embassy seems our only course of action." Moril lowered himself, his brown eyes to the ground, perhaps considering this a defeat to his life's work.

Giving the man a private moment, Favik glanced about, noting a wheelbarrow with a small mound of dirt in its bed and a long, level, excavated area along one of the fortress's walls. Though curious about it, he instead asked, "How many people are here?"

The Ambassador returned his attention to the present. "Six Soldiers, four Eskalinder staff, including Bafnil and myself, and also my wife and my son. So, twelve."

"That's all?"

Moril's lips puckered slightly. "Our Havadran personnel disappeared at the same time as our ample rations. They had made tunnels. We dug up half the courtyard to plug them, as you can see."

"I'm glad we're escorting you home." He placed a hand on his compatriot's shoulder. "We brought food, and can carry documents or belongings that will fit in our satchels. Is everyone well enough to walk?"

"Walk? Aye. Oh Favik, thank The Powers you came. I'll gather my family and staff."

Whilst Moril attended to his charges, the former Ambassador saw that First Sergeant Avnil's group removed the red and white flags of Heedlich First King from the rooftop flagpole, leaving only the violet and black pennants of Dalich King. This signaled their ship in the harbor that they had arrived safely. As though The Powers smiled on their venture, a slight breeze rose and rippled the cloth. The Lord of Eskalind's banner flew straight and proud.

One Soldier stayed as lookout, the white and red pennants of the First King resting by her feet, ready to be flown again to indicate their departure and signal for the ship to return to the harbor. With her dark hair and uniform, she appeared almost a shadow against the bright sun, standing watch over bustling activities inside and the quiet streets outside.

Entering the foyer, Favik found a dusty scent lingering in the air. Soldiers rushing in all directions crossed paths in what appeared a choreographed chaos. Bafnil approached with an armful of parchments and papyrus. "Records from the last two years, Ambassador Favik. Everything else will have a copy in Eskalind."

"Good. See which of my people can stow them. And ask them for food, we brought enough to share."

"Aye, Ambassador." Bafnil grinned, a spark of joy animating his eyes. "Ambassador Moril requests you come to his office."

Favik grinned in return. "I know the way." He found Moril at his desk, a stack of documents burning on a large brazier in the middle of the room and the Eskalinder determinedly prying a nail from an object resting on his desk.

"Finally!" He sounded victorious. "I would not leave this behind." Noticing his colleague, he beckoned him close and tossed aside an empty wooden frame not much bigger than a book. A square sheet of canvas lay facing the desk. Moril turned it over, and a painting of his wife gazed at the two men. "Kostaza's perfect likeness. I had the best female portraitist in Capitola paint this."

Favik bent closer to examine the work. The outline of a gold square rested in one corner, a tiny letter *S* in its center. It recalled to mind the pendant Deenofts wore. "Who painted it?"

"I know not her name, just her mark and reputation. Kostaza might know, they got along like long-separated sisters. She was quite sad when their sessions were over."

Someone entered the room, and both men raised their gaze to see Moril's blond wife, whose expression mirrored the mood he just described. Clad in black, in her pale hands she bore a wooden coffer painted with purples and blue zigzag designs: the mark of Kaymif royalty. She clutched the casket like it was a babe almost too weighty to lift. Favik bowed slightly to her.

"Kostaza, not that. It's too heavy to carry to the harbor." Moril rolled the painting upon itself.

"It was my mother's." His wife's cheeks went red. "I never thought I would want it, for that very reason."

Moril left the desk and approached her, his free hand outstretched. "It still contains her jewelry, yes? Bring that as lighter-weight remembrances of her." He touched her arm as she lowered her blue eyes to the box. "I'm sorry it has come to this, 'Staza, but we are going home to safety." Moril reached with one arm across her back to bring her close, while with the other hand he helped bolster her burden. "It's very heavy. Let me hold it."

"No, I will."

Favik shifted on his feet. His movement had the desired effect, for the couple raised their eyes to his. "My apologies for interrupting, but time is short."

Moril released his wife. "Yes it is. We should not tarry a moment."

Kostaza turned to leave, but Favik stayed her with a serious gaze as he said, "Your husband showed me the lovely portrait of you; might you recall the name of the woman who painted it?"

"Oh yes." Her fair forehead creased for a moment. "Samathe was her name. I adored her. The only Havadran woman I could truly talk with." She lowered her mother's coffer to the desk with a thud, as though frustrated with her losses. "Moril, have you a small bag or cloth for the jewelry?"

Favik bowed and made his leave.

———

The flags of Heedlich First King fluttered again from the Embassy's flagpole; the sun had risen to its highest point. The air felt hotter than one would expect at the end of the third month of the year, but Capitola was the desert city by the sea, and the current temperature aimed to live up to that description.

The Eskalinders were assembled under the sun's unblinking gaze in the courtyard: three abreast, Soldiers at the perimeters and civilians in the middle. Moril and Favik reviewed the group. The last Soldier hurried to her position, after raising the pennant that signaled their departure.   Absent only was Bafnil, who stood atop a ladder watching the street outside.

Two brown-haired women Favik had not seen before were amongst the gathering, one hefting Moril's son Elai over her wide hips. The satchel across her back drooped, misshapen around its bulky contents, though given her broad shoulders and worn but determined countenance, he did not doubt she could bear both it and the child. The boy was less than six months shy of his third Naming Day, with pudgy cheeks that marked him as the only member of the Embassy's population who appeared well nourished. His mother, standing behind him, leaned toward her son to place a toy in his hand and stroke his arm. Like everyone else, she bore a satchel upon her back.

No one spoke a word; it was as though the only language that existed was made of gazes and hand signals. Bafnil climbed down the ladder, gesturing that he saw no threats. It was safe to depart.

First Sergeant Avnil raised a silent hand for the Soldiers to draw arms. The women donned beige veils. Kostaza helped her son's nurse adjust hers as the boy playfully tugged at the colorless fabric. Two Soldiers, their mouths set in a grim line, strode forth and removed the timber blocking the doors. Bafnil pulled one side of the gate inward. It scraped the hard dirt, not quite opening fully. Still, the group began their progress. With a curt motion, the Ambassador gestured to the former Page to merge with the rest. Bafnil drew blade and did so.

The last of the Soldiers passed through the opening, eyes darting back and forth as they entered the Havadran side of their gate, followed by Favik and, lastly, Ambassador Moril. Two Soldiers lingered to shut the gate, but Moril waved them away. "It's our charge," he murmured, nodding to Favik. The pair tugged the gate closed whilst the Soldiers stood guard, long knives gleaming as though proud to be unsheathed and of use. Then the four walked at a brisk pace to catch up with their group. The passageways were narrow and sunbaked in this area, but soon they came to a wider, cooler patch. The diplomats made to move to the front of the line, but Kostaza stayed her husband and the two walked together.

The streets narrowed again. Heat pressed upon them like a smothering, living thing, rebounding against the colorless walls.

The child whimpered in his nurse's arms. "Mama?"

Kostaza reached for her son. "Here, Elai, let Mama carry you a while." The boy nestled against her shoulder, one hand clutching at her veil.

"Halt!" barked First Sergeant Avnil in an aggressive grunt.

In the middle of the passage stood a Havadran man with a short sword, broader near the hilt, tapered at the end. Two more men stood behind him, similarly armed. The leader's brown eyes glanced amongst the group, accounting all the weaponry, till they alighted with a lecherous glare upon the womenfolk, just as Kostaza's son yanked off her veil. She inhaled, a wisp of a sound, and gripped her child tightly, fumbling with the fabric to cover her fair face.

Moril stepped forward, Avnil advancing with him. "Leave us or die," the Ambassador growled.

The Havadran's lower lip protruded, perhaps in disdain, perhaps in agreement, but he waved his men off and walked backward, nearly tripping on the body Favik's group had passed that morning. The trio disappeared around a corner.

Avnil signaled two Soldiers to pursue, and they also disappeared behind the wall, returning a few moments later to report all was clear.

The Eskalinders continued on, eyes and ears alert for further danger. Kostaza had restored her veil and covered her son's face with her hand to spare him the sight of the speared man dead in the dust. They passed the blue-tiled fountain, the only spot of color in this beige city. A dirty-faced boy drinking from it spied them and dashed away.

When they reached the dock, cooler air wafted toward them from the sparkling sapphire water. The group of clamorers from earlier, their numbers swelled with more people, sat or stood in varying postures of defeat or weariness. Save for one short man, who had cupped his hands around his mouth and was calling to the approaching Mavoldian ship.

The dark-hulled vessel approached from the open harbor, crew readying the anchoring lines to be cast. Avnil shouted for half the rank to secure the ship's landing area. Six Eskalinder Soldiers, blades still drawn, motioned the Havadran aside.

The ship docked, and the rest of the Embassy party stepped onto the platform, their anxious footfalls thundering on the wooden dock. Mavoldian sailors, surrounded by Eskalind's Soldiers, secured the lines. From the deck, the captain's eyes roamed mechanically from one Eskalinder to another. One could almost hear his tally. The armed Eskalinders ushered the three women on board, little Elai still snuggled against his mother. Captain Madain introduced himself with curt aplomb to the women. Kostaza doffed her veil and looked over her shoulder at her husband, who gestured for her to continue.

Once the diplomats were aboard, Favik touched Moril's arm to stay him. "I must tell you, now that we are all safe on board, I have another mission here in Capitola, by our Lady King's Mother's bidding."

"You are going back out there?" Behind the Ambassador, the last

Eskalind Soldier boarded the ship and sheathed his long knife.

"Stay the gangway!" Favik shouted to Madain. Below, the Havadrans on the dock cried and clamored. The former Ambassador lowered his gaze and spoke softly. "It would please Lady Marna greatly to have any word of a missing dye merchant who supplied her Scriptorium. If I were to find him, it would please her even more to bring him with us. But he may have family that he would want to include on the voyage."

Moril waved Madain to their quiet conference. "Captain, how many more passengers can you carry?"

"Besides my crew, you and your men were fourteen. You brought twelve, but one was a small child. I calculate the ship can hold eight, maybe nine more passengers. Eight adults more to be safe; count two children as equal to an adult in weight, three if they are very young."

"Favik must return to the city—"

Madain interrupted, "The tides will be against us if we do not leave in three hours. We can sail a short distance into the harbor and wait as before, but you must be back before the tide turns."

"I understand."

"Favik, do you know where to find this man?"

"I thought to ask at the fortress of the Dye and Cloth Merchants Guild."

Moril smiled, the expression of a man with a far better idea. He turned to the deck railing and called to the Havadrans assembled below. "Dye Merchant!" he hailed. One man raised his head to the Eskalinder, who called again, "Are any of you dye merchants?"

The first man and two others raised their hands. "No you aren't," spat one of the latter at the other. The accused pulled a long knife at the face of his accuser. The first man stepped away from the arguing pair, waving his hands as he trotted to a box. Unlocking the container, he held aloft vials of various colored liquids. "Dyes!" he called, as breezily as though selling them at market.

"Let us speak with that man," Moril said. "Avnil, call your Soldiers to send the other two away. Favik and I will speak with that dye merchant."

Moments later, a light rank of Eskalinders disembarked and herded away the pair of supposed dye sellers. Then they surrounded the round-faced man holding the vials, who identified himself as Safish. The Ambassadors came for a word.

Favik asked, "Do you know a fellow merchant named Deenofts?"

Safish wiped sweat from his wide brow. "I do. Short chin, prominent eyebrows. A most flamboyant individual." He seemed about to say more but stayed himself.

Favik looked to Moril with a nod to convey his belief in the Havadran. "Where can I find him?"

"Will you grant me passage on this ship?"

"Perhaps. I require more information first."

Safish's small brown eyes narrowed. "I have not seen him in many months, but I know where he lives. He stored dyes for me. I have been there. It is here in Capitola. Eastern side of the city." He leaned close. "If I bring you to his fortress, grant me passage on this ship. That is my price for showing you the way."

The Eskalinders regarded one another, Favik's eyes keen on Moril. He said in a clear voice, "If I do not return with Safish, I will give him a token that will signal you what to do next."

"I understand." Moril spoke as firmly as if issuing orders to a rank of Soldiers. "Merchant Safish, we will grant passage for you and your goods, but only upon your return with my man or the correct token. We will hold your goods on our ship to protect them whilst you make this journey." He watched the Havadran closely.

Safish's brown eyes squinted slightly. "Agreed."

Whilst Safish gathered his belongings for transport to the ship, Favik quickly boarded and changed his clothing, leaving the purple and black of Dalich King behind. Emerging dressed in a beige Havadran robe, the former Ambassador whispered to the present Ambassador, "A black ribbon means depart without me, purple to wait as long as you are able."

"Bring some men with you," Moril breathed, eyes on the merchant.

"Much as I would like the company, our King has not authorized it. If any were injured—"

"Or killed. Yes, I know, I know. By The Powers do I know." Moril faced his colleague. "I hope this is worth it."

"As do I," Favik said, turning and murmuring to himself, "More than you can imagine." For if he found Deenofts, he might find his son as well.

———

At a quick pace, the unlikely pair threaded wordlessly through the empty streets of Capitola. Safish pointed the direction; Favik followed. This eastern side of the city was a gentler place than the passages from the harbor to the Eskalind Embassy. Here, the streets were free of bodies and debris, indicating perhaps that the most recent coup had not touched the area. Quiet reigned, as though the inhabitants held their breath in silent anticipation. Favik pondered how best to gain entrance once they arrived. If Deenofts was there, it would be easy. If he was not, then Favik must gamble that Samathe was indeed the sister's name. A Havadran woman would not meet with an unknown man, unless he claimed kinship and knew what she was called.

Rounding a corner, Favik's guide gestured to a fortress door. "This." Nothing remarkable about the structure evidenced itself. The wooden door exhibited a design of a large square, which could be a reference to Samathe's maker's mark—or be simply another example of the Havadran love of equilateral shapes of four right angles. The Scholar nodded, sheathed his long knife, then hammered on the door.

The usual long quiet after a knock. Eventually, a voice came from above their heads. "What do you want?" They craned their necks to see a thick-jawed man leaning slightly over the top of the wall.

Safish displayed his hands, empty palms skyward. "We seek Deenofts. I am a guild brother of his."

"I recognize you. Who is the other one?"

Favik stepped back to allow the man to see him better and spoke imperiously. "I am cousin to Deenofts. I would name another of this household, but will not shout that name from the street." Safish turned to him with a quick snap of his head, while the man at the wall called into the fortress, "Bring the whore to the door."

The pair waited. Safish leaned close to his side. "I bought you to Deenofts's fortress. Give me the token."

The Scholar cautioned, "Deenofts may come with us. Wait." Both let their eyes roam the empty passageway while they listened for passersby.

Several minutes later, a small piece of the fortress's door opened at about neck height, blank cloth appearing on the other side. A veiled woman. "Whisper to me this name," she said. Given the authority in her voice, he wondered if it was Deenofts's sister behind the veil.

He walked toward the opening, his eyes intent, hoping he was making eye contact and looked truthful. She backed away slightly, as though fearful he might hurl a sharp weapon at her face. Shielding his mouth from Safish's view, he muttered, "Samathe."

"One moment." The door shut.

———

The list of accounts before her bore a sad tale. Each column testified to substantial diminishment as the months progressed. "Less work, less coin. Only four servants left. No brothers, no family." Samathe looked away.

"Fine Lady," came the whore's voice.

Rolling the papyrus quickly, Deenofts's sister replied, "Enter." She stowed her accounts in a lower drawer as the veiled woman came into the studio.

Her servant pulled aside her veil. "There are two men at the outside door. One has visited before, a member of the dye merchants' guild."

The painter rose. "Has he word of my brother?"

"No, Fine Lady, he wants to meet with your brother."

"Ah."

After a slight pause, the servant continued. "The other is your cousin. He knows your name."

The portraitist raised her eyes abruptly. "Is he brown or fair-skinned?"

Her servant's head tilted ever so slightly. "Fair but sunbrowned, with blond hair. A nose like the young cousin who stayed here, at least from the brief moments I saw him." She folded her hands before her beige robes.

Samathe studied her. "I want to view him. Send them both to the reception room, give them cool wine. Are there still some sweet nuts from the rear courtyard tree?"

"Cook roasted some this morning, Fine Lady."

"Good. Serve them to our guests; I'll linger behind the screen wall and ring for you."

The whore nodded and left, replacing her head covering. Samathe's hands shook, but she brushed her own veil past the curls framing her face and hurried from her studio.

From the dark passage behind the wooden viewing screen, she spied a short Havadran man entering the room, led by the whore. Behind the pair trailed a man so alike in face to young Anish that she gulped, her hands flying to her mouth as if they could somehow stuff the sound back inside. "I know who *you* are," she breathed. "Thank The Powers King Sirish is dead." Samathe placed a steadying hand on her chest, then rang the bell signal for the whore to meet her again in the painting studio.

There, Samathe gave her commands. "I will meet with my cousin privately. First, bring my thinnest veil. It has been quite a while since I've seen him; I'm not comfortable being barefaced." She chided herself for making excuses to a servant, but the thought spilled from her mouth in her nervousness. Once the colorless veil was in her hands, she stared at its transparency: thin enough to make out the dark paint lodged in the dried cracks of her fingers. The shimmering spun silk had been a present from her mother, years ago, meant to be worn at Samathe's signing of the joining contract, when a Havadran bride meets her husband for the first time. Then her mother died and her father realized that Samathe's portraits brought more coin to the household than the menfolk's wages combined.

A creak at the door alerted her of entry. Deenofts's sister placed veil over head. The whore came forward. "Should I present your cousin Favik?"

"Just let him in. I want you to stand outside the door and sing."

"Sing, Fine Lady?"

"As our musicians are gone, I require you to sing. Anything that comes to mind."

"Oh. Yes, Fine Lady." She departed and allowed the man to enter.

"Samathe," he said, his voice warm as though he had known her since childhood. It made her deeply uncomfortable. The stranger closed the door behind him. Outside, her servant began a tentative warble of a nursery rhyme.

"Favik." It was such an odd name, it almost hurt to say it. He stood by the door. She studied him: the planes of his face, those strange but familiar eyes. She guessed him to be about thirty-five, close in age to her younger brother.

"I am very sorry to intrude." He lowered his voice. "Would you speak with me about Deenofts?" he asked, an air of urgency in his Eskalind-accented voice. She gestured to the small table with chairs for two, where she had often conferred with her beloved sibling. They both sat, though it still seemed wrong to have an unknown man this close, in private quarters.

Samathe pushed her chair farther from the table and avoided looking at him. "Have you word of my brother?"

"Not since the beginning of the sixth month of last year."

"Oh." She paused, sick in her gut, for that was a month before Deenofts departed their fortress. He waited. "What word did you have then?"

"That he was coming to Eskalind with someone dear to me."

"Your son." She did not care that it sounded like an accusation.

He nodded. Her servant sang a new tune, an attempt to mimic a fiddler's melody, using "La la la" as the lyrics.

Stretching her arms forward, the portrait painter placed both hands on the table. "At the start of the seventh month, Deenofts and Anish left here to buy dromas and journey to Eskalind. As it turned out, it was the same day the first Santris brother overthrew King Sirish. I have had no word since." Her voice cracked at the last. "Almost nine months. Alone alone." Her eyes shut, she collapsed into misery.

Something warm touched her arm. The stranger knelt by her side, a gentle hand on her sleeve. Tears wet his eyes. "We have both likely suffered a great loss, but there is still hope. If they escaped in time and made the overland journey—"

"No. Deenofts knew the desert. He would have crossed it by now. I would have had word. Even with all the strife in Capitola, he would have written me several letters. One of them would have made it through. They always did before." Samathe lifted her feet from the floor and curled into her chair, her back to him. "He wanted to bring me to Eskalind. Was always asking me to go with him."

"I can bring you to Eskalind. I have a ship in the harbor as we speak, heading for Mavold, where we will make the overland journey to Eskalind."

She stared at her vacant easels, not a single painting in process. An accusing entourage of loss. Or perhaps they hinted at anticipation, of works to come. "I want to go to Guerland," she said to them.

"Guerland?" the odd-looking man replied. "But Deenofts and Anish would go to Eskalind, if they got through. And if you were in Eskalind already—"

Samathe turned to him, lowering her feet to the floor. "You hold hope still. I do not. I have made a plan. I have—" It wounded her to disclose such personal details, but she let the words tumble forth: "An aunt joined with a Guerlander. I would live with her."

He stood, a hand to his breast. "Much as I might wish to do so, I cannot ask my ship's captain to detour to Guerland." He sounded like a weakling outerland diplomat in a children's story. "But if you come with me to Mavold, we could find a Guerland-bound ship for you—"

The portraitist stood. "I want to leave for Guerland from Capitola, and I want you to escort me." He opened his mouth, but she continued, drawing close to him. "I am a woman alone, with no family here to shield me." She spoke low and cool. "My brother and I sheltered your son in our fortress for two *months*. Two months that Sirish's men were looking for him. My brother saw banners in the markets seeking his return, with a large sum of coin offered. We hid your boy, in our household, even from our servants, for fear they would turn him in. Turn us in. We could have lost everything." She fixed him with a look that commanded silence. "In those two months I grew a great and genuine affection for Anish, but there was always the fear, always the terror under the surface that at any moment armed men would storm the walls and seize us all." She hoped he could feel the terror of those days in her voice. "The least you can do for me now is see me safe to Guerland."

Favik backed away, but his strangely colored eyes remained steady on hers. "I will do this for you, but I must first send word to my ship and write a swift note to my Lady Marna, mother of the King of Eskalind. It was she who tasked me with this mission to seek word of your brother."

The mention that a royal sent him surprised her, and it must have shown on her face, because he continued. "King's Mother much admires your brother and would undoubtedly admire your artistic skills as well in her magnificent Scriptorium, if you were to seek such employment. And there are many rich and noble Ladies in Eskalind who require portraits for display in their family halls. I assure you, many profitable possibilities await you in Eskalind."

"I will consider this." She walked to her desk and opened the top drawer. "You will find papyrus, ink, and wax here for your note. And drying sand."

"My ship is the only vessel in the Capitola harbor at this moment. Another coup has plagued the western parts of the city. It may be many days, or weeks, before we can leave."

Samathe reached for her quill. "I can wait. Besides, I must hang the white sheet over the entrance."

"I don't understand."

"I must sell this fortress first. The white sheet announces that the fortress is for sale; brokers will come and make offers."

"How long might that require?"

"Depends." Deenofts's sister fanned herself with the quilling feather, then walked toward the Eskalinder. "You may want this as well." Placing the quill in his hand, she departed with, "I will have Deenofts's room prepared for you. It is where your son stayed." Samathe opened the door, raised a hand for her servant to stop singing, gave her instructions, and departed for her private chamber to lie abed and grieve.

———

Favik rolled the smooth part of the quill between his fingers, aiming it at the closed door like a dart. Turning abruptly, he went to the desk and slapped a pair of blank papyruses upon it. Two notes he wrote, one to Ambassador Moril and the other to his Lady, telling her what he had learned of Deenofts's departure from Capitola and of his own upcoming journey to Guerland to escort Deenofts's family to safety. The former Ambassador softened the blow of this extension to his absence with a promise to seek out Scholar Kermon whilst in Guerland, though he referred to the man as "Lady Reader's blood cousin" in his message. Sealing the notes shut, he fished in a deep pocket for the sable-colored ribbon, the token for Safish the dye merchant to bring to Moril. The Eskalinders would depart without him.

Soon thereafter he placed the two notes and the ribbon in Safish's eager hands, and the man bolted from the fortress like a penned animal freed of its cage.

Only then, as the go-between woman of the household led him to the room where his son had resided, did Favik realize a serious flaw in his plan. For if he met with Scholar Kermon, a Guerish Merchant Master Gifted with the ability to discern truthfulness in others, then

Kermon would know of Favik's lies, his forgeries, his impersonation of a man who did not exist, all committed in the service of rescuing his son and Melande. His secrets would be laid bare, and his fellow Scholar would undoubtedly report them to Marna King's Mother. He might never be able to return to Eskalind.

It was from the top of the dune that Anish first espied his new land: a hill crested with dark rocks on the western horizon. The sun shone full upon the land below him, merciless as a Shinglo drawing blade across a snub nose's throat. Specks that were likely men moved back and forth atop the hill. Anish paced the downward slope of the sand drift into a boiling heat, the air hot as the worst summer day in Capitola. His hands felt heavy and dull; his pack seemed to gain weight with each step. Hot air stung through the worn elbows of his long shirt. Eskalind seemed farther and farther away, but raising his eyes, he could see a break in the wall above, and he made for it. Beige Havadran sand covered his shoes, and his hands itched. Glancing at his skin, he saw that the lingering rash and scars from Deenofts's potion had reddened and darkened as though the heat was a personal affront to them. His fingers stiffened toward his palms, but he trudged forward.

The dune sloped slightly upward then to a broken, blackish stone wall, a yellowish dirt issuing from the wide opening that the road passed through. Above, he could see Guardsmen in dark uniforms pacing the inside of the wall that barely rose to their knees. One stood in the opening, holding a spear, still as a statue as Anish approached. The Havadran turned around, half expecting to see one last glance of the Shinglo. But seeing no one, Anish faced forward and paced toward his destination, toward freedom and a life of his own making.

"Halt," called the stone-still Guard.

"Is passage not free to all who would enter Eskalind?" Anish called, trying to sound confident.

"Aye, but identify yourself."

"I am Anish of Havadra."

"You don't look like a Havadran."

"It is the land of my birth, though I would rather have been born in your country."

The Guard grinned, lifting a finger from the dark wooden shaft of the spear. "I was born in Kursak."

"I don't know much about Kursak, but if Eskalind will have me, by The Powers, I will serve the Strange King."

"Then come and speak with our Records Keeper." The man held out an open hand in a universal gesture of goodwill. "The first lesson in becoming an Eskalinder: hold your heart hand palm toward the ground when entering the country. It is a sign of respect to The Powers, who guard this land." Anish approached, stiffly uncurling his cramped digits. But when the man saw the angry red rash on the youth's hand, he withdrew. "You need healing."

"Yes," Anish kept his eyes steady on the man. "Will your King grant me relief?"

"That's for The Powers to decide. But you'll have to be quarantined. We can't risk whatever *that* is spreading." Still, he beckoned the blond refugee through the entrance. The air immediately felt cooler, temperate even, as though an invisible barrier had been crossed.

Anish addressed the Guard. "Would it help if you knew the rash is from an irritant I applied so I could pass freely through Havadra?"

The man's eyes narrowed. "Sounds like a Havadran trick."

"It was, but a trick used against Havadrans. My intentions here are honest. Truly. I just want a new home, where I can build my own life." He realized he sounded like a whining child, but he spoke truth.

"Tell the Records Keeper. And the Healer. Over here." He led Anish along a row of buildings pitched low on one side and rising on the opposite, perhaps a former stable. A babe wailed inside. Another Guard trotted over to escort them. The first Guard knocked, and the door swung open to reveal a dim hallway running along the taller side of the building. "In here." The man pointed to another door that Anish could barely discern in the murky light. "Leave your satchel on the table."

He turned to see an empty table by the main door. He did not want to leave the bag, but obeyed. The second Guard opened the inner door and beckoned the youth forward. He saw a darkish room, lined with straw. A milking stool was the solitary piece of furniture, its presence forlorn as though hoping for company. Anish paused on the threshold.

"Laddie," the first Guard said, "you need to go in, and I don't want to touch you."

Anish paced forward as the babe in the stall next door howled again. The door behind him shut with a trembling clank, and the room darkened except for a thin ray of sun that struggled through a split board in the high rafters. "Wait!" He turned around, spinning on the straw. "When will I see the Records Keeper?"

"After the Healer comes for you."

"But when will that be? Hello?" The outer door shut, and he slumped to the straw. "So this is the Strange Kingdom. Another prison." He groaned for his lost life.

Someone stepped along the hall outside Anish's door, someone with quiet footsteps. "Hello?" he called.

"In a moment," came the response, in a woman's voice. Another door opened, and he heard the babe next door squeak, an expectant, almost questioning sound. Quiet whispering followed, and another woman's voice, husky as though she had cried for days: "By The Powers!" Then she began weeping. He shuddered, his thoughts thick with the possible torments befalling them. His hands clawed out before him and he pawed the straw hoping for a hidden weapon, a loose board, a long splinter, something to defend himself with.

A creaking, then more shuffling sounded in the hallway, the second woman sobbing, "All will be well now, little one." More whispering. He feared they were killing the babe.

He could do nothing but rattle his door. "Let me out!"

"Please." The first woman's voice again. "Calm down, you're frightening everyone. I will explain if you let me in peaceably. Or should I call a Guard?"

"I won't hurt you if you don't hurt me." Anish glowered from behind the locked door.

"Good." She unlocked the door, and he slunk far away from the entrance, his back flat against the back wall as though anchored to the construction. The woman entered. "They didn't give you a lamp? Deplorable." He could not make out her features in the darkness. "I'll be right back." She left, not closing the door. Anish eased across the room's perimeter, listening, trying to determine how far she had gone, but he heard nothing. He reached for the door, but before he could slip out, she was in the doorway, striking a match, nearly in his face. "Oh!"

He jumped back, blinded for a moment and shielding his eyes, pointing his elbows in her direction, half expecting to block a blow.

When he could see again, she had lit a lantern and had a beam of light aimed at his face. He still could not discern her features. She exhaled loudly, the same expression his mother made when displeased with him. "I know you're scared, but please understand, the Guards feared you might infect them with whatever contagion afflicts you. We're nearly full here, there's been a sudden influx of people seeking healing." She marched into the room and hung the lamp. "People were transferred here from the other borders, as this one does not usually see much traffic. It's more than ever before, and there was no time to set up decent rooms for our patients." The woman fiddled with the lamp's shades.

"You aren't afraid of me?"

The last shade open, a kind glow showed the room. The woman had brownish hair and a nose like his own and wore a floor-length scarlet apron dress over a long-sleeved white tunic. "No. The Guards are overly cautious, as one would expect, but I'm a Healer, protected by Dalich Strange King." The Eskalinder tapped a white flower stitched over her heart. He wondered what it meant.

"How're you protected?"

The woman tugged the stool near him. A strand of straw stuck to the hem of her bright red garment. "Our King is Gifted by The Powers to heal a person merely by thinking about them and their affliction. He healed that poor babe in the stall next to you. Poor child was struck with an atrophying disease. Now her legs are straightening and she will grow into a healthy girl, thank The Powers."

The Healer gestured for him to sit on the stool. The young Havadran did so, looking up at her. "The King is here?"

"No. We send word to his Halls by Swift Rider, telling of each person's affliction and their name. Once he learns of their condition, he can heal them. Now, let me examine your rash and we shall write the King to heal you."

"I'm not contagious."

She held out a hand. "I told you, that doesn't worry me."

"But it's true. The rash came from a potion I applied."

Her brown eyes scanned his hands and arms. "Remove your robes."

Anish stammered, sliding off his seat, "Isn't there a male Healer? Please, I've never been undressed before a woman besides my mother or her whore."

"My!" She exhaled again. "How did you come by this potion?"

"Deen—, um, someone gave it to me."

"Why?"

"It was to protect me, whilst we were traveling together, if we got separated."

The Healer's expression mirrored that of his strategy tutor when he had concocted a dubious plan. "Is that the whole story?"

"I wasn't finished. My, um, companion thought the potion would scare away anyone who tried to harm me. He was right, but I didn't use it in time. When he came to rescue me, he was killed."

Her expression likely echoed his own at the moment of the tragic event. "That's awful."

"It's all my fault."

The Eskalinder woman regarded him as though considering that it might be. Standing over him, her brown eyes narrowed, which made the freckles on her cheeks more prominent. "When was this?"

"A few months ago? I'm not certain. I've been…in the desert a long time." He sat again, an immense weariness seeping into his muscles. The threading on his trousers was so thin, he felt the wood grain of the stool.

"Well, we haven't been introduced properly. My name is Morya." The Healer waited.

"I'm Anish." He spoke the name with pride.

"How old are you, Anish?"

"Thirteen. Oh, maybe fourteen. Um, what month is it?"

A flash of surprise and perhaps sympathy crossed her features. "It's the twenty-fifth day of the third month, of 2915."

He straightened his neck as though his swordmaster were examining his posture. "I'll be fourteen in the fifth month."

"Let me see your hands, Anish." The Healer's voice was softer when she said his name. Morya reached to him, the gesture reminding him of his mother. Instinctively, he lifted his hands to hers. She grasped his stiff digits, her touch warm, with a gentle pressure. The first human skin he had felt in months. He fought a sob as she bent closer. "Am I hurting you, Anish?"

"No."

"Good. No pain?" He shook his head. "Hmm, this looks more like a burn, like burn scarring, though there is some rash present. But I don't think it's contagious." The woman dropped his hands, and water fell from his eyes. He leaned away, eyes to his feet. "Anish, what's wrong?"

The youth shook his head, finding it hard to breathe. "No one has touched me in a long time." He sank to the straw and wept into his hands. The Healer encircled his shoulders with her arms.

"Shh, you are safe here. It will be all right, Anish. You're safe in Eskalind." Under her breath she swore, "Powers take those cruel Havadrans."

The rumor in Capitola was that the eastern side of the city was the safest, and it had some credence. Opposite the city from the king's palace and its attendant households—large, ambitious, perennially plotting to pounce—the eastern section was seen by many as budding with overlooked potential, a safe harbor to wait out civil unrest. This brought many brokers to Samathe's sheet-draped gate. As the supposed sole male member of the household, Favik represented the family, anticipating the quick conclusion of these irksome dealings with thinly concealed impatience. This was read by the Havadran brokers as a clever tactic, and each one, supposing a more generous bid had bested his own, increased his offer on the desirable property.

Just before Favik formally accepted a final offer, the fortress adjacent also hung a white sheet. Now Capitola's builders saw an opportunity to merge the properties and create one large, double-walled dwelling for a wealthy family. More offers poured in, and the bidding escalated. There was even a skirmish outside the gate when a broker and builder drew long knives upon one another. At the last, the former Ambassador negotiated a price high enough that Samathe could easily spend the rest of her days draped in all the accoutrements of a fine lady with no need to lift a brush again. The proceeds also effortlessly funded their current sea journey to Guerland and would see his return sailing to Mavold in well-appointed comfort. That was, if he could return to Eskalind.

Standing near the ship's prow, Favik gazed at the sunlit Guerish tidelands. The sun itself, in sixth month, was standing nearly overhead. Slightly inland, shimmering mounds of the famed gray Guerish salt twinkled, a sharp contrast to the deep-shaded skin of the workers skimming the edges of a shallow, briny, salt pond with fine nets to retrieve the savory treasure. The Guerlanders' hair hung straight, in long, tightly wrapped ponytails trailing their spines. Clad in the blues and greens favored by Guerlanders, they bent long and lean to their task, ferrying nets full of crystals from atop a series of shallow ponds to piles resting on waxed cloths. Others pushed red wheelbarrows, empty or laden with sparking salt, along eggshell-colored paths that snaked amongst the clay-lined ponds. A picturesque sight of industry and landscape, captured by Samathe's sketching pencil as she stood near the back of the boat, the bottom edge of a drawing sheet resting against her stomach.

"Sir?"

He turned to face Samathe's maidservant, whom he now knew to be named Malthe. Unlike her mistress, at this moment she was not wearing her veil, but rather holding it. The Havadran woman's pale forehead and small nose evidenced a bit of reddening from the sun. "Admiring the view, Malthe?"

The blond woman glanced back to her lady, then to him. She tucked her veil into her beige robes. "I wanted to thank you for bringing us to Guerland."

"I am glad to see you both here safely."

Malthe paused, with a distracted look, as though making a decision. "There's something else I wanted to tell you." Another quick look at Samathe. "The young cousin who stayed at my fine lady's fortress." Now her brown eyes held his. "Not long after he came to us, I was out in the city during one of the lulls, and I saw ... banners seeking the return of a youth who matched his description."

"You did."

Turning her heavy-lidded eyes to the salt workers, she stepped forward a pace and gripped the ship's polished brass railing. "I . . . considered seeking the reward. It was . . . substantial." Favik stepped to her side, studying her. "I would have become a fine lady on my own. But then I overheard some of King Sirish's men debating how they would kill him, how their lord stabbed his mother and sister." Closing her eyes, Malthe said, "I made the decision to stay silent. I wanted you to know."

Before he could speak, she bolted toward her mistress, donning her veil as she strode. Keeping silent and distant from his charges, Favik stumbled to the opposite end the boat, bile in his throat and tears burning his eyes. "A sister. Our child was a daughter. Oh Melande . . ." He coughed, then spat into the water to clear his mouth, unable to articulate a thread of thought.

Perhaps an hour later they arrived at the western entrance to the main harbor of Guernain, the largest city in Guerland and the crossroads of trade between the seafaring nations to the south and west and the eastern interior lands. In the middle of the bay, a slender cylindrical tower stood, improbably, in the softly lapping water. A long, slender causeway of ivory sand stretched from the tower to the mainland.

"Excuse me, sir." One of the vessel's Guerish sailors stepped to the prow of the ship and splayed several short-poled signal flags on the ground before him, hoisting two aloft to announce to the harbormaster their intention to dock.

Favik cleared his throat, glad for the distraction. "Do you know anything about how that tower was constructed?"

The man's eyes did not waver from the harbormaster as he said, "It's quite a sight." He bent and switched his flags, then raised them in a graceful swirl. Completing the pattern, he added, "It is said that long ago, there was a large rock there that was connected to the land.

The Powers struck it down, but left enough for Guerlanders to build that tower." The harbormaster raised more colored pennants. "That means we will dock past the white piers." The sailor nodded to the captain, who had seen the signals and responses and gave directions to his crew. Their craft passed a pier of stone construction, which was packed with boats painted white, bleached pennants drooping on their poles, and crowds of people of every description.

"Quarantine boats," the sailor explained, perhaps feeling it was his duty to teach Guerish ways to the outerlander. "People seeking healing from Dalich Strange King come here from all over the world. They sail for Mavold, then make the inland journey to Eskalind."

Favik leaned forward, noting a plethora of bandage-wrapped limbs on people limping or leaning on crutches as though a battlefield hospital had turned out all its patients. "Gergelt would be closer than Mavold," he mused.

The sailor grinned, his perfect teeth a generous white flash. "In miles, yes. But traversing Gergelt is slow, their people see no need for haste in anything and are very generous, wanting travelers to linger. So I am told."

"It is true. I have made the journey through Gergelt," Favik grimly replied. The captain's mate shouted orders for the boat to sail toward their designated dockage.

On their arrival, many Guerlander men bustled along the wooden pier with bulging burlap bags of cargo. All were clothed in the tight breeches and tunics popular amongst the male population, a skirting of material hanging from their waists to render the coverings more modest. Blues and greens, the colors of sky and sea and the plentiful vegetation growing on distant hills, were echoed in the people's clothes, though at this moment, the landscape and sky stayed steady and immovable in opposition to the buzzing human activity. Yet one shorter man stood still at the end of the pier, hands on his hips as though perplexed but determined to deny the emotion. Thin gray hair capped his dark head, and his eyes scanned the scene as though searching for something on the cusp of discernment. Then he locked eyes on Favik.

Despite the distance between the pier and the ship, Marna's man recognized him and nearly fell overboard. "Kermon." The last man in Guerland he wanted to see. The Merchant Master Scholar.

The Powers take me.

A slow smile spread on the distant Guerish Scholar's face. He raised a hand and beckoned, laughing. He was still laughing when Favik, forcing a smile, walked the steep gangway a few minutes later and came forward to embrace him.

"By The Powers!" Lady Saralya's blood cousin exclaimed, slapping Favik on the back, for he was not a tall man and the Eskalinder's shoulder blades were a reach for him. "I felt they led me to the dock today, and I knew not why. My feet began walking on their own. And look who I find!"

Favik attempted a grin, amazed at his poor luck. "I see They have not failed you."

Kermon's bright expression fell. "We must speak alone soon. I have much to tell. The Bladesmith's Daughter sent you to me, yes?"

"In a way—" The younger Scholar gestured to the ship. Samathe and her maidservant descended to the dock, shrouded in their beige robes and veils. "I'm escorting Deenofts's sister and her maid to their new home, then I must swiftly return to Eskalind." Favik spoke quickly and quietly. "I will tell you more soon of him, but please do not mention his name to her. She is an extremely traditional Havadran."

"Ah, no mention of family. A shame, but I am familiar with the practice." His forehead furrowed, the rows extending into the gray of his hairline. "Why does she come to Guerland?"

"She has a blood aunt, joined with a merchant—"

"I likely know them. Did she tell you their names?"

"She told me to seek direction to the house of Merchant Onas."

"Yes, yes. Onas and his Havadran wife, Semise." Kermon lowered his round chin. "Semise is an expert negotiator. Has made their family much coin. Please, I know the way and will accompany you there."

"There is no need to trouble yourself. We may meet later."

"I insist." He raised a hand straight in the air, which caught the attention of one of the workers on the dock. Soon Kermon had commandeered a wagon with generously padded seats for the passengers and a large bed for the myriad household baggage. Favik introduced the Merchant Master as the blood cousin of a Lady of Eskalind, explaining that they had met at her ennobling ceremony, years before. Malthe, more comfortable in the ways of the outside world than her mistress, offered her hand as well as her name for the traditional Guerish greeting, though when she did so, she stepped slightly forward of her fine lady, as if to shield her. Samathe stood, stiff and wary, but murmured thanks as Kermon offered to help her into their transportation.

Once all were seated, two large oxen heaved the cart forward, and the four passengers and the driver lumbered through the crowds. Kermon insisted the women sit behind the men and the driver, to shield them from dirt or dust kicked up by the animals. He then encouraged the Havadrans to remove their face coverings with the zeal of one waging a campaign to convert them to the ways of their new land. "This is Guerland; the sun wants to see your face. It is healthy!"

Malthe complied with a slender smile, but Samathe replied, "I will wait till we arrive at the fortress." She turned her veiled face away.

Perhaps hoping to make amends, the Guerish Scholar halted their procession a moment later when he saw a vendor selling small bouquets of a sweet-scented herb, calling her over and hastily negotiating a pair of nosegays for his female guests. As he settled the transaction, a line of Guerish children paced by, holding a rope to stay together. They were led and tailed by a pair of minders, womenfolk dressed in calf-length, scoop-necked tunics of an ashy green shade, belted with blue ribbon. The children's dark eyes surveyed the pale outerlanders with curious interest, especially the completely covered Samathe in her beige drapes. Malthe nodded, and some of little ones smiled.

One boy reached an ebony finger to touch her ivory hand on the side of her seat.

For Favik, it was refreshing to see women and children in the public mix, after the intense concentration of adult males in the streets of Capitola, but he had little chance to enjoy the scenery, as his stomach churned over Melande's fate and what would befall him next. Sensing that the women were distracted by the sights around them, he whispered the sad news of Deenofts's disappearance to Kermon. He would endeavor to keep any word of Anish from the Scholar's ears. If it were possible to do such a thing in the presence of a Guerish Merchant Master.

Arriving at Samathe's new home, the quartet and their baggage waited a moment in the unpopulated courtyard, lush with festive greenery and bold-scented flowers trailing from trellises on the two upper stories of the house. Then her blood aunt and Guerish uncle burst forth from the house with open arms, greeting them gladly and calling for refreshments from their servants, then countermanding those requests with calls to send for the rest of the family, to hastily unpack the wagon, and to draw warm baths for their guests. Some of this happened, but as Samathe's blood cousins began arriving with their wives and young children, the happy chaos was complete, and nothing was accomplished except embraces, smiles, and joyful tears.

At last, with bellies full from the impromptu feast that wondrously emerged from the household's kitchen, Kermon whisked Favik to his own home to lodge for the night and converse privately on Scholarly business. The blond man claimed fatigue from the journey, but the Merchant Master countered, "If you must return to Eskalind as swiftly as you say, we must speak together alone first, for I have much to tell that cannot be trusted to writing, unless you have come to tell me Lord Radil has at last discovered a way to code messages." Thus, despite the late hour, they sat for tea beside the fountain in Kermon's torchlit courtyard. The music of the water served to cover conversation as the elder Scholar began.

"A joyful reunion today, for Samathe, sister to our departed Scholar Deenofts. May she find peace and happiness here in Guerland with her blood family." Favik nodded and saluted the sentiment with his teacup. Kermon continued, "I'm also relieved at The Powers' direction in guiding me to the dock at the time of your ship's arrival."

"Yes, that was most fortuitous." Favik tried to sound pleased, though he guessed that this would lead into questions of why he had defied Eskalind's orders.

"But Favik, it most truly is. They have not advised me in a long while."

"What do you mean?"

The Merchant Master shook his head, deep brown eyes sad. He placed his teacup on the flat rim of the fountain with a slight clank and placed his hands together like a book. Favik mimicked the gesture. "When you return to our Lady Marna, you must tell her this, though it is a deep and unfathomable pain to me." He inhaled and spoke low. "I have not been able to discern truthfulness in an individual since the very end of last year. I have lost my Gift. And I am not alone." The elder Scholar pointed to an eye. "Not one of my guild has breathed of it, but I can see it in all the Merchant Masters, in their masked, lost faces. They too have lost this Gift. One even lost her life, when a man she deemed trustworthy turned against her."

"You mean you cannot tell, at all, with anyone?"

"No one. As surely as the sun sets each day, it is gone."

"But you felt The Powers lead you to the dock today…"

"Yes. It gives me hope." He reached and squeezed Favik's forearm. "You alone, I can trust with this information. You must tell Dalock's Queen. She may know what it means."

"Gladly." Never had he meant the word more. Kermon's brow furrowed, and he withdrew his hand. Favik continued, his tone light, "I was afraid you would have detected that I have absconded with half the treasury of Eskalind."

Then the Guerlander laughed, a deep sound that ascended from his chest and rebounded from the courtyard's wall. "Well, one might be forgiven for considering it a possibility, given the sums you tell me the sale of Samathe's fortress garnered. Deenofts would be glad to know his sister will never want for anything."

Favik nearly grinned, amazed at his luck, but his fellow Scholar's mood dimmed into a soft melancholy.

"Deenofts's sister wanted a family, children in her life. Even I, in my diminishment, can see that." Kermon smiled wryly. "Now she has what she wished." Looking to his hands. "My wife died, long ago. I never considered another. She was everything to me. Hmm." He retrieved his teacup and sipped. "She died birthing our child, who must have loved my wife more than me, for he went with her into death."

"How horrible," Favik stated, his mouth dry, for the circumstances mirrored his own in its outcome.

The Guerish Scholar lowered his tea to the ledge and again placed his hands in the signature gesture. "But I believe we can make our own family, and determine who we are akin to in spirit, based on common interests and pursuits." Kermon's eyes shone with purpose. "The Bladesmith's Daughter is a conduit to The Powers, and she chose us. Us, Favik. To preserve, to protect, to prevent. To be her eyes and ears in the prevention of strife and conflict between the nations. To guard against the development of new weapons. To safeguard all nations. What better purpose can a man serve? The Scholars are my family now." He rose. "Come, Favik, embrace me as a son."

Weary with relief, the blond man did so.

Kermon released him and clapped him on the arms. "And tomorrow I will introduce you to a merchant, one I would count amongst our secret number and call daughter, if my Gift returns." The Guerish Scholar grinned. "I met her just after I realized it was gone. But I will not make a Scholar until it returns. Today gives me hope it will. Or you," he tapped his hand quickly on Favik's chest, "will help me decide without it."

———

The next morning dawned to the scent of a fresh-brewed, earthy tea, wafting into Favik's room from a cup on a tray of minute blue and green tiles carried by a barefoot young man. The servant left the tea by the Scholar's bedside as Favik slowly roused himself to sit upright and sip from the thick-rimmed glass bowl. A tiny cup of fine-ground gray crystalloid salt rested on the tray as well, testament to Guerland-ers' love of adding a pinch of salt to all consumables. The Eskalinder was grateful that his host left to his guests' discretion the addition of salt to morning beverages. The sparkling crystals would fetch several coins in the faraway markets of Nordak, Ofsha or Eyfia, and whilst Favik appreciated the luxury, salt in tea had no appeal.

Arising and dressing, he met Kermon for the morning meal, which was followed by a short walk to the courtyard fountain where they sat the previous night. As they approached the tinkling waters, a woman with long, curly black tresses stood to greet them. The moment she turned to him, he saw her clad in a long red belted tunic with a curved neckline, and matching leggings, but when he blinked, her attire was entirely in shades of blue. He paused for the briefest of moments, and her brown eyes met his like a spark, as though judgment were rendered and a sentence pronounced. Favik sensed that this one bore the Gift of Guerish Merchant Masters; she knew his deceptions, his transgressions. The blood shivered in his veins as he approached her. He felt again the newly made Eskalind Ambassador to Havadra, trembling under the general's raptor gleam. But he was no longer a young man possessing only tutored knowledge. The deeds he would have to answer for had been made by his own choice, with the best intentions, to protect the people he loved. A reasonable, compassion-ate person would understand that. The thought gave him courage.

"Ambassador Favik, I present to you Naynarp of Guerland, please." Kermon placed their hands together in the traditional Guerish manner of formally making acquaintances. The woman's skin, whilst brown, was much lighter than Kermon's. It felt feverishly hot.

The woman spoke as though making a royal pronouncement. "Favik of Hudiksland." It had been years since anyone addressed him as a Hudikslander. Again, an icy feeling permeated his core.

"Yes, I was born in Hudiksland when King Hudik reigned, though now the land is called after his son, King Humik." He glanced at Kermon, who beamed.

"She did not learn that from me. You see, Favik? Naynarp has a way of finding out things."

Favik smiled, though it required calling upon all his Ambassador's skills to do so in a seemingly genuine manner. The potential Scholar released his hand, which tingled with heat. "How did you learn that about me?"

As though dismissing an overly inquisitive child, she replied, "It was known to me."

He risked what might be construed a rude question. "Might I inquire after your origins?"

The corners of her lips lifted slightly as Kermon chuckled to her. "Favik has just returned from Havadra and is perhaps still smothered by their customs. Of course, of course." He waved a hand for her to continue.

"Kermon knowns me for a Guerlander, but as you can see," she lifted a hand to her fawn-colored cheek, "my family is from a paler line." A look of serene disdain inhabited her brown eyes.

He continued pleasantly, despite the chill in his being, sensing that he was undergoing a strange assessment. "What manner of goods do you trade?"

"Broadly defined, anything that makes light. Wicks, candles, lanterns. Guerlanders love lanterns." Her gaze alighted on the elder Scholar with warmth and intention. "Kermon, thank you for your hospitality, but this talk of trade reminds me of an appointment I must keep."

The Guerish Scholar's graying eyebrows rose. "So short a visit? But Naynarp, you have only just been introduced."

"Business calls," she said, a hint of weariness mixed with playfulness in her tone. "Good to finally meet you in person, Ambassador."

"And you, Merchant Naynarp of Guerland."

She lowered her eyes and smiled as though a private joke had passed between them. After a long embrace from Kermon, the woman departed the courtyard, a discernible sway in her hips even under her shapeless garment. Kermon watched her depart. Favik watched him watch her.

Once she had left their view, the elder Scholar turned to the Eskalinder, his expression bright with expectation. "Well, what do you think?"

"I think it was a very brief visit."

"Yes, but what do you think of *her*? I had hoped you would spend more time together." He gestured for them to sit on the fountain's ample edge, and the pair lowered themselves onto the cool tiles. "Do you sense that Naynarp would make a Scholar?"

Favik curled then stretched the fingers of the hand she had touched. "It seems a wise course of action to wait until your Gift returns to make that decision."

"But what if it doesn't?" Kermon rolled his lips. "You should spend more time with her. You will grow to like and trust her."

"Alas, the tides dictate I must depart this afternoon." As he spoke, he dipped his aching hand into the water. It felt cool and soothing, a much-needed balm against the heat that plagued only this small part of his body.

"Favik, we must find more Scholars. The Powers only know how much time I have left. There must be a Guerish Scholar to fill my position when I am no longer able. To preserve our works, we must prepare." Lady Saralya's blood cousin gripped his knees, then leaned close to the Eskalinder. "With Deenofts gone too, our numbers shrink. None of us grow younger. The Scholars must continue. Our work is very important."

"I agree, yet I cannot clearly say to you that I agree with your assessment of Naynarp."

The elder Scholar placed a hand on Favik's shoulder. "Stay longer.

Meet with her again. You will grow to like her. It is how it was with me."

"Much as I would linger, I must return to our Lady Marna. I was very much delayed in my stay in Havadra, though I am glad to see Deenofts's sister and her maid safely settled." Kermon squeezed his shoulder, and the younger man continued, "Please, I would ask, on behalf of the Bladesmith's Daughter, to wait to decide until your Gift returns."

The Guerlander removed his hand. "What if it does not?"

"Think on it this way." Here warmth retuned to Favik's voice as he made a plan. "There must be a reason The Powers withdrew your Gift. Withdrew the Gifts of all the Merchant Masters. When that reason is removed, it will return. Give it time." His host stared straight ahead. "Consider, Kermon, what if your coming to the dock yesterday is a sign, from Them, that your Gift may be restored soon?" He brought his hands together like a book. "As your fellow Scholar, that is my counsel."

Kermon shrugged, his shoulders bobbing with the movement. "We shall see."

One could always count on a Records Keeper arriving at the appointed time. It was one of the many traits of their profession that Morya found appealing. The Records Keeper's black-robed Apprentice had no sooner sat the Healer at the small table in the private room and departed when the dark-robed official entered. He placed his portable writing desk upon the table with barely a sound.

"You're punctual," she said, tapping a hand on the red fabric draping her knee.

"I'm Brisnil."

Morya smiled, but knew he would not—not during an official conference. It was a good thing, for when this man smiled, she found it difficult to concentrate on official business.

"You were slightly early," Brisnil said, his keen blue eyes alighting upon her for an instant as he unpacked his writing desk with regimental efficiency. The Healer watched him stack papyruses and a half dozen quilling instruments in precise order across the polished table. Then Brisnil sat, folding his hands before his chest. Even in his voluminous black robes, she could discern strong shoulders. For a man who spent most of his days hovering around scroll stacks and desks, he had the musculature of a sturdy Soldier. It was a shame his locks were completely tucked under his purple headwrap, for they were a glory of chestnut and looked to be soft to the touch.

She fingered the King's Flower emblem stitched over her heart, the mark of her profession. He began, "I, Brisnil, Records Keeper at the border with Havadra, on this twenty-eighth day of the sixth month, in the year since the founding of Eskalind 2915, am present with Healer Morya. We are gathered to discuss the problem of the Havadran youth Anish. As he seeks political refuge, I am referring to him as X in my records." Brisnil tapped a smoothly filed fingernail upon one of the papyruses. "First, the child claims he left Capitola with an adult companion during the seventh month of 2914. He arrives alone at our border on the twenty-fifth day of the third month of 2915. Can you explain the time discrepancy?"

"How he survived months in the desert after his companion was killed is a mystery to me. All he told me was that he found shelter and that he did not harm anyone during his sojourn there."

The Records Keeper nodded, cool and perfunctory. "Just as he claimed when I questioned him. Second, he claims that he is an outstanding Copyist, that he has sold many copied books for coin."

"I examined the scars on his hands. They attest to a severe injury—"

"Which accounts for why he could barely write a legible sentence when I tested him. Or he never had this ability in the first place, which would make him a liar."

Morya crossed her arms.

The Records Keeper did nothing to acknowledge her gesture. "Lastly, you and I have each, individually, written Dalich King asking him to heal the lad's hands. Two requests with no results, though other healing requests sent in the same letter pouch yielded healthy, healed patients."

"I affirm this to be true," the Healer replied, albeit reluctantly.

"The Havadran arrives at our border dressed in rags, and yet in his satchel bag, he possessed . . .," Brisnil retrieved a papyrus with the account, "five fine quality drawings, a pearl-handled dagger, a long knife hilted and scabbarded with round pale green stones set in gold, fifteen gold coins, a gold pendant in the shape of a square, and," he drew a breath, "a fine linen tunic with gold embroidery about the cuffs. As I noted, X came to Eskalind dressed in rags." He lowered the papyrus. "I put forth that he is a thief."

She shook her head. "I understand your suspicions, but as a Healer, my evaluations make it clear to me that this boy has suffered great traumas. Of those items you list, he told me the dagger was a token intended for his mother and the long knife was a Naming Day present from his parents. The fine tunic is his size. He says the drawings were of his own hand, portraying people he knew. The gold pendant and coins came from the deceased companion."

"I affirm that he tells us both the identical story about these items."

Morya tapped the table. "Consider this likely hypothesis: He was a member of a family of high standing that lost their influence during one of the Havadran uprisings. He and a relative fled into the desert."

Brisnil paused. "It is possible. These possessions would attest to luxurious circumstances, but as he will not tell us anything about his family either—"

"Havadrans never talk about their family to strangers, and rarely with companions."

"I am fully aware of that." The Records Keeper sounded aggrieved. "But it does not help his situation."

The Healer pressed, "My counsel is that Anish isn't contagious, thus he poses no disease threat to anyone. I counsel that he requires rest in a comforting, safe environment to heal his mind. Living quarantined here at the border under our current pressed circumstances does not provide that. As he is only fourteen and has no family or companions in Eskalind, I recommend transferring him to a King's House to recuperate."

"I'm considering sending him back to Havadra."

Morya stood. "No."

Brisnil's gaze rose to hers, though he remained in his chair. "There must be a good reason why Dalich King is not healing him. I believe the youth is hiding something."

"The boy's a refugee from a treacherous, dangerous country. There may be much he does not want to reveal, perhaps even his name, out of fear of being found."

"Yes, that is why I am referring to him as X in my reports." Brisnil's tone sounded as though Morya were the dullest person he had ever dealt with.

"Anish is safe here in Eskalind, and he wants to be a citizen of Eskalind. Thus he must convalesce first, then be allowed to serve his five years. His service will prove his intent and character. During that time he can be judged worthy, or not, to stay."

The Records Keeper intoned, "The fact that he has not been healed, despite two requests, could be interpreted as a message from The Powers that They do not want him to stay."

"It is your decision in the end, I know that." She sat. "But I'm Anish's Healer, and I have spent much time with him. My evaluation is that the youth has promise. Have a heart. Let the poor lad stay." She stared hard at him, wishing she'd never considered showing him her feet.

Brisnil gazed at the table and inhaled. "If this Havadran is healed by Dalich King, I will grant him application for citizenship by beginning his service, with convalescent time first at a King's House." Looking to her, he continued, "But not until The Powers see fit to heal him. Until they do, I must insist he stay in quarantine. I know of no other case where Dalich King and thus The Powers have declined a healing request, so I must interpret this as a sign that the youth is *not* wanted inside our borders."

Morya placed her fingertips on the table, feeling the wood yield to her nails. "Then I propose that Anish, rather than us, quill the King, in private, and see what follows."

"His handwriting is barely legible."

"Let him try."

The Records Keeper stood, and the floorboards creaked as he rose to his toes. "I approve this course of action: the Havadran, or X as the records will show, will compose his own letter to Dalich King, and we await the results. If he is healed, he may apply for citizenship. If not, he will be expelled. I grant him three months from this date." Nodding to her, he said, "I will record the notes of this meeting and expect your signature tomorrow if we are in agreement."

"Aye." She turned on her heels, hoping with all her heart that this plan would buy the youth enough time to recover. If hope were a tangible thing, she would fill the largest basket she could carry and bring it to the young Havadran. And if Brisnil were transferred to another posting tomorrow, after he completed the requisite documents, she would rejoice.

"Anish, may I come in? It's Morya."

The door groaned open and the lad beckoned her inside. As she closed the door, it pleased her to see the progress in the room's acquisition of furnishings: a candlelit desk with an open map scroll upon it, a bed with a plump, straw-stuffed mattress, neatly dressed as though for military inspection with crisp sheets and two feathered pillows, and a pair of wooden chairs. Lastly, the original occupant, a three-legged stool, glowering in a dark corner as though banished to the fringes by the others.

Anish, standing, regarded her with his blue-rimmed irises as he touched the gold pendant around his neck. "Did you bring me some food?"

She shook her head. "Haven't you been served the midday meal?"

He looked to his feet, cracking his toes. "Yes, but I'm hungry again."

Morya patted his tunic sleeve, cheered at his healthy appetite. "You are likely still growing. I will see that a hearty snack is brought, but I must speak to you first." Swiftly she imparted the Records Keeper's judgment, keeping her tone sunny even as she saw despair growing in his eyes. "Once you are healed, you can continue your plan for citizenship." She lifted the two chairs, placed them facing one another, and sat. "All you must do is quill the King yourself, in your own hand, and request healing."

"But my writing is terrible. I can scarcely read it anymore." The blond youth faded into the seat opposite her as though the chair would absorb him.

"Do the best you can, Anish. And, oh, one thing that may differ with Havadran ways." He raised his head slowly, but his eyes held interest. "In Eskalind, children are named by both parents. It is one of our most important customs." The youth clutched his pendant with coiled fingers. "I realize it may be different in your birthland, but it might be useful, in your letter, to call yourself by any name or names your parents called you."

"Oh."

"Now, I realize it may be a bit frightening for you to write that down. As one fleeing a perilous country, hiding your identity may feel safer. It is entirely understandable."

The refugee opened his mouth slightly but said nothing.

"I will quill a letter myself asking that no one but the King read your request. I will ask that your letter be destroyed before anyone else reads it. Your note will be sealed inside my letter."

"Oh."

"Can you do this for me?"

"Um, yes."

"Good." She leapt to her feet. "I will send an Apprentice Healer to bring you quilling instruments and food. When I return, I will have my letter written, and we will seal your note inside mine." Anish looked at his lap as she bent to touch his shoulders. "I will also write King's Mother, for she too is a great Healer. I'll request a formula for a salve that might relax your fingers."

"You are making two plans," he said weakly.

"Don't worry, this will work, Anish."

"I hope so," he murmured as she left the room.

——

Weeks passed, as slowly as they can when one accounts for every merciless hour. The beginning of the eighth month of 2915 arrived. Whilst on one of his limited, supervised times outside his room, Anish paced along the Eskalind side of the borderwall. Healer Morya and her Apprentice stood a dozen feet away, discussing the supplies they would need to make yet another iteration of King's Mother's salve.

"No no no, we did that last time, and it didn't bind properly," the Healer scolded, rubbing a finger over her freckled forehead.

"Why don't they just give up?" he said quietly, turning away from the bickering women. Looking beyond the crumbling wall into the sea of sand, he wondered if it might be better for him to scramble over the porous rocks and walk back into the desert, suffering what fate might come next. Then the thought of facing the Shinglo again sent a shudder through his being. But nothing he did here in Eskalind seemed to work. Nothing anyone else did for him worked either. Perhaps it would have been better if his father's men had found him. Then none of this would matter.

Anish sighed. He held his curled left hand over the rocks, leaning, reaching across into the hot Havadran air, his knuckles stinging with the heat but his wrist cool on the Eskalind side of the border. Such an odd phenomenon. It surprised him Deenofts had never mentioned it, for surely the man had experienced it. If he ever had a companion again, far from the cursed border, he would be sure to relate this fantastic fact.

A Guard he did not recognize marched by, surprisingly close to him, thick lips twisted in a scowl. "Palm open, facing down, when you cross the border. Show some respect for The Powers."

The youth spun to face the Soldier as he passed, angry that the man thought him rude and seething at his malady. With one curled hand, the general's grandson attempted to pry straight the stiff fingers of the other. For once the digits yielded. Anish held that hand flat over the borderwall and reached into the land of his birth, admiring the unfamiliar sight of his fingers even, though the skin was thick with scars like miniature ropes. He raised the other hand, which mimicked the flat position of the first. He wanted to wiggle his fingers. He did. They flexed as easily as the air passing unnoticed through his lungs. "I'm healed? I'm healed. Healer Morya! Look!"

PART TWO
2921–2923

Morya's husband's voice woke her from deep slumber upon the soft pillows of their couch. "A letter from an old patient for you, my dear Healer." Outside, a Mavoldian sparrow shrieked repeatedly, a most annoying high-pitched E-E-E sound. She wished the irksome bird would stay on the other side of the border, or fly to Kaymif. Living at the intersection of Eskalind, Mavold, and Kaymif, the bird had its pick of lands, though the borders were likely invisible to avian eyes.

Morya hefted herself up as best she could, feeling drowsy and heavy. The babe in her belly rolled, perhaps displeased with the sudden motion. Its father tapped the short side of the envelope on the low table before the divan. He pinched the corner of the thin papyrus.

"I fell asleep again?"

"I'm not surprised," Brisnil said. "You would not cease tidying the house yesterday, despite my protestations."

Ignoring the veneer of criticism in his tone, she squinted at the delicate, inked flourish alongside the quilling of her address. "From Anish?"

"Aye." He slipped the letter into her waiting hand.

"Good. I have not heard from him since just after our joining." The Healer tore a thin strip of the envelope and retrieved the missive. She read aloud,

2nd Day, 9th Month, 2921

"So, two weeks to reach us," he said. She cast him a quick glare and continued,

Dear Healer Morya,
I hope this note finds you and Brisnil well, hopefully with the
newbabe in your arms.

She laughed lightly. "Soon, I do hope."

I write glad news. Having completed my five years' service, I am
now officially a citizen of Eskalind. My plan is to continue in
the army and pursue a military career. I find it suits me, and
dare I say, it runs in my family. Again I want to thank you for
all your care and letters, and kind words affirming my decision
to not pursue work in King's Mother's Scriptorium. My quilling
skills find much use with my company.
I hope to be made Secretary to my Captain, Lord Marnil, when
his current Secretary retires. It is a position that can lead to a
leadership role, as the current Secretary is also a First Sergeant.

"He sounds like a Havadran there," her husband remarked with a smile, coming to sit in the chair beside her.

"Oh Brisnil, he is just a young man who's thinking ahead. There's nothing wrong with planning one's future." She leaned further into the pillows.

Please write as soon as you are able with news of your health
and the name of your babe. I would like to quill the Naming
announcement for you, if I may.
Fondly, Anish

"How sweet of him. Our child will have an enviably beautiful Naming announcement. We can hang it there," she gestured with the letter to a bare spot of wall beside the window. "Unless we are transferred to another border crossing again."

Brisnil reached for the rough envelope. "Let me see the direction," he said, tugging the papyrus from her fingers.

"You know he cannot quill his company's location on an envelope." She released it.

"That is not what I'm curious about." From the letter, Brisnil read,

Citizen Stander Anish, Sixth Company

His sharp blue eyes alighted on her. "Morya, why is his rank still Stander? He is twenty, if my memory is correct."

Morya nodded. "Yes, he's old enough to be our adult son—if we had met when I was just of age, and if I had found a fondness for you the first time we met."

"But you did like me the second time we were stationed at the same border."

She gestured to her belly. "Apparently."

The Records Keeper continued, in a tone befitting his vocation, "If he is twenty, then his rank should be Soldier, unless he has not earned his sword yet." Brisnil leaned toward his wife. "Which would be very odd."

Draping a hand across her stomach, the Healer looked away. "You're right, he's never mentioned earning his sword. But he must have. Force of long habit might have made him mistakenly write his old rank."

"I would think he would be proud of any elevation in his status—as he is with being a full citizen—and thus would not make that mistake."

His wife rubbed the unfamiliar protrusion of her belly button. With a hint of a sigh in her voice, she said, "My, how you sound like a Records Keeper."

"You told me your heart always favored Records Keepers." Brisnil reached for Morya's hand.

"And especially the one I call husband."

The Lady Saralya closed her eyes, lowering the Legend scroll she had been reading onto her lap. This beloved text by Haarshil had belonged to her father and exhibited his favored way of marking the passages he enjoyed most. Rather than dipping quill to ink and drawing on the surface, he had impressed into the parchment a thin, invisible vertical line with his fingernail. She could feel it on the underside of the beige surface. A slight smile traced her lips at this nearly imperceptible reminder of his presence once in this world. Nearly every passage of this dear volume possessed that line, and for the most favored sections, two or even three lines ran in parallel. She now kept this scroll in her study at King's Halls, along with other precious texts that warmed her heart when the absence of her husband felt heavy in the quarters they shared for many dear years.

A knock outside her study door summoned her attention to the present.

"Grandmother?" came a young voice.

"Yes, Kaloft," Saralya responded. "Open the door." The lad did so and entered at a heavy pace, as though weights anchored his black leather shoes. He closed the door and turned his dark head to her, an exaggerated sadness in his nine-year-old gaze.

"Kaloft, what is wrong?" She placed the scroll on a side table and held her arms open for him to approach. With a glance back at the door, he shuffled toward the head of his noble house, leaning against her chair and placing his brown hands on the crimson skirt covering her leg.

"Mother says I have to play with King's Son again." The seriousness of his voice reminded her of how her elder son imparted ill news.

"Well, that sounds like fun to me." She ran her fingers over her grandson's thick locks.

"I do not wish to."

"Why not?" The Acta Sua brought her hands together.

The boy looked away. "Please do not make me, Grandmother." He pushed his fingertips into her leg. "If you tell Mother no, she will have to do what you say."

Smiling at his understanding of familial rank, Saralya replied, "Can you tell me why you feel this way? Did he hurt you?"

Kaloft paused, withdrawing his hands to the arm of her chair. "No. It is just, he is bigger than me, but he acts like a, like a babe sometimes."

"You must remember he is younger than you, only seven. Why, our young Lord has barely left the nursery."

Her grandson puckered his lips together. "You are siding with Mother."

Saralya reached for the short sleeve of his linen tunic and stroked his arm. "I need you to be a good example to King's Son. Show him how a more mature boy conducts himself. Be fair and patient with him. Offer him guidance and counsel him, like your Uncle Saril does with the King." The lad lowered his forehead. "And companionship, as your Mother does to our Queen."

The youngest member of her noble house raised his head, a spark of hope lighting his expression. "Can I stay here and you will read to me?"

"Ah, alas, I was about to depart to read to King's Mother."

With a sad nod, the boy stepped toward the door, opening it and stopping. With a last glance to her, Kaloft solemnly observed, "We each have our royal." He closed the door.

"Thank The Powers," Saralya said to herself. "My grandson is as smart as his sires."

———

"My dearest Reader." Marna greeted her old friend into her Library Study. Saralya carried a laden scroll basket, the polished stone finials of the scrolls glistening in the orange slant of late afternoon sunlight. "Come, come sit by the window with me."

The two women settled into the cushions, and Saralya set the basket near their feet, her dark brown eyes darting to the smooth wax tablets resting on the window ledge. The Scholars' Mistress began.

"Before you read, and while we have a moment alone, I must tell you the news from your blood cousin. Some of it is highly unusual."

"Is Kermon well?"

"He quilled that he is in fine health. Sometimes he neglects to report his condition, which sets my mind to worry over our Guerish Scholar. He is close to seventy, after all." The side of Marna's mouth quirked upwards; he was but four years older than herself. At least she knew how much time she had. Well, she believed she knew. "He knows I possess some knowledge of herbcraft," here she raised an eyebrow at her companion, "and I have told him he should always inform me as to his fitness. Ever since, he makes a point to mention his wellness or lack thereof."

Her Reader nodded. "Has he lost his Gift again?"

"No, he mentioned that 'all is well with the Merchant Masters,' which is how he conveys that his Gift feels intact. But he was not as clear in his main news." She cast her companion a knowing look and reached for the wax tablets. Saralya inhaled slightly as the Bladesmith's Daughter wrote the Guerish Scholar's news: reports had reached his ears of people in the distant southern lands speaking with strange sounds that no one could comprehend, and writing with strange symbols.

The part-Guerish woman leaned toward the tablet to read, the crimson of her gown casting a warm glow onto the white wax. "I do not know what to make of this," she said at last, drawing back as though the tablet were some fearsome creature.

"Mmm, I think I do," said the former Queen. She scraped her wax writing into the small trough at the bottom of the tablet, then traced the stylus across the smoothed wax to impart that she believed this was a sign that The Powers' rules were being broken again.

"Oh, my Lady. This cannot happen."

"Indeed. But consider, I may be misinterpreting what Kermon wrote. He was not very explicit, as one would expect in a written communication that might be read by others. If word of this propagated—" She wiped away her words. "My first thought was to send Favik to speak with him in person."

"But Favik is still across the Kursak border, yes?"

"Indeed, far to the north. Since he is traveling, I do not know when my message might reach our blond Scholar. And I do not trust such news to writing."

The Acta Sua nodded, her gaze thoughtful, as her Lady reached the crux of this meeting.

"Saralya, it pains me to ask, though I deem it necessary. Would you consider journeying yourself to speak with Kermon?"

The Reader's eyes were downcast. "My Lady, I am not certain my house could bear the expense at the moment."

"Do not trouble yourself with the expense. I will fund the journey."

The Acta Sua knit her fingers. "I deeply appreciate the offer." She raised her gaze. "More and more people have crossed my estate's border from Kaymif, desperate people seeking healing from my Lord Dalich King. They come not just from Kaymif but from Vikmere and Swedfia and the lands west. They do not travel the main roads; they come across open fields, through the woods, whichever way is closest. They are desperate to enter Eskalind for healing." Her Reader paused. "I understand their plight, but I could not allow them to camp in the open. They often come with so little means—the sanitation, the conditions, it was deplorable. Inhumane. Thus, I engaged Builders."

Saralya rubbed a thumb over her knuckles. "Every five or so miles, along the border, we built enclosed shelters with beds and small kitchens, we drilled wells and dug outhouses. It is enough to be comfortable, whilst they await healing."

"Every five miles? That must be at least ten structures."

"A bit more, my Lady."

Marna sat in silence, calculating the number of people required for such an endeavor. After the initial requirement for Builders and laborers, then Healers to attend those in need. Scribes to write the King, Messengers to carry the notes requesting healing to the nearest Swift Riders' office. Caretakers for the shelters, to say nothing of supplying food for the people and their animals. The amount of coin would drain even a noble household. Her friend's generosity warmed her heart. "Well, your estate must not bear the entire burden of this expense. I will speak with my son about this."

"Please, my Lady, I would rather do this quietly, without reward or compensation. By your leave, without the knowledge of Dalich King. Even Saril does not know." Here she smiled slightly, perhaps pleased to keep another secret from her eldest son, who counted himself all-knowing. "My family has been immeasurably honored and enriched by this land, by your family. It is the least we can do."

The former Queen shook her head. "Then I must insist on financing a comfortable trip by sea to Guerland, via Mavold of course, if you will go. I will not argue the financial point, I will simply make it so, if you deem to make this journey for me."

Saralya was quiet a moment. "Then I thank you. I know I have mentioned how I hoped to never depart Eskalind again, but Kermon has been much in my thoughts lately. I deeply relish the chance to see him again, my sole blood relation besides my children and grandson. I will bring any reports of import to your ears."

"Excellent."

"How I hope to The Powers I return with good news." She gestured to the tablet; King's Mother handed it and the stylus to her. "My Lady,

I hope to The Powers that this is another instance of a strange event dissolved by Their doing. Like the…" She wrote as she spoke:

Havadran weapons that flew through the air, and the Guerish Merchant Masters temporarily losing their Gift.

Marna scanned the words. "That is my chief hope as well. Your blood cousin also quilled that he is still making inquiries about the missing Merchant Naynarp, whom he hoped to make a Scholar. I still find it odd that she disappeared just before his Gift was restored." The former Queen fell silent a moment, considering again Favik's report about Naynarp, how his opinion about her was in direct opposition to Kermon's, as though they had met different people. Five years had passed, and it still troubled her. Then again, it had happened during the period when the Merchant Masters' Gift had been removed, which could account for Kermon's troubling fondness and trust of the strange woman.

"Well, dear Reader," she patted her companion's arm and grinned, "putting aside this talk of coin and travel for just a moment…" Marna stood, and Saralya did as well. "Come look at what was also just delivered to King's Halls." With her pale hands she reached to a nearby table and lifted the open scroll she had laid over the elaborately quilled document to conceal it from view. "The Naming announcement for Lord Radil's second child." She passed the crimson parchment to her fellow Scholar, whose bountiful smile conveyed her pleasure at the news.

"A girl. And what a lovely name." She read the gold lettering aloud:

Lord Radil and Lady Mayva, along with their son Lord Amril, welcome Lady Alayna, born and named on the Fourth Day, Seventh Month, 2921.

"Radil wrote apologizing for the two-month delay in sending the announcement; he was hoping to invent a new style of quilling to commemorate the birth." Marna chuckled.

Saralya replaced the document upon the table. "Oh my Lady." Her dark eyes turned to the former Queen's. "Seeing the date just makes me realize how much time has passed since Jinilya was born, since Jinil died. And since you and I first met…" The thought of adding up the years showed for an instant in her deep gaze. "That was thirty-five years ago."

A sudden sadness gripped Marna, and she squeezed her friend's arm. "Ah yes, we are no longer young." She looked at her hand. "But we still have time, and purpose."

"I hope that to The Powers, my Lady."

Dalich King leaned forward on the cushioned window seat and placed a gentle hand on his mother's shoulder. The sadness in his gaze and the aura of stillness about him served to enhance his handsome features. His long dark locks tinged by gray belied his thirty-three years, lending him the commanding but compassionate look of a King out of Legend.

His mother closed her eyes, shutting out his sympathetic expression, her Library chambers, the blue twilight outside. "Go on, say your news." Marna thought better of telling her son that they sat in the same spot where Favik, long ago, had comforted her upon delivering the news of her husband's death. The former Queen of Eskalind prepared herself for the worst as a myriad of horrible scenarios swirled through her mind. She barely heard her son's next utterance, which began with a sigh.

"Saril just received news about his mother." He paused and she opened her eyes to see his brow knit as he glanced to the window, a thin streak of gray hair perfectly framing his ear. An amethyst stud twinkled in the lobe. "I am very, very sorry to impart this to you, Mother, but The Powers have claimed her. I know how close you were to your Reader."

The Scholars' Mistress's breath caught for a moment, and she fought to use her reason to stay in the conversation. "How did it happen?"

"She left our borders and thus my protection." He withdrew his warm hand from her shoulder. "It seems she was journeying through Mavold, with the intention of sailing to Guerland. Saril had no knowledge she aimed to return to her mother's homeland ever again."

"I did."

His countenance changed to a look of surprise. "You did? But why was I not informed?" He seemed to catch himself. "Or Saril, at the very least?"

"Oh Dalich, must you truly trouble yourself with the comings and goings of the old women in your life?"

Her son pressed his long fingers against his smooth forehead and slumped back into the window seat's cushion. "I do not understand. Saril told me that finances were poor on their estate. His mother insisted on spending a great deal on building comfortable facilities to house the refugees seeking healing. She said they are crossing the Kaymif border in great numbers." The King shook his head slowly. "A journey to Guerland for a Lady alone by ship would be a great expense. She would require bodyguards and servants and—"

"I gave her the funds."

His gray eyes raised. "But why did you do that, Mother?"

"Saralya was my friend, and she wanted to go. Do you know how difficult she was to do anything for, to give anything to? She never wanted jewelry or cloth and her passion for rare old scrolls was well satisfied in her own vast library. Funding her trip was the least I could do. Oh Dalich, she wanted to see her blood cousin again. You recall him, from their ennobling ceremony? He is her elder by at least a decade, and she knew it might be the last time she saw him. Can you not understand that?"

"Of course, but where did you get the coin?"

Her jaw dropped. "I have *always* spent less than my allowances." Anger at his questioning rang in her ears, and she murmured, "I cannot say the same for other members of this family."

He sat straight. "My wife spends less than you think. Most of her cloth and adornments come as presents from the borderland rulers and their ambassadors."

"And my Scriptorium and Library make do with the scraps." Marna inhaled slowly, watching the cool glare in her son's eyes. How it reminded her of his father, when they had their rare, stupid arguments. "Dalich, ours is the most prosperous land in the world; there is no reason to be quarreling over this. The Powers provide for Eskalind most handsomely." She placed her hands on the embroidered pillows by her side.

The King flicked his manicured fingers on the onyx-studded closure of his belt. "You leave me in a difficult position. How am I to tell my Second *you* funded the journey on which his mother died?"

King's Mother gripped the pillows, a rough-edged fingernail snagging the fabric. "You make it sound as though her death were my fault!"

Dalich leapt to his feet as though they had decided to leave without him. "If Lady Saralya had not left our borders, she would still be alive, under my protection." Her son was nearly to the far door when he spun on his heels and all but spat, "You have no idea what a burden it is, Mother." He lowered his voice. "You who can come and go as you please, yet choose to remain here," he gestured to the room around them, "all of your days. It is not by *my* choice that I must linger in these Halls, within our borders, for the rest of my life. I make this sacrifice for the good of my people. What do you do with your days? Nothing."

"Silence your tongue!" She rose and approached him, her tone cool and low. "I am at constant work to protect and preserve our land, our people, our way of life. I," she pointed to her chest, "I speak with Those above us, my son. You understand me? I wish you had an ounce of the trust in me that my Reader did."

"Do not ask that of me." With that he yanked the door open, then yanked it closed again with a deafening boom.

Marna seethed, settling into the nearest chair. Then she slid her fingertips across her cheeks and clawed into her long hair, leaning forward to groan, "Oh, Saralya, why, why did I encourage you to go? My dear, beloved Reader…"

Lady Athla lowered the papyrus letter before her and closed her eyes. "Your brother Saril is not coming."

"Too many duties at court?" Jinilya rose to gaze out the window, her green eyes following the stone path from the seat of their estate to the road beyond, imagining its length stretching all the way to Dalich King's Halls. Then her thoughts turned toward the southern route from their house, along the way to Mavold, following Mother's last journey.

"Yes." Athla paused. "By The Powers, I hoped this letter would not come." She draped herself into a deep chestnut colored leather seat. "I never wanted this responsibility."

"What is Saril asking you to do?" She watched her saister's expression reflected in the window.

Athla looked away, her neatly proportioned face in profile against the dark brown of the chair. "Saril wants me to go through your mother's estate papers and her locked pyx, and deliver what I find to him." Marnil's wife shook her fawn-colored locks and dropped the letter to the carpet. Both were caramel colored, and the missive seemed to fade into the floor covering as though it had never existed. "May The Powers forgive me," Athla continued. "It still seems unreal that she is gone. Can Saril not just wait until he can journey here himself? He is the Acta Sua now. It is his duty, not mine."

Jinilya turned to face her saister. "But Athla, you are the eldest present in the house."

"Perhaps we could recall Marnil, home from maneuvers, and have him do it. I miss my dear husband so. It would be wonderful if he could come home again." She rubbed a hand over the tucked sleeves of her crimson blouse.

The younger Lady bit her tongue, not wanting to point out, again, that her brother Marnil was unlikely to respond well to a summons from his wife when no true crisis presented itself. She must give her saister something else to focus upon. Saralya's daughter softened her face into a sad expression. "Would it be helpful if I was with you when you went through the estate documents? I would like to be of some comfort, if I can."

"Oh, my young saister, I am sorry. Here I am blathering about my trepidation, and it is you who have lost your dear mother. I remember when my parents died, how sweet you were. You made me a ribbon wreath in my birth house's colors. Do you remember that?" Athla smiled sadly, and Jinilya nodded as she paced toward her brother's wife. "I still treasure it. The orange has faded slightly, but the blue looks as fresh as the day I received it." A tear slipped from her eyes as she raised herself from the chair and stood. "Yes, let us go through the documents together." Under her breath she whispered, "I will be brave," and the younger woman wondered what she meant. "But first I must see how Kaloft and his new tutor are faring. And the dressmaker is coming for a fitting. Perhaps after luncheon?"

Jinilya nodded her dark head, certain that this would be the first of many delays.

———

True to her saister's suspicions, Athla made excuses until Jinilya proposed that she alone would examine the documents, to spare her saister the odious chore, though she feared this might violate Saril's wishes and the rules of a noble house of Eskalind. Cornered, Athla sighed and at last agreed to help. Inside Lady Saralya's rooms, the pair unlocked the red-lacquered pyx to find it crammed with documents. Her saister inhaled slowly, blue eyes upon the mass. "Jinilya, you read faster than me; you look at all the loose parchments." She sorted them and handed the stack to her saister. "There are a few slit envelopes too. I will go through them. Tell me what the loose ones say."

Jinilya leafed through the two dozen or so sheets. "Recently paid bills, contracts of engagement for the current servants. Ah, at the bottom, here are more important documents. The ennobling papers from Dalock King…"

"We should place that in a frame for the main hall. Between the portrait of your parents, as founders of the house. I think that would look lovely. We will engage a framesmith, and if we want cloth for one of the inner frames, my dressmaker has fine scraps we could use, and that reminds me, we must commission a new portrait of Saril now that he is Acta Sua…"

Whether Athla's voice trailed into a murmur or Jinilya's attention faded against the onslaught of tangential shopping lists, the younger woman was uncertain. Thus she interrupted with, "Here is a note from your mother congratulating our house on Kaloft's birth—"

"Oh, do let me see that." Athla reached for the sheet. She read every word on the page, of blue ink darkened to almost black against the orange parchment, her eyes misting. "Mother's writing was quite lovely. How I hoped Kaloft would inherit her talent."

Meanwhile Saralya's daughter had completed her scan of the sheets and turned her eyes to the dead hearth of the fireplace. No one had shoveled it since her mother departed, and a heap of ashes lay within. She spied a few fragments of charcoal-shaded papyrus and wondered what had burned there.

Athla lowered her parent's note as Jinilya said softly, "The rest are copies of the inventories sent to the Records Keepers of the estate and furnishings, from the time of its granting to last year."

Her saister nodded and turned to the stack of slit envelopes, which she began perusing. "This one is odd." Athla held up a plain brown papyrus envelope, sealed with a messy blob of red wax.

"What is it?" Jinilya asked as her saister turned the object over.

"I thought it was opened, but it is not, and the seal is without a signet imprint. It is addressed to Marna, Queen of Eskalind. It must be old. But what is it doing in your mother's pyx?"

"Perhaps it was mislaid. May I look at it?" Jinilya reached a slender hand forward, and Athla laid it on her bare palm, then turned her blue eyes to the remaining stack of envelopes.

"You should open it, Jinilya. I am curious what it says."

"It is not for us to open if it is addressed to King's Mother."

"But it is old. Whatever it says can no longer be important."

"Our Lady Marna should decide that." Saralya's daughter peered hard at the quilling, the impression of a thought coming to her that the writer who had inscribed the direction did so at the behest of another person—her mother.

This was very strange. Clearly Mother did not want even her to know the contents. "Hmm, the seal is completely plain, not even the hint of an imprint. I think." She pulled the envelope close to her chest and bent her head, examining the smooth wax closely, and hoping to discern a word inside.

Athla sat back in her chair. "Truly, Jinilya? You act as though I would snatch it from your hand."

"What?" The younger Lady turned over the envelope. "But Saister, it does not look like Mother's script. And the papyrus is very rough, like a pauper would use. It is very curious."

"All the more reasons to just open it."

Jinilya stood, clutching the mysterious item, eyes on the door. "This must be delivered to our Lady at court. Then we can bring the other papers that Saril requests as well."

"A journey to court?" No better suggestion could sidetrack her saister.

"It will be a week or more before I can be ready. I must wait for my new dresses to be finished, and Kaloft must come with us, thus his tutors must come along. And ah, since it is King's Halls, I will order a new fancy gown and—"

"Then I will go on my own, Athla, with the light carriage, and meet you there when you arrive." Her saister opened her mouth, but Jinilya pressed on. "Think how pleased Saril will be that you sent me ahead to hand deliver the important documents he requested, sooner rather than later. I must pack." Jinilya quit the room in a swirl of her ruby-hued skirt, the envelope safe within her grasp.

Halfway up the Royals' Tower was the large circular room that served as King's Son's Nursery. Much differentiated this room from others throughout the world intended for the use of young children. First, its capacious size, which occupied the entire circumference of the tower, which at its top housed spacious quarters for both the Queen and the King. Second, the stones curving along the walls were windowless and pierced only by two doors, one opposite the other. These doors stood on a landing at the exact point midway up or midway down the stairs, depending on one's direction. Whilst the designated child no longer slept in this room, his mother enjoyed keeping it as a private play area for her beloved boy. The pair could often be found there.

Thus Marna huffed and puffed up the stairs to the landing, breathed a moment, then entered her grandson's candlelit playroom to find the Queen sitting on the other side of the round room, the glossy black candelabra at her side illuminating her needlework. By her side, her son stared at one of the candles. Marna approached, and the lad turned to her with an expression of relief, as though she offered a respite from some difficult circumstances.

"Hullo, Grandmother." He leaned away from his mother as though about to approach Marna, but his mother lowered her embroidery and embraced the lad.

"Oh my pet, I wish you were still a wee babe so I could cuddle you." Whilst there were three years to go before his tenth Naming Day, Namlich's form was indeed more akin to a youth of fourteen: large of feet and long in the leg as though his body grew from the earth up. Damina clasped her son on the cheeks, kissing his forehead. The straw-haired youngster then turned to Marna for a tight embrace, his strength nearly knocking the wind from her lungs.

"What a joyous greeting." Marna pulled away from the lad and patted his shoulder. Spying a leather-clad wooden ball resting nearby on the floor, she reached for it and lifted it up. It nearly slipped from her grasp, for it was much lighter than expected. "Here, Grandson, show us how you play with this."

King's Son accepted the sphere. Dashing to the other side of the carpeted room, he dropped the ball, which bounced poorly.

King's Mother leaned toward her son's wife. "Daighter, a quick word." Behind her, Namlich kicked the ball against the wall. "I just received notice that Lady Jinilya will arrive here tomorrow around noon."

"Oh, that is wonderful news! Athla too, yes?"

The thud of the ball pounded. Lady Marna drew closer to her daighter's ear. "Jinilya travels alone. Athla will follow later."

"Ah. Well, we have not seen Saril's sister and both her brothers all together in years. I am glad to hear she is coming to court." The Queen stood and retrieved her embroidery ring. "We must plan a grand welcoming and reunion with her brothers to cheer her. They all need cheering since their mother's death."

King's Mother smiled as best she could manage at this off-hand reminder of her dear friend's demise. "I see we follow the same thinking."

She stepped alongside her daughter as Namlich's foot propelled the ball against the wall again and again. "Like a drum!" he called. Marna hoped his enthusiasm would not lead to a drumming tutor.

"But Damina, we must consider Jinilya's nature. The young woman is shy, like her mother in this regard." Marna placed a light hand on the sable silk of her daighter's sleeve and spoke wistfully, trying not to grit her teeth over the echoing din. "Saralya was never one to enjoy public ceremony or attention. As Jinilya is alike to her mother in disposition, I can imagine at this delicate time, she is even more likely to wish for privacy. "

The Queen's voice rose with dismay, or perhaps to account for the volume of Namlich's play. "But we must do something special to observe her arrival."

"I am in full agreement. A private dinner of just our family and hers would be an intimate way to celebrate her visit to court. And to perhaps persuade her to stay for a long while."

"And if we can convince her that Athla and Kaloft should visit too, sooner than later, it would be perfect. I would love for Namlich to have his friend Kaloft here." She smiled at her son, who had grown tired of sending the ball such a short distance over and over again and just then kicked the dark orb in their direction. The round object sailed long in the high-raftered room, toward the two women, who ducked. It passed over their heads.

"Oops," squeaked the boy, eyes startled.

"King's Son," scolded his mother, "show some care."

"I will make the arrangements," Marna called as she bolted for the closest door.

A mere few hours later, the former Queen paced through the King's Library, relishing the quiet, industrious sounds of Apprentices shuffling by and the soft clank of scroll knobs in their carrying baskets. Approaching the long tables, she saw rows of Apprentices sitting, their violet cloaks draped over their chair backs to free their arms and hands to open and sort the stacks of healing request letters for Dalich King. Pausing, she admired their efficiency and dedication; all were dutifully intent on their work. King's Mother also wryly considered how her presence might intensify their industriousness. An

Apprentice walked by just then at a pace worthy of a solemn ceremony, the bright glow of the lit taper in her hands in stark contrast to the dark wax of its long shaft.

It seemed early for the candelabra to be lit, but she decided against scolding the young woman. From another aisle, the faint scent of smoke wafted to her nose, its scent putridly acrid. Rounding a corner, she spied the source of the foul smell, a burnt-edged scroll being shoved repeatedly into a candle's flame by her grandson.

"You foolish boy!" Marna cried as she rushed toward him, snatching the parchment scroll from his hand and grabbing him by the shoulder. A quick glance revealed that the scroll was not alight. "Why were you—"

"No!" Namlich yelled, jerking away and shaking his blond head, tears streaking his face. "I was trying—"

"You," Marna raised her eyebrows, "are a foolish boy to be doing this. Henceforth, you are forbidden from my Library."

The child puffed his cheeks in a caricature of rage, then turned and ran away shouting, "Mama! Make her stop!"

"Would that his mind grew at the same rate as his body," King's Mother muttered as she examined the scroll. "I know of no herbcraft for that."

A crowd of Apprentices had gathered, and one scooted forward with a pail of sand, brown eyes bright with concern under thin eyebrows. "May I assist, my Lady?" he asked.

"Yes." She plunged the scroll into the sand. "Let it sit a bit to be certain it is not burning, then see that this scroll attended to by Scriptor Vinil." The Scholars' Mistress marched away to report the incident to her daighter.

Proving that punctuality was a family trait, Lady Jinilya's light coach approached King's Halls moments before noon that next day. Inside, the seventeen-year-old closed her eyes and gripped the window tightly, hoping to The Powers that Favik might be there and see her finally as more than a child. Ever since she could remember, he had been in her thoughts, though he was old enough to be her father. But she knew her father only through the memories of others: wise, intelligent, and, Mother always added, handsome. Favik was all of that, with a gentleness about him too.

Someone called a hello to the driver, and she peered from the window, surprised by the changes in the scenery since her last visit. Half the structure retained its incohesive mishmash of architectural styles and textures, with the only unifying element the charcoal-shaded paint that toned the mass. But Dalich King's building schemes had yielded a pleasing unifying form to the other half of his Halls. New crenellated rooflines and towers dotted the edifices. Workers clattered atop the facade of a timber-sheathed section, setting up scaffolding for the next area to be updated to their Lord's grand plans.

The glossy chestnut coach entered the main courtyard, and the young Lady clutched her wine-colored gown with smooth hands, noting how her fingers and the folds in the fabric made a repeating *M* shape. Then she spied King's Mother standing alone, still as a statue, her face alabaster against the jet of her smock. The pair made eye contact and did not break their gaze until they were in each other's firm embrace.

"Dearest Jinilya. How grateful I am to see you again."

"And I you, my Lady. I thank you for coming to greet me."

"Let me look at you." They separated, and the elder woman surveyed the younger, a fond smile upon her lips. "Ah, you are the embodiment of my beloved husband's reign. I miss the brown and the red, but Dalich is a good King and I am a proud King's Mother." Her kind gray eyes misted. "How I feel the great loss of your Lady mother. She was my friend, my confidant, and the person closest to me after Dalock died."

Jinilya could not help but look away. "It has been hard to bear." They embraced again for a long while, and she fought tears, warm in the cozy embrace of a beloved person. Somehow she felt more at home here than at her house, and she silently thanked The Powers for the peaceful feeling that enveloped her.

"Now, dear, let us get you settled. I will see that a Records Keeper comes to your quarters to record your arrival." King's Mother turned to call two servants. "Bring Lady Jinilya's baggage to her house's quarters." As she spoke, four young, tan army men rode into the courtyard, their horses dripping sweat. The young woman strained to read their regiment insignias as one called to the others, "Ha! Outdone by the Havadran. We Eskalinders must watch our backs."

All the men laughed except the sole blond one, who turned his head toward Jinilya as though her voice called him. He locked eyes on her, and she nearly exclaimed at the intensity of his gaze, a light gray against a tan face framed with fair locks.

"Is that a member of the House of Jinil, Dalock King's Friend?" the man who had spoken before called.

She broke her gaze with the other. "It is," Lady Jinilya responded, holding her head high, still craning to decipher their emblems as the men jostled and dismounted their horses.

The inquisitive man approached, smoothing his deep brown hair with a black glove. His black tunic was trimmed with purple, marking him as a Sergeant. "I thought I recognized the colors. We are of the Sixth Company, under the command of Captain Marnil, of your house?"

"He is my brother. I am Lady Jinilya."

"Fair Lady Jinilya." The man dipped his head as the three others congregated alongside him. Above their hearts she could now see the lilac threads stitched in the shape of a six. "I am Sergeant Tarnil, and these are my men, Soldiers Sanil and Gafnil"—the two other dark-haired men bowed—"and Anish of Havadra, the oldest youth to earn his sword ever. Ha ha!" The blond Soldier stepped forward, and his eyes were even more striking at close range, for the irises were not merely gray, but encircled with a border of dark blue. He lowered his eyes and forehead in deference to her, and for a moment she forgot to breathe.

"Ahem," said a voice by her side. She turned to find Lady Marna, lips set in a straight line, glaring at the young men. "You start a tale, you will finish it, Sergeant Tarnil."

The Sergeant blinked frantically. "My Lady King's Mother, your pardon."

"I am waiting. Do elucidate, young man." She narrowed her gaze at the talkative one.

Tarnil stammered, "My Lady, I am not certain what you are asking."

The former Queen raised an eyebrow, and the man looked to the Havadran, who said smoothly to his commanding officer, "Elucidate means to explain, Sergeant."

"Yes. Of course. You explain to the Lady, Anish. It is your tale, after all." Tarnil stepped aside, King's Mother's eyes still hard upon him.

"My Ladies," his voice was mellow but insistent. "Sergeant Tarnil refers to my recent Sword Earning. With all respect, in the country of my birth, a youth is not a man until he reaches his twentieth year and earns his sword in fatal combat."

The young Lady could not help but blurt, "You fought a man to the death to earn your sword?"

He looked at her, sad and distant though they stood close enough to touch. "Yes. Though now that it is over, I am not proud of it."

King's Mother interrupted, "That is because it was completely unnecessary. You are a citizen of Eskalind, aye?" She directed her gaze to the top of his head, as though his face were unworthy of her acknowledgment.

"Yes, my Lady. I earned citizenship by serving five years and still continue in my Lord King's service." His eyes subtly roamed the elder Lady's face, studying her.

"Then you should have had a normal Sword Earning combat like other youths during peacetime." The former Queen had already turned to Sergeant Tarnil. "Our Ambassadors do not work for concord between the borderlands only to have our young males kill each other to prove they are men."

Jinilya was in accord with her Lady's thinking. "But where did this happen and how?"

Anish replied, "We just returned from Amkland, where I earned my sword, thanks to Captain Marnil."

"My brother had a hand in this?" Her green eyes darted to her Lady, who folded her arms before her as though considering a punishment for a troublesome Apprentice.

"Come, Jinilya, enough of this. Marnil is here, and we will hear the full, no doubt sordid tale from him at dinner tonight. Jinil's son will doubtlessly suffer my disapproval for allowing this." She turned and strode toward an arched doorway lined with dark stones.

"I'm sorry to trouble you, my Lady." The Havadran placed a hand to his heart, the flesh below his fingers a shocking mass of curdled scars. He bowed.

She felt an unfamiliar rush of light-headedness, revulsion, and something else she could not name. Uncertain what to say, she resorted to, "I thank you," and dashed after King's Mother.

Sergeant Tarnil appraised his companion. "You upset the young Lady, Anish."

"That was not my intention." The Soldier hardened his gaze on his commanding officer. "But I spoke truth."

"A truthful Havadran. What is the world coming to?" Tarnil tossed his head with a grin at his other men, who chuckled. Gafnil shook his head. "Well, men, to the stables and then to the Records Keepers to register our arrival." In pairs, the foursome led their horses to the stables, hooves clattering on the cobblestones.

The blond Soldier joked, "Do elucidate, sir."

"Ha! You had me with that. Elucidate. Well, The Powers know I have learned a new word and will never forget it." Tarnil's horse paused, and he shook the reins just as a lanky youth sped by them at a gangling gait, his head flopping from side to side as he called, "Pretty Lady!" in a singsong voice befitting a very young child. He passed the quartet, his clothing a blur of black under his fair head, bounding in the same direction the Ladies had departed. The refrain of "Pretty Lady! I am going to see Pretty Lady!" decrescendoed in his wake.

Anish's horse tossed its head as though annoyed by a fly, and the Soldier steadied the animal with a gentle stroke of its gray mane. "What, who was that? The jester?"

"Ah," said Tarnil, his tone as serious as though reviewing his rank before their Captain's inspection. "I forgot this is your first visit to King's Halls." He turned his face to the broad-beamed stable as they approached the entrance. Straw spilled from the doorway, and a young lad paused with his broom to let them pass. "That was King's Son."

"*The* King's Son?"

His Sergeant did not reply, but turned to the lad with the broom. "Where shall we stable our mounts?"

"On the far end, Sergeant, sir." The boy pointed. "There are at least four open stalls there."

"Thank you," Tarnil replied. He leaned close to Anish. "That stable boy I just spoke with?"

"Yes?"

"He is how old, would you guess?"

"Nine, ten."

"And what age would you guess our young Lord to be?"

"I could barely see his face…" Tarnil's features sharpened to a look of keen scrutiny befitting an officer. "Well, sir, I would guess that given his height, he would qualify to be a Stander."

"I believe he is seven." The Sergeant led his mount into an open stall whilst Anish paused in his tracks.

"Hey!" Gafnil cried from behind, as he nearly plowed into the suddenly path-blocking form of the blond Soldier.

"Sorry," called the new man. He steered his horse to a vacant stall, worrying over his new country's future should that strange child ever claim rulership.

———

Steps from the entranceway to the House of Jinil's chambers, King's Son caught up with Marna and Jinilya. After a few moments of excitement and antics, the elder Lady moved to extract the womenfolk. As her grandson clung to Jinilya's arm, cooing, she fussed, "Namlich, do stop. Enough with the greetings and embracing."

"But pretty Lady is back." He nestled the top of his head against the red fabric draping the young woman's bosom, leaning against her as though his head were anchored to her chest, and gazed up at her with a fond light in his gray eyes.

Jinilya, for her part, stood rigid against the continuing barrage of affection. A stiff smile on her face, Saralya's daughter reached to steady the lad's uncomfortable position, stuttering, "My, you have grown in strength, my Lord. You lean heavy."

Marna folded her arms over the inky dark cloth of her smock. "Grandson, do something useful; go find your Mother and let her know Lady Jinilya has arrived."

Namlich elevated himself from what had become an awkward backbend to his full height, nearly as tall as the object of his affection, and bounced away along the corridor, shouting, "Mama! Pretty Lady is here!" and sounding for all the world convinced that the volume of his outburst would draw her to him. His voice echoed at a deafening pitch across the stones.

"Well," the former Queen breathed as the ringing in her ears subsided, "that will occupy his attention for some time. I am sorry, my dear. You must want to rest after your journey and greet your brothers. I see the servants have stowed your bags in your family's quarters." She nodded in thanks to the two men as they exited the doorway. The statue-faced Guard outside the entrance maintained an air of unflappable composure befitting his station.

The young woman murmured quietly, "I thank you, my Lady. I do want to rest and see my brothers, but I had hoped you and I might speak in private as soon as possible."

"Certainly, my dear. Come, let us go to my Library chamber." King's Mother led her in the opposite direction from where the boy had disappeared. "My grandson will not follow us there; he is forbidden it."

"Forbidden, my Lady?"

"As well he should be." Her cheeks flushed as she continued at a brisk pace, hoping to outpace any changes in Namlich's direction. "Yesterday, I caught him sticking a scroll in a lit candle. A beautiful, irreplaceable scroll. There was quite a fuss, and Damina became incensed with me."

Given her young companion's suddenly stricken expression, Marna thought it best to refrain from further discussing familial discord. Leading her young friend by the arm, they strolled to their destination. "But tonight your family and the *adult* members of mine will dine in the Queen's chamber. I have prepared my roast chicken."

"Oh, how wonderful—might Favik be here at King's Halls too?"

Nodding to a passing Library Apprentice, Marna replied, "No, dear, he is away at Lord Radil's estate, in the north."

A knot of gatherers, including the ambassador from Eastlant, with blue strips of velvet tied into her long black hair, blocked the passage ahead but made way for them, bowing to King's Mother as she passed. Steps later they arrived in the former Queen's spacious study. Closing the door behind them, the Scholars' Mistress turned to face Jinilya, who held in her hands a plain papyrus envelope with two dark seals upon it. Marna wondered where the young Lady had stowed it, for its abrupt appearance was a trick worthy of a Scholar.

"My Lady, this is what I wished to speak to you about. I found this in my mother's private papers, addressed to you." The hesitancy in her tone hinted that there was more, but she remained silent as she placed the note in Marna's hand.

King's Mother read the direction. "Addressed to me as Dalock's Queen?" She sat and gestured for Saralya's daughter to sit across from her. "That was a long time ago."

"But the quilling, my Lady, it does not look like my mother's hand. Though I sense it was written … for her."

It was an odd statement, and all Marna could conjure was, "Mmm." She hoped that sounded noncommittal, for indeed she recognized the style as close to her dear Reader's hidden hand, used only for the Scholars' missives. Roving her eyes over the plain seals, she split them asunder, inhaled, and read silently.

My Dearest Lady,
It is strange to write of this matter, for what I write I hope to say
in person one day.

"Oh," Marna breathed. Jinilya leaned forward slightly. "No, I am all right." Despite the weakness creeping into her knees, she rose and paced to the window to read the rest of the single sheet, with her back toward her companion.

I swear to The Powers that my daughter possesses a unique talent. She can read any written script, even utter gibberish, as long as it was written with clear intent. I tested her with all manner of quilling and content suitable for a child her age, and she told me the meaning of each with merely a glance. I further examined her by creating missals of nonsensical characters, and still, if I had quilled them with a firm message in mind, she could discover and reproduce that message in words. Thus, I asked a servant to quill the direction on this note.

My Lady, her Gift will be useful to our cause, yet as her mother, I do not wish to expose her to any text that may be traumatic or harmful to her delicate young mind. She has found scrolls I would have hid from her eyes, and torturous nightmares are the aftermath. I now keep those volumes under lock and key. May The Powers reveal to me when she has the strength and maturity of mind to weather this distress, but if They claim me before then, I trust that They will show you when the time is right. I am entrusting no one else with this knowledge, not even any member of my family.

With grateful affection,

Your Lady

Behind her Jinilya asked, "May I ask what it says, my Lady?"

Marna lowered the letter, folding the writing from view. She faced the young woman. "Jinilya, when did you first learn to read?"

She fumbled for words, glancing out the window as she spoke. "I … it seems I always knew how, but that must be because Mother taught me from a very early age." Saralya's daughter smiled. "I remember crawling over the bars of my barrier bed once to retrieve a soft toy in the shape of the letter *J* because I wanted it next to the letter blocks that spelled the rest of my name. I must have been younger than two, as when I recounted this memory years later, Mother insisted that I did not use that barrier bed after my second Naming Day."

She looked to the former Queen, who said gently, "Do you recall reading anything unsettling when you were quite young?"

"Um, yes." She paused, her front teeth creeping cautiously over her bottom lip. "I was not certain I really read it, yet I must have. It seemed like I was in a horrible Legend, at a terrible battle with streams of bl—" She stopped and swallowed. "For a long time after, I could not sleep in peace, until Mother quilled the King to heal me." Her green gaze fell to the carpets. "Does the note say something about that? Who wrote it?"

"I am sorry, dear. Here, come." Placing her free hand lightly on the young Lady's back, Marna led her to a window seat and the pair sat. Gazing again at the folded note, the Scholars' Mistress continued, "I do recognize this as your mother's hand. It is in the style she used when we wished to communicate most privately."

"Oh." This seemed to surprise her.

"In this note, Saralya did indeed write of the incident of which you speak."

"But my Lady, why would Mother write you, in a different hand, in a sealed note? Why not tell you in person?"

The former Queen folded the papyrus again. "She wanted me to know about it, eventually. But she was uncertain when to discuss it." Marna placed the note into its envelope. "Jinilya, I would be your protector, would look after you as I would my own daughter, had I ever borne one. Your mother entrusted you and your care to me." She smiled steadily at the young woman, whose features tightened. "Of course, you are of age, a full woman who can make her own decisions. But when we are young, there are times we may look to our elders for wisdom or guidance. I know you have your brothers, and your saister, but there may be times you desire close-by female companionship and perspective. I would be this person for you, if you wish."

"I, I thank you, my Lady. You are most kind." Tears threatened to spill from the young woman's eyes, and Marna caught her in a tight embrace.

"Dear girl, it will be all right."

After a few sniffles, Saralya's daughter whispered, "I think I am just … tired."

Releasing her, Marna offered, "Rest here if you wish; the pillows are comfortable to recline upon. Now I must attend to some business in the Library. Stay as long as you desire." She smoothed a hand over the young woman's brown cheek and, clutching the letter in her other hand, rose for the door.

Chapter Forty-Six—By the Queen's Request

As promised, that evening found the adults of the royal family and the grown children of Jinil and Saralya dining in the Queen's Quarters. The chicken, bread, and sauces devoured, some wine drunk, King's Mother turned to Captain Marnil, holding him in her gray gaze. "One of your Soldiers shared an outlandish tale with me today," King's Mother began, "about his earning his sword in the Havadran manner, and with your permission."

"Indeed."

Lady Damina asked, "What is the Havadran manner of earning a sword?"

"Killing a man," Marnil answered, in the matter-of-fact tone in which he dispatched orders. The Queen blanched.

His brother said, "That is indeed outlandish."

"Truly?" King's Wife asked, eyes keen upon her husband.

"Indeed," the Captain replied. He could feel his Lord's gaze on him, intent and curious.

King's Mother began. "To The Powers, I cannot comprehend why you would allow such a thing." He opened his mouth to reply, but the former Queen's pale cheeks pinked. "I will speak!" She cut her eyes to her son as though addressing him. "Our Ambassadors work mightily to ensure the outer peace." Now gazing to Jinil's older son, "Your brother and my family labor in King's Halls to do the same. Diplomats from the borderlands and outerlands come to King's Halls to meet and negotiate and to admire our peaceful ways." Her attention returned to Marnil. "What you have done goes against our customs."

His sister looked at her plate.

"My Lady, it grieved me to do so, but I felt I must allow it for a number of reasons."

"Then set them forth." King's Mother drew her napkin across her mouth as though a lingering crumb offended her.

Marnil lay a hand palm up upon the table, the signet on his Lord's ring flat against the table linen. "As Eskalinders, we are taught from a young age to honor the customs of those beyond our borders."

"This is a case where reason begs to differ."

"Please," and his voice rose to a tone he did not wish to use with the beloved womenfolk in his life. Calming himself, he continued. "I can vouch for the Soldier in question. Anish is twenty and Havadran born. He served five years for Eskalind citizenship. When he turned sixteen, there was no likelihood of battle, as there has not been for these many years—"

"Thank The Powers," Damina breathed, with a quick glance to her husband. King's Mother's expression bordered on a smirk.

Marnil leaned forward. "But Anish asked to not participate in the Sword Earning trials that season. Or the next, or the following. Over the years, all his peers became men, whilst he stayed a Stander."

"Fine. Then he stays a Stander till he is eighty."

The Captain of the Sixth Company held his Lady King's Mother's eyes. "It showed me conviction, and dedication to his birth land's customs. I had to respect that."

"Even though it meant killing another?"

"Let me explain, my Lady. This young man serves as my undersecretary, thus I am better acquainted with his character than most under my command." Marnil leaned back, tugging his purple Captain's tunic to smooth out a wrinkle. "We are freshly returned from a diplomatic mission in Amkland, where the ideal situation presented itself. A prisoner, after a just trial, was condemned to death for his odious crime." He considered saying more about the heinous Amklander, but continued, "The offender was offered a chance to live out his sentence in an Eskalind prison were he to prevail in single combat against Stander Anish. He accepted. Anish defeated him. Amklander justice was served, Havadran custom honored, and Eskalind gains a solid Soldier." He glanced at the other Ladies. "After that match, there is no doubt in my mind that Anish can defend his country, if he is called upon to do so."

"And your armyfolk witnessed this blood sport?"

"Indeed. Which brings me to my next point." Nodding to Saril and the King, who had studiously leaned away from King's Mother, the Captain continued, "Many years have passed since any companies of Eskalind's army faced battle."

"*That* is a good thing," King's Mother said. Her son glared at her, then looked to his goblet, nodding, his dark eyebrows lowered slightly.

"Very much agreed, my Lady," continued Marnil. "But it also means that the people under my command, who are trained to defend and to fight, have not fought, have not defended."

"They have no doubt excellent training under your command." Her tone bordered on a question.

"Mother," muttered the King.

"Yes, my Lady, but training is no substitute for actual battle. No substitute for killing, which is what battle is." Inclining his head to the Queen and his sister. "Your pardon, Ladies, but that is the sad truth, and thanks to Anish's Sword Earning, my Soldiers have now seen killing firsthand. An experience they are not likely to forget. There is nothing glorious in it, despite what the Loremasters may tell us."

His dear sister spoke, her innocent eyes still cast to her crumb-flecked plate. "The young man told me that afterward, he was not proud of what he had done."

Saril stiffened slightly. "*You* spoke with this Havadran degenerate?"

Something sparked in Jinilya, and her green gaze shone alike to their father's when anger kindled. "Is he not a citizen of Eskalind?"

"Havadran-born degenerate then," Saril countered, swirling his wine goblet with a nonchalance that indicated it did not bother him to concede such a trifling point.

"King's Second and I are in accord in our thinking." King's Mother placed her elbows on the table and her hands flat upon its surface, the dark ink stains on her first finger blending against the sable-shaded tablecloth so that her finger looked oddly truncated.

"Well," began Damina Queen, running a fingertip over the onyx beads threading her necklace, her violet gaze darting from her husband to her maither. "I want to meet this young man."

"To share your disapproval?" Lady Marna queried.

"To decide for myself about this incident." There was a hint of defiance in her voice. Her husband raised his eyebrows, and their eyes locked for moment.

"I do not think it requires much deciding," huffed King's Mother, though the Captain felt that her continued harping on the point might turn others in his favor. An odd silence held the room as the royal pair discussed the point in their silent mind talk. Jinilya, less familiar with this phenomenon then the others, looked to Marnil questioningly, and he shook his head slightly to avert any questions that might exit her mouth.

———

The conversation the group could not hear went as follows.

The Queen: "*I want to find out more about this incident and the young man.*"

"*If you wish, but Marnil is my Captain, and I trust his judgment and reasoning, though this is vastly unusual. Anything that follows is not an investigation. I do not wish to undermine his authority.*"

"*Yes, but Dalich, do you not think it curious that a sixteen-year-old boy would decline to earn his sword? That he waited till he was twenty? It shows serious dedication. Surely he must have been tempted to jump into bed with someone during those years."*

"Well, perhaps he did not come across your sister Pamina's path."

"Ha! Perhaps he is too ugly even for her." The Queen's cheeks pinked. *"Or he prefers men, like Saril."*

His wife shrugged. *"Even if he does, by our laws he must wait till he has earned his sword."*

"Indeed. Speak with him if you like, my heart. Have Yamina and Jinilya present, so it does not appear to be a private meeting, but is still amongst our most trusted circle. Saril's sister seems curiously shy about the young Soldier."

"I agree. I think she may fancy him, which is all the more reason to plumb his character. I would see her with a good and gentle man if The Powers allot me any sway in these matters."

———

Saril cleared his throat, simultaneous to the eldest Lady in the room heaving a sigh. Damina laughed and stretched her arms before her, the amethyst jewels on her wrist sparkling in the candlelight. "Marnil, you said you vouch for Soldier Anish?"

"Fully."

"Then I will require no Guards. My young Lady, will you introduce me to Soldier Anish?"

"Why her?" King's Mother posed.

"Oh Maither. Because she has spoken with him before, and he is a member of her brother's company." The Queen's rosy lips parted in smile. "And, I doubt he would refuse her." Saril's jaw twitched ever so slightly. Marnil recognized that as a struggle to hold his tongue, an action Saril had little cause for as King's Second. It was the Captain's turn to smile.

Jinilya's voice was soft, diffident. "Yes, my Lady."

The next morning, the youngest Lady of the House of Jinil stood speechless near the formally attired Soldier Anish. They were facing the same direction, though another person or even two could easily fit between them. To an onlooker, it would seem each had staked a fainthearted claim to their separate sides of the corridor. Jinilya kept her eyes upon the passageway, silently hoping to The Powers that her Queen would arrive swiftly at this, their designated meeting spot. Or that the blond man would speak. Or that she could think of two words to say.

She cut her eyes quickly to his hands. One still clutched the note she had sent to summon him, the other rested on the bejeweled scabbard of his long knife. Had he turned to face her, he would have seen the surprise writ on her features at spying such a rich weapon on a non-noble Soldier's hip. Well, here was something to inquire about. "I have never seen a long knife like yours, Soldier Anish."

"It is a product of Havadra, my Lady." He seemed finished with the tale.

She glanced to the ground, then decided to press on. "It is very lovely. How did you come by it?"

"It was a present from a family member to me, a long time ago."

That begged more questions, but a swish sounded nearby as the Queen rounded a corner, the scent of Lamorda perfuming the air and the Queen's sister Yamina by her side. The Lady of Eskalind wore a gown of pale lilac silk, bedecked with tiny, glossy black beads in patterns of interlocking *D*'s for Damina Queen and Dalich King. Jinilya recognized the fabric and its adornment, for the women of her house months ago had received a trunk of this cloth and others, as well as the same beads, as a present from their Queen. Only Athla had transformed the bolts into new gowns to be worn at King's Halls, in her case employing the small orbs into quill-shaped patterns. Saralya's daughter felt very aware of her unembellished crimson and brown attire. Perhaps she should spend more time with the dressmakers.

"Jinilya." The Queen beckoned to the younger woman with a pale, elegant hand, a ring set with a glistening purple jewel entwined about her middle finger. "Introduce me to this young man."

Jinilya complied, studying the graceful formality of the Soldier's bow to the royal Lady. Damina Queen led him to a cushioned window seat, and the pair sat upon the sable-shaded cushions whilst Yamina and Jinilya watched, elbow to elbow. A rapid pitter-pat echoed in the corridor, and a Page approached the Queen's sister, brown eyes alight with worry. The lad reported that Yamina's younger daughter had scraped her knee and was calling for her mother. Yamina rushed away to attend to her child, leaving Jinilya to watch as Anish unbelted his long knife's scabbard. For a moment she thought he was granting it to the dark-haired Queen, but the royal Lady regarded it with the curious eyes of one investigating an unusual specimen, rather than receiving a gift. Green stones of a cool hue glimmered on the hilt as she rotated the scabbard.

Tromping feet further along the corridor drowned their quiet speech, but Jinilya could admire the handsome Havadran-born Soldier looking serious and respectful. At last the Queen retuned the weapon to his care, calling to her, "Come, I must make advantage of your Guerish heritage. Help me with a custom lesson. I wish to practice a traditional Guerish introduction. I shall properly introduce you and Anish here for the first time."

"But my Lady, we have already been introduced."

The Queen rose, a hint of a smile in her violet eyes. Anish stood as well, belting his long knife. "Humor me. Now this part I am familiar with." She reached for the Soldier's wrist and Jinilya's, bringing their hands together. His fingers had a slight roughness about the edges, and she could feel the dense scars atop his hand. "Now, who is introduced to whom?"

The young Lady gazed at her Queen's mouth, not wanting to make eye contact. "The person of higher rank to the person of lower rank."

"Ah, I must decide. I see there is risk for the introducer in this endeavor." She seemed to find this greatly amusing. "Thank The Powers it is clear in this case. Lovely Lady Jinilya, this is Soldier Anish." King's Wife pulled her hand away and regarded the pair.

"Lady Jinilya, a pleasure," the young man stated, and she looked to him to find his eyes warm upon hers. Again she found herself unable to speak, and without meaning to she squeezed his hand, then dropped it in embarrassment.

"I thank you for engaging in this folly with me," stated their Lady, all but grinning. "Now, Jinilya, Anish tells me he has never visited the Scriptorium. Would you be so kind as to give him direction and a tour?"

Somehow the words came. "Certainly, my Lady. Oh, your pardon, your sister left to attend to her youngest girl, who hurt herself."

"Ah." The Lady of Eskalind stood still, her eyes clear and intent upon nothing the younger people could see. After a moment she said, "She is better now." The royal smiled and gestured to them like a mother shooing children out to play.

"Would you accompany me to the Scriptorium, Soldier Anish?" Jinilya said politely. He agreed, and they bowed to Damina Queen to make their leave. The pair walked along the stone passageway and after rounding a corner, he asked her quietly, "My Lady, do you know what happened back there when the Queen said 'She is better now'?"

"I think so. She and her husband can speak with one another in thought. My guess is that she asked him to heal her niece."

The former Havadran did not reply. After a moment he said, "When I first learned Eskalind 's Legends, I never thought I would witness the royals' Gifts in person."

"If you stay at King's Halls, you may see it again."

"Then I have many reasons to hope my rank is stationed here for a long time."

A smile slipped onto her lips. "This way." Jinilya gestured for them to turn. "It is a very pleasant approach through this garden." They passed through an open door into the sunlight, squinting in the brightness. Even in this eleventh month of the year, four-petaled King's Flowers splayed their crimson centers and white blooms to the sun, their spiky, leafless red vines trailing alongside the stone path, a hazard for her silk slippers. As they walked, she stepped closer to Anish to avoid the thorns, conscious of the closeness of the black sleeve of his fine uniform.

He gestured to the vine with his other arm. "I have seen these flowers at every borderwall where I have been stationed, but nowhere else in Eskalind until now."

"Have you been stationed by Kaymif?"

"No."

"Well, King's Flowers grow along the borderwall with Kaymif too, on my estate. My saister tried to plant their seeds in the garden at our seat, which is farther from the border, but they would not grow." The path meandered toward an unoccupied bench, and she was tempted to invite him to sit, as a myriad of things to converse about suddenly flooded her mind. But ahead she saw people bowing. Wondering if the King was passing by, and she touched Anish's arm to stay him. The personage generating the respectful gestures was none other than her eldest brother, Saril, clad in a long, formal purple tunic and walking with the red-faced Amkland ambassador, who wore a densely dot-patterned shirt draped open to his navel. The Amklander's sprawling, fluffy beard concealed most of his chest, but not the clink of the many necklaces and pendants of Amkish gold beneath it.

Behind him, his pale female attendant trailed at a measured pace, her hair a mass of a tiny golden-orange braids styled in clusters and bound with shiny yellow metal ornaments. The trio approached, and the blond Soldier by her side halted, eyes lowered as he tucked his free elbow to his side, flexing his wrist, palm outward, to salute his commander. Jinilya dipped her chin to the borderlanders and her brother, her hand still upon the Soldier's arm. Saril's gaze cut between her and her companion, lingering on Anish with distasteful recognition.

"Sister."

The word sounded like a claim and a warning.

Then King's Second and the Amklanders passed the pair. Fighting a shrug, Jinilya placed her hands together, breathing to her companion, "My, that was unpleasant." He said nothing, though there was a withdrawn stiffness in his posture as though he fought the urge to cower. By The Powers, Saril did not need to be that intimidating. She was of age and could converse with whomever she chose. Spying her destination ahead, she spoke. "The Scriptorium is just inside that passageway, there." As she led him toward the open door, Anish paused.

"I can smell the ink."

The expression of sudden delight on his face warmed her chest, and the dark-haired woman grinned. "Not much farther." The large wooden doors stood flung wide on their metal hinges, and the two entered the broad room. Filling the cavernous space were rows of tables, a pair of tabletop lecterns atop each. On a platform overlooking the desks was the Chief Scriptor's station, though she was not in her seat at this moment. In fact, only one scribing station in the entire room was occupied. A lanky man with thin lips and broad, dark eyes glanced to them, a blank parchment resting before him. An array of stoppered ink pots and quill cutters bordered his station with the precision of an army unit drilling before the King.

He called as they approached, "Are you Lady Saralya's daughter?"

"Yes, I am Lady Jinilya."

He inclined his thin locks toward her, then raised his head. "My Lady, I see both of your parents in you. My sorrow for your loss."

"I thank you, Scriptor—?"

"I am Vinil. My specialty is restoration and repair of texts, though of late I have begun quilling original designs." He swept a hand at his station. "I have been a Scriptor here since Marna Queen rebuilt the Scriptorium after the windstorm and fires of 2904. I attended the ennobling ceremony for your house, when you were a wee babe. How time flies." She smiled as he squinted and asked, "And who is this young Soldier who studies my inks so closely?"

Jinilya introduced them, and Anish shook Vinil's hand with vigor, asking, "Scriptor, some of your colors, I have never seen such shades before. And that red there, does it contain ochre?" He pointed to the third pot in the row, which exhibited a powdery yellowish-red crust of dried ink about its spout.

The Scriptor nodded. "Indeed, but a type only known to come from the far southern regions."

"From Ofsha?"

"Indeed. You are schooled in inks or copying work?"

"Mainly copying and drawing. But it has been many years since I did either for, er, coin."

"Both copying and drawing? And you are so young."

"I am twenty."

"My. Tell me, what do you think of this?" Vinil handed the Soldier a metal knife with a thick blade.

"The shape is right for a—but the heft—this cannot be a quill cutter?"

The Scriptor raised a finger, eager to make his point. "But it is. Before you question it, study the blade closely."

Anish peered at the knife, turning it slowly in the light. "I see an odd pattern. Was there powder in the metal, when it was forged?"

"Why, yes. A hard stone powder, my own invention, and wait till you see how clean it cuts the shaft." The elder man reached for a canister of ebony-shaded quills.

And thus began a very very long conversation.

At first Jinilya found their exchange interesting, but after the men discussed rare ink materials, quill cutters of new and old invention, and materials for smoothing raw parchment, they delved into the esoterica of the hardness of graphite best used for initial tracings, which varied depending on whether one quilled upon parchment or papyrus, while vellum was another discourse altogether, which Vinil promised to visit in depth and offer his full opinion upon. The Lady found her attention, and feet, wandering. Entering the passageway outside the Scriptorium, she heard distant laughter traveling from one side of the corridor, while on the opposite side stood young King's

Son alone, staring intently at a lit candle in a wall niche. She paused, holding her breath, and stepped backward to hide in the Scriptorium. But something in his gaze kindled her attention. She stepped forward.

"Is it speaking to you?" she asked.

For once the boy ignored her, gray eyes intent upon the flame as if it imparted a message of great import or promised the fruition of his fondest wish. A cold fear crept into Jinilya's being. "King's Son?" He did not respond. The young Lady reached into the burning wick and painlessly pinched the flame dead.

The boy blinked, turning to face her as though noticing her for the first time. "Was it speaking to you, my Lord?" she whispered. It had been years since a voice had come to her in the fire, and she feared that voice had transferred its malicious intent to King's Son.

He nodded, eyes wet with impending tears.

"Do not listen to it," she counseled, lowering her chin slightly to face the lanky lad at eye level.

He was quivering, but held her gaze. "It, it tells me things, to do things I do not want to do. Once I tried to put it out, to make her stop."

"Try not to listen, my Lord. It speaks untruths."

"You hear it too?"

Jinilya nodded, wondering to The Powers why they shared this affliction and how she might help him.

King's Son reached for her hand. "Did it hurt, when you touched it?"

"No, fire never hurts me." She allowed him to examine her fingers, turning them over.

"When I touched it once, it hurt." The boy squeezed her hand, hard.

"Aw, that hurts." She pulled her hand away.

He looked up at her. "Please, give it back."

She did not want to, but he was King's Son and thus her Lord. Yet he was also a child, despite his size, who had just crushed her delicate fingers in a grip tight enough to leave her nerves tingling. Perhaps he did not know his strength. "If you promise not to squeeze again. You are very strong."

"No, I want you to squeeze my hand. As hard as you can."

"I am not as strong as you, my Lord."

His eyes pleaded as he said, "Please, try."

The Lady inhaled and reached for King's Son's hand, clasping it tighter and tighter, pressing hard to the bones, waiting and wishing for him to tell her to stop. "Harder," he begged. Jinilya dug her fingernails into his flesh, but the lad neither flinched or shuddered. His fingers drained of color as she continued to hold fast.

"You do not feel anything? No pain?" she whispered.

"No. Only fire hurts." There was a calm disappointment in his expression, as though he long expected this outcome. In this moment he seemed more youth than child.

She released her Lord's hand. "Have you told your parents?"

He shook his disheveled blond locks. "You think I should?"

"My Lord King's Son, this may be a Gift from The Powers. Your mother and father should know."

"I do not want to tell them." Namlich studied the brazier, then faced her, a childish pout returned to his features. "I will not tell them fire does not hurt you if you do not tell them about this."

Surprised that he bargained with her in this manner, Jinilya replied, "Then I will not tell your parents."

King's Son's smile was the cunning expression of a seven-year-old inhabiting the body of a youth who believed he had gotten his way. "I thank you, pretty Lady." Then Namlich dashed away.

The young Lady smiled as well, for although she had promised not to tell the King and Queen, she had agreed to no such restriction on telling King's Mother.

"Lady Jinilya?" It was Soldier Anish, returned from his immersive discourse with the Scriptor. "There you are, my Lady." He dipped his blond head. "My apologies for falling fast into conversation with Scriptor Vinil." He raised his head, his expression bright. "This has been a most auspicious day: speaking personally with our Queen, then meeting a fellow Copyist. It has been many years since I was able to talk with anyone who had such deep interest in inks and quills, how to cut them correctly, what type to use for…" His cheerfulness dimmed as his eyes traced her face.

Perhaps her disappointment, that his list of the day's highlights did not include time spent in her company, showed.

The young Lady stated, "I admire the work of the Scriptors, but I find my interests lie more in the tales themselves." He looked wounded, and her heart sank to see such a sad expression on his fair face. "Though without the efforts of Scriptors, our Legends would not be preserved in such beautiful forms." She was not certain she truly conveyed what she meant. "It is just that I think I prefer reading scrolls and books to making them. My quilling tutors were rather, mmm, strident." She paused. "Though even King's Mother says I have a lovely hand."

"I agree with her." He lifted Jinilya's note from his uniform's pocket, a fond light in his captivating eyes. "My Lady, I would like to quill a book or scroll for you, if you would like that?"

His offer astonished her. "Oh, that is most generous of you."

"Please, I would enjoy it greatly. It has been a very long time since I quilled a tale. Which is your favorite?"

"Oh no, something short. My favorite would consume years, and you have your army duties…" She rubbed her hands together.

The Soldier grinned. "There's a great secret about the military that perhaps your brother Captain Marnil has not shared with you."

"What is it?"

"We often have a lot of free time that needs occupying. I would like to spend it making something beautiful, for you." Anish looked to her hands. "If I may."

Inside, she felt like a child bobbing in expectation of a favorite treat, but she kept her feet flat to the stone pavers. "I love the tale of Seerlich King and Maayla Queen, do you know it?"

He gazed to her. "I do not."

Something in his look made breathing difficult, yet her words came in a torrent. "It is very, very romantic and tragic. But beautifully written. Maayla was a Records Keeper before they joined, and Seerlich King courted her in many elaborate ways, and then he died in battle when their son was still in the nursery, but she was an able and wise Queen famous for—Oh, I am going on."

"I know none of it and appreciate the education."

"But truly, a single passage in your hand would be a great kindness."

"Then you shall have it, my Lady Jinilya."

If they had been of longer acquaintance, The Powers knew she would have embraced him in thanks. Instead, she murmured a soft, "I thank you."

The Queen entered her maither's Library chamber in a swirl of violet fabric. Later that day she was to meet with the ambassador from Eastlant, and her attendants had adorned her dark locks with embroidered strips of purpled velvet in the fashion of that country, as well as a long voluminous gown becoming Eskalind's reigning Lady.

"Damina, what a lovely ensemble," called King's Mother from her desk at the far end of the lengthy room. From the doorway, Lady Marna appeared a petite woman, shrunken by grand surroundings, clad in a plain black smock one would think better suited to a craftswoman at her labors. The Queen glided through the lengthy room upon dainty slippers, with purposeful steps, one hand lightly touching the pale amethysts studding the pendant of her long necklace. The sable silk of her bodice contrasted with the stones to magnificent effect. The elder Lady lowered her eyes to a document on her desk. "Eastlant-style hair today, I see. Is your father coming to visit?"

Dalich's Queen sighed, for she had numerous times related to her maither that even though her Innkeeper father hailed from Eastlant, he possessed a convert's zeal for insisting his children lived and dressed in accordance with Eskalind customs, as though the family had been Strange Kingdomers for many generations. "No, just an audience later with the ambassador from the land of Father's birth." At last approaching the thick oaken table, she sat in a plumply stuffed chair. "Speaking of family—"

"Yes, how fares your son?"

Well, her maither had divined the purpose of this visit quickly. Damina looked to the tea table, anchored by the last window, with its canisters arrayed in neat rows that belied the teetering stacks of scrolls, parchments, and books littering the rest of the room. Returning her gaze to her maither, she said, "Namlich is sad, as am I, that he has been forbidden the Library."

The elder woman's eyes did not leave the sheet before her. "You do know I saw him push a scroll into flame."

"He tells me he thought the candlewick too bright and feared the fire spreading. He did not consider that a scroll might catch fire. He is only seven." Her maither made no comment. "Nevertheless, Namlich has been disciplined. He will not make that mistake again."

"I am glad to hear it."

Silence followed, and when the former Queen made no effort to continue the conversation, her daighter, after a lengthy examination of the patterning of the dark metal thread decorating her skirt, began, "Maither, I have been thinking, if Namlich cannot enter the Library, how will he ever develop a love for the place?" She turned the band of the black opal ring that graced her index finger, a bit of violet luster in its depths. "He is still very young and he can be mischievous," here King's Mother raised a dubious eyebrow, "but if he is well supervised on his visits, any further mishaps can be prevented. Though I truly think he has learned his lesson." The Queen glanced to the haphazardly filed scroll shelves and caught herself before she sighed. "It must be hard on Namlich, growing at such a fast pace. How he gangles about, especially when he first wakes up." Damina rubbed a hand over her forehead. "His lack of coordination is a great worry to me. I know the poor boy gets frustrated." She looked to the elder Lady. "I asked Dalich if he could do something to slow Namlich's growth, but his healing Gifts have no effect in this matter."

The former Queen's features softened as she at long last gave her visitor her gaze. "My dear daighter, I understand your concerns, for they are my own as well." She rolled the scroll before her closed as she spoke. "Of course I want the best for my grandson, and I hope this was a temporary aberration in his behavior. If there is someone you trust to look after him in the Library, by all means arrange it, and I will amend my order to the Librarians."

"I will watch him myself."

Her maither tied the scroll closed with an embroidered ribbon patterned with stylized King's Flowers. "Do you have the time?"

For once, Damina allowed herself to exhibit her disappointment that the eldest family member lived mainly on the periphery of their lives, despite residing in the same Halls. She had longed for a convivial and confiding mother-daughter relationship, one denied to her at birth by her mother's death. Whilst she and Dalich's living parent had shared some close moments, those occurrences were likely outnumbered by the hair combs forgotten and buried under papyruses in this very room. "For my *family*, yes, of course I have the time."

Her maither smiled. "I am glad to hear it. Are you and I speaking alone, or are you in current communication with Dalich?"

"It is just you and me."

"Let us speak in private conference then. How does my son fare?"

"Dalich?" The question surprised her; she had no answer ready for her maither, though had anyone else asked, she would have answered with a positive affirmation. But Lady Marna demanded a thoughtful reply, not a rote response. Damina ran a finger over the soft plum-colored fabric of her chair's arm. "Why do you ask, Maither?"

The other royal placed her scroll aside and folded her hands. "I believe, from time to time, he finds it a heavy burden that he must stay within our borders, by the Will of The Powers. But that is just this mother's supposition. Have you any thoughts on the matter?"

Her immediate thought was that she did not, but a moment's

pause yielded an inkling that her maither was on to something. "Dalich does become moody when he is not immersed in diplomacy or a building project." Damina smoothed a ribbon of the fabric tied in her hair. "With his master design plan for King's Halls complete, I sense that he feels at a bit of a loss." She glanced at the other Lady.

"Perhaps a change of scenery might be in the offing."

"Oh, please do not suggest that. I do not think I could tolerate the sound of Builder's hammers thundering away inside King's Halls. It is enough of a racket as they work to complete the exterior. Besides, the interior of the building has been functional for generations. Though perhaps some new furnishings or decor—Lady Dara was just telling me about an inventive weaver she discovered who creates lovely wall hangings."

"Perhaps, yes, but what I was thinking of is a sojourn away from King's Halls, yet still inside the border. Perhaps Dalich could journey about the land, healing people and visiting the noble houses."

"Ah, a King's Progress? If only I thought of it last year, in honor of the tenth anniversary of Dalich's reign."

The Queen instantly felt remorse for this off-handed reference to her faither's death, but her maither made no reaction. "It need not be tied to an anniversary," she said. "It could simply be the royal family visiting different regions of the land."

Family. That meant she expected Namlich to go with them. Whilst Damina did not want to leave her boy behind, the thought of bringing him as a guest into the households of others—she would need to enlist an army of child minders.

The bell rang. "That would be Jinilya," said her maither, rising to pace to the bellpull.

"The pattern sounds familiar."

"It is the same as her mother's." King's Mother gave a tug on a worn-looking cord to ring the answering signal. "Well, think on this journeying notion. I am pleased that you and I have come to an agreement on Namlich's Library visits."

The dismissal in her maither's tone niggled at the Queen's mood. She turned in her seat to see Saril's sister entering the room, dressed in a long unembellished scarlet dress that the dressmaker should have fitted closer to her body's curves. "Jinilya," Damina called, rising slowly, for her skirt had entrenched itself in the chair's cushions. "How did you enjoy the rest of your day yesterday with that handsome Soldier Anish?"

The young woman approached, eyes to the carpet. "Very well, my Lady." She stopped nearby and curtsied.

"I am glad to hear it." With a flounce of her gown, Damina extracted the last of her attire from the chair. "I must depart. I thank you, Maither, for the visit." She stroked Jinilya's smooth sleeve as she passed by. "Do come to my quarters for supper tonight if you are free." Behind her she could hear King's Mother questioning the young woman about the blond Soldier. Damina grinned as she exited the chamber.

———

After the Queen withdrew, Saralya's daughter turned to Marna, her lips parted. "But perhaps The Powers were at work, my Lady, for if the Queen had not directed me to lead Soldier Anish to the Scriptorium, I would not have witnessed this." What followed was a remarkable tale of King's Son staring at a candle, unresponsive till Jinilya pinched the flame out. The Scholars' Mistress felt her heart sink at this news, and she glanced to her desk where The Powers' parchment lay under several tomes.

"After the flame was gone," the young Lady continued, "my Lord King's Son acknowledged me and we spoke. He asked to touch my hand, and squeezed it hard. I told him he knows not his strength and it pained me. Then he wanted me to squeeze *his* hand, which I did, hard as I might, till his fingers turned yellow. He felt none of the pressure."

"Namlich said he felt nothing?"

"Nothing. He said he never feels pain, that only fire hurts him. I counseled that this was a Gift from The Powers, that the King and

Queen should know. He refused to tell them and made me promise not to reveal it to them." Her green eyes twinkled. "But he did not say I could not share it with you."

"Smart girl." King's Mother patted the young Lady's arm. "I thank you. You did the right thing in telling me. Dalich and Damina must know at some point, but when they do, the word will come from my mouth, not yours. I will set about discovering this on my own."

———

It pleased the Queen greatly to encounter, by chance, her son and his reading tutor in a nearby passageway. Perhaps The Powers smiled on her endeavor.

"I will instruct my son in the Library," she told the man, a rotund Humikslander who looked about to raise an objection, but deferred to his Queen. Touching her boy's fair cheek, she said, "Come, Namlich, Mama will read to you. Would you like that?" The lad beamed at her, such an expression of pure love she wanted to scoop him into her arms for an everlasting embrace. Thank The Powers this member of the family freely exhibited affection. She would enjoy every moment of its radiance.

Hand in hand, the royal pair entered the area recently forbidden to her son. Librarian Synya, prematurely gray in her early thirties, rose to greet them as her flock of Apprentices stood to bow. A pained expression fell upon her long face, and all the Apprentices' eyes to their shoes surely signaled that apologies about the restriction on King's Son's presence would follow. Thus Damina interrupted. "Synya, I have come to read to my son. King's Mother and I have made an agreement." She bestowed her most gracious smile upon the Librarian. "Where might I find the plain copies of Braashnil's work?"

Synya acquiesced, and gestured for the Queen to follow. Passing shelves stacked with scrolls and loose papyrus sheets, she led them toward a sunlit area by an open double door that connected to a corridor.

"Here, my Lady. Braashnil is an excellent choice. Very suitable for youngsters." Synya examined the tags dangling from the scrolls, and with her bony fingers partially extracted a few of the plain-knobbed volumes. "Were you searching for a specific tale by Braashnil?"

"Not particularly."

Namlich held fast to his mother's hand, staring about the tall cases. With her free hand, the Queen flipped through the tags, the string of one catching on the setting of her amethyst signet. Dashing it off, she decided to let this be a sign from The Powers to choose that scroll, and she pulled forth the volume, the papyrus a faded red. It felt rough under her fingertips. "This will do. I thank you, Synya."

"Very good, my Lady." The Librarian bowed and gestured to two chairs of adult proportions anchoring the ends of a table, with four smaller chairs hugging the long ends. "This is an area for reading aloud, if you wish to sit here. Or I can see any other area of the Library readied for you and King's Son, if you wish."

"This location is fine. I thank you." Damina smiled pleasantly and led her boy to the table. The Librarian departed. The Queen sat whilst Namlich squeezed into one of the small chairs. "My pet, bring the other big chair over here and sit in it." The lanky lad pried himself out of the little seat and did as she bid, scraping the larger chair's legs across the wooden floor in a hideous grating that surely did damage to the floor's finish. Exhaling, Damina unrolled the scroll to its beginning as her sole child sat beside her, snuggling against her arm, eager eyes close to the quillwork. "This is the tale of Kaarnlock King and his *Wonderful* Sword," she began, tracing a finger under each word as she read it. "My dearest pet, before I begin, know that this is not a fine scroll, so we are allowed to touch it. Understand?"

He nodded. "Why was his sword wonderful, Mama?"

"Well, let us find out." She began the tale, allowing her boy to read a line or two if a sentence suited his abilities. He trailed her finger with his, and her heart warmed at his engaged expression. She made a mental note to thank his reading tutor for a job well done.

Then she noticed her sister Yamina, standing by a scroll shelf, eyes mirthful, beckoning to her royal sister.

Damina scanned the next section of the tale, the margin illustrated with the figure of Kaarnlock King clad in orange and white, holding aloft a sword, orange as though dipped in fire. At his feet, a short vine of King's Flowers. "Namlich, I want you to read the next part on your own, all the way to the flowers in this drawing. I will be with Aunt Yamina, right there, if you require help." His gray eyes never left the papyrus, and she was not certain he heard her. She stood and went to her sister, keeping a watchful eye on the youngster.

Yamina leaned forward, whispering, "I just received word; Pamina is coming to King's Halls!"

"Our sister is coming here? Has she run out of male guests at Father's inn?" They leaned in, foreheads nearly touching. Damina whispered, "Remember the last time she visited?"

Yamina's cheeks lifted with her huge smile. "When she pursued both the Amkish and Kursak ambassadors?"

"Nearly causing a diplomatic crisis."

"I will never forget the look on King's Second's face."

"Yes, Saril was incensed." The Queen grinned saucily, an expression worthy of their much discussed sister. "And Pamina concludes the incident by showing her feet to the Kursak's valet—"

"The incredibly handsome valet who she said could not perform—"

"In bed."

The women giggled, clutching their hands over their mouths to stifle the sound.

"Thank The Powers," Damina exhaled. "Since the Amkland ambassador just departed, our only visiting ambassador now is female, otherwise Pamina would be incensing Saril again." As often happened, the laughter of one sparked the laughter of the other until tears coursed from their eyes.

———

Behind the Queen, an Apprentice Librarian, tasked with candle lighting, passed by, for it was approaching the hours of darkness and a darkened Library is useless for reading and research. He carried a black wax candle stiffly before him. Not only were the Queen and her sister in the same room, but King's Son as well. Even if he went unnoticed, he wanted to perform his meek duty well.

———

Namlich, King's Son, closed his eyes, imagination swelling with the tale of Kaarnlock King and his victorious sword. Whilst he could not read all of the words on the scroll before him, enough of the tale simmered in his thoughts that he could almost smell the grasses of the battlefield, hear the thudding beat of Soldiers stamping upon the earth, see the King raising his bright sword high—so bright the lad could see it now before him, approaching. But it was not a shining sword but a flame coming closer and closer, advancing, rushing toward him with lethal speed. A voice murmured, but Namlich would neither listen nor obey its lies again. He shrieked, emboldened by Kaarnlock King's battle courage, and tackled the darkness around the flame, trying to beat it out.

———

A sudden sound startled the Queen. She turned to see her son leaping toward a candle-carrying Apprentice and knocking him to the wooden floor. The lit taper slipped through the air, rolling to rest inside a scroll case laden with loose papyrus sheets. Flames curled outward, climbing the case. Below them, Namlich pummeled the black-tunicked youth beneath his knees, screaming over the Apprentice's protestations.

"Fire! Bring sand pails!" she shouted to her sister, gathering her violet silk skirt and rushing forward to separate the two boys. "Namlich, stop, stop!" Her son looked to her, fury writ upon his reddened face but in his eyes a startling, animal indifference. Cinders rained behind him, and the Apprentice tried to wiggle away from the lad's clutches, his purple Apprentice cloak lying crumpled near the fire.

With strength she did not know she had, the Lady of Eskalind yanked her lanky son by the collar to his feet, finding to her horror that the cuff of his tunic was alight. She batted out the flame with her bare hands as the boy bent his head, whimpering, "It hurts." Yamina and another Apprentice came forward with sand buckets, flinging dirt to smother the rising flames. The first Apprentice scrambled to his feet just as the second tossed soil toward the burning papyrus, launching the dirt directly into the first Apprentice's eyes.

Blinded, disoriented, the first Apprentice turned and flailed right into the smoking, burning papyrus. Then, his black tunic afire, he backed toward them as Yamina screamed.

Someone yelled behind the Queen, "Get back!" She turned to see King's Mother calling for help as Jinilya strode forth, fists clenched, stern as a warrior out of Legend lacking a sword but determined to fight bare-handed. Her scarlet silk gown echoing the flames, Jinilya surged past the Queen and her son, between the burning Apprentice and the fire. Damina looked away, prodding her transfixed son to run, to escape, her eyes scanning for more sand buckets.

"Thank The Powers," Yamina cried, clutching an empty pail, a dusty trail of earth along its metal side. Damina turned to see the fiery blaze completely extinguished, a smoking stack of scrolls and a pungent, nose-curdling scent the only evidence of the flames. Then her eyes traveled to the floor, where the Apprentice lay in a quivering heap, a wreck of a body, shuddering. Lady Jinilya bent toward his face, whispering softly. The Queen approached and sank down by his back, her slippers nearly slipping on the dirt-laden wood floor. Along his arm, the dark fabric of his tunic and his pale skin were charred together. His face was wet and sticky, with burns or blood she could not tell. The scent of cindered flesh was unbearable. Damina fought the constricting feeling in her throat that heralded vomiting. She spoke and thought,

"Dalich, please, please heal this man."

Jinilya looked to her with green-eyed woe. The King did not reply.

"Husband, husband! Please heal this man before me. He is burnt terribly and it is my fault."

Thank The Powers, her husband's voice appeared in her mind.

"What has happened? Heal who?"

She whispered to the fallen Apprentice, "What is your name?"

He sputtered a bloody foam from his lips, but formed no words she could comprehend. Jinilya shook her head. Damina turned, looking to the crowd standing behind her. Her maither's fingers clutched sad-faced Namlich's shoulders, a gaggle of Apprentices stood on tiptoe, narrow-chinned Librarian Synya holding a sand pail; all standing, watching. Some Soldiers and a kerchiefed kitchen worker, Soldier Anish among them, rushed into the room toting buckets of dirt, and the new arrivals stopped and stared at the scene.

"Who knows his name?" Damina demanded, fearful that the Apprentice might perish at any instant.

His fellow Apprentices muttered together. "I didn't see who it was."

"It's not Karvil, is it?"

"Is it Karvil?"

"No no, he went to the kitchens just before…"

"Where is Athril?"

"It's Athril?"

"Athril!" called the Librarian, her voice clear and authoritative over the debating Apprentices.

"Athril"

The mute figure before her slackened. "Athril?" Damina peeped. Jinilya's brown hands darted to cover her mouth as the Queen tentatively rolled the Apprentice to his back. Athril's face was tan and smooth, completely unblemished. He raised his eyes to her.

"Thank you, my Lady, thank you. The pain was…incredible. Powers forgive me, I wanted to die." Athril's brown eyes were moist and his lips trembled.

"Thank The Powers you are healed," Damina sighed, placing one hand upon his shoulder, the other reaching forward to embrace Jinilya. Then the Ladies rose, together helping Athril to his feet. His tunic sleeve was shredded and tattered; the clean skin on his arm beneath showed no sign of disfigurement.

The King's voice in her thoughts interrupted.

"Damina, what happened?"

"Thank The Powers, you saved Athril."

She looked to their son. *"I will explain it all later. Your mother was right. I will never ever let our son in the Library again. Oh Dalich, can you heal Namlich? There is truly something wrong with him."*

"My heart, you know I have attempted many times to slow his growth and moderate his behavior. Please, if this immediate crisis has passed, let us speak later. I have an Ambassador's letter before me and Saril is waiting."

The Apprentice waded across the sand-strewn floor toward his fellows, who welcomed him with outstretched arms and embraces.

"Yes, we will speak later."

The Queen felt weak in her knees; she stayed Jinilya. "I thank you for putting out the fire. That was quite brave of you to step forward. And you were so quick, I never saw you grab a sand pail."

The young Lady stammered, her face visibly losing its color. "It happened very fast."

Soldier Anish stepped to their sides, his gray eyes bright and sympathetic. "Your pardon, my Ladies, might I be of any assistance?"

Jinilya spoke before Damina could utter a syllable. "Would you bring me away? I think I might become ill."

"As you wish, Lady Jinilya." He glanced to the royal Lady and noted her nod of approval. The blond young man then placed a gentle hand on the younger Lady's shoulder, drawing her close while with his other hand he kept the crowd at bay. "Make way for the Lady." He led her through the crowd, the authority in his voice parting the gatherers.

Damina sighed, wishing her beloved by her side and solicitous of her needs. Yamina approached. "Oh, my Lady Sister, your gown..."

The Queen gazed down to the dirt encrusting the folds and stitched threads of her skirt. "A small price to pay," she murmured. "Yamina, see Namlich confined to his chamber till I come speak with him. And fetch me another dress. I must speak with my maither." She brought her lips together for a breath and then murmured, "To apologize."

The next day, at King's Mother's request, Jinilya presented herself in the Library, hands fidgeting in the pockets of her scarlet dress and sending tremors to her hemline that shuddered over her slippers. The pleasing scent of Lamorda flowers, hastily hung from the scroll cases, made a valiant attempt to overcome the lingering stench from the fire yesterday. The Library felt unnaturally quiet, as though the volumes it contained awaited a grand pronouncement, or perhaps it was just that she and King's Mother were the sole occupants of the enormous room, which usually creaked from the steps and hummed with the breath of its patrons.

The former Queen sat at a long wooden table, an unfurled scroll before her, gold lettering glimmering on brown velum. "I have a task for you, Jinilya. With my keys, I unlocked each of the locked cabinets. I want you to retrieve one scroll from each and every cabinet here and bring them to me."

"Which scrolls do you wish, my Lady?"

"You choose which scroll. It is solely your decision." King's Mother turned her gray eyes to the parchment before her, her lips moving ever so slightly as she read.

Jinilya's brow knit at the odd request, but she reached for an empty scroll basket and made long strides to the first cabinet, where she opened the doors and grabbed a scroll at random. The panoply of colors in the Library always surprised her, as much of the decor and dress at King's Halls followed solely the current King's colors. But here, faded and strong blues, soothing greens and striking reds, the tarnished smoky shades of silver, all resided upon cabinet shelves together. Even the cabinets themselves wore the shades of the Kings who reigned at the time of their completion: the green and gold of Farlich King, sunny yellow with bright red accents for Palich King, warm orange and red for Trelich. How many glad hours one could spend in this place. The thought brought a smile to her face as she gathered a scroll from each of the cabinets, placing them into the ebony-colored basket and presenting them at last before her Lady's table.

The former Queen laid the parchment she perused aside. She reached for the basket. Pulling it before her, she curled her fingers around a scroll of orange parchment capped with green marble finials, then spread the spindles apart to read a passage. "Ah, you chose the personal chronicle of Bravna Queen, wife to Palock King. How fitting."

"Oh no. A private royal scroll? It must have been misfiled."

"No."

"But my Lady, I thought the chronicles of the royals were kept locked in Trelich King's cabinet."

"They are." Gone was the fondness in the gray eyes of her Lady, replaced with a hardened expression Jinilya could not decipher.

"It makes no sense to me, my Lady. Please help me."

"You, dear Jinilya, unlocked Trelich's cabinet."

"But I thought you had unlocked all the cabinets?"

"Only the cabinets that unlock with a key. But one lock opens without a key."

She must have been staring blankly, for Dalich King's Mother continued, "The Cabinet of Trelich King, which only members of the King's family—or future members of his family—can open."

Still searching for the answer to the riddle, or perhaps distracted by her thoughts wandering to the tale of Bravna Queen, Jinilya looked hard upon the scroll in her Lady's hand. "Our Legends tell that Bravna Queen opened the cabinet as a young girl."

"And later she joined with King's Son."

Now she understood. "I cannot."

Her mother's closest friend raised an eyebrow. "You do understand that The Powers' Will decides who can lock and unlock Trelich's cabinet. They Willed that *you* unlock it."

Jinilya looked away, scouring her mind for the right words to explain her plight. The former Queen rose from her seat, but before she could speak, Jinilya placed both hands on the table and knelt to the ground. "Please, please my Lady, you must not think me ungrateful or rude or unwilling or mad. It is just that—" How hard it was to say the words.

"Tell me what your thoughts are."

"Will you believe me if I tell you the strange truth?" The word hurt her throat, but she must reveal her quandary. "I hear it, like King's Son does. There is a voice sometimes, a woman's voice that speaks to me, in my head, when I am near fire…" The older woman's gray eyes brightened as Jinilya continued: "Do you hear it too?"

"Tell me what she says."

Jinilya closed her eyes. "She tells me things, horrible, the worst things, then she says I will be joined with King's Son, and she laughs and laughs…" She laid her forehead on the table, her breath smothering hot against the wood. A warm hand touched her shoulder, and she wept till tears left her.

"Jinilya, dear, raise your head, look at me."

"I am sorry, my Lady. I must be an awful sight."

"Never. Though when you were born, you had the cord in your mouth. It was a great concern for a moment. I thought it was some deformity, and how to tell your mother…" This was information Jinilya had never heard before, and she lifted her head. A clean handkerchief was pressed into her hand, and with it she wiped her eyes.

"Jinilya, could you tell me more? About what the voice says to you."

"Yes. But it is awful." She sniffed, dabbing her nose. "She told me that Mother would die in great pain." A sob escaped her dry lips but she continued, "She told me that my nephew Kaloft and I would never have issue, that our house would die with us, that no one would ever love me." Anger rose in her heart, for the sympathetic, motherly look on her Lady's face told her that here indeed was someone who did love her.

Her Lady nodded, gray brows knit. "If you did join with King's Son, you can be assured that you would have a son, as it has always been." Her voice quivered a bit, and she placed her hands on Jinilya's elbows, helping to raise the young woman to her feet.

"But my Lady, what if I were the one Queen who was childless? Oh, how she laughed when she said I would be Queen. Such a maddening, piercing laugh. My only thought when I hear it is to escape."

"And how do you escape it?"

"I quench the fire and it stops." Jinilya dried her eyes again, feigning a smile. "I spend a lot of time at night in the dark."

There was a gravity to her Lady's nod that assured the young woman all would be well, but Jinilya felt tears, unbidden, returning to her eyes. Lady Marna asked, "When did this start?"

Jinilya held the drenched handkerchief to her cheek. "At the banquet to celebrate the royals' joining. I was seven." Gazing at the former Queen, she whispered, "What she says is not true, is it? None of it?"

Her Lady squeezed her arm. "I do not think I have sway with The Powers." The King of Eskalind's mother paused, her gray eyes sharp in her pale face. "Did you know, though, before your mother got with your oldest brother, she told me she dearly wanted a child, so that she and your father would join." Here she smiled. "And I told her I would ask The Powers to send her a child."

"And then Saril was conceived."

"Saril followed, yes." King's Mother lowered her gaze. "We do not know what The Powers have planned for us, but we have Gifts in our possession that will protect us and prepare us for our hour of need. Eskalind must be a preserve of peace and safety, a haven and beacon for all the world. You must help me with this, Jinilya."

"Me? Help? How can I help?"

"Stay here at King's Halls, and don the black and violet to work in my Library." She gestured to the room. "You will discover there is much purposeful work to be done."

Jinilya did not understand how Library tasks would keep Eskalind safe, but in the former Queen's presence she felt an authority and sheltering presence akin to her mother's, and something more. "I thank you, my Lady. I will stay and help as much as I am able."

"And I thank you. You cannot know how pleased I am that you will stay." King's Mother walked to her desk and reached for a quill. "I shall order an Apprentice Librarian's cloak and dress for you, but your main role will be as my personal assistant." She sat, reaching for a papyrus sheet. "We shall work together in this endeavor. During daylight hours." Her eyes brightened at her jest. "Now, spend the rest of this day in rest or recreation as you see fit, and return to me first thing in the morning."

"Yes, my Lady." Jinilya bowed and left the room, hope blooming in her chest at this unanticipated new direction. Breezing past a flock of purple-cloaked Apprentice Librarians, she felt elated that soon she would be one amidst their numbers. With Athla arriving in the next few days, she would tell her saister in person, perhaps already wearing her violet cape so there would be no debate on her chosen path. And Saril, as Acta Sua of their house, could not trouble her on this matter, for King's Mother would not hear of it. Marnil. Dear brother Marnil. He would see her on any path she found suited her; that was his nature, for he trusted The Powers to lead each person to their best use.

As though the thought of her brother conjured his men, before she had gone far, she spied Soldiers Gafnil and Sanil, followed by Anish. The three young men bowed, and the first two continued along the passage, but Anish lingered. "Lady Jinilya, might I have a private word?" There was a distraction in his expression she had not seen before.

"Yes." She wondered if her eyes were red and puffy from crying, so she turned her head from him but touched his arm, pulling him toward a door that shielded a storage area. It opened, and no one was inside, the only objects stack after stack of neatly piled black chairs. Some of the legs bore nicks and scratches that bared oak hearts. The soft glow of sunshine filtered from the sole window. She entered, beckoned for Anish to follow, and stepped to the side, away from the door, to face him.

The young Soldier glanced at the chairs that surrounded them like an audience and fidgeted with the handle of his long knife, which he gazed at as he spoke in a tentative, unsure tone. "Perhaps your brother, Captain Marnil, told you? We're to depart day after tomorrow to return to our company."

Her hand flew to her mouth. "No, oh no, he did not. And his wife and son are to arrive here at King's Halls shortly." The young Lady lowered her hand. "They will miss him." Her gaze traced along the walls as she imagined how upset Athla would be, how sad Kaloft would be to miss his father.

"It was a surprise to us all. At first the order was just for the Soldiers and our Sergeant to return—"

"What? Who ordered this?"

The Soldier stammered, "Your Lord brother, King's Second—"

"Saril," she seethed, contemplating that he engineered such an order, to distance her from Anish. By The Powers, she could choose her companions as she wished. Neither Saril nor that woman's voice in the fire would rule her.

"No, please, my Lady, you misunderstand. I have more to say," Anish continued, his gray eyes insistent and pleading. "Lord Saril only delivered the order." She must have looked disbelieving. "You see, the order came through King's Second, but was from the King. I—" He swallowed. "I believe there was an Ambassador's letter, and that is why the Captain's presence is required. Please do not mention that last fact to anyone. I don't think I'm supposed to know it."

"I see."

Anish smiled weakly. "I'm sorry. I didn't mean to cause any discord with your brother."

"He is the one who causes discord." She could not help but think back to when Saril called her cold-acting toward their mother. Jinilya had been a child at the time, distracted by an exciting visit to King's Halls. Now she was a woman who felt anything but cold. Heat flowed in her veins. The young man before her emanated a different heat, one that drew her, offering the promise of a life of her own choosing. She acted upon what felt right and placed a tentative hand on his chest, just above the lilac-stitched insignia for his company. "Anish, I am sad to see you go."

His clear eyes scanned her face. "I'm sad to go. To … depart from you, my Lady." His fingers reached to lightly touch her hand. He smiled at her. For a moment she felt it was Favik looking at her with such a look of sweetness her heart would break. Closing her eyes, she bit her lip and raised herself on one foot to drop a slipper to the floor. She hopped, ungainly, to the other foot, leaning against him, almost losing her balance, and opening her eyes only as she set free the other shoe from her foot. He reached to steady her with his other hand. Gazing at Anish's questioning expression, she stepped back, pulling her hand from his to gesture at the floor and raising her scarlet hem to reveal her bare toes. He glanced to her feet and his bottom lip dropped slightly.

"My Lady?" Perhaps the custom of a woman baring her feet to a man she desired was not something he had learned about during his time in Eskalind.

Suddenly shy, she whispered, "Would you be my lover?"

"I would be anything you would ask of me."

She drew close and raised her lips to his.

How many glad times Marna had welcomed her favorite former Ambassador into her Library chambers, she could not tally. Today, midway through the twelfth year of her son's reign, King's Mother and her former Queensman once again were reunited after a long absence. An absence which was, once again, of her own bidding.

When a smile lit his face, Favik still maintained a youthful glow, but when his face settled to a serious matter, one would not be surprised to learn he was midway through his fourth decade. For now, he was grinning, standing before her as she sat to crush the herbs for his favorite tea, the bold scent of the dark tea leaves mixing with the citrusy herbals. "Tell me, Favik, how fares Lord Radil and his family?"

"Very well. Lord Amril, at a mere thirteen years of age, already has a strong, quick arm. He will make quite a swordsman, I gather." Favik inhaled slowly, his eyelids lowered, savoring the deep aroma as Marna chased the herbs under her pestle. "Radil has long told me that scholarly pursuits and military careers alternate generationally in the men of his family. I see it for myself in the living generations."

She spooned the herbs into tea cups. "Hmm, I believe Radil had an ancestor who was King's Second."

"Two, he tells me." King's Mother beckoned for the hot water pot and he passed the speckled, glazed purple pot to her. "Also, his young daughter Alayna is growing fast."

Marna poured the hot water, nearly choking on the steam. "Not as fast as King's Son, I hope. Sit, Favik, sit."

He settled into a chair. "Ah, my Lady, it is good to be returned to King's Halls and its kitchens. I don't know how Radil and his family stomach the bland Nordak food his maither concocts."

Marna chuckled as she slid his cup toward him. "Shall I call for some bread and sauces?"

"Thank you, my Lady, but not for me." Favik patted his belly. "I made straight from the stables to the kitchens and stuffed myself."

They laughed together, though her joy was cut short by the realization of what she must tell him. She nearly sighed as she lifted the loose papyrus sheet draped over clean wax tablets. Retrieving the tablets, Marna placed one into Favik's hands. His gray eyes questioned as she began, "There is much to tell, and it cannot be spoken aloud for ..." And she wrote,

> *The Powers are listening. Not all of Them have our best interests at heart.*

He almost smiled. "Well, that would explain some things."

She shook her head solemnly at his attempt at levity, a niggle of doubt prodding her as to whether or not she should reveal these secrets to him. But with Saralya gone, he was the person she trusted most. Thus, moving the stylus across the wax, she wrote,

> *The Powers established rules long ago: All peoples speak the same tongue.*

She paused as he wrote a reply:

As Lord Radil's ancient parchment stated.

"Indeed, but there is more," she said aloud, then returned to writing.

No weapons of a range farther than a person can throw.

His gray eyes narrowed slightly as he impressed his question into the wax.

But the Havadrans accomplished this?

"One moment." Marna waved a hand to stay him, writing,

Ice confined to most northern and southern regions.

She laid down the stylus. Favik's lips tightened.

Are there more rules?

She held her hands up helplessly, then retrieved her stylus:

Perhaps, but none I have discovered. They made these rules, and now They allow some to be broken. As you mentioned, the Havadran weapons research. Also, Kermon had reports of people who speak incomprehensibly, yet are understood by their fellows. Last, I believe that Kermon and his fellow Merchant Masters temporarily losing their Gift is somehow related.

The tablet exhausted, she showed it to him. Favik read without expression, though the lines around his mouth seemed to deepen. He wrote on his tablet as she scraped hers clean.

My Lady, how did you find out?

She impressed her answer into the wax:

One of Their number revealed it to me.

He studied her with that steady Ambassador's gaze. When Favik looked at her in that appraising manner, she felt she did not truly know him, as though all their years together evaporated and before her sat a mystery, a man of unknown agendas and loyalties. Dismissing this ridiculous thought, she considered mentioning The Powers' parchment, but it had failed to respond to her quilling for years.

Again Favik moved stylus across wax.

Do you know why the rules were broken? Why one of Them would communicate with you?

The Scholars' Mistress shook her head twice, then wrote,

But She told me the Scholars must continue to act, and that she is at work.

Aloud she said, "I felt the time was ripe to impart this to you, which is why I requested you return to King's Halls rather than travel to Eyfia to research their ancient scrolls." She placed her tablet on the table between them.

"Your timing was superb, as I was delayed in leaving for Eyfia. Lord Radil had word of profound unrest there after the death of their king; there's uncertainty about the succession." He paused. "My Lady, this," he tapped her tablet, "is incredible news to digest."

"Indeed. But now you understand my great interest in ancient scrolls and documents that reference the time before the founding of Eskalind, as well as these many years of sending you to research beyond King's Halls on my behalf. Any knowledge of what life was like, how people lived and coped, would be useful if we are to prepare for living in those circumstances again."

"Very wise, my Lady." He brought his hands before him, his gaze indeterminate, perhaps upon the place where his thoughts lay.

"Yes, I just wish more information were discoverable." She noticed a stray flake of black wax stuck to her finger and brushed it aside. "And there is one more thing." Marna reclaimed her tablet.

One of The Powers inhabits fire and speaks evils to Jinilya.

Favik's eyebrows lifted. The Bladesmith's Daughter touched a finger over her closed lips. Favik nodded slowly.

"Well, my Ambassador," she began, scraping away her words, "there is an amusing letter I wanted to show you. Stay seated, enjoy your tea."

She put the tablet down, stood, and patted the linen draping his shoulder as she made for her desk, leaving her man in thoughtful silence. But he turned to face her, asking, "My Lady, I meant to inquire, how you are faring with your new assistant?"

"Lady Jinilya has been a boon to my days."

"I'm most glad to hear that."

The Scholars' Mistress fussed with the sheaves littering her desk. "Yes, my only disappointment is whom Jinilya chooses to bed, but he seems to treat her well despite my initial misgivings. Thus, truly, I should not complain." Marna heaved a book out of her way. "He is a Soldier, currently stationed at the Thislin border with Marnil's company, and so is not often at King's Halls. There was a threat to Thislin from the Askvits, but it came to nothing. For a while, two companies were stationed there. Now it is just the Sixth."

His voice carried clearly across the chamber. "A relationship over such a long distance, that must be difficult on young people. But I'm assuming he is young."

"Young indeed. Everyone is young to me, except me. Ha." Dalock's

Queen lifted a scroll aside. "Jinilya says he is a few years older than her. What I do know about him is he is a Havadran-born Soldier named Anish." Her man turned away and she fumbled with the papyruses before her, still seeking the missive she wanted him to read. "That is the best description you can hope for, as I have never looked him in the eye."

Favik's back was toward her, which must explain why his next utterance was muted. "Know you anything about his family?"

"Hmm, no, I do not." King's Mother paused, frustrated that the missive she searched for eluded her. Hands on her ample hips, she scanned the desk and nearest table. "Point of fact, the only complaint against her young Soldier that Jinilya has shared with me is that he will not tell her anything about his background. He says it is of no importance." Her man stood and stepped close to a window. She continued, "Saralya's daughter is still quite young, immature emotionally, I would say. I blame that on her hardships. Besides losing her mother, also what you and I have just discussed." King's Mother sighed. "But family means everything to her, and it troubles her that her lover finds his own not worth discussing."

"Perhaps it is a sad tale."

"Given he is Havadran, I do not doubt it. I told her such." She sighed again, wishing she could right the wrongs of the world. "Yet I can tell she finds the matter troubling."

Marna shuffled to another table and peeked under a stack of lose parchments as Favik asked, "What was your disappointment in the young man?"

"That he is a citizen of Eskalind yet chose to earn his sword in the Havadran manner." A strand of loose silver hair glistened on her sleeve. She snatched at it. "Killing another man. Inexcusable. And Marnil, of all people, approved it." She dropped the hair to the carpet.

"Your pardon, my Lady." Her blond Scholar paced to the door. "Something I ate is not agreeing with me." One hand on the door handle and the other on his belly, he turned to her, his face difficult to discern given the distance and the darkened doorway.

"Oh Favik, I will prepare you a healing remedy. Something with—"

"I'm most sorry, I must go immediately." Her man opened the door, sunlight in the exterior corridor illuminating his pained expression.

"I will send it to your quarters!" Marna called as he shut the door behind him. She exhaled, turning her head to the nearest table, where she saw, finally, the missive she had sought. "There you are. Near the door. Of course. So I could hand you to Favik when he came in. By The Powers." She sat heavily. "Too much to attend to, at times. Well, it was of little importance."

Sighing, the Scholars' Mistress glanced across the long room to her desk. A shaft of sunlight appeared upon it. She shot from her seat and raced toward it. Opening the lowest drawer, she retrieved The Powers' parchment with one hand and with the other swept aside a clear area in the light. Laying the sheet there, she dipped her quill in ink and wrote,

You visited me in 2902. You wrote me in 2913. It is over eight years later; why are you silent? What are you doing? What should I be doing?

She hovered her quill over the parchment. Nothing happened. Dipping the nib in ink, Marna wrote, pouring forth her anxieties,

Why does my grandson grow too swiftly? Is it the herbs I gave his mother? Will he die prematurely aged?

She sucked air through her nose, grit her teeth and inked her instrument again, quilling,

Flames speak in a woman's voice, to him and to she who unlocked the Cabinet of Trelich King.

And lo, writing appeared below hers.

> *Does she speak aloud to them*

Scared and furious, Marna quilled,

> *Will you answer anything I have asked?*
>> *King's Son is needed to serve*
>> *when the time comes*

Marna waited, heart pounding, then scrawled in a hand worthy of one new to the craft,

> *What of his rapid aging?*

Fresh writing appeared.

>> *It will be dealt with when the*
>> *time comes*
>> *Do the flames speak aloud to*
>> *King's Son and the Flame Quencher*

Marna blinked. She knew something a Power did not. The Scholars' Mistress inserted her quill nib into the narrow opening of the ink bottle, withdrew it, and admired the translucency of the shaft, the glimmer of light upon the pendulous curve of black ink at the nib. She dabbed the excess fluid against the bottle's mouth, then quilled with a flourish,

> *Why is that important? Will you tell me what is the fourth rule*
> *of The Powers?*

The desk lurched forward as though shoved in anger. Marna yelped, drawing back as quilling appeared on the smooth parchment surface.

> *Do not play with me*

Answer

She swallowed, stretching her elbow straight to write,

The voice speaks in their minds, not aloud.

She waited.

Then Fire acts alone and
Air does not know

The Power's script had reached the bottom edge of the page. After staring a moment, Marna flipped the sheet into the shade, then replaced the now blank leaf before her. A message instantly appeared:

Fire seeks to unmake this world
That will be The War between
The Powers
Events unfold slowly
You have been given the Vision of the
Moment of Death
You know how much time you have

Marna whispered, "I meant to ask about that."

The Flame Quencher will temper
King's Son
I am at work

Dalock's Queen breathed a moment, for she had seen this phrase before as a conclusion to their correspondence. Thus she wrote,

I too am at work.

She passed the parchment into the erasing shade.

Enshrouded in a floor-length beige veil, the portraitist Samathe peered at Dalich King's gardens, the wide paving stones hard under her slippers. "I should bring my sketch pad to record these lovely blooms. Red vines and four white petals. I've never seen anything like them." A young boy passed by, shaking his wrists like her brother Deenofts had when he had been quilling too long. The boy's expression was merry, his eyes bright, as though he relished a secret prank. A deep sadness filled her. Samathe minced toward a cushion-topped stone bench set in shadow and sat, stone heavy. Violet-petaled Lamorda flowers bobbed in clusters near her seat. Two purple becloaked women, their hair that common shade of Eskalind brown that required just a hint of red to render true in paint, breezed along the sunlit path, carrying baskets of letters. Intent upon their errand and conversation, they did not notice her. Then a Soldier in his sable army tunic approached. His hair was light, which always garnered her attention in this land. But it was not his face but his eyes that commanded her gaze, for as he stepped into the sunlight, the clear gray color shone in the midst of a ring of dark blue.

"Anish?" she called, her voice tight and rising. He stopped cold; his head swung toward her as she stood, bringing a hand to her veiled mouth. His eyes darted toward her hand, scanning it minutely.

"Who are you?" he queried, as though he spoke to a dream.

"It is Samathe." She doffed her veil, water in her eyes, and for a moment his expression threatened to collapse into disappointment, before he smiled hugely and embraced her. "You are alive, in Eskalind! Thank The Powers!" she breathed against his ear as she hugged him. "And my brother. What of Deenofts? Where is he?"

His embrace weakened, then his hands trailed from her back to her elbows, and he held her kindly but steadily as he gazed at their feet.

"I'm very sorry. He did not…survive the journey out of Havadra."

Samathe shook her head. "I thought as much. He never wrote. He always did in the past." She swallowed. "Did your father ever find you?"

"Um, no." He raised his eyes to her, innocent and puzzled.

"Oh, Anish, why didn't *you* write and tell me about Deenofts?"

"I did, but I couldn't quill at first. I hurt my hands." Anish released her arms and turned the tops of his hands toward her. She gaped at the threading of scars on his skin, evidence of horrible burning, she guessed.

"What happened?"

"I was held in quarantine in Eskalind for a very long time; it was nearly a year after Deenofts and I left your fortress in Capitola."

"So you did escape the city together?" Anish nodded. "How, where did he die?"

"In the desert, we were separated in a dust storm. Bandits found me. Then Deenofts," the young man looked away, "came, into the cave where they held me. He tried to save me. They murdered him."

She felt cold, even though death by bandits was a scenario she had considered many a time. "But you escaped?"

"I did, thanks to a potion Deenofts gave me." He paused, turning his gaze back to her. "That's what scarred my hands. It frightened the bandits away, as they thought I had the scourge. I made it to Eskalind and am now a Citizen Soldier."

Samathe was not certain what the term meant, but pressed, "You said you did write me?"

"I did, at least four times. Twice as soon as I recovered, and again later, once or twice more after that, it's been quite a long time now. But I heard nothing in return. Are you still in your fortress in Capitola?"

Quietly she said, "I removed to Guerland. I lived and painted there for many years but recently decided to travel to other, safer countries to further my … renown." Her ambitions felt worthless as she again mourned her beloved brother. The nearby flowers bobbed on their stems uselessly. She tried to speak calmly. "Deenofts said you were to work in the Scriptorium."

"I could have, after my hands were healed, but I decided for a military career. Partly because of the helplessness I felt when he came to save me. I wished I had been able to fight the bandits and save him." His eyes watered. "I thought I could defend myself; I was trained for it, but against grown men, and I was scared—it was stupid, stupid letting them catch me. I regret it every day."

She said nothing, and he descended in her vision. Then the painter realized he had fallen to his knees, his head bowed and hands at the nape of his neck. "Here," he offered, pulling a shining thread over his head. "You should have this, I want you to have this." In his bare hand he held the open square pendant she had given her brother, dangling from a finely crafted gold chain she did not recognize. Samathe reached for it, held it. It felt heavier than she remembered, as though it carried a weight in memories. Or perhaps it was the gold chain. The young man continued, "There are coins that were his too that I have; they should be yours as well. I have them locked away safely, but not here."

"Stand up," she murmured. "Anish, please." He did so, hesitantly.

After several moments of silence, he leaned toward her and murmured, "I'm most sorry, but I must go. My rank is leaving, and I was on my way to say goodbye to someone who awaits me. But please tell me where to quill you. There is more to tell, and I hope we may correspond."

"I am here for a while, at King's Halls, painting the Queen, and later other fine Ladies, I hope. Just as Deenofts always wanted." The portraitist smiled weakly. "Do write me, Cousin Anish." He smiled, and she raised her arms and embraced him again.

When they released one another he blurted, "Oh, there she is. Lady Jinilya!"

Samathe turned to see a black-haired woman's back as she trotted away from the pair.

"I must catch her. I'm with the Sixth Company, if you were to write me." He grinned, a bit sadly, then dashed off after the woman.

———

"Lady Jinilya!" Anish called, but she did not stop, weaving her way around sculpted hedges, shoulders held high. A pair of kitchen workers carrying trays of sauces crossed his path and he nearly plowed into them. Making quick apologies, he picked up his pace to reach her. "My Lady Jinilya?" At last his lover stopped, and rounded on her heels, fury in her eyes. The young Soldier stopped short, as though his Sergeant barked an order. "What's wrong? I was calling to you, but you kept going."

"Do you have two lovers?" she fumed.

"What?" He could not comprehend what she was asking.

"I saw you embracing another woman. Giving her jewelry." Jinilya crossed her arms tight against her bosom.

He stuttered, "N-no, that was a fine lady I knew in Havadra."

"Truly?" Her brows and eyes lowered in accusal.

"Yes, truly. Jinilya!" He raised his hands to her, reaching. "She recognized me and called me by name. She was veiled, and for a moment, I thought my mother was there, under all the cloth. I felt faint."

His lover stepped back. "She was not veiled when you held her."

Anish gaped and shook his head. "You truly don't believe me. Did you not see her face? She must be fifty, at the least."

"And here I was, happy you came to King's Halls for my eighteenth Naming Day. Then I catch you giving jewelry to some other woman."

It seemed impossible that she would accuse him of this, that she could not understand the situation. He lowered his voice. "I just informed her of her brother's death, that I saw the man killed before my own eyes back in Havadra, and for this you accuse me of being her lover?"

Jinilya turned slightly to the side, green eyes on the hedges as though she spoke only to them. "You have never told me anything about Havadra, about killing or a single thing. You would not even tell me who in your family gave you your rich long knife. How am I to know anything?" Her eyes darted to his neck. "And you gave her the pendant you always wear."

"It was her dead brother's. I wanted her to have it. It's the least I can—" He stared hard at her critical expression. In that moment it seemed inconceivable that she had ever looked at him tenderly, whispering words of endearment, of love. "It's plain you don't trust me, my Lady. I've done nothing to deserve such disservice. Goodbye." He nodded curtly and passed her by.

———

"Havadrans!" Jinilya seethed, and she made straight for her family's quarters, fury and confusion in her heart at her lover's betrayal and dismissal. The only inkling of a pleasing notion was finding the rooms unoccupied—Saril was elsewhere, thank The Powers. In her chamber, the sheets still testified to her former lover's presence, and she gathered them hastily, stuffing them in the hamper and kicking the basket in anger, then feeling a fool for punishing an inanimate object. A mute witness. She sat at her desk to quill furious missives, littering the smooth wooden surface and the carpet with exhausted papyruses till daylight failed. Then she bolted from her chair, washed her face, and emerged to haunt the corridors, restless and uncertain of her destination.

Ahead, a crowd, their backs to her, gathered, hunched and intent on what, she could not see. Odd, hollow staccato noises echoed. One of her fellow Apprentices stood nearby. "What is it?" Jinilya whispered.

The young woman did not look at her, but teetered on her toes, bobbing like the flames of torchlight in the corridor. "King's Son and his Swordmaster. I could see them myself, before all these people came. He's becoming very handsome."

"What are they doing?"

"Sparring. It was quite a sight."

"Disperse, disperse," came a strong male voice. Some of the people fluttered away.

"Oh well," said the other Apprentice as she turned to leave. Jinilya stood her ground. As more of the crowd departed, the Mavoldian Swordmaster came into view, brown tunic and linen leggings recalling the comforting color of her house.

"Everyone move along," ordered the man in clipped tones, waving one hand and, with the other, pointing his wooden practice sword to the stones paving the hall.

Blond King's Son stepped to his side and locked his gray eyes on Jinilya. He was perhaps an ear short of the man's height. A slight smile lit his features, and even in the torchlight, she could see a bit of beard fuzzing his cheeks. "She can stay," he commanded, in the voice of a youth eligible to earn his sword, despite being in truth only half that age.

The Swordmaster seemed to notice her for the first time. "You are too unskilled to be showing off before womenfolk, my Lord. You must concentrate. It is of utmost importance to your training."

"Master, please, I wish for her to watch."

"Then we go to the royal sparring area. No more commotions in public areas." He gestured Jinilya forward with a curt wave, turned his shoulders, and marched away, leading his charge, who followed with a slow glance to her. She trailed them. Once there, the young Lady leaned against a column just outside the sparring ring, watching the pair fight.

"Try to hit me if you can, Master Edvain," Namlich goaded, his feet executing complicated steps as though commanded to dance as fast as they were able. The man, on the other hand, shook his head wearily, as though the pair had played a game too long. Edvain feinted to the right, then struck the youth cleanly on the left. The force sent King's Son to the ground, but he leapt to his feet instantly, as though The Powers themselves righted his position.

"That did not hurt at all," bragged the youth, stepping as sveltely as before.

The Swordmaster said mirthlessly, "You asked your father to always heal you?" Namlich glanced to Jinilya with a conspiratorial grin. Several more parries and thrusts followed, surprisingly well executed on Namlich's part. She found herself impressed with his coordination and skill.

"Pause," the Mavoldian called, laying his practice blade aside and moving toward a glossy black water pitcher.

King's Son approached his audience, wiping sweat from his brow. "See how brave I am, my Lady?"

His tone hinted at jest, but his words kindled her spirit. "Maybe you should fight against something that can hurt you," Jinilya taunted in a quiet voice. That drew him closer.

"What, a lit candle? A hanging brazier?" King's Son tapped his dull sparring blade against the chain of one of the metal lamps lining the courtyard.

"There were fighters with flaming swords and spears at the Battle of Delant." King's Son opened his mouth, but she interrupted, "Maybe your tutors have not let you read that tale yet, the version by Baavnif."

"I read what I wish." The young Lord stepped close enough for her to feel heat radiating from his body. He gazed down his nose into her eyes.

Jinilya folded her arms across her chest, realizing for the first time that the action lifted her bosom, giving her cleavage. "I read it when I was nine. I needed healing from your father to recover."

Namlich turned, casting her a sidelong glance, and she found something in that gaze oddly compelling, as though it could pull her to him. It was difficult to remember that he was only eight when he looked at her like that. She stood with her feet firm upon the floor.

King's Son bowed his forehead, his voice soft. "Then I am most glad Father helped you."

The Swordmaster called, "Come, my Lord."

As Namlich walked away, the braziers flickered, as though anticipating their next taunt. Jinilya marched away before they could speak to her.

Samathe sat at her easel in the studio loaned to her, dabbing a paint brush on her palette, wishing she had purchased more black paint before arriving at Dalich King's Halls. She should have believed the stories that told it was the commonest color at court. The shade consumed light and made it difficult to distinguish the sitter's body from the plain dark background that was a hallmark of her portraits. For this preliminary color sample sketch it did not matter, yet even at this stage she wanted to convey the character of the sitter in the height of the shoulders. Such details carried into the final painting when incorporated at the beginning. One of the many lessons learned from her mentor that still served her well.

Her subject was none other than Marna, King's Mother of Eskalind, seated in sunlight softened by a white sheet draped over the long window, a look of disinterest writ upon her elderly features. Years before, that man Favik had told her this was the woman who had sent him to Havadra to find her brother. The portraitist had a plan to endeavor to find out if this were true. But at the moment, her trade required concentration to render the skin and hair tones correctly. Gripping the brush handle, Samathe caressed the bristles into a creamy plop of paint, thinking to add perhaps a flattering hint of red or brown to warm the tones so the Lady did not appear as sickly pale as she was in life.

Someone entered the room behind her, and the older woman spoke. "Ah, Lady Jinilya, I am glad you found us. Come, meet Painter Samathe from Guerland, via Havadra."

A brown-skinned woman with a Guerish look about her features entered, an ovoid cup of tea in her hands. Dressed in the dark uniform worn by the Librarians in training, a violet cloak draped over her shoulders, she bent at a slight angle to present the cup to the seated royal, who accepted the tea and sipped.

"A pleasure to meet you, Lady Jinilya."

So this was Anish's former lover. Ah, how one came by such information. The portraitist had heard Anish call Jinilya by name that day she encountered him in the garden, then later, during her portrait sessions, Damina Queen gossiped about the lovers breaking, though it should be noted she had considered the pair a good match.

Lady Jinilya nodded her long black locks and went to stand behind King's Mother as though the elder were a shield. "Damina Queen showed me your portrait of her," she said. "It is a beautiful likeness." Despite the complimentary words, there was no warmth in her voice.

Samathe responded in like tones. "Thank you, my Lady."

The smooth-faced woman pursed her lips. "Soldier Anish mentioned that he was acquainted with you in Havadra. Is that true?"

"Yes." Despite having achieved the desired shade, Samathe continued blending her paint, casting an indifferent eye to her commission's skin tone.

Her subject's light complexion colored. "Are you related?"

Such personal questions still pained her, but Samathe had spent enough time beyond the land of her birth to realize that in most nations, it was an innocent, normal inquiry. That, and she truly could not deny an answer to a royal personage quizzing her. Especially if she hoped to find favor and win more commissions at King's Halls. "No my Lady, we are not." She switched to a smaller brush.

The young Lady, perhaps emboldened by her superior's line of questioning, asked, "Was he a student of yours?"

Here Samathe smiled. "Not formally." Both Eskalinder nobles gazed at her intently, the darker Lady with a questioning curiosity and the former Queen with a critical hardness that recalled the attitude of a Havadran head of household warning the portraitist not to reveal whom she painted in his fortress.

The elder spoke in a leading tone: "From my understanding of Havadran customs, this sounds most unusual."

"Yes, my Lady, it was." She laid her brush aside, choosing her words with care. "Anish was born to a family of high standing. They lost their position when he was but a youth. He became a hunted fugitive with a high price upon his head." The brown-skinned woman brought a hand to her mouth. "I and my brother sheltered him in our fortress, for months, telling the servants he was our cousin the copyist. Anish and I would spend our time together drawing and discussing our crafts." She glanced at her easel, her jaw involuntarily tightening at the recollection of those tense days. "Then, for safety reasons, my brother decided he must smuggle Anish out of Havadra." She looked to King's Mother, as shyly as she could manage. "My brother hoped Anish would be safe in Eskalind; he thought Anish's talents might lead to an Apprenticeship in your Ladyship's Scriptorium." The gray-haired woman raised an eyebrow, an intimidating gleam in her eyes.

"Well," continued the painter, looking away, fearing she had over-stepped some invisible boundary. "That was my brother Deenofts. He believed the lad to be talented enough to perhaps qualify for service. The end of the tale is that they departed my fortress and I never saw either of them again. Until I encountered Anish in the garden here." Samathe looked to her hands.

The younger Lady had sat, whilst the former Queen inhaled slowly, then asked, "Your brother's name was Deenofts?"

"Yes."

"What was his profession?"

"He sold dyes."

Lady Marna spoke. "I knew a Deenofts from Havadra."

Samathe glanced up to find the older Lady's gaze on the younger, who was shaking. The portraitist asked, "You knew my brother, my Lady King's Mother?"

"Describe him."

The request surprised her, but she complied, nearly fumbling for words as the emotional effort of conjuring his image, even after these years, saddened her. Afterward, no one said anything for a long moment. Then Lady Jinilya, quivering in her seat, hands over her face, whimpered, "Anish told me he saw your brother … slain … right before his eyes and … I did not believe him."

King's Mother had placed a hand on the young woman's arm. "Anish told you this?"

The noble nodded, face still shielded behind her brown fingers. "Yes, but he never said a name. I did not realize it was Deenofts."

The former Queen turned to her portraitist. "Painter Samathe, I apologize for asking you to describe your brother. I could see you found it difficult. I merely wanted to be certain he was the man we knew."

Lady Jinilya sobbed, murmuring, "Anish saw … Deenofts—" She lowered her hands, tears streaking her face. "Your brother was always very kind to me." This begged more questions, but the young woman seemed incapable of speaking more.

The royal Lady whispered calmly, "Jinilya, dear, if you wish to go—"

The young Eskalinder stood quickly, as though her feet would launch her to the door. "I thank you, my Lady." In a swirl of violet-colored cloak, she departed.

Samathe weighed the conversation in her mind, fathoming the depth, or rather the height, of her brother's foreign connections. King's Mother spoke, squeezing a hand on the arm of her chair. "Painter Samathe, this is a great shock to her. She and her mother were very fond of Deenofts. As was I."

This confession astonished the Havadran. Samathe wondered if her brother had a deeper interest in women, especially older women, than she had ever realized. "My Lady, I had no idea my brother was highly connected." It was not entirely true, for Favik had told her that the very woman seated before her had assigned him to seek word of her disappeared brother. Of course, she had not believed him. She had no reason to believe that vile Eskalinder. If Favik had not tasked Deenofts with sheltering Anish, with bringing the lad back to Eskalind, her brother would still be alive.

The royal lifted her chin slightly. "Deenofts never mentioned his associations here at King's Halls?"

"No, my Lady. I knew he traveled a great deal, to Eskalind and farther, but he told me nothing of those he met of high standing." Here Samathe smiled. "It was something we had in common, as in my profession I met members of the highest households of Capitola, but could say nothing about them to anyone."

"So you met only the womenfolk?"

"The women to paint, and the men to warn me not to reveal whom I painted." Her tone veered toward grim. "My painting mentor, she was accused of breaking that silence, and one day she left her fortress and never returned. I vowed that would never happen to me."

King's Mother only said, "I understand." She looked away.

The portraitist considered a moment. The royal Lady seemed genuinely surprised to hear that she was related to Deenofts, which meant either that Favik had never reported her name to the former Queen or that the Lady had forgotten. The lingering question of why Anish did not know Favik was his father also troubled her. What seemed clear was that King's Mother did not favor the young Soldier. But Anish was not the one who deserved the royal's disdain. "My Lady, there was one person who had hinted to me that Deenofts found favor with your Ladyship."

The gray eyes returned to hers. "Oh?"

"Ambassador Favik."

"I see." The Eskalinder Lady pulled the cuff of her gown as though it irked her. "It was Favik who escorted you and your household to Guerland?"

"He did, my Lady." She added, gesturing to herself, "for which I am most grateful. As a woman without family, in Havadra, I would not have been able to make the journey without his assistance."

"Then I am glad my man could be of service to you." It sounded like she considered Samathe in her debt. "How did you and Deenofts come to shelter Anish?"

The painter could feel her face color at the memory. "My brother arrived at our fortress with Anish, calling him our cousin, which he is not." She paused, wondering how best to continue. "I immediately went along with Deenofts's story, as it would have looked suspicious to the servants if I had not. Then Deenofts whispered he encountered armed men searching for Anish with murder in their eyes, that there was a large reward offered for the lad. It was thus imperative that no one discover he sheltered with us, or who Anish was."

The former Queen ever so slightly raised an eyebrow. "And who was he?"

Samathe looked the woman straight in the eye, acting decisive even though she battled within herself whether she would truly answer this question until the very moment the words left her lips. "Your pardon, my Lady. I mean no disobedience, but I feel that question is better answered by Anish himself."

A slight smile appeared on the countenance before her. "But you know."

"I do." She dipped her head respectfully.

"I admire your discretion, Painter Samathe. Your brother possessed the same talent."

"Thank you, my Lady. I hope you will find my service as satisfactory as his." She waved a hand toward her sketch of the woman, but wondered if there might be other duties she could perform.

After this exchange, Samathe departed, seeking time for thought. But when that time ended, she presented herself at the door of Favik's quarters and knocked, expecting a servant to answer. Instead, the man himself opened the door, his odd gray eyes calm, as though he had expected her.

"Painter Samathe. To what do I owe this visit?"

"Allow me entry and you'll find out."

He gazed at her with that awful studied neutrality of his, then gestured her inside. Samathe entered, rather surprised at the spareness of the room and furnishings. No carpets nor portraits adorned the chamber, only a papyrus map hung from one wall, its corners curling upon itself as though ashamed of its current circumstances. Here was a former Ambassador, who served as King's Mother's hand, and yet he quartered in dull, pauper-like chambers. A sparsely populated scroll stack gloomed in the corner; beside it, a desk with a worn chair. The austerity made her like him even less.

Favik looked about to speak, but she carried over him, "You know your son Anish is here, in Eskalind?"

"Yes."

"Was here at King's Halls not long ago?"

"Yes."

"Yet you play no part in his life."

He paused. "Circumstances are such that we have never met face to face. I would rather not reveal—"

"Reveal? What are you hiding?"

He drew his lips together. "This is a deeply personal matter. I appreciate your silence on the topic."

She doubted that he ever used that tone with King's Mother. The portraitist crossed her arms. "You sent my brother on a death mission to bring you your son, and now you cannot even acknowledge that same son?"

———

Favik inhaled slowly, the first technique every Ambassador Apprentice learns in calming oneself in tense situations, even before they arise. "Samathe, know that every day I grieve for your brother. And for my son who does not know me. For his mother, who died a violent, cruel death. For his newbabe sister who met the same horrible fate, moments after she first drew breath." He could not help it, his voice broke on the last word. For a moment Deenofts's sister seemed to shrink within herself. "You and I have both suffered terrible losses. Nothing either of us can do now will change that."

Her brown eyes blazed; her small nostrils reddened. "I cannot believe anything you tell me. You are all lies. My brother did not deserve to die for your lies." The portraitist marched to the door, her beige robes swirling about her, an angry whisper on her lips. "I'm telling Anish all of this."

Oh, he had once served as an Ambassador for Eskalind, immune to threats and demands, but this was a challenge unprecedented, for it would alter the course of his life as he decided to live it. He must persuade in order to precipitate the outcome he desired. "Please Samathe, do not do this. Do not make me your enemy or the fixation of your anger." Favik raised his open hands to his side, the classic gesture in Havadra of showing one did not possess weapons, was harmless. "I tried to help you as best I could. Think what might have befallen you if I had not stayed in Capitola to help you sell your fortress. If I had not arranged passage for you to Guerland, if I had not accompanied you to safety on that journey."

Her hand darted to a chain about her neck, the pendant hidden under her robes. "If Deenofts had been alive, I would have needed nothing from you."

Favik approached slowly. "How does telling Anish change the past? Someday I hope he and I will meet face to face, just the two of us, and I will tell him, I promise. But why impinge or even destroy any chance of my having a normal relationship with my son?"

"Deenofts's death destroyed any chance of his having a family. I will destroy any chance you have with yours." She yanked the door open, stepped outside, and shut it firmly behind her.

The former Ambassador exhaled, long and loud. "Then I know what I must do," he said quietly, casting a searing glare to his quilling desk. "My letters have priority with the Swift Riders, which yours, Painter Samathe, do not." With a tight grimace, he stepped to his desk.

It was quiet in Captain Marnil's commander's tent as both of its occupants bent before their desks, sable quills in hand. Sunlight illuminated the white walls of the tent and provided even light for Soldier Anish's work. He studied his freshly inked copy of the Eastlant border region, their position marked by small violet and charcoal hued *X*'s. A woman's voice was heard outside, an authority in her tone as though she were a First Sergeant, but her words were lost. He glanced to Captain Marnil, who tapped a dry quill nib against the sheet before him. Moments passed. Anish wondered how much longer till the break for their meal.

The tent flap moved aside and ginger-haired Stander Haknil entered, hands clasped upon a thick letter pouch that perhaps dated to the beginning of Dalich King's reign, for it was no longer a pure black but shaded gray about the creases and stubbed edges. "Captain Marnil, sir, Swift Rider just brought the post. She reports there was a mix-up and some letters were sent in the wrong direction. Envelopes coming from the south or King's Halls might be older than usual."

Marnil raised his eyes to the youth. "I see. Sort out the missives for the occupants of this tent, then see the rest distributed."

"Already done, sir." Haknil flipped the pouch open. "Two for you,

Captain." The young teen came forward and deposited a red envelope and a cream-shaded one upon his desk, "And three for Secretary Anish." The Stander paced to the blond man, who offered his hand to accept the identically pale envelopes.

"Thank you," said the Soldier, though when he saw Lady Jinilya's handwriting on the direction of the topmost letter, his expression soured. He placed the letters aside and returned to his work.

"Any for you, Haknil?" asked the Captain.

The youth's bright brown eyes shone as he clutched the pouch. "Yes, sir. From my father."

"He is stationed with the Tenth Company, yes?"

"Yes, sir. On the border between Kaymif and Mavold." The Soldier found this tidbit of interest, for Healer Morya and her family were stationed there as well.

"Indeed." There was a smile in the Captain's tone. "Dismissed, Stander." Haknil gave the Eskalinder salute and left. Marnil spoke. "Anish, a break for reading is in order." He slit the seals on his first envelope and pulled forth the papyruses inside.

The Soldier looked to his stack of three letters and fanned them apart. Lady Jinilya, Samathe, and Morya. He opened the latter, finding it dated from almost a month ago.

5th Day 10th Month, 2922
Dear Anish,
Just a short note as the babe is asleep and at last I am able to
quill you. Was wonderful to receive your letter and learn you
had finally convinced a woman to show you her feet—and a
Lady no less. You worry needlessly. We understand this will lead
to less visits from you, but want you to enjoy your life as much
as you are able with all of your duties.
Recall what I told you when you left my care: "Duties first but
do not neglect your heart." At the time, I meant your copying
work, but the same rule applies to lovers and companions.

*Yes, despite at last having a babe, I will still mother you if
you allow it.*
*We will all come visit you sometime, though our journeying
must wait till the little one is older. Saysha has learned to
smile and is charming beyond belief. Ah, but now she is awake
and wailing. Thank The Powers for my Apprentices, they are
receiving an extra education in caring for newbabes.*
Love,
Morya

He had not the heart to write her immediately and disclose his breaking with the Lady. Anish turned to the other two envelopes, debating which of the pair to open first. At last he opened Jinilya's, his eyelids lowering as he prepared for a barrage of invectives. Best to scan quickly. But from the first sentence, she spoke of apology, of the severe offense she had caused him and, incredibly, that Deenofts was a colleague of her mother and she had known the merchant in childhood.

He could hear weeping in her voice as he read her quilling. Shaking his head, Anish leaned away from the papyrus. One thing he knew; he had no intention of leaping back into her arms or bed. Why, since the Lady had made no reference to being with child, he was free to find a new lover the next time a woman showed him her feet. He would need to think on his response.

But there was a third letter to attend to, Samathe's.

Splitting the seal, he read of the Havadran's joy in encountering him again in good circumstances. Next followed an impressive listing of the Eskalinder Ladies she was engaged to paint, then a reassurance that she did not want her brother Deenofts's gold coins returned to her. Samathe instead requested Anish save them to purchase a large enough home for his future wife, their armfuls of children, and a private room for the portraitist to occupy during her visits. He nearly smiled at her plan. She ended her note by saying she had more news to impart, but would wait until next they met in person. She signed her note, *Fondly, Samathe, 29th Day of the 10th Month.*

Her generosity surprised him, and he folded her letter upon itself thinking of how best to thank her. The energies he had once planned to devote to copying Lady Jinilya's favorite tale would be better served in a work for the Havadran portraitist.

———

Captain Marnil tucked his wife's letter back into its envelope, pleased that all was well on their estate and their son's tutors reported his progress to be exemplary. At ten years of age, Kaloft would likely be ready to begin Ambassador Apprenticeship schooling at King's Halls in a couple of years. Even Athla thought the lad exhibited the aptitude of a diplomat and would follow in his uncle's, and grandfather's, footsteps.

Closing his eyes a moment, he pictured his wife and child walking the horseshoe-curved drive leading to their home, with the small red-barked tree in its crook. Marnil wondered if the years since his last visit had endowed the unusual plant with some measure of growth, for it had always seemed scrawny, underdeveloped, lacking in the sturdiness and spreading growth his mother had anticipated when she planted it in its prominent position nearly two decades ago, when he was but fourteen. He must remember to ask Athla about the tree's development in his reply.

Renewing his attention to his field headquarters, Jinil's youngest son glanced to the second letter, which came from King's Halls and bore the seal of an *F.* The envelope most certainly had been delayed in the Swift Riders' misdirection of the mails, for upon opening it, Marnil saw that it was a nearly a month old.

7th Day, 10th Month, 2922
My Lord Captain Marnil,
Word has reached me concerning a family matter of the

*Havadran-born Soldier Anish, of your company. The
information is such that it is best delivered in person, privately,
to him. The matter is timely.*
*By your command, might you grant Soldier Anish leave to
journey to court? I understand that he is of great use to you and
do not ask this lightly.*
Servant of Eskalind,
Favik

Marnil looked to his Soldier, currently engrossed in one of his own letters. Loathe to part with his young Secretary, but also fair-minded and thus unwilling to delay whatever news his assistant might learn of his family, he set himself to quilling leave papers and a Swift Riders pass.

King's Halls was nearly 365 miles away, though. Whilst the roads were mainly flat and well maintained, even with the Swift Riders' horses, the journey would consume at a minimum five days in each direction. Likely six days or a week. As Favik had stated that the matter was timely, yet not urgent, the Captain would not normally issue the highest priority pass. Without that pass, the Soldier could be delayed if more pressing orders superseded his needs. But as the summons had been written a full month before, and then delayed in reaching the Sixth Company, Marnil thus opted for the most urgent pass. He hoped to The Powers that the news awaiting his Soldier would not lead to a lengthy furlough of his valuable man.

The fourth day of his journey concluded with Anish walking bandy-legged into the Kayna Queenstown Records Keepers' office, hoping there might be a Healer on call with an ointment to soothe his chafed thighs. It amazed him that the army-issued fabric of his trousers had not worn through; never had he ridden so far so quickly over so many days. Not once in the more than a dozen Swift Riders offices he had visited thus far had he waited for a horse. Each time, once his documents passed the Records Keeper's scrutiny, the next leg of his journey commenced upon a fresh mount—or he was granted a sleeping bunk in the Swift Riders' office.

Thus the young Soldier was now only seventy miles from King's Halls. Were he offered the option of walking the rest of the way or even lying on the slats of an unpadded wagon that only traversed a gravel path, he would have accepted. Anish half hoped some urgent business of his betters would supersede his departure tomorrow. In the meantime, his only desire was a horizontal surface to lie upon and a clean bucket of water to wash. Food had no appeal.

A Records Keeper received him at the ubiquitous counter that partitioned officials from plebeians, though in Eskalind such wooden walls were short enough to serve as writing desks. Under her purple headwrap, impassive brown eyes studied his pass, the creamy papyrus stained dark about its veins from his own sweat and the countless hands which had examined and handled it over the last few days. She recited the same words he had heard over and over again on his reports to these offices. Only the date changed. "On this eighth day of the eleventh month of the year 2922, I approve a horse for you. There should be one ready in the stables."

"I'm very tired. Bunking at the Swift Riders for the night is most appealing." She raised an eyebrow, and he continued, "If there is a bunk in the male quarters." The official reached under the counter, pulled forth a short piece of sable-shaded ribbon, tied two knots in it, and handed it to him.

"Present this to the Swift Riders for your bed." She turned and left, and he thought to stay her and ask about a Healer, but given her determined manner, he thought it might look like weakness. On occasion such Havadran instincts needled him, but this time he obeyed them and departed stiff-backed, nursing his thoughts.

Spreading his feet farther apart than normal, Anish walked to the adjacent building, which housed the Swift Riders. The door was flung open to the wall as though the room anticipated his arrival with keen eagerness. Entering, he passed a low table with six post baskets upon it, four marked with the cardinal points, the fifth labeled "King's Halls," and the sixth "Local." All were empty, which signaled that the office would be minimally staffed as the Riders were abroad running their errands. A large papyrus map of the local area hung above the post table, denoting the nearby noble estates, towns, farms, and even a quarry.

He approached the counter and called, "Hello?"

The door in the back of the room opened, and a petite Eskalinder wearing the Swift Riders uniform of black riding pants and a hip-length tunic approached him, her shoulders alert and brown eyes with a quick notice about them. "Yes?"

Anish found the energy to smile and placed his ribbon and pass upon the counter by the open log book. She glanced at them, and before he could speak, she asked, "Family leave? Is your wife heavy with child?"

"Um, no, I'm not joined." Her face held a neutral expression, but her eyes surveyed his physique in a hawkish appraisal. A bit wearily, he said, "I'm hoping there might be a bed for me."

"There is. Sign the log." The woman placed a quill and ink bottle on the counter, then turned and paced to a cabinet along the back wall, bending to open a drawer, her bottom superbly displayed by the cut of her trousers and the extra padding sewn in the seat giving her a generous shape. The Swift Rider fumbled about in the drawer, shifting her weight to her other leg. There was something hypnotic in her movement. Or maybe he was more tired than he thought. Anish scrawled his name and designations on the papyrus.

Drawing forth crisp sheets and a blanket, she returned and laid them upon the counter. "The bunk closest to the window has the most headroom. If you require it." Her lips did not part but she smiled.

"Thank you."

He gathered the items as she added, "Are you hungry? There's a small tavern on the other side of the Records Keepers' office."

Anish considered, but still craved rest. "No, I think I will wash and head straight to bed. But thank you. Again." Exhaustion made it difficult to talk.

She nodded and pointed to the door. "The male quarters are on the right."

The spent Soldier made his way to the room, grateful to find a fresh pitcher of water, a bucket, and even small towels on a stand in the room. Stripping completely, he hung his satchel on a peg, draped his uniform on a chair, and set to washing with one end of the cloth and drying with the other. Dropping the used towel into the hamper, he flung one bedsheet over the bunk under the window and laid the blanket by the footboard in case he grew cold later. Tossing himself onto the bed, he pulled the second sheet over him and passed into unconsciousness upon the stiff pillow.

It was dark and the air slightly chilled when he struggled from a fathomless sleep to a woman saying, "Is your blanket keeping you warm enough?" Her voice sounded akin to the Swift Rider.

"I didn't need the blanket," he mumbled, wiping his eyes though it did not improve his vision in the darkened room. "But it's chillier now—"

"You still don't need it." His sheet lifted, and a warm and definitely female form slid over him with the soft press of unclothed breasts upon his chest. He reached tentatively and touched her unclad buttocks.

"Oh," he said. Once, twice, and then it became one long word as she took command of the situation.

Anish awoke alone in his bunk at first light the next morning, not certain if he had dreamed the night's activities. Inhaling, he found his sheet was not mute; it spoke of a woman's presence. He grinned, recalling how tired he had been when he went to bed. Rising, he washed and dressed. Now he was hungry.

The Soldier did not see the Swift Rider in Kayna Queenstown again. He arrived at King's Halls on the fourth horse of the ninth day of the month as the sun dove for the horizon. He blew the dust from the road out his nose and slid his eyes left and right, wondering if he might see Lady Jinilya along the way. Not a word of this visit had he quilled her, and not only because he would likely arrive before a note reached her.

Anish finally presented himself at the crowded King's Halls' Records Keepers' office, amongst dozens of people costumed in the manner befitting their citizenship: a Gergelt man in a floppy long tunic purposefully stained with more colors than a double rainbow; an Eastlant family, the mother and two young daughters with ribbons in their hair that echoed their dress colors, neat and fresh as though they had just come from the baths; Kursaks in their plain straight robes, necks and cuffs bedecked with ivy-patterned imprints; a woman from Humiksland in a bodice taut at the waist, giving an expression of rounded plenitude to her bosom and hips. He would not be tempted by his former lover if such a view remained long before him. Perhaps that Swift Rider had unleashed something inside him.

Dark-robed Apprentices greeted each person or group at the wide-arched entryway, asked their business, and directed them to the appropriate counter, but the Apprentice Records Keeper Anish spoke to seemed befuddled by the Soldier's situation and directed him to a line for borderlanders. The Mavoldian standing in front of him then questioned why Anish wore an Eskalind Soldier's uniform yet stood in this line. Hearing that Anish was an Eskalind citizen, the Mavoldian shook his head, muttering of ineptitude. Loudly he summoned another Apprentice, a meek young woman pale in her black robes and easily cowed by the borderlander. That Apprentice led Anish away to a waiting purple-headwrapped Records Keeper, standing behind the counter with clean sheets of papyrus lying before her.

Her rapid assessment of his documents concluded with, "I'm not certain of Ambassador Favik's schedule. Tell me where you plan to be the rest of the evening; an Apprentice will be sent to inform you of more details."

Anish grit his teeth, feeling stupid for not considering his evening plans. He was starving. "I'm going to the kitchens, then the baths." The Apprentice by his side made a quiet murmur and nodded her approval. He wondered how badly he stank.

The Records Keeper shot her Apprentice a stern glance at this display of opinion. "And where will you quarter, Soldier?"

"In the military dormitory, if there's room for me."

"There should be, but check with them." She dipped her quill in ink and began recording their exchange. "On your way then."

En route to his meal, he passed Scriptor Vinil, who waved an amiable greeting but continued on in a hurry. Once seated at his destination, Anish devoured bread and sauces of a stunning variety of flavors and textures. The cooks at King's Halls enjoyed access to a wider variety of spices and ingredients than those of his company. A few sauces exhibited a robust level of spicy heat that recalled his birthland. This unexpectedly flavorful abundance was brought to him in an array of bowls by an eager-to-please flaxen-haired Stander, who assured him that ample unclaimed bunks awaited in the dormitory. The lad even offered to see to his uniform's laundering and brought him a sleeping robe, along with a towel, for the baths. Laden with a full belly, Anish all but waddled to the cavernous baths in the bowels of King's Halls, bright candles illuminating the barrel-arched ceilings carved from bare rock.

As he was undressing in the men's area, the Stander darted under his elbows, dodging the other occupants, to claim Anish's dirty clothing. The lad whisked his satchel, sword, and sweat-stained uniform away. At last soaking nude in the earth-heated, deliciously warm waters, Anish wondered if he might find a way to be stationed at King's Halls to prolong such luxuries. Perhaps when he met with Ambassador Favik, the man might find favor with him and could arrange something. Then he chided himself on such Havadran plotting, for he knew not what news awaited him. Until now he had relished a measure of mental will in keeping speculation from overriding his days. In truth, he had thought such conjecture would consume his thoughts as he rode, but galloping along roadways necessitated extreme concentration upon negotiating the road surfaces and the other travelers, on foot, horsed, driving carriages or lumbering carts. Even now, when he closed his eyes, he could see the pale yellow track before him as though he still sat a horse.

No, the best news he could hope for would be that a member of his family still survived, and the worst that his death was sought by a powerful Havadran faction. Or that Eskalind sought him as the general's heir, a calmer of chaos and muter of unrest. It would be advantageous to his adopted country to sponsor a Havadran leader with such qualities. If he had them. Anish laughed at himself and closed his eyes, resting his head against the smooth stone bordering the water's edge and counting the sounds echoing from the bare rock walls: water splashing, a distant conversation, his own breathing.

"Citizen Soldier Anish?" He opened his eyes to view a stiff-backed Apprentice Records Keeper standing near the steps leading into the pool, his body-shielding long black robes odd looking as a comfortably nude man entered the pool behind him. The Apprentice darted his gaze amongst the heads bobbing in the water. Anish raised a hand and the young man nodded, hands folded before his uniform in an attitude of constrained patience and expectation. Stepping out of the water, Anish considered that this Apprentice must be near the end of his training, given his reserve.

"Soldier Anish, Ambassador Favik will be waiting for you in a private room in the Library. I will show you the way."

"Now?" Anish asked as he wiped a drying cloth over his head.

"Indeed."

"But I have only a sleeping robe to wear." He toweled the water dripping along his chest. "My uniform is being laundered."

The man's eyes were as coyly neutral as a First Sergeant inspecting a rank known for concealing trouble. "It will have to do. *You* cannot keep an Ambassador waiting, Soldier."

Anish stared, while he proceeded to dry his male parts and bottom in an exaggerated manner. Someone in the pool snickered. The Apprentice waited, watching with an imperious gaze. Finally donning his donated sleeping robe, the Soldier flung the towel aside and followed the black-robed young man away from the baths, heat rising from his skin and slickening it with perspiration.

Not fifty steps from the Library's main door, Lady Jinilya came into view, a purple Apprentice Librarian cloak about her shoulders, her expression beaming and bright as she approached. "Anish! You came back to me!"

How pretty she looked, her stunning green eyes glossy with reflected candlelight, but he disdained her notion that she was the focus of his orbit. "No, my Lady. I was summoned on other business." Anish nodded and continued walking, pulling the sleeping robe tighter across his chest.

"Oh." It was as though joy were a tangible thing she had mislaid, unfathomable that it had vanished. Then she dashed to his elbow, hovering like a tame bird expecting a treat. "Did you receive my letter?"

"I did." Her lips parted as he continued, "Excuse me, my Lady, I am required elsewhere." He made to turn away, but her hand grasped his arm, the tender weight of her touch swaying him to stop. Ahead, the Records Keeper Apprentice entered the Library through its main door.

Jinilya spoke, quiet and sad, drawing close to his ear, eyes downcast. "Please know how sorry I am for my terrible mistake. I hope The Powers will help you to forgive me."

He shrugged, and she released his arm.

It hurt to see her, to speak to her thus. He felt a burning coolness inside himself, as though a long-denied confirmation affirmed itself that he was akin to the worst of Havadrans.

Anish moved mechanically into the Library, following his guide to the appointed room. Entering, the Apprentice presented him to Ambassador Favik, a graying blond man with thin lines etching his face, remnants of past scolds and smiles. He was standing near a lit candelabra and wearing a quiet and sad expression remarkably similar to Lady Jinilya's. The Apprentice departed, closing the door behind him.

The elder man did not lower his gaze from Anish's to survey his inappropriate attire, but still the Soldier made his excuse. "Your pardon, sir, for my appearance. The Apprentice insisted I come as I was, with no provision to dress respectfully."

"Don't be troubled by this, it is I who should apologize for requiring your immediate audience. Please, sit with me." He lowered himself into a chair. Anish mirrored his action. "I was sorry to call you in such haste, but the matter is timely. Have you received any startling news of late?"

"No sir."

Anish must have looked puzzled, for the man continued. "Any correspondence from the portraitist Samathe?"

"Yes sir, but nothing beyond some pleasantries and where to quill her in future." There was a simmering expectation in the man's gaze, compelling him to continue. "Samathe wrote me on the, um, I believe the twenty-ninth day of last month. I have her letter in my satchel, but it's in the military dormitory." Anish paused. "Should I send for it?"

The Ambassador had looked away. "There is no need."

Anish waited, feeling that perhaps the man was counting something unseen. The Soldier settled into his chair just as Favik spoke. "Let me relate to you some things you already know." Anish nodded, curling his thumb around the chair arm. "Your grandfather was General Yirlofts. Yes?"

He felt a small lad under that beloved but keen scrutiny again, and he spoke as calmly as he could. "Yes."

"Your mother's name was…Melande." Her name on his lips hinted at a sigh.

Anish whispered, "How…can you possibly know that?"

Favik's eyes rested upon his own. "Because I, not Colonel Sirish, am your father."

Anish must have stammered out a question, for the man began describing secret meetings and the inside of his grandfather's fortress—images that brought overwhelming memories. "And the babe your mother carried was your full sister," he was saying.

It was as though the air had turned to water and Anish was drowning. "Stop," he sputtered. "Please stop. I need, need to think." He dragged his fingers over his face, leaning into them. If this man was his true father, than no part of him was of Sirish's line. He shared no part of that vile man's blood. That was a relief, if it was true.

Anish exhaled, lowering his hands and facing the Ambassador. Looking into those odd gray eyes, another thought came.

If Sirish *had* fathered him, and Mother's newbabe, then Sirish would have had no cause to slay them. If Sirish had truly been his father, none of that would have happened.

Anish never would have been in the desert, he would not have gotten lost, captured by bandits.

Deenofts would not have died by a thief's knife.

The Shinglo's very existence would be unknown rather than a recurring nightmare.

Words were coming out of his mouth. "Were it not for you, Mother and the child she carried would still be alive."

"Please know, Anish, I did everything I could to try to pull you, Melande, and your sister safely away from Havadra. Everything. And though it pains me to point to this fact, were it not for me, you would not be here."

"Then I would be no different than I am now. Nothing." He stood. "I have no family. My family is dead."

Perhaps the Ambassador said something else, but Anish exited the chamber in a daze, walking unconscious of where he was going. But his feet knew. They found the shortest course to the door that quartered the House of Jinil, and he knocked boldly, ignoring the Guard's cutting eyes, not considering that anyone other than his object might answer. Answer she did, lips open and eyes soft, a hopeful expectation about them. He wished he weighed nothing, that he could fall into her and be absorbed, forgetful of all things save her warmth and beloved being. "Jinilya," he whispered, "I need you."

———

Gentle kisses awoke Anish the next morning. Disappointingly they tapered into words. "I will be back soon," Jinilya whispered. "I wrote a note requesting time away from service so we might be together as long as possible before you depart."

Well, for the promise of the comfort of her bare skin, he *might* be able to bring himself to release her from his arms now. Allowing his lover to slip away, Anish watched her wrap her violet Apprentice's cloak over the wine-colored sleeping robe she must have donned whilst he slept. "Back soon." As she departed, his sweet beloved waved the note as though it were a tasty morsel to lead a hungry horse.

Food would be a good idea.

Her chamber door closed, and Anish sat upright, rubbing his forehead. He half hoped that meeting Ambassador Favik had been a dream. Well, without that, the evening would not have concluded so favorably. Something for which he could thank the man, not that he intended to speak with him again. But now that he and Jinilya were reunited, he would be returning to King's Halls again, and his and the Ambassador's paths might intersect. Much as he might wish it, he could not spend every waking moment in his Lady's chamber. Anish lowered his hands to the smooth, crimson sheets, planning how to respond next he encountered his supposed father.

Easy: a deferential nod as he would offer to any superior, as though none of it happened. The Ambassador had his version of events; Anish had his own. His own included being a captive of the Shinglo, his grandfather dead, a father who killed a mother near childbed. Best to put the woes of the past aside, to tell no one, ever. Besides, the Shinglo had demanded his silence, he had made an oath.

The notion came easily, as though a part of him decided long ago upon this course of action and his awareness just now grasped this perfect fact.

A muffled, high-pitched squeal sounded. His stomach, demanding nourishment. Spying his sleeping robe strewn under a fine-grained mahogany chair, he reached for the garment and donned it as he marched to the door. All the future awaited outside that door: his military career, the fond eyes of Lady Jinilya, and most immediately, breakfast.

He patted his belly, then swung open the wooden door and stepped into the corridor, only to face at last a countenance he had studiously avoided. The other occupant of these chambers, Lord Saril, King's Second, former Eskalind Ambassador to Havadra.

It was as though Anish were transported back to Grandfather's office, as though he shrank to the height he had been as a lad of ten, watching as this brown-skinned man turned toward him for the general's introduction of his grandson. This was the first time their eyes had met since then, for the young Soldier had deliberately lowered his gaze when making his deference to King's Second, the excuse of being an underling most convenient for his aim of avoiding eye contact. For if Lord Saril recognized him as the general's grandson, who knew to whom he might relay this news in Havadra. Surely the former Ambassador maintained contacts there, even with the frequent overthrows of leadership. Anish could chance nothing pulling him back to Havadra. That fear was like a dagger of ice in his heart.

"Sir." Anish looked to the floor and raised his arm, flexing the wrist in salute to his superior, dressed alike to himself in a sleeping robe.

"What are you doing in my family quarters?"

"Your pardon, sir. I was with Lady Jinilya last night—"

"So I heard. You are?"

"Soldier Anish, sir." He stared at the man's bare feet, the slight wisp of dark hair near the big toe joint.

A long pause before the order came. "Look at me."

The young man complied. He could see King's Second thinking, the slight jitter of the eyes as they studied his face, the slightest pucker in the bottom lip. The act of observation calmed him, for he knew his course, even before the Lord said, "You look familiar. Did we meet before, in Havadra?"

"No sir."

"Are you certain?"

"Yes sir."

"You answered quickly. Was your answer formed before I asked it?" A slight compression in the eyelids, a lifting of the corner of the mouth.

"Sir, with respect, I had little conference with outsiders whilst I lived in Havadra. And it was a long time ago."

The Second to the Eskalinder King probed, brown eyes intent, so different from the softness of his sister's. "No private meetings, arranged by close family members?"

He did not hesitate. "No sir." How Grandfather would have been proud of the certainty in his voice, even though his words meant denying their relationship.

"Why do I not believe you?"

"With respect, sir, only you can answer that question." His superior officer stared hard into his eyes.

The main door to the chamber opened and Jinilya stepped forth. The Lord glanced to her, then went to the dining table and sat as though answering a pleasant summons to meal. He pulled an empty plate before him and tore into the bread basket.

Jinilya's gaze swung from Anish's face, to his upraised arm, the palm still raised in salute, to her brother, who had dipped bread in a sauce bowl. He munched loudly.

"What is going on?" she said.

Saril smacked his lips. "Sister, be cautious with this Havadran." He gestured with the bread as a crumb dropped from it. "He is a liar."

"How can you use your rank to make him stand in salute in our private quarters?" She marched to Anish and cupped her fingers over his fingertips to lower his taut wrist. "It is behavior unworthy of an outerland lord." With that, she pulled Anish into her chamber and shut the door with seething restraint, once again providing solace after a confrontation with a man best avoided.

A note from Jinilya arrived first thing in the morning, asking if King's Mother might grant the young Lady some hours free from service. Her former lover had unexpectedly returned to King's Halls and the pair were reunited. Marna's gray eyebrows lowered as she read the note.

No, she would not require Jinilya's presence this day. Rather, she would summon the Havadran for an audience. There was much she wanted to ask him after her conversation with the portraitist Samathe.

Thus, when the bell signal rang announcing her visitor, she lay her palms flat upon her desk, still debating whether to hold a formal conference with him from behind her imposing desk, or visit more companionably in one of the sets of stuffed chairs mid room. Prominent on her mental list was the question of why he engaged in completely unnecessary mortal combat to earn his sword. But given the first item on her agenda *should* be an assessment of his character in regards to his relationship with the young Lady, she opted for the more casual setting. Best for it to seem a companionable visit, at first.

Rising from behind her desk, Marna walked at a regal pace to the center of the room and rang the answering signal from the bellpulls by the new black curtains, which were studded with purple buttons.

She seated herself as the doors opened. A familiar face stepped into the room, but dressed as a military man. He bowed and paced toward her. "Favik?" She squinted, for he had shaved away his beard, his chin line strong and youthful.

"My Lady?" By The Powers, he even sounded like her man, though his bearing was a bit timid. "I'm Soldier Anish, you sent for me."

"For a moment I thought—" She had to look away and gather her reason, for all her plans for this conversation dissipated like smoke in a drafty room. Many chances she had had to look upon his face, but in her disgust over how he earned his sword, she had not. It was a shock to now behold his resemblance to her man. Years ago, Favik had told her he had a son who died. If the child had lived, he would have appeared exactly thus.

Before her the young man stood, quiet, with an uneasy expectation in his aspect. Formulating her next utterance, she returned her gaze to his blond eyebrows, for she could not concentrate when looking into those familiar eyes.

"Jinilya tells me your family hails from Havadra, but you appear to me more akin to the people of my birth country, Humiksland."

"I was…born and raised in Havadra, though I was told I resembled a grandmother whom I never met. She was descended from a…" He seemed to lose his thought. "Descended from a northern line." The Soldier swallowed audibly as the color in his face pinked.

"Well, that explains it," Marna said, not quite convinced herself, especially given his odd reaction. "And Painter Samathe tells me you knew her brother Deenofts?"

"Yes."

When he did not add any further information, she asked, "And how did you come to know him?"

Anish could have been a traveling player reciting well-worn lines. "Deenofts and I met by chance when we were caught out-of-walls during a coup."

This was most odd. "He did not know you, yet sheltered you in his household?"

"Yes, my Lady."

"Do you know why he did that?"

The young man bowed his head, voice quiet. "He told me his lady had sent him to find me. I thought he meant my mother."

The last word was on the threshold of her hearing. A moment passed as she replayed the sound in her mind to ascertain what he had said. If he thought Deenofts had called his mother "my lady," then his family must have been highly placed. Gently she stated, "Though she has spoken much of you, Lady Jinilya has told me nothing of your family."

Her assistant's lover spoke slightly louder, but a hint of shame tinted his words. "I have told her nothing of them, for they are all gone."

He had raised his eyes to her, and in them she saw the pleading expression of a young boy, so alike to Favik when he entered her life as an orphaned Page that she nearly stood to embrace him. Perhaps he read the sympathy and concern in her eyes, for he continued, "My Lady King's Mother, I must ask your forgiveness and beg your confidence before I tell you more."

Again she settled her vision on his eyebrows, for the sight of his eyes clutched at her maternal heart. The Powers must have aided her, steadying her voice. "Beg my confidence. Why?"

"I promised myself to tell no one, ever, but Lady Jinilya trusts you and—I know much time has passed, but I still fear—I was hunted and helpless when Deenofts found me, an experience I hope never to repeat." She nodded for him to continue, trying to find the thread of his tale. "My family lost their standing; I was the sole survivor with a high price on my head. No one in Eskalind knows, not even Lady Jinilya. I fear being hunted again."

He was silent as though words had abandoned him. She waited, then replied, "I see. Then tell me what you will and I shall keep it to myself."

There was nearly a sigh in his voice. "My mother's father was known as the general."

Dalock's Queen raised an eyebrow. "Ah, she was very highly placed."

Anish said nothing, holding a respectful pose with a dejected quality as though he wished to flee, an image entirely antithetical to the imposing impression she conjured of the renowned general. "And what of your father?"

Ever so slightly, the Soldier's shoulders hunched forward. "The man I was raised to believe was my father killed my mother and her babe."

Slowly a trickle of memory of this heinous event rose in her mind. "But was he not your father?"

"I don't know, my Lady." He raised his head but glanced away. "Last night I met a man who claimed to answer to the deed." Now he gazed at her with a cool detachment, worthy of an ambassador from his homeland, or one shielding himself against the cruel vagaries of others. "But it would explain why a man would slay his entire family and hunt the sole survivor, me."

Marna studied her assistant's lover, formulating her thoughts. "Who is the man who claims to be your father?"

"Ambassador Favik." The Scholars' Mistress was glad to be sitting, for her head felt light as though it might float away from her body. Long ago, when Favik told her his wife and son were dead, he had cried before her. To comfort his distress, she had embraced him close, and Dalich had entered her chamber at that moment and accused her of being lovers with Favik. Then her son had tumbled into an emotional pit of despair, and the two of them were estranged for months, leaving all the responsibilities of rulership upon her. How angry she had been at Dalich, but it was Favik who deserved her repudiation, for his lie caused that breach. Yet she could not fathom why he would lie to her. If he lied about that, other falsehoods surely must plague their interactions.

"My Lady?"

Marna blinked, realizing some time had passed as she pursued her tangled thoughts, coherent as a basket of scrap yarn. She lifted her shoulders and felt tiny pops in her back as she straightened her spine. "Soldier Anish, do you accept what the Ambassador told you as truth?"

"My Lady, if it is true, I want nothing to do with him."

Well. He seemed very firm about that. "Will you tell Lady Jinilya, or anyone else, of Favik's claim of paternity?"

"By your leave, my Lady, I plan never to do so."

She wanted to stand, but did not trust that her feet would serve her at this moment. "Then carry on. Ask the Apprentice outside the door to send the Ambassador to me immediately."

This younger twin to Favik bowed and departed her chamber. Marna rose slowly, scanning the room. "By The Powers, any Records Keeper with eyes would judge them to be father and son. The face proves the father, as we say in Eskalind. " She moved to her desk to sit and brood and wait.

She shut her eyes until the bell rang, then pretended to read the papyrus before her as her man entered the room and approached her desk. There he waited, standing patient and quiet, on the same patch of floor where he once imparted news of Dalock's death. Her heart heavy at the thought, she raised her eyes. "I just spoke with your son."

A slight nod of the head. "Soldier Anish." It was as though he expected her to know and was not displeased.

Folding her fingers together, she stated, "I recall, years ago, when you confided that your wife and son were dead."

Gone was the Ambassadorial calm. "My Lady, they were dead to me in that I thought I would never see them again. They were sequestered in Havadra, in heavily guarded fortresses. Anish's mother was—"

"General Yirlofts's daughter? Yes, he told me." She nearly uttered what she thought, that his trips to Havadra had been less onerous than she had been led to believe. Rage swelled her heart at his treachery. Marna pressed her elbows and arms firm against the desk, as though building a scaffold to hold herself steady. "Anish seems displeased with your revelation."

"He blames me for the death of his mother and his sister."

He was trying to confuse her. "This makes no sense. They were killed when General Yirlofts lost command, in 2914 as I recall? But it was some years prior, before Dalich finally went to Damina, when you told me your family was dead." He looked lost. He was likely trying to fabricate an excuse, but she did not care, instead aiming for her final objective. "What else have you told me that was not true?"

There was a pause, and he looked directly at her, his voice an odd monotone. "I am Portnil, the Eskalinder whose family was held against their will in Havadra. I appeared before a Records Keeper under that false name to petition for my family's rescue. I forged documents to create that identity." The Scholars' Mistress brought her hands to her ears. When she realized her reaction, she pulled them away slowly, catching a finger in her long hair. She yanked it free as the former Ambassador continued. "My Lady, I did this only to protect my family when they entered Eskalind. I could not use my true name on the documents, for I feared assassins from Havadra would pursue us. I needed them to be safe. That meant untraceable, with new names."

"You lied to a Records Keeper. And to me. Oh Favik." Marna leaned forward into her hands. Her voice a bit muffled by her palms, she asked, "What of the scroll, the scroll about ancient weapons that was stolen from the Library and found later in Havadra?"

His speech was low and thick, as though he had run up the stairs of the Royals' Tower to make a dire report. "My Lady, my sole role in that was returning it to your hands. General Yirlofts gave the scroll to me. I had never, ever seen it before then."

Marna's thoughts overlapped. "If any of this were to out—faking an identity for your own gain—I can no longer have you at King's Halls. You must go."

"But, my Lady—"

"Go where you will, as long as it is away from here." She rotated in her chair, turning her shoulders to him, eyes shuttered hard as though she might blot out the very existence of the world.

"My Lady—"

"Just—go."

She sat immobile, listening to the pad of footsteps retreating behind her. "My Lady, please hear me. I have been ever faithful to *you*, and to the Scholars. That I told you none of this plan earlier was to shield you and the Scholars in case you were questioned. I wish, how I wish I had been more precise when I told you my family was gone. Know that I did what I did *only* for them." His voice quavered on the final word. "Ask The Powers themselves if that is true. If they truly are The Powers, then They know my heart." The door opened and closed with a whisper, as though he did not leave. She waited, but the room was silent. Marna turned to see if he was there, but he was absent, as though death unexpected claimed him.

"And this." Lord Radil led his son Amril around the crowd of laden tables in the spacious study. The elder Lord uncovered a shabby wooden box. "This is where I keep the gold toasting cup for First Day of the Year. Thus, when I send you to fetch the box tomorrow, you know where it is hidden."

The thirteen-year-old grimaced. "Father, the lock is half attached."

Radil smiled. "It is. Has been for years." He placed a hand on the lad's shoulder, his fingers just below the dark blond of his locks. "You see? This way it looks like nothing of value."

"But we do not have thieves in our house."

The Lord nodded. "Thankfully, no. We live in Eskalind, which by The Powers' Will is considered free of such vices. But." He used both hands to part the halves of the box, revealing the thick gold cup nestled amongst red velvet, a pure rendition of the colors of their house. "It is important for you to learn the *concept* of hiding in plain sight."

Amril peered at the polished sheen of the sunlight-hued cup. "You keep it in an old box that appears to have no worth. Thus it is overlooked?"

"Indeed." The Scholar lowered the box onto a cluttered table, directly atop a large portion of the latest note from his Lady Marna. It was an odd missive: the first paragraphs in her tortured quilling recounted some borderland news of little importance, but the last paragraph, a mere sentence, was written roughly and almost illegible, as though dashed in angry haste. It read,

> *Our former Ambassador has permanently departed*
> *King's Halls.*

She signed her title, and that was all. The words resided there on the papyrus, just at the foot of the box, for Amril to read. If he noticed.

Instead, the young noble reached forward, asking, "May I hold the cup, Father?"

"Not until you are Acta Sua." The lad's expression was one of utter surprise, and Radil chuckled. "No need to wait that long. I want to see you enjoy it." He pulled forth the treasure and laid it in his son's slim hands, studying the transfixed expression in the blue eyes as the boy tilted the shiny surface, reading the names of their ancestors who had been Acta Sua, back to the founder of their house, Valip, ennobled by Palich, the 117th King of Eskalind. The names crowded the shimmery surface, but room remained for generations more.

As Amril admired this bit of family history, a tentative knock sounded on the door. Radil paced to the redwood portal and opened it slightly to face his Steward. "Yes?"

The man spoke in hushed tones, as though Radil were a nursery maid attending to sleeping toddler Alayna rather than at the door of his private study. "A private message for you, my Lord, from Ambassador Favik. He is horsed, upon the entrance road, and comes on urgent business. He hopes for a brief visit to meet with you alone, if convenient for you."

"Ah." It was not an entirely unusual request given the needs of Scholarly business, though King's Mother's letter portended something else was afoot. Best to speak to Favik in person, away from the household. "See my horse prepared. I will leave shortly. I thank you." His man nodded and departed as Radil shut the door. "Son, stow the cup away. We will raise it tomorrow night."

Amril pretended to drink from the cup, eyes mirthful as his father laughed, then replaced the heirloom in the box. Radil smiled then, his mood lightening at his son's antics. Perhaps Favik's errand was such that he might be persuaded to stay a night or two and divulge the reason for his sudden departure from their Lady's service.

Not long thereafter, the Acta Sua and his chestnut mount trotted the road leading away from the house. Just around the bend, the long line of pine trees bordering the road flickered their bright green needles in the breeze which also stirred the grasses shielding their thick roots. There, still as though quilled upon a fine Legend scroll's parchment, Favik sat astride his gray horse, his head angled toward the dark leather of his saddle. Whether his attitude was that of defeat or he was merely a rider attending to his mount's need for a snack, Radil could not discern. The gelding was nose deep in the waving grass, feeding in one spot as though the ground yielded a satisfying abundance only in the area just under his muzzle. The gray paid no heed to the approaching rider.

Radil called in a glad voice, "Your mount looks hungry."

Favik raised his head, eyes reddened, distant, tired. "My Lord, we both are."

The Scholar steadied his horse as it sidled away from the pair. "Then pause on your journey, however urgent, and sup with us tonight."

"Much as the offer deeply appeals, I cannot." Favik paused.

Radil tugged his reins to come alongside his fellow. "What is the matter? How might I offer assistance?"

"I am cast out." The lack of emotion in Favik's tone made the utterance even harder to believe.

"What has happened?"

His next utterance did little to explain things. "Do you recall when your wife's maid showed me her feet?"

The Acta Sua raised his head. "Wh—why, yes. And you declined, to her great disappointment. Mayva says she still asks about you. She is a smart lass and well read; we thought you and she might find things in common."

"It was not long before she showed me her feet that I discovered I had a son."

"What? That was quite some time ago, Amril was still in the nursery. Favik, why did you not mention it?" His companion was silent. Another thought crept forward. "Would you tell me why you did not join with your child's mother?" Radil wondered if this was why his companion had left King's Halls. He awaited the key that would solve this puzzle.

"After we conceived, she was forcibly joined to another."

"By The Powers, that is horrible." Radil silently thanked Them that none of his family was nearby to hear this horrific news. "Favik," he breathed, "this did not happen in Eskalind?"

"No."

The Lord of the House of Valip was certain his relief showed on his face, as the former Ambassador continued, "She and her husband parented no children, and when I saw her a dozen years later, we conceived again. A daughter."

A son, and a dozen years later a daughter. By The Powers, the gender and age difference was identical to that of his own family. Radil spoke with the authority of his position. "Then that was another clear sign from The Powers that you and she were meant to be together. Did you petition a Records Keeper to bring her and the children to Eskalind?"

"I did." Now Favik spoke urgently, "But Radil, I could not use my true name or theirs. Her husband was highly placed. What if he had sent assassins to seek them out? I'm convinced he would have; later he proved himself that type of man. So I lied. I lied to a Records Keeper, I forged documents about my family's identities and my own." He looked to the pines, which had stilled. His face was reddened, from the sun and from anger. "I did it to shield them, to protect them, so my family could flee to Eskalind, live here and know peace."

Afraid of the answer, but compelled to ask, Radil whispered, "Where are they now?"

The former Ambassador turned to him, eyes moist. "The newbabe and ... Melande, they were slain by her husband. He found out." The words sent a chill through the noble's body. It was the worst outerlander outcome one could imagine. He imagined that happening to Mayva and babe Alayna. But they were safe in their home just a few minutes' ride behind him. And Amril too. "What, what of your son?"

Favik shook his head. "He lives, he is safe, but he blames me for their deaths."

"How could he?"

"He's right. Were it not for me, her husband would not have killed them." A corner of his companion's lips lifted slightly. "It is all a great sadness to me." Favik looked to the reins in his hands. "My son revealed my deeds to King's Mother. She questioned me, I confirmed it. Then she told me to leave King's Halls and her service." A resigned sigh in his voice. "She cannot trust one who lies to a Records Keeper for his own benefit."

"But, you did it to save your family."

Favik's expression did not change; he lifted his reins slightly as if to turn to leave. His horse raised its head. Radil continued in urgent tones, "I do not want to second-guess the Bladesmith's Daughter, but truly, I would have acted the same in your circumstances. By The Powers, I would have."

His companion was quiet a moment. "Then you, my dear Lord Radil, are the only party sympathetic to my circumstance in all of Eskalind."

The Acta Sua's horse tried to shy away as though it too was incapable of empathy toward the man's plight. Radil yanked the reins to steady his beast. "I and all my house welcome you to stay with us, as long as you wish."

Favik's voice was quiet, as though already far away. "I had thought to ride to Swedfia and Eyfia and study the old scrolls there."

"You still wish to pursue the Scholars' work?"

The former Ambassador paused. "The Scholars have been my family. Despite what has happened, theirs is still the work I would contribute to, if I am able."

It warmed his fellow to hear this, for the thought arose that he must find a way to preserve their bond, despite this ill situation. Thus Radil spoke. "The weather in the upper mountain passes will be too cold for travel by the time you arrive there. Stay at my estate through the Spring. That sojourn will give me time to quill introductions for you to my contacts in Eyfia, Nordak, and beyond."

"Your kindness is a boon." Exhaustion had crept into Favik's voice. He bowed his head.

"Come, my brother, we shall work together to preserve and protect Eskalind from the cruel circumstances of the borderlands and outerlands. Tonight let us feast together, and tomorrow raise a glad cup for First Day, and separate you from the miserable happenings of this passing year." Radil angled his chestnut mount toward the house, leading his fellow Scholar home.

Anish answered his Captain's summons and stood at attention before his commander's desk. Captain Marnil watched him with an exacting sharpness in his gaze, as if he were preparing to deal out a reprimand. "Soldier Anish, you are called by the Records Keepers to appear at a paternity trial in Dayna Queenstown on the second day of the ninth month."

"What? That's less than a week from now—" Catching himself, the Captain's Secretary asked, "But why, sir?"

"I was hoping you could tell me." The dark-haired man tapped his signet ring on a folded papyrus that bore a purple Records Keepers' seal.

"Your pardon, sir." He hated to reveal that Favik sought him as his son, and spoke vaguely. "There's a man who claims to be my father. I hope he isn't. By your leave, I would rather not go, especially as the date corresponds with my next leave to visit Lady Jinilya at King's Halls."

"Hmm." His superior officer's demeanor softened, even as he said, "You cannot deny the Records Keepers, nor the laws of Eskalind."

"Yes sir. I know that. I will go. Your pardon again, sir."

Here his Captain smiled, reaching for his quill. "Anish, I am quilling your leave papers and wish you an outcome you can live with. To soften the hardship, I will allot a bit of extra time so that you may visit my sister at King's Halls, as you planned." Pulling forth a plain papyrus, he added, "By The Powers, it is I who should ask your pardon. My first thought when I received this notice was that the Records Keepers wanted your presence in determining the father of someone's babe." He chuckled. "Go, go pack for the journey, and I will have a Stander bring the pass to you. Dismissed."

Anish saluted, making his leave as the Captain's words triggered a memory of a Swift Rider sliding into his bed. He gulped and for once hoped to The Powers that he was not a father.

Despite the inevitable nightly rain, he elected to leave immediately, departing the Sixth Company's camp at the Eastlant and Humiksland border that night. Traveling due south along the main road, with only one lengthy hiccup in obtaining a fresh horse, he entered Dayna Queenstown a few hours shy of the trial time. This large village lay about midway between King's Halls and the borderwall where East-lant, Thislin, and Eskalind intersected. He would face a ride of 125 miles west to reach King's Halls and his lover. Unless this trial saw him joined to a Swift Rider.

A freshly painted sign along the road announced in red and brown lettering the locals' pride that Haavlock, ninety-fifth King of Eskalind, chose Dayna, a Brewer from this very place, as his Queen. Anish hoped that the coincidence of Haavlock's colors being identical to Lady Jinilya's boded well. Skimming his gaze about the town, the Soldier eyed the smaller women to see if any resembled his memory of the Swift Rider. Not seeing her, a lump of hope grew in his thoughts that indeed it was Favik who had called him, though he thought it odd for the man to call for a trial this far from King's Halls. He entered the Red Door Tavern and Inn. The establishments in Dayna Queenstown incorporated Haavlock's colors into their decor and even their food, thus he lunched on bread and dipped sauces from earth-hued ceramic bowls and plates and drank from a scarlet-glazed cup. A small, crudely hand-lettered but framed sign on each table offered these wares for sale, as a souvenir of one's visit. After arranging accommodations at the Red Door for that night, Anish wondered if he would make use of them or would rather be rid of the place.

The hour of judgment approached. Traipsing to the Records Keepers, Anish presented himself and was led to the trial room by an Apprentice. A door anchored each side of the rectangular chamber. A grim-faced Guard stood near each door, though the young man was fairly certain he had seen the same four people leaving the tavern earlier, laughing in convivial company. Dalich King's colors were draped on the white-plastered walls. Upon a dais, three chairs sat. Below, a long desk with three matching chairs.

The Apprentice Records Keeper directed him, with a flourish worthy of a traveling player, to sit upon one of the dais seats. Anish chose the middle position, pushing the chair back slightly to better scrutinize the room and anyone who would sit beside him. Moments later, a fat-cheeked man without a hair on his head, but roughly Anish's age, entered, dressed in the reddish brown that Thislin people wore. He sat to the Soldier's side, not acknowledging his presence. No one said anything, as though speech were foreign to them or they were beasts incommunicable. The former Havadran studied the newcomer, noting his dark eyes. He wondered why a man who looked nothing like Favik would be called to sit at a paternity trial. Then he realized Captain Marnil's initial supposition might have been correct. They could be summoned to determine the father of a babe. He hoped the child had dark eyes.

A shuffling outside one door, and a flabby blond man entered, eyes to the ground as he made for the dais. A black-headwrapped Chief Records Keeper, clad in long purple robes, followed, along with an Apprentice of slender build. The last man to arrive sat on the other side of Anish, who shifted his gaze between the two men flanking to him. This newcomer might pass for a younger, paunchier version of the Ambassador. Anish's heart nearly stopped as he debated which outcome he would prefer. He imagined Lady Jinilya's accusation of mistrust leveled back at him with justified vengeance were he indeed judged the male parent of a newbabe.

The Records Keeper stood, lifting her heels from the ground. "I remind you all that you must truthfully answer any questions asked here by me. Failure to comply will lead to loss of Eskalind citizenship or banishment from Eskalind." She coughed away a catch in her throat. "Now, which of you is Citizen Soldier Anish of the Sixth Company, born in Havadra?" He waited, as he alone was attired in a Soldier's uniform, expecting that to answer for him.

"Raise your hand, please." He obeyed, briefly.

She continued. "Citizen Taknil, Groomsman for the House of Wenil, Farlich King's Friend?"

The other blond man lowered his head respectfully.

"Lastly, Avath of Thislin, merchant of…hair combs."

The lockless man replied, "With your permission, I prefer the term *hair ornaments*. It conveys the variety of my wares, which range from ties to barrettes to wreaths for the head, cloth for wraps," Avath gestured to the Chief Records Keeper's headgear, "as well as combs."

"Indeed." The woman snapped her chin up and walked to the platform. She stared at each in turn, her impassive eyes shifting slowly across their faces, then stepped to the side to study their profiles, their necks, ears. Anish could not discern what held her interest. The Soldier held silent, still as if undergoing a lengthy inspection by a nearsighted Sergeant.

The official returned to her desk, still standing, heels raised. "These three men are called for me to stand in judgment…" She gestured to the one of the door Guards. "To determine the father of a nameless babe." Anish nearly swallowed his teeth as the flame Guard opened the door and the petite Swift Rider he feared to see paced into the room, sad-faced, plumper, and with a babe-sized bundle in her arms. The child's head appeared bald, but as the mother drew closer, he saw a hint of wispy blond locks. He may have stopped breathing, may have swayed in his seat.

The Records Keeper walked to the Swift Rider and gathered the child and its swaddles into her arms, holding the head rather stiffly and aiming its face toward hers. The babe peeped a squeak of displeasure at this uncomfortable orientation as the official approached the three men. The Thislin made a sound as though he'd swallowed a large egg. The Records Keeper's gaze fell to each man and then the child in turn, but she gave Anish and the groomsman special interest. "Avath of Thislin, you may go." The hair-ornament merchant stood and strode away, thudding the platform with his steps. The babe whimpered at the sound, and the Records Keeper nodded to its mother, who came to collect the child.

"Soldier Anish," the official stated, rising to her toes, "I call you to serve as witness to the joining of Swift Rider Ana and Groomsman Taknil, for I deem this child to have his face and features, even to the unusually wide notch in the ears. The face proves the father."

"Gladly," exhaled Anish, his head light as he rose.

"But first, this nameless child must be named. I call the parents to stand side by side and gaze at their babe." This seemed odd to Anish, but then he recalled it was a custom of Eskalinders to never name children until their birth, and to require both parents, if living, to be present. He found himself curious to watch.

Taknil rose to his feet with the enthusiasm of a prisoner treading to his execution. "Um, is it a boy child or girl?"

The Swift Rider answered, a bit harshly, "She's a she."

He shambled to her elbow as the Records Keeper intoned, "The custom is for you both to look at the babe, and the same name will come into your minds."

"Truly?" asked Anish. Everyone ignored him.

The groomsman gazed at his daughter for the first time. "She's so small."

Swift Rider Ana glared at her future husband. "She didn't feel small when I birthed her."

The Records Keeper urged, "Please look at your child."

They obeyed. Ana's brown eyes widened, whilst Taknil gaped.

"Have you a name?"

Taknil looked to his bride, who nodded, though her forehead wrinkled. "It's…unusual."

"Gergeltish," said the mother.

"Very," said the father.

The official intoned, "Please state the name simultaneously."

The couple both said, "Petal?"

"Very Gergeltish," murmured Anish.

The groomsman placed a wavering hand on his bride's back, as though she might steady him. "By The Powers, they are both beautiful." He gazed at his daughter and her mother with a fond, affectionate smile that bordered on goofy. One of the Apprentices wiped away a tear. Anish found himself struck by the sudden profound emotion of the new father. A twinge of envy crept into his heart.

"Well," began the Records Keeper, keeping to her agenda. "Swift Rider Ana, Groomsman Taknil, by the Will of The Powers, I declare you joined on this second day of the ninth month of the year 2923. My Apprentices will draw up the records for the joining and the Naming of your daughter. This concludes our business together. Thank you all." She lowered her heels to the floor.

PART THREE
2929–2938

Chapter Fifty-Seven—Changes Afoot
Ninth Month, 2929

It was the ninth month, and the crests of the oak trees blushed to russets and reds above their green-leafed hearts. Six more peaceful, healthful years under the reign of Dalich King had passed.

Something made Damina Queen pause in her progress through a quiet corridor in her husband's halls. Perhaps it was the wet, smacking sound that lured her attention to the alcove. Inside, beyond the rounded corner, a man-sized, velvet-tunicked back greeted her, the person inside enraptured with the woman whose cream-colored fingers tousled his dark blond locks.

"Namlich," Damina said. Her son turned to face her, complexion reddened, lips glistening. At fifteen, his build could easily pass for that of a man of thirty, but his eyes betrayed the shallow life experience of his true age.

The woman who had been the object of his tender administrations stared loose-jawed at the Queen. "Lady Fayna," Damina began, "and Namlich. Must I remind all present that King's Son has *not* earned his sword yet?"

The woman's green eyes darted to the Heir of Eskalind, who crossed his arms and glared at the stone floor as if it had insulted him. Lady Fayna peeped a sound that was perhaps an apology.

Dalich's Queen pointed a perfectly polished fingernail at her son. "Come with me." He dropped his arms to his side as though they were laden with stone and loped to her elbow at a leaden pace. She spun on her silk-clad heels toward the Royals' Tower, calling in her mind, *"Dalich, are you in your chamber?"*

"Yes. Is it something quick?"

"We must speak, you and I, with Namlich. This is the second time in a week I have caught him kissing a woman. A different woman than last time." Damina cast a sideways glance at the youth. He avoided her eyes. *"His sixteenth Naming Day is not for months, and I fear he will be bedding someone before that. We cannot allow it, there must be something we can do."*

They had reached the foot of the tower, and she nodded distractedly to the King's Guard at the base of the many stairs as her husband spoke again in her mind.

"Send Namlich to his quarters. You and I must speak face to face without him first."

"But—"

"Please, Damina."

She sighed aloud, just then realizing the Guard was her sister's husband, Trevil. Shaking her head at her daftness, she gave him the instructions. "My braither, see that King's Son remains in his quarters until I return." Trevil nodded his graying locks and called up the rising, curved corridor of stairs in his resonant voice, "The Queen approaches."

To her son, she ordered, "Wait in your chambers. Alone."

Namlich groaned and yanked open his chamber door by its carved handle. Entering, he turned to face her, speaking in a low whisper. "Mother, you do not know what it is like." His words surprised her, but before she could inquire what he meant, he slammed the door shut, hard enough for the reverberations to be felt on the stairs. She trod up up up to her husband's door.

"By The Powers," she muttered, caught between irritation and sympathy, "First Namlich gallops his poor mare till she breaks her leg, next every unjoined woman at court wants to show him her feet and he cannot refuse." How she wished for the days, not that long ago, when he would clamber into her lap and beg her to read him a tale.

The King's Guard stationed at her husband's door bowed, opening the portal for her. She seldom entered from this direction, usually using the convenient door that adjoined their quarters. Damina entered, finding not only Dalich, but King's Second and King's Mother also, seated around the larger table. A few tan-colored sheets of papyrus lay upon the wood surface, a black envelope emblazoned with two wax seals to the side as though it had birthed its contents and languished exhausted and forgotten. Saril stood and dipped his chin, the action exhibiting the slight hint of gray at the crest of his dark curls. "My Lady."

The King stared wordlessly at the missive, upon which she could just discern the date. *Sixteenth Day, Eighth Month, 2929.*

"Have a seat with us, dear," her maither invited with a sad smile. In her seventh decade now, her features looked worn above her shapeless black smock.

"What is going on?" the Queen asked, touching the smooth oval jewel of her pendant necklace as she sank low into the plush cushion of a vacant chair at the table.

Dalich flicked his wrist toward Saril, who seated himself across from her. The Acta Sua began. "An Ambassador's letter," and there was nearly a sigh in his voice, "from our Ambassador Fornil in Kaymif. He writes that King Moulai is seeking to unjoin from his childless wife and join with a Swedfian noblewoman he has gotten with child."

"Unjoin?" As Queen, she had become more aware of distasteful borderlander customs than most Eskalinders, but this form of disgraceful conduct made her want to tear her dress. Betraying one's spouse and getting another woman with child, then seeking to end the joining? She silently thanked The Powers for protecting Eskalind from such entangled domestic situations.

King's Second continued, "King Moulai's joining was for an alliance.

His wife is the daughter of the queen of Vikmere, and Vikmere threatens to invade Kaymif if Moulai, forgive the term, unjoins."

Looking to her Lord, the Lady of Eskalind asked, "Is Moulai calling for military aid from us?"

"Yes," he replied, gray eyes never leaving the Ambassador's letter.

Saril spoke again. "Moulai cites Eskalind custom in joining with the woman who carries his child."

"Perhaps he forgets another Eskalind custom: not lying with others once one is joined." Damina adjusted the black spinel stones of her bracelet to hide the silver clasp that had rotated to the top of her wrist.

"My thoughts as well, but my Lady, and I say this with the utmost respect, it is not for us to impose our morals on the borderlanders." King Second's brown eyes were steady, a calm, kind firmness in them.

Her throat grew tight. "Yet King Moulai cites our customs to justify his actions."

"His logic is imperfect, I wholeheartedly agree."

The Queen leaned toward her husband. "What will you do?"

Dalich raised a hand to stroke a long finger down his forehead to the bridge of nose. "As we are charged by The Powers to defend our border allies, I must send companies of the army into Kaymif to defend it." The King closed his eyes.

King's Mother said, "This will be the first time in many years that Eskalind has sent its army beyond the borders. The Long Peace ends."

The Queen glanced to her maither, who was looking at Saril. "Who will lead them?" Damina asked slowly, a chilling fear rising in her chest.

Her husband replied, eyes opening to glance at his Second. "Since The Powers forbid I go, I will send Saril. And Namlich."

"Our son?"

King's Mother spoke. "I do not like it."

Dalich folded his fingers together. "Mother, The Powers protect him. As they did me when I was King's Son without an heir." Her maither looked about to speak, but no words followed.

Damina gaped at her husband, unable to form a sentence aloud or in their minds. While she knew their Legends and tales were full of Eskalind Kings and King's Sons coming to the aid of besieged and invaded borderlanders, the thought of sending her boy to fight clove her heart. And for such a cause. Namlich in battle, defending a loathsome lord undeserving of Eskalind's aid.

Another thought came: if he had already lain with a woman in secret, and she were with child, he would no longer enjoy The Powers' protection.

"My heart," Dalich whispered to her, attempting a smile, "do you not see? This will solve our other problem. For if Namlich goes, and his sword is needed, he will earn his sword and thus his manhood."

Her words came forth as a quiet plea. "But he is only fifteen."

Dalich reached for her hand. "Fifteen, but grown into a strong frame that befits the Heir of Eskalind." Her husband's gentle gaze brought a lump to her throat as he tenderly squeezed her cool fingers with his warm hands. "He will be fine."

"If it is any comfort," King's Mother began, a hitch in her voice, "you all must know that Namlich is Gifted by The Powers to feel no pain."

Damina exclaimed, "What?"

Dalich released her hand as Saril asked, "Might I inquire how you know this, my Lady?"

"Dalich, you do not seem surprised." The observation softened the former Queen's demeanor, rendering her expression tenderly maternal.

"I long suspected it, Mother." He looked to his friend King's Second, who seemed to withdraw into himself. "When I heal people, I have a momentary insight into their body, their mind, how they feel." The King smiled sadly, returning his gaze to his wife. "I have never felt that with Namlich. As though he did not need me."

The Queen parted her lips, but the quiet sob she heard came not from her own throat. All eyes turned to King's Mother, who brushed a sable-shaded handkerchief over her eyes. "Maither?" The Queen rose and rushed to embrace her.

"I am sorry, Damina, for this … display. I know, how I know, what a difficult moment this is for you as a mother, to send your son to battle." She drew away to loudly blow her nose.

Her daighter settled next to her, a gentle hand on the smooth black linen of the elder Lady's shoulder. "I know you, of all people, understand exactly how I feel, Maither." She managed a smile, the empathy of comforting another swelling her breast as she consoled the former Queen.

Namlich leaned against the open tent's corner post, watching one of the kitchen workers as she bent to stir a pot steaming with savory mushroom broth. The dreaded voice murmured from the cooking fire, but he honed his attention on the bead of sweat sliding along the woman's long, creamy neck. A drop disappeared into the warm-looking curves below the neckline of her tucked bodice. By The Powers, she looked as delicious as the broth-tinged air smelled, and not even the fire's voice could steal this delightful moment from him.

"King's Son, a word?" His father's Second beckoned. He managed to speak in a tone that was both respectful and commandfull, which deeply annoyed the teenager.

"Powers," he grumbled, trudging toward Lord Saril. He had half a mind to steal a kiss from the kitchen worker as he passed her, knowing full well that Saril watched his every move. It was bad enough to be trapped in the body of a grown man while denied the pleasures of an enticing woman, let alone to debate this restriction with one on whom such charms were wasted. The blond youth stopped before his father's closet companion, relishing the fact that he was a few hairs taller than the dark-haired man.

"My Lord, I have the feeling you know what I am going to say." The noble began walking as he spoke, which compelled Namlich to follow alongside.

"Mmm." King's Son's eyes roamed the neat rows of tents, his father's banners flying from poles marking the intersections of the main pathways. Everywhere were Soldiers and Standers passing to and fro on their duties, carrying bundles and scabbards, stacks of bedding, ewers for water. A pair of stout men rolled an ale barrel, their faces humorless as they called forth gravely, "Make way," as though participating in a solemn ritual. Sergeant Lamon, a native of Guerland with a hint of the facial proportions of Lady Jinilya, saluted the noble pair as he cut by them.

Not a single woman, be she camp worker or Soldier, strode into his field of view, as though all had been ordered to stay away. Muffled clangs rang forth from a nearby smithy. King's Son realized his overseer was not talking and glanced at him. Which turned out to be a mistake.

"My Lord, do you truly not know what I was about to say?"

Namlich groaned, trapped into replying. "You were going to say I need to stay away from the women."

Saril looked straight ahead, a pleasant expression about his permanently tan features as he nodded to Captain Sakil, passing by in his violet-crested helm. "I see your deductive abilities have not left you. I feared they had."

The fifteen-year-old smirked, replying in breathy courtier's voice, "But my Lord Saril, if no women, then how about men?"

"Neither, until you *earn* your sword." King's Second paused, brown eyes regarding the youngster with studious aplomb. "Remember, my Lord, that I speak on behalf of your Lord father and Lady mother—"

"And my grandmother too, I suppose." He would almost prefer to return to the kitchens and chance the fire's voice.

"You are most fortunate to know a grandparent, my Lord. None of mine lived to see my birth." Saril stepped forward again while Namlich, chastened, trailed at his heels. He felt like a useless oaf.

That night, King's Son sat alone atop the smooth sheets of his tent's bed, the dark a tangible thing about him. Outside the fabric walls, the soft plods of footsteps came and went, as though the night might impart a secret message through frequency and pattern. He listened, but nothing came. At least there were no candles lit, no fire, no fire's voice taunting him. Only Lady Jinilya understood; only she could put out that pain. But he was too young for her. Too young for any woman.

Falling back into his pillow, the young royal sighed. He was the 125th sole son of an Eskalind King. His life was about waiting. Waiting for the important moments that Loremasters would record, that future King's Sons would read and dream about.

He was tired of waiting. He sat up.

A brightness flared outside, and he flinched in his bed sheets. "My Lord?" came a male voice as the tent flap parted. A blond man entered, clad in the purple-trimmed dark tunic and plain black trousers of an Eskalinder Sergeant, and bearing a lit lantern. "Your pardon, sir, it is urgent. King's Second calls you immediately."

Now he recognized the man. "Sergeant Anish." The man whom Lady Jinilya chose to bed. A kindling envy sped his blood.

"Yes, my Lord. Please come swiftly." The Havadran bowed his head, eyes on his Lord, holding the tent flap open expectantly.

Namlich rose to the soles of his feet, hurling aside his sleeping robe. Naked, he stared at the Sergeant, who cut his eyes away as King's Son dressed. Once clothed, Namlich belted his long knife and loaned sword, then wordlessly departed the tent with his escort. The silent pair arrived at Lord Saril's tent to find a wheeled cart, draped with purple and blue zigzag pennants, parked outside. A clutch of Kaymiflander soldiers, all men, all wearing short betasseled caps, stood nearby. They bowed at Namlich's approach.

Entering the spacious but sparsely furnished tent alone, he found Captains Sakil and Marnil standing, conferring with King's Second and Kaymif's King Moulai. A soft light came from the two lit candelabras in the tent, but the flames were quiet. A Kaymif aide stood near one, thumbs tucked into his belt.

"King's Son," called Lord Saril, a hint of dark circles under his eyes. All the men turned to the young royal, tall Sakil's locks brushing the fabric ceiling though he stood near the loftiest section of the structure. "Our scouts send word that the Vikmeres are setting camp just three hours march from here. Battle will commence in the morning."

King Moulai's blue eyes flashed under narrowed brows. "They will be march-weary and easily defeated."

Saril continued, a slightly pinched quality in his tone. "That is my hope as well." The two Captains glanced at one another.

Moulai laid bejeweled fingers on the youth's arm. "I am glad you are here, King's Son, to earn your sword as your father did, here in Kaymif." He nodded at the end of the last sentence, a quick snap of the head that shook his chin-length blond hair and the cloudy white stone earring dangling from his earlobe. "An honor for my country, again."

King Moulai's tone made it sound like Namlich was bestowing a personal favor. Captain Marnil's upper lip lifted slightly. Sakil crossed his arms. Only King's Second looked unperturbed.

Dalich's son regarded the other royal with a cool nod as the man withdrew his hand. "As Kaymif is an Ever Ally of Eskalind, it is my duty."

The Kaymiflander lifted his lips into a smile, the look of a man convinced his fellow wholeheartedly agreed with him. "I anticipate the day, soon, when my new queen brings forth my son and disproves my mother's rebounded curse."

"I do not understand your meaning."

"It was a most unfortunate incident." Moulai tapped a finger upon his neatly trimmed beard, gazing for a moment at the carpet. "She wished it upon my sister to bear only daughters." He glanced to the younger royal. "Yet my sister mothers a son, while my previous wife brought forth no children. A small matter, soon corrected."

A clarity of thought entered the youth's mind, and whether it came from himself or The Powers, he knew not. Namlich turned his gaze to King's Second and said softly, "No, this will not correct it, and many will die."

At his side he could feel the Kaymif king staring hard, whilst that royal's aide's shoulders lifted into a menacing bearing befitting a vigilant Guard protective of his Lord's person. King's Second raised his eyebrows and tilted his head, a gravity in his gaze as though he agreed with King's Son's utterance. Behind Saril, Captain Sakil nodded in approval, placing a tan hand upon his broad chin.

Captain Marnil spoke. "My Lords, if there is battle to be done tomorrow, we must prepare our fighters."

"My Lord Brother, I am in agreement," said King's Second. "King Moulai, I thank you for your visit. We shall meet tomorrow at first light, and by The Powers' Will, again later in the day as well."

Moulai departed without a word, his adjutant in his wake. The Eskalinders exchanged glances and good nights, with Sakil first to leave. But Saril waylaid King's Son with his hand and a quiet, "Stay a moment." He gestured to a small table with a glossy ceramic wine jug set beside two short goblets that echoed the pitcher's sable-colored materials. Marnil must have heard, for he paused and regarded his elder with suspicion. King's Second's eyes hardened. "Good night, Brother. You are dismissed." The last Captain filed away.

Lord Saril poured a quiet slosh of deep red liquid into each cup, handing one to the youth. "Do not tell your father," he said, in a quiet, scheming tone, his mouth disappearing behind the cup as he swallowed.

"Not tell him what?" Namlich drew closer.

King's Second lowered his cup. "What I am about to tell you. But have a drink first." He touched Namlich's cup hand and lifted it slightly toward the youth's mouth. King's Son drank. The wine tasted plummy and cool.

Saril lowered his brown hand and gazed into his own cup. "You know how your father earned his sword in single combat, in Kaymif against the king of Ghemif." It was a question, but presented as a statement.

"Of course." King's Son looked to the tent ceiling, hoping a long recounting of that tale was not in the offing.

"I was there, I saw it."

Namlich gazed back to see Lord Saril's dark eyes narrowed as though he sensed the teen's ennui and viewed it with keen disapproval.

"It was a thing to behold." Saril raised his cup slightly. "But that is not what I want to talk to you about now." His voice softened. "Your parents wanted me to wait until you earned your sword to tell you this, but I will tell you now, because I believe it will aid you in your Sword Earning." He stepped to Namlich's side, close enough for the youth to feel the heat of his breath.

King's Second whispered, "Your father cannot leave Eskalind. If he crosses the border, disasters happen." Saril's eyes perfectly reflected the flames of the nearby candelabra. Namlich inhaled, fearing the fire would speak, or that perhaps it had already spoken what he just heard. But only Saril's voice continued: "Fires, windstorms, and floods, akin to those seen in the borderlands and beyond. Every time Dalich King left Eskalind." King's Second placed his free hand on the youth's shoulder, eyes keen and intent. "That means you, you must defend, you must lead our army in the borderlands, as your father is forbidden by The Powers to do so."

"But," and the teen's voice quavered though he sought to steady it, "Father is the Lord of Eskalind. Why would The Powers—"

The older Lord released his hand from Namlich's shoulder and put a cool finger over King's Son's lips. "It is Their proven Will, and thus not for us to debate. Yes?" His gaze was solemn but kind. He withdrew his hand and Namlich nodded, still feeling the slight pressure of the man's touch as though it lingered invisibly upon his lips. "Now," said his father's friend, turning away, "get some rest. I will call for you in the morning."

But Namlich did not rest. He sat abed through the candleless night in silent questioning and swirling thoughts till the sun crested the horizon and two male Pages appeared at his tent flap. Both entered, one with a laden plate of bread and aromatic sauces, and the other with anxious reports that the Vikmere army was on the march, and Lord Saril required King's Son dressed for combat. King's Son forgot to eat and flew into his battle clothes. The Stander sent to assist him found his Lord cinching the last of his gear into position, the scabbard and sword borrowed for this day from Dalich King.

All the years of rehearsal, by many masters, but especially one particular Mavoldian Swordmaster, Edvain, who insisted on timing with a sandglass how quickly the youth could dress and prepare his kit, at last came to fruition. The time of waiting was over. Excitement and terror flowed in King's Son's veins. Standing by King's Second in the shorn field, he watched the horizon for the enemy's approach. Saril's scouts reported that the Vikmeres marched as one body toward them, then a messenger gave tidings of the Vikmere general's agreement to battle at this place. The Eskalinder and Kaymif armies waited. A group of Standers, hoping to earn their swords today as well, stood near Namlich, casting quick glances at the royal youngster who, while close to them in years, stood strong muscled and lean as a man twice their age.

Despite it being the tenth month, the day grew hotter, as though the tension in the combatants fed heat into the air. Scouts fanned forth to ascertain the enemy's approach. Captain Sakil gave leave to his people of the First Company to sit. The Sixth Company followed suit. Officers remained on their feet. Namlich sat.

Kitchen workers came forward with water and bread and sauces. Someone whispered that roast chicken would follow shortly, but Namlich shook his head to the offerings, gray eyes on the horizon, waiting for what would manifest.

There in the distance, he saw what appeared to be an approaching, glowing band of light, thin and flickering. Fear propelled him to his feet, and it was unmistakable, the glow brighter now that he had risen: a trailing of light above the rim of the land. "Do you see that?" he asked a nearby Sergeant, not attending to who it was.

The man squinted and raised a hand riven with scars to shield his eyes. His blond brows knit. "I see only empty land, my Lord." It was Sergeant Anish.

"Do you see it? The fire?" King's Son begged a seated Stander, who leapt to his feet as though commanded, doffing his black cap.

The youth peered at the horizon. "Um, I think I see some dust, my Lord?"

"She is coming," Namlich murmured. He closed his eyes, wanting to shut out the red glow, wanting to run, ashamed and surely trembling.

Then an unknown, authoritative, but gentle, female voice came into his mind.

King's Son

Namlich saw the deeds of his ancestors relived before him in a race of time, so fast he felt the breath stolen out of him. Heedlich First King setting the borders, Talva the Battle Queen protecting her injured husband from swordsmen, Kaarnlock King and his undefeatable sword doing its work, his grandfather Dalock in single combat against a fork-bearded, gold-armored king. Namlich's eyes flew open and the Vikmere army was on the horizon, their standards red and emblazoned with black birds, curved talons outstretched, swooping for prey. The soldiers bellowed and sang as was their battle custom. Along the Eskalind army's line, shouts and orders rang as his people marched forth as one body, responding to commands given long before. They flowed past Namlich like water coursing around a rock in a swift-flowing stream. King's Son neither spoke nor moved, for he saw about each Vikmere soldier a clinging silhouette of rippling red fire. His heart quaked.

They cannot harm you
King's Son
Put out the lights

As he watched, the flames lost their heat and cooled to a calming green, soft as a garden viewed in heavy rain. Namlich's blood kindled.

He drew his loaned sword and marched toward the lights, then broke into a run, outdistancing the Eskalind Soldiers and slashing at the green lights. Something crumpled heavily before him and he yanked his foot free as more glows charged him. Long knife in one hand, sword in the other, he cut, he hacked, he swiped and stabbed, shrieking and roaring, wild, unleashed, for the voice spoke true: they could not harm him, and no pain entered his body, even when he touched the green fire itself. The lights charged him, and he smote them into darkness.

———

King's Second, Commander of the Eskalind Army in his King's stead, surveyed the spent field of battle, Captain Sakil at his side. Dozens of Vikmere fighters lay blood dry and slain in the dirt where King's Son had charged them, their fur and leather uniforms torn and filthy, unredeemable as their lives. A pair of red-aproned Eskalind Healers bent to help one moaning man, the white sleeves of their undertunics sloshed with blood. In the distance, the dead littered the landscape like forgotten rags, twisted and clotted in haphazard groupings. In the midst of the destruction, Dalich King's banner billowed proudly, staked by Eskalinders against a pile of dented Vikmere shields.

A rider approached, her horse delicately picking its way through the corpses. "My Lord Commander," the woman called, "King's Son has been located."

"Where? How is he?"

"Mire splattered but uninjured, about two miles distance."

"Thank The Powers. Soldier, send him a horse." Lord Saril waved her aside as a light-haired Eskalind Sergeant sped toward them. "Now to find the Vikmeres' leader."

Captain Sakil's tone was wry. "I believe this will be an unconditional surrender."

"If there is anyone left to surrender." Saril paused and surveyed the sad scene. "By The Powers, the youth must have slain a thousand." The Sergeant stopped and bowed, his eyes to the ground. "Ah, Sergeant

Anish. Do you have word from my brother?"

"Yes, my Lord. Captain Marnil's Soldiers found the Vikmere leader dead, along with his fighters." The Sergeant raised his head, gray eyes holding an astonished reserve. "There are very few Vikmere survivors, my Lord. King's Son brought down their entire army."

"Yes," said Saril, looking to his Captain, "The Loremasters will have much to tell about this day."

———

Namlich trudged through the field, stepping over bodies and across dropped spears and shields, the lowering sun at his back as he approached the ordered tents of the Eskalind camp. His shadow grew before him, a thin, brooding form stretching further and further away from its maker. Perhaps it wanted to distance itself from him. How odd and small he felt, as though his body were a foreign entity.

Standers and Soldiers spied him and stood crisply at attention; a Healer rose from her position next to a prone Eskalinder and bowed. In the eyes of his people he saw caution, as if a warning had been issued. He wanted to hide. No one spoke, and only the distant sounds of voices whooping at an ale tent and the soft clop of horseshoes upon the dirt disturbed the wary stillness. A small delegation fluttered toward him, Lord Saril at its helm, and Pages bearing torches against the coming night.

"My Lord King's Son." Saril made his obedience, his followers echoing his movements. Raising his head, he whispered, "Were you not brought a horse?"

"I ... did not need it."

"Ah." Louder Saril announced, "Today you have proven yourself a man before The Powers and Eskalind." More onlookers gathered, closer, the same odd quietude cloaking them like a blanket worn against chilly weather. "When do you wish to celebrate your Sword Earning ceremony?"

The youth cast a glance at the torches, but they were as silent as the assembling body. Perhaps he was freed from their vile murmurings forever. Which would indeed be a cause for celebration. "Now?"

Lord Saril drew close, and for a moment he thought the man might touch him as familiarly as he had last night. Instead, his father's advisor murmured, "My Lord, you come battle-soiled. Perhaps a bath first?"

Namlich considered, cutting his eyes away a moment. There, amongst the farther bystanders, he spied the comely, buxom woman from the kitchen tent. She held his gaze, and nothing in her expression indicated that she found his appearance distasteful. Quite the contrary.

Namlich looked back at King's Second, who said merely, "Understood." Lord Saril pointed to one of the Pages, then raised his hand as though to silence a crowd. "I am sending for King's Son's Sword Earning sword. Go." The boy sped away. "Once it arrives, the Sword Earning ceremony will be held here, immediately."

This reinvigorated the crowd. About half the gatherers dashed away to alert companions. Animated babbling enlivened those remaining, whilst Pages and Standers brought more torches to combat the growing dark. Namlich watched the silent flames closely, alert to any thin whisperings of doubt. Saril sent another boy after the first.

The crowd increased in number, a swelling ring of men forming about him. Namlich's fingers twitched, but still no ill words from the fire.

A Stander called forth, "My Lord? How many Vikmeres did you kill?"

He hesitated, for he had seen only light and fire. If they were people . . . . It felt like a stone fell from his throat to his stomach. But The Powers had guided him. Or at least, *a* Power. Now he understood the sadness, after giving battle, that some Kings told of in their private chronicles.

"Twenty?" the Stander whispered.

"No, hundreds," Namlich breathed, fighting a constriction in his windpipe. The fire was right, he truly was a monster.

"Twenty hundred!" the Stander reported, and excited murmurs echoed through the crowd, the number propagating amongst them like ripples from a rock dropped in water. Namlich wanted to shout a correction; he raised his head tall, seeing the kitchen woman and trying to catch her attention. But her gaze was turned away as she chatted with a dowdy Healer. Before he could move, a Page approached him with a basin of water held in his small hands, a cloth draped over one arm. "My Lord, King's Second said, if you wash, that the women…" He paused and glanced to his chest as though he might find the words he sought written on his tunic. "That the women will be able to see your handsome features better."

King's Son nodded, thankful for the distraction, and dipped his hands into the bowl, sloshing the perfumed liquid onto his face. It felt cool, like a revitalizing salve that washed away all woes. He thought to sip from it, until he saw coppery brown vortexes swirling within the bowl. Instead he splashed more water upon his clothes and hair until the basin was empty. Another Page had appeared with his dress tunic, and King's Son grudgingly stripped and changed his attire. The first Page handed him a cloth and set to straightening the tunic hem whilst King's Son toweled the last drops from his face and hair. A quick glance at the woman found her eyeing him. Holding her gaze, he drew the drying cloth lingeringly down his neck. Heat swelled his veins. He hoped to The Powers the ceremony would be concluded swiftly.

As it came to pass, more and more men gathered, so that in the end, instead of an orderly circle about the Sword Earner, a serpentine, meandering ribbon of Eskalinders stood about King's Son as a Page delivered the designated blade to King's Second. Lord Saril said, in a carrying voice, "I thank The Powers to be with you all tonight, to grant sword to Namlich, Dalich King's Son." Some cheered. "Twenty-five years ago, Dalich King received his sword for saving my life." Some looked to King's Second with surprise writ on their features, whilst others nudged them for their historical ignorance. "Today, this sword is granted to Dalich's son for saving the lives of untold many Eskalinders, who by his deeds stand with us tonight."

"Hear, hear," murmured the gathering, as others called, "Thank The Powers."

Saril raised a scabbarded blade, rounded onyx stones set into the rich metal of the scabbard in the pattern of the letter *N*. He spoke the traditional words every male youth longs to hear: "As is our long custom, since before Heedlich First King, before Eskalind was Eskalind, we let the sword pass through the hands of all men present." King's Second passed the scabbard to Captain Sakil, who passed it to Captain Marnil, and from there into the hands of Soldiers and Sergeants, blacksmiths, wheelwrights, a Records Keeper, more Soldiers, messengers and scouts, the sole male Healer in the army, horse drivers, aides, and adjutants. Standers and women looked from over the shoulders of the shorter men, and a few female Soldiers reached into the circle to touch the hilt or scabbard as it passed, whilst Pages crouched by the feet of the men in the circle, peeking between their knees.

The last man passed the scabbard back to King's Second, who grasped it and completed the customary pronouncements. "This night, Namlich, King's Son, proved himself before The Powers to be fully a man by defeating"—his voice dropped—"or rather, annihilating, the Vikmere army." Saril then spoke loud: "My Lord, wear this sword in defense of yourself, your family, our Kingdom, and the borderlands."

At long last, the youth whose body, for years, had been that of a man's could live the life of a man. Namlich raised his head and reached for the scabbard, drawing forth his very own sword for the first time. A glittering amethyst sparked at the end of the pommel, the hilt metal smooth, polished, reflective. His parents' initials were inset in darker metal across the shining blade. Namlich could not suppress a smile as he admired the reflective surface in the torchlight, his own face mirrored back at him. Then a dark-haired woman's face appeared where his should be and she spoke again in his thoughts.

I am not finished with you

The blade threatened to slip from his grasp, and she vanished, leaving King's Son staring at his startled reflection.

Sunshine streamed gladly through the windows onto the crisp papyrus scroll Healer Morya held in her lap. Beside her on the couch, her chestnut-headed daughter peered at the quilling. "Read more, Mama," the girl encouraged.

Morya chuckled. "Saysha, despite having lived all your life at our borders, you are a true Eskalinder. You never tire of our Legends."

The girl wiggled from her position and sat straight, back to the window and the rolling farm hills of Thislin beyond the borderwall. "But Mama, I don't know this tale yet, I want to find out what happens."

Morya teased, "Perhaps we will wait till your Naming Day tomorrow." The girl's expression grew serious. "Your father should not have opened Anish's present for you until the day arrived."

"But Father said it was not wrapped like a Naming Day gift. That's why he opened it."

The Healer sighed. "Yes, that is what he said. My, you will make quite a Records Keeper someday."

"No, I want to be a Healer."

"I thought you wanted to be a Records—"

"That was last week." Then Saysha smiled, bright and happy as she giggled, poking her mother's leg. "I'm teasing you, Mama." The pair laughed, and the girl put her head in her mother's lap, reaching around her waist to embrace her.

"Dear! Mindful of the scroll." Hastily the Healer rolled up the scroll and hugged her sole child, eyes alighting on the date on the framed Naming announcement, also quilled by Anish, that was hanging just next to the front door. "Hard to believe you will turn ten tomorrow," she breathed, squeezing her girl tightly.

"Seventeenth day, ninth month, 2931, tenth Naming Day," Saysha recited, her voice muffled in the folds of her mother's Healer's robes.

"You do have a Records Keeper's mind for details. Here, come up before you suffocate."

Sharp knocking sounded on the door. "Healer Morya, Healer Morya!" a woman called. Saysha bolted upright as the Healer scooted off the couch.

Morya opened the door to find her Apprentice's face as red as her apron, one of her normally neat braids dangling down the side of her head, sweat on her brow. "What's the matter?"

"There's an injured man coming up the border road, from Thislin. He's bleeding, he looks very hurt…"

Morya darted back into her home, the Apprentice at her heels. "Saysha, fetch my smaller Healer's pouch. In the kitchen." The girl dashed away. To the Apprentice, she barked, "Did you send Soldiers with a cart for him?"

"Yes, but the wheel broke off, so I sent the Soldiers to get a litter." As the Apprentice spoke, the Healer retrieved her larger herb bag from beside the couch.

"Good thinking." Morya accepted the smaller satchel from her daughter with a quick kiss on the forehead. "Saysha, stay here and wait for Father or me to come home." The two women raced away, hefting the hems of their aprons and skirts from the ground to speed their progress.

———

Saysha sat on the couch on her knees, watching her mother and the Apprentice running toward the border, her small fingers on the window glass like she could touch them. She considered going after them, but she had done that once before when Mother was called away, and a horse nearly trampled her. The girl's ears still rang from the scolding she'd received; she could almost hear the horse's hooves pounding the earth again. "Maybe I will be a Healer," she said to the empty room. "They're very important." Saysha sank into the couch to read her new scroll.

———

Jinilya leaned close to Anish as they walked the corridor outside the Library. "I have something amusing to share with you."

Just the whisper of his lover's breath near his ear thrilled him. How glad it was to be back at King's Halls, by her side, near to her embrace and bed. He wished Eskalinders celebrated their Naming Day more than once a year so he could visit on each occasion. Then again, the army might not grant leave for such celebrations if they occurred too often.

"Anish, shall I tell you?" His Lady had stopped, green eyes upon him with a hint of merriment in her fond gaze.

"How can you tell me anything when I'm kissing you?" He moved closer, but she pulled him to her side as a babe-faced Apprentice passed by, stacked letter baskets in her hands and brown eyes intent on her path as though she faced a superior's scrutiny.

"That," Jinilya nodded to the brunette youngster, "just makes my tale even more amusing." She led him to a door that accessed the garden. "I overheard a group of borderlanders discussing their time in Eskalind." The couple exited King's Halls into warm sunshine and spied an occupied bench just as the Mavoldian man upon it rose and walked away. The pair settled onto the flat stone, its seat still heated from the previous occupant. "The borderlanders jested about the constant bustle of healing notes and letters moving through King's

Halls. One said that Eskalind should be renamed Letter Carry Land. Another said it must be a requirement of Eskalind citizenship to have a person in one's family employed at bearing healing notes."

"Hmm," said Anish, smirking to himself. "Do you know the nickname Havadrans have for Gergelts?"

She tilted her beautiful face to him, eyes lit with suspense. "No?"

"Weak."

Her eyes narrowed slightly. "And what Havadrans call Thislins?" he continued.

"With your permission, allow me to guess," she said, imitating the Thislins' way of expressing themselves. "Do Havadrans call them weak too?"

"Indeed. You are a very intelligent woman."

They both laughed, and she leaned to kiss him as a voice interrupted their revelry.

"Sergeant Anish, a letter for you." That same Apprentice stood before them, a thin papyrus envelope in hand. He pulled away from his lover, and the youngster placed the note in his hand.

"Thank you." The Apprentice nodded and departed. Jinilya watched as he turned the envelope over.

"Who is it from?" She inched closer to his shoulder.

"The Records Keepers' office at the Thislin border, but I don't recognize the quilling." Anish frowned, retrieving his short knife. He split the seal.

He laid the knife upon the bench in its sable sheath as she asked, "Healer Morya and her family are stationed there, are they not?"

"Yes, but it's not her husband's hand either." He flipped the papyrus note from its encasement and they both read,

1st Day, 10th Month, 2931
Sergeant Anish,
It is with great sadness I write to inform you of the deaths of
Healer Morya and her husband, Records Keeper Brisnil.

"No," he breathed. Jinilya's hand shot to her mouth. The pair read on:

> *On the sixteenth day of the ninth month of this year, Healer*
> *Morya was called to assist a gravely injured man on the Thislin*
> *side of the border. When she crossed, she was seized with a*
> *sudden illness, and The Powers claimed her*

"Oh," cried Jinilya. "That is how my mother died." Anish placed his free hand upon her back but could not pull his eyes from the papyrus.

> *before she reached the patient. Her husband, Brisnil the*
> *Records Keeper, was called, but as often happens in Eskalind,*
> *was sadly found to have perished at the same time as his wife.*

"By The Powers!" Jinilya wept into her hands. "Their poor little girl."
Anish read aloud, thick in his throat as he rubbed the fabric of the Librarian's robe draping his lover's back.

> *As there is no other family, their daughter Saysha will be placed*
> *in the King's House at Pleasanton. She will likely be there by the*
> *time this letter finds you.*
> *Saysha asked that I write you, requesting that you visit her*
> *there. I advise that you quill her and visit as soon as you are*
> *able; kind words and a familiar face would be a boon after this*
> *great and sudden loss.*
> *Acting Records Keeper at Thislin Border, Apprentice Onamil*

Anish dropped the letter and pulled his lover close, their heads touching. A long while they stayed thus, and he was not certain he thought of anything comprehensible, the news was too unbelievable. At last Jinilya whispered, "When can you go see her?"

He blinked, as though the action would cause thoughts to form. "I will ask for family leave immediately."

Jinilya wiped away a tear streaking her cheek and inhaled, turning to him. "But your Captain is on nearly the opposite side of the country from Saysha's King's House. You will not have an answer from Marnil before you are due back with the Sixth Company."

"That is why I will appeal directly to Captain Marnil's superior." He trailed his hand from her back to her elbow, released her, and folded the letter.

"Saril? You will count on him to honor a special request from you? I do not think that too likely."

"The borders are calm at the moment. What reason can he give to deny it, given the circumstances? And even if he does, I will appeal to the Records Keepers for their judgment."

"It sounds as though you have made a plan."

He grimaced. "Indeed."

They sat a moment in silence, till Jinilya said, "I would like to go with you, if you do not mind. But King's Mother must agree to grant me a leave."

"I hope she can spare you." Anish touched the smooth linen draping her knee. "I would like that very much."

Chapter Sixty—A King's House
11th Month, 2931

The road curved past a strand of late Autumn stripped white-barked trees, though the sun beamed full and unseasonably warm as Lady Jinilya and Sergeant Anish trotted their mounts. Ahead, upon a slight rise, sat the King's House of Pleasanton, its gardens trailing down the slope to their path. The bent backs of a trio of workers faced the sky as they toiled, pulling potatoes from the earth and tossing them into short baskets. One laborer rose to greet them and gestured toward the building as two laughing, suntanned girls ran by, clad in red dresses with matching ribbons entwined in their braids. A stiff-backed, pale-faced boy stood on the porch watching their approach. He came forward and with a curt Mavoldian accent offered to stable their horses. The pair dismounted and thanked him just as a red-tressed, cream-complected woman in white emerged from the open doorway and introduced herself as Minder Perka, director of the house.

"Thank you very much for coming. Please come inside. Saysha will be down in a moment." The Minder led them into a wide entry hall, populated by Lamorda flowers in large pots. "Saysha has been numbering the days until your arrival, though I kept telling her you might be delayed. One never knows when one travels. But it is good that you arrived on No Lessons Day."

They had entered a small room set with a leather couch and chairs, the furnishings in First King's colors of red and white, with only the portraits of Dalich King and Damina Queen over the fireplace draped in the current King's colors. How odd it was to see this flat representation of the royals, for to Jinilya they were as robustly familiar as her brothers. Yet this was how most Eskalinders knew their rulers.

A delicate pitter-patter echoed along the hallway, and Saysha entered the room, her blue eyes alighting upon Anish, a sad smile upon her pale complexion. The Sergeant bent at the waist, holding his hands toward her, and she approached wordlessly, then dashed herself into his arms and clung to him as though drowning.

"Dear Saysha." He embraced her, one hand upon her long chestnut curls as Jinilya and the Minder traded sympathetic looks. The girl whimpered something, and Anish replied, "I miss your mother too. She was a wonderful woman. Here, let us sit down and visit, and you can open the present I brought for you." He looked to the women as Saysha raised her head.

Jinilya whispered to the Minder, "Might you be able to show me about the house?" Perka agreed and the women left the room as Anish and the girl settled onto the couch. The Minder led the Lady along a clean-scented corridor, pointing to the various chambers: a schoolroom set neatly with wide desks, wax tablets, and eight seats, then further along, a spotless dining area, then the kitchen where a cheerful woman pulled piping loaves from the oven. They passed a large playroom populated with balls, toy swords, a rocking horse, and hoops. Lastly they stepped up to the dormitory floor and entered a nursery with two cribs and a bassinet. All the babe furniture was draped in white cloth. "But where are the other children?" asked Jinilya. She touched the fabric covering the dome of the bassinet, feeling a slight layer of clinging dust on her fingertips.

Perka nodded. "They should all be out on the grounds. There are only five with us at the moment. No babes or wee ones, but two sisters from Eastlant, a boy from Mavold, another from Guerland, and Saysha."

Jinilya's first thought ran to inquiring about the Guerish child, but it surprised her that none of the other children hailed from Eskalind. "Saysha is the only Eskalinder?"

The Minder led her past a bedroom with an open door, saying, "Yes, my Lady. The foreign-born children are here because their parent or parents who brought them to Eskalind perished here." A soft swish sounded, as when one opens a Legend scroll. Perka paused, a practiced instinct in her movements, her brown eyes shifting along the corridor. "Mamon," she called, "is that you?"

A boy's voice replied from another room, in the universal tone of a child caught in the act. "Yes, Minder Perka."

"Reading again instead of getting fresh air?"

"Yes, Minder Perka."

She shook her head. "Come here, then. There is someone I want you to meet."

Perka winked at Jinilya as an umber-skinned boy of about eight or nine years entered the corridor, his hands behind his back. He wore Guerish-style trousers of red hue and a white tunic that hung to his thighs. He saw her and immediately gaped. "You are brown too."

"I am," the Librarian replied, smiling. "My mother's mother was from Guerland." For a moment she considered asking Minder Perka to introduce them in the proper Guerish manner. Instead, she held out her hand; he reached for it and clasped it as an Eskalinder would. The sight of his darker skin touching hers brought a sharp memory of her mother grasping her hand. "I am Lady Jinilya."

His eyes were a deep brown, and there was concern in them. "Do you have a longer name?"

"I do, but tell me yours first."

He opened his mouth but paused a bit before saying, "I am Mamon of Guernain in Guerland." She released his hand. "May I ask what is the rest of your name, my Lady?"

How he reminded her of a little Ambassador. She wondered if her brother Saril had been like this at the same age, a youngster who related to adults as though forgoing childish things and full ready to be a part of the grown-up world. "I am Lady Librarian Jinilya of King's Halls. My family is the House of Jinil, Dalock King's Friend."

The lad pondered. "Dalock King was the father of Dalich King?"

"Indeed."

"I'm learning the histories of Eskalind, so if I stay here I will be a good citizen." Here he smiled expectantly at Perka, who patted his dark hair.

"You are a model pupil, Mamon. Soon you will be giving the other students their lessons. But you should get out more and enjoy the fresh air."

He grinned. "Yes, Minder Perka."

It puzzled Jinilya that Mamon thought he might be leaving Eskalind. "You might return to Guerland soon?"

"If my father is found." The Guerlander looked down. "Mother was ill, so we came to Eskalind, but her healing note didn't reach the King in time." Before she could utter a condolence, he continued, brightly, "But the Records Keeper has written back home to try and find my father."

"Your father stayed behind, in Guerland?"

"Um, well, we don't know where he is. I have only seen him twice. But Mother said he saw me as a newbabe, so truly three times." With each utterance his voice grew softer.

"Is he a merchant?"

"Yes, a salt merchant. He's in the far south a lot. Most of the time. All the time." Mamon's gaze grew sad and he seemed to shrink within himself. Her heart urged her to scoop the lad into her arms and whisper comforts.

Instead she dropped slowly to one knee to face him at his eye level, laying a gentle hand on his shoulder and speaking with kind conviction. "Mamon, the Records Keepers of Eskalind are very good at their jobs. With The Powers' help, they should find your father."

He nodded, dark eyes slightly wet. "They told me it could be a long long time."

"It might be. Now tell me, can you quill?"

The Guerish boy looked at her intently. "I'm not very good, but I'm learning."

"That is excellent. I will send you a letter when I return to King's Halls. Would you quill me in return?"

He glanced to the Minder, then back, his eyes wide. "Would you? I promise I'll improve my quilling so you can read what I write."

The women laughed as Jinilya rose to her feet. "Well, Mamon, Sergeant Anish and I will be staying here a few days. I could give you and the other children lessons, if Minder Perka agrees."

The redhead dipped her locks. "Certainly, Lady Jinilya."

The next days passed in a pleasant flurry of activities as the visitors immersed themselves in the daily schedule of a King's House: meals, studies, games, and gardening. After the last meal of the day, the pair would sit with the children in the candlelit parlor and tell tales of military life or about King's Halls, answering questions. Thank The Powers, the flames were mercifully silent. Still, Jinilya kept alert.

This night, Minder Perka leaned against the wall, observing the group. An inquiry about army service from the Mavoldian boy generated a particularly lengthy monologue from Anish, during which he gave the two boys in the chamber his keen attention. One of the Eastlant girls yawned. Jinilya watched Mamon's face as he listened to her lover, and she felt a keen warmth in her heart that the lad's talents would be better used elsewhere. When Anish ended a sentence, she said, in a tone worthy of King's Mother, "There are other ways males can serve Eskalind and earn citizenship, without military service." She waited until everyone looked to her. "Our Apprentice Ambassadors study the customs and ways of the borderlands and outerlands, learning diplomacy and negotiating skills. Once they pass their assessments, they travel to the borderlands in service to the Ambassadors of Dalich King. Many become Ambassadors in time."

Mamon piped, "Even those born in the outerlands?"

"It matters not where one is born, just that he, or she," and she looked to Saysha and the other girls, "is deemed loyal and qualified. There are many examinations and assessments to determine who is best suited to serve. Eskalind is nearly unique among nations in awarding its positions of trust based on merit, not family standing or position."

Minder Perka cut her eyes at Anish as Saysha said, "But you are a noble Lady, and your brother is King's Second."

"That is true. But my father, the founder of my house, was not born a noble. In fact, he was raised in a King's House." The older Eastlant girl, Merlina, tapped the arm of her sister. Mamon moved forward in his seat. "There was a Healer at his King's House who sensed his talents," Jinilya said, while Saysha's head bowed slightly, "and she mentioned my father to their Records Keeper." The girl looked up again, tears brimming in her blue eyes. "In the end, my father came to King's Halls to study as an Ambassador, which he became, based on his own merits. Later still, he rose to be King's Second."

Saysha's fingers bunched in her white skirt. Turning to face the Minder, she whispered, "May I be excused?"

"Yes, dear." The Healer's daughter bolted from the room, her dress a light blur as she departed. Jinilya looked to Anish, wishing she had omitted some of the details of the story.

Minder Perka spoke. "Well, let us all thank Lady Jinilya and Sergeant Anish for their tales tonight. Then, children, it is time for bed. Tomorrow's special lesson will be bread baking with Cook." Her hands reached for the shoulders of the youngest members of the room as they murmured good nights and gratitude, then filed from the room.

"Thank you, Lady Jinilya," the Guerish boy beamed as he left.

"Goodnight, Mamon," Jinil's daughter called with a smile, happy that he seemed to find some worth in her tale.

Anish placed his hand on her leg as Perka turned to face the pair. "My Lady," the Minder said in a whisper, "I appreciate your tales greatly and can see the hope it gives the children. But I worry they may set their dreams too high."

The Sergeant added, "And not to be indelicate, but anyone

considering Ambassador studies must know that if one does not pass the final assessments and provide five years' service for citizenship, payment is owed for the education."

"Anish, you know I am aware of that." The other woman in the room raised her thin eyebrows slightly as Jinilya continued. "Minder Perka, I should explain. My nephew Kaloft departed his Ambassador studies prior to completion and thus was compelled to serve in the army for the standard five years. Kaloft was fortunate that his parents repaid the coin due for his studies, so he was not left in great debt." The hint of a smirk appeared on the Minder's lips. "So yes, I know into what waters I tread, which is why, Minder Perka, if any one of these five children were accepted for Ambassador's studies, I would sponsor them."

Even Anish looked surprised, and Minder Perka said, "Forgive me, my Lady, but what does that mean?"

"That from my own purse I would repay the coin for their education if they do not complete their studies and are unable to serve." Anish was smiling.

Perka sat, stupefied. "That is most generous, my Lady."

"Your Acta Sua," began her lover in a low voice, "will not be pleased."

It was Jinilya's moment to grin. "Another thing about me with which he can be displeased." She touched his cheek fondly, warmed by the thought of the young people in their lives. To The Powers, she hoped she and Anish would one day parent a child, but if they did not, he had Saysha and she, she hoped, had Mamon.

Lord Lachmir clanked his tall cup onto the slate top of the high table in his great hall. A bright plume of mead erupted from the cup and splashed the table with eccentric curved patterns like a copyist exhibiting her finesse. The Eyfian lord stood, his belt buckle striking the table and a small piece of the stone flaking away, unnoticed by the man, as he bellowed, "Come, Favik, to the window!"

The former Ambassador of Eskalind raised himself to his feet, swayed, shouldered his woolly cape with one hand, and lifted the nearest mead jug with the other. The libations safe in the crook of his arm, he staggered to the window as the Eyfian pushed back the shutters. A blast of frigid air flooded their faces like a spray of cold water.

"The sobering breezes sober our minds so we can drink more!" Lachmir laughed as he spotted the jug in Favik's embrace. He reached for it, cackling. "Good lad." Perhaps he had forgotten that Favik, now approaching sixty years of age, was easily half a decade older than himself.

The Eskalinder gazed across the broad, moonlit valley below, the chimneys of the Cast Outs' huts yielding thin plumes of smoke. In the distance, the easterly peaks of Eyfia ringed the wide valley, pinnacles wrapped in downy snow, bluish under the white orb's glow. The silver sheen of a river coursed through the heart of the lowlands.

The gray jug was before his eyes again. "Drink, Favik," coaxed Lachmir. "You're returned to Eyfia, the land of cups, copying, and copulating!"

Favik waved a hand. "But, my lord, Eyfia has more charms than three."

Lachmir tilted the bottom of the jug toward the ceiling. A stream of amber liquid escaped along his chin before he lowered the jug to the windowsill. Favik rescued it before it plummeted from the thin ledge to the stone floor.

"Ha," said Lachmir. "You cannot tell me you missed thistle tea?"

"No." Favik gestured to his shoulder. "The sheep."

The Eyfian wiped his eyes. "Oh Favik, I missed you, lad. Thank The Powers you're back." He clasped his hands on the Eskalinder's shoulders. "The sheep! The howling woolen monsters of Eyfia, crying to be trimmed, so round with wool they roll down the mountain. And the Cast Outs, running across the flatland, shearing knives ready, empty wool bags flopping—"

A woman hollered, "Close the window!"

"I'll be opening the windows and leaving 'em open in my own castle." Lachmir turned to the main room and locked eyes on the shouter, then looked to Favik, aghast. "Me wife. Can't believe I didn't recognize Heida's voice. She'll be having my eyes for this." The lord reached for the shutters and pulled them tight as a gentler female voice rose in song behind them. Then the men turned to the room behind them, the lord pulling the pitcher from his guest's hands. "Goodbye to what you Eskalinders—ha ha—to what we all call 2936. The new year approaches." He looked into the jug and shook it from side to side, his voice dropping. "May The Powers keep us safe still from King Rothbur." He drank again, likely emptying the jug this time.

Favik murmured, "Is there new cause for concern?" A young man blended his voice with the first singer's in a lovely harmony.

"Rothbur's alive and he's half our age. That's concern enough for me." The stout Eyfian lord tapped the mead pitcher. "No one believes his elder brother died naturally. By The Powers, ambition is a young man's game. May Rothbur set his sights eastward."

"To Amkland?"

Lachmir's cheek puckered. "Hadn't thought it like that, but given he's on the eastern edge of Eyfia, Amkland would be a good place for him to go and run into a sword." The Eyfian's chins bobbed in agreement. "I meant east of my castle, far, far away from my domain here in the wonderfully woolly westerly reaches. Let him have all the gold in Amkland." The jug slipped from his fingers, shattering upon the floor. "Oops."

Several faces turned to look at them; a couple girls tittered. The lord's wife barked a curse.

"It was empty, Heida. I'll buy you another." She folded her arms over her ample bosom as another woman bent to speak in her ear.

A boy sprang toward the men and the destroyed jug, rustling the shards onto a cloth. Favik bent to help him, noting a light-haired woman he did not recognize observing him with eyes that appeared brown in the candle's glow. A shadow of Melande, perhaps. He looked to the broken pieces of pitcher tottering uselessly on the floor, at the boy's swift hands claiming them as deftly as though this were a well-practiced game.

"Husband!" boomed a voice. Lady Heida sailed across the floor with swift steps toward her intended goal, Favik and the youngster stepping aside at her majestic approach: she was nearly as stout as her husband, but when propelled into action, infinitely more graceful in her movements. "Dance, my lord." She twirled by, sweeping her husband along to a tune not yet voiced by the musicians. Lachmir laughed, stumbling by her side.

A fiddler struck a tune, and Favik withdrew from the revelry in the hall to his chamber, away from the warmth and company and into his wool-blanketed bed, a sleeping cap his only companion.

The next morning he returned to the hall. A few prone and snoring forms huddled over the tables or sprawled on the wall-lining benches, wrecks of the previous night's antics. A few others sat alone, eating at the common tables. Lord Lachmir chewed on a hard cracker, bits of white flecks decorating the silvery threads of his short beard. He motioned the Eskalinder to sit with him. "That one there." He pointed with the jaggy crust to another table's sole occupant. "She's been watching you ever since you came into the hall."

Favik sat, training his eyes in the direction the lord's breakfast directed. Melande's shadow gazed back at him. In the daylight she lost the youthful glow that drink or candlelight—or both—had granted her, for the skin about her neck was no longer smooth. Though she wore a neutral expression, the remnants of past smiles and frowns were lightly etched upon her face. There was a hint of acknowledgment as their eyes met. He looked away and murmured to his host, "Does she have a name, my lord?" Favik tugged the deep gray wool of his cape snugly across his chest.

"Fastest copyist in Eyfia. Accurate too." The stout lord sank his teeth into the dried bread with a crunch, then reached for his thistle-tea mug. "Quite a story, that lass."

"What brought her here?"

He expected the tale to consume their repast, but Lachmir said gruffly, "The fact that I don't tolerate inscribers, or men who take women."

The second phrase required no explanation, but the first term was unfamiliar; Favik inhaled slowly as he reached for the bread basket. "Inscribers?"

The Eyfian raised both of his furry eyebrows. "You don't know? After all these years coming and going in Eyfia?" Favik shook his head. "Mmm. Well, then, you've never lain with a copyist." The lord glanced to the woman. "Some of my countrymen write their names on those they consider valuable property. It was an ancient atrocity, which is for some reason now reserved for copyists." He spat on the floor. "Soldiers cut their allegiances into their left upper arms, here," and Lachmir gestured to just below his shoulder joint. "You've seen that, yes?"

"On Eyfian soldiers. And Swedfians as well."

"Old tradition, goes back to when Eyfia and Swedfia were the same land." He coughed. "Grown people doing it to themselves, I pay no heed. But with copyists, some thug lords cut into their copyists' backs." He gestured to someone, but Favik kept his eyes intent on Lachmir's expression. "Our fast copyist there labored in our last king's copy halls. Rothbur inherited her." His tone was of utter disgust, as though the food in his mouth had turned to rot.

Favik digested this unsavory morsel. "Rothbur's castle is on the opposite side of Eyfia from yours. How did she come to your halls?"

A woman said, "Rothbur lost a bet. I was the prize." The subject of their discussion stood before the table. At closer range, her slim figure was apparent in her stark cheekbones.

"Ha!" The Eyfian lord rose to his feet. "What amazes me still is Rothbur honored the bet."

She inclined her head, dexterous fingers clutching her cape. "Honor had nothing to do with it, my lord. He was outnumbered."

"That explains it. Let go the fastest copyist in the land—" A boy had appeared with a serving tray set with a squat tea pot, two mugs, and bowls with steam trailing above their mounded contents. "Good lad. I'll bring it from here." Lachmir stood, accepted the tray, and winked at Favik. "Heida's Naming Day. Breakfast in bed, ha ha!" He wandered away, leaving the strangers alone and awkwardly unintroduced.

The Eskalinder stood and gave her his name.

"What brings you to this quarry?" Melande's shadow asked, using the Eskalinder term for a castle.

He nodded slightly in acknowledgment of her word choice. "To study scrolls of ancient source for my Lord Radil of Eskalind. Also to commission and purchase copies of those that meet his interest, as Lord Lachmir allows."

"I can assist you." At close range, her eyes were not brown but a deep, compelling blue above the light gray of her worsted wool cape. "My name is Kala."

"How do you find life here in Lachmir's domain?"

Without a change in expression, the copyist gestured him away from the table, replying, "Our lord is eccentric, but generous. No one here goes hungry or cold." Kala pinched the deep pile of her cape. "I can tell you that is a unique experience in over thirty years among Eyfian lords."

The woman's forthrightness intrigued him.

The copyist led him down a spiral of stone stairs to the main scroll room. None of this terrain was new to him, but he wanted to hear her perspective on this tour. Eyfians locked their scrolls in small trunks nested inside larger, locked strongboxes made of sheets of metal or stone, to keep out both vermin and thieving hands. The appearance of the room was similar to the hold of a merchant ship, for the ceiling was low and it lacked shelves. Lit lanterns hung from posts. Coffin-proportioned trunks lined the walls, and Favik found himself considering the way these units housed and protected the stories within, much as each person holds tales and experiences within himself or herself. He wondered what Kala's history encompassed, besides the events that Lachmir's remarks referenced. Their bodies were separated by perhaps the width of the large lord's stomach, and studying Kala, he guessed her to be into her fourth decade, perhaps close in age to Damina Queen. He recalled the Lady of Eskalind as a young girl, just eight when he had first met her. He wondered what she looked like now.

"We do not have many books, mainly scrolls," the copyist said. "An Eskalind Queen was the first to make a book. Did you know this?"

Favik withheld a grin, although references to his Lady Marna still saddened him, even after these many years. His thoughts were populated with more memories than there were breathing people in this room.

"Yes," he answered. "I was her Page at the time."

The Eyfian turned to him with renewed interest, pausing her steps. "I thought it was legendarily long ago."

"You make a man feel old."

"Look at us. We are old." He grinned at her remarks.

Kala continued, "I would be a grandmother had I mothered children. So, how long ago?"

"Nearly fifty years."

The copyist absorbed the number without reaction. "What was it like to be there?"

"Well…" Favik scratched his forehead; some lingering dust in the air was causing an itch. "Rather amusing. No one was quite sure her invention would be that useful at first, until they tried it."

Kala laughed. "I'm still fighting that fight. My countrymen wish to stick with scrolls, but look at all these heavy trunks. We could store many more books in the same space, as long as the covers are not made thick with rich ornaments."

"Indeed, but I am curious. Lord Lachmir calls you the fastest copyist in the land. How did you earn such a distinction?"

A distinct smirk puckered her thin lips. "I know how to keep warm." He lifted an eyebrow at her seemingly flirtatious comment. "If one stays warm, one can work longer."

"That makes sense, but does not explain—"

The copyist spoke matter-of-factly. "It's a secret of my craft. Forgive me, I must return to work." With that Kala turned and left him, the wool of her cape stretched tight over her back. He wondered what was inscribed upon her skin, but mostly he wondered what he might do to win her favor.

———

Months passed, and Favik might catch a glance of Kala across the great hall or see her ahead of him in a passageway. A young male copyist was assigned to bring the scrolls he requested, often accompanied by Uldrik, Lord Lachmir's tall and silent sergeant-at-arms, whose muscles easily bore three times more load than the youngster's.

One long afternoon of reading caught the Eskalinder blinking away sleep at the tedious tale before him. Radil would find nothing of interest in this document. No one likely would.

Favik snuffed his reading candle and made for the great hall, thinking a spot of tea would warm his belly and invigorate his thoughts. An unseasonably cold wind buffeted the rock walls outside, and the eerie sounds floating through the passageways were punctuated by Lachmir's call for silence. On the pads of his feet, Favik tiptoed into the great hall to find a cautious crowd gathered, the tables pushed to the walls. Lachmir stood in his boots atop a wide bench before the high table.

"Quiet!" thundered the head of the household in a rumbling roar, the final syllable punctuated like an explosion.

"What's happening?" the former Ambassador whispered to a nearby man.

"A trial," was the soft reply.

A blond head a few feet away turned, and Kala's deep blue eyes gazed at him with a hint of distant sadness. Favik nodded in acknowledgment, and she retuned her gaze to the lord.

Near Lachmir, a young female voice sputtered words the Eskalinder could not apprehend, though he saw a head bobbing that he suspected was the speaker. The Eyfian lord's eyes were keen upon the woman. Then he muttered, "You will be seen to."

His wife stepped forward: "I'll tend to her." Lady Heida lifted her woolen cape and placed an arm around the young woman's shoulders, leading her away. A brief glimpse of her face revealed her to be a serving woman known for being quick with a jest and a smile. Not at this moment, however.

"Uldrik, bring the messenger here. And send for my sword." The sergeant-at-arms dragged a male form forward whilst calling to a boy to bring the blade.

Lachmir leveled his gaze at the accused, who doffed his cap. "You took a woman of my household. Here. In *my* castle. Did The Powers make you such a fool as to think this would go unpunished?"

The man groveled, "My lord, I did not. She was willing."

"Then why did three witnesses hear her shout, 'No'?"

The man coughed and dropped to his knees. He murmured something, perhaps a plea. A boy approached his master and lifted the scabbard to him. Lachmir gripped the pommel, drew the blade, and dropped the scabbard to the table with a hollow clank. "Strip," ordered Lord Lachmir. A hint of whispering propagated through the crowd. The man let drop his cape, then pulled an outer tunic over his head, shoulders rising in defiance. He undid the laces of his inner shirt and let it fall to the floor. The crowd before Favik stretched and leaned to view the scene, leaving him to strain on his toes to see if any writing marred the accused's back. It appeared scarless. The messenger removed his boots, socks, and long trousers.

"Everything." Lachmir's eyes did not waver.

The man complied, standing naked before the crowd, shivering, but with a calmness about him as though resigned to his fate, whatever it might be. The Eyfian lord stared hard at him, dipping his sword slightly. Perhaps hoping to nudge the verdict, someone whispered, "Cut it off!"

Lachmir spoke. "Uldrik, lead him to the gate, and not to become a Cast Out either; see that he finds the short route over the precipice."

"Death!" cried a woman, joyful as though a victory were won. Others cheered. The man before Favik uttered, "Yes." Some surged forward as Uldrik jerked the guilty man from the room. Lachmir clambered down from his perch with a thud and departed toward his quarters, calling for his best inks as he waved his blade. Favik paced toward Kala, hoping for a word, but she darted to the opposite side of the room as though an urgent duty called. The hall emptied noisily as most eagerly ran to follow the progress of the condemned man to the gate.

Kala sat with another woman, sorting a stack of envelopes. Favik decided to approach. The copyist was speaking. "We'll send another messenger to deliver the notes not meant for this castle." She placed the envelopes on the table, pushing aside a yellow-hued one. She turned as though expecting him. "Ah, Favik, this is addressed to you." Into his hand she placed the yellow note, sealed with a single red blob of wax. He knew the quilling and inhaled as he studied the seal. An *M*: Lord Radil's wife, Lady Mayva. The worst reason she alone might write him plagued his thoughts. But if Radil were dead, she would be Acta Sua of their house, and would seal the note with two seals, one for her name and the second for the title.

Kala had stood and was reaching for his wrist, her fingers hovering just above his skin. "Would it be best to read this note in private?"

"I would be most grateful."

She nodded to the other woman and led him away. "Here." She steered him toward one of the alcoved passageways adjoining the hall. It led to straight stairs and a lower level where the copyists had their cells. A single lantern lit the dim, narrow corridor as they entered. With a key, Kala opened the third door and motioned him inside, striking a match to light a trio of candles in a dish dangling from a chain in the corner. The former Ambassador stopped cold at the screen that blocked entry deeper into the room, for it reminded him of similar barriers found in Havadran private chambers. Lifting a candle, Kala said, "Stay here. I will be on the other side; call if you require me." She disappeared behind the screen.

Favik breathed slowly and tore the seal. The date was the first surprise, for it was three months ago, and Radil's estate was less than five hundred miles away. Once again, the messengers in the outerlands had proved far less fast and reliable than Eskalind's Swift Riders.

Fifth Day, Third Month, 2937
Dear Favik, Brother to my husband, Uncle to my children,
Please forgive the brevity of this note but it is with great joy I
quill our glad news; Amril's lover Samsa has gotten with child
and they will be joined by the time this reaches you, the babe to
arrive late in the ninth month.

He did not intend it, but a sound akin to a relieved sob escaped his throat.

"Are you all right?" called Kala.

"Yes, yes." He scanned the rest of the note.

Radil hurt his hand in a very clumsy and embarrassing
accident, which he asks I do not commit to ink. You must ask
for the tale when you are with us again. He awaits healing
from Dalich King, but wanted our wonderful news conveyed to
you swiftly.
We all miss you and hope you are staying warm and welcome
in Eyfia.
Fondly,
Lady Mayva

The copyist had poked her head around the screen. "You're smiling; I thought I heard you weep."

Favik was indeed grinning, feeling bright and light with delight. "My benefactor writes with happy word. His family expects their first grandchild soon." He folded the note and placed it in a pocket.

She paused a moment, then came nearer. Her height seemed to have diminished. "I like how you look when you smile." A calm deliberation resided in her eyes as her face came close to his. The copyist lifted a finger to touch his beard.

He was not certain he was breathing, but said, "Tell me, if we were in Eskalind, would you be showing me your feet?"

"Have you looked at my feet?"

He cut his eyes to the floor and saw her bare toes. "You must be freezing," he murmured, crouching and reaching with his hands to cover her cool toes.

She beamed down at him. "I know how to keep warm." Offering her hand, she led him to the other side of the screen. The Eskalinder nearly tripped on her discarded slippers. Something dark blocked the way, and as she parted it he realized it was a wall of deep gray wool. They stepped through into an enclosed room chambered within the stone-walled cell. Another bowl of candles illuminated the bed, as well as a cabinet of shelves, a chair, and a desk cluttered with parchments and inks. The temperature was a great deal warmer than on the other side of the enclosure. Favik stood in his boots and gawked as Kala slipped onto the bed, rubbing her icy feet with the blanket.

"A room within a room." He petted the fabric wall closest. "This keeps you warm?"

She grinned. "It does. Besides quilling next to a brazier, it's the best way to keep the fingers nimble and cozy. Though I was hoping to have your assistance with that this night."

He was more than happy to be of service that night. And the next. Until nights became weeks and months.

Lord Radil's grandchild must be born and named by now, Favik considered one morning by Kala's side. Their inner chamber nearly glowed from their body heat, and most nights they slept nude. His lover rolled to her side, and he shut his eyes, not wanting to read her back, the words visible even in the dim illumination of the single lit candle.

Possessed by Lathbur

And beneath it:

Possessed by Rothbur

He wondered, if he could bring her to Eskalind, would Dalich King's healing extend to scars inflicted by lunatics? Given how Lord Lachmir felt about inscribers, the odds seemed good he would approve of such a journey, though traveling across Eyfia with a valuable copyist, one inscribed with a former master's name—the king's name, no less—would be risky. Perhaps she would be willing to pose as his wife to escape close inspection. It was possible, too, that even in an outerland like Eyfia, a former Ambassador of Eskalind might enjoy less scrutiny when crossing borders.

But there remained a great problem. Once they reached Eskalind, he would need to explain his relationship with Kala to Lord Radil. Radil knew Favik fathered children with Melande. By Eskalind law, and thus Radil's way of thinking, Favik was joined to Melande alone and always. Though she was dead, he was by law unable to join again, or even to have a lover. No, his benefactor must never know. Favik could not bring Kala to Eskalind. He would leave with only his memories and the copious copies she had made for him.

He found this most displeasing.

Perhaps he would not return to reside in Eskalind, but merely shuttle copies and knowledge to the noble Scholar, while making his home in Eyfia, with Kala. Lord Lachmir welcomed his company and companionship. Lachmir's castle could easily become his permanent home.

Favik opened his eyes to a room that was brightly lit, as though the sun shone through windows. But it was not the room within a room that he shared with Kala, but rather a silk-blanketed bedchamber as one might find in an Eskalind noble household, with embroidered ruby coverlets under his hand. At least, a hand that was shaped and formed like his hand, but with skin that was nearly gray and a heavy gold ring he did not own encircling the circumference under the thick knobbed joint of his index finger.

He squinted and choked. Sitting upright, eyes wide in panic, he was back in the copyist's chamber.

"What is it?" Kala said, turning to him, her expression lit with concern.

"I don't know. A bad dream. Yes, that's what it was."

But during the day, the vision returned again and again, once when he was upon a stairway and nearly lost his footing, forgetting where he was. That night in bed he could not sleep, and his restlessness kept Kala awake as well.

His lover murmured into his ear, "I hear you breathing like you ran around the castle thrice without stopping. I'm calling the herbsmith." The Eyfian lifted herself upright, feet swinging out of the bed and into her slippers.

"No, stay with me." He made a conscious effort to steady his inhalations. It worked. The old Ambassador tricks still were of use. Favik smiled at his lover. "I'm feeling better. Please, Kala, stay here with me."

She regarded him with a critical eye, similar to her appraisals of him when they first encountered one another. Slowly she slid under the sheets. They lay abed a long time, his ears alert to her breathing as it shifted into the rhythm of sleep. The copyist rolled over, and he chanced a peek at her back. As he followed the puckered edges of her scars, the letters dissolved, all except for the name of the king of Eyfia. New writing appeared after it.

> *Rothbur aims for Eskalind*
> *Warn Radil in person*

Lady Jinilya lay abed alone in her private chamber nestled within her family's quarters at King's Halls. For half her life, the Scholar had resided here. Memories of home prior to her seventeenth year, of childhood at her family's estate, were a soft fog, as though not lived by her, merely familiar from the stories told by others.

Morning sun illuminated her gauzy curtains, which were a light tan color that passed for her house's designated brown when a pale, subtle shade was required. An unfamiliar feminine voice echoed faintly in the private corridor connecting the family's rooms. The tone was playful and husky, and certainly not the voice of their young substitute Chamber Keeper. Jinilya slipped from the crimson sheets, tightened the belt on her sleeping robe, and opened her door a crack to view the back of a honey-haired woman exiting Saril's room. "Until later," she heard her brother say. The woman patted her tight braids and turned, cheeks flush and eyes lowered. She exited the main door into the corridor.

Well, this was most unusual. The Librarian opened her door fully and walked to her brother's door. She knocked.

"Back so soon?" he called lazily.

"It is your sister."

"Come in."

She opened the door to find Saril sprawled naked and sleepy-eyed in his large bed. "Ah, it truly is you."

"I did not think we lived in Gergelt." Jinilya tossed a bit of loose sheet over his crotch as he grinned. She sat on the bed, facing him, noting a low-burning candle on the night table. "Saril, were you just lying with an Amklander *woman*?"

King's Second stretched his arms, placing his hands behind his head. Whilst she was used to the bits of gray at his temples, it surprised her to see a hint of gray in the tufts under his arms. "I am of age, you know."

She laughed. "You have been of age nearly as long as I have lived."

Saril sat upright. "Amklander women are of special interest. Not all are as they seem …" His voice trailed away as he gestured to a water glass by the bed, too far for his reach. She smirked, not wanting to procure it for him, but wondering what he insinuated. Jinilya stretched to the glass and handed it to him.

The Acta Sua of her house sipped, then spoke. "Besides, if Madix gets with child, our house will enjoy the increase in population." Ah, now she wished she had doused him with that water. "Or does my Lady Sister not approve of an Amklander saister?"

The years had taught her to recognize this tactic: misdirection before he doubled back to his main topic. "Well, Brother, our nephew writes from Teffle that he has a lover. A fellow Apprentice Builder, who hails from Nordak. Perhaps she will be part of our house someday."

He looked to his glass. "That is possible. What is not possible is our brother's wife conceiving again."

"Mother was forty when she bore me."

"Athla is more than a few years past that. What would truly have helped matters is if she and her husband had resided on the same side of the country for more than brief visits."

Jinilya said nothing, for the situation duplicated her own and Anish's. Perhaps if they were together more often, different results would follow. But neither wished to leave their trade, for she would not leave King's Mother, nor the Scholars, and for some years now Anish had been a First Sergeant, devoted to his duty. He aspired to captain a company someday, and thus must follow the dictates of his commanders on that path.

Saril drained the glass and set it against a pillow. "And what of you?"

"I am a servant of The Powers." She smiled, the same expression she used when assigning an Apprentice an unpleasant task and wanted to evaluate their reaction.

"Then you await joining your future husband when They speak by granting you a babe."

The Librarian felt she was giving something away but said, "I do. It is one of the many characteristics I favor about our homeland."

"How long have you and your First Sergeant been lovers?"

Ah, now he bared his mind.

"Many years."

"Over fifteen?" She did not reply, though he was right. "All those years of opportunity with no child."

"King's Mother tells me her husband's parents waited thirteen years for his arrival."

King's Second shook his head. "The Powers make the royals different from us, my sister. You should know that by now. Here you have spent your irretrievable youth with the same, faraway man and ... ?" His voice slipped away with the air of a question. She gazed at him blandly, as though he spoke of the weather. Then Saril added, "Perhaps another approach is called for."

"Oh, perhaps I should bed women?" Jinilya stood, tapping her lips. "My Lord Brother, do mind your appearance when you step out. There is a short hair caught in your teeth." She marched forth from the room.

The day found her bustling about with her varied tasks, administering an organizing examination for the Library's Apprentices, and enjoying a stop by the Scriptorium to confer with Chief Scriptor Palika as to the progress of a set of books commissioned by Damina Queen.

The vivid quillwork with its intricate designs, created by one of the seniormost Scriptors, never failed to awe. She wondered if Anish's talent would still flourish when he reached an advanced age. How present he was in her daily life despite being hundreds of miles away.

"Such a rich joining present for the son of King Homik of Humiksland," Palika said. Her blue eyes scanned the gold-edged frontispiece, displayed by itself upon a lectern, for the book was not yet bound and covered. "To think his great-grandfather, King Hudik, ruled when I was born there." Her gaze remained upon the parchment, but Jinilya felt that something in the Scriptor's aspect studied her minutely, as though anticipating a particular response. It reminded her of when two Scholars were uncertain if the other was truly one of their number and so hesitated before speaking their motto or displaying their hands in the secret ways. As she had no response for Palika, she thanked her and departed to continue her errands.

Passing from the Scriptorium, she heard her name called in voice that cracked mid sentence.

"Lady Jinilya, I'm sorry." Mamon greeted her with a bow, one hand to the bare skin of his throat just above the sable cloth collar of his Apprentice Ambassador's uniform. "My voice keeps changing."

She smiled fondly. "You are fifteen; it is the normal course of life for a male your age." He stood nearly to her shoulder and perhaps would never be as tall as she, but full Guerlanders did tend to be shorter than Eskalinders. She chided herself for wanting to make him a complete Eskalinder; it was still possible his father might be found and that Mamon would return to his native country. Still, if Anish must be far from her side, it was a comfort that Mamon resided in the same halls and she saw him near daily. "Any news for me?"

"I just learned I passed the Customs Assessment."

"Well done." She hugged him. "I am proud beyond words, Mamon, that is wonderful." What she did not tell him was her nephew Kaloft waited until he was seventeen for the Customs Assessment and still did not pass. How disappointed Saril had been, but to his credit he concealed it before Kaloft, offering only steady encouragement when their nephew elected to complete his service to Eskalind as a Soldier, not Ambassador.

Mamon continued, "The Master Ambassador will send you a full report, but I wanted to tell you in person. Thank The Powers I found you swiftly—I thought I might burst with the news."

"Well, containing one's personal emotions is another Ambassadors' assessment."

His expression blanked into complete neutrality. "As you say, my Lady. But not until I receive the proper training." For a moment she wondered who this studious, unreadable person before her was, then his dark eyes brightened and he lapsed into a grin.

Jinilya laughed, "Oh Mamon, I think you need not worry about passing that assessment either."

"Thank you for your confidence, my Lady Sponsor." The Guerish youth spoke crisply and clearly, as though reading to his master. "I will endeavor to absorb as much in that regard as possible prior to the examination."

"My, you do sound like an Ambassador." She smiled. "I am off to see King's Mother."

Mamon bowed as though she were that royal personage herself, and the pair departed one another, each with a bright joy in their heart.

Arriving in Lady Marna's Library Chamber, Jinilya found the Scholars' Mistress seated in a window seat, eyes closed against the gleam of direct sun upon her face. Her pale brow furrowed, she looked so still that for a moment Jinilya feared her elder was not breathing. But the gray eyes flashed open. "Come, my dear Reader's daughter, sit and give me your opinion on a letter." She patted a mustard-yellow envelope resting atop the black cushions. King's Mother's hand covered the direction, but given the color, Jinilya guessed the sender to be Scholar Lord Radil.

"Are you well, my Lady?" Jinilya settled into the window seat next to her Lady.

"Yes, just a wee bit tired. But I require nothing more than your eyes, voice, and mind."

"That is all I possess, my Lady," she replied in a delicate, teasing tone.

"Ha!" guffawed the former Queen. "You are infinitely more than that, my Librarian Scholar." A smile lifted her cheeks. "Oh, but first would you slit the seals on these other letters?" She handed over a short stack of tan envelopes. "The wax is quite sticky and has gummed my seal-slicing knife."

The younger woman removed from her pocket sheath the pearl-handled envelope opener Anish had given her. Its thin blade might be called a dagger, but its excellence shone in the peaceful use of seal breaking. The white gleam of its shaft glinted with all the colors light revealed, but particularly rubies and violets, well suited for a woman whose noble house possessed red as one of its colors and who worked at Dalich King's court. She clove the seals on the envelopes as her Lady instructed. "Just place them aside when you are done and read this one aloud."

Completing her task, Jinilya picked up the yellow envelope, which indeed bore the familiar quilling of their Scholar in the northwest of Eskalind. It was dated just less than a week ago. She read in a soft voice,

Last Day, 2937
My Lady Marna, King's Mother,
It is with great urgency that I write. My researcher in the
outerland of Eyfia has news of import.

"Researcher," interrupted the former Queen. "Who is he thinking of when he quilled that?"

Jinilya hesitated, for though she could feel Radil's thoughts as he wrote the letter, it was not a name she thought her Lady wanted to hear. Not a name that had been uttered between them in years. It still saddened her to think of his sudden dismissal from their lives. King's Mother must have had her reasons, but not a word had she spoken of them.

The Scholars' Mistress raised a gray eyebrow.

"My Lady, Radil is thinking of Favik."

"Hmm." The sound had an angry flatness to it, but melancholy lingered in the eyes. They sat in silence a moment. "What else was Radil thinking?"

Jinilya reread the lines, replying, "That he trusts no one else to be as reliable as Favik in this matter."

The elder Lady stroked a finger across her gray hairline. "Please read more."

As you may recall, King Lathbur of Eyfia's designated heir, a nephew, perished not long before the ailing king himself, leaving a younger nephew, Lord Rothbur, the successor. Rothbur, after turbulent years as king in Eyfia, at last solidifies his rule amongst the Eyfian lords.

He now seeks to spread his reach and territory and makes a loud claim of it, recruiting an army which my researcher saw personally when he traveled to Eskalind. He also has word from a strange source

"What strange source?" King's Mother interrupted.

It was hard to believe, but Jinilya voiced Radil's thought. "Favik saw writing appear on someone's skin."

"Ah." It was an unmistakable tone of recognition. Jinilya looked to King's Mother, who said, "Continue."

The Librarian found her voice.

He also has word from a strange source that Rothbur aims for Eskalind. Geography and caution dictate setting a watchful eye upon Rothbur's future aims that may cross his border.

King's Mother raised her head. "Rothbur may set his sights on our borderlands Kaymif or Amkland. Our Ambassadors there should be apprised of this situation."

Jinilya lowered the note. "My Lady, shall I mention to King's Second that this word comes from our Library guests?"

There was an bitter urgency to King's Mother's tone. "No, I will. And if your brother asks you, corroborate the source as such."

"I will." Jinilya waited, hoping to learn more.

"And a bit of news about Kaymif, to be shared just between ourselves." King's Mother inhaled as though about to begin a lengthy exposition. "I had a letter from Samathe; you recall Deenofts's sister the portraitist?"

It was a mild surprise to hear more names from her youth mentioned. Jinilya nodded.

"Scholar Samathe wrote from Kaymif. She accepted commissions to paint the Kaymif queen and the king's sister, Princess Kostaza. Samathe knew the princess previously in Havadra." Lady Marna's lips pursed slightly. "When the time of payment came, the exchequer gave Samathe coin for the princess's portrait, but not for the queen's. Now, why would that happen?" King's Mother's tone made it clear she had come to a conclusion.

"The Kaymif queen did not care for her portrait?"

King's Mother sounded like a Records Keeper outlining a case at trial. "Samathe writes that the queen thought it a lovely likeness and ordered copies sent to her family in Swedfia."

"Then the king did not care for the portrait?"

"Ah-ha!" Lady Marna had raised a hand in the air, a gesture worthy of Deenofts. "The king of Kaymif does not care for his queen's portrait, or he does not care for *her*?" She lowered her hand to the black linen of her smock. "Given Scholar Samathe's time spent at the Kaymif royal court, she suspects the latter led to the former. And thus the nonpayment." The Scholars' Mistress reached for a wax tablet. "We shall see what comes of it. Please read the rest of Radil's letter, but not aloud." She placed the tablet in her wide lap and waited, her posture that of one bracing herself for unwelcome news.

Jinilya studied her Lady's bearing, but the elder woman gave no explanation. Thus, she turned her eyes to Radil's quilling.

Also, my latest experiments with secret writing yet again ended in failure, the last nearly disastrous to my poor daughter. As I have attempted previously, I made new symbols for each letter of the alphabet, quilling a message with those symbols and sealing it in an envelope. This time I gave Alayna the envelope along with the list to interpret the symbols. When she opened the envelope, it burst into flames in her lap.

Jinilya exclaimed, "By The Powers!"

King's Mother sighed. "Very distressing. The poor girl."

The young Scholar scanned the rest of the note.

Thank The Powers Alayna was not hurt, as this happened in the presence of her tutor and a maidservant. The adults doused the flames before any harm came to my dear child, though she is still upset with me for the shock and the ruination of a favorite dress. Needless to say, I ended my experimentations after the incident. I intend to quill a more detailed report later, but that is the plain heart of my news.

Yours,

Lord Radil

The fear in his nerves as he wrote the words was palpable. Jinilya lowered the papyrus to rest atop the dark fabric draping her legs. Lady Marna grasped a stylus and wrote on her tablet. She showed it to Jinilya.

I asked Lord Radil to invent a code for our Scholars to use to send cloaked messages to one another. This letter proves to me that The Powers will not allow such a device.

Jinilya felt like a little child, and could only say, "Oh." Gathering her wits, she gestured to the tablet. "Might I inquire why you use this?"

Her Lady scraped away the writing. "Some things must not be spoken aloud." She pulled on her earlobe as though inspecting it to see if an earring was still present, though she wore no such jewelry. Her gray eyes cut to the younger woman. Gathering that the former Queen suspected someone was listening to their conversation, Jinilya tapped her own ear and nodded.

It was all very curious, but the Bladesmith's Daughter often conveyed information piecemeal; one needed only to be patient and wait for the next nugget. In most matters. Patience was a trait the young noble shared with her brother Saril, and like his wont, she made an off-topic inquiry. "My Lady, I spoke with your niece, Scriptor Palika, today. I felt that she was studying me closely at one point in the conversation."

"What were you talking about?"

"She was speaking of King Hudik, the great-grandfather of the current crown prince of Humiksland."

"Ah." Her Lady eyed her with similar interest. "And?"

"Nothing more than that King Hudik had ruled when she was born. It was the way she said his name ... I did not understand how it might be important, but something in her tone made me think it was significant."

Dalock's Queen smiled. "Well, it is old news. Palika's father was a son of King Hudik."

"I did not know her father was a prince." All these years, she had thought her Lady's relatives commoners; it was a shock.

"No, dear. Palika's father was a secret son. His mother was a lover to King Hudik, not his wife."

Now this was a circumstance hardly ever spoken of in Eskalind. "Truly, my Lady?"

"Indeed. But that leads me to another tidbit." King's Mother leaned close. "When I am gone, if you ever speak face to face with," she paused and her next utterance was tinged with a reticence akin to regret, "Favik, most privately, mention this all to him." Before Jinilya could ask why, her elder turned and raised herself to her feet with an "Umpf! Now, I promised Lady Dara I would meet her for the evening meal. Two old Ladies reminiscing about old times. I am certain we will bore the poor servants to tears." She guffawed, leaving the younger Lady to wonder.

After supper, but before dark, Jinilya sat in her day clothes at her writing desk in her chamber, quilling a letter to Minder Perka of Mamon's former King's House, to apprise her of his progress. A slight tap at the door, and a voice called, "May I bring fresh water, my Lady?" The voice was timid, as one would expect from a servant fresh to her trade, for she was just past her sixteenth Naming Day.

"Yes, Saura, come in."

Behind, the new-to-her-service maid entered and replenished the pitcher on the night table. Then, unnoticed by Jinilya, Saura departed, returning with a flame to light the dusty-wicked candles on the candelabra adjacent to the bed. For Jinilya, the tall candle-holder was merely an ornamental piece of furniture, but Saura had not been instructed in this unusual practice of her Lady's. It was still light enough in the room that the candles made it no brighter. Saura considered that she might have lit them too early, but decided against dousing them. She left.

Jinilya completed her letter and closed her eyes a moment. Perhaps she would quill Anish next. Then a delicate whisper came from the flames behind her, so quiet she did not distinguish the thought from her own:

She would write her lover that she would break with him, for she was not with child and hoped to be a mother someday. Clearly their pairing would never yield a babe.

The Lady opened her eyes and, unconscious of her actions, quilled these thoughts upon a fresh papyrus, signing the bottom of the letter in her fluid hand. A bell rang in the corridor, heralding that someone waited at the main door. Placing the letter next to an envelope previously addressed to Anish, she rose and went to her door, finding the new Chamber Keeper stepping from Saril's room, a lit taper in her hand. "Do not trouble yourself, Saura. I will answer the door."

She passed the large table in the main room, the lit candles clustered in its center calm and quiet under her appraising glance. Then Jinil's daughter pulled the main door open to face Saril's lover, the honey-haired Amklander woman, who seemed startled. She recovered, saying, "Your pardon. I believe Lord Saril is expecting me." Her blue-green eyes darted to the Librarian's insignia over Jinilya's heart, the gesture made more pronounced by the dark makeup outlining her eyes.

The Lady replied, "We have not met. I am Saril's sister, Jinilya."

The Amklander seemed relieved to learn this. She offered her hand in greeting. "I am Madix, chief assistant to Ambassador Lalis."

Jinilya grasped only the woman's fingers, as was traditional for Amklander greetings. She found herself captivated by Madix's unusual eyes. "Saril is not yet returned to his chamber, but do come and sit with me if you like." She released the woman's warm hand.

"Thank you for the invitation. I am most pleased to accept." A smoky depth tinged her voice.

Jinilya led the Amklander to the family's main table, motioning for her to sit as the Chamber Keeper passed by with the burning taper in her hand. "Saura, do not trouble yourself with lighting the candles in my chamber. I sleep best in darkness."

"Oh," said the very young woman, blinking. "Um, may I bring you any refreshments?" The maidservant gazed expectantly at the Amklander. "Bread and sauces, or?"

Glancing at her potential saister, Jinilya ventured, "Wine?"

"I would be most pleased to drink wine with you, my Lady." Madix's tone was formal, but her irises sparkled, the dark makeup that traced her eyes rendering her visage dramatically lovely. The color of her robe was a close match to her eyes, the embroidered dots decorating the fabric composed of shiny gold thread that caught the light to stunning effect. Small wonder Saril found her enticing; even Jinilya, who had always been attracted to men, felt her appeal.

"Bring us wine then. I thank you, Saura." Jinilya sat.

The servant nodded, but rather than leaving, she returned to her Lady's chamber as the pair commenced conversing. The Amklander's natural charm and intelligence was quite compelling in close quarters; one could study her eyes and find mystery. Then the Lady's gaze lowered to Madix's neck, which exhibited a projection at mid span, as commonly seen in males. She peered closer at the woman's chin. A hint of shaven stubble barely visible. By The Powers, she suspected that this enthralling woman was truly a man! That would explain why Saril found it easy to bed her.

It also made it explicitly unfair of him to claim a sacrifice for lying with a woman in the hopes it might increase their house, and to berate her for staying with the same lover for years. She was incensed.

Madix's husky voice sent a shiver through her. "Is everything all right?"

Knowing she had no quarrel with this person, Jinilya inhaled. "My brother—no, I wondered at something about Amklander custom. Perhaps you could assist?"

"I would be most pleased to." Madix's gaze was calm and open.

"I have never visited your land, and have met only a few of your people here at King's Halls. Thus something my brother said recently I do not understand." She paused; Madix was quiet and waitful in her aspect. "Saril mentioned that Amklander women are not all they appear to be…" A slow smile grew on Madix's lips. "Please do not think me impolite for asking or disloyal for repeating this. I am uncertain what he meant and would like to know more about your customs."

The eyes remained steadfast and welcoming upon her. "Some males of my country choose to live as females. I am one of them."

"I see." Having never encountered such a circumstance before,

Jinilya fumbled to speak as her mind tumbled with this information. Other than Saril's deception, she found no fault with it. Still, she was uncertain what to say next, until she recalled that King's Mother often said that compliments bridge conversational gaps in any land. Thus she started with, "I must tell you that you have the most lovely eyes I have ever seen."

Now Madix was grinning. "Without this dark ink," and she gestured to the black paint tracing her eyes, "how plain they would look." The Eskalinder laughed as Madix laid her hands upon the table, a gentle seriousness inhabiting her manner. "May I confide in you, Lady Jinilya?"

Echoing the familiar Amklander phrase, she replied, "I would be most pleased."

Madix nodded and began. "When I was a child, I found myself drawn to the life women lead. I felt out of place with the menfolk and how they live, dress, and behave." She looked to her hands. "Those not from my country will tell you that women in Amkland are subservient to men. As I have traveled beyond my homeland, I see how our ways can be viewed that way." A playful look enlivened her face as she gazed full upon the Eskalinder Lady, her hands rising to gesture with her speech. "But Amklander men are *worthless* without their women. Truly. They march around with their big bushy beards as though The Powers smiled upon them only, but without a woman or two or three to mind them, most could not even feed themselves."

The Eskalinder answered, "I never thought of it that way."

"It's true. There's a reason The Powers see that in Amkland, three births out of four are female. Without all the women, the men would be helpless." They both laughed, Jinilya feeling lighter, happier, and more intrigued than ever with this fascinating person. Madix continued, "So you see, I wanted to live a life of purpose, to add something to my society rather than lie back and live off the labors of others. Thus, here I am."

The Lady nodded. "I think I understand."

The Chamber Keeper returned from Jinilya's chamber, waving

envelopes in her hand. "My Lady, I am off to get your wine, and I sealed these with the plain seal. Shall I post them or wait for your seal, my Lady?"

Jinilya considered, trying to bring her mind back to what letters she had quilled. No, nothing in her dispatches required her personal official seal. Besides, she did not want to interrupt this enlightening conversation. "Just post them. I thank you, Saura."

Smiling the satisfied smile of one who believes she has rendered a good deed, the young woman departed the chambers of the House of Jinil to complete her errands.

———

Saril returned to his quarters to find his sister and his lover giggling together, each grasping a cup in one hand and covering their mouth with the other. A glazed pitcher stood solemnly over its spent, prone twin as though dubious of the goings-on about it. He doubted the two were imbibing water and opened his mouth to say so aloud, for they had not yet noticed his presence. Then a sad thought entered his mind—never had he seen Jinilya and their saister Athla enjoying a convivial moment akin to this.

"Brother!" his sister called, spying him. "Oh, tell us how long you have stood there, then I will know how much I must apologize for." She laughed while Madix playfully patted her arm.

"I heard nothing," he said in a facetious tone, which elicited a peal of laughter from the pair. "My, I never thought I could be the source of such copious amusement."

Jinilya stood, placing both hands on the table. "Well, I thank you for the excellent company—by which I mean Madix." She kissed the Amklander on the head, chortling like a drunken outlander, then lumbered to her chamber, swaying. Saril watched her progress, wanting to assist her but wagering she would rebuff his aid. The door closed behind her as though it were embarrassed. Saril feared they would hear her losing her stomach. But a different sound reached his ears.

Deep snoring, emanating from Madix, whose head lay facedown upon the table where long ago he and his parents and brother had breakfasted every morning. Without a word, the Acta Sua scooped his lover into his arms and bore her to his chamber.

CHAPTER SIXTY-THREE—AN UNUSUAL MENU
8TH DAY, 1ST MONTH, 2938

An inventory listing every item on the breakfast table would lead one to suspect that a very important personage was to enjoy the diverse repast of fruits, meats, breads, and porridges. In fact, just two important diners sat together, but apart, at this feast, though the number of servants awaiting their orders tripled the room's population. No orders were spoken, the only sound to break the silence was the chewing of the still childless queen of Kaymif and the occasional clank of her knife upon the engraved zigzag patterns of her plate as she sawed into a morsel. The native of Swedfia's deep brown eyes were lowered to her task, though the veil beads draping her forehead made it difficult to discern just where her gaze fell. Usually in private quarters she did not wear the beads, for women in her birth country endured no such impediments, as she called them. But of late she had added this part of the costume of Kaymif, whether to please her husband or hide her gaze in her grief at losing another child in the womb, one might only guess.

On the opposite side of the repast from his second wife, quite far down the long table, flaxen-haired King Moulai glanced at an overturned letter. He had slipped it between a platter of grilled asparagus topped with a chunky, roasted-nut sauce and a bowl of stewed mushrooms of the most enticing scent. That note contained an offer beyond his deepest ambitions, for in it, Batmis, king of Amkland, pledged not just one of his many daughters to Moulai, but an army to aid him should his current wife's home nation threaten war over their unjoining. This time, he would not need to rely solely upon Eskalind for aid, though he would still petition for the Strange Kingdom's assistance, as was his right. The Powers themselves charged Dalich King's land with protection of its borderlands.

Moulai pondered as he bit an asparagus tip. Many of his people found his Swedfian wife mannish in her ways; he doubted they would show much concern over the change of queenship. Especially for a dainty Amklander princess. Even more importantly, Eskalind's King's Son was a one-man army unto himself, so little Kaymiflander blood would be spilt in the process. Would that The Powers granted to Kaymif royal warriors of like breed to the Eskalinder in the next generation, for Moulai's designated heir, his sole nephew, Elai, was more inclined to scholarly pursuits of debates and diplomacy. The young man's Eskalinder father was to blame for that.

A parcel of miniature gold-framed portraits of the three young Amkland princesses waited in Moulai's chambers for his perusal. Amkland's king spiced his proposal with one last gem, a suggestion that if more than one of the princesses should meet the Kaymiflander's fancy, he should choose a second and even the third to serve as their sister's companions. Moulai considered that these extra women could serve as mistresses; if one got with his child, he would join her to his nephew. Most convenient.

There seemed no reason the king of Kaymif should refuse, for which he silently thanked The Powers. Next he would call guards and order his wife to pack her trunks. She likely would not obey without a physical struggle, which normally was quite enjoyable. But first he would need time to digest, and to devour more of the tasty mushrooms.

Lady Jinilya sat relishing a lengthy soak in the soothing waters of the baths at the foot of King's Halls. She could think of nothing more relaxing, when her lover was absent from her side, than a visit to the hot waters after a day on her feet in the Library. For years she had been afraid to even enter the fire-illuminated baths. Now, thanking The Powers for the severing of the woman's voice that used to emerge from the fire, she lingered long in the spacious pool, watching the soft flames glimmer on the rough-hewn stone walls, illuminating their odd textures and rendering flickering patterns that slipped from one's mind before an interpretation could shape itself.

Later, returning to her family's quarters, Jinilya nodded to the Door Guard and entered, aiming for her pillow, as night had already drawn the sun past the horizon. Upon the dark brown table in the main room, the red candles threw steady light upon the smooth wood, revealing a thick pouch and an envelope. Glad for the light to read the direction on the two objects, she found both were addressed to her from the Sixth Company, the letter from Marnil and the package from Anish. Well, it had been some time since Anish had written; perhaps he was compensating by sending a volume. She hoped it contained more pages from the tale of Seerlich King and Maayla Queen. She smiled and, deferring the pleasure of Anish's words for a few moments, tore Marnil's letter open first.

> *Eighth Day, Second Month, 2938*
> *My sister,*
> *I trust this note finds you well.*
> *I just received a letter from Kaloft. He wrote thanking us for the letters celebrating his 26th Naming Day, which reached him swiftly despite the usual slowness of the post in Teffle. He did not wait until the fourth month to open them, but after last year's letters were delayed by five months, that is understandable.*
> *Then he told the surprising tale of breaking with his lover after nearly joining with her. She claimed to be with child, but when her cycle began copiously, Kaloft was most distressed at the thought that she was losing their child. Thank The Powers she then admitted her lie or our house would have welcomed an immoral cheat as a daighter and nayce.*

"My poor nephew." Jinilya shook her head, wondering what words she might quill to soften Kaloft's troubles. Nothing came easily for him. Her green eyes scanned to the next line.

> *Kaloft says nothing of how he feels about the matter, but his tone is more somber than usual. He pours himself into his Builder studies and sends fond greetings to all our family. Teffle may be renowned for its Builders, but by The Powers, I wish he would leave the treacherous outerlands and come home. But that is his decision.*

She turned to the next page.

> *Now I can no longer restrain myself and must opine, though

*the subject is none of my business. It came as a great surprise
to learn that you quilled First Sergeant Anish to break
yourself from him.*

"What?" Jinilya gaped. Her eyes flew over the next words.

*I must respect your decision to end with your lover, but I do
wish you had told me in your last letter. I did not believe Anish
at first. It was an unpleasant and awkward interaction with
one of my most trusted people, before whom I do not wish to
appear ignorant.*

"Is this a miserable jest? I would *never* write that to Anish. Who could
have done this?" the Librarian asked the empty room, her eyes alighting in the direction of her elder brother's door. Then the flames in the
candles spoke, a cruel, confiding murmur.

You did

She gaped in disbelief and reached for the pouch from Anish. Breaking its three seals, she withdrew sheets of parchment, some entirely
covered in his exquisite quilling, others only partially, as though he
had stepped away from the task and never returned. "What is this?"
A drawing of a woman's head, her hair wrapped in a Records Keeper's head covering—styled as those of the present reign, but blue in
color. "Oh no." A thin sheet of papyrus fluttered away from the mass.
She hefted the parchment onto the table and snatched at the thin,
undated sheet. Anish had lettered upon it,

*The tale of Seerlich King and Maayla Queen, as completed as it
will ever be by my hand.*

The fire spoke.

> *You obeyed my whispers*
> *and wrote him*

"No."

> *Only now the memory returns*
> *Because I allow it*

Jinilya dropped her lover's note as the recollection grew in her mind. The voice continued.

> *Your servant posted the*
> *letter without your seal*
> *But that did not matter*
> *For he knows your hand*

She howled, smashing her palms flat into the candle. Molten red wax ejected onto the table, splashing the parchments and her purple Librarian's robe, dousing the fire and its voice together. To the main door she rushed, grabbing a firm purchase on the handle despite the wax slicking her hand. She yanked it open. The Door Guard stood to the side, next to a lit torch. He greeted her good evening, but her aim was upon the fire, and she crushed it with a bare hand. Along the corridor she raged, bringing darkness to one passage then the next. A clamor rose around her in the endarkened walkways, but she carried on. Then strong hands seized her waist and lifted her into a silvery night, the moon shimmering over wet roofs as clouds raced to veil its disk. Something cool dripped on her cheek, on her forehead, on her lips, and she blinked into the gray eyes of King's Son.

"Lady Jinilya." His kind voice was a comfort, and she realized that he held her in his arms, in King's Garden, in a light rain. She could feel the shape of his honed muscles through the wet fabric of her clothing. "Are you free of the voice now?"

She nodded. A strand of her long hair somehow stuck to her chin and tugged on her scalp as she moved. She pushed it aside and raised her hand to Namlich's chin, admiring the pleasing proportions of his face as though she had never seen him before.

"King's Son," called a stern, familiar voice. The pair turned away from each other to see Marna, King's Mother, striding toward them, her pale face oddly silver in the moonlight, drips of rain cascading along the sagging skin of her jaw. She came not from the direction of her chambers, but from Jinilya's family's quarters. The elder woman stopped beside her son's son and patted his arm, as if to direct him to release the Lady. At such close range, the echoing similarities of the two blood relations was evident in build and facial structure. Despite King's Mother's near eighty years, she was still an imposing woman of strong stature, wife and progenitor of warriors. "I thank you, my grandson. Your timing was Powerfully fortuitous."

Jinilya felt Namlich's fingers curl, claiming her flesh. "I will not say the same for yours, Grandmother."

Lady Marna lifted an eyebrow. Acquiescing to her rank, or perhaps something else, Namlich lightly tilted Jinilya forward onto her slippered feet.

"Come with me, my Librarian, I must show you something." The Scholars' Mistress laced her arm through the younger woman's and led her across the garden as casually as though the sun shone full on a clear afternoon. "We will find you a dry sleeping robe and you will stay with me tonight."

Jinilya looked back to Namlich, who watched her departure with a calm but intense nod as though he could impart peace to her through his gaze. There seemed to be a silent understanding amongst the royals. Leaning closer to King's Mother, she whispered, "How many people saw me, my Lady?"

"Shh, do not fret. I think only the Guard who chased you and a pair of our Apprentices. Ha. Those two will never give you any trouble."

"But how did you find me? And how did King's Son?" They reached a closed door that led to the Library.

Dalock's Queen turned to her. "I was summoned. Perhaps he was as well."

"Summoned?"

"Yes. Come." She opened the door and stepped over the threshold. Water pooled from their clothing as though each had brought a lake's share of liquid. "There is much to reveal to you."

The voluminous sleeping robe was cut for the older woman's larger proportions, and Jinilya draped it about her thinner frame as modestly as it allowed. Her long hair was wrapped in a towel, her cast-aside Librarian's robes puddled in a heap by the door. She seated herself upon a window seat in the former Queen's candleless room, lit merely by moonlight, which is itself the reflected light of the sun back to earth.

Her Lady Marna approached, she, too, attired in a sleeping robe with her head wrapped like a Records Keeper. Even her current task mirrored their office: she was carrying a stack of perhaps half a dozen parchment sheets. The top sheet was without quilling.

"Here." She placed the slight load into the younger Lady's hands and sat beside her. "Glance through these and tell me if you discern anything."

Many years had passed since her Lady had administered any type of examination to her, yet her tone carried that air of appraisal. Jinilya wondered if the sheets might contain writing visible only in moonlight, as some Legend Scrolls related. She lifted the top sheet, leaned toward the windowpanes, and shifted it at slight angles in the light. No words became apparent. The second sheet, too, was blank and yielded the same result. Her judge's attention wandered. Jinilya moved to the third spotless sheet. Nothing happened. As she peeled the fourth sheet without quilling away from the fifth, her Lady's shoulders lifted and her gray eyes cut to watch.

Jinilya inhaled, pinching the fourth parchment between her fingers, turning it to the moonlight. She did not see, but rather felt, words on top of words, in both the endearingly sloppy quilling of her Lady and another, elegant, vine-like hand with an authority and Will in its messages that left her without breath. She dropped the sheet, her lips quivering. A warm hand touched hers.

"What did you see?"

The Librarian felt blind, bound to the mortal world only by the weight of her Lady's hand. Jinilya saw not what was before her, not the light of the moon, nor the room, not her Lady or the parchments. She saw, nay, lived quilled conversations between the Scholars' Mistress and a benevolent Power, one who strove to right the wrongs of the voice who hid in the candles. For it was another Power in the flames, identified as Fire. Why she chose to vex King's Son and Jinilya, no explanation followed. Air and Water too were names of Powers, and there was a fourth whose name began with *E.*

The benevolent Power, whom Lady Marna addressed as the Green Lady, had directed the Scholars' Mistress to find Jinilya that night. Even as the candles began whispering in the House of Jinil's family quarters, Dalock's Queen, at the bidding of the Green Lady, rose from her desk to seek the Flame Quencher.

Flame Quencher. That is what she called Jinilya.

Even more incredibly, this kind Power identified Jinilya as Namlich's future Queen, meant to temper his damage by Fire's voice. The young Lady's vision cleared, and fresh writing appeared upon the parchment, directing her to close her eyes. Then the Green Lady shared her mind with the Eskalind Scholar, revealing solely to her visions the Librarian could not explain or interpret. The Powers' protection held Eskalind apart, and oh, The Powers' laws were staggering and strange, but their existence had lifted this world away from rougher violence, from hor- rific, unimaginable destruction. Baavnif's retelling of the brutal Battle of Delant had revealed merely a mote of the unspeakable cruelties humans could visit upon one another; far worse weapon-wrought deeds could happen, for they had happened, in the long ago past.

"My Lady?" Jinilya breathed the words like a frightened child, squeezing the kind hand. When she blinked her eyes open, her Lady's face came into view, replacing the cinders, the fear, the screams dampening into silence.

"Yes, dear, I am here." The Scholars' Mistress moved closer. "Did you see something?"

"I did."

"Tell me, what did you see?"

"Things. Terrible things. Flame that disintegrates huge villages. Weapons . . ."

"A way to defend against these weapons?"

She looked away. "No."

"Shh, shh, shh. Try not to think on it now." Dalock's Queen patted her hand. "I will ask my son to heal you of these thoughts, if you wish."

Saralya's daughter was quiet a moment. "No, I must keep this in myself. I need to understand what I have seen." She withdrew her hand and hugged her arms tight over the sable-shaded sleeping robe draping her torso as though the room had chilled. An odd quiet came over her thoughts, calming her. Jinilya gestured to the sheet. "She sent you for me tonight."

"Ah yes." King's Mother adjusted the belt of her sleeping robe. "After years of no communication from Her, this night She told me of your immediate trial."

"But, why?"

"To save you." A cord of the elderly Lady's neck tightened. "How grateful I am that Namlich was able to stop you. I shouted, over and over, but you could not hear me."

Mortified, Jinilya bowed her head, causing the cloth holding her hair to slide forward. She tipped it aside, her hair flopping like a rag atop her shoulder. She turned to stare skyward to the moon. "When I returned to my quarters tonight, I found a letter from Marnil inquiring why I had broken with Anish." It seemed an eternity ago.

"I did not know you had done that."

Jinilya looked to her Mistress. "Neither did I." She lowered her voice and whispered the story.

"How distressing!"

"If I explain to Anish what happened, he will never believe me. Only King's Son understands the voice." Her voice trailed as though she were far away. "When King's Son held me tonight, I forgot everything that had happened. As though he were all my world." She wanted to cry but her eyes were dry. She wondered why a Power would torment her so.

The former Queen was quiet. After a moment she said, "Much has happened this night. Rest now."

"But my Lady, she wrote that I was meant to be with him? With King's Son?"

"Well, you did open the Cabinet of Trelich King." A slyness crept into King's Mother's voice at that utterance. Then she softened. "My dear, if you are, then it will be so, but let me say this to you now," and her voice changed from companionly to commanding. "News from Kaymif foretells battle coming. Namlich will be called upon to fight. He must not get any woman with child before that, you understand?" The Scholars' Mistress lightened her tone. "But if, when he returns, you become lovers and join with Namlich, I would rejoice." The elder Lady's smile was a welcome sight amidst all the turmoil and fears welling in Jinilya's chest, but still the horrible visions lingered, like a gauzy, shadowed curtain blinkering her vision.

"My Lady, I am sorry, but I am afraid. What I have seen—"

The smile fell and the gray eyes narrowed. "Then use that fear to work for the Scholars. To preserve and protect the orders established by The Powers long ago. That is our course."

The Flame Quencher said nothing, but her thoughts conjured the idea that yes, preventing the worst was a plan of action, though no idea on how to accomplish it could penetrate the fearsome haze.

Chapter Sixty-Six—King's Son Is Required

20th Day, 2nd Month, 2938

"Again to Kaymif?" Namlich brooded, his gray eyes shifting between his father and Lord Saril. The three sat clustered at the end of the long table in his father's chamber.

"Yes, to King Moulai's aid. Though I want both of you," and the King's eyes darted between his son and his Second, "to assess, once you are there, if perhaps it might be better for all concerned to find a new ruler upon the Kaymif throne. Prince Elai is the designated heir?"

"And half Eskalinder," Saril added. "His father is our former Ambassador Moril, since retired."

"I earned my sword nearly a decade ago. I don't need a Minder," Namlich scolded. The elder men gazed at him, his father with a look of surprise and Lady Jinilya's brother with caution. "Father, let me go alone. Without Lord Saril. I want to command the army, to make decisions on my own."

"Of course you do, and you will, as my representative." Dalich King smiled. "But you may need to fight, if it comes to that. Then you will need a man as trusted and rich in experience as Saril to monitor the field while you lead our Captains in combat." His father folded his long fingers together. "And to advise you and offer insight into the matter of whether King Moulai continues to deserve Eskalind's assistance."

Cutting his eyes to his Second, he said, "To The Powers, I do not wish to aid that serial unjoiner Moulai, but I am even less keen on exposing the Kaymif people to another onslaught by an invading army."

Namlich spread his fingers across the violet tablecloth, his fingers snagging a moment in the black metal embroidery as he ruminated upon a host of thoughts. "Our Soldiers should not fight and suffer for such a king."

"That," intoned his Lord, "is why you must lead the charge, if there is battle. You and Captains Marnil and Narnik. Let it never be said that Eskalind's officers lead from the back." He lowered his gray eyes, with a slight dip of his graying locks, then unexpectedly reached to clutch his son's hands. "Namlich, I would go, if The Powers would only allow me to cross our border. Do not make this more difficult for me." He gazed at his son with such an expression of sorrow, Namlich found it difficult to meet his eyes. For years he had wondered why The Powers had cursed his father so, wondered why They would restrict a royal of Their own lineage. Just as he wondered why the voice in the fire taunted him in secret. Best not to mention that to anyone here. Only Lady Jinilya knew. Besides, the voice had been silent to his ears, for years now, ever since its last taunt just after he earned his sword. Perhaps something had changed, and Father could indeed cross the border now.

The King was talking. "Understand, Namlich, it is the bane of my life that I must remain forever trapped inside our borderwall, never to defend again. You," and he lifted and squeezed the young man's fingers, "you are my sole son, graced by The Powers with invincibility until your son comes." There was both a sigh and a conviction in his words. "You alone are Eskalind's best hope and its future. You, Namlich, must go and do this in my stead." The elder royal released his son's hands, as though they were a great weight.

His throat constricting with emotion, King's Son rose to embrace his Lord. "Do not doubt that I will, Father." The royal pair shared a long moment in this state, Dalich rubbing his child's back as though he were still a small boy and not taller and a bit broader than his parent in size. Then the King released him and sat wearily. "I see my father in you, Namlich. He too was a great warrior."

Lord Saril nodded, with an unusual gentleness in his gaze that recalled his sister's sweet face. Then Namlich made his leave to prepare for the journey. The next two days would be busy.

———

On the twenty-second day of the second month of 2938, all of King's Halls arrayed to farewell King's Son and King's Second as they journeyed to meet the Sixth Company at the Kaymif border. Captain Narnik and half of his Tenth Company, currently stationed at King's Halls, would accompany them, the officers atop their black horses, their manes knit with ribbons and beads of violet hue. A line of young women watched, chins dipped to their chests, for King's Son would soon depart, and they had missed their chance to show him their feet for The Powers knew how long. Not that any captured his interest.

Whilst the last couple days had seen a flurry of activity for most, the Flame Quencher had slept and napped, resting in sequestration in King's Mother's quarters, her sole companions warming blankets and a variety of comforting teas. Still she struggled with the terror of the terrible visions the Green Lady had revealed to her, yet her feet led her to the awaying ceremony for King's Son and his company. She hoped no one saw anything amiss in her demeanor. But the collective group concentrated outwardly upon the departing parties, and, as is normal in human circumstances, inwardly upon each's own small problems.

Thus, Namlich hugged his grandmother, his cousin Scriptor Palika, his aunt Yamina, her two daughters, all the women with eyes wet and handkerchiefs at the ready, but none as sad-faced as his mother the Queen. Behind the royals' embrace, Lady Jinilya farewelled her brother as he stood by his steed. Dalich King approached, gray eyes glinting in the sunshine as he reached a hand to his friend's shoulder. "We shall meet again, Saril, soon."

An uncommon tenderness inhabited her brother's voice. "It is my fondest wish, my Lord." The Acta Sua of her house bowed.

The King smiled, turning to his son, who had come to his side. Dalich clasped hands with his sole child. "Defend Eskalind, King's Son," he said quietly. "May The Powers keep you."

"And you, Father." Namlich dipped his head, his lustrous blond locks cascading over the dark brocaded fabric of his riding cloak. A groom led the Heir of Eskalind's horse to the pair; a Page bearing King's Son's scabbarded sword came and stood near.

Behind Jinilya, Saril climbed into his saddle, a grim smile upon her. "Beloved sister," he murmured, and she nodded, speech having left her at this unexpected endearment. Then her brother's sharp eyes cut behind her. Following his direction, she turned to face King's Son standing before her, gazing calmly at her. He raised a black-gloved hand. In his grasp, a single King's Flower, white petals sharply outlined in contrast to the dark leather. Jinilya accepted the token gingerly, for the red-vined plant was notorious for its sharp thorns. But this flower held no such perils, and she bowed her head low to her Lord in thanks and confusion as to the intention of the gesture, for still her thoughts were clouded and leaden.

"No," Namlich murmured as she tilted her head down, his voice soft. "Let me see your face." The Librarian raised her eyes to him, and he gazed upon her wordlessly, then turned and leapt onto his horse.

The days after King's Son's departure, King's Halls felt dampened of joy and activity. Despite the arrival of a new company of traveling players, a heavy mood troubled the royals as they awaited word from King's Son and Saril. The journey to Kaymif would consume three weeks to reach the front; word from inside the borderland would not arrive as quickly as was customary in Eskalind. Like most other nations, Kaymiflanders had no messenger system with the speed of the Swift Riders.

The first week after his heir's departure saw a heavy schedule for the Lord of Eskalind, as he continued to send supplies and Eskalind Swift Riders into Kaymif to bolster his companies. This coordination, and the necessary orders given, was accomplished by the second week. With nothing else to be done, Dalich King fought the clawings of melancholy and uselessness on a long solo ride far from his Halls. How he wished his wife could accompany him, but the royal Lady's schedule exhibited less flexibility.

———

In her chamber atop the Royals' Tower, Damina made ready for her late afternoon appointments, pale hands resting on her dressing table where she sat. Her newest attendant, Lady Navla, pinned her hair with a thin strand of pearly amethyst beads. She had shaped the Queen's black locks into a scalloped pattern that would impress even Lady Dara. This noblewoman had a Gift for hair styling, twisting tresses effortlessly into beautiful designs. Damina thanked The Powers for the distraction, and was eager to show her husband how pretty it looked. Perhaps it would cheer him.

Yamina presented her sister with a black velvet tray laden with glimmering necklaces of amethyst and onyx for her selection. A soft pattering flush of footsteps racing up the stairs floated to Damina's ears. At any moment she expected to see a beet-faced Page panting in the doorway. Instead, Saril's sister came into the room, her brown face flush with perspiration.

"My Lady, I come with news from King's Mother." She placed a hand to her chest, which swelled and contracted from her rapid breathing.

"Oh, those stairs." Damina gestured to Navla to bring a chair. "Come in and sit, Jinilya, catch your breath." Navla brought a seat forward as Yamina laid the jewelry tray atop a table and rose, leading the part-Guerish noble to sit by the Queen.

"I thank you all." Her green eyes alighted on Damina. "Lady Marna has word from the northwest border of Eskalind, from Lord Radil"— the Queen nodded; she knew the name—"that an army of Eyfians is sweeping across Amkland. They intend for Eskalind."

Yamina gaped. Navla dropped her hairpin cushion.

Dalich's Queen asked, "How comes Lord Radil by this news?"

"First as witnessed by former Ambassador Favik." Now that was a name she had not heard in years. Thank The Powers he was alive, and presumably healthy.

Jinilya was still speaking. "And after that report, a second from a swift horsewoman of the Lord's household. Radil sent her to scout across the border; she saw villages emptying and homesteaders trudging toward Eskalind before the advancing Eyfians."

Damina conveyed this knowledge to her husband in their silent mind talk as Saril's sister divulged more. "Lord Radil also sent word to the Ninth Company, as they are the army unit closest to his estate, stationed between Amkland and Kursak."

"Wise," breathed Damina.

Yamina asked, "Can't the Amkland army stop the Eyfians?"

The Lady of Eskalind gripped the hair comb in her lap. "Dalich just told me that the Amkish king sent the bulk of his fighters to Kaymif to war against the Swedfians."

"Oh no," was the only reply.

Jinilya spoke in a tone worthy of her brother on advising their Lord, "My Lady, King's Mother believes that your husband should ride to the Amkland border and direct our army from the Eskalind side. She asks that you convey this to him." Jinilya bent her neck in a subtle bow.

"Yes," whispered the Queen, gazing toward her husband's chamber door. "He has already decided to do that."

———

The day after next, the ninth day of the third month, saw Dalich and a light rank of his black-clad Soldiers departing King's Halls for Lord Radil's estate, at a quick pace. Swift Riders raced ahead to prepare the way, as the Lord of Eskalind and his party traveled light. A report sent to the Ninth Company would see them camped and ready for the King when his group arrived. All along the way, the citizens of Eskalind were alerted to expect their ruler's passage and provide food or shelter to his retinue as required. Many turned out to line the main road, cheering and waving small flags in the colors of Dalich and Damina Queen and the national colors of First King.

Thus it was just a week later that, upon the main road, a woman faced the King upon his stable steed, his dusty cadre of troops trailing behind him. In her arms she held a swaddled babe, and she beckoned, anguish squeezing her voice. "My Lord Dalich King, I beseech you!"

"Let me see what she wants," Trevil King's Guard muttered.

All his life the King had known Trevil, and he mostly appreciated the man's attentive protectiveness, but Dalich saw the woman's desperate eyes and sensed a deep emotional pain within her. "Hold, Trevil. She needs healing. I will speak with her." He dismounted and handed the reins to his man.

Tears wet her plump cheeks as he approached, asking, "What is the matter, good woman?"

"Please, my Lord, this is my grandson. He was born two days ago. My daughter—" Her voice croaked into a sob. "She died." Dalich reached for her shoulder, and she leaned toward him, panicked, whispering as though conveying an unspeakable horror. "The babe is unnamed. His father is a Soldier. Soldier Haknil, with the Sixth, in Kaymif. Please, my Lord, would you name my grandson?"

The King gazed at her, hoping to will calm into her being. She sobbed again, but her brown eyes remained open as though she caught herself in an action she did not wish to do.

"Tell me your name?"

The woman clutched the babe tight. "Ayda."

"Ayda," he said in a soothing voice. "When the child's father returns, when Soldier Haknil comes back, he will name his son on that day."

It was the slightest voice that responded, "But what if he doesn't? The babe will be unnamed, never have a Naming Day, never earn his sword…" Ayda's face lost its color, becoming as gray as her hair, and Dalich feared she would swoon.

The Healer King grasped her elbows with both hands. "Steady, Ayda. Let me see your grandson." She lifted the newbabe toward the Lord of Eskalind.

"Please, my Lord, you are the King. By The Powers, you can name him, yes?"

The child's eyes were closed, the tiny mouth set in a frown. One small fist hovered in the air as if ready to ward away a blanket thief. Dalich smiled. "You are Bayril."

"Bayril?"

"Yes, he looks like a Bayril. Do you not think?"

The Eskalinder woman blinked at him, then at her grandson. "Yes. Bayril King-Named. I will quill his father and tell him. Thank The Powers he is named, my Lord, thank you."

One last matter troubled Dalich. He touched Bayril's round cheek and spoke. "Ayda, why was your sain sent to battle when his child was due?"

Her eyes not leaving the babe, she said, "Haknil wrote that they needed everyone, and Bayril came very early, my Lord. He was not due until late in the fifth month." Her lips sputtered. "I told my daughter to write you, my Lord, for your healing protection in childbed, but she…she put it off. Was always too busy." She hugged her swaddled grandson. "I should have done it for her. Why did I not do it?" The wee babe peeped a whimper of displeasure as though he concurred. "Nothing can be done. Nothing."

"That is not true. I will send a Healer and a helper to attend to you both, and I will keep you, Bayril, and his father in my thoughts." In his mind he called to his wife, grateful to have a distracting tale to relay. *"My heart, I just named a babe."*

"Named a babe?"

Dalich smiled to himself, relishing conveying the story to Damina on the weary road to war.

The battle in Kaymif commenced not a full day after Namlich, Saril, and Captains Marnil and Narnik established their war camp alongside the Amklanders and Kaymiflanders.

Eskalind, as Ever Ally to both Kaymif and Amkland, gave final orders for the borderlanders to line the front with their forces, with Eskalinders behind. Neither Namlich nor Saril wanted to risk their people's lives in the initial attacks. Only King's Son marched with the borderlanders.

The Swedfians were swift and brutal, Eskalinder reinforcements were needed but in the end Namlich and his grim sword ruled the field. Few Eskalinders perished, but a few was more than too many in King's Son's mind.

As the sun set, Namlich gazed across the verdant hills, dotted with haphazard small dark mounds as though some diminutive tunneling creature had worked its way under the earth in an arbitrary, careless mapping of its terrain. Smoke rising from the burning burial mounds of the enemies' bodies smudged the horizon. No voice arose from the fire, but rather from Lord Saril standing by his side.

"Amazingly, I believe we are very near the battlefield where your father earned his sword." King's Second glanced at his boot, flicking mud away. "Though it was slightly drier that day."

Namlich was silent, simmering in his ruminations.

"I thank you, King's Son."

He turned to Saril. "For again winning the day and sparing many Eskalinders? You said this to me last we were in Kaymif."

The Acta Sua of Lady Jinilya's house cleared his throat, "I thought to say that, but … " A grin formed with his next words. "This time I thank you for allowing me to see all of my fiftieth Naming Day."

It was King's Son's turn to smile, his heart warming. "Today? Had I known, I would have had the kitchens prepare my grandmother's roast chicken."

Saril dipped his head, eyes on Dalich King's heir. "There is still time, my Lord." He pantomimed making a toast. "And raised glasses, brimming with wine, would be welcome."

"We will toast your Naming, and that we never set foot to fight in King Moulai's Kaymif again."

"Very much agreed, my Lord. We must consider our next course of action here."

"My Lords," a male voice called. They turned to see an Eskalind Soldier threading his way toward them, something held aloft in his hand. "Make way," he called. Reaching the commanders, he bowed, standing between them to present a purple envelope sealed with the King's signet in ebony-shaded wax. "A Swift Rider, she just brought this, my Lords."

———

Namlich's eyes cut to Saril, who stepped back half a pace with a nod to King's Son. Namlich grasped the letter and tore it open, turning aside. As he read, Saril said, "I thank you, Soldier …?"

"Haknil, Soldier Haknil. Of the Sixth Company. Under Captain Marnil's command."

"Very good." He dismissed the man and turned to his friend 's son, who gazed no longer at the letter but straight ahead.

Stepping closer to the younger man, Saril opened his mouth, but Namlich spoke first. "Eyfian invaders are sweeping through the southern parts of Amkland, which are offering little resistance."

"Because most of the Amkland fighters are here." Oh that Eyfian king was clever.

Namlich continued. "Batmis, king of Amkland, sent those who remain to defend his seat, in central Amkland." Those keen gray eyes were upon him. "Father says the Eyfians make for Eskalind."

Saril felt as though he were dipped in an icy lake. "When was this letter written?"

"The seventh day of this month." By The Powers, that was a full week ago. "Father intends to make a war camp at the Eskalind-Amkland borderwall, at the westernmost part of the estate of Lord"—he glanced at the letter—"Lord Radil."

"Then we must gather our sturdiest uninjured Soldiers to pack and rest. We will make for our border before dawn."

King's Son nodded.

How Saril pitied Dalich, standing at the borderwall, expected to lead his army but unable to cross without risking The Powers-knew-what fate.

———

Eight times the sun rose and set as the uninjured warriors of the Sixth Company, led by their Captain Marnil, King's Son, and King's Second Lord Saril, broke as many as forty miles a day in a mad rush toward Dalich King's war camp. They rubbed the crust from their eyes before first light and rested the horses well at midday while putting food into their faces. During the early part of their journey, they fed at Kaymif farmhouses, later at temporary kitchen stations established along their route by Dalich King's orders.

King's Second felt as though his rump had knitted to his saddle, his bones clattering in a bag of skin. He and his party slept in bed-rolls wherever exhaustion found them, in the last days resting their heads mere feet from the Eskalind borderwall as they approached the northwestern corner of their land.

Just before noon on the twenty-third day of the third month, Dalich

King's war camp greeted their weary eyes. At a slight crest in the terrain rested the expansive purple-striped pavilion of their Lord, topped with pennants in his colors and the red and white of Eskalind's First King. A banner for the Ninth Company flew nearby, staked to the north of the pavilion. Orderly rows of black tents paralleled the rocky borderwall, with a gulf of foot-trammeled green grass between. Eskalind Soldiers marched through that divide in columns, attired in full battle gear. Standers ran forward to greet the new arrivals, shouting in a clamor of anticipation like a pack of hounds contesting a prize.

A mounted officer rode forward, his uniform of sable-colored cloak and breeches and purple tunic announcing his rank before he identified himself: "First Sergeant Lord Amril, son of Lord Radil, who is Acta Sua of the estate upon which this war camp resides." Amril called a Stander to alert the King. "Thank The Powers for your arrival, my Lords! We plan to march into Amkland within the hour. The Eyfians approach."

Behind Saril, his brother groaned. King's Second glanced to King's Son, then behind him to their dirty, tired Soldiers. Only First Sergeant Anish sat his mount straight-backed, as though only beginning a journey. Ah, to be fifteen years younger again. Saril's horse sidestepped and he steadied the failing beast with a gentle tug on the reins. "How close are the Eyfians?"

Amril's blue eyes darted to the west. "Some miles. Our scouts saw several on horseback, heading this way." He gazed back to Eskalind. "Many Amklander refugees are sheltering here on my estate. My father and the King agreed they should be brought a few miles away from the borderwall, in case—"

"They need not fear. King Rothbur's men will not cross our border," purred King's Son. "I will see to it." He prodded his horse past Amril and trotted past the marching armyfolk.

Saril spoke. "First Sergeant Amril, our group comes direct from battle and a hard eight days ride. See them to the kitchen tents so they might eat and rest a moment while I confer with Captain Marnil and our Lords."

"Yes sir. With me," Amril ordered. The Sixth Company followed the blond Eskalinder.

"Anish," called the Acta Sua of the House of Jinil, "accompany me and my brother." The former Havadran shadowed the older men's horses as they plodded up a short rise. Soon the trio found the leader of Eskalind standing before his tent, flanked by his son and two bright-burning braziers. He was arrayed in a stunning battlefield ensemble: a long tunic of sable-shaded pleated brocade, with his scabbarded sword hilt, studded with purple jewels, glimmering like a weapon out of Legend. Dalich looked every inch the hale, tried warrior, with the confident gaze of a victor—ready to direct his Soldiers to glory and deeds of great doing. Saril found himself wanting to gape at his oldest companion like an outerlander peasant of the lowest station.

By Dalich's side, King's Son grinned at their approach. Trevil King's Guard stood at attention by his Lords. He held a spear in one hand and a shield in the other, a slight menace in his green gaze. It was the same expression he had worn when he guarded King Dalock's door, when Dalich was a child and the young brothers Saril and Marnil sought ways to sneak him away from his chambers.

They halted their mounts before the King, who called, "How I wish I could offer you rest, my friends. But another trial awaits."

"Seeing you again is no trial, my Lord," Saril jested as he dismounted, his heart lifting. With a fond laugh, Dalock's son embraced him, and then Marnil as well. A Stander came forward to claim the brothers' horses, whilst Anish held the reins of his own mount and bowed to their Lord.

"To the wall," King's Son ordered, pointing a black-gloved hand.

"A moment," Dalich commanded, looking to Marnil, who met his gray gaze with an alertness and attention that recalled the brothers' father Jinil. "My Captain, I realize your people are exhausted, but we have no choice but to press ahead. Eyfia is close at hand." The King glared hard into Amkland as though its spacious fields offended his person. "Our scouts fully expect the brunt of the attack to come from the north. Thus I instructed Captain Tarnil of the Ninth Company to lead the bulk of his fighters from their position just north of here into Amkland. They await the horn's signal." He appraised his man with a look of sharp intelligence. "Marnil, you and Namlich will lead half your Soldiers of the Sixth and five full ranks of the Ninth, from here."

"Yes sir." The Captain nodded, calling to Anish, "Pick our freshest fighters. Order them to return here and prepare for battle. Hold the others as reinforcements." His sister's former lover dashed to do his bidding.

"May The Powers preserve us all." The King turned and placed a firm hand on Saril's shoulder, as if to stay his friend. "Saril, you and I will stay on this side of the wall, to observe and send reinforcements as necessary." He turned to his son. "Namlich, this is your command. Ready the army and go forth. I await your return."

King's Son's smile was as bright as the sun upon an unsheathed sword. He made no utterance, but waved a hand to Marnil. The pair departed as the ruler of Eskalind murmured to Saril, "And now, we watch." His voice carried the sentiment of regret, at odds with the commandfull utterances of a moment ago.

Dalich lowered his hand to Saril's elbow, who leaned close. "My Lord, The Powers protect King's Son. It is truly a sight to see, even from this side of the borderwall." His King glanced at the braziers' flame. For a moment Saril thought he heard a soft whisper, and he made to mention it, but Dalich raised watering eyes to the sky, and his Second considered it best to allow him a quiet moment.

A velvety white cloud lazily floated by, drifting in serene blue in calm counterpoint to the earthbound marching Soldiers, the roving Standers, the Pages leading horses to commanders and Sergeants yelping orders. The two men stood silent, watching King's Son ride to the front of the line of Soldiers arrayed several paces back from the crumbling dark rocks of the borderwall. The Soldiers stood side by side, some with spears, others with sword and shield, all kitted with long knives scabbarded on their dark leather belts. Their faces represented the panoply of Eskalind's population, most with deep brown hair, a few blond or gray, some dark-skinned, others browned by the sun, women and men, all forming a human wall far more formidable than the short-stacked, porous stones that marked Eskalind's border. They stamped their feet in answer to Namlich's rallying cries and marched over the rocks. Those with an unencumbered hand showed a palm to the earth, a gesture of respect to The Powers. Those unable to exhibit the sign bowed their heads as they clambered over the wall and murmured thanks. Thus the army of Eskalind, charged by The Powers with protection of the border nations, marched into Amkland to hammer their might upon King Rothbur's army.

A Page brought the King and his Second a pair of violet-glazed teacups. Another Page followed, her hands clutching a tray topped with a tea canister and a short pot suspended over a small, licking flame. Saril contemplated how serene and civilized the ceramicware seemed against the backdrop of dust and deepening clamor. It felt odd to stand with his feet upon firm earth, watching motion in the distance, freed of the rocking and jumbling of horse riding. He imbibed the beverage in one thirsty gulp.

"Have mine, Saril," his friend offered. "You need to maintain your strength." Here his Lord grinned, but his eyes kept their attention upon the front. Saril downed the second cup and passed both to the Page. A horn blast rose, and hearty shouts broiled in a rumble to the north. Dimly in the distance, the Soldiers of the Ninth Company could be seen striding forth, departing Eskalind. A single-file line of troops remained on the Strange Kingdom's side of the wall.

An advance of Eyfian foot soldiers rose from a low point in Amkland and engaged them. "They were closer than we thought," breathed the King. Even as he spoke, Namlich galloped from the Sixth Company's forces toward the invaders, sword brandished, bellowing.

"But your son saw them."

Dalich did not move; only his eyes roamed to the brazier by his side as though it had issued a command. After a time he said, "Let us go stand closer by the wall."

He paced away, his Pages and Guard in his wake. Saril paused, a bit surprised by this sudden decision. He followed, calling, "But my Lord, the rise affords a fuller view."

The King countered, "Send for a pair of horses for us to observe upon. Meet me at the wall." Dalich was already a quarter of the way down the rise, one hand on his sword's pommel and the other drawing his long tunic to his side as if to sweep away an unseen opponent. The two Pages scampered behind him, bearing the cups and tray. Trevil King's Guard ran ahead, armed with his shield and spear, with focused and fluid movements that belied his years.

King's Second grimaced and strode back to the pavilion, the muscles in his legs stiff and aching from the effort, ungrateful for this unexpected call to duty. Once there, Saril ordered a red-haired Page to fetch horses, then directed a lean Stander to wait by the pavilion's entrance in readiness to relay any messages delivered to King's pavilion to the King. Before he turned to face Amkland, a Healer stayed him, asking if he required any salves or potions.

"I saw your face when you came up the hill, my Lord. It was the look of a man in pain." Her steady brown eyes appraised him like an Ambassador Tutor judging an assessment.

Laughing lightly, Saril replied, "I go directly to meet the King and will seek healing from him if I am in need. I thank you for your concern." A curt nod of his chin dismissed her, and she made her way elsewhere, a Healer once again unneeded due to the presence and protection of Dalich King.

Saril's dark eyes cut toward the borderwall. On the Eskalind side, the Pages flanked their Lord like tiny sentinels. Opposite the wall stood Trevil, spear and shield in hands, neck panning as he scanned the Amkish terrain. A gray, weathered structure, perhaps once a barn, now collapsing into the earth, lay perhaps a hundred yards from the King's Guard's position. From Saril's vantage tromping down the rise, he detected movement by the structure. He opened his mouth to shout as a couple of wild-haired Eyfians on horseback cut from behind the wrecked barn, charging toward Trevil with swords drawn. Each bore a vertical red stripe from forehead to chin.

The King shouted to the Pages to flee. They ran toward Saril, the girl's teapot clattering on its tray as though embodying their terror. Dalich called to Trevil whilst pulling forth his shimmering steel. He heaved a foot over the wall.

Saril's chest tightened. "No. Stop!" King's Second yelled, and he ran, flailing his arms in the air like a crazed bird beating its wings. The riders were nearly upon Trevil, who had stationed himself behind a pair of knee-height rocks, shield held high and shrieking savagely at the horses. The Lord of Eskalind hoisted his sword aloft with one hand and held his other palm flat to the borderwall as he departed Eskalind.

For a moment the sun felt hotter and the air heavy-still, as though some immense thing found sudden, silent interest in these events. Saril scrambled to the borderwall, heart straining, eyes intent on the charging royal. Then he was across. Trevil had dislodged one of the Eyfians from his horse, which limped away as the King's Guard skewered the prone man with his spear. The other Eyfian wheeled her mount toward Trevil, blade brandished, her back to the King, who raced to assist his man.

Trevil hefted the spear from the male Eyfian's ribs and arched his arm back, casting the weapon toward the one ahorse. She ducked, and it missed as she pulled the reins to angle the horse along Trevil's side. He tried to block her with his shield, but did not raise it in time. As she passed, her sword sliced at his neck and face. Trevil fell. The Eyfian's mount galloped away, and she turned to look back, just as her horse tripped on rock. She pitched forward and tumbled aside, foot caught in a stirrup. The horse dragged her at breakneck pace over the rocks, toward a group of her countrymen skirmishing with Soldiers of the Sixth.

The King was nearly to his Guard, with Saril close behind. Then

Dalich dropped to his rear as though the earth had yanked itself from under his feet. His sword left his grasp.

"My Lord!" Saril called, at last at his friend's side, kneeling.

Dalich King's eyes darted about as though tracking an enraged wasp zigzagging through the air. "She is gone." The King appeared not to see Saril, his gray gaze far away as he sat upon the dirt.

"Yes, the Eyfian woman is gone. I think Trevil—"

"My heart—" Dalich grasped his chest with a stiffened hand.

"Here, lie down," Saril commanded, lowering his King flat to the ground in a smooth motion.

"Saril…"

King's Second brought his face close to his beloved Lord, one arm bolstering the prone ruler. "Shh. Can I convince you to heal yourself?"

The King did not respond to the jest, but his gaze grew in focus upon his friend. He murmured, "She came into my mind, and called my name." He made a choking sound. "Then she disappeared. She is gone. My heart, Damina…" A horrible rattling sounded in his throat.

"My Lord? Dalich?" Saril shook his friend, who stared emptily ahead. He clutched the King's shoulders, tight enough to feel their bones against one another. "No. No, you cannot. I cannot live without you." Saril pressed his forehead against Dalich's and howled to The Powers.

———

Marnil scanned the front as a light rank of Eskalind Soldiers, together with Anish and Namlich, hacked at a thin stream of Eyfian warriors rushing toward them. The enemy's woolly shoulder coverings, above their twisted, scowling faces, gave them the aspect of a blend of human and beast. He turned to survey the land behind him and gaped, spying bodies. An Eyfian, a King's Guard, and his King—grasping his chest as Saril sat on his knees beside him.

"Fall back to the King!" the Captain shouted, whirling his sword overhead. In the near distance, he watched Anish swipe the Eyfian closest with his blood-drenched blade, sending the man to his knees. Anish circled tight, giving a final thrust, and gravity did its work, pulling the man to the dirt. The First Sergeant then repeated the order to his Soldiers and called to King's Son, who heeded him not but charged ahead on foot, attacking. Some of the Eskalinders followed the First Sergeant.

Captain Marnil rushed toward his brother just as Saril leaned to the dirt as though it summoned him.

Reaching his elders, Marnil knelt by the fallen pair, calling to them, squeezing their arms. No response. He looked for punctures, rips in their clothing. Not a wound gaped; no hint of blood showed on their persons. The Captain stared disbelieving at their vacant gazes, Dalich's gray eyes acknowledging nothing but the sky's reflection, Saril lying by his friend's side, frozen gaze locked on his Lord. "By The … Powers."

His warriors approached, panting, Anish again calling over his shoulder to King's Son, shouting to hurry. Marnil reached for his brother's hand. It felt unnaturally still. Raising his eyes, he watched the new King of Eskalind dispatch more of Rothbur's soldiers to The Powers. His eyes cut to the fallen King's Guard, realizing it was Trevil, ayncle to Namlich. He too was dead. Marnil felt encircled by death, as though it were a rope coiling tighter and tighter. He pulled away.

Finally Namlich jogged toward him, two more Eskalinders by his side. Marnil stood and found himself speaking. "My Lord, The Powers have claimed them."

The King's gray eyes burned, surveying the sad scene. "What? Who, who did this?"

The Captain shook his head. "The Eyfian, there?" Two of the Soldiers prodded the limp man as another bent to the King's Guard. "I do not understand. I thought Dalich and Saril had remained behind in Eskalind, and then I saw them here."

Namlich shut his eyes, the muscles in his neck trembling. "Why did Father cross the border!?" the new Lord of Eskalind roared, eyes ablaze, his long sword rising to point at his Captain's chest.

Marnil held his hands aloft, pleading, "My Lord, I know not. All I saw was the King, hands to his heart, and Saril by his side, steadying him…then they fell together." Behind Namlich, First Sergeant Anish locked his gaze on his Captain. Marnil shook his head. "Please, my Lord, I would have defended them both with my life—"

"Then do so now." Namlich King lowered his blade.

The Captain looked to the bodies, whispering, "This must be, it has to be, some strange work of The Powers."

Namlich craned his head as though hard of hearing, or perhaps he attended to faraway shouting. "I will put out their lights," he murmured. "All their lights. To me!" he ordered the Soldiers. They charged away, thundering down the hill. Only Anish remained by his commander.

"Go, protect King's Son," Marnil choked.

The blond man sputtered. "My Captain, I cannot leave you here, alone, undefended."

"It is an order, not a point for discussion. Go!" An Eyfian armed with a stout shield was charging in their direction. He butted the leftmost of the Eskalind Soldiers trailing Namlich to the ground and ran toward the two officers, sword aloft, his eyes gashes of blue against the blood coating his face.

Anish flew at him, screaming, "Come back! King's Son! King's Son!" over and over as though it were a battle cry. The First Sergeant hacked and sliced at the Eyfian as more came toward him, a pair of Eskalind Soldiers chasing them. Farther down the hill, Namlich was a blur of glinting sword and blade, mowing through another cadre of enemy fighters, howling as though he could give voice to all the air on the earth. Anish calls meant nothing to him, as though he could no longer hear his former title and would not answer to it.

"I was supposed to ask New King to choose his colors," Marnil murmured in a daze, the action seeming to shrink away. "That is what the Legends tell—" A sound behind him snapped his attention to the moment. A trio of Eyfian horsemen charged along Amkland's side of the borderwall, the first two turning their mounts toward him, the third falling from his horse, a spear planted in his back. The lead man wore a pelt of purest white about his shoulders and brandished a sword detailed with gold.

"King Rothbur." The Acta Sua of the House of Jinil raised his sword.

———

Lady Athla gazed into the compelling green eyes of the founder of her house. Had she never seen Jinil's daughter in the flesh, she would have thought the portraitist a bit imaginative in the mixing of the paints. But when she walked down the line of family members, Jinilya's portrait exhibited the same hue, perhaps confirming for future generations that luminous green eyes ran in the family, perhaps to return again. With a glance at the most recent portrait, that of her son, Marnil's wife recalled that when she carried Kaloft, she had hoped that he might inherit the color. But it pleased her that he looked alike to his dear father.

She stood between her husband's image and her own. Athla hoped to see Marnil soon, though the war in Kaymif intervened, he with his army duties and she tending to their estate. Thank The Powers the war was in the northern part of Kaymif, as their estate bordered its southern flank. Far fewer people had sought refuge in Eskalind than expected, but it was best to be home and prepared to help any refugees who might cross into the safety of the Strange Kingdom.

She breathed out, loud and long, the sound echoing in the tall hallway and the breath ruffling a bit of dust that had settled on Marnil's portrait. "A feather duster is called for," she murmured as a door opened behind her. The Lady turned.

"My Lady?" panted the servant, burly arms hoisting a large wooden chair. "Where did you wish this to go?"

"Oh Sunil, just put it down there for now. It is quite heavy." He complied, then leaned limply over the carved chair back, breathing as labored as though he had carried the hefty object up the full flight of stairs to the Royals' Tower at King's Halls. "I will find someone to help you," Athla stated, noting the perspiration wetting his tunic.

"Carrying that chair is a two-person task."

As if his whole body wanted to show wholehearted agreement, the man slumped to the floor. "Sunil?" She lifted her hazel-colored skirt and dashed to his side where he lay collapsed in a curled heap by the chair. "Help! Help!" Athla shouted, her voice a clamor in the long room. "Someone come!"

Sunil's chest heaved, and he gulped air like a forlorn fish tossed by a fisherman onto streamside grass. A pair of maids entered, the clatter of their footsteps upon the stone floor adding to the cacophony. Athla directed the women to help her roll the stout man to his back, but as she rose, blackness crept into her vision, tunneling to darkness, her last blink catching the steadfast gaze of Marnil's portrait.

Turning briefly from the battlefield, Anish saw his Captain fall, alone against an Eyfian on horseback, the man's shoulders swathed in a white pelt. A few feet away, a horse rolled upon the ground, wounded and screaming, its master crushed beneath it. Anish cursed, swinging his head forward, fighting on against the enemies near him, anger swelling his strength. Far ahead, Dalich's son mowed a swath through Eyfia's warriors, the zeal of bloodlust upon him, slaying and screaming. Eskalind Soldiers backed away from him, warning their comrades-in-arms out of his path. Against this onslaught, the Eyfians' press toward the borderwall ceased, some of the attackers turning to run homeward, others standing their ground and fighting where their feet were planted.

Namlich King came to claim them all.

With the threat of imminent attack abating, Anish turned and climbed the hill. The horseman who had felled his Captain galloped away, leaning hurt in the saddle, hopefully heading directly to Namlich's blade. Anish found his commander slashed, bled out, perished with sword in hand. The First Sergeant cursed again, eyes wet at the loss of his Captain, sinking to Marnil's side. "I should have disobeyed your last order," he murmured. Then he looked about, wary for another approaching enemy even as his thoughts turned to his former lover and how she would fare upon learning of the deaths of her brothers. He half desired it be she instead who lay dead upon Amkland soil. If The Powers existed, they would forgive a forsaken man his ire.

It would fall to him as the company's Secretary to write Jinilya and her family the news. "You were a good man, my Captain. The best man of our company. Fair-minded. Even-tempered. Loyal. A true Eskalinder." Perhaps that was what he would write her.

Several Eskalind Soldiers and a Sergeant trudged toward him, one man leaning on the arms of his companions, blood coating his face, drops glistening on his dark uniform. Anish stood, barking orders. "You who are uninjured, cross the borderwall. Send Healers and attendants for the wounded." To the Soldiers assisting the hurt man, he bade them lay him upon the ground, but the man refused. "Sir, if I die, I die in Eskalind. Please, not here."

"If you die here, you die mere feet from where the best of Eskalind fell." The First Sergeant glanced to the dead King and his companions, which drew the Soldiers' eyes and elicited sobs. "For now, this sad earth is part of Eskalind, for Dalich King lies here until we bring him home." He called for the deceased Lord's banner to be brought and planted nearby.

By the time this was done, their new Lord had returned, was halfway up the hill, a few of his Soldiers following behind. Anish hardened his demeanor to deliver the harsh news of Captain Marnil's demise. An old Havadran saying surfaced: "May this day end soon," he muttered. He bowed to his living Lord.

Eskalind's New King wept at the report, contrite as a man under a Records Keeper's pronouncement of a judgment he knew he full deserved. "Marnil, you should not have died. None of you." He sat by the body, "Were I a better, swifter warrior—" He put his teeth together, a flash of white against the mire coating his face and lips. "I tried." Tears chased the blood and mud in streaks down his face. He seethed,

"What to do? What to do what to do?" The King repeated the phrase as though the words would compel his course, a maniacal motto.

"Get up, my Lord," began Anish, reaching for the younger man's shoulder, wanting to shake him. "Your orders are needed."

The Lord of Eskalind leapt to his feet, gray eyes narrowed upon the First Sergeant as if ready to pounce. But the words he spoke came gently. "You are right, Anish. My orders, my colors, my symbol." He glanced to the gathered Eskalinders, injured Soldiers, a Healer rubbing salve onto the head wound of a man, Standers dragging a prone Soldier upon a litter.

Namlich King proclaimed, "I choose as my colors, blue and gold, and my symbol . . ." His words tightened into a menacing tone. "A sword, cutting a candle. A lit candle's wick." He pointed his bloody blade at the First Sergeant. "I make this man Captain of the Sixth Company. Captain Anish, confer with Captain Tarnil of the Ninth for his battle report. I want my father and his friends guarded here in this place until I return."

"Yes, my Lord." Anish bowed his head slightly, his eyes not leaving the ominous royal but daring to ask, "Where, my Lord, are you going?" He could not yet bring himself to call this man King.

"To slay Eyfians. Any left alive in this land." Namlich marched away, pausing briefly to hover his blade by the neck of an Eyfian's corpse.

The new Captain started to shake his head, but as he did so, his gaze was drawn to the slain Lords. A strange grayish mist rose from the earth around them. It lingered close about the noble fallen like a shroud. For a moment, a slight tinge of palest green colored the thin fog draping the King. Then the vapor vanished.

"Did you see that?" Anish asked the Soldier nearest him.

"See what, sir?"

"The cloud on the King, on the Captain?"

The man gazed at him as though he were a puzzlement. "No, I didn't see anything, sir." Anish dismissed him and his fellows to see if an embalmer could be found.

It was the third day after the battle in Amkland, and word of what had befallen had not yet reached King's Halls, for nothing was as it had been.

Marna turned her head to the wall. At her feet, all along the corridor, lay the bodies of the fallen—those of King's Halls who had succumbed to whatever malady The Powers rained upon them. So many dead, their faces hastily covered with whatever cloth could be found: a Healer's crimson apron, a dish towel from the kitchens, banners from the Great Hall draped across multiple bodies, even a pillow cover with its plain, denuded pillow lying listlessly between two of those who had succumbed. A downy feather fluttered as she reached and hesitantly tugged the cloth away to see who lay beneath. Scriptor Vinil. She dropped the cloth, sick in her heart at the loss of such a talented restorer.

Years ago, when Dalich left their border to earn his sword, a windstorm caused fires that consumed a section of the Library, resulting in a great loss of scrolls and a couple of deaths. But this was a great loss of her dear craftspeople, those skilled in copying, preserving, and perpetuating the knowledge of the Library. Vinil, her beloved niece Palika…She was too lost in grief to make a full account.

"My Lady?" a young female voice called. The scent of Lamorda rose in the air.

She turned to see a blue-eyed Apprentice Healer, her eyes stark above the white scarf tied over her nose and mouth. Her forehead was pale and smooth as a babe's. She was flanked by two other Apprentices whose faces were similarly covered. As they approached, their shoes stirred the strewn purple flower wands littering the path between the soles of the feet of the dead. The rosy citrus scent of Lamorda punctuated the air. The trio's white tunics and red aprons testified to long days of use without laundering. Finally, the three young women stopped before the former Queen as she slowly raised herself as tall as her back would allow. Ever since this outbreak it seemed she was in a perpetual state of bending forward. Or perhaps her spine had crooked.

"Lady Jinilya gathered you to come to me?"

"Yes. We are all that remain of those training in healing." The Apprentice continued without pause, as though one utterance led naturally to the next. "My Lady, there are more bodies. Should we have them brought here, away from the sick?"

Dalock's Queen rubbed the aching joints on her hand. "For now. As we do not know what has caused this outbreak, we must burn all the dead as soon as possible."

One of the other Apprentices exhaled sharply, but the woman in the lead gazed as steady as a Records Keeper in the midst of a judgment. "Even the Queen, my Lady?"

How her son would fare after his beloved wife's death, The Powers only knew. Then again, if he had left their border, then this was The Powers' punishment for his trespass. She hoped to the Green Lady she was wrong in her suspicions.

"Yes, even Damina." It hurt to speak the words. "Her ashes must be saved. The King will determine what to do with them."

One of the Apprentices whimpered.

"You three." She leveled her eyes at the trio. "While you are in the midst of your Apprenticeship, you are the only Healers at King's Halls besides myself, and my skills have not been needed since before any of you were born. Nevertheless, we must offer care and comfort to those who are ailing." Marna reached for the hand of the crying woman. "Go to the Library and find copies of my herb book, one for each of you and one for Lady Jinilya. She absorbs knowledge quickly; she will assist you." She tried to smile. "Consult it as you need. I will help as well."

The Apprentice croaked, "Yes, my Lady." Marna squeezed the young woman's hand and released her to her task. She dismissed another to the patients' halls, leaving only the blue-eyed leader remaining. "What is your name?"

"Saysha, my Lady."

The name sounded familiar, but in the haze of the events, no connection raised itself to her consciousness. "I value your steadiness, your calm. It is most admirable, especially in one so young." She lifted an eyebrow slightly. "How old are you?"

"Seventeen, my Lady."

"A mere babe." Marna would have shaken her head but feared the motion would cause a twinge. "Saysha, I need you to gather laborers to dig a pit for the dead. Have them cover their mouths and noses, as you do. It is very important. Tell them to wash their hands in clean water after touching the dead. We cannot risk contagion spreading. Can you oversee this?"

"Yes, my Lady." She glanced away. "May I ask why you do not cover your face?"

Here the Scholars' Mistress smiled. The vision of her hand resting on a crimson coverlet, of shadows reaching a wall, surfaced. Last she had experienced it, and gazed at her hand afterward, she had seen that the similarities had come to fruition: her end was near. Red might be one of First King's colors, but she now made it a point to avoid any cloths or blankets in that shade. But that would not keep away the inevitable. "My time here is short."

The young Apprentice seemed to shrink in the manner Eskalinders exhibited when faced with the strange behavior of their royals. Marna nodded dismissal. A hesitant curtsy, and the young woman dipped the long curls of her chestnut hair and departed.

Marna turned her gaze toward those lying near her feet. Spying a very dark-skinned hand, a body dressed in dark trousers, she inhaled, fearful it was Jinilya's brilliant Guerish Apprentice Ambassador. "No, not Mamon." She lifted the violet-shaded banner covering the head. A peaceful expression about the features of a Verangan man. Dropping the cloth, she clutched her heart and exhaled with relief. Then remorse chilled her, considering that his companions and family back home knew not of his demise. She wondered what circumstance had led him to King's Halls at this disastrous time.

Dalock's Queen spoke softly to herself. "I must tend to the sick. The living require me, not the dead." Turning toward the passageway. "But first to the kitchens to prepare King's Mother's Recipe roast chicken. We must eat well, to preserve our strength and stave away the gloom and trial of these days."

Favik slid his documents across the Records Keeper's desk, a gentle swoosh the sole sound in the office occupied only by two adults of near age.

"You are a former Ambassador of Eskalind, I see," stated the official in the dour tone of her profession.

Favik's neck creaked as he nodded slightly, a budding impatience in his chest.

"Currently residing at the estate of Lord Radil, Acta Sua of the House of—"

"Yes, my Lord Radil is a great collector of old scrolls, and my business in Amkland was to research such for him."

Her green eyes shot to his. They were a lively contrast to her purple headwrap, but carried the glare of one who did not appreciate interruption. "Researching scrolls despite the threat of war?"

"I left Eskalind for Amkland unaware of that. I became very aware when I saw the Eyfian army crossing into Amkland. Thus I detoured south, deep into Kaymif, for safety."

"And you work for Lord Radil of the House of Valip, Palich King's Friend." The Records Keeper paused, laying her hands atop the papyrus documenting Favik's credentials. "Where is his estate?"

Favik replied in the tone of one aggrieved at the test. "In the north-west of Eskalind, bordering Amkland." He adjusted the red sleeve of his tunic over the yellow undersleeve. "I wear his colors."

"Are you aware of reports of Eyfians sweeping through Amkland, that they are not far from our borderwall?"

"I was not." Had he believed in The Powers' direction, he would have thought that was why he had felt such a keen anxiousness to return to Eskalind. In truth, though, something strange was at work, for a gnawing compulsion whispered that he must go to King's Halls and speak with his Lady Marna, if she would hear him. All his thoughts curved toward this undesired visit as though he were pressed into a slotted passageway bordered with high walls, with no means of escape save the thin way laid before him.

The official was speaking. "I see this news makes you anxious."

Let her believe that. "I'm concerned for my Lord and his family. They are dear to me."

It was the closest he had ever seen to a smile on a presiding Records Keeper's face as she shuffled his papyruses into a neat stack. "Yes, we must all look after those who are dear to us." Handing them back to him, the woman stated, "You may go. In my records, I will document your return to Eskalind on this twenty-sixth day of the third month, 2938."

Again feeling a test in her tone, he replied, "Is recording not the duty of your Apprentices?"

She placed her hands together, the knuckles bony and enlarged. "They are both ill, since three days ago. My husband as well." The Records Keeper stood, her black robes a cascade of fabric, as though the cloth had anticipated more body to drape than was present.

The former Ambassador rose as well. "Then I wish them swift healing from Dalich King." He departed into the bright afternoon sun and made for his horse, a sturdy bay gelding, fresh in years, from Lord Radil's stable. The beast had served him well on his journey. Yet as he departed the border station between Kaymif and Eskalind, the thought grew that speed was needed on this trek, that he must make use of his former status to procure a Swift Rider's horse at the next town that housed such.

A few hours later he arrived in the next hamlet, a quiet village where even the wandering chickens seemed mute. After securing his horse, with swift steps Favik made straight for the pennants of Dalich King marking the Records Keepers' office and Swift Riders' station. Inside, an odd silence met his ears.

"Hello?" He rang the bell, its sharp *Ting! Ting!* a punctuation in the air. He adjusted the strap on his leather satchel and waited. A shuffling from deep within the structure yielded a weary-faced Apprentice Records Keeper, a young man with dark marks like half moons under his brown eyes. His sable-shaded robes accentuated his woebegone countenance.

"What do you require?"

"Is there not a Records Keeper available?"

"No, she died the day before yesterday. The other Apprentice is sick too." He seemed uncertain what to say next and lowered his eyes to the desk between them.

The elder man spoke as gently as he could. "I'm very sorry to hear that, but I must ask your assistance. I'm former Ambassador Favik." He reached into his satchel and procured his documents, speaking the truth in his heart. "I ask for a horse as I make my way to deliver an urgent message to King's Mother." He placed the papyruses on the table.

The young Apprentice touched the top document. "No Swift Riders have come in the last couple of days. Their office is unattended; I've been looking after the horses." He swallowed, reached in a drawer, and pulled forth a violet-colored ribbon. "You travel toward King's Halls?"

"Aye."

He tied four knots in the ribbon. "Ambassador, sir, just pick a horse." The Apprentice laid the ribbon over the papyruses.

Not quite believing his luck, Favik nodded. "Thank you." He scooped the ribbon into a pocket and his identifying records into his satchel and departed in haste. Soon thereafter, he left the town upon a chestnut gelding, with Lord Radil's horse roped to its saddle. The pair trotted at a good pace as their master set a course for the next town, some fifteen miles on, where he tried to leave Radil's mount at their Swift Riders' stable.

"I'm sorry, sir," the young woman behind the desk apologized. "You may switch your Riders' mount with the only horse in my stable, but I can't accept your horse into my care for more than tonight." She shook her head slowly as she spoke, as though not quite believing her circumstances. "I'm alone here, and our supplies were supposed to be restocked yesterday. If the supplies don't come and your horse stays, the feed may run out."

It was a situation more common to the borderlands and outerlands than Eskalind. One glance at Radil's flagging gelding nosing the ground, and Favik knew he could not force the horse onward without a long rest. He bedded that night in one of the two bunks apportioned to the small office. The next day he rode the Swift Riders' horse, again leading Radil's horse with a rope. But at the next office he found the staffing akin to the last, and an empty stable. Reports of ill health plaguing Eskalinders abounded. Taverns were shuttered, and markets too. Procuring food became difficult, lengthening his journey as he sought scarce supplies.

As he entered Anya Queenstown, word of Dalich King's passing reached him. Despite their estrangement, his heart fell with sympathy for Lady Marna. Favik wondered how his own son fared. Onward the former Queensman pressed, east, to King's Halls, switching horses at the Swift Riders as he could, Radil's bay wearily trotting beside, saddleless to lighten his burden.

Namlich King was not seen by his people on either side of the Eskalind border for days. Reports of his furious sweep across Amkland came sporadically, while Captains Tarnil and Anish oversaw the care of the wounded and the burial of the fallen, all except the bodies of the slain Lords. While some Healers were also skilled in embalming, their services were found unnecessary, as day after day the fallen nobles exhibited no sign of decay. They appeared as though air had flowed through their lungs and blood in their veins mere moments ago. Even the blood on Captain Marnil's wounds looked wet to the touch.

The born and bred Eskalinders accepted this as normal and made no great remark upon it, but the native Havadran Captain wondered if the strange mist he had witnessed draping the bodies was the cause. Perhaps the people of his adopted country were correct in their belief in The Powers' protection of the royals and their favorites.

Still, he ordered the Healers to examine the bodies where they lay. No sign of injury was found upon Dalich King, nor on his Second. Their deaths were a great mystery, but as news arrived of a sudden illness felling many in Eskalind, concern grew that a pestilence brewed amongst them.

Anish spent his nights crafting letters to the next of kin of the fallen.

Given Namlich King's absence, it rested upon him to write his Lady the Queen of her husband's death. King's Halls must know, and better to have firm word in writing of the circumstances than the fever of rumor inundating the land. He doubted that the energy he poured into quilling beautiful words of condolence would soften the blow.

Nearly a week after the battle, on the twenty-ninth day of this accursed third month, a Stander spotted Namlich King riding toward the Eskalind border camp. Captain Anish was called, and he met his Lord by Dalich King's pennants, where the three bodies were guarded and arrayed as heroes on biers laden with Lamorda flowers. The King reeked of battle, sweat, and blood, his fine clothes cut, torn, and muddied, but no visible injuries slowed his pace or movements. His first task, reporting that he had slain 960 Eyfians, including their King Rothbur, with the survivors running for their border, their backsides to Amkland and Eskalind, hopefully forever.

When informed of the pestilence in Eskalind, Namlich King roared for help to carry his father over the borderwall. So insistent was his order that the task was done with minimal ceremony and much heavy-handed lugging and lurching of the bier, so that all who watched feared their dead Lord might tumble forth. Once the bier rested upon the yellowish soil of Eskalind, Namlich King asked for direction to the Healer's tents, where the sick resided. He beckoned Anish to come along. There they found many of the ill sitting upright, startled to find themselves alert and awake, their pains vanished. Namlich laughed, thumped backs, and slapped arms mirthfully at the glad sight.

That was when the Swift Rider arrived bearing messages from King's Halls that reported his Lady mother's death.

The new Captain feared this sad word would send the young man on another killing spree into Amkland, to hunt more Eyfians. Or—worse—to Kaymif to settle with King Moulai, for Namlich muttered curses of blame upon the Kaymif king as though words would deliver the man's demise.

Unaware of the situation, a dark-haired Healer of about forty approached, her voice proclaiming loud thanks to The Powers for returning Namlich King to Eskalind, for his presence had healed the sick and surely he was as Gifted as his father.

"Were I Gifted at healing," Namlich replied with sudden humility, his gaze to the crusts of blood still upon his hands. Then he turned toward the woman and gathered her in his arms for a filial embrace, head bowed against her shoulder as though she were his departed mother.

The sun streamed through the tall windows of King's Grandmother's chamber, unimbued with any inkling of the events of the last month, for it shone as brightly as if everyone who had ever loved and lived still walked the earth. Lady Jinilya leaned into the window seat's cushions, eyes slitted against the glare. The letters informing her of the deaths of her brothers and of her saister lay abandoned upon the sable fabric where she had dropped them in a fog of misery. No one had tidied them away. The dust glooming on the stone sill kept silent watch upon them, day after day.

Lady Marna sat quilling behind her desk on the far end of the long room, the furious scratching of her writing unremitting. She had spoken little of her son's death, as though she had expected it and her plans marched forth regardless. At present, she had no use for the younger Lady, who minded it not as she sank into dark thoughts. Even closing her eyes she could see Anish's elegant characters detailing the demise of her beloved Marnil, could recite from memory her former lover's impassioned words of commendation and tribute to his Captain. She opened her eyes, moving that letter beneath the one from her estate.

Someone knocked on the door, and Jinilya feared another letter carrier, bearing the worst news about her only surviving family member.

Almost all of the terrible things Fire had told her would happen, had happened. If only Kaloft would quill her.

Glancing to the elder Lady for instruction, she heard the knock again. The Scholars' Mistress gruffed, "No more interruptions. I have little time left—must finish this letter." Jinilya rose and trod on silent slippers, half wanting to flee her Mistress's poor mood. When she opened the door, Mamon's dear features looked to her. He bowed his head, stretching both arms toward her. In his thick-gloved hands, the Guerish youth held the metal handle of a small, lidded cauldron.

"Wax soup, my Lady Librarian?" he asked, in the buoyant voice of a fifteen-year-old with a clever notion in mind.

She placed a finger to her lips to soften his volume. "Is that the sealing wax for my Lady?"

"Indeed," the youth whispered back, beaming at her with clear glee at his quip. It pleased her that life had returned enough to normal that her favorite Apprentice would venture a silly jest with his noble sponsor. Mamon's dark eyes cut to his side, where something blue protruded from a high pocket in his black tunic. "Oven mitt for you, my Lady. The pot handle may still be hot."

"Ah, I thank you." She retrieved the mitt and placed it over one hand, admiring the unfamiliar shade against her skin for a moment, finding it a pleasing distraction. "Made in New King's colors."

"Indeed it is."

Jinilya accepted the pot handle from the Apprentice as he spoke. "Merlina is being fitted for her new Apprentice Ambassador clothes today. Also in blue."

He seemed very eager to tell her this, as though Merlina held special interest to him. Well, the young woman was two years his senior and had developed a very attractive figure since coming of age the previous year.

"That will be a lovely shade on her," Jinilya said. "Your studies will be resuming shortly?"

"Yes, the latest word is our new Chief Tutor, Ambassador Moril, will arrive at King's Halls from Kaymif in a couple of days. Our lessons begin just after that."

"Excellent news." Jinilya smiled and placed her free hand on his arm. "Now, I best bring this to Lady Marna before it cools. I thank you again, Mamon."

"You are most welcome, my Lady. It's … good to see you in better cheer." He bowed before she could reply and departed. Closing the door, the Acta Sua made for her prior seat, acknowledging to herself that she did indeed feel her mood improved.

The Scholars' Mistress was speaking. "There. Thank the Green Lady. The last one is finished and I date it today, the twenty-fourth day of the fourth month in the two thousand, nine hundred, and thirty-eighth year of Eskalind. Spoken like a Records Keeper." Lady Marna heaved her backside against her chair back, arms stretched before her upon her desk, the posture of one at last finished with a monumental task. "Is that the sealing wax?"

"Indeed, my Lady. Shall I bring it forward?" She walked toward the imposing piece of furniture. Were the King's grandmother a smaller woman, she would look like a child behind its wooden mass.

"Yes yes, and the ladle is on the long table there, the one with the most envelopes upon it." She sighed, smoothing a hand down her long white hair. "Come, come and use my signet to seal all these letters." Dalock's Queen shimmied the thick bronze ring from her stout finger and placed it into Jinilya's hand when she approached. "But first look at the stone, mark its face." The younger Librarian squinted at the clear red stone. "Look closely at the first tall point of the *M*. What do you see?"

"Mmm, a small dark spot."

"Yes, a mote of something else, some other substance. An inclusion, my father would have said." The elder Lady tilted her head toward the sunlight. "Mark it well, Jinilya. You may be called upon to identify this stone in the future."

"Yes, my Lady."

She hoped to learn more, but the Scholars' Mistress continued, "Now, seal them all for me, but mind! Do not turn them over until we return from our walk."

"We are going for a walk, my Lady?" It surprised her how sunny her voice sounded. On the envelope-laden table rested a trivet, and she placed the ponderous weight of the cauldron upon it. Jinilya then retrieved the ladle and tipped pools of wax upon the closure of each envelope. The wax smelled of heat and tallow. Not for the first time she silently thanked her Lady for not lighting candles in her presence. The Scholars' Mistress had long ago grown tired of the notion of Jinilya's gratitude for this, and the part-Guerish Lady knew better than to express the sentiment. For some reason, that thought made her smile. Perhaps the mantle of despondence was slipping away.

"Yes, my dear young Librarian, let us stroll to the garden. Come, I want to sit in pure sunshine, unfiltered by window glass. And breathe fresh herbs." She inhaled as though the moment she described was upon them.

Jinilya impressed the signet into the cooling black wax, which oozed under the brownish rim of the ring's face. She glanced at the deep carved *M* in the ruby-hued jewel, checking to see if any wax stuck to it. "That sounds like a wonderful notion, my Lady." She continued impressing the seal against the backs of the beige and delicately hued purple envelopes. Her Lady had insisted upon using up their stock of stationery in Dalich King's colors, though some of the Scholars' missives called for plain, colorless envelopes.

"Yes yes, and when you are finished there, be sure to seal the letters here on my desk. But do not use my signet on this one." She waved a thickly stuffed beige envelope. "It is for Lord Radil. No word from him has reached us since everything happened, and I want to make sure he is fully informed of how things stand."

"Certainly, my Lady." Her task at the long table complete, Jinilya carried the cauldron to her Lady's desk as King's Grandmother stood and shuffled toward the center of the room. The younger Lady continued ladling the sealant upon the missives that awaited her, then impressing the signet into each circular glob, except on Radil's note.

After a while, the royal Lady said, "Jinilya, was that Apprentice Mamon at the door earlier?" She nodded and made to speak, but Lady Marna continued. "It is good to have young people in our lives. Are you finished?"

"Just finished, my Lady."

"Then let them cool and come, my dear, dear Reader's daughter." The elder Lady advanced toward the door, her long hair a white slash against her black smock. The Librarian hurried to her side, returning the ring to her and stepping ahead to open the door. The royal Lady paused at the desk by the exit, fiddling with a drawer for a moment. Upon leaving the chamber, the Scholars' Mistress's gray eyes gave the room a long look, and Jinilya closed the door slowly, thinking her Lady pondered a final request. But no, she said nothing as Jinilya locked the door, then offered her arm. The pair made their way together along the unpopulated corridor.

King's Halls felt empty since the passing of so many, and every person who happened by received a warm acknowledgment from the Acta Sua of the House of Jinil, while the former Queen at her side looked straight ahead as though maintaining her momentum demanded keeping sight of the stones lining the passageway.

Not fifty paces from the garden door, Lady Marna sank onto a carved bench, her face incredibly pale.

"My Lady?"

She was waved away. "No no, I am fine, just a bit of a rest. Here, sit with me." Then she gazed at her hands and sighed. Jinilya sat and knit her fingers, wondering if she should call the sole Healer, who had just arrived at King's Halls. A list of herbs that might be efficacious scrolled through her mind. Absorbing Lady Marna's herb book had been quite an education.

An Apprentice Librarian walked by and bowed to them both, the young man's eyes wide on the former Queen as he passed, as though he had never seen her before. Then a voice rang out, "My Lady Marna?" Lady Dara, the seniormost noble at court, swept toward them. In her wake followed a tall, sad-faced girl clad in a purple gown trimmed in emerald. The girl's deep brown hair was coiled and looped above her ears in an unusual style. Jinilya rose and offered the elder Lady her seat, noting a line of gray at the roots of her dyed-dark hair. "I thank you," the Lady said.

Dalock's Queen's face and voice recovered its warmth, her tone one of sharing happy news with a fond companion. "Ah, my Joining Day attendant. A day over fifty years past."

The elder women shared a seated embrace, then faced one another. Dara spoke. "My Lady, I thank The Powers still for that day." She placed both her hands on the royal Lady's arm, a sparkling green signet prominent beside her smaller rings. "My servants are packing my trunks, the coaches are engaged, and I have come to say goodbye."

Here the Scholars' Mistress smiled, the expression of a person who knows more than she reveals. "It is the time of goodbyes."

"And introductions!" Lady Dara beamed, her voice rising and falling dramatically as was her manner. "This," she motioned to the girl who accompanied her, "Is my great-grandniece, Meera. She is just of age and had come to King's Halls from our estate to serve with me." Meera curtsied, her thin lips slightly pursed, brown eyes serious and woeful. "You see, she still wears the colors of our house."

Marna appraised the young woman with a glance. To Jinilya's eye, the girl looked well shy of her sixteenth Naming Day, but there was no reason to doubt her great-aunt's account. "You have pretty hair, dear," Lady Marna said.

Dara beamed. "Yes, Lady Navla did an exquisite styling for Meera as a goodbye treat. A shame we must depart, but it is all my doing. I want to return to my estate one last time."

"I knew the story would out," the royal stated, her tone both sly and confiding.

The Acta Sua had risen to her feet, which were slippered in a violet fabric crisscrossed with ebony beads. "Goodbye, my Lady. It has been an honor to serve you and your family, these many, many years. I thank The Powers for your wise rulership, your family's protection of Eskalind, and for the continuation of my house." She bowed, her niece mirroring the action.

Lady Marna's lips stretched but did not open, barely covering her teeth. Oddly, she appeared to fight tears, nodding. The women of the House of Naymil, Merlich King's Friend, departed. Watching their backs, Jinilya's Lady murmured hoarsely, "We have known one another a very long time. Best to not linger on goodbyes." She paused a bit as the pair left their view. Her gray eyes dimmed, then she lifted a hand to her Scholar. "Here, dear, help me up."

Jinilya obliged, but the former Queen did not, for she slumped forward, to the floor, with a heavy thud, escaping the younger woman's grasp. Jinilya inhaled sharply and called for help, dropping to her knees to support the heavy white-haired head in her arms. The Librarian Apprentice who had passed earlier ran to them, accompanied by a Scriptor and his Apprentice. The four able-bodied Eskalinders lifted King's Grandmother, calling to her, but she did not respond.

"My quarters are nearby," Jinilya barked to the men. "Let us bring her there." The quartet struggled with their weighty burden, huffing and puffing in single-minded effort toward their goal. They did not pass a single person until they reached the door. A Guard no longer stood there, for King's Second did not reside within, but a Page had drawn himself against the door to let them pass, not realizing that opening the door was their intention.

"Step aside and run for the Healer," Jinilya ordered, fumbling in her pocket for the correct key, for locking the door was still an unfamiliar habit. The boy gaped. "Go!" She slid the metal into the lock and the door swung open. "Toward the back," the Acta Sua panted as she held her Lady's shoulders. "Did the boy leave?" No one was certain.

They lugged the Lady Marna to Saril's chamber, placing her upon his bed with a large tea-colored pillow under her head. Afternoon sun showed full in the long row of diamond-paned windows.

"She's speaking," reported the Scriptor.

Jinilya pushed to her Lady's side. "Send for the Healer," she ordered the others.

They departed as she clutched her Mistress's hand. "Can you hear me? Are you cold?" She lifted a crimson coverlet to her Lady's chin.

"Where am I?"

"In my mother's chamber, my Lady." She hoped the reference might be a comfort.

The gray eyes fluttered open, gained focus, and darted to the windows. "No, this is not her chamber. Her windowpanes were square."

"They were replaced during Dalich King's building scheme. Please, my Lady, how do you feel?"

The pale hands pawed the blanket. "Red."

"Yes, the red and brown of Dalock King. The mud and the blood, as you have joked." She aimed to keep her tone light, hoping this would be a comfort. But the more she spoke, the more distressed the royal Lady became, closing her eyes and sinking into the pillow.

"Rest now," Jinilya said. "The Healer is coming." She hoped to The Powers it would help.

Into the next day, the Scholars' Mistress lay abed in the House of Jinil's quarters. As the sun descended and the afternoon light fell through the windows, she avoided looking at her hand or the windowpanes, for the time she had long foreseen was upon her. Like many things in life, dying was not as she had thought it would be. To The Green Lady, she had thought that the next mistress or master of the Scholars would share her last Gift, to see their own death, and would find the courage to tell her. Her Reader's daughter hovered over her. "Jinilya, dear, is there anything…"

"May I bring you something, my Lady? Water? Broth? More blankets?"

The effort of speech was exhausting, as was finding enough will to draw breath. "No no, I was hoping…you had something to say to me…something you needed to tell me?"

Jinilya smiled weakly. Her eyes were such a lovely shade of calm green, like the memory of a garden in Spring. "I wish you were better, my Lady."

"That is not going to happen. Are you certain, there is nothing?"

Lady Jinilya shook her head, her forehead creasing, deep concern in her eyes. She seemed to diminish for a moment, as though transforming into the old woman she would be someday. "My Lady, I am most sad to see you in this condition. I wish I could help." Marna closed her eyes and shook her head. "I am not certain what you want, my Lady. I will do anything you ask, but perhaps resting a bit will help you feel better?"

Someone entered the room on tiptoes, quiet as air, but the voice carried true to the Bladesmith's Daughter's ears. "My Lady Jinilya, Ambassador Favik has just arrived. He deeply wishes to see our Lady."

Marna lifted her head. "Favik? Favik is here?" She thought her heart had stopped at this incredible news, that her Queensman had returned unbidden.

Jinilya leaned close, "He is. Do you wish to see him now or after your rest?"

"No no, now, it must be now!" Her eyes darted to the lengthening shadows, now making their crisscross pattern across the bed covers, gliding in invisible, steadfast increments to the far edge of the bed. "Send him in!"

The Scholars' Mistress closed her eyes and leaned back into her pillow. She breathed. By The Powers, he had come to see her. Thank Them, thank Them. Muffled sounds reached her ears and she could not make out the words, but if she could, she would have heard Jinilya in an urgent whisper briefing Favik on her state.

Marna opened her eyes to see her man approaching. It was as though she saw his young face at a distance, and he aged as he came closer, for his hair and beard were full gray as he drew near to her, the skin under his eyes swollen from the years. Some of the sun's shadows still clung to the bed, though she guessed only for a few more minutes. "Hurry!" she whispered. "Hurry." Oh the trouble in his fond eyes as he knelt by the bedside.

"My Lady, thank you for seeing me." She reached for him and he grasped her hand. How warm it felt. "Do you require more blankets? You are very cold."

Here she smiled. "Not as cold as I will be." He opened his mouth, but before he could speak, the former Queen of Eskalind asked, in a voice caught between a command and a plea, "Have you something urgent to tell me? Privately? Do you?"

He hesitated a moment. "I do."

"Send Jinilya outside."

He turned and said something. She could not hear the response, though she felt a reverberation like a door closing.

"Oh Favik, I wish I had never sent you away. I am certain She influenced me. I have nursed such anger at myself." Marna was not certain if she uttered the thought aloud. He turned back to her.

"My Lady, we are alone, and there is much I would say, but what I am compelled to say immediately is unexplainable to me. A phrase has come to me unbidden and repeats and repeats, unceasing these past months, through endless delays to reach you. I sense the only relief I will have is to utter it to you." He swallowed, clutching her hand. "I know when I will die."

"You have seen it?"

He seemed surprised she did not question him. "Yes, the bed, the light…"

"Thank the Green Lady. A peaceful end for you." She lifted her head slightly, finding it easier to breathe and speak in this position. Noting his puzzled expression, she said, "I too know my end. It is near, when the shadows leave the bed and their pattern covers the wall." She gestured with their linked hands. His gray eyes followed, and he may have said something as he turned to her. "Favik, this means you will be the Master of the Scholars. My dear Favik. I grieve the time lost to us. I was a fool to send you away. The fire…"

He said something, but her throaty inhale caused her to miss the words.

"In my Library chamber, there is an ebony desk by the door. A… hidden compartment in the back of the top drawer, the side toward the windows. My signet ring is inside." He rotated the position of their hands and looked at the ring on her finger. She nearly smiled at his silent question. "This is a duplicate. The true ring is in the drawer."

He lowered their hands. "I see." He leaned to her, his dear eyes close.

"Also in that hidden place is a blank parchment. Write the Green Lady and she may—" Marna paused, for her breath nearly stopped, but the shadows still fell upon the bed. "She may answer your questions. Not always, but sometimes, when you need it most."

"But who is—"

"One of—" She raised a thumb upward.

His lips mouthed the words, *The Powers?*

Marna answered aloud. "Yes."

He drew away slightly. "Will She allow me to use this Gift?"

"You are revealed as my successor." She pressed his hand hard as she could and tried to sit straight. A warm arm encircled her back. "As she has given you the Gift of the Vision of Death ... I believe She will." The Scholars' Mistress inhaled slowly. "But Favik, always quill on the parchment in direct sunlight, and never, ever expose the parchment to candlelight."

"Quill by sunlight, never by candlelight. I will do this."

"In that drawer also is a letter for Jinilya, written when I thought she would be my successor." Her breath caught in her throat, but she managed to utter, "Destroy it."

"Is there anything else, my Queen?"

She would have acknowledged his endearment, but a glance at the shadows showed them nearly to the edge of the bed. "No. Call Jinilya, quick. I want her here too." He lowered her gently, released her hand, then shot away. In a moment both her hands were warming in the grasp of the two living people she loved above all others. "Jinilya, Favik will lead the Scholars until his death."

"As you say, my Lady." How bright her green eyes glistened from withheld tears.

"Ah, it was not my decision, but I thank you, my beloved Scholars." Marna squeezed their hands. "Protect Eskalind."

"But my Lady," began Jinilya, but either her voice faded or the world was snuffed out, for the shadows had reached the wall.

"Now?" exhaled the dying woman.

Thus passed Marna, Dalock's Queen, born a Bladesmith's daughter.

———

Favik the Scholars' Master reached across the bed with his free hand and grasped Lady Jinilya's. They wept into the coverlets.

Even the key made a mournful sound as it slid into the lock. Well, one would expect his late Lady's Library chamber to exhibit a funereal presence, given her death yesterday. The new Scholars' Master, accompanied by Lady Jinilya, entered the tall room which, in his thoughts, was populated by more memories than people that bustled outside the thick door. Meanwhile, all those who remained at King's Halls zigged and zagged through the corridors: servants and Apprentices toting furniture and draperies, Pages bearing yellow flowers, Ladies in new blue and gold gowns, all in a frantic quest to ready King's Halls for New King's anticipated return tomorrow. As his people strove to usher in his succession and his person, Namlich would find much of the familiar violet and sable replaced with his colors or the red and white of Heedlich First King.

Favik's agenda involved a relic from another reign. He shut the door behind his colleague, latched it, and turned to the dark wood desk near the threshold.

There, as his Lady had told him, his fingers found a compartment hidden above the vacant and shallow topmost drawer. Amidst the finely sanded wood, his fingers caressed the slight gloss of a parchment, which he pulled forth, a virgin sheet. A clunk sounded, and lowering the blank parchment, he beheld a note addressed to Jinilya and a bronze signet ring lying perfectly centered inside the previously unpopulated drawer as though placed there by a scrupulously orderly hand. Favik withdrew the ring as Jinilya asked, "What is it?"

"Her signet." He placed it in his hand and admired the carved ruby stone. How perfect and smooth it was against the rivulets crossing his weathered palm. "I was there when Dalock King presented it to her. I stood by her side, though my head was just to her elbow." The corners of the former Page's lips lifted. "The perfect stature to view a handsome ring."

"May I see it?" He passed it to her slim brown fingers, making advantage of her distraction and sliding Lady Marna's letter into a pocket. Jinilya scrutinized the ring close to her eye like an outerland merchant appraising a purchase. "This is the ring with which she bade me seal her last letters. But, I thought she was wearing it now as she lies in state in Saril's chamber?"

Favik raised his head and looked deeper into the room, not knowing that he spoke in the same tone as their Lady when she had uttered the same words to Jinilya. "A duplicate." He paused and retrieved the signet from her. "This is a symbol of the Scholars' Master. Our work must continue." He lifted the parchment sheet. "Have you seen this before?"

The gravity in her eyes would sink a ship. "Lady Marna showed it to me. Did she give you instruction?"

"She did."

"The instructions are of utmost importance." A heaviness tinged her voice, akin to a great disappointment. Then she brightened as though forcing a cheerful mood upon herself. "The letters—" She turned her head and at a brisk pace went to a table, her dark Librarian's robes a soft swish as she walked.

"Letters?" He followed, rolling the parchment into an inner pocket sleeve.

She was at the longest table, gathering horizontal columns of sealed envelopes into stacks. Some were the lavender color of correspondence from Dalich King's court and others the plain beige favored by the common folk and foreigners. The perfect shade for Scholars' business. "The last letters of the Scholars' Mistress." As he drew closer, she flipped the papyruses over and read the addresses of several, setting a few aside. One she held a moment before saying, "Favik, this message is for King's Son."

"You mean Namlich King?"

"No, I saved his. This," she raised the envelope, "is addressed to Namlock King."

Favik's eyebrows rose slightly. "That *will* be King's Son's name, if his father follows the tradition."

"Our Lady wrote her great-grandson . . ." Her green eyes stared intently at the envelope's inscription.

"I'm certain she had her reasons," the Scholars' Master intoned. Then he uttered gently, "May I see it?" She passed the undyed papyrus to him. It was heavier than he expected. Rubbing it with his fingers, he guessed that the sheet inside was vellum or parchment, for he sensed a smoothness under the veins of the papyrus envelope. But without opening it, one could not tell with certitude. "Hmm."

"I know Lady Marna's thoughts as she addressed his name." Before he could inquire as to how, she responded, "Call it my Gift." Here the Acta Sua looked at him like a person who knows she possesses authority of an uncommon breadth. Given that he had witnessed her, as a child, comprehend an upside-down scroll written in Thislin quilling, he was not completely surprised. Favik maintained an aloof demeanor before her claim. "Favik, the Bladesmith's Daughter wanted this envelope hidden by her Scholars until Namlock comes to his last title." She watched him, and he felt an Ambassador again under scrutiny of a foreign lord who awaited a single specific answer.

His response was obvious. "Then we must hide it."

"But not here, not at King's Halls," she whispered, her smooth face close to his. "If Namlich King finds it, he will open it. He may resist, he may desire to withhold, but forces will work against him to undo the seal." How certain she seemed. He nodded, waiting. Jinilya lowered her eyes. Her next utterance came quiet and casual, one companion ascertaining the plans of another. "Favik, are you staying at court?"

"I planned to return to Lord Radil's estate."

She was still close to him, and she pushed his hand with the envelope to his chest as she raised her gaze. "Then you stow it away there, in a hidden place." Her breath was near and warm upon him. "It cannot remain here. It must be kept secret until it is required for King's Son."

"Then I will bear it to Lord Radil's estate and keep it safe." He slipped the missive into a pocket, beside the special parchment and the letter Lady Marna bid that he hide. "You are quite insistent, my Lady."

"Oh Favik." She sounded like a young girl again. Then, pacing to another long table, Jinilya again began gathering envelopes into neat stacks, like an Apprentice readying healing notes for Dalich King. "We must post these. There should be letter baskets here somewhere."

"At your feet," he said, instantly realizing that calling attention to her feet might sound like a flirtatious invitation. Not once in the day since he arrived at King's Halls had she mentioned Anish, or any lover, though in their mutual grief at their Lady's death, conversation was most often replaced with quiet thought. She bent to procure a basket and he fought his natural urge to assist, for instinct told him to remove himself before her childhood fondness for him yielded a display of her bare toes. "I plan to leave for Lord Radil's by tomorrow."

Jinilya stood to her full height, an envelope fluttering unnoticed from her grasp. "So soon? I thought with the long weeks of travel to reach King's Halls, you would want to rest."

"I was in Amkland on Radil's business prior to coming to court and have been away from his estate for months." His voice became wistful. "His first grandchild was a babe when I left. They grow so much at this age, he may be a little boy when I see him next if I delay." Favik gave his most persuasive smile.

The Librarian's expression was thoughtful. "Lady Marna told me that Radil's son joined near the end of last year." She went to the large oaken desk and gathered more letters into the basket. "Ah, this one is for Lord Radil." She gazed to Favik with a lingering sadness as she held a fat missive. "Now I recall that Lord Amril and his Lady were expecting a child."

"Yes, a joining babe." Not wanting to linger on family or joining talk, he continued, walking toward her, "I will deliver that." The Scholars' Master lifted the heavy letter for Radil from her hand without looking at her and paced away, retrieving the note she had dropped and laying it on the table. "Sending and receiving letters and messages has been difficult this past month, given the Strange Plague. All the more reason for me to return as swiftly as I might. After all, Radil's estate is my home now. I shall direct the Scholars from there." He stopped by the first couch, smiling, eyes firm on the young Lady, his bearing that of a man who will not be swayed. "Many letters will still come here for Lady Marna. I will need you to forward them to me."

"I have had no word from my nephew Kaloft," she began, quiet-voiced, in a bent posture behind the desk as though she would slump against its seat.

"If I encounter any word or sight of him along the road, I will quill you immediately."

"Favik." Her voice quavered, her eyes rose. "Would you stay? The King brings my brothers' bodies here tomorrow. There will be some type of ceremony, before I send their remains to my estate. I need, I would like, you to stand by my side."

The former Ambassador felt heartless for pausing even a breath in response. "My Lady, no man of quality who calls himself a man could refuse such a request." He dipped his head.

"I thank you." It was barely a murmur.

"Now," he said softly, reaching for the basket, "I shall fulfill this last duty to our Lady by seeing these letters posted swiftly."

———

After Favik departed, the Lady Librarian paced to the windows, their black curtains gathered to the sides like wings waiting to enfold her. "Thus Favik becomes the Scholars' Master. How he hardens to the task." She wiped an errant tear with the heel of her palm. "Why did our Lady choose him? I thought for certain I would be her successor." She regarded the vacant desk. "Does he know what forces of evil await us?" The images the Green Lady had showed her played in her mind. Jinilya stood in silence she knew not how long. Then the air pressure in the room altered slightly and she realized the chamber's door was open. She turned to find Namlich King crossing the threshold, gray eyes surveying the long room with a fevered glance as though he expected a piece of furniture to attack him.

"My Lord?" Not quite believing his presence, she stepped forward. "But you arrive a day before we were told you would come."

He swiveled his blond head toward her, then, with a tone of dismay, stated, "Lady Jinilya. I find my grandmother laid out in your quarters and you afoot in hers."

Jinilya bowed her head to New King. "You came early to see her, my Lord?"

"I received word she was ill and tried to ride here yesterday. But the torrential rain last night made it impossible." He closed the door and turned to her, his sable-shaded brocade cape making a gentle swoosh.

"Oh my Lord, it breaks the heart that The Powers claimed my Lady before you could speak with her again." When he made no reply, she raised her head. Seeing his gaze directed at the tables, she moved closer to the last remaining Eskalind royal. "Your grandmother was nearly a second mother to me, after my mother passed."

How still he seemed, taller than she remembered, as though becoming King had conferred a loftier stature and a tranquility to his bearing. Yet he smelled of the road and weary travel, his blond locks merely finger-combed back so as not to cloak his clear eyes. A trail of Eskalind's yellow soil lingered between his eyebrows and hairline, likely the result of a towel hastily swept over his skin after splashing water upon his face.

"This chamber is different than I expected. My mother always told me what a mess it was, parchment and scrolls draping every surface. I can hear her words in my mind as though she were here speaking them." He glanced about as though expecting to see Damina Queen. "Yet I find the room tidied to perfection. It must be your doing." The hint of a smile graced his eyes.

"No, my Lord." Jinilya looked to her hands, her personal signet askew on her finger. She straightened the bronze band. "In the days before her death, Lady Marna seemed to have an urge to order her things and—"

"Like she knew when she would die." The phrase garnered the Lady's attention and she glanced back to him. "Would that she had considered quilling to inform me…" She could not tell from his tone if he were jesting or not.

Jinilya fluttered to the nearest table, upon which she had set the missive addressed to New King. "She quilled a letter for you, my Lord." Gathering the pale purple parchment envelope, she passed it to Namlich. His eyes stayed upon hers as he advanced toward her, stopping but an arm's length away to accept the message.

"I am very grateful to see you, Lady Jinilya, standing here before me. It has weighed upon my thoughts that you might… not be here." His nearness contained a presence on its own, as though someone occupied the space between them, or perhaps some foreknowledge that he would claim her in his arms alerted her nerves. Given the calm maturity he exhibited in this moment, it was a pleasurable idea. He smiled full, perhaps reading her thoughts. "Would you share a private cup with me?"

"A cup? Will you not read your letter?" He was already moving for the door, tucking the parchment into his tunic.

"I want to salute you." He laughed, pulling the door open. "A moment, my Lady." He departed as Jinilya stood dazed.

"All the males are behaving strangely." She sank into an upholstered chair. "But these are strange times."

Many moments later a slender Page stood before the King, holding a gold serving tray with quavering hands as she announced her Lord. The royal followed the girl as the pair stepped into his grandmother's Library chamber.

Lady Jinilya rose from her seat. "My Lord, this is a surprise." Namlich appreciated the hint of mirth in her tone, glad to The Powers for her cheerful voice and beautiful face.

"I hope a welcome one." He gestured for the Page to place the golden tray and the wine ewer with its two small matching cups on a low table before a deep plum colored couch.

"Of course."

The child completed the task, and the Lady's lustrous eyes seemed to enlarge as she approached and surveyed the elegant drinkware.

He dismissed the girl, and the pair settled next to each other atop the plump cushions. Namlich poured the wine, the liquid coming forth in a great ruby rush, an almost embarrassing *glug glug glug* sound echoing in the chamber.

He passed the glossy cup to the Lady's smooth fingers, the red stone of her signet a keen echo of the wine's hue. His eyes traveled to her wrist, the slight throb of her pulse apparent as she accepted the cup, waiting as he reached for his own. Her lack of speech unleashed his tongue. "I want to toast you, Lady Jinilya, to toast the living. Our immediate days ahead will be about the dead. For now, it is the two of us." He raised his glass, lifting his eyebrows. "To you."

"I thank you." They both drank.

By The Powers, simply sitting beside her felt good, as though her presence were a balm. But there was much to discuss, much of it unpleasant. "My Lady, it pains me to speak on this, but I would rather do so now than wait. It has been much in my thought on the journey home how to honor my father's and mother's bodies." Once he had begun, the words poured forth as eagerly as the wine. "I thought first to build them a tomb as my father did for his parents, but the more I considered, the answer came clear: a magnificent funeral pyre on the hill overlooking King's Halls."

"Fire?"

He understood her concern, but pushed on. "Yes." His voice deepened and quieted. "My parents were intertwined throughout their lives. I believe only through fire can they be commingled forever. I also feel," he looked to his signet, "directed by Them that a remnant of Father's healing Gift will spread across the land if we do this." It felt odd to say this out loud, but she alone he could trust. He glanced to her again. "It will also show that we do not let the voice hinder us."

The dark-haired Lady rolled her lips together, eyes to the desk anchoring the other end of the room. "Do you know, your grandmother thought it best, given the contagion, that all those who succumbed be burned?"

"I do. She wrote me that Mother's ashes were kept apart. As if she knew." He drank from his cup. Speaking quickly numbed the grief, as though speed were a blanket to smother unwanted sensations. "I also want…" The King reached to touch her arm, the motion bringing her eyes back to his. "If you allow it, my Lady, I want to include your brothers' remains in the pyre so that they too are eternal companions to my father, as they were in life."

Her lips opened, colored a deeper red from the wine. "You have thought much upon it." It may have begun as a question, but the last syllable dropped low in the register of her voice. Namlich nodded. She sipped the wine, the bottom of the cup seeming to hover over her mouth as though she were frozen a moment. "It would be a great honor, but please, you must understand, it is quite fearsome to me."

"I will stand by your side." How lovely her eyes were. "Together, you and I, we are a force against Her." He felt an expansive sense of dominion at speaking the words aloud, as though issuing a challenge that would go undisputed.

Yes, together they could subdue the voice. It was their Gift. "We have been all our lives." He thought he detected a trace of confusion and charged on. "Recall when I was a lad, helplessly listening to a candle. You heard it too and stopped it?"

"I pinched the flame out."

"Yes, and again later, I heard it in the Library and knocked that Apprentice down. You," Namlich gently grasped her sleeve, "came and put out the fire his candle started."

"I remember." She seemed to be warming to his plan.

"You see? Together we will make it stop, and the love between my parents, the love between your brothers and my father," he squeezed her wrist, "will be preserved forever and rain upon the land. I sense it will make Eskalind stronger than ever."

"I see." A brave smile followed, for there was fear in her gaze. He wanted to wrap his arms around her or kiss her, but his hand still held upon her wrist. Namlich withdrew it for fear he was hurting her.

She watched his hand retreat to his lap. "Then, my Lord, it is settled." The Librarian eyed her cup, holding it with both hands, her elbows akimbo as if to ward him away. "I thank you for bringing such a fine wine in these rich cups." She turned the gold slightly, a hitch in her voice. "Is it from the reign of Farlock King and Treya Queen? I see an *F* and a *T* carved on the side."

"Ah, I believe so." Namlich admired her attention and knowledge of their land's history, a glad distraction. He cleared his throat. "King's Storage is being plundered by the Steward for any items that are in my colors." He looked to the tray, then to the sable and violet furnishings in the room. Black was the predominant color, soon to be swept aside by the blue and gold. "May I tell you something?"

Lady Jinilya turned to face him, reluctance in the gesture. "I am here to listen, my Lord." He wished there were more pleasant subjects to talk about. Yet to her alone could he bare his heart.

"So many deaths. My parents, my cousins, my aunt, my ayncle." He drank.

"I underst—"

Namlich interrupted. "And do not think me weak, but it is an ache to my heart to see my parents' colors stripped away." Dalich's son swallowed more wine. "Even in the short time since I arrived today," he gestured with his cup, "when I passed through the corridor to your quarters, then returned to come here, in that short time my father's banners were removed. When I went, just this moment, for the wine service, I saw a servant replacing a purple vase with a blue one." He drank.

"It is your rule now."

"I know. I prepared my whole life for it. I wish things had gone differently."

Namlich poured more wine into his empty cup as she spoke: "I keep asking myself, how could The Powers allow this to happen?"

The King regarded his cup, his reflection in the wine, accusing. "I think She made Father cross the border." The Lady shook her head as she placed her half-full cup onto the gold tray. "The voice, in the fire," he said.

"But, what would it matter for the King to depart Eskalind?"

"Your brother never told you? My grandmother never told you?" It was clear from the confusion in her green eyes that neither had ever revealed that truth. "Ah." He realized he alone, among all those living, knew that secret. Namlich swirled the red liquid in his cup, nearly spilling it. His thought upon how to smother the fact he had just admitted, the fault in the royal line, the weaknesses The Powers bestowed upon his family. Their restrictions. Their taunts.

He had always assumed Lady Jinilya knew. Saril must have had opportunity to tell her; they quartered together. She might as well have quartered with Grandmother, as the two had been inseparable. Then again, what did it matter now, except to expose the royal line's impotence to the Will of The Powers.

A quiet, whispery sound came from the main door of the chamber. The pair turned, glancing toward it. A thin brown envelope, sealed with red wax, slid under the door. A dim voice called from the other side, "Letter for Lady Jinilya."

His companion leapt to her feet. "The colors of my house?" She raced to the threshold like an eager Page and retrieved the missive, flipping it over to read the directions. "It is in Kaloft's hand." She tore it open in feverish haste, laughing, as though she already knew glad contents awaited inside. The King leaned an arm over the couch back to watch her. "Thank The Powers." The lovely Lady grinned at him, eyes alight. "Kaloft is alive. My nephew is alive! He knows what has happened." She placed her fingertips on her forehead, shielding her face, laughing or crying, he could not tell. "He is quitting his studies in Teffle to journey to King's Halls to see me, to stay."

"What welcome news!" Namlich stood, hoping this signaled the end of this trial of tragedies. He went to her with open arms.

On such a historic day, a Lady at King's Halls would be expected to attire herself three times, once for each formal ceremony. In the morning, the national colors of red and white, those of Heedlich First King, would clothe her for the awaying of Dalock's Queen's hearse as it rolled northward to their shared tomb at the Kursak border. At noon, for the lighting of the funeral pyre of that Lady's son and daighter, Dalich King and Damina Queen, the familiar black and purple would drape members of court. Lastly, the gold and blue of Namlich King would be donned in honor of his inaugural feast as Lord of Eskalind.

This manner of dress was prescribed to all Ladies except one. Lady Jinilya, who as Acta Sua of her house on the occasion of her brothers' joint funeral with Dalich King, wore the red and brown of the ruler who had granted her family noble status. Pinned to her gown above her heart was the bronze brooch in the form of a sword laid over a book, the symbols of Marna Queen and her King. The brooch rattled to the touch, for it had been a babe toy as well as a Granting Present to her house by Dalock King over thirty years ago.

She sat alone in the Library, for it was approaching midday and preparations for the pyre ceremony consumed everyone but her, who had no requirement or desire to alter her jewelry or hairstyle for the next occasions. The warm oak of the floor reflected the vibrant red of her gown about her, giving the area a rosy glow as she ruminated on why, of all the letters Lady Marna had written, not a one was addressed to her.

Glancing about to pairs of small chairs, she realized she was in the children's reading area, where Namlich as a boy had attacked a candle-carrying Apprentice, causing an inferno that she had extinguished with her bare hands. Yes, the King was correct, she had done that. Jinilya held her slim fingers before her, the signet glimmering, wondering if she had enough Gift to smother a funeral pyre if the voice in the fire dared harm Namlich or the crowd.

A familiar voice, pitched high with excitement, called, "Lady Jinilya, are you within?"

She closed her eyes, not wanting to break the peace of the room a moment, then stood, eyes unshuttered. "I am, Mamon. Are you ready for your role tonight?"

Footsteps bounded toward her, though she thought she saw two heads through the scroll shelf as the youth came forward, sable clad in his dress Apprentice Ambassador robes, a gleeful smile upon his face, lips stretched wide and dark eyes bright. "My Lady, I have the greatest surprise for you." Before she could reply, he swept his arm with a flourish as someone else rounded the scroll case. "My father, Narmen of Guernain."

Jinilya's hands flew to her mouth. One need not be a Records Keeper to see in the son a true copy of the sire, though Mamon stood a finger's width taller.

The elder Guerlander wore the traditional blues and greens of his people, a tunic and tight leggings, though the fabric looked to be a soft, silky material. Narmen's long dark locks, peppered with gray, were tied behind his head, and his eyes were kind and as black as though her Lady mother again gazed upon her. A smooth gem of swirled shades of sea green and blue, set in silver, adorned his neck.

"Lady Jinilya, Acta Sua of the House of Jinil, Dalock King's Friend, and my sponsor here in Eskalind's King's Halls, this is my father."

Halfway through the introduction, she recovered enough from the shock to offer her hand to Mamon's father for the traditional Guerish greeting of clasping hands together.

"I am astonished to meet you at last, Narmen," she sputtered as they broke hands, the man bowing to her. Mamon continued to grin as though his face knew no other expression. "We did not know you were coming?" She looked to the Apprentice, but his father spoke.

"My Lady, I give thanks to The Powers for granting me the length of life to see my son again. How I mourned the loss of his mother when word reached me." He placed a hand over his heart, the tip of the index finger missing. "I have traveled south, as far as Ofsha, and returned to Guerland a rich man, only to find my wife and son," he placed his free hand around Mamon, "gone to Eskalind for healing years before and never returned. I wept." Narmen shook his head. "Then a fellow salt merchant showed me a letter, from Eskalind. A Records Keeper writing about my son, my son alive and well. The letter came to the Salt Merchants' Guild, and my colleague kept it in hopes that I would return. Thank The Powers he saved it for me."

Mamon nodded, interrupting, "Then Father boarded boat and sent letters to King's Halls, but he arrived before his notes did."

"I came through Mavold, but suspect my letters are still in Gergelt." The elder Guerlander patted his son on the back with a joyful thump as he flashed a toothy grin.

"What glad news that you are reunited!" Jinilya breathed, basking in their happiness.

"You were right, my Lady, do you recall? When we first met, at the King's House, you told me the Records Keepers were very good at their work and would find my father?" Her response was to embrace him to her heart.

Narmen watched, nodding and murmuring, "Thank The Powers."

She released him. "Oh Mamon, have you discussed what you will do next?"

"I, we, have." The joy drained from his face. "My Lady, I would return to Guerland. With your permission."

It felt as though her heart had been tugged out of her body, but the calm part of her had expected his words. "You do not need my permission."

His father was speaking. "My son told me you sponsored him, that it is a great expense, his education here. I have the coin. I will repay you for your great kindnesses to my son." His hands flew behind his neck, and the silver chain around his neck slumped on his chest as he undid the clasp. "Please, let me begin with this token, Lady Jinilya." He held the cool-colored gem'd pendant before him with both hands.

"Narmen, there is no need. The greatest repayment is that father and son are reunited." Mamon's black eyebrows lifted ever so slightly, a gesture worthy of Saril's subtlety. She did not resist embracing him again.

———

As the sun approached its zenith, a sad procession departed King's Halls, the living Lord of Eskalind in his parents' regal black and purple, accompanied by Lady Jinilya, clad in the colors of his grandfather's reign. Together they led Captain Anish and former Ambassador Favik, along with the entirety of the King's household, foreign visitors and ambassadors, citizens and Soldiers of Eskalind, arranged at first in orderly lines, then clumping and crowding as they processed up the short rise overlooking the seat of the Strange Kings. Atop the hill rested three pyres, set upon thick branches stacked chest high for the lowest, the last resting place of Lord and Captain Marnil. Next, his brother King's Second, on the opposite side of the middle and tallest pyre. On that pyre, draped about the sides with vines of First King's Flowers and bunting of violet and black, the body of Dalich King. In his hands, a basket spun like an open bird's nest composed of Lamorda flowers and stems, cradling a violet Mavoldian linen scarf in which lay wrapped the ashes of his beloved Damina Queen.

Coal-colored clouds gathered high above, blotting the sun, as Jinilya contemplated the top of Marnil's head and waited for everyone to advance up the hill and gather a safe distance from the pyres. She had not wanted to view her brothers' bodies, despite reassurances that they merely looked asleep. But the stillness of Marnil's distinctive gently curly locks brought a catch to her throat, for she could see plain it was her beloved brother and that he would not rise again.

Marnil's sister touched the red fabric swathing her chest, feeling the green and blue gem pendant Narmen had given her underneath the cloth. Her insistence that no repayment was needed for Mamon's education led to his father's insistence that she keep the sea-colored cabochon. That in turn led to a delicate explanation by Mamon of how each noble house represented the reign of the King who granted the house, and that said house's members must wear only those colors, especially at official functions.

Jinilya settled the matter by accepting the jewel and promising to wear it underneath the swaths of her gown. This pleased Narmen, and all were satisfied. She glanced now at the elder Guerlander, who gave a solemn nod to her, touching his hand with the short index finger to his heart.

Now all were gathered, and she risked a quick glance at Anish, on the King's other side, finding his expression impassive, chest and shoulders held high as one would expect of an Eskalind Captain. How she wanted to explain to him that her last letter had been a fault of the voice of the fire, but alas. A gentle hand touched her opposite elbow, and she turned to face Favik, his eyes kind as he had once been to her. Or as the moment required.

"Are you all right?" Favik murmured. The torch bearers came forward to pass their flambeaus to the King and the Lady.

"Yes, I thank you," she replied, thinking that she would be better when the rite was over, if all went well. Perhaps the dark clouds heralded rain. She distracted her anxiety by gazing at the flambeau bearers, chosen as symbols of the future that honored the distinctions of the dead.

For Dalich, the Healer King, Healer Apprentice Saysha bore the torch to Dalich's son.

Jinilya's firebrand was placed into her hand by Mamon, the Guerland-born Ambassador Apprentice, a nod to the heritage of Marnil and Saril and to King's Second's first profession. No one but she and the two Guerlanders knew the youngster would soon depart King's Halls, for the Lady insisted the trio keep silence until after the ceremony. The Librarian trusted no one but Mamon to place the fire into her hands.

The flambeau's handle was wrapped in cord, and she grasped it firmly, the flames' heat and the smell of soot loud in the air . . . but no voice rose from the fire. She and Namlich King stepped forward and thrust the brands into the wood, stepping back in tandem as a blaze grew and crackled in the tangle of horizontal tree limbs. They watched in silence.

Favik's chest rose and lowered in a deep but silent sigh, calling Jinilya's attention. His eyes were on Anish, who glared at him as though the former Ambassador himself had caused the tragic end of the dead they honored. Saysha, slender and still, blue eyes reflecting the burning pyre, stood beside Anish, leaning slightly toward the Captain as though he were a shelter.

Warm fingers slipped into the Lady's as Namlich encompassed her hand in his. The fire puffed outward slightly, and all made a step back. A murmuring rose. But it was merely some in the crowd, speaking softly. The King tightened his gentle hold on her hand. She looked to him, his gray eyes watching the topmost bier crumble amidst the flames, black smoke rising skyward, a dusting of ash tracing it. There was a resoluteness in his bearing, as though the mantle of Kingship were a physical object wound about him. His majestic demeanor invigorated her spirits, lifted her shoulders, filled her with certainty: he was right, together they were a force against the voice. She felt a Queen out of Legend, capable of conquering any trial The Powers laid before her.

A mote of a cinder ascended from the apex of the fire, flashing bright amidst the dark smoke. Then the glow spiraled to earth in a widening trajectory, targeting the King, growing larger, aiming for his face.

Sweeping her free hand before him, Jinilya seized the palm-sized ember from the air and quenched it in her fist.

Namlich turned his blond head to her, the slightest smile lifting his lips as their gazes met. She returned the expression. They both glanced to her fist as she opened it. There, the cinder glowed anew, a woman's face in its shape.

I am not finished with you

Jinilya inhaled as Namlich turned fully to her, eyes wide, for he too heard the voice. He reached for her open hand and gently closed her fingers again around the ember. She did not dare breathe as he removed his hand. She uncurled her fingers. Featureless ash floated away.

1   **Heedlich King**
Queen: **Said to be a Power**
Colors: Red and White

2   **Heedlock King**
Queen: **Maarva**
Colors: Red And Yellow

3   **Heedalich King**
Colors: Gray and Red

4   **Haadlock King**
Colors: Brown and Red

5   **Haadlich King**
Queen: **Braanya**
Colors: Blue and Red

6   **Heenlich King**
Colors: Green and Red

7   **Heenlock King**
Colors: Black and Red

8   **Breenlock King**
Colors: Black and Silver

9   **Breenlich King**
Colors: Gold and Silver

10   **Baanlich King**
Colors: Purple and Silver

11   **Baanlock King**
Colors: Green and White

12   **Taanlock King**
Colors: Blue and Yellow

13   **Taanlich King**
Colors: Green and Yellow

14   **Praanlich King**
Colors: Green and White

15   **Praanlock King**
Colors: Gold and Orange

16   **Daavlock King**
Colors: Blue and Gold

17   **Daavlich King**
Colors: Green and Silver

18   **Saavlich King**
Colors: Green and Orange

19   **Saavlock King**
Colors: Black and Yellow

20   **Taamlock King**
Colors: Gold and Gray

21   **Taamlich King**
Colors: Blue and Gray

22   **Taaylich King**
Colors: Blue and White

23   **Taaylock King**
Colors: Brown and Green

24   **Steevlock King**
Colors: Green and Purple

25   **Steevlich King**
Colors: Orange and Red

26   **Keelich King**
Colors: Black and Yellow

27   **Keelock King**
Colors: Brown and Gold

28   **Kaanlock King**
Colors: Orange and Silver

29   **Kaanlich King**
Colors: Red and Silver

30   **Raamlich King**
Colors: Black and Blue

31   **Raamlock King**
Colors: Red and Yellow

32 **Aarklock King**
Colors: Blue and Gold

33 **Aarlich King**
Colors: Black and Blue

34 **Aavlich King**
Colors: Green and Yellow

35 **Aavlock King**
Queen: **Talva of Eskalind, The Battle Queen**
Colors: Green and Red

36 **Maamlock King**
Colors: Black and Red

37 **Maamlich King**
Colors: Blue and Gray

38 **Paarlich King**
Colors: Blue and White

39 **Paarlock King**
Colors: Orange and Red

40 **Aamlock King**
Colors: Green and Purple

41 **Aamlich King**
Colors: Green and Silver

42 **Plaanlich King**
Colors: Gray and Yellow

43 **Plaanlock King**
Colors: Black and Yellow

44 **Maarlock King**
Colors: Red and Silver

45 **Maarlich King**
Colors: Yellow and White

46 **Faanlich King**
Colors: Blue and Brown

47 **Faanlock King**
Colors: Brown and Red

48 **Kaarlich King**
Colors: Black and White

49 **Kaarlock King**
Colors: Blue and Orange

50 **Hoolock King**
Colors: Green and White

51 **Hoolich King**
Colors: Blue and Purple

52 **Taablich King**
Colors: Green and Red

53 **Taablock King**
Colors: Gold and Red

54 **Slaalock King**
Colors: Orange and Red

55 **Slaalich King**
Colors: Black and Green

56 **Aaplich King**
Colors: Brown and White

57 **Aaplock King**
Colors: Purple and Red

58 **Haanlock King**
Colors: Red and Rose

59 **Haanlich King**
Colors: Brown and Orange

60 **Kaastlich King**
Colors: Silver and White

61 **Kaastlock King**
Colors: Blue and Orange

62 **Keernlock King**
Colors: Black and Silver

63 **Keernlich King**
Colors: Red and Yellow

64 **Kaarnlich King**
Colors: Blue and Red

65 **Kaarnlock King**
Queen: **Asda of Eskalind**
Colors: Orange and White
Emblem: Sword

66 **Haaydlock King**
Colors: Black and Orange

67 **Haaydlich King**
Colors: Blue and Violet

68 **Meedlich King**
Colors: Blue and Orange

69 **Meedlock King**
Colors: Gray and Orange

70 **Aablock King**
Colors: Black and White

71 **Aablich King**
Colors: Yellow and Green

72 **Laaylich King**
Colors: Blue and Brown

73 **Laaylock King**
Colors: Black and Silver

74 **Vaalock King**
Colors: Purple and Red

75 **Vaalich King** *Queen*: **Anya**
Colors: Brown and Red

76 **Aadlich King**
Colors: Green and Orange

77 **Aadlock King**
Colors: Green and Red

78 **Seerlock King**
Colors: Gray and Red

79 **Seerlich King**
Queen: **Maayla**
Colors: Blue and Brown

80 **Saanlich King**
Colors: Blue and Red

81 **Saanlock King**
Colors: Gray and Green

82 **Maavlock King**
Colors: Blue and White

83 **Maavlich King**
Colors: Gray and Red

84 **Daylich King**
Colors: Brown and Gray

85 **Daylock King**
Colors: Blue and Black

86 **Kraalock King**
Colors: Green and White

87 **Kraalich King**
Colors: Brown and White

88 **Maaylock King**
Colors: Black and Silver

89 **Maaylich King**
Colors: Blue and Red

90 **Stelich King**
Colors: Blue and Brown

91 **Stelock King**
Colors: Blue and Brown

92 **Husklock King**
Colors: Blue and Gold

93 **Husklich King**
Colors: Purple and Gold

94 **Haavlich King**
Colors: Black and Orange

95 **Haavlock King**
Queen: **Dayna of Eskalind**
Colors: Brown and Red

96 **Kilock King**
Colors: Black and Brown

97 **Kilich King**
Colors: Silver and Gold

98 **Kerlich King**
Colors: Blue and White

99 **Kerlock King**
Colors: Red and Yellow

100 Kamlock King
Colors: Brown and Green

101 Kamlich King
Colors: Blue and Orange

102 Karlich King
Queen: **Treeva**
Colors: Green and Yellow

103 Karlock King
Queen: **Faya**
Colors: Purple and Blue

104 Kalock King
Queen: **Tiya**
Colors: Green and Yellow

105 Kalich King
Queen: **Kayna of Eskalind**
Colors: Green and Red

106 Salich King
*Colors:*Blue and Red

107 Salock King
Colors: Green and White

108 Mavlock King
Colors: Blue and Orange

109 Mavlich King
Queen: **Elya of Eskalind**
Colors: Blue and Gold

110 Trelich King
Queen: **Deke of Guerland**
Colors: Orange and Red
Emblem: Tree and two conjoined leaves

111 Trelock King
Queen: **Karel of Salmand**
Colors: Gold and Red

112 Tremlock King
Colors: Black and Red

113 Tremlich King
Colors: Green and White

114 Narmlich King
Colors: Green and Purple

115 Narmlock King
Colors: Brown and Yellow

116 Palock King
Queen: **Bravna of Eskalind**
Colors: Green and Orange

117 Palich King
Colors: Red and Yellow

118 Narlich King
Colors: Black and Green

119 Narlock King
Colors: Blue and Red

120 Merlock King
Colors: Blue and Red

121 Merlich King
Colors: Green and Purple

122 Farlich King
Queen: **Merva of Eskalind**
Colors: Gold and Green
Emblem: Gold beaker on green field

123 Farlock King
Queen: **Lady Treya of Eskalind**
Colors: Black and Gold
Emblem: Black horse on gold field

124 Dalock King
Queen: **Marna of Hudiksland**
Colors: Brown and Red
Emblem: Initially red sword on brown field or shield. Later altered to red sword upon brown book, in honor of his wife's invention.

125 Dalich King
Queen: **Damina of Eskalind**
Colors: Black and Violet
Emblem: Blank parchment and a quill

LIST OF FINAL CHARACTERS

Note: This character list includes some spoilers. Eskalinders preceded by 🖋

🖋 **Abya**, *Records Keeper*

🖋 **Alayna**, *Lady of the House of House of Valip, Palich King's Friend, daughter of Radil and Mayva*

🖋 **Amril**, *Lord of of the House of Valip, Palich King's Friend, son of Radil and Mayva*

🖋 **Ana**, *Swift Rider*

Anish, *born of Havadra, serves in 6th Company (see Yirish)*

Astofts, *king of Havadra*

🖋 **Athla**, *Lady of the House of Jinil, Dalock King's Friend*

🖋 **Athril**, *Apprentice Librarian*

Avath of Thislin, *merchant*

🖋 **Avnil**, *First Sergeant of the Eighth Company*

Ayda, *maither of Soldier Haknil, formerCook's Assistant Eskalinder*

🖋 **Baavnif**, *born of Thislin, famous Eskalind Loremaster*

🖋 **Bafnil**, *Secretary of Ambassador Moril*

Batmis, *king of Amkland*

🖋 **Bayril**, *son of Haknil, grandson of Ayda*

🖋 **Brisnil**, *Records Keeper*

🖋 **Dalich**, *125th King of Eskalind, husband of Damina, father of Namlich*

🖋 **Dalock**, *124th King of Eskalind, deceased, husband of Marna, father of Dalich*

🖋 **Damina**, *Queen of Eskalind*

🖋 **Damnil**, *Tavernkeep at the Orchardton Tavern*

🖋 **Dara**, *Lady and Acta Sua* of the House of Naymil, Merlich King's Friend*

Deenofts, *Scholar and dye merchant of Havadra, brother of Samathe*

Edvain, *Mavoldian Swordmaster*

Elai, *son of Moril and Kostaza*

Falina, *born of Eastlant, orphan of King's House** at Pleasanton*

🖋 **Favik**, *born of Hudiksland, now Humiksland, Ambassador of Eskalind*

🖋 **Fayna**, *Lady of the House of Mavnil, Trelock King's Friend*

Feethe of Havadra, *household whore*** of Yirlofts*

🖋 **Fornil**, *Ambassador of Eskalind*

🖋 **Gafnil**, *Soldier of the Sixth Company*

🖋 **Haknil**, *Stander, later Solider of the Sixth Company*

Homik, *son of King Humik and later king of Humiksland*

Humik, *king of Humiksland*

Jinilya, *Lady of the House of Jinil, Dalock King's Friend, daughter of Saralya, sister of Saril and Marnil*

Kala of Eyfia, *copyist*

Kaloft, *Lord of the House of Jinil, Dalock King's Friend, son of Marnil and Athla*

Karvil, *Apprentice Librarian*

Kayvil, *Engineer*

Kermon, *Merchant Master of Guerland, Scholar, blood cousin of Saralya*

Kostaza, *princess of Kaymif, wife of Moril, sister of King Moulai, mother of Elai*

Hamvish of Havadra, *Engineer*

Hazish of Havadra, *trusted man to Sirish*

Heida, *a lady of Eyfia, wife of Lachmir*

Lachmir, *a lord of Eyfia, husband of Heida*

Laglil, *Apprentice, later Records Keeper*

Lamon, *born of Guerland, First Sergeant of the Sixth Company*

Lathbur, *king of Eyfia*

Layda, *Apprentice Librarian*

Madain of Mavold, *ship captain*

Madix of Amkland, *Assistant of Amkland Ambassador*

Malthe of Havadra, *household whore*** of Samathe*

Mamon of Guerland

Marna, *born of Hudiksland, now Humiksland, Scholars' Mistress, King's Mother of Eskalind, wife of Dalock, mother of Dalich, called the Bladesmith's Daughter by the Scholars*

Marnil, *Lord of House of Jinil, Dalock King's Friend, brother of Saril and Jinilya, husband of Athla, father of Kaloft*

Mayva, *Lady of the House of Valip, Palich King's Friend, wife of Radil*

Meera, *Lady of the House of Naymil, Merlich King's Friend*

Melande of Havadra, *daughter of Yirlofts, wife of Sirish, mother of Yirish*

Merlina, *born of Eastlant, orphan of King's House** at Pleasanton*

Moril, *Ambassador of Eskalind, husband of Kostaza*

Morya, *Healer*

Moulai, *king of Kaymif, brother of Kostaza*

Namlich, *King's Son of Eskalind, son of Dalich and Damina*

Narmen of Guerland, *salt merchant*

Narnik, *born of Hudiksland, Captain of Eskalind, nephew of Marna, cousin of Dalich*

Navla, *Lady of the House of Albina, Mavlich King's Friend*

Naynarp of Guerland, *merchant*

Onamil, *Apprentice Records Keeper*

Onas of Guerland, *merchant, husband of Semise*

Palika, *born of Hudiksland, Chief Scriptor of Eskalind, niece of Marna, cousin of Dalich*

Pamina, *sister of Damina Queen and Yamina, daughter of Gamin*

Perka, *Minder of the King's House** at Pleasanton*

Radil, *Lord and Acta Sua* of the House of Valip, Palich King's Friend; Scholar, husband of Mayva, father of Amril and Alayna*

Rothbur, *nephew of Lathbur, later king of Eyfia*

Safish, *dye merchant of Havadra*

Sakil, *Army Captain*

Samathe of Havadra, *portraitist, sister of Deenofts*

Sanil, *Soldier of the Sixth Company*

Santris family of Havadra

Saralya, *Scholar, Lady and Acta Sua* of the House of Jinil, Dalock King's Friend, Mother of Saril, Marnil, and Jinilya, called Queen's Reader*

Saril, *King's Second and Lord and Acta Sua* of House of Jinil, Dalock King's Friend*

Sastofts, *prince of Havadra, son of King Astofts*

Saura, *servant in King's Halls*

Saysha, *daughter of Morya and Brisnil*

Semise of Havadra, *aunt of Deenofts and Samathe*

Sirish, *a colonel of Havadra, husband to Melande*

Synya, *Librarian at King's Halls*

Tarnil, *Sergeant of the Sixth Company*

Taknil, *Groomsman at the House of Wenil, Farlich King's Friend*

Trevil, *Dalich King's Guard, husband of Yamina*

Uldrik of Eyfia, *Lachmir's Sergeant-at-Arms*

Vinil, *Scriptor at King's Halls*

Werna, *midwife of Humiksland, sister of Marna, mother of Palika and Narnik*

Yamina, *sister of Damina Queen*

Yirish of Havadra, *grandson of Yirlofts, son of Melande (See Anish)*

Yirlofts, *general of Havadra, father of Melande, grandfather of Yirish*

***Acta Sua,** *title given to the eldest member of a noble house of Eskalind*

****King's House,** *an orphanage*

****Female go-between servant of a Havadran household*

Royal Family of Eskalind

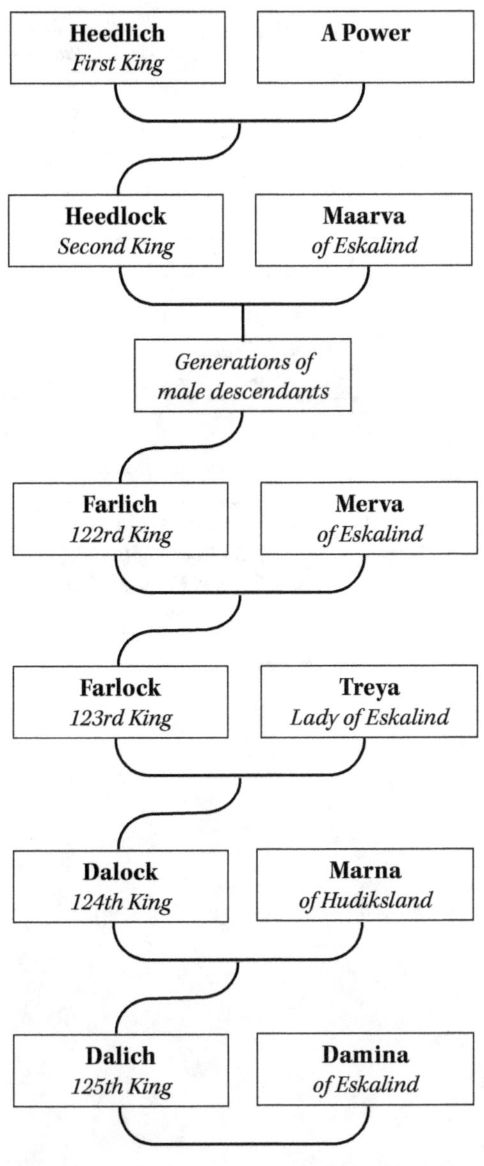

FAMILY TREE : HOUSE OF JINIL, DALOCK KING'S FRIEND

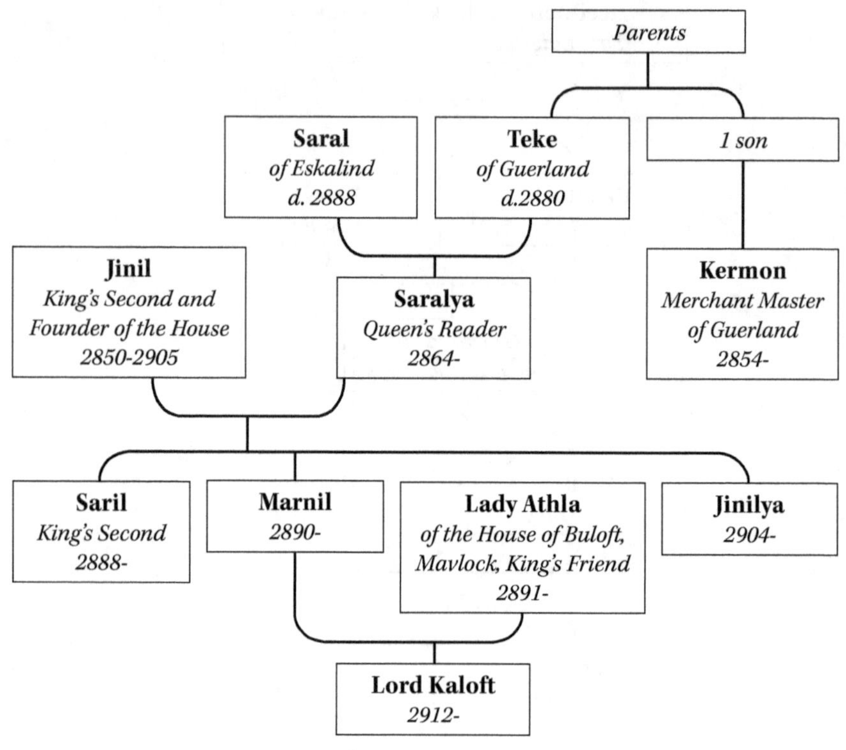

Note: *Designation of Lady or Lord indicates noble at the time of birth*

www.ingramcontent.com/pod-product-compliance
Lightning Source LLC
Chambersburg PA
CBHW060808120726
47909CB00006B/1830